THE
USURPER

TELNARIAN HISTORIES
BOOK FOUR

JOHN NORMAN

OPEN ROAD
INTEGRATED MEDIA
NEW YORK

Copyright © 2015 by John Norman

Cover design by Andy Ross

978-1-4976-7926-9

Published in 2015 by Open Road Integrated Media, Inc.
345 Hudson Street
New York, NY 10014
www.openroadmedia.com

THE
USURPER

THE
USURPER

NOTES, IN THE MANNER
OF A PREFACE

"The sky was dark with the coming of ships." The Annals

It is difficult in our enlightened era to understand the dark and troubled times. How terrible they were, how fearful to live then! How fortunate that they are past! And yet, then, one suspects, men, and women, were alive, as they are not now. Perhaps something was lost with their passing. But one should not speak such thoughts. Indeed, one should not even think them, lest they be inadvertently spoken. Have not many been sentenced, for words spoken in sleep, monitored by the electronic listeners?

What is one to make of the thousand sciences, of the thousand worlds?

The ant has his world, the vi-cat his, and we ours.

Some believe that time is the creature of clocks; yet it seems there was a time before clocks; if clocks stopped, might they not have stopped for a *coding* or less; some believe that length is the child of marked sticks; yet it seems that a length lay in wait, so patiently, for the stick. It is fortunate we have discovered the end of space. We are informed, and wise. One wonders what lies beyond that end, and where our space might be. Some say the world had a beginning, but how could it begin? Would it

just appear? Were things not lonely then, so empty, nothing-
ness, without even space? A universe contained in a spoonful
of energy? And whence that spoonful of energy? How wide and
deep that spoon? Was it far from here? Perhaps there are tides in
worlds, as universes breathe, expanding and contracting.

We are fortunate to live in a quiet, stable, equable world. Science has sounded our world, and tamed it, made it fit for habita-
tion, by such as we. We graze peacefully. How grateful we must
be. Our science is one of the thousand sciences. How fortunate
we are that it is the one truth, as we are told. What, I wonder, do
the thousand false sciences tell their populations, or herds. Do
they proclaim their falsity boldly? Perhaps not.

Surely the world is a mysterious place, this world, and
perhaps others. One puzzles on the dark selections of nature.
Would it select equivalently on a heavy world, and a light
world, on a hot world, and a cold world, on a dry, barren world
and on an aqueous world? One supposes not. On one world a
termite prospers, on another a wolf. In the dark and troubled
times who would prosper? I think men and women were not
then as they are now. In our world what place would there be
for such men and women, or, in their world, what place would
there be for such as we? Might not they turn their back on
our world? Might we have survived in theirs? Perhaps, if we
became as they, those who could. One wonders if one could
become as they, impatient, alert, agile-sinewed, far-trekking,
keen-sighted, enduring, wary, sustaining hunger, and heat and
cold, hardy, ready to hunt, and be hunted, ready to kill or be
killed. They were the dark and troubled times, times in which
life was noticed, not overlooked, times of threat, difference,
and risk, times in which life was simpler and more raw, times
in which life was perilous, but lived.

I am different from many others; I am much alone, with my
studies, and my memories of lives I never lived, or do not think I
lived. I frequent ruins, and old buildings. I am found in obscure

libraries, I peruse crumbling manuscripts, not seen fit for pre-servation. I am one with chroniclers I have never known. I sift through their accounts, often so laconic. This manuscript, fol-lowing, is based largely on the Valens manuscript, 122B, details concerning which I have supplied elsewhere. It is unusual amongst such manuscripts as it deals largely with individuals, and not institutions, federations, and states. I effect nothing crit-ical on this score. Is it not one way to understand a time, seeing it as those saw it, whose time it was?

As our story begins, the wings of the Telnarian empire spread over thousands of worlds. The empire was eternal, and, I fear, dying.

I think there is a particular reason I have attended to these supposedly antique matters, and it has to do with the mysteries and intricacies of time, and the interlacings of dimensions. Sci-ences, here and there, doubtless the false sciences, as we are told, have supposed a multiplicity of worlds and dimensions, suggest-ing that reality is less prosaic and constricted than commonly sup-posed by small animals such as we, bred not to understand but, in the midst of dark sanctions, to survive. Are we, whom it took millennia to discover the stone club, the planted seed, and the bronze knife, ready to understand the possible births and divi-sions of worlds?

I wondered, long ago, if Telnaria might not lie at our elbow. How is it, for example, that certain troves of manuscripts lay so long, not merely neglected, but, apparently, undiscovered? Is it possible that they were not there, until recently, in the historical past? But surely that is absurd. But one wonders. As I once men-tioned, long ago, when I was very young, once, for the briefest instant, while wandering amongst ruins, my sleeve brushed a column, but it was not worn with age, weathered by centuries of wind and rain, sheeted with moss, blackened and scarred by lightning, but fresh and golden, lofty and deeply carved, and then it was gone. But I had glimpsed Telnaria.

*   *   *

Our story continues, at the edge of a forest on the world of Tangara, at a small camp far from the provincial capital of Venitzia.

It is the month of Igon, a month of bitter cold in the northern latitudes of Tangara.

It is dusk.

CHAPTER ONE

"Prepare yourself, Cornhair!" snapped the brunette, who was first girl, and carried a switch.

"'Filene'!" said the blonde.

"Why 'Filene'?" said the brunette.

"It is my name!" said the blonde.

"Why is it your name?" laughed the brunette.

The blonde was silent.

"Speak," said the brunette, "or my switch will play a merry melody on your silken hide, and, as you are, you will feel it, and keenly!"

"Because it is the name Masters have given me!" said the blonde, tears in her eyes. Almost without thinking, she lifted her hand to her throat. She wore, as did the brunette, a Telnarian slave necklace, of the sort favored in some of the provinces. It was all she wore.

"Kneel, Cornhair," said the brunette.

The blonde knelt. Instant obedience is expected in a slave, to any free person, and even to another slave, if possessed of authority over her.

The blonde touched the light, small chain locked about her neck, with its pendant metal disk. The disk, in three languages, including a Herul pictograph, identified her as a property of the Telnarian empire, to be returned, if found, to

the office of the provincial governor, in Venitzia. In her transportation to the camp, her naked body bundled in a thick fur
sack and hood, the chain had been housed in a soft, leather
sleeve, which is not uncommon in the cold, or in a situation where the slave might be exposed to cold. Indoors, or
in warmer areas, sleeves are removed from such "necklaces."
The reason for this is simple. Men like to see the chain on a
slave's neck. Metal against female flesh is sexually stimulating. It is even more so when it is understood that the woman
is a slave, and the device is, in effect, a slave collar, which she
cannot remove. It does not take long for an enslaved woman
to gather that she is now, is expected to be, and must be, a
stimulating sexual object.

"You look well on your knees, Cornhair," said the brunette,
"—as any slave."

The blonde and the brunette were in a rearward portion of a
long tent, one of four at the camp, inside the defense perimeter.
These four tents were designed for imperial occupants, even
of rank; accordingly, they were floored, insulated, and heated.
They were small oases of comfort in the wilderness outside
Venitzia, even in the month of Igon, even at the edge of a forest,
into which not even Heruls would penetrate, a forest rumored to
be roamed by Otungs.

"For what am I to prepare myself?" asked the blonde.

"The camp has a visitor," said the brunette.

"The sought barbarian, he has been found?" exclaimed the
blonde. "He, Ottonius!"

"The Master, Ottonius," said the brunette.

"Yes," said the blonde, "the Master, Ottonius!"

Slaves do not address free persons by their name. They
address free men as "Master" and free women as "Mistress."

"It seems he recalls you from the *Narcona*," said the brunette.

The blonde felt giddy.

"You served him on the ship," said the brunette.

"He did but interrogate me and use me for a servile task," said the blonde.

"What task?" inquired the brunette.

"Polishing his boots," said the blonde.

"That is all?" said the brunette, skeptically.

Putting the slave to a servile task, particularly if she has recently been free, before putting her to one's pleasure, is often thought to be instructive. It helps them better understand what it is to be a slave. Interestingly, the performance of such small, homely tasks, caring for a Master's quarters, cleaning his garments, preparing his food, expectantly awaiting his return, and the opportunity to welcome him, kneeling before him, and such, can be sexually stimulating to the slave. Many a free woman fails to understand the joys of submission, and the yielding totality and warmth of a woman's bondage, for slavery, for the slave, is a wholeness, a mode of being, a way of life, a life of surrender, of serving, of love, and devotion. In helpless bondage, choiceless, mastered, and owned, she is contented, grateful, and fulfilled; she is as she would have herself.

"Yes, Mistress," said the blonde.

As first girl, the brunette was as Mistress to the blonde.

The blonde recalled how the barbarian had taped her mouth shut and bound her, kneeling, at the foot of his bed, and then slept. How her feelings had wavered, and disturbed her, how she had wanted to hate him, and had, at the same time, helpless at the foot of his bed, longed for his hands upon her body, holding and caressing her, with thoughtless, severe, possessive authority, as a slave may be held and caressed. How well the slave knows herself, nothing, and owned, and trembles with a responsiveness no free woman can understand, save in her dreams, thrashing in bonds, or grasped in the implacable might of her Master's arms.

"Why then would he wish you at the supper?" asked the brunette.

"I do not know," said the blonde.

"Your lineaments are acceptable," said the brunette. "That is probably enough."

"Four will serve," said the brunette, "you amongst them. Perhaps, if you beg prettily enough, he may, after the men are done with their business, as the conclusion of an evening's collation of wine and tarts, bed you for his pleasure."

"What is wrong?" asked the brunette.

"Nothing, Mistress," said the blonde.

The heart and body of the blonde churned with tumult. It was with difficulty that she restrained herself from reaching to the floor, to steady herself. It would be unwise, of course, to break position before a superior.

It was as though she suddenly found herself on a plank, unsteady, frightened, precariously located, a yawning abyss disappearing, leagues below.

The time was at hand, for which she had waited, for so long, enduring such hardships, and humiliations, as though she might be naught but another meaningless slave.

Surely no more than one or two in the camp, those who would supply the tool of assassination, whose identity or identities were unknown to her, knew her true identity, that she was not a slave, at all, but, rather, was a free woman, the Lady Publennia Calasalia, and a free woman not merely of the *honestori*, but of patrician stock, indeed, one once of the Larial Calasalii, before being disavowed, because of waywardness and debts, even to the obliteration of her name from the relevant rolls of lineage. Long ago, in a private audience, late at night, with sober, cunning Iaachus, the Arbiter of Protocol in the court of the Emperor Aesilesius, he aware of the miseries and nigh destitution of her lot, she had been recruited to perform a tiny task, in which no more than a single drop of blood need be shed, but a drop on which might ride, so delicately, breaking not even the surface, the fate of worlds, and the winds of power, reaching to the ten thousand sectors of an empire, for small things in a single palace, or court, or audience room, or hallway, an order given, a glance exchanged, a nod, might be eventually felt, borne on the wings of light, and piercing the charted thresholds and passes of space, to the farthest outposts of the *limitanei*, verging on the remote, threatened perimeters of the empire itself.

"Perhaps he will find you of interest," said the brunette.

"'Of interest'!" exclaimed the blonde, angrily.

The brunette looked at her, puzzled. What an odd cry, she thought, from a slave. "You had best hope so," she said, "lest you be whipped, discarded, sold, or slain."

"Of course, Mistress," said the blonde, lowering her head, humbly.

Soon, she told herself, this dreadful matter, with its humiliations and degradations, would be done. The chain then, with haste and abject apologies, might be removed from her neck.

She could not remove it herself, of course. It was on her, as much as on the neck of any slave. How fearful it would be, she thought, to truly be a slave! How she might then pull at that chain, helplessly, wildly, fearfully, and know it truly on her, signifying to all who might look upon her what then she would be, a property, as much as a pig or dog!

Happily it would soon be removed, when her task was done.

Again she touched the necklace.

How fearful to think of being truly a slave, a helpless, lovely, purchasable object, one no stranger to thongs and chains, to gags and blindfolds, to hoods and harnesses, to cells, kennels, and cages, a creature which must kneel, submit, obey, and strive to please, something to be ranked as loot, something to be listed as cargo, something which might be routinely vended from a thousand, indifferent platforms on a thousand, indifferent worlds.

But she would soon be rich, and once more highly placed, with position, and power.

How she would enjoy a hundred vengeances. How she might then buy the brunette, and others, who had slighted or abused her, and teach them then what it might be to be the slaves of a free woman!

But who would supply the delicate knife, light and slender, needlelike, so finely ground, with its transparently coated blade? Might it be blond Corelius, so handsome, and ironically polite, who had so often treated her as though she might be free, perhaps knowing she was truly free? Or had he been merely mocking one he deemed a helpless slave? Might it be severe Ronisius, who treated her no differently than he did others, assumed slaves, or was this part of a subterfuge on his part, that little attention be brought to her? Or it might be a higher officer, say, Lysis, supply officer of the *Narcona*. The knife would not be entrusted to a lesser figure, surely. It must be he, then, a higher officer! Certainly it could not be short, ugly Qualius, with his shuffling gait, his porcine countenance and porcine manners, a tender of livestock on the *Narcona*, that being brought to Venit-zia, who had occasionally brought her her gruel, and feasted his eyes upon her as she crouched hungry, wishing to be fed, in her cage. But Phidias, himself, the captain of the *Narcona*, was in the camp! How anomalous that was! Why should one such as he brave the long trek to the forest, a dangerous journey through frozen terrain, perhaps under the eyes of furtive, lurking Heruls? His post was surely on the ship.

It must be he, then, she thought.

How could wise, cunning Iaachus, Arbiter of Protocol, who, it was said, was depended upon by the empress mother herself, and was perhaps the mind and will behind the throne, have chosen a better agent to transport a small, black, flat leather case between worlds, thence to bring it from a rude provincial capital to a mysterious rendezvous at the edge of a dark forest?

It must be he, she thought.

But perhaps not!

He may know nothing of the knife.

She did know matters of moment were afoot, as perhaps many in the camp did not, recruitments and alliances, matters supposedly of political and military consequence.

Would not an agent less conspicuous be more judicious?

"Clean and groom yourself, Cornhair," said the brunette. "You are to sparkle."

"Yes, Mistress," said the blonde.

"Slave cosmetics, and slave perfume," said the brunette.

"Such?" inquired the blonde. They were, after all, in a wilderness camp, far even from the modest comforts and amenities of a provincial capital.

"Surely," said the brunette. "You are not a free woman."

Little did the brunette know, thought the blonde. How she would pale, and cringe, if she knew she were free.

We would then see in whose hand the switch reposed!

The blonde thought of the subtleties of the dressing table, before which she might kneel, and avail herself of the assorted pencils and brushes, disks and vials, on its surface, and in its tiny, shallow drawers. How different those articles and supplies were from those with which she had once been familiar, ordered at great expense from a dozen worlds, long ago, before she had fallen on straitened times. How little she had thought of such things then, the *darins* slipping through her small fingers like water, before the glistening, spinning wheels and the tiny plates on the marked tables had turned against her. She had fled creditors on more than one world, only on another to once more drain family resources and accounts.

How she despised that miscellany, suitable for slaves, on the low table.

Even the mirror was small, and cheap, mounted in its unpainted frame. How different it was from the large, broad, ornate, expensive mirrors she had had installed in her various boudoirs, particularly before falling upon her straitened times.

"How are we to garb ourselves?" asked the blonde. "In serving gowns, as at the captain's table, on the *Narcona*?"

They were ample, flowing, long, tasteful, and modest.

"You are no longer on the *Narcona*," said the brunette.

"How, then?" said the blonde.

"In tavern tunics," said the brunette.

"Surely not!" said the blonde.

"Why not?" inquired the brunette.

"They are so tiny, so short, there is so little to them, they are too revealing."

"They are fit for slaves," said the brunette.

"One might as well be naked," said the blonde, petulantly.

"If the men grow drunk, you may well be," said the brunette.

The blonde shuddered.

"Accustom yourself to what you are," said the brunette. "You are a slave, a property, to be exhibited, or displayed, in any way Masters might wish."

"Still!" protested the blonde.

"Do not fear," said the brunette, "there will be no free women present, to beat you, because you are beautiful and owned by men."

"Such tunics are disgraceful," said the blonde.

"Not on a slave," said the brunette.

"They are too tiny, too short, too revealing," said the blonde.

"You will wear them," said the brunette.

"As Mistress wishes," said the blonde.

"Men like them," said the brunette, "and do they not excite you, as well, the display, the revealing to all who look upon you what you are; do they not well impress upon you your helplessness and vulnerability; do they not mark you as a mere property, an object whose very *raison d'être* is to delight. Have not women been bred over millennia for the pleasure of men? And what is an enslaving but putting the confirmation and seal of legality, of implacable law, on the decree of nature? And surely the touch of such things on your skin, a rag, a rope, a leather strap, a collar, heats your limbs and belly."

"Please do not speak so!" cried the blonde.

"And is there not a reciprocity here, between women and men, between slaves, and Masters?"

A tiny cry of anguish escaped the blonde.

"Have I dismayed Cornhair?" said the brunette.

"Of course not," said the blonde, looking away, adding, "—Mistress."

"You are a slave," said the brunette, "a plaything for men. Make them cry out for the having of you. What other power do we have?"

"Where are the others?" asked the blonde.

"They prepare themselves elsewhere," said the brunette.

"I am then different, special?" said the blonde.

"Apparently," said the brunette.

"How so?" asked the blonde.

"I do not know," said the brunette. "But I do not think you are surprised."

"Mistress?"

"There are subtleties here," said the brunette, "things I do not understand."

"What sorts of things, Mistress?" said the blonde.

"Do not concern yourself," said the brunette.

"Has it to do with a Master, or Masters?" asked the blonde.

"Do not concern yourself," said the brunette.

"Perhaps I have been spoken of, or you have noted my behavior being unusually observed or monitored?"

"The things are subtle, hard to place," said the brunette.

"Perhaps you have seen one with a closed package, a small, flat box, one storing it, one who might have glanced at me?" said the blonde.

The brunette regarded her, puzzled.

"Perhaps I am to be given something, a gift?"

"A gift?" said the brunette.

"Yes," said the blonde, "a gift, in a small, flat, black, leather case, perhaps an anklet, a strand of beads, a bracelet."

"What are you talking about?" asked the brunette.

"Nothing," said the blonde.

"Are you mad?"

"No, Mistress."

"You smile?" said the brunette.

"Forgive me," said the blonde.

"Consider our group," said the brunette, "shipped from Lisle on the *Narcona*, brought to Venitzia on Tangara, and then carried here, into the wilderness."

"Mistress?" said the blonde, uncertainly.

"Are we not a very unusual group, an anomalous group?"

"How so?" asked the blonde.

"There are twenty of us, twenty," she said.

"Mistress?"

"Surely you are aware of what we all have in common?"

"We are all slaves," said the blonde.

"Other than that," said the brunette.

"What?" asked the blonde.

"Not one of us is branded," she said.

"So?" said the blonde.

"An unbranded slave is extremely rare," said the brunette. "Many markets will not handle an unbranded slave. Many ships will not transport them between worlds. You can understand the commercial and societal wisdom of marking slaves. It is an almost universal practice. On many worlds, it is required by law."

The blonde smiled to herself. She was not a slave, of course, but, if she were the only unmarked girl in the group, that would have surely excited undue speculation and interest. Accordingly, brilliant Iaachus, in his cunning, had arranged that she would not be conspicuous in her group on account of the absence of an expected slave mark, perhaps the tiny, tasteful "slave rose." If she was not to be marked, for she was free, then let the others, true slaves, lowly and owned, be unmarked, as well.

"Perhaps we are too beautiful to mark," said the blonde.

"Do not be absurd," said the brunette. "All slaves are to be marked, and the more beautiful the most of all, for they are the more costly merchandise. One does not wish to lose them."

"I see," said the blonde.

"So why are we, slaves, not marked?"

"I am sure I do not know," said the blonde.

"I long for the brand," said the brunette.

"You long for it?" asked the blonde.

"Yes," said the brunette. "I want to be a slave. I have wanted to be a slave since I was a young girl. That is why I want to be marked, to have my nature, destiny, and meaning proclaimed publicly on my body. I am not ashamed to be a slave, for it is what I am, and want to be. I revel in it, I exult in it! It is my joy! I want to love a man so deeply that I will accept nothing short of utter bondage at his hands. I want to submit to him, and love and serve him, wholly and helplessly. And I want him to want me so fiercely that he will be content with nothing less than my categorical possession; I want him to want me so much that he will be satisfied with nothing less than putting me to his feet, in his collar, as his indisputable property."

The blonde began to tremble.

Why should the words of the brunette, a mere slave, concern her, she, a free woman?

"What is wrong, Cornhair?" asked the brunette.

"Nothing," said the blonde.

"You are disturbed?"

"No."

"I suspect," said the brunette, "that you are in some way special. But how is it that you, if you are, might be special?"

"Perhaps I am particularly attractive to Masters," said the blonde.

"You do not yet know your collar," said the brunette. "You are still much like a free woman. Your body is stiff, and wooden. You lack the modalities of the slave, her sensuousness, her fluidity, her subtle movements, her grace, her vulnerability, her sense of being owned, and desired, and desired as the slave she is, her pleasure in such things, and her joy."

"The barbarian asked for me!" said the blonde.

"Perhaps he recalls you from the *Narcona*," said the brunette.

"Doubtless," said the blonde.

"But why should he choose you?" asked the brunette.

"Why not?" asked the blonde.

"You are beautiful," said the brunette, "but you are not yet a suitable slave."

"Perhaps I will never be a suitable slave," said the blonde.

"Perhaps not," said the brunette, "but I assure you that you are eminently suitable for the condition. I have seldom seen a woman, even at a glance, more obviously suitable for slavery."

The blonde stiffened, in fury, hating the brunette, but felt uneasy, rejecting the sheet of flame which had suddenly flared in her belly.

How fearful it would be, to be truly a slave!

"Why you?" said the brunette. "There are others, several others, better slaves."

"But nonetheless it was I for whom he asked," said the blonde.

"He is a barbarian," said the brunette.

"No matter," said the blonde. "He is a captain. He is charged to recruit *comitates*. He is no simple bumpkin from the forests, lost when separated from his sty of pigs or patch of roots. He is an officer. He was held in honor on the *Narcona*. Surely he has visited cities, frequented markets, perused slave shelves and cages, been in the brothels and taverns, and is no stranger to marked chain-sluts."

"So why would he want you?" asked the brunette.

"Because of my extraordinary beauty," said the blonde.

"Perhaps he is curious about you," said the brunette. "He may be wondering if you, despite your seeming inertness and rigidities, have the makings of a slave."

"I am extraordinarily beautiful," said the blonde.

"There are things in this camp, and things about you, I do not understand," said the brunette.

"It seems that I am to prepare myself alone," said the blonde.

"I think it is just as well," said the brunette. "You are not popular with the other girls. You hold yourself apart from them. You behave as though you were superior to them. This is resented. Many times, were it not for my switch, they would have dealt roundly, and effectively, with your impatience, your lofty manners, your impudence."

"A slave is grateful," said the blonde.

"You are not," said the brunette, "but you should be." The brunette then turned away, but, before exiting that portion of the long, warm tent, turned back. "Prepare yourself," she said. "See to it! Be ready, soon!"

"Yes, Mistress," said the blonde.

"When the gong sounds," said the brunette, "proceed to the kitchen, to be given your flagon or tray."

"Yes, Mistress," said the blonde.

The blonde, naked save for the tavern tunic, knelt before the mirror, and returned the tiny tube of lip coloring to its place on the table.

She hooked her fingers over the chain on her neck, with its disk, and drew against it, once or twice.

Hateful thing, she thought, but it is, in its way, attractive.

In her days of liberty and wealth, of travel and extravagance, she had had high collars of rows of jewels closed about her neck, nine such rows, collars worth fortunes, and these had been well matched by the bracelets on her arms, the rings

on her fingers, the diamond tiara fixed in her bright hair. She
was well aware, so bejeweled, in her off-the shoulder gowns,
lengthy, silken, and shimmering, of her striking appearance
at the gaming tables. How beautiful she was, and yet she suspected that many of the men present might have been more
struck by the glitter of jewels and the brandishing of position
and station, than the lovely, living manikin which served as
the cabinet of their mounting, and the tray of their display.
Few, it seemed, in such precincts, looked past the blaze of taste
and wealth to the model by means of which such things were
exhibited. Lady Publennia Calasalia did not much care for
men, save for what benefits might be derived from them. She
had, of course commonly seen through and scorned a variety
of suitors, most of whom, clearly enough, even of the *honestori*,
were merely interested in accruing to themselves the advantages which might appertain to an alliance with a patrician,
particularly a wealthy one. But these advantages, eventually,
muchly diminished, as various accounts became unavailable
to her. No longer could she draw on her family's wealth on a
dozen worlds. Later, her very name was excised from the Calasalii's rolls of lineage. For better than a year she had lived in
nigh destitution, supported only by a pittance begrudgingly
extended by her outraged family. Soon she had been reduced
to marketing her jewels, her goods, and slaves, to inhabiting
humble quarters in poor districts, even to patronizing the
women's public baths, and had but one slave left of her former retinue of slaves, a small, exquisite, redhead, Nika, whom
she had often beaten, perhaps because there was little else at
hand on which to vent her anger and frustration. Men who had
sought her hand now avoided her, and would not extend her
loans. Then, somehow, it seemed, eventually, her plight had
come to the attention of a sympathetic, mighty figure, Iaachus,
the Arbiter of Protocol in the court of the emperor, Aesilesius.

   She looked at the simple, plain, light, attractive chain on her neck. Any beast, even a dog, she thought, might wear such a collar.

And the fools who saw it on her would think she was a beast, a slave! How little did they know! How wrong they were!

She recalled her jeweled collars. How conveniently they might be affixed, or removed.

How different from the chain, with its disk, now fastened on her neck!

She wondered if the men who had looked upon those jeweled, sparkling collars had more seen her, or the collars. Were they not dazzling, so bright, so calling attention to themselves as to blind a vision which might, otherwise, have noted a woman? Did they not divert an attention away from what was incidental to their display, a rack, a platform, a woman? What was most important here? What would be the prize? How would one see the woman, as a woman, or as an instrumentality by means of which a putative treasure might be secured? Which, jewels, or woman, would be the essence and motivation of some projected quest? Or had she affected such displays that she might conceal herself behind them, fearing to be looked upon simply, primitively?

In the case of a slave, things were muchly different.

Slave goods are presented objectively, directly.

In the case of the jeweled collar, the woman displays the collar; in the case of the slave collar, it is the woman which is displayed.

She jerked at the chain on her neck. She could not remove it. Men had put it on her, and she would wear it.

But it was attractive.

But one of the things she sensed about chains, and collars, far transcended the provinces of aesthetics, and bespoke itself of cognitive matters, of meanings. Did not the collar on a woman's neck say, "I can be owned," or, if she is a slave, "I am owned"? Does it

not say, "I am goods," "I can be purchased," "I am a slave," "I can
be yours"? "Would you not care to own me, Master?" One does
not see a slave as one sees a free woman. One steps aside for the free
woman; one is heeled by the slave; one notes the free woman; one
seeks the slave; one honors the free woman, one wants the slave;
one defers to the free woman; one commands the slave; one courts
the free woman; one buys the slave; one admires the free woman;
one puts the slave to her knees; one esteems the free woman; one
puts the slave to one's pleasure.

How is it, wondered the blonde, the fine Lady Publennia Calasalia, that men prefer a half-naked, collared chit to an exalted,
splendidly robed, noble free woman? How is it that they bid so
avidly in markets for a lascivious beast, writhing to the auctioneer's whip? What is wrong with men, she wondered, that they
do not see the superiority of a free woman, any free woman, to
the weeping, moaning, and thrashing of a slave in her chains,
begging piteously for at least one more caress, even a tiny one?

The Lady Publennia Calasalia, with anger, recalled an incident
in one of the opulent gambling palaces whose portals were once
open to her, perhaps one in Lisle itself, seat of one of the imperial palaces, in which a fellow near her had brought his slave with
him into the hall, in defiance of proprieties, and knelt her near the
table, head down. "She brings me luck," he had explained, insouci-
antly, responding to her acidic reminder of his indiscretion. Surely
he knew there was a room off the main vestibule where such beasts
might be shackled, for a small fee. Indeed, even small bowls of porridge were provided, included in the cost of the temporary housing. Indeed, there were even poles outside the gambling palace to
which they might be chained, free of charge, awaiting the return of
their Masters. "She brings me luck," he insisted, "like a lucky piece,
or charm." Lady Publennia had then, muchly irritated, returned
her attention to the table, and the dizzy orbits of the tiny golden
sphere spinning about in the bowl of the large, shallow wheel. She
had later looked down at the slave, a girl with light brown hair,

kneeling, head down, with her knees closely together. How uneasy was that pathetic creature! She knows she does not belong here, Lady Publennia had thought. She is afraid she will be whipped and ejected, perhaps to one of the poles outside with its waiting, now-opened ankle manacle. I hope it will occur! And then she discovered she had lost another fifty *darins*. It was small comfort that the insolent recreant at her elbow, he so apparently oblivious of his breach of indisputable decorum, had not fared any better. Later, when the troublesome fellow prepared to withdraw, and somewhat worse off for the evening's play, she had remarked that the slave, as her presence had failed to bring him good luck, might be beaten. "Would you do so?" he had asked. "Certainly," she had said. How the girl had then trembled. "No," he had said, "there are better things to do with a pretty slave than beat her." "I see," she had said. "What are they?" she asked. His demeanor had then changed, alarmingly. He had seemed to loom over her, his mien displeased, and she had become suddenly aware of her smallness, and slightness, before his powerful height, and frame. She had the sense he might, had he wished, have broken her in two. "If you were not a free woman," he said, quietly, "I would show you." Her knees suddenly felt weak, and she feared she might actually be struck, indeed, disciplined. She almost sank to her knees before him, trembling, her head down. Then he was again a light-hearted gentleman, ingratiatingly frivolous. He snapped his fingers, and the slave sprang to her feet, keeping her head down. How quickly she obeys had thought the Lady Publennia. But then slaves were to obey, instantaneously, unquestioningly. Certainly she had switch-trained her own little Nika to do so. "You have brought me luck, little Nutmeg," he said. "Without you I would doubtless have lost far more." She looked up at him, smiling. Why is she happy, wondered the Lady Publennia. Why is she not unhappy? Does she not know she is a miserable, meaningless slave? She seems so pleased, so radiant! How dare she be happy! The fellow then turned away, and the girl followed him closely, a bit behind, on his left side. What a silly name,

'Nutmeg', thought the Lady Publennia. But she doubtless answers
to it quickly enough. Slaves, of course, are named as the Masters
please. Perhaps she had once been free, and had had a fine name,
but now she is only 'Nutmeg', clearly a pet name, a slave name, but
now her name. Then the Lady Publennia recalled, kneeling before
the cheap vanity mirror, before a small table, in a tent in the wilderness of Tangara, that there were those in the camp who referred to
her as 'Cornhair'. She had noticed, during the gambling evening,
to her annoyance, that the attention of many of the men about had
often fallen on the kneeling slave. Certainly the slave was a distraction. Why did the men bother to look upon her; she was only a
slave! There were many free women in the room, many bejeweled as
richly as she, the Lady Publennia, but it seemed it was the slave to
which the attention of the men had often strayed. The Lady Publennia had watched the fellow, and his slave, leave the room. Several
of the men had also witnessed their departure. "The lucky dog,"
remarked a fellow. "I wager she is a hot little thing," said another.
Lady Publennia watched the pair until they had left the room. The
slave did not walk like a free woman, but, of course, she was not a
free woman. Lady Publennia felt disturbed. There seemed subtle
differences in the slave's movements, and walk, something different
from that to which she was accustomed in free women. She did not
understand it at the time, but the slave, as she is a beast, owned, and
a sexual creature, is free to move naturally, gracefully, sensuously, as
a woman's natural, feminine body moves, innocent of the body language implicitly expected in, and prescribed for, the free woman.
The tunic the girl wore had clearly identified her as a slave, as did
the collar on her neck, but the tunic had been clean, well-pressed,
tasteful, and relatively modest, as such garments go. Indeed, it had
fallen below her knees. Her arms, of course, had been bare. That is
common in slave garments. In a sleeve a knife might be concealed.
I wager, had thought the Lady Publennia, that that single, simple
rag is all she has on. And in this wager the Lady Publennia would
have been successful. The slave is often denied certain forms of

undergarments, particularly those which might have a nether closure. They are for free women. The slave is to be conveniently at the disposal of the Master, at any time he might be inclined to make use of her. She is, after all, a slave. The fellow who had exited with the slave had lost something like seventy-five *darins*. The Lady Publennia, that evening, had lost more than a thousand.

The Lady Publennia again, in the mirror, regarded the light, simple chain fastened on her neck. Yes, she thought, it is attractive, and she had little doubt but what, if a man should look upon her in such a device, that it would be she, she herself, who would be seen.

She thought of the barbarian, remembered well from the *Narcona*, he, Ottonius, for whom a small dagger was to lie in wait, laden with its venom, not unlike the fang of a viper.

Who would bring her the dagger?

What would be her opportunity to strike?

Presumably, even now, a hoverer was being readied to transport her safely, swiftly, after the deed, to Venitzia, whence the shuttle would carry her to the waiting *Narcona*, in orbit, and then she would be wafted away, presumably to Lisle, the *Narcona*'s port of registry, or another world, to bask in new riches, exult in renewed station, and revel in the perquisites of power, accompanying wealth like a golden shadow.

She flushed with anger.

How furious she was that he had put her, a free woman, even of patrician stock, to the polishing of his boots, and had then taped her mouth shut, and tied her, for the night, unused, at the foot of his bed!

He was a barbarian, not even of the *honestori*!

How she hated men, and what they could do to women, if they pleased!

She recalled the brunette.

"Perhaps he will find you of interest," had said the brunette.

"'Of interest'!" she had exclaimed, angrily.

How horrifying that would be for a free woman! But is a free woman not a woman, and, if her freedom were torn from her, like her clothing, and she were put to her knees, naked, in the shadow of a whip, with a marked thigh, and that lovely, light, locked chain on her neck, with its pendant disk, would she be different? I do not think so. She, too, would now be a slave, a property, merely another stimulating sexual object.

Bring me the dagger, someone, she whispered to the mirror.

She thought of her slave, small, exquisite, red-haired Nika, whom she thought was awaiting her, in a tiny, dingy room in Lisle. As she recalled the slave in the gambling palace, and had been muchly displeased with her, she decided that, upon her return to Lisle, Nika would do nicely as a proxy for that other slave, and would receive the switching which she was in no position to administer to the other, a switching Nika would long remember. Her other slaves, many highly trained in a variety of domestic tasks, the dressing of free women, the marketing and preparation of food, the care of garmenture, the singing of songs to the lyre, and such, one even a specialist in the carving of meat to music, she had disposed of, one by one, in various markets, but she had retained Nika, who would have marketed for the fewest *darins*. A free woman, and certainly one of station, requires at least one slave, even in the throes of near destitution. We mentioned earlier that the Lady Publennia frequently beat Nika, and had speculated that that might have been because there was little else at hand on which to vent her anger and frustration. On the other hand, Nika's back and legs had not been immune from attention even in the Lady Publennia's more halcyon days. First, the Lady Publennia, as many free women, was a most impatient, demanding, and exacting Mistress. The slightest perceived imperfection in service, a supposed tardy response, a brief lapse of attention, a wrinkle in a garment, a disk of rouge out of place, slippers misaligned in a closet, a bath ill drawn, improperly heated, or wrongly perfumed, many such things, would earn a woman's serving slave the admonitory sting of her Mistress' switch. Too, as is well known, it is always easy to find reasons to strike a slave, even the most frightened, zealous, and desperate-to-please slave, if one wishes to do so. Perhaps the Mistress is not satisfied with the arrangement of flowers in a vase, perhaps she is not pleased with the view from her terrace on a cloudy day, perhaps she did not care for a party or theatrical event recently attended. But, second, in the case of Nika, there seems to have been an additional, and subtler, matter involved, something beyond the typical domestic hazards of a slave's trying to please a temperamental, impatient Mistress. On the streets, the Lady Publennia had noted that Nika was often noticed, even regarded, by free men. This attention, accorded a slave, had muchly displeased the Lady Publennia. They might admire herself, if they wished, but surely not Nika, a mere slave. How stupid are men! Can they not see that a free woman, in her robes and hauteur, in her noble dignity and arrogance, resplendent in the raiment of station, is a thousand times more beautiful than a helpless, needful, half-clad slave? And once she had caught Nika inadvertently, naturally enough, I suppose, apparently without thinking, returning the smile of a free man. How dared she? What a reflection on the dignity of her Mistress! This wantonness had cost the slave much. Did she not know that she was a woman's slave? Thereafter Nika often accompanied her switch-bearing Mistress on a leash, blindfolded, with her hands tied behind her. "She is naughty," the Lady Publennia had explained to one or another free woman encountered in the street. "I do not know what to do with her." "Switch her," was the usual suggestion. After all, this sort of situation was not wholly unprecedented amongst Mistresses and their serving slaves. "Excellent," the Lady Publennia would say, and then give the slave two or three swift strokes on the back of the thighs. But now, unbeknownst to the Lady Publennia, Nika was no longer in Lisle, on Inez IV, but on Tangara, and, even now, in the traces of a sled, drawing it for two men, Julian of the Aureliani, a minor naval officer but kin to the emperor, and Tuvo Ausonius, a former civil servant on Miton, and was approaching the camp.

The Lady Publennia again recalled the slave in the gambling palace. How she had scorned that simple tunic in which the slave had been garbed. And yet, clearly, she noted, it was far more ample, tasteful, discreet, and modest than that which she had been forced to don, a tavern tunic, fit for tavern slaves hurrying about in the half-lit, low-ceilinged rooms, serving their Master's customers, whose use, at the patron's discretion, might accompany, say, a second drink.

Who would bring her the dagger, that proposed, convenient article of assassination, with its slender, yellow, oval handle, and slim guard, and fine narrow blade, with its invisible coating, as unseen as air, as patient as acid?

She had seen it only once, in a small room late at night, in the imperial palace on Lisle.

Then it had been returned to its case.

It was well the implement had a guard. It would not do at all for the hand which would dare to wield such a thing to slip onto the blade, even to the tiniest break in the skin.

She doubted that he whom it might strike, or scratch, would suffer much, or long, perhaps no more than a moment, one of comprehension and misery, not that such matters would be of much concern to those who might mix and brew the coating. The important thing was that the matter would be quickly done, that there would be no time to search out an antidote, even to cry out, or summon help. This would allow the assassin the time to slip away and board the waiting hoverer.

She knew the blade need not be driven into the victim's body. It would be enough for it to touch the skin or be drawn across it, just enough to open the skin. Indeed, the blade was so sharp that, if things were lightly done, the victim might even be unaware, for a moment, that he was dying.

But she hated this Ottonius, for he had put her to a slave's work on the *Narcona*, she, of the patricians, and had silenced her with bands of tape, and tied her to the foot of his couch.

Perhaps she might drive the blade into his body to the hilt!

The blade's guard would permit this. It would protect her.

But she wondered what it might be, to be taken into the arms of such a man, to be held there, helplessly, crushed with the same passion, possessiveness, and indifference which might be accorded a slave.

She did not understand the likely repercussions and consequences of her task, but she gathered it was important.

It had to do with politics, and power, and perhaps even with the fate of an empire.

She knew the empire was eternal, but there were rumors, far off, of crumbling walls, of crossed borders, of lapsed, lost, or surrendered worlds, of transgressed spacelanes, of remote smithies in which alien ships, in their hundreds, were being built and fueled.

Who, or what, might stand against the darkness, like night, rising over far worlds?

What forces, what men, in a thousand effete worlds, devoted to luxury and pleasure, might be strong enough to stand against storms of hungry wolves, their eyes burning in the night, now prowling just beyond watch fires of civilization?

She knew her task.

That was enough.

Its implications were for others to assess.

We have little reason to suppose that she knew, or much cared, what might ride on the stroke of a tiny blade, and a drop of poison.

The empire was eternal.

At that moment, a gong sounded, and she rose to her feet, turned, and hurried to the kitchen.

It would not do to dally.

The brunette, the first girl, carried a switch.

CHAPTER TWO

"We are surely lost," said Tuvo Ausonius.

"No," said Julian, he of the Aureliani, kin even to the emperor.

"The snow has concealed the tracks of the tractor sleds, of the expedition trying to make contact with Captain Ottonius," said Tuvo.

"I am not now concerned with the tracks," said Julian. "In Venitzia, I determined the route of the expedition. The sky is unfamiliar, but I am using the appropriate star sighting."

"That is why we have moved primarily at night," said Ausonius, "after the snow."

"Yes," said Julian.

I gather from the manuscript that Tangara lacked a magnetic pole.

"How close is the forest?" said Tuvo.

"I do not know," said Julian. "I hope it is not far. There may be little time."

It may be recalled that Otto, now king of the Otungs, to the consternation of many, had left Venitzia alone to make contact with the Otungs, even though it was the Killing Time. This had been in direct contradiction to the clearly expressed, urgent wishes of Julian whose departure from Lisle had been delayed, quite possibly deliberately, that he wait in Venitzia before proceeding. Julian fully expected that he would do so. But he had left, alone. Before the arrival of Julian in Venitzia, an expedition had been hastily organized to follow and, presumably, support Otto, an expedition, as far as we know, nominally under the command of Phidias, captain of the *Narcona*. Julian, being apprised of these matters, once he had arrived in Venitzia, had set forth almost immediately with his aide, Tuvo Ausonius, and a slave, Nika, on the trail of the expedition. It was not a coincidence that the lovely young slave was in his party. Two strands of evidence had been intertwined in such a way as to excite the apprehension of Julian; on the quay at Lisle he had been troubled by an unusual group of slaves being prepared for shipment to Tangara. Surprisingly, none were branded. In particular, he was disturbed by one slave, whose behavior seemed anomalous for that of a slave. Furthermore, he had the sense that she was familiar. Could it be that he might have seen her somewhere before, perhaps in a plaza, a theater, a market, perhaps at an entertainment, a reception, or ball? Curious he had made inquiries and found that the slave's supposed background and antecedents were spurious. He had then had, from memory, a drawing, colored, prepared. A number of inquiries, conducted largely by Tuvo Ausonius, with the drawing in hand, at local slave houses, and slave-holding facilities, proved unilluminating. This drawing, however, was later interpreted by a number of free persons, particularly those of note and station in Lisle, as possibly being a likeness of the disreputable, notorious Lady Publennia Calasalia, putatively of the Larial Calasalii. The second strand of evidence was woven into the cord of suspicion when it was discovered that she was no longer in the city. Her personal slave, Nika, was seized, and, confused, took her captors for being those who, or enleagued with those who, had expressed an interest in her Mistress, presumably wishing to utilize her in some project or other. As a slave, or pretended slave, would be an unlikely spy, given her supervision and the restrictions on her movements, Julian had surmised her role, if role she had, would be something other than espionage. And who but a slave would be likely to be alone, wholly alone, with a Master, fondled and unsuspected, in the warmth and darkness of a night?

"Behind these rocks!" hissed Julian.

"Master?" said Nika.

"Silence," whispered Julian.

Tuvo Ausonius, aide to Julian, drew Nika by her harness, fastened to the sled, behind the rocky outcropping, the sled half turning in the snow. He then pushed her down, to her knees in the snow.

"They can follow the sled tracks," said Tuvo Ausonius.

"I do not think they have seen the tracks," said Julian. "I do not think they are aware of our presence."

"Bells," said Tuvo Ausonius.

"Sled bells," said Julian.

"Who would dare mount bells on a sled here, in this region?" asked Tuvo Ausonius.

"Those without fear, in what they take to be their own country," said Julian, "Heruls."

"Men?" said Tuvo.

"I think not," said Julian, "but manlike, a rational species, with the common symmetries, found on many worlds, a pairing of limbs, a pairing of certain organs, and such. They are aggressive and territorial. They are warlike and dangerous. They commonly kill male humans but capture and enslave human females, whom they enjoy or sell."

"Are they cross-fertile with them?" asked Tuvo.

"No," said Julian, "but that does not preclude pleasuring themselves with them, no more than certain humans, interestingly, derive pleasure from lower animals. They do occasionally keep a healthy, stalwart male slave, chained by the neck in a hut, to whom a number of selected female slaves, hooded, are brought for impregnation. The females are treated in such a manner, by means of a drug obtained in trade, that the offspring are invariably female. In this way more female slaves are obtained, most of whom will be sold as children to slave farms."

"I see," said Tuvo.

"Heruls differ from humans in a variety of ways," said Julian, "physiologically, and, certainly, culturally. For example, they are occasionally cannibalistic, and frequently, within their own group, kill the old and weak."

"The bells grow louder," said Tuvo, whispering.

"You hear the snorting of the horses, and the scratching of their claws in the hard snow, too," said Julian.

"Yes," said Tuvo.

In my editing of the manuscripts, I frequently speak of diverse animals in terms of a familiar nomenclature, for example, I might speak of horses, pigs, dogs, and such. I do the same here. I think this is easiest, on the whole, as the animals in question occupy similar ecological niches. I suppose I could, accordingly, also, call the Heruls men, but, on the whole, it seemed to me best not to do so. In such matters one craves the reader's patience, and indulgence.

"They are close," said Tuvo.

"I fear they are stopping," said Julian.

"They have seen us, or the tracks?" said Tuvo.

"I do not know," said Julian.

Nika, even in her furs, shuddered.

Julian unslung his rifle, as did Tuvo.

Great pains are taken by the empire to keep rifles, and other formidable weapons, out of the hands of such species as the Heruls, and such tribes and communities as the Otungs, the Wolfungs, and such.

"Look," whispered Julian, raising his head slowly, the smallest bit, above the rocks.

"They are stopped, yes," said Tuvo.

There was a small sound of harnessing, the tiny sound of a bell or two.

"They are removing the bells from the harness, from the sled," said Julian.

"Apparently they wish to approach their destination silently," said Tuvo.

"It seems so," said Julian.

"I thought you said they had no fear," said Tuvo.

"There are five horses," said Julian, "one to draw the sled, and four others. Consider the four riders and he who holds the reins of the sled horse, their helmets and furs. Heruls."

"One rides the sled, bundled in furs, who is different," said Tuvo.

"Not a Herul," said Julian.

"That is why they will now proceed silently," said Tuvo.

"I think so," said Julian. "Here, in the vicinity of the forest, its edge perhaps only hours away, I suspect the passenger is an Otung."

"One who chooses to return silently to his community," said Tuvo. "But why should an Otung, if he be such, be in the company of Heruls?"

"I do not know," said Julian.

"I cannot see him clearly," said Tuvo. "It is too dark."

"That is most unfortunate," said Julian.

Shortly thereafter the sled, silently now, sped on.

"We must resume our journey," said Julian.

"Nika is still," said Tuvo, looking down.

Julian bent down. "She is asleep," he said. "Let us unharness her, and put her on the sled. We two can draw it more swiftly."

"How can she fall asleep, with danger about?" asked Tuvo Ausonius.

"She is exhausted," said Julian. "Do not awaken her. She will do us little good in the traces. She has labored long and had little sleep."

Tuvo Ausonius regarded the slave.

"Many men," said Julian, "have fallen asleep even under fire."

"It seems a shame to have brought her here," said Tuvo.

"You have never seen the Lady Publennia Calasalia," said Julian. "If we should be separated, either by accident or design, she can identify the impostor we seek."

"There is the drawing," said Tuvo.

"It is only a drawing," said Julian.

"True," said Tuvo Ausonius.

"And," smiled Julian, grimly, "is it not appropriate to reunite a slave with her Mistress?"

"I do not think she would be pleased to see her, here, on Tangara," said Tuvo.

"Perhaps not," said Julian. "Help with the sled, we must press on. I fear there is little time. We may already be too late."

"Will you not again examine the night sky?" asked Tuvo Ausonius.

"No," said Julian, "I think we need only follow the tracks before us. I suspect they will lead us more readily to our destination than the night sky."

CHAPTER THREE

"You remember Filene?" asked Lysis, the supply officer of the *Narcona*, of the blond giant, Otto, at the table.

"Yes," said Otto, "from the *Narcona*."

"Stand straighter," said severe Ronisius, a minor officer of the vessel's commissioned officers.

"Forgive me, Master," said Filene, straightening her body. She carried a small, shallow tray of cakes.

She had been entered into the room later than the other three, for some reason. The meal was now nearly done.

"You were once a free woman, were you not, my dear?" inquired polite, blond Corelius, a handsome young officer, also, as Ronisius, one of the vessel's lesser commissioned officers.

"Yes," she whispered.

"'Yes, Master'," corrected Ronisius.

"Yes, Master, forgive me, Master," said the blonde, Filene.

She feared Ronisius.

She felt helpless, and slave before him.

What would it be if she were truly a slave?

"You are no longer a free woman, Filene," said Corelius, kindly. "So you may no longer be slovenly and clumsy. You may no longer be stiff and wooden. It is not permitted. You must be soft, feminine, inviting, attractive, ready, lovely, graceful. You are now no longer yours. You are now another's. You are owned."

"Yes, Master," she said.

"Note how Filene is painted," said Phidias, captain of the *Narcona*.

"I see," said Otto, "and scented, as well."

"We have arranged that she is prepared for you," said Phidias.

"My thanks, Captain," said Otto.

"Presumably it will be pleasant to pluck and crush that flower," said Ronisius.

Filene shuddered.

"She is new to the collar," said Lysis. "We hope that you will much improve her. Let her learn her bondage in your arms."

"There are others, of course," said Ronisius. "These three," he said, gesturing to the other slaves, "Lira, Faye, Rabbit, and there are sixteen others in the tents, whom you may inspect and have your pick, if you wish, any one, or two, or three."

Otto smiled at Ronisius. "I am sure this one will do," he said, nodding toward Filene.

"As you wish," said Ronisius, smiling.

Otto had arrived in the camp near dusk, from a hall of Otungs deep in the forest. He had had retainers with him who were now encamped nearby, in amongst the shadows of trees, not far from the wired perimeter of the rude imperial enclave. It had been deemed unwise to mix soldiers of the empire with Otungs, for fear of hasty words, even angry glances, which might lead to drawn blades and the flash of discharged weapons.

Otto was now in a long, silken dinner robe.

Slaves had sought to bathe him, hoping to touch such a man.

Yesterday night, however, it might well have been different. Yesterday night they might well have fled from a terrible figure which, gaunt and hungry, might have emerged from the darkness.

Yesterday night Otto had arrived at the great hall of the Otungs, that of the King Naming, half naked, stinking and bloody, the skins of dogs, Herul dogs, tied about his body. He had survived the "running of the dogs." He had had with him, however, the skin of a giant, white vi-cat, and a weighty long sword which few but such as he could wield. The skin of the vi-cat was that of a beast he had earlier killed, and the sword was that which he had carried toward the forest before his capture by Heruls. These were returned to him by the Herul, Hunlaki, who, by Herul means, utilizing a sensory organ foreign to humans, a form of touch, had recognized him as the Otung infant he had once, several years earlier, delivered to the brothers in the *festung* of Sim Giadini. When Otto, later, apprehended by Otungs in the forest, was brought to the great hall, it was the "Killing Time," and the time of the King Naming, a yearly ritual imposed on Otungs, disunited and bickering amongst themselves, by Heruls, issuing in the naming of a temporary king, a political device well calculated to subjugate and demoralize an enemy. Long ago, it seems, on the plains of Barrionuevo, or the flats of Tung, as the Heruls will have it, the Otungs had been defeated by Herul horsemen, and driven into the forest, to be thenceforth a scattered, jealous, divided people. Then he, Otto, a stranger, but bearing the pelt of the giant, white vi-cat, traditionally taken as a mantle of kingship by the Otungs, had come to the great hall and claimed the hero's portion of the mighty, roasting boar. In the hall much blood was shed but before the fire in the long pit had turned to ashes a new king, one defiant to Heruls, one who would be subject to no limitations imposed by enemies, was lifted on the shields.

"You may serve the cakes, Filene," said Phidias.

"Yes, Master," she said.

"To our guest, first," said Ronisius.

"Yes, Master," she said.

"She is stupid," said Ronisius.

"No," said Corelius, "merely ignorant."

"But pretty," said Lysis.

"Like the others," said Phidias.

"They are lovely things, slaves," said Lysis.

"True," said Corelius.

Earlier in the evening Otto, or Ottonius, as those of the empire will often have it, had arrived at the encampment, with several retainers. He had arrived, of course, not then in the skins of Herul dogs but in other skins, and boots, and leg-wrappings, soft, and well-tanned, from the hide of the *hroth*, a beast indigenous to the forests of northern Tangara, and resembling the *arn* bear, often encountered in beast fights, in imperial arenas. Now, however, as noted, he was in a dinner robe.

The serving had proceeded apace, with dessert wines, followed by steaming *feldis*.

Otto removed a cake from the Filene's tray without glancing at her. A slave is an instrument whose presence need not be noticed.

She would presumably be sent later to his quarters, doubtless to await him, naked, in the furs of his couch.

"I am surprised at the garmenture of the slaves," said Otto.

"They are slaves," said Ronisius, which seemed, one supposes, an adequate explanation for the matter in question.

"How is it, Captain, that you are surprised?" asked Lysis.

"This is an imperial camp, even though in the wilderness," said Otto. "I would have expected serving gowns, as at the captain's suppers on the *Narcona*."

"Do you object?" asked Phidias, captain of the *Narcona*.

"Certainly not," said Otto. "I was merely curious, as to why the difference."

"No free women are present," said Lysis.

"Nor were they on the *Narcona*," said the barbarian.

"True," acknowledged Lysis.

"The tunics," said Otto.

"They are tavern tunics," said Lysis.

Tavern tunics are designed to display the charms of a slave and arouse the passions of men.

"Yes, or such," said Otto.

There are many varieties of slave tunics, of course. Some are reasonably discreet, such as those often imposed on women's serving slaves, those suitable for doing a marketing and running errands, those likely to be worn, if not gowns, in mixed company, and such. Others are less discreet, of which there are many varieties, one such variety being the sort commonly referred to as a tavern tunic, which sort of tunic, of course, is not restricted to taverns, brothels, and such. Tavern tunics are usually of plain, cheap material, usually *hevis* or cotton; they are seldom of silk, *corton*, or *leel*. Some tunics are "work tunics," "house tunics," and such, for slaves who are permitted clothing indoors. Different sorts of tunics tend to be favored on various worlds. And, naturally, there are many forms of slave garments which are not tunics, at all, such as the long, scarf-like *keb*.

"I fear that Captain Ottonius may have taken offense," said Corelius.

"How so?" said Phidias, concerned.

"He may resent, if not the garmenture of the slaves, the fact that it has been arranged so tonight, perhaps suspecting that he is being patronized, being confronted with a condescending concession to the simple tastes and rude manners so often ascribed to individuals of his origin."

"And what are your origins?" inquired Lysis.

"I do not know my origins," said Otto. "In the imperial records, I would be regarded as of the low *humiliori*, even of the peasants. I was raised in a small village, at the foot of the pass leading to the *festung* of Sim Giadini, on the heights bordering the plains of Barrionuevo. I departed from Tangara. You need not know why. On Terennia, a prisoner, condemned, I was consigned to the gladiatorial school of the landowner, Pulendius. I fought many times. I won my freedom. I became one of the bodyguards of Pulendius. Later, I came to the chieftainship of

the Wolfungs, on Varna, and yesterday night, here, I was lifted
on the shields of the Otungs."

"King?" said Phidias.

"Yes," said Otto.

"The Otungs are understood as barbarians," said Lysis.

"Surely, as you see them," said Otto.

"You, too, then," said Phidias, "as their leader, their chieftain, or king, would be understood as a barbarian."

"Yes," said Otto.

"I trust you take no offense," said Phidias.

"No more, I hope," said Otto, "than you, when I regard you
as citizens of the empire."

"Citizenship has been granted to almost everyone in the
empire now," said Lysis. "One need only be born."

It might be noted that at one time citizenship, with its privileges and benefits, except for those of the original, inner worlds,
had to be earned, commonly by ten to twenty years of military
service. When citizenship became free, so to speak, it ceased to
be respected and prized. Recruitments in the military declined
sharply, this imperiling borders and worlds. Alternative avenues
to citizenship, too, particularly those involving danger or hard-
ship, such as laboring in the civil bureaucracy in remote venues, were also less frequented. In the meantime, migrations of
new citizens, of various species, many dispossessed by large-
scale economic transitions, in particular, the formation of the
great industrial farms manned by slaves, flooded toward major
population centers to claim the entitlements of citizenship, such
as free food, shelter, clothing, and access to massive entertainments, spectacles and pageants, beast races, arena sports, and
such, these wisely provided to distract and pacify idle, restless,
dangerous crowds. In the meantime the wealth of the empire,
drained from better than a thousand outer worlds, accumulated
in the coffers of a smaller and smaller number of individuals,
on fewer and fewer worlds, producing a discrepancy between

abundance, even luxury, on certain worlds and a desert of scarcity on others. These political and social developments, on various worlds, were exacerbated by the widespread exhaustion of
the soil, the diminution of precious and base metals, and the
crumbling of infrastructure, such as roads, bridges, aqueducts,
and sewerage systems. Predictably, portions of several worlds
were afflicted by both famine and disease. In some areas nature
reclaimed deserted cities, and dry canals, with inert locks,
were filled with wind-blown sand and dust. Dangerous animals
prowled in the ruins of towns. There was also, on many worlds,
the collapse of a viable tax base, which seems to have been the
primary motivation for the imperial binding laws, attempting to
hold peasants to the soil, sons to the crafts of their fathers, and
such. On many worlds currency was now almost unknown, and
exchange was largely in terms of barter. On other worlds the currency was multiplied and debased to the point that it was substantially worthless. On some worlds it was a capital offense not
to accept printed paper or stamped wooden blocks for goods. On
another world where a *darin* might once have purchased a thousand arrow points it was now cheaper to melt the *darin* itself and
pour the bright, coarse metal into the appropriate mold. In the
meantime, on many worlds, the high *honestori*, and, in particular, the patrician classes, once the mind, shield, fiber, heart, and
sword of the empire, now wealthy, indulgent, and degenerate,
were failing to reproduce themselves. "No children are born in
golden beds," had become a saying on several worlds.

"In any event," said Phidias, captain of the freighter, *Narcona*, "the garmenture was thought appropriate, not because of
your origins, which may be other than ours, or because your
tastes might be other than ours, if they are, but because there are
men and women and we, as you, are men."

"Good," said Otto.

"I am not satisfied," said Corelius. "It is as though we invited
him to supper and served not the delectable *Safian* wine he

expected, and had reason to expect, but a rude bowl of Terennian field beer."

"Surely not," said Phidias.

"Be at ease," said Otto. "I am not offended by the garmenture. I relish it. Indeed, if it were prescribed on my account, I am appreciative. I would take it as a token of thoughtfulness, not as an insult, irony, or mockery, but as a credit to the sensitivity of a generous, attentive host."

"It improves the appetite of all," said Ronisius.

"Doubtless," said Lysis, the supply officer.

Filene's body stiffened, in anger. She hoped no one had noticed. She feared Ronisius had noticed.

"It is true," said Otto, "that I am a man of simple tastes and, I suppose, uncouth manners."

"You are esteemed, Captain Ottonius," Phidias assured him.

"On a thousand worlds," said Ronisius, "the empire needs allies."

"These slaves," said Phidias, "there are twenty of them in the camp, are a picked lot."

"They are imperial slaves, obviously," said Lysis.

"That makes no difference," said Otto. "Imperial slaves, as other slaves, are women. There are slaves who are more expensive and less expensive, more beautiful and less beautiful, better slaves and worse slaves. But that is all. There is little difference between a tavern tunic and a fistful of expensive slave silk. What matters is the slave herself."

"True," said Phidias.

"Imperial slaves," said Otto, "as other slaves, are women, and I enjoy seeing them so presented, imperial slaves, in this way, no different from the lowest of slaves on a thousand worlds."

"But these slaves are quite good, quite attractive, do you not agree?" asked Phidias.

"Certainly," said Otto.

"They are high slaves," said Lysis.

"I thought they were trade goods," said Otto.

"But excellent trade goods," said Phidias.

"Surely," said Otto.

"And none, not one of the twenty, is marked," said Lysis.

"Interesting," said Otto, glancing at Ronisius.

"Yes," said Ronisius.

"All slaves should be marked," said Otto.

"Surely you would not wish such fair skins to be marked," said Corelius.

"The brand," said Otto, "enhances a woman's beauty a thousand times. It puts the slave mark on her. One then sees her as slave, and she knows herself as slave. How could she be more exciting, or more meaningful, or more beautiful, than as marked slave?"

"Barbarian!" said Corelius.

"Quite," said Otto.

"Please, Corelius," protested Phidias, captain of the *Narcona*.

"Filene understands that she is to be soon sent to the couch of Captain Ottonius," said Ronisius. "But one supposes we could heat an iron and have her marked first."

"Do not drop the tray, Filene," snapped Ronisius.

"I do not think there is time, Master," said Filene.

"Were you given permission to speak?" asked Ronisius.

"No, Master, forgive me, Master," she said.

"It seems," said Ronisius to Otto, "that this slave, perhaps in several respects, is in need of instruction."

"Perhaps," said Otto.

"I will have a whip sent to your quarters," said Ronisius.

"Excellent," said Otto.

"You are a barbarian, indeed," said Corelius.

"Yes," said Otto.

"Esteemed ally," said Phidias, "I beg you to take no umbrage at the remark or tone of my junior officer."

"None is taken," Otto assured him.

"I trust," said Corelius, "you can tell the difference between *Safian* wine and beer."

"I believe so," said Otto.

"These slaves," said he, "are *Safian* wine, not beer."

"Beware, Corelius," said Phidias.

"But," said Otto, "they are in tavern tunics."

Corelius looked away, angrily.

"I grant they are *Safian* wine," said Otto, "but is not *Safian* wine especially interesting and enjoyable when it finds itself served in the way of beer?"

Filene clutched the tray. She would not dash it to the floor of the tent. She must not reveal her imposture. She must cleave to her role. Who would bring her the knife?

"Perhaps," said Corelius.

"A tincture of humiliation," said Otto, "a helplessness, even a tear of frustration, can make a slave oil more readily. A touch here, a touch there, and then, later, when one wishes, if one wishes, one may, perhaps gagging her first, command forth her surrender spasms."

"You are a barbarian, indeed," said Corelius. "Perhaps, apart from considerations of serving gowns, and such, we should not have bothered with the mockery of a tunic. Perhaps we should simply strip them."

"That will not be necessary," said Otto, glancing at Filene.

She stiffened, stripped by his glance.

"Whatever you might wish," said Phidias.

The slaves exchanged glances.

"That, of course, dear friend, whose name, I take it, is Corelius," said Otto, "is how women of the empire, even high women, often serve the feasts of their barbarian Masters."

"Shameful!" said Corelius.

"Not at all, it is delectable," said Otto. "Surely you do not mean to tell me that you would not like seeing these slaves, here, serve our supper naked?"

Corelius looked down, reddening, angrily.

"I see you would," said Otto.

"The free women of the empire are not slaves," said Corelius.

"You would be surprised," said Otto. "They make excellent slaves. And what is the purpose of a free woman's clothing, even the richest, finest, and most abundant, but to conceal a slave? And many of your noble free women, their trappings removed, I assure you, would do well on an auction block."

"I see," said Corelius.

"Surely," said Otto, "you would enjoy seeing some of your exalted free women, and their spoiled, curvaceous brats, if they have them, stripped and put to work, marked and collared, laboring fearfully, subject to the whip."

"Captain Phidias," said Corelius. "I beg to be excused."

"And I assure you," said Otto, "they leap well, crying out, as other slaves, in the arms of their Masters."

"You may withdraw," said Phidias to Corelius, and Corelius, rising, with a curt nod to those at the table, including Otto, took his leave.

Ahh, thought Filene to herself, it is Corelius who will bring the knife! How well he has managed matters, pretending to resent the barbarian's remarks, Corelius, who now withdraws, seemingly disconcerted, thereby winning the interval, unsuspected, necessary to fetch the knife. How natural and appropriate everything seemed now, and clear, his consideration for her on the *Narcona*, his concern, his politeness, and such! Too, as a gallant and refined gentleman of the empire, so different from harsh, blunt Ronisius, he had, courageously, and brazenly, dared to let be known his disapproval of the person and views of the barbarian, and his sort. Captain Phidias would surely be too highly placed and conspicuous to perform so sensitive and covert a task as supplying an assassin's tool. The purport of his seemingly anomalous presence in the camp was now obvious. Only one of his rank would be empowered to conduct subtle negotiations having to do with the recruitment of barbarian *comitates*. Ronisius could be discounted, as he had, in his ignorance, known no better than to treat her as merely another slave. She did fear him. Why does he look at me in that fashion, she had once asked Faye. Tremble, my dear, had said Faye, he is considering your price. How ignorant he was! He had even been so ignorant as to speak of her, the Lady Publennia Calasalia, of the Larial Calasalii, or once so, in relation to a slaving iron, she, the agent of Iaachus, Arbiter of Protocol in the court of the emperor, Aesilesius! And Qualius, in his gross ugliness, and simplicity, a tender of livestock on the *Narcona*, had not even been at the supper. Let him swill with other pigs, she thought. There was another, of course, Lysis, the supply officer of the *Narcona*, but he, she thought, might, like the captain, Phidias, be too highly ranked, too conspicuous, for the errand in question. A lesser fellow, less likely to be noticed and observed, would be a courier better suited to transport and deliver that small artifact on whose action so much might hang. Too, Lysis did not leave the table. He had not seized an opportunity, as had Corelius, in which one might place that small, light artifact in the quarters of the barbarian, in such a place that she would find it, and he would not. Where would that be, she wondered. Presumably it could not be simply handed to her. And how would it be concealed if she were naked, or even tunicked? A tiny, brief, form-clinging tunic affords little concealment for even so slight and modest an object. Too, what if it should crease her skin as she moved, and it prove not her means to victory, power, wealth, and station, but her doom? Of course, she thought, it would be beneath the furs, where she, invitingly curled in repose, would be awaiting him!

But would Corelius have time to place the dagger, she wondered.

Surely this supper is at its end, she thought.

Be swift, Corelius.

I trust that all is in order.

Had Corelius had time to place the dagger?

Was it done?

Outside the tent she heard the whirr of a hoverer's engines, one of two light, circular craft, air sleds or air vessels, in the camp, and then the sound, too, came from its matching vessel.

"You warm your hoverers," said the barbarian.

"Against the cold," said Phidias.

"An excellent precaution," said the barbarian.

"Our treaded conveyances," said Phidias, "will be similarly warmed.

"I hear the ignitions," said Ronisius.

"It takes but a few moments," said Lysis.

"Excellent," said the barbarian. "Thus all may be activated without delay."

"Heruls may be about," said Phidias.

"This close to the forest?" asked Otto.

"Possibly," said Phidias.

On the approach to the camp, in addition to the several horse-drawn sleds, and the hoverers, there had been two armored, treaded vehicles. Corelius had piloted one of the hoverers, Ronisius the other. Lysis had driven the first armored vehicle, and Qualius the other, which had brought up the rear of the column. Phidias, captain of the *Narcona*, had ridden in the first of the two armored vehicles.

"More *feldis*," said the barbarian to Lira, holding forth his cup.

"Yes, Master," responded Lira.

"I, as well," said Ronisius.

"Yes, Master," said Lira, then carrying the two-handled, silver vessel to his place

Shortly thereafter all four engines were shut down, those of the hoverers and those of the two armored vehicles.

They are now prepared, they are ready for departure, thought Filene, in the background, with her tray of cakes. All is in order, all proceeds apace.

She looked, anxiously, to Phidias, to Lysis.

Were they party to the evening's projected deed?

"You are excused, Filene," said Phidias.

"Yes, Master," she said. "Thank you, Master."

"Proceed to the quarters of Captain Ottonius, and await him, naked, in the furs."

How humiliating, she thought. I am a free woman!

"Yes, Master," she said.

It seemed the knife then, as she had thought, would be concealed in the furs.

She handed her tray to Rabbit.

The barbarian would not know, of course, that this was the first of the night camps in which the hoverers and treaded vehicles had been so warmed.

They will be ready, she thought.

A departure is anticipated. All, indeed, proceeds apace.

The knife, by now, must have been placed.

As she exited, her wrist was seized by Ronisius.

"Master?" she said, stopped, startled.

"Our guest is to be well pleased," he said.

"Yes, Master," she said, catching her breath, relieved.

"If he is not well pleased," said Ronisius, "you will muchly regret your failure in the morning."

"I will do my best," she said.

"I trust that will be sufficient," he said.

"Yes, Master," she said.

"Do well," he said.

"Yes, Master," she said.

She then hurried from the room.

She was determined to do well, indeed.

CHAPTER FOUR

For those who live on full, generous worlds, worlds of plenty, worlds of blue water and black soil, it is difficult to conceive of want, save in limited ways, as in, say, an exhaustion of *vessite* or copper, or the extinction of a given food animal. And if one world is exhausted, its oceans gone, its soil barren, its star a cinder, one might, with an appropriate means, discover, colonize, and plunder another world, just as one who ruins one farm might move to another, and another. But even light takes time to plow its passage amongst stars, and there may be but a limited number of thresholds, and passes, in the mountains of space. It is recognized that, for a given civilization, housing massive, covetous populations, exploiting even ten thousand worlds, or millions of worlds, for a million or more years, nonrenewable resources, however abundant, will prove finite. That had come about in the empire, producing paradoxical discrepancies betwixt worlds, worlds which clung to a remnant of sophistication, refinement, technology, and power, and worlds which had relapsed into primitive savagery. There were worlds on which the sight of an airship, even a simple hoverer, would excite storms of disbelief and superstition, and worlds on which starships routinely departed from spaceports. On some worlds there existed power which could split planets and explode stars, while, on others, creatures of diverse species would do war with stones and sharpened sticks. And on many worlds the mixes of technology and simplicity, of machines and horses, of civilization and barbarism, existed side by side. Venitzia, on Tangara, the provincial capital, for example, had its electronic defenses and its occasional visitations by imperial ships, with their shuttles, or lighters, descending to the surface, while outside the perimeter Heruls rode, with their slender lances, and Otungs hunted in dark forests. Accountings in the empire had become erratic. Many worlds, marginal and now isolated, continuing to regard themselves as members of the empire, had faded, unbeknownst to themselves, from the records of the imperial administration. Others, rebel worlds, had declared their independence from the empire, several unnoticed by the empire. Over the past ten thousand imperial years, years measured in terms of Telnaria's orbital periods, borders had contracted. Yet, in many of the inner worlds, life went on much as usual. Frivolous gayety reigned in palaces, mansions, and villas, while, sometimes but streets away, brutes and savages prowled amongst tenements and hovels, claiming domains, ruling their tiny kingdoms of hunger, fear, want, and scarcity. On some worlds, a single Telnarian rifle drew the distinction between king and criminal, between rogue and hero, between tyrant and rightful lord, between noble and base. A dozen women might be exchanged for a handful of charges or cartridges. There is little doubt that, at the time of our story, and doubtless for many years earlier, for such things take time, there had existed, amongst many worlds, fear of, distrust of, and surely resentment of, the empire. For example, consider taxation. It is natural to resent taxes, which deprive one of a portion, considerable or not, of the fruits of one's labor, and particularly natural to resent them if one sees little personal benefit consequent upon their exaction, and if they seem to be imposed by a remote, almost anonymous, almost faceless authority, an authority one suspects of corruption and exploitation. In such a situation a spark of disgruntlement, perhaps occasioned by a fresh law, a new confiscation, an unpopular bureaucratic ruling, can ignite a torch of hate which can, in turn, set a continent or planet ablaze. In such a situation there are always beasts who can recognize, encourage, feed upon, and utilize discontent. Masses, ignorant and weighty, properly stimulated and guided, constitute a mighty force. Powerful indeed is he who, by means of golden promises, holds the reins of the masses.

We have noted, earlier, in reporting the observation of Lysis, supply officer of the *Narcona*, the current pervasiveness of citizenship in the empire. No longer was it prized; no longer, for most, needed it be sought, and obtained, if at all, only by a considerable expenditure of time and effort; now, freely bestowed, it had become meaningless; it had become worthless. The relevance of this sociological development would become obvious. The vast, seething, restless populations of the empire, without identification, without allegiance, like cattle, might be herded with impunity. Once men would die for the empire; now they lived for nothing. Once the empire was the sun of their day and the star of their night; its standards and anthems were now neglected or forgotten; the temples of former gods were unfrequented; altars crumbled; weeds intruded into sacred groves; holy springs ran dry. Coin ruled in precincts where patriotism and love had once held sway. Man, in a great and impersonal world, now deemed himself small, alone, and lost.

It may help to understand certain impending developments if one contrasts the restless populations of unhappy worlds, hitherto referred to, strangers to one another, united by little but a nominal citizenship in a vast, scarcely understood hierarchy of power, with a quite different societal arrangement, that of tribality. Those referred to by the civilized as "barbarians" tended, almost universally, to belong to sociological groups which might be, for lack of a better word, called tribes. This is what men were, a Drisriak, an Otung, or such. In the earlier days of the empire these tribes had been robbed of worlds; where they had resisted, they had been, in large part, exterminated, or banished and relocated, permitted to live here and there on the peripheries of civilization, perhaps to supply raw materials to the civilized worlds, such as produce, timber, hides, fur, and animals for arena sports. Indeed, some of these individuals were recruited for the games themselves, or for bodyguards to men who could afford them. While the men of the empire tended to grow weak and soft, the barbarians, in their isolation, in their harsh climes and dangerous wildernesses, continued to wax hard and strong. In times, some of these tribes were recruited as *federates* and permitted to settle within the empire, largely to supply soldiers for the imperial military. In this fashion, several of these tribes, and collections of tribes, gained a foothold within the empire itself, and access to the training and discipline formerly reserved to regulars in the Telnarian armed forces. It was rather as though one might invite vi-cats or *arn* bears into one's home, that they might serve as guard beasts.

One looks into the night sky.

The passage of light, as is well known, is very swift, but its velocity, as is also well known, is finite.

One sees, in many instances, the consequence of a journey begun thousands of years ago.

The star, even the galaxy, may no longer exist.

Several of the passes, and the thresholds, in space have been charted. Some are guarded by imperial forces.

What if a pass should be breached, a threshold forced and its garrison overcome?

It is not impossible that strange ships might ply such a river.

But there may be other geodesics in the gravitational mountains of space, as well, and even, as in the case of the passes, and the thresholds, other passes, other thresholds, undisclosed gaps, crevices, in space.

Might not such things be scouted? Might not probe vessels seek them out? Might not some small ship, poised, look upon such a sea, and some account of its adventure, later, be heard in some tavern, or hall?

It must be understood that borders shift, expanding and contracting, and may be crossed. Certainly several worlds, at the periphery of the empire, and not always at the periphery, have known raids. And some of these worlds, we fear, have been settled by invaders, who have mixed with the indigenous population, absorbing their culture, industry, and technology. Some such worlds remain, officially, imperial worlds. Other worlds, it is rumored, in order to escape the burdens of the empire, surrendered to the fleets of armed, barbarian kings, exchanging one lord for another. Yet other worlds, to further consolidate the fruits of their own rebellions, supplied barbarians with training, ships, and weaponry, that they might discomfit the empire.

And so we have a beleaguered empire, with far-flung, brittle walls, defended by a diminishing military, with ever-diminishing resources, and a soft, vulnerable center, the inner worlds, muchly defenseless if those far walls should be breached, and foreign ships should pour through, darkening the sky.

At the edges of the empire wolves prowled, their fierce, gleaming eyes alit with hatred, envy, and greed.

One of these wolves we have met before, Abrogastes, the Far-Grasper, lord of the Drisriaks.

CHAPTER FIVE

It was warm, and soft, lying within the furs on the great couch.

Filene's heart was beating rapidly.

With delicate care, and circumspection, she had felt beneath the covers for the implement. Her fingers, ever so lightly, had touched the smooth, yellow, oval handle, locating it. It would not do to touch the blade, lest the tiniest bit of its transparent coating, invisibly painted on that razor-sharp edge, might open her skin, even slightly. She had found it muchly where she had anticipated it might lie, beneath the furs, toward the head of the couch, where it might be convenient to her right hand.

Even during the supper, she had heard the warming of the motors of the two hoverers and the two treaded, armored, motorized vehicles. She doubted that more than one hoverer would be utilized in her escape, extracting her from the camp, hurrying her through the cold, clouded night to Venitzia, where she would be taken aboard the lighter, and carried to the *Narcona*, in orbit, to be returned to Lisle, to wealth, dignity, honor, and power. The other three devices, or, at least, the two motorized vehicles, would have been warmed merely that the barbarian, who seemed a clever, cunning fellow, might not note the peculiarity of but one, or two, of the devices being readied for departure. She recalled that Corelius, who had doubtless placed the knife, had piloted one of the hoverers. That, most

likely, would be utilized in her escape. It now seemed clear
to her, as well, that Phidias, captain of the *Narcona*, must be
privy to the plot. Otherwise, one of a comparable, or higher,
rank, and one with similar skills, would have to be involved,
one whom the staff and crew of the freighter would accept,
and obey, a second in command possibly, or a hitherto obscure
figure, who would then disclose his credentials and take command. That was possible, surely, but unlikely. Phidias must be
one of us, she thought, as Corelius, and perhaps others.

"Hold, Cornhair," had said Nissimi, the brunette first-girl,
intercepting Filene on her way to the barbarian's quarters.

"Mistress?" had said Filene, apprehensive, immediately
kneeling, having been addressed by her superior.

"You are on your way to the bed chamber of Master Ottonius, are you not?" asked Nissimi.

"Yes, Mistress," said Filene.

"You are rather heavily garmented, are you not?" asked
Nissimi.

"Mistress?" said Filene.

"Get it off," snapped Nissimi.

Filene slipped the tavern tunic over her head, and handed it
to Nissimi. She felt Nissimi's switch under her chin, lifting her
head.

"Hold still, straighten your back, hands palms down on your
thighs," said Nissimi, who then, slowly, walked about Filene,
and then stood again before her.

"You are a pretty thing," said Nissimi. "Men will like you.
You might go for as much as fifteen or twenty *darins*."

Filene gasped, furious.

To be sure, given the chaotic economies of the worlds, even
several of the inner worlds, the value of a *darin* was problematical, ranging from less than its metal value on many worlds to the
equivalent, or better, of a workman's daily wage on others. We
may suppose that on the worlds with which Nissimi was likely

to be familiar fifteen to twenty *darins* was a plausible price for a comely slave. The rhythms of markets, of course, also fluctuate, as would be expected, even with a stable currency, given the time of year, and the exigencies of supply and demand. As a consequence, independent of market conditions, it is idle to speculate on what a given slave might bring on the block, as is the case, obviously, with other forms of merchandise, as well. Other factors may also exert their influence, such as the prestige of the vending house, the care and quality with which a given sale is organized, advertised, and conducted, the skills of the auctioneer, some of whom command high salaries or commissions, and so on.

"Why did you not seek me out, to be inspected?" asked Nissimi.

"I did not know it was necessary," said Filene, acidly.

"It is not," said Nissimi. "But one would have supposed that a new girl, perhaps timid, fearful, hesitant, and uncertain, might have wished to solicit the views of her first girl."

"I may be new," said Filene, "but I assure you that I am not timid, fearful, hesitant, or uncertain."

"You are fearful, Cornhair," said Nissimi. "It is easy to see. You are upset. You are afraid of something."

"I do not wish to be late, to report to Master Ottonius," Filene had said.

"Many slaves," said Nissimi, "would be frightened to be sent to the furs of a barbarian. He is not of the empire. He is different. You were of the empire. Perhaps he will beat you, or break an arm."

"I am not afraid," said Filene, and felt a bit of blood at her lip, where she had inadvertently closed her small, fine white teeth on that soft tissue.

"You are a virgin!" laughed Nissimi. She had had, of course, no access to the blonde's slave papers.

Filene looked away, angrily.

"I wondered about that," said Nissimi. Virgin slaves, of course, are quite rare.

"It improves my price," said Filene, petulantly.

"I doubt that it did," said Nissimi. "The virginity of a slave is of no more interest than that of a pig."

"I see," said Filene.

"You expect him to be considerate on that score, to be understanding, sensitive, patient, kind?"

"That would be my hope," said Filene.

"He is a barbarian," said Nissimi.

"I see," said Filene. If all went well, of course, she would carry her virginity to the *Narcona*, and to Inez IV itself.

"It seems Mistress lay in wait for me," said Filene.

"I am unwilling to send an unkempt, unprepared slave to the quarters of a guest," she said.

"Of course," said Filene. "Do I pass Mistress' inspection?"

"Your attitude," she said, "is less that of a slave than that a free woman."

"I was free," said Filene.

"So were most slaves," she said. "Few slaves are the issue of the breeding houses, the produce of the slave farms, and such. Why spend years breeding and raising slaves when one can pick them up, and ones quite as good, or even better, on the streets?"

"But seldom legally," said Filene.

"Many men," said Nissimi, "believe that all women are bred slaves, the product of lengthy natural selections on thousands of worlds."

"Men are beasts," said Filene.

"And our Masters," said Nissimi.

"No man is my Master!" said Filene.

"True," said Nissimi, "your Master is the empire."

Filene wondered what it might be, to have a Master, to belong to a given man, to be his owned animal. This thought disturbed her, and made her muchly uneasy, that for no reason she clearly understood.

Filene struggled to recover herself. She should not have cried out, certainly not in such an exasperated manner. She must recall her role. She must do nothing which might jeopardize her business, her evening's dark work.

"Alas," said Filene, putting down her head. "I am only a poor, and miserable, slave."

"I have heard," said Nissimi, "that on some worlds subtle and pervasive conditioning regimes exist, the products of social engineering, emplaced to extract the Master from the hearts of men."

"I have heard so," said Filene.

"I trust I will never be on such a world," said Nissimi, "one so unnatural and pathological."

Certainly Inez IV and Tangara were not such worlds.

"Such worlds exist," said Filene.

"I think so," said Nissimi, "Same Worlds, and such worlds, where men are taught to resent and repudiate the Master in their hearts. They are taught to fear the Master in their hearts. They are taught to betray him. They are taught, even, incredibly enough, to be ashamed of the Master in their hearts. It is demanded that they deny him, that they do treason to their blood. If vi-cats, lions, the *hroth*, and such were rational, doubtless we could also divide them from themselves, and ruin them with self-doubts, self-conflicts, and shame, stunting their minds and shortening their lives. The lion who pretends to be a lamb is a hypocrite; the lion who tries to be a lamb is a fool; the lion who thinks he is a lamb is insane."

Filene was silent.

I am a free woman, she said to herself.

"You are to please the barbarian well," said Nissimi. "If he is not pleased, and well pleased, you may expect to be punished."

"I understand," said Filene. "Do I pass Mistress' inspection?"

"You have the appearance of doing so," said Nissimi.

"Then," said Filene, "that is all that is required."

"What a naive little fool you are," said Nissimi.

"May I proceed?" asked Filene. "May I be on my way?"

"Yes," had said Nissimi.

"I will hope to do well," had said Filene, rising.

"And I," had said Nissimi, "have a hope, as well, that you will survive."

It was with trepidation, indeed, that Filene entered the tent chamber of the barbarian, reached by means of closed, warmed tunnels from the main tent. It had, she noted, an opening, twice sealed, as she determined, to the outside, as well. That she did not doubt was to facilitate her withdrawal from the chamber, without again traversing the passages she had followed to reach the chamber. Corelius, or a confederate, she supposed, would be stationed outside that opening, to spirit her quickly to the waiting, warmed hoverer. She could grasp a fur about her, and make her way, barefoot, through the snow, the few yards to one of the hoverers. Then, wrapped in a fur, she would be on her way through the winter night, over the dark, leafless treetops, to Venitzia.

At that point, she had no more than conjectured the likely location of the knife.

Her heart was beating rapidly, and she fought to breathe normally.

Was she, upon reflection, she wondered, the appropriate instrument of Iaachus, to accomplish this act?

She must rely on his judgment, his astuteness and cunning.

The barbarian, aware to some extent of the weight and danger of imperial matters, the hazards of intrigues, the possibilities of plots, the menaces likely to be found in the corridors of power, might well be on his guard against a male of the empire, or, perhaps, even another barbarian, particularly if not of his own tribe.

Surely a man would be better suited to this business, thought Filene to herself. Why not Corelius, Lysis, or another?

Could not a man, with one blow, sink even a long, broad blade to the hilt in a back or chest?

She was not sure she could drive even so slim and fine a blade to the hilt in a man's body, not that it would be necessary.

The slightest scratch would suffice.

But Iaachus would know best.

Who could bring himself to suspect a naked, unarmed slave girl, introduced so naturally, as a furnished pleasure, a gesture of hospitality, into a guest's bed chamber?

Too, perhaps Corelius, Lysis, Phidias, and such, if all were fellow conspirators in this business, must avoid, to the extent possible, being implicated in the matter. Indeed, her pilot to Venitzia might not even be one of them. Another, a lesser fellow, would do, assigned to deliver her to Venitzia. In that way, Phidias, Corelius, and others, might pretend to dismay and consternation when, in the morning, the results of her work would be discovered. She could even be secreted on the *Narcona*, awaiting their return to the ship. She did not know how matters might proceed. She knew only her own part, what she must do. Perhaps all conspirators might flee the camp, disabling other vehicles, abandoning their fellows to Heruls or vengeful Otungs.

She regarded the couch; it was broad, and deeply furred. Two furs, as well, were scattered on the floor, at its foot. Could the knife be hidden there? Surely not. It must reside beneath the furs on the surface of the couch, where the barbarian would doubtless expect to make use of her. Was she not extraordinarily beautiful? She was not the sort of slave, surely, who would be used merely at the foot of a couch, on furs strewn on the floor, as might be a common girl, one not allowed the privilege of a couch's surface. She did note, uneasily, a heavy metal ring fixed in the base of the couch, some six inches above the floor. It was a slave ring, a common convenience in a slave culture, the sort to which a girl might be fastened. That might not do at all.

But, was the knife there?

She scurried to the furs at the foot of the couch and then, kneeling, looking about, fearing the barbarian might appear any moment, lifted and shook the furs. No knife was there!

The chamber was lit by two small, hanging lamps.

A chest was at one side of the chamber. Doubtless it was from that receptacle, clearly unlocked, the padlock dangling, with its inserted key, that the barbarian had removed the dinner robe.

Someone was coming!

She had not yet found the knife!

She knelt, with her head to the furs, at the foot of the couch, the palms of her hands at the side of her head, a common slave position.

She dared to lift her head, a little.

It was Qualius, gross Qualius, the porcine tender of domestic animals, recalled from the *Narcona*.

She thrust her head down again. She did not dare address him.

He paid her no attention. The explanation of her presence there was obvious enough. She was a slave. She heard some object, stout, leathery, dropped on the lid of the unlocked, closed chest.

Then he was gone.

She rose to her feet, and went to the chest. It was as she feared. "I will have a whip sent to your quarters," had said Ronisius. "Excellent," had said the barbarian. She regarded the supple, inert object lying on the chest. How she hated Ronisius. "Excellent," had said the barbarian.

She was uneasy, regarding the whip, its coils now quiescent. She could scarcely conjecture what it might feel like, wielded by a man, on her soft, bared skin. She did not, of course, expect to feel it. The whip is seldom used gratuitously. Its end is discipline, not meaningless, wanton cruelty. There would be no point in that. It would be easy to avoid its whistling, hissing, lashing kiss. She was determined to do so. It would not be hard. She would be careful, and watchful. She need only, as other slaves, be obedient, attentive, zealous, and pleasing, wholly pleasing. Besides, the knife would be at hand, she trusted. And how could even a massive, formidable brute like the barbarian defend himself against the coated blade, where even a scratch on a lifted hand, or a fending arm, would wreak an almost instantaneous doom?

She gazed at the instrument lying on the lid of the chest.

How pleased she was that she was not as other women, not a slave.

What would it be, she asked herself, looking at the coiled leather tool on the lid of the chest, coiled like a viper, ready to strike, to be truly a slave?

The slave, she knew, is subject to the whip.

If she were a slave, she would be subject to the whip.

For a moment she swayed, giddy.

Did she sense then, if only for an instant, the meaning of the whip, the thrill and joy of being helplessly subject to command and discipline, the thrill and joy of being owned and mastered, the thrill and joy of being a kneeling, submitted slave?

No, no, she cried to herself, and spun away from the chest, and the quiet, coiled thing, which rested on its smooth surface.

The knife, she thought. I must find the knife. There may be little time!

She then approached the couch.

It was warm, and soft, lying within the furs on the great couch.

Her heart was beating rapidly.

With delicate care, and circumspection, she had felt beneath the covers for the implement. Her fingers, ever so lightly, had touched the smooth, yellow, oval handle, locating it. It would not do to touch the blade, lest the tiniest bit of its transparent coating, invisibly painted on that razor-sharp edge, might open her skin, even slightly. She had found it muchly where she had anticipated it might lie, beneath the furs, toward the head of the couch, where it might be convenient to her right hand.

Where was the barbarian?

Did he linger, for conversation, matters of moment not to be discussed before women, or slaves?

Why did he not hasten to her side?

Why had he not put aside business and rushed, breathless and trembling, to join her?

Did he not realize the inestimable worth of what awaited him?

But he had not hurried.

He had made her wait.

How angry she was!

Did he think she was a slave?

Yes, of course, he thought her a slave.

She recalled how he had put her to the polishing of his boots on the *Narcona*, how he bound her, kneeling, to a post at the foot of his bed, and how he had taped her mouth shut, that he might not hear from her, and then, ignoring her, had slept.

Was she insufficiently desirable?

Did he regret that she had been prepared? Did he prefer another? Would he put another to his pleasure?

No, she thought. Qualius had not summoned her back to her chain in the girls' quarters. Rather, he had delivered the whip.

Was he making her wait?

If so, why?

Because he thought her nothing, only a slave?

Did he suspect a plot?

Did he think this delay might make her churn with fear, with an apprehension that she might be insufficiently desired?

Did he really think this dalliance would heat her, as it might a slave, a yearning beast, hoping for the caress of its Master?

One hurries quickly enough, she thought, to the couch of a free woman. How anxious men are to please such a lofty one! How they will tumble over themselves to win one of her smiles! Well could she remember such things, on several worlds! See them hurry! Are they fearful that a whim may change her mind, a shift of mood occur, precluding a liaison, that an alleged discomfort will cloud her mien? How skillful are free women, how well they tease and taunt, how well they play games forbidden to the slave!

It was a craft which she had well mastered.

Many were the favors, the invitations, the introductions, the dinners, the trips, the small loans, the perquisites of one sort or another, she had garnered in virtue of such skills, until the invitations, and such, had ceased, and she would move to another world, leaving behind her another train of debt.

Suddenly she heard a sound.

Someone was approaching.

Her small hand closed on the handle of the dagger beneath the furs.

CHAPTER SIX

In the cold light of the moon, amidst the black shadows of leafless branches on the snow, the two tracks of the Herul sled were fresh, deep, and sharp, and black on the side shielded from the light, and the edges of the craters left behind by the paws of what we, for want of a better word, will call horses, had not yet crumbled.

"Might the Heruls not return by the same route?" asked Tuvo Ausonius.

"I think not," said Julian, of the Aureliani, putting his shoulder to the harness of the small sled. "Heruls are clever. Tracks may be seen, and a return by the same route might facilitate an ambush. Little love is lost between Heruls and Otungs."

"Otungs range outside the forest," said Tuvo.

"Undoubtedly," said Julian, "and, I suspect, though less often, Heruls enter it."

The explanation for this seems to be that the Heruls are a horse people, so to speak, and ill at ease afoot, and certainly amongst the darknesses of the forest, where archers might lurk undetected in the shadows. Heruls would prefer expanses, such as the plains of Barrionuevo, or, as they will have it, the flats of Tung, venues congenial to the sudden appearances, the rapid movements, the feints, the charges and withdrawals, the encirclings, of light cavalry, seldom choosing to close with a set, prepared enemy.

"The trees grow more frequent," said Tuvo. "Surely the forest is near."

"It may be hours away," said Julian.

One gathers that little has prepared denizens of sparser, more open worlds, denuded worlds, so to speak, those unfamiliar with original, natural worlds, to anticipate the nature, the breadth and density, of the forests commonly found in the northern latitudes of Tangara. Indeed, the Otungs, the Wolfungs, and such, as earlier noted, were all tribes of the Vandalii, the etymology of which term is apparently related to "van land," or "forest land." The Vandalii, then, despite the more recent semantic accretions, perhaps unfortunate, of the word, and related words, are perhaps best understood as the "forest people," or "people of the forest," such things.

The unwillingness of Heruls to penetrate the forest in large numbers, to transgress it in force, so to speak, aside from its preclusion of their common tactics, is understandable. The empire had lost divisions in such locales.

"When the tracks turn," said Julian, "the Heruls will have discharged their mysterious passenger. At that point, the forest, or an Otung enclave, at least, will be near."

"There will then be danger," said Tuvo.

"There is danger now," said Julian.

"Our most pressing need," said Tuvo Ausonius, "is not to encounter an Otung enclave, which might prove our misfortune, but to make contact with the expedition sent to support Captain Ottonius."

"It is the intent of the expedition to make contact with Otungs," said Julian. "Thus, one hopes the two matters will coincide."

"There may be many Otung camps, or halls, or villages," said Tuvo.

"True," said Julian, grimly.

"Presumably the imperial camp will now be in place," said Tuvo.

"Almost certainly," said Julian. "And it need not search out Otungs. Otungs will recognize its presence, and, doubtless, make the first contact."

"A bloody one?" said Tuvo Ausonius.

"Perhaps," said Julian.

"The expedition, in place, camped," said Tuvo, "will be relatively impervious. It has armored vehicles, and hoverers. It will have a defensive perimeter. The area will be guarded, and flooded with light."

"One expects so," said Julian.

"At the camp we will be safe," said Tuvo.

"We do not know that," said Julian. "The danger there may be greater than here, in the forest."

"We are not assured," said Tuvo, "that we will find the camp."

"No," said Julian.

"The expedition may not have followed the course set in Venitzia."

"Possibly," said Julian.

"Perhaps we will not find it," said Tuvo.

"Perhaps, not," said Julian, leaning forward, straining against the harness.

"It might have been attacked, and overrun," said Tuvo.

"Pull," said Julian. "Pull."

The two men continued to press forward, in the still-fresh tracks of the Herul sled.

"Masters," said a woman's voice, behind them.

"She is awake," said Tuvo.

"Masters draw the sled," said the voice.

Nika, bundled in her fur, and in her boots, slipped from the sled. She struggled to match the pace of the men.

The shallow, brittle snow continued to crackle beneath the boots of Julian and Tuvo.

"I remember nothing," she said.

"You slept," said Julian.

"I am awake," she said. "Harness me."

For much of their journey, Nika had drawn the sled. This was appropriate, for she was a slave.

"Remain on the sled," said Julian.

"Masters?" she asked.

"Or you will be left behind," said Julian.

"Yes, Master," she said, taking her place on the sled.

Julian and Tuvo continued to follow the tracks of the Herul sled.

"Masters!" said Nika.

"We hear them," snapped Julian.

In the cold, frosty air, the baying, even far away, was clear. It was most dangerous when the baying stopped, for then they were close, and approaching silently.

"They may alert others," said Tuvo Ausonius. "They will arouse suspicion. They will mark our position."

"We will proceed," said Julian.

"Otungs, or Heruls," said Tuvo Ausonius.

"Or imperial troops," said Julian, "anticipating our presence, and intent to intercept us."

"To bring us safely to the camp," said Tuvo.

"Or guarantee," said Julian, "that we will never reach it."

"The baying is louder now, closer," said Tuvo.

"Continue on, pull," said Julian.

CHAPTER SEVEN

"You are here?" asked the barbarian.

He had just emerged from the comparative brightness of the tunnel. The chamber was not much illuminated by the two small hanging lamps.

He looked about the chamber, and to the foot of the couch.

Was the slave not present? Such a lapse might call for punishment. Surely then she must be in the chamber.

"I am here, Master," said Filene.

"You are on the couch, concealed within the covers," he said.

"Yes, Master," she said.

"What are you doing there?" he asked.

"Awaiting Master," said Filene. "In my collar I am heated, and filled with longing. Remove your robe, and join me."

"Do you think that you are a free woman?" he inquired.

Filene's heart skipped a beat. "No, Master," she said. "Certainly not, Master!"

"How is it, then," he asked, "that you would have me remove my own robe?"

"Master?" she asked.

"I am to disrobe myself," he asked, "and hope to be invited to your furs?"

"I do not understand," she said.

"You are indeed new to your collar," he said.

"Hurry to me, Master," she said. "Join me, within the furs. I wait!"

Her hand, moist, was tight on the handle of the knife.

He must approach. He must be closer.

"A slave," he said, "is not a free woman, on whom one might attend in darkness, beneath covers, as though in modesty, or shame. A slave is to be seen, not hidden. Every bit of her is to be exposed, displayed for the Master's perusal. Every one of his senses, his touch, his hearing, his sight, everything, is to be stimulated in the feast of the furs."

"But I am new to my collar, Master," she said. "Take pity on me! I am afraid! Be kind! Join me here, within the furs!"

The barbarian strode to the chest at the side of the chamber, lifted up the whip which lay upon its lid, shook out its coil, meaningfully, and snapped it once, sharply, in the chamber.

Filene cried out in misery.

The barbarian pointed to the floor before him. "Here," he said.

"Master!" she cried out, in protest.

Again the whip cracked.

Filene then, in consternation, loosed her grip on the oval handle of the knife, leaving it well concealed, and slipped from the furs, and hurried to kneel before the barbarian. She was not at all sure she could have, knife in hand, its menace in sight, sprung from the furs and crossed the distance between them. And what if the blow of that terrible device in his hand should arrest her progress, coiling like fire about her, perhaps binding her very arm to her side?

"An ignorant slave begs forgiveness," she said, head down.

"You are very pretty," he said. "Do you require the instruction of leather?"

"No, Master," she said.

"Good," he said.

One regrets putting a lovely slave to the leather, but sometimes it is appropriate, quite appropriate.

One desires perfection in the service of a slave.

He coiled the whip, and tossed it to the foot of the couch. This action much relieved her apprehension. She did not wish to experience the excruciating pain of a punished slave, and she was not sure, were she lashed, that she could muster the strength or will to fetch the knife. She was not sure she could have managed to rise to her feet. She might have found herself foiled and defeated, before him, lying at his feet, scarcely able to move, alone and helpless, in the misery of her beating.

"May I remove Master's robe?" asked Filene.

"Sandals, first," said the barbarian, and he sat on the edge of the couch, rather near its foot.

Filene wished that he would have taken his position closer to the head of the couch, where she might the more easily regain the knife.

She removed the sandals, one at a time, and placed them near the couch.

She did not know enough to put down her head and kiss each first, for they were the sandals of a free person, and then remove them, and then lift them to her lips, one at a time, and kiss them again, and then place them beside the couch.

"Unbraid my hair," said the barbarian.

It had been braided in the hall of the King Naming, by the slave, Yata, whom he had earlier sold to one of his liegeman, one named Citherix, for a pig.

Long hair is common amongst barbarians.

It is unusual, of course, among bodyguards, gladiators, and such, and he had once been a bodyguard of Pulendius of Terennia, a rich merchant, proprietor of a gladiatorial school, and a lord of estates. It was said that four thousand *coloni* tilled his fields. As many rich men, he maintained a small, private army, his of some five hundred men. The barbarian had not had his hair cut even when he had fought in the arena. This length of hair was unusual, as mentioned, for bodyguards, gladiators, and such. Short hair, or hair bound back, tightly on the head, often knotted, not easy to grasp, is common. Similarly, bodyguards, gladiators, and such, men who may be involved in hand-to-hand combat, are generally smoothly shaven, or have their beards cut short. A hand knotted in long hair, or a beard, might draw a throat to a knife. Regular troops in the imperial military, incidentally, were required to be clean-shaven, but probably, mainly, for purposes of uniformity and discipline. The matter was more lax amongst troops enlisted as *comitates*, or those in the *limitanei*. In any event, wisely or not, the barbarian had commonly worn his hair long. Perhaps it was a challenge to enemies, to try to grasp it, that they might be brought within his reach. Perhaps it was a matter of a dimly sensed propriety, harking back to suspected origins. Perhaps it was merely a matter of idiosyncratic preference. In any event, it was appropriate enough, one supposes, for a projected commander of barbarian *comitates*, men who might follow such a leader more readily than one whose appearance reminded them of the authority and oppression of a hated empire.

"It is done, Master," said Filene.

She was now behind him, kneeling on the couch, toward its foot. Given his height, had both stood, it would have been difficult for her to reach up and perform this simple task. She glanced to the place, beneath the furs, where the knife, with its transparent sheathing of poison, lay concealed. It was beyond her reach. She considered whether or not she might throw herself to the place, sweep back the furs, seize it, and put it to its dark employment. But she feared a sudden move would alert the barbarian. She might not live to reach the knife.

She must wait.

He stood up.

She slipped from the couch and stood behind him.

She feared to touch the dinner robe without permission.

He turned to face her. She felt small and weak before him. She went to her knees as was appropriate for a slave in the presence of a free person. She castigated herself. How right she suddenly felt, placed so before him! Were there not men and women, and they were so different, so profoundly and radically different! She hoped he would not ask her to widen her knees before him. How helpless she would be then! She was not sure she could control herself, should he do so. How conscious she was of the chain on her neck, with its dependent disk!

"You should have waited, kneeling, at the foot of the couch," he said. "You should not have ascended the surface of the couch without permission."

"Forgive an ignorant slave," she said.

"Nor should you have concealed your body before the Master," he said.

"Forgive me, Master," she said.

"The girl kneels, that at the foot of the couch, on the left side, as the couch is faced, she waits; she might be permitted to turn back the furs," he said.

"The girl hopes to be found pleasing," she said.

"Have you earned the surface of the couch?" he asked.

"I hope to be granted it," she said.

"One such as you, a new slave, a substantially worthless slave, would expect," he said, "to be thrown to the floor at the foot of the couch, perhaps chained to the ring. You see the ring?"

"Yes, Master," she said.

"In the chest to the side," he said, "there are thongs, and chains, in which you would be quite helpless."

She put her head down.

"Have you learned to thrash in chains?" he asked.

"No, Master," she whispered.

"Can you conceive of lying on your back, absolutely helpless, your limbs tied, or chained, widely apart, at the mercy of a Master?"

"I fear to do so," she said.

"Are you ready for the unspeakable ecstasies your body may be forced to endure, if the Master pleases?"

"Please be kind to me, Master," she said.

"You will moan, cry out, thrash, weep, and beg for more, and hope that the Master will accede to your pleas."

A soft cry of anguish escaped the girl.

"He may not," said the barbarian.

"Could he be so cruel?" she asked.

"Perhaps you will try to be a good slave," he said.

"Yes, Master!" she said.

"I do not think that you now desire to be a good slave," he said.

"Oh, no, Master," she said. "Filene desires to be a good slave!"

"Filene is a liar," he said.

"Master?" she said, frightened.

"But it does not matter, now," he said.

"I do not understand," she said.

"It is my understanding," he said, "that you are not marked."

"None of us are," she said, "those in the camp."

"Surely that is unusual," he said.

"We were thought too beautiful to be marked," she said.

"That is absurd," he said. "Slaves should be marked. A collar might be removed. The mark is a useful identification."

"Undoubtedly," she said.

"Without the mark one might mistake you for a free woman," he said. "Once you are marked, we need not be concerned about that. Once marked, everyone will know you are a slave."

"Yes, Master," she said.

What a dreadful thing, she thought, to be marked, to be designated for all to see as goods.

But the very thought, too, thrilled her.

She could then be owned, possessed as a helpless object, a beast.

I would then, at last, be something, she thought, something

real, something societally recognized, accepted, and sanctioned, something with a meaning, and a place, something with a country and a home. What is a free woman, she wondered, but a loose and empty thing, a stray thing, an abstraction without content, a sound without meaning, a movement without purpose, an empty page, a bark without course, a vessel without its summoning, guiding star. I would have an identity. I would know how I must be. I would know how to speak. I would know what to do, how to act, how to behave. I would then, at last, be something, however trivial and unimportant, something of value, something real.

Do I long for a Master, she wondered. Am I incomplete without a Master?

No, no, she thought.

Filene's mind raced.

Somehow she must obtain the knife.

"As I understand it," he said, "you are a virgin."

"Yes, Master," she said.

"That is very rare amongst slaves," he said.

"I was purchased with that in mind," she said, "that I might be presented so to some high and worthy person, perhaps an ally, or guest, of the empire."

"An interesting forethought," he said.

"It seems so," she said.

"Perhaps," he said, "to one such as I?"

"I know not, of course," she said.

"Of course not," he said.

"In view of my newness to the collar," she said, "and the comity with which I am sure you would hold a former free woman of the empire, I would crave your indulgence."

"In what way?" he asked.

"You are not unfamiliar with the ways of the empire," she said. "You learned them, at least, on the *Narcona*. You must have observed the manners of gentlemen, such as our noble officers,

Lysis and Corelius. I petition then, though I am naught but a miserable and lowly slave, to be accorded, for moments at least, in view of my antecedents, some respect and civility."

"You wish to be treated somewhat as though you might be a free woman?" he said.

"Yes," she said.

"At least for a moment?" he said.

"Yes," she said.

"*Civilitas*," he said.

"Yes," she said.

"Not *barbaritas*," he said.

"No," she said.

"You have seen your gentlemen in certain settings, incidentally, not others," said the barbarian.

"I am sure they are gentlemen," she said.

"Some gentlemen," he said, "know well the purposes and uses of slaves. Some gentlemen are cunning, shrewd, dangerous, intelligent, and powerful, superb and uncompromising Masters. The empire, I assure you, in all its wealth, in all its expanse and depth, in all its might and terror, was not founded by, nor enlarged and maintained by, weaklings."

"Still," she said.

"You do not wish to be whipped, or used as a pig?"

"No, Master," she said.

"Though a slave?"

"Though a slave," she said.

"Some women find it instructive to be used as a pig," he said.

"Please, Master!" she said.

"What then would you have me do, and how would you have me be?" he asked.

"Be kind," she said. "Realize my fears, and feelings. Permit me to ascend the surface of the couch, as might be permitted a high or preferred slave, and permit me, too, in deference to my shyness, modesty, and timidity, to conceal myself within the furs, as might a free woman. And then join me there, tenderly and sweetly."

"I see," said the barbarian, skeptically.

"Please, Master!" she said.

"How then will you learn your collar?" he said.

"It need not be taught to me tonight," she said.

"You must learn it," he said.

"Not tonight, not now," she said. "Please, please be kind to a lowly, frightened, miserable slave."

"I am to remove my own robe?" he asked.

"No, no," she said. "I will do so."

She rose to her feet, and, going behind him, lifted the long, flowing, white dinner robe from his broad shoulders.

She was uneasy, gazing on the breadth of that back. She resisted the impulse to lean forward, and touch it gently, timidly, with her lips.

No, she thought, no!

How terrible it would be, she thought, to be a slave!

She looked to the side.

The knife, beneath the covers, was close.

She was holding the robe before her, in two hands. She considered casting it down and darting to the knife. It would take a moment to throw back the furs and get her hands on the implement.

He turned to face her.

She must wait!

"Why are you clutching the robe so?" he asked. "You might wrinkle it."

"Forgive me, Master," she said.

"Are you all right?" he asked.

"Yes, Master," she said. "Thank you, Master."

"You may fold the robe and place it in the chest," he said.

"Yes, Master," she said. "Thank you, Master."

She then folded the robe, went to the chest, opened it, and placed the robe within it, carefully. Uneasily she noted certain

articles within the chest, thongs, coils of cord, some lengths of
chain, such things. Too, she noted, dully gleaming, reflecting
the light of the nearest lamp, slender and attractive, metal slave
cuffs. How easily, she thought, and how effectively, a slave might
be rendered helpless!

She was facing away from him.

"I plead to be permitted the surface of the couch," she said.

"Very well," he said.

"Master is kind to a poor, miserable slave," she said.

"Perhaps," he said.

I have won, she thought, elatedly. What a fool he is! How
could a simple, crude barbarian, a boor of the fields or forests, from some tiny village or remote farm, but succumb to
the wiles and cleverness of a woman of the empire, one of the
honestori, one even of the patrician class, even of the senatorial
class itself!

"Hold," he said.

"Master?" she said.

"Turn about," he said.

She did not think she could run to the couch. She must be
patient.

He went to the chest, now behind her, which was still open,
and withdrew something from it. It was a short thong.

"Master?" she said, uneasily.

He was now before her.

"Master?" she said.

He bound her wrists together, crossed, before her body, at
the center of the thong, and, with its loose ends, tied them about
the chain on her neck. Her hands, then, bound closely together,
were fastened before her, just below her chin.

She tried to separate her hands, fruitlessly. The chain pulled
against the back of her neck.

"Master!" she protested.

The barbarian then lifted her, easily, and threw her, feet

away, to the surface of the vast couch, where she tumbled, and rolled amidst the furs.

She scrambled to her knees on the couch. She feared to stand, lest she lose her balance, and fall.

She felt a mighty hand grasp her hair, and jerk her head back. She cried out. She tried to free her hands. The chain shook on her neck, the pendant metal disk, with its three languages, including its pictograph, shook, and rattled against the sturdy links of her collar, the slave necklace. Then she was touched as a slave may be touched. She shrieked with dismay. Her knees moved, wildly. Her body shook. Her fingers twisted. She jerked at the thong and chain holding her hands together, helplessly, at her collar. She could scarcely move. She could not defend the sweet, exposed latitudes of her vulnerable beauty, no more than a slave. Then she was touched, again. Again she shrieked, with dismay, and misery. She wanted to cry out, "Desist! Desist! I am a free woman! I am a free woman!" but she knew she must not do so. Too, she was in the hands of a barbarian. Would such a cry deter a man, any man, from the prey designed for him by nature?

"*Civilitas*!" she cried. "*Civilitas*!"

The barbarian then did desist.

"*Civilitas*!" she wept.

The mighty hand was removed from her hair.

"Free my hands, Master," she begged. "Free my hands, if not for my sake, for yours! I am bound! So tethered, so helpless, how can I please you? I would touch you. I would hold you! I would caress you! I long for you! I want you! How can I, so bound, please you, and caress you? Free my hands! Free my hands!"

He then reached to her throat, to free her hands.

CHAPTER EIGHT

"There!" cried Tuvo Ausonius, pointing.

A blast of fire rushed forth from the rifle of Julian, of the Aureliani, and one of the large beasts spun a dozen feet into the air, twisting, and howling, alit with fire, the darkness of the now heavily clouded night suddenly blinded with light, an incongruous instant of heat and noontide in the cold, bitter darkness.

"Another!" said Tuvo, discharging his own weapon, brought from Venitzia.

In the moment of brightness, the men had seen two of the creatures tearing at, and devouring, one of their own, struck by earlier fire.

A hundred yards away a tree burned in the night, where a charge had carried past its intended target.

"How many are there?" said Tuvo.

"Few, ten, twelve," said Julian.

As will be understood there is, depending on several conditions, primarily the nature and abundance of game, an ideal pack count. A pack may be too small or too large. Too large a pack is hard to feed, and likely to overhunt the available game. A smaller pack needs less food. On the other hand, too small a pack may not be adequate to bring down certain large animals, such as the Tangaran *hroth*, the field stag, the forest bull, and certainly the Tangaran *torodont*, scarcely smaller than the

Thalasian *torodont*. In times of plenty a pack waxes; in times of
scarcity a pack wanes. Kinship relations commonly determine
pack membership, except when game is abundant, a time which
coincides, as one would expect, with the common mating season. In times of starvation, male pack members become irritable
and intragroup attacks may occur, dominance competitions, and
such, the result of which is cannibalism. Needless to say it is the
older and weaker animals which tend, statistically, to be elimi-
nated. Also, as would be expected, save for the mating season,
packs tend to be territorial, which tends to distribute the packs,
which enlarges the hunting areas for each pack.

"There!" said Julian.

"My charges are gone," said Tuvo.

"I have two left," said Julian.

"Each is precious," said Tuvo.

"I think they are waiting," said Julian.

The men stood almost back to back. Between them, kneeling
in the snow, was the small, exquisite, red-haired slave, Nika.

"Burn the sled, the provisions," said Julian.

"Is that wise?" said Tuvo.

"It is necessary," said Julian.

"They may have no fear of fire," said Tuvo.

"Then let them regard it with circumspection, with puzzlement, with wary curiosity," said Julian.

Tuvo Ausonius applied the tiny camp torch to the small sled,
and its freight.

Nika cried out in fear, pointing.

Two pair of eyes, intent, and gleaming, burned in the
darkness.

"I see another," said Tuvo.

"I, as well," said Julian.

"There may be others," said Tuvo, "farther from the fire."

"I fear so," said Julian.

The wolves on various worlds, for we shall call them wolves, are almost invariably related to the animals which we have been accustomed to refer to as "dogs." Except on some of the inner worlds, where they may be bred in almost any way for almost any purpose, "dogs" tend to be territorial, dangerous animals. On the outer worlds, they are bred almost exclusively for hunting and war.

"The tracks turn," had cried Tuvo earlier, shortly before the storm of blackness in the sky had begun to hide the pale, white moon, and the shadows of branches on the snow had fled, returned, and fled again.

This discovery informed Julian and Tuvo that, in all likelihood, the Herul sled had discharged its passenger, presumably an Otung, that he might return, presumably in stealth, to some Otung village or holding. This suggested the possibility, as well, that the imperial camp might be near, as its expedition had hoped, in its pursuit of, and support of, Captain Ottonius, to meet and deal with Otungs. In any event, it seemed clear that they had now arrived, for better or for worse, in the vicinity of Otungs, the largest and most formidable tribe of the Vandal nation. Shortly thereafter the hurrying darknesses in the sky had intermittently obscured not only the moon but the stars, this rendering more precarious and uncertain Julian's capacity to keep to the expedition's original course, that allegedly determined for it in Venitzia. Nonetheless, he and Ausonius had pressed on to the best of their ability, assisted by occasional glimpses of the stars, as the clouds would break, muchly in the same direction, certainly as nearly as they could determine, in which they had been moving. It was an hour or so later that the baying of the wolves had ceased.

"They are here, they are about," had said Tuvo Ausonius.

"Do not move," had said Julian, unslinging his rifle.

The flight of prey, of course, tends to stimulate pursuit. Too, a running animal does not defend itself. The pack tries for the hind legs, or slashes at flanks, crippling and bleeding the prey,

until it slows, turns, and is set upon by the entire pack, and
devoured alive. On the other hand, a wary, stationary prey is
approached more tentatively, more cautiously. A blow from the
paw of a *hroth* can break a wolf's neck; the antlers of the field
stag, the horns of the forest bull, the tusks of the *torodont* can
shatter rib cages, impale, and disembowel wolves. The *torodont*
is a particularly dangerous prey for a pack as it is commonly
gregarious, and forms a defensive circle, with the females and
young within the circle.

"I have two charges left," said Julian.

"There are at least four about," said Tuvo Ausonius.

"If they maintain their distance, I will not fire," said Julian.

"Do not miss," said Tuvo.

"I am unlikely to miss at this distance," said Julian.

"Why do they not charge?" asked Tuvo.

"The fire, the fire, I think," said Julian.

"It will not last, Masters," said Nika.

"Then they will attack," said Tuvo.

The men heard a low, rumbling growl, from somewhere
beyond the flickering ring of darkness and shadows.

"That is another, another out there," said Tuvo.

"Yes," said Julian.

"One creeps forward," said Tuvo.

"I see him," said Julian.

"The trail is lost," said Tuvo. "Provisions burn. Charges are
few. Beasts abound."

"The fire grows less, Masters!" said Nika.

"We are lost," said Tuvo.

"I will expend one charge," said Julian. "At this distance, I
will not miss. Hopefully others will feed. We have seen that. We
might then, with good fortune, withdraw."

"To withdraw, wandering into cold and darkness, substantially defenseless, lost and facing starvation," said Tuvo, "seems
to me, dear friend, a surprising concept of good fortune."

"Be of good cheer," said Julian. "We might be soon set upon by Otungs or Heruls."

"There are too many, they are too close," said Tuvo. "Farewell, dear friend."

Julian swung the rifle about, assessing the proximity of the beasts, and then, selecting the closest, that which Tuvo had earlier noted, which was presumably the most aggressive and most likely to suddenly hasten forward, pressed the trigger.

The beast exploded in fire and blood; the snow was melted for yards about, where it had crouched; the cold, clear night air, bright with sparks and drifting, scattered, flaming hair; was freighted, befouled, with the ugly, sweet stench of incinerated tissue.

"They do not feed!" said Tuvo. "They approach."

"So, farewell, dear friend," said Julian.

"Iaachus is triumphant," said Tuvo Ausonius.

"I have one more charge," said Julian.

"Expend it," said Tuvo.

"It is for Nika," said Julian.

"No, Master!" she screamed, looking into the short, wide muzzle of the rifle.

"I will not have you fed upon by ravening beasts," said Julian. "You will not be torn to pieces, and eaten alive. I will spare you that."

"No, Master!" she cried.

"It will be quick," he said.

"Please, no, Master!" she cried.

His finger rested on the trigger.

At that point there was a bounding, hurtling furred shape which, rushing past, buffeted Julian about, spinning him to the snow, the rifle lost to the side. Nika screamed, and Tuvo staggered back, another, lengthy, furred, humped, crested thing bounding past, out of the darkness, in the wake of the first. "Wolves!" he cried, in dismay. "No!" cried Julian. "Dogs!" A few yards from the fire there was a whirl of tearing, snarling shadows rolling

in the snow. Almost simultaneously two of the pairs of threat-
ening eyes gleaming outside the fire ring disappeared, as the
beasts turned and fled into the darkness. One may have been
pulled down in the darkness, as a horrid wavering cry, clear
in the cold, dry air, carried back to the glowing embers of the
almost extinguished fire. Another pair of eyes suddenly gleamed
in the darkness as a shape approached, a dark, crumpled shadow
inert in the snow behind it. Nika cried out, and seized the sleeve
of Julian, who shook her hand away. "Wolf," whispered Tuvo.
"No," said Julian, "do not move." The shape emerging from the
darkness went, as though curious, to the remains of the beast on
which Julian had recently fired, thrust its snout into the burned
meat, and, a moment later, began to feed. It was joined, shortly,
by its companion, and they fed together. Occasionally they lifted
their blackened, bloodied snouts from the feeding and regarded
Julian, Tuvo, and the slave, and then returned to their feeding.

Tuvo regarded the two nigh beasts. "Surely those are wolves,"
he said.

"No," said Julian, "dogs."

"They are feeding," said Tuvo, "on your kill."

"Such things are familiar with cooked meat," said Julian.

"I do not care how they look upon us," said Nika.

"The margin which separates such things from their wild
brethren is, I fear, narrow," said Julian.

"We are in danger?" said Nika.

"Not now, perhaps soon," said Julian.

"Surely they are wolves," said Tuvo.

"No," said Julian, "they are dogs, bred for size and ferocity,
bred to hunt, bred to attack on command, bred to kill wolves."

"Dogs?" said Tuvo.

"Yes, dogs," said Julian, "and here, Otung dogs."

"The wolves are gone," said Tuvo.

"Probably not far," said Julian. "They have probably
returned, to feed on their fellows."

"If those are Otung dogs," said Tuvo, "then we must be in the country of the Otungs."

"Yes," said Julian. "We have arrived. We are now in the country of the Otungs."

Tuvo recovered the fallen rifle and handed it to Julian. "You still have one charge not expended," he said.

"I think we have little to fear from the wolves at present," said Julian. "They fear the dogs, and there is enough feeding about for them. I think they will eat, and then drift away, and, in a day or two, range forth again, seeking the scent of possible prey."

"Then we are safe," said Tuvo.

"Not from the dogs," said Julian, "nor from Otungs, if they are about."

"Let us be on our way," said Tuvo.

Then, warily, backing away for a time, regarded occasionally by the monstrous dogs, lifting their heads from the burned, blackened, half-eaten carcass, they turned, and moved into the darkness, away from the dying fire, inside its ring of dark earth, where the snow had melted.

"Heel us," said Julian, to the slave.

"I heel, Master," she said.

They had not gone far when, in the distance, they noted a spot of light, incongruous in the darkness, not far from a partly illuminated, thick border of looming trees.

"Look," said Tuvo.

"I see," said Julian.

The party stood in the darkness, in the snow, amongst trees, regarding that surprising, tiny, far-off point of illumination.

"Otungs?" said Tuvo.

"No," said Julian. "That light, so cold, so bright, so bleak, so steady, is artificial."

"Here, then, in the wilderness," said Tuvo, "it can be but one thing."

"Yes," said Julian. "We have found the camp."

CHAPTER NINE

"Your hands are now free," said the barbarian. "Perhaps you do not know what to do with them."

"Forgive me, Master," said Filene, "but I have recently been free."

She slipped quickly, gracefully, beneath the furs.

"You conceal yourself," observed the barbarian.

"Permit me to do so," she said.

"Why?" he asked.

"I am still timid, and modest," she said. "Much of the free woman remains in me."

"It could be whipped out of you," said the barbarian.

"Be kind," she said.

"The slave is not a free woman," he said. "It is a mistake to lavish consideration on her. Soon, as the free woman, she will not appreciate it, but expect it, and take it for granted. Thus, a slave should be kept on her knees."

"I see," she said.

"That is what they want, and where they belong," he said.

"I see," she said.

"They are women, slaves," he said.

"Join me within the covers, Master," she said.

"No woman is truly happy," said the barbarian, "who is not in her collar."

"Hurry, Master," she urged.

"You are an extremely pretty slave," he said.

"That is why you give me my way," she said.

"Your hair is long, your eyes blue, your features exquisite, your lips soft," he said.

"And my skin is smooth, and my thigh fair, and unmarked," she said.

"As unmarked as that of a free woman," he said.

"That is interesting, is it not?" she asked.

"I find it so," he said.

"It is my hope that I will please Master," she said.

"Your hands," he said, "are small, soft, and fine."

"Thank you, Master," she said.

"I freed them," he said. "I would see them."

"Join me," she said. "And let them, within the furs, unseen, concealed, touch and caress you, addressing themselves to your pleasure."

"I have heard that some call you 'Cornhair'," said the barbarian.

"Please do not do so," she said.

"You wish to please me?" he asked.

"Yes, Master," she said. "And you will be well pleased, I assure you, with how I shall please you."

"Are you trained?" he asked.

"I do not need to be trained," she said.

"Why is that?" he asked.

"I am beautiful," she said.

"That is pleasant, but, for a slave, far from enough," he said.

"Master?" she said.

"Are you trained?" he asked.

"I have had little, or no training," she said.

"Are you trained?" he asked.

"No, Master," she said.

"No woman," said the barbarian, "should be sent to the selling platform without some training."

"But many are," protested Filene. "Cities fall, space liners are seized, ships are captured at sea, caravans are intercepted, girl tributes are levied from subdued communities, taxes may be levied in terms of female flesh, edifices are raided, women's baths are plundered!"

"Who would wish to purchase an untrained slave?" said the barbarian.

"Surely much depends on the slave," said Filene.

"When one buys a slave, one expects a slave," said the barbarian, "not simply a piece of chained meat."

"I have heard, Master," said Filene, "that some men prefer a hitherto-unowned slave, that they may train her with perfection to their personal tastes."

"Every slave is trained to her Master's tastes," said the barbarian, "but one expects them to know something or other before they are introduced to the whipping ring in their Master's domicile."

"Still," protested Filene.

"And what then," he asked, "when she is sold to another?"

"I see," said Filene.

"It is dangerous to the woman to be sold untrained," said the barbarian. "What if she does not know how to please a man? Some Masters are impatient."

"I trust that Master is not impatient," said Filene.

"For you do not know how to please a man?"

"I fear not," said Filene.

"You are an interesting slave," he said.

"Every slave hopes to be of interest," she said.

How horrid, she thought to herself, how dreadful, how humiliating, to be of "interest." I am a free woman. We do not wish to be found of interest. We are not slaves! How insulting to be found of interest! And yet, too, she recalled, on a dozen worlds, at a hundred entertainments, on the street, in restaurants, in theaters, at races, at arena events, in the gambling palaces, at the tables and wheels, in her gowns and ensembles, she had been smugly thrilled to be found of interest. How she, delighted and keenly aware, had relished the heedful, furtive glances of men, the striking impression she had made, the stir for which she was responsible, had sensed their notice and attention, had basked in their commendatory regard. How she despised men, and yet thrived on their discomfort. Yes, she thought, she had wished to be found of interest! Keenly so, very much so! Could it be, then, she wondered, that in every woman there was a slave? Could it be, then, as the barbarian had asserted, that no woman could be truly happy who is not in her collar? No, no, she thought. But there was a pleasure, doubtless, an exceedingly pleasant gratification, in being a tumult-engendering, exhibited, inaccessible treasure. Let them suffer the starvation and denial of their nature, the frustration of their blood, the pangs of unrequited desire! How horrifying then, she thought, to be a slave, to be owned, to be available and resistless, to be wholly and instantaneously subject, at any moment, to a man's least wishes, to be the helpless, defenseless source of a thousand pleasures which might be reaped at will from her body, to be at the mercy of a Master! I am not a slave, she cried out to herself. Not a slave! I am a free woman! And yet here I am, she thought, wildly, hidden in the furs of a barbarian's couch, as stripped as a slave, a chain locked on my neck!

She closed her hand on the handle of the knife beneath the furs.

"What is wrong?" asked the barbarian.

"I languish, Master," she said. "Join me, in the soft warmth of these inviting, sheltering furs."

"You beg it?" he asked.

"Yes, Master," she said.

Why was he not with her, beneath the furs, where the knife, concealed, might move so quickly, like a striking viper, into his side or thigh? A scratch would suffice. He sat upon the edge of the couch, regarding her.

"What is wrong?" he asked, once more.

"Nothing, Master," she said.

At that moment, they heard, outside the stout tent, beyond the twice-sealed private exit to the chamber, away from the entering tunnel, the hum of a hoverer.

"How is this?" asked the barbarian, as though to himself. "These machines were warmed earlier. What would be the point of doing it again, so soon? And, strange, I hear only one engine."

Filene was suddenly terrified. Sweat burst forth from her fair skin, heated beneath the furs. Her heart pounded, her breath came quickly. Her hand clenched on the handle of the knife, so tightly it hurt.

"I shall investigate," said the barbarian.

"No, Master!" she cried. "Stay! Stay! Do not leave me!" He remained on the couch, beside her, regarding her.

Why, she asked herself, frightened, wildly, is the hoverer activated? Is it being warmed for my escape? Should I have managed this business by now? Is this the signal to act? Are my confederates, whomsoever they may be, preparing for departure? Do they think I have finished the business? Surely they wait for me. Surely they will call for me. They must now be outside the private exit. Are they impatient? They must not leave without me! Am I to be abandoned? I must act!

"What is wrong?" he asked, again.

"Nothing, Master!" she said.

If only he would turn away!

"Surely something is wrong," he said.

"Oh, misery, Master!" she said. "I fear I am a disappointment to a free man! I fear I must be punished!"

"How so?" he asked.

"I hide, I tremble, I am unworthy," she said. "Correct my behavior! Improve me! I beg it. Beat me! I would be a good slave!

Inform me I am a slave! Leave me in no doubt! Lash the free woman out of me!"

Why did he smile?

"Seize up the whip," she said. "Draw me by the hair from under the covers, throw me to your feet, and lash me!"

The whip, as might be recalled, had been put at the bottom of the couch. It was to the barbarian's left, as he sat.

Filene almost moaned with fear, for the hum of the hover-er's engine had become an intense whine. Every indication was given of an imminent ascent.

Do not leave without me, she cried, in her heart.

"The whip, the whip, please, Master!" she cried.

He turned away, as though to reach for the supple tool of instruction, and she thrust aside the furs, springing to her knees, the long fang of the knife raised in her right hand, but to her horror she found herself looking into his stern, blue eyes, her right wrist helpless, held in a grip as obdurate, unforgiv-ing, and merciless as a manacle bolted flush to a common market wall. He had not truly turned away, then, but had given no more than such an indication, and had turned back, quickly, easily, to seize her wrist, even before it could begin its progress toward his body. She struggled, on the furs, on her knees, twisting, weep-ing. "Oh!" she cried in misery, her small fingers opening, her wrist in danger of being crushed in such a grip, and the lovely knife, with its yellow, oval handle, and its slender blade of some seven inches, fell into the furs. He then drew her from the sur-face of the couch, holding her by the wrist, and, as he sat on the edge of the couch, forced her to her knees before him, her wrist extended toward him, still in his grasp.

"Unless a slave's hands are fastened behind her, cuffed, chained, thonged, or such," he said, "one commonly expects to see her hands. A girl tunic provides little concealment for a weapon, or for the girl herself. And even less opportunity is afforded a naked slave. You see it need not be merely for the simple pleasure of it that one might deny a slave clothing and keep her naked, as the property and beast she is."

The whine of the hoverer was now shrill.

He then released her wrist, and she sprang to her feet, turned, and tore at the closures on the private exit, and, as she swept them aside, and hurried into the darkness, a blast of cold wind from the night swept through the chamber, and she spun about, in the opening, now pelted by scattered snow and gravel as the hoverer rose into the air, and, amidst the shouts of startled men, sped over the wires of the defensive perimeter.

She stood in the opening, stunned, and shivering.

"You were never to accompany them," said the barbarian. "I know not what you were offered, but there was never an intent to pay it. Why should there have been? Too, you would know too much, and would thus be a threat to dangerous, higher men. What if you were suspected, caught, and tortured? Would you not speak on the rack, or under the glowing metal slivers? Too, who would trust one such as you? Might you not intimate catastrophic revelations, that you be further enriched, in gold or position? Perhaps you would like a world? No, you were to be abandoned, left here to our mercy. Perhaps those who fled, and I think I know who they are, think you were successful. Let us hope so, for that might buy time, in which a large *comitatus* may be secretly formed. If they learn not, that you were not successful, they might justify their flight by the claim they were pursuing you. Perhaps they will claim they found you, and disposed of you. If they do apprehend you, I do not think you need fear being surrendered to a suitable authority."

Filene cried out with misery and, naked, and barefoot, ran out, away from the portal, into the freezing, brightly lit, snowy yard, weeping, her hands lifted to the sky, to the course pursued by the now-vanished hoverer.

She fled then toward the perimeter of the yard, but stopped short of the lethal wall of wires that enclosed the camp.

Two men, brightly illuminated in the glare of the flood lights, approached her, one from each side.

The barbarian went to the chest, donned the dinner robe, and slipped into his sandals.

"Here she is," said Ronisius, thrusting Filene ahead of him. Behind him, Qualius refastened the closures of the exit. The heating sheets incorporated in the walls of the tent began to glow.

Filene stood before him.

He sat, rather as before, on the edge of the couch.

"I am a free woman," she said.

"I am sure you have supposed so," said the barbarian.

"I am free!" she said.

"There are papers on you," said the barbarian, "suitably certified."

"False papers!" she said.

"Names may be false, details might be false," he said. "But the woman herself was enslaved. The measurements and descriptions, the toeprints, and fingerprints, the body codes, were all registered, and checked."

"But I am free!" she said.

"Not at all," he said. "Unbeknownst to yourself, you have been as much a slave as the others, the nineteen others, brought with you from Inez IV on the *Narcona*."

"No!" she said.

"You are a slave," said the barbarian.

"No!" she said.

"Rest assured," said the barbarian. "All is legal, all is in order."

"No," she said. "No!"

"Do not fret," said the barbarian. "You are not unique. Many women are made slaves. It is a common fate for them in thousands of societies on thousands of worlds."

"No!" she cried.

"Kneel," said the barbarian.

"As though I might be a slave?" she said.

"As a slave," he said.

She knelt before him, shuddering. Her fingers were locked inside the chain on her neck.

"Palms of your hands down, on your thighs," said the barbarian.

She complied.

"You will now be silent," he said, "until you are given permission to speak."

"Let me cut her throat," said Qualius.

A tiny sound of fear escaped the kneeling slave.

"Who fled in the hoverer?" asked the barbarian.

"Phidias, Lysis, and Corelius," said Ronisius.

"It seems they did not trust the matter, arranging the slave, and such, to a single man," said the barbarian.

"It seems not," said Ronisius.

"Why was there no pursuit?" asked the barbarian.

"The other hoverer, and the two treaded vehicles," said Qualius, "were disabled."

"It is perhaps just as well," said the barbarian. "Perhaps they will believe the business was accomplished to their satisfaction."

"Let us hope so," said Ronisius.

"Attend to the camp," said the barbarian. "There will be fruitless speculation, much confusion. Consternation will abound."

"Officers," said Ronisius, "were suddenly recalled to Venitzia, due to some unforeseen emergency."

"Excellent," said the barbarian. "That will do nicely."

"The slave," said Qualius, "may be taken outside the perimeter, and bound naked to a tree. Earlier in the evening I heard, far off, the baying of wolves. There must be such brutes about."

"Attend to the camp, my friends," said Otto.

Ronisius, standing, looked to the surface of the couch. "Captain," he said.

"I know," said Otto.

The dropped knife lay amongst the furs, half hidden.

The two men then withdrew, taking the tunnel exit which led to the main tenting.

"On whose behalf did you engage in your enterprise?" asked Otto.

She shook her head, frightened.

"You are not a free woman," said Otto. "A slave may be punished terribly for not telling the truth."

"I am afraid to speak," she said.

"He is elsewhere," said Otto. "You are here. I would expect you to be more afraid not to speak."

"Have mercy," she whispered.

"It would be easy to turn you over to Qualius," said Otto.

"—Iaachus," she said, "Arbiter of Protocol."

"So high a personage?" said Otto.

"Yes," she said.

"So close to the throne?"

"Yes."

"Are you sure?"

"Yes," she said.

"'Yes'?" said Otto.

"Yes," she said, "—Master."

"Perhaps you find it surprising that one so highly placed, so exalted, might deal directly in this matter," he said.

"Yes, Master," she said.

"It is not so surprising," he said. "Who would he trust with such a charge? Too, he would not expect you to return."

"I fear so, now," she said, "Master."

Otto stood up, facing the frightened, kneeling slave.

"On the couch," he said, "you will find a knife. It is there, amidst the furs. Obviously you are familiar with it. Fetch it, and bring it to me."

"It is dangerous," she said. "It is painted with poison."

"Must a command be repeated?" asked Otto. That, of course, can be cause for discipline.

She crawled to the surface of the great couch, ascended it, made her way to the knife, and returned, holding it by the handle, careful not to touch the blade, to the vicinity of the barbarian.

"Stand," said Otto.

She was small, standing before him.

"Perhaps you would like to drive it into my body?" he said.

"No, Master," she said, handing it to him.

"On many worlds," said Otto, "it is a capital offense for a slave to touch a weapon."

"Has Master tricked me," she asked, "that I may now be slain?"

"No," said Otto.

"A slave is grateful," she said.

"One punishes a slave for disobedience," said Otto, "not for obedience."

She put down her head, trembling. "Thank you, Master," she said. "Master is merciful."

"Perhaps not," he said.

"Master?" she said, apprehensively.

"On your knees," said he.

Swiftly she knelt, before him.

"Straighten your body," he snapped, "belly in, head up, hands down, palms on your thighs; shake your hair behind you; it is not to interfere with my looking upon you. Do you not know where you are? You are before a man. You are not a free woman. You are a slave, a commodity. Be beautiful!"

She looked at him, frightened.

"Good," he said. "That is how a slave kneels, beautifully."

"Master!" she wept.

"It is true, you are pretty," he said. "Yes," he said, "quite pretty. And you are doubtless aware that a pretty woman is even prettier, far prettier, with her neck in a collar. Yes, the noble Iaachus chose his agent well, an inviting, lovely, supposedly unarmed naked slave. Who would suspect a source of mischief so unlikely? And is this tiny, lovely dagger not a surprising instrument by means of which to address oneself to the commonly crude work of assassination?"

"Beware the blade, Master," she whispered.

"Beware this unportentous thing," he asked, "this inauspicious, slight piece of metal, tapering to so negligible a point?"

"Unseen death," she said, "inhabits its small terrain of steel."

"Dangerous, this tiny needlelike blade?" he asked, poising its point at her left cheek.

"Yes, Master," she whispered. "Death reclines there, in covert secrecy, ready to spring forth. Through the smallest portal put ajar swift death rushes in."

"Shall we see?" he asked.

"No, please!" she wept, drawing back a tiny bit.

"Only a crease, only a scratch?" he suggested.

"Please, no, Master!" she begged.

"Very well," he said, removing the point from her cheek, under the left eye, drawing back.

"Behold," he said. He thrust back the sleeve of the dinner robe.

"Master!" she cried.

He had drawn the blade across the inside of his left forearm, and, where it had taken its short journey, there was a thin, bright line of fresh blood.

He wiped the blood away with a small cloth.

"I do not understand," she said.

"It was clear to several of us, certainly to Ronisius, Qualius, and myself, even on the *Narcona*, that you, though a slave, did not take yourself to be a slave. What, then, was to be your role on Tangara? It was not difficult to speculate. What was not known were your confederates, one or more, who would abet you in your business. The weapon then, presumably, would be poison. Given the time involved, and your recent freedom, we supposed you were not a poison girl, prepared over a period of years, whose bite would be venomous. Too, in your medical examination, it was determined your teeth were sound, none hollowed to hold poison, thence to be discharged, as though by a fang, into a wound. This suggested, then, either poison to be administered in food or drink, or by a knife. If the deed were to be done secretly, as you fully expected to be extracted from the camp, it would presumably be administered in a private collation or by means of a blade or point. It was easy, even on the *Narcona*, to determine that no collation would be accepted in circumstances which might favor a conspirator or conspirators. Things became simpler here, in the camp. Ronisius, surreptitiously investigating the gear of officers, discovered the case, with the knife, amongst the belongings of Corelius. We did not know, of course, if others were in league with him. If there were others, and who they might be, had to remain undetermined for at least a time, until the assassination would be attempted. Their identities and number, of course, became clear with the flight of the hoverer."

"The blade was poisoned," said Filene.

"That was supposed so," said the barbarian, "given its slightness, and the strength, nature, and weight of the presumed assassin, a slave not likely to be trained in death skills, skills such that, in the hands of an adept, a needle or sliver can function as a lethal weapon."

"You removed the poison from the blade," said Filene, numbly.

"Certainly," said the barbarian. "The blade was stained, to reveal the poison, which was then scoured away, with coarse cleansers, even acid."

"You knew all the time," said Filene, softly.

"We surmised all the time," said the barbarian.

"Ronisius, then, replaced the cleansed blade in its case," she said.

"Of course," he said.

"You let me address myself, futilely and foolishly, to the deed," she said.

"It was important that the attempt be made, in order, if possible, to flush out the conspirators. I was even prepared to pretend being stricken, to observe the consequences, but the obvious preparation of the hoverer for departure rendered that ruse unnecessary."

"Yes, Master," she murmured.

"This is a pretty dagger, a lovely thing, a woman's weapon," he said. He regarded the implement, turning it over in his hand.

"Master?" she said.

"Please do not, Master!" she cried.

"Why not?" he asked.

"I do not want to die!" she said.

He then snapped the blade from the handle, and cast the pieces to the side.

She swayed, and gasped with relief.

"May I speak?" she asked.

"Yes," he said.

"I am in your power, wholly," she said. "What is to become of me?"

"By your own will, thinking yourself free," he said, "you would have struck at me with a weapon you deemed of lethal import, though you were in fact naught but an unpleasant, nasty little slave."

She was silent.

"Slaves are to be pleasing, wholly pleasing," he said.

"Yes, Master," she said.

"Do you think," he asked, "that you have been wholly pleasing?"

"I fear not, Master," she said.

"Your crime," he said, "for a free person, would be heinous. What do you think it is for a slave?"

"I know not," she said, trembling.

"It is a thousand times worse," he said.

"Spare me," she said.

"Why?" he asked.

"I am beautiful!" she said.

"Your body would sell," he said, "but your heart is worthless."

"Have mercy," she said. "I have known, since the *Narcona*, since being at the command and mercy of men, since kneeling before men, since having a collar on my neck, that it is a slave's heart!"

"I think," he said, "that I shall turn you over to Qualius."

"Please do not do so, Master," she said. "I do not want my throat cut, I do not want to be put forth, tied to a tree, naked, for wolves."

"Do you plead for your life?" he asked.

"Yes, yes!" she cried.

"What do you offer?" he asked.

"My body," she sobbed, "and its pleasures!"

"I see," he said, his arms folded, looking down upon her.

"I know men have desired me!" she said. "I have been aware of this since puberty, how they look upon me! I have seen their eyes, their interest, their expressions, how they have positioned themselves to see me, how they have sought to frequent my whereabouts, how they have sought introductions, how they have endeavored to win my smiles, how they have striven to please and serve me! I have twisted and diverted many men to my purposes."

"You are selling goods?" he asked.

"Yes!" she said.

"But you are not a free woman," he said.

"Master?" she said.

"A free woman can sell her body," he said. "But you cannot. You are a slave. You own nothing. It is you who are owned. You do not sell goods. Rather it is you who are goods. You have nothing to sell. Rather, it is you yourself who may be sold."

"Please, no, Master!" she said.

"Do you desire to be a good slave?" he asked.

"Yes, Master!" she said.

"I did not think it true before," he said.

"It is true now, Master," she said.

"Whether you are a good slave or not," he said, "will not be decided by you, but by Masters."

"Yes, Master," she said.

"I gather you wish to live?" he said.

"Yes, Master!" she said.

"Then you will strive zealously to be a good slave," he said.

"Yes, Master," she said. "I am changed now. I would hope to be granted the privilege of polishing your boots, as on the *Narcona*. I would be pleased, if it were my Master's will, to have my mouth taped shut, and be tied, kneeling, neglected, to the foot of his couch. I am my Master's toy, the mat on which he wipes his feet, his towel and footstool. I am nothing! I am worthless! I belong to him! I am his!"

At this point, clearly audible throughout the camp, and well into the forest beyond, like a sudden, alarming, cold flame of sound, pronounced and disruptive, tearing apart the silence of the winter night, came the shrill, oscillating shriek of a klaxon.

"You know the camp," said the barbarian. "What is this sound?"

"The alerting signal, Master!" she cried. "Something obtrusive has occurred, an attack, an animal at the wire, unannounced visitors or envoys, Heruls or Otungs, a party from Venitzia, some contact from the outside, anything!"

"When I approached the camp," he said, "no such sound, no such warning, was heard."

"They were watching for you, anticipating you," she said. "You were recognized in the floodlights, as you approached the wire."

"Who is now high in the camp?" asked the barbarian.

"Ronisius!" she said.

"'Ronisius'?" he snapped.

"Master Ronisius!" she said. Had she not understood that such a lapse might call for a switching?

The klaxon's disturbance of the night subsided, almost as quickly as it had begun.

The barbarian looked to the slave, fiercely.

"It cannot be an attack, Master," she said.

"Someone," he said, "may have been recognized?"

"I know of no one," she said.

The barbarian whipped away the dinner robe and kicked the sandals to the side. In moments he had gathered together, and drawn on, the hides and furs, the soft boots, which he had worn when first approaching the camp. He then strode to the tunnel exit from the chamber, that leading to the main tenting, that of the headquarters tenting.

"Otto!" cried Julian, elatedly, meeting him at the threshold of the bedding chamber. "You live!"

"I live," said Otto.

Behind Julian were Tuvo Ausonius and a small, exquisite slave, bundled in furs, whom Otto did not recognize.

"Captain Ottonius!" said Tuvo Ausonius. Behind him, the slave knelt.

"Be greeted," said Otto, grinning.

"Be shamed, friend," said Julian. "You were to wait in Venitzia, to proceed in safety, accompanied by trade goods, and imperial troops, to contact Otungs in the forest."

"I did not do so," said Otto. "I deemed it best to approach Otungs alone, not accompanied by imperial troops."

"I was delayed, surely deliberately, in Lisle," said Julian.

"When I arrived in Venitzia I discovered, to my dismay, not only that you had departed alone, but that the supporting expedition, then intent on locating and supporting you, had also departed."

"You followed, through the wilderness, alone?" said Otto.

"We three, no others," said Julian.

"You might have encountered Heruls," he said, "or Otungs."

"We were pursued from Venitzia," said Julian, "by enemies, sent from Venitzia."

"You survived," observed Otto.

"They did not," said Julian.

"We heard wolves," said Otto.

"We fought," said Julian, "but owe our lives, I fear, to Otung dogs."

"You are fortunate," said Otto. "Such dogs are trained to clear the vicinity of wolves."

"We count ourselves fortunate," said Julian.

"More than you know," said Otto. "Such dogs are close to wolves. Occasionally they set upon men."

"You are all right, dear captain?" inquired Tuvo Ausonius.

"Certainly," said Otto. "How is it that you ask?"

"We observed women, putative slaves, trade goods, being boarded on the *Narcona*," said Julian. "I was troubled. None were marked. It seemed to me that one knew not yet her collar. More troublesome was the sense I had that I had seen this woman before, somewhere, and not on a leash or chain. Curious, we investigated, and found discrepancies involved, falsity of claims and such. Alarmed, I had, from memory, a portrait prepared. Inquiries were conducted in Lisle, at markets, in slave houses, and such. No one recognized the woman. Then similar inquiries were conducted in more prestigious venues, from which I might have recalled the woman. These inquiries bore immediate fruit. Several citizens, particularly high citizens, citizens of the *honestori*, of the patricians, suggested it might be a likeness of a fallen, nigh-destitute patrician, even of the senatorial class,

a Lady Publennia Calasalia, formerly of the Larial Calasalii. We
had little doubt that such a person, disreputable and unscrupulous, eager to recoup wealth and power, might prove of interest
to men with much to hide and much to protect. Would conspirators not find such a person a likely recruit to further their ends
and schemes? And if assassination were in the offing what would
better assure its likelihood of success than ensconcing an assassin amongst slaves, a slave who, unsuspected, sooner or later,
would be almost certain to be alone with the intended object of
her work, and might have hours afterward in which to be sped
to safety, and presumed riches."

"An excellent plan," said Otto. "May I see this portrait?"

Julian reached within his furs, and, from the inside pocket
of his naval jacket, handed the putative likeness of the Lady
Publennia to Otto.

"Interesting," said Otto.

"We feared she might be here, in the camp," said Julian.

"Have you seen her, captain?" asked Tuvo Ausonius.

"One similar," said Otto.

"Beware!" said Julian.

"Look," said Tuvo Ausonius, pointing to Nika, kneeling
behind the men, to their left.

"Brush your hood back," said Otto.

The slave complied. A shake of her head spread the wealth of
her bright hair about her face and shoulders.

"Pretty," said Otto. "Where did you buy her?"

"We acquired her by the right of imperial seizure, exigency
of the empire," said Julian. This right, apparently, authorizes a
suitable imperial authority, by fiat, to acquire any given slave for
the empire, and, interestingly, well beyond this, to reduce free
women to bondage. We may speculate that this was the fate of
Elena, a brown-haired, gray-eyed former lady-in-waiting to the
empress mother, Atalana. She apparently, in some way, a careless action, an unwise expression, or such, had displeased the

empress mother. Iaachus may have suggested the discipline. In any event, Elena, it seems, soon learned what it is to be a female collar-wearer, having received this instruction at the foot of the couch of Iaachus.

"She was the serving slave of the Lady Publennia Calasalia in Lisle," said Tuvo Ausonius. "Interrogated, it was determined, as we had feared, that the Lady Publennia was no longer in Lisle. We brought her with us, then, in case an explicit identification of the mysterious Lady Publennia should prove necessary, or appropriate. I, for example, had never seen the woman in question."

"I understand," said Otto.

"If we should suspect deception or subterfuge," said Julian, "she will be killed on the spot."

"Come into the bedding chamber," said Otto, turning about. "There is a slave here you may be interested in meeting."

"Mistress!" cried Nika.

She then resumed her kneeling position, appropriate for a slave in the presence of free men.

"I gather," said Otto, "the identification is made."

"Indisputably," said Julian, with satisfaction.

"Hold position, you collared slut," warned Otto.

"One seldom finds women of the *honestori*, of the patrician class, even of the senatorial class," said Julian, "so positioned, naked, and neck-ringed."

"It is not unusual, in the halls of those whom you would speak of as barbarians," said Otto.

"I feared we might not arrive in time," said Julian.

"She was suspected, even on the *Narcona*," said Otto.

"Who enlisted her?" asked Julian.

"Iaachus," said Otto.

"Of course," said Julian.

"I fear," said Tuvo Ausonius, "there will be no way to prove that."

"I fear you are right," said Julian.

"It is dangerous to levy charges against powerful men," said Otto.

"It could be death," said Julian.

Otto regarded Filene, or Cornhair, the former free woman, Publennia Calasalia.

"She is pretty in her nasty way, is she not?" asked Otto.

"Indeed," said Julian.

"Shall I have her split her knees before you?"

"No," said Julian.

"Why not?" said Otto. "She is less now than a tavern slave, or brothel slave."

"She is unworthy to spread her knees before a free man," said Julian. He then unslung his rifle. "I have one charge left," he said. "Draw her out into the yard, into the snow, and I will do justice."

"Do not waste a charge on her," said Tuvo Ausonius.

"True," said Julian. "Such things on Tangara are valuable. We will take her into the yard and throw her across the wire."

"Hold position," Otto warned Filene.

She remained in position, that position in which Otto had placed her, one common for female slaves.

Otto turned to the exquisite, kneeling, red-haired slave.

"What is your name?" he asked.

"I have been named 'Nika', Master," she said.

"Rise, and stand here, beside me," said Otto.

"I am uneasy to stand," she said. "Free men are present."

"Here," said Otto, indicating the spot.

"You are sure this is your former Mistress?" he asked.

"'Former'?" she asked.

"Yes," said Otto. "She is now a slave."

"Yes, Master," said Nika. "She is my former Mistress."

"Doubtless she was a kind, patient, thoughtful Mistress?"

Nika trembled. She did not speak.

"Not at all," said Tuvo Ausonius. "Inquiries were made. The Lady Publennia Calasalia was an unusually demanding and exacting Mistress. She was noted for her short temper and lack of patience. Frequently did she subject this slave to needless castigations and gratuitous torments. The slave was frequently demeaned, mocked, berated, and ridiculed, even publicly. No matter how desperately the slave sought to please, the Mistress was never satisfied. Fault would somehow be found. Any pretext, or no pretext, would serve to elicit reprimands. The slave was frequently and well acquainted with the admonitions of her Mistress' switch, openly, publicly, even in the marketplaces, in the squares, and streets. Her life was made a veritable misery."

"But now," said Otto to the exquisite, red-haired slave, "you have priority. You are as first girl. That is why you are standing."

"Master?" asked Nika, frightened.

Otto then turned to Filene. "It seems," he said, "you abused your freedom."

"No, Master!" protested Filene, frightened.

"Perhaps you did not realize that the collar would one day be on your own neck."

Filene regarded him, wildly.

"On your belly!" snapped Otto. "Crawl to this slave who is as Mistress to you, and cover her boots with kisses. Now! Again and again, more, more, as the worthless slave you are! Now, tongue work. More! Lick, and whimper! Kiss those boots, head down, again and again! Cover them with your tears of fear and contrition!"

"Forgive me, pretty, lovely Nika," wept Filene.

"Oh!" cried Filene, kicked by the barbarian.

"Do you dare soil the name of one who is to you as first girl, letting it escape the portal of your slave lips?" he inquired.

"Forgive me, Mistress!" begged Filene. "I was intemperate and cruel! I muchly wronged you! Be kind! Forgive me! I am afraid! Do not hurt me, Mistress!"

"Shall I call for a switch?" asked Otto.

"No, Master," said Nika.

"The whip is at hand," he said. "You could use it, with two hands on the staff."

"No, please, Master," said Nika.

"Forgive me, Mistress!" begged Filene.

"I forgive you," said Nika, "poor, neck-ringed slave."

Weeping, Filene pressed the side of her face on the fur of Nika's boots.

"You must be hungry," said Otto to Julian and Tuvo Ausonius. "Return down the corridor. Make your wants known. If it is in the camp, it will be prepared for you. Take your lovely red-haired slave with you. She will kneel beside you, and see if you choose to feed her."

"First," said Julian, bending down and seizing Filene by the hair, and yanking her up, she crying out with misery, to her knees, "we will take this slave into the yard and throw her upon the wire. I know such things, the wires will slice through her, burning, leaving little but shreds of tissue on the snow. Such wire would resist the charge of a *torodont*."

"Seek the kitchen," said Otto. "Feed."

"The slave!" said Julian, angrily.

"She is my prisoner," said Otto. "I have a suitable disposition in mind for her."

"As you will, my friend," said Julian. Tuvo Ausonius, heeled by Nika, had withdrawn. Julian paused in the threshold. "The *comitatus*?" he asked.

"It will be formed," said Otto.

"The matter is arranged?"

"Yes."

"You can speak for the Otungs," said Julian.

"The voice of the king is the voice of the Otungen," said Otto.

"You have bargained with the king?" said Julian.

"I am the king," said Otto.

"How is this possible?" asked Julian.

"It has come about," said Otto, "in the ways of the Otungen."

"In dark ways, I suspect," said Julian.

"Civilized folk need not inquire too closely into such things," said Otto.

"The Otungs is the largest and most formidable tribe of the Vandal nation, the Vandalii," said Julian.

"I have heard so," said Otto.

"Will not the tribes of the Vandalii follow the lead of the Otungs?" asked Julian.

"I do not know," said Otto.

"Have you heard," asked Julian, "of the medallion and chain of the Vandal council?"

"No," said Otto.

"I had thought you would await me in Venitzia," said Julian.

"I did not think it advisable," said Otto.

"After my arrival on Tangara," said Julian, "I did not proceed immediately to Venitzia. I went, instead, to the *festung* of Sim Giadini, situated in the heights of Barrionuevo."

"I was raised in the *festung* village, at the foot of the pass," said Otto.

"I know," said Julian.

"And what did you seek there?" asked Otto.

"The origins of a friend," said Julian.

"Then you heard of a human child, a newly born infant, rescued from the plains of Barrionuevo, after a battle, delivered by a Herul rider to the *festung*, many years ago," said Otto.

"Yes," said Julian, "an infant, suckled by a dog, an infant who would be called 'Dog', who would grow to manhood in that place."

"It was I," said Otto.

"I met there," said Julian, "Brother Benjamin, a salamanderine."

"I remember him with fondness," said Otto. "He was kind to me, much as might have been a loving father. I am told it was into his arms that I was given by the Herul rider."

"Found near the infant," said Julian, "was a medallion and chain."

"I know nothing of that," said Otto.

"Both were given to the salamanderine," said Julian.

"Did you see this medallion and chain?"

"Yes," said Julian.

"What do you think it is?" asked Otto.

"The infant may have been of royal blood," said Julian.

"Unlikely," said Otto. "Tell me of this medallion and chain."

"It is of rich stuff, of gold," said Julian. "It is large, heavy, and loose, and closed, with five great links, each link fastened to others, with no opening, no catch, or lock. It bears an emblem."

"What do you think it is?" asked Otto.

"I do not know," said Julian. "I think it may be the symbol of the union of the Vandal tribes."

These tribes, it may be recalled, are five in number, the Otungs, the Darisi, the Haakons, the Basungs, and the Wolfungs.

"Brother Benjamin would not give it to you?"

"No," said Julian. "He may hold it for you. He may destroy it."

"Why would he do that?" asked Otto.

"The brothers are gentle creatures, creatures of peace," said Julian. "The Vandals, like the Aatii, or the Alemanni, as we know them, are feared. Security in the empire largely hinges on the jealousies and divisions of its enemies. Who knows what might ensue if, say, the medallion and chain were found, if the tribes of the Vandals were to become once more, after a thousand years, a single nation?"

"Then let the chain and medallion rest easy, forgotten, undisturbed, in the *festung*," said Otto.

"The *festung* itself may be destroyed," said Julian.

"It has stood for centuries," said Otto.

"Sects grow numerous and powerful," said Julian.

"I know little of such things," said Otto.

"The *festung* may be threatened," said Julian.

"The *festung* is a holy place, a retreat," said Otto. "The brothers are holy creatures."

"Few holy creatures are regarded as holy creatures by other creatures who think themselves holy," said Julian.

"I do not understand," said Otto.

"The brothers of the *festung* are Emanationists," said Julian. "By many, Emanationism is regarded as a heresy."

"What is a heresy?" asked Otto.

"A view with which one disagrees," said Julian.

"I do not understand," said Otto.

"The empire is tolerant," said Julian. "Fanatics are not tolerant."

"What is involved here?" asked Otto.

"Power has many faces," said Julian. "Too, it may wear many masks."

"It is hard to understand you, my friend," said Otto.

"You understand the ax, the sword," said Julian.

"Yes," said Otto.

"Not every sword is seen," said Julian. "Not every ax is visible."

"Do not speak strangely," said Otto. "I am a simple man, with simple thoughts, raised in a *festung* village."

"You are not simple," said Julian. "You are cunning and your thoughts are deep, and secret. You have the strength of a *torodont*, the quickness and agility of a vi-cat, the mind of a mover of men. Sometimes I fear you."

"And I the empire, and what is hidden in its thousand lairs," said Otto.

"*Civilitas* is the hope of the empire," said Julian.

"And yet," said Otto, "you would recruit a *comitatus*."

"Allow me to take this slave," said Julian, "and I will cast her on the wire."

"She is my prisoner," said Otto.

"She is nasty, disreputable, vicious, shallow, treacherous, and heinous. She would have killed you."

"She tried," said Otto. "She did not succeed."

"The wire," said Julian.

"I have another disposition in mind for her," said Otto. "Go, join Tuvo, and the little, red-haired slut. Get her out of those furs, and into a tunic. To see her so should improve the digestion. You could probably get good coin for her."

Julian, angrily, seized the kneeling Filene by the hair, and contemptuously threw her to the floor.

She looked up, from her side, frightened.

"You look well, fine lady," he said, "with a chain on your neck."

She averted her head, fearing to look into his eyes.

"She is at your feet," said Julian.

"That is where women belong," said Otto, "at our feet."

"We shall discuss the *comitatus* later," said Julian.

"In the morning," said Otto.

The men then clasped hands, hand to wrist, wrist to hand.

"I am pleased that you live, my friend," said Julian.

"And I am pleased, too, that you live, my friend," said Otto.

Julian then withdrew from the chamber.

Otto turned back to the slave who, trembling, lay prostrate at his feet.

"Master?" she said.

"You realize, lovely conspirator," he said, "that you have been discovered and apprehended, that you have failed in your murderous project, that you have been caught, like a pig in a trap, that you are alone, without succor, here in the remote, cold wilderness, far from civilization, that you are wholly and helplessly at the mercy of he whom you sought to treacherously slay."

"Yes, Master," she whispered.

"You were a high lady of the empire," he said.

"Of the Calasalii," she said, "of the patricians, even of the senatorial class."

"How came you to this, lying naked, at the feet of a free man?"

"I was wayward and reckless," she said. "I misspent resources. I abused my position and station. I lived extravagantly, wildly. I accumulated debts. I courted ruin. I defied creditors. I fled. I betrayed friends. I scandalized my family. I was cast out."

"You have betrayed the honor of your class," he said. "You stooped to accept a charge which might have been rejected by the most worthless churls of the *humiliori*."

"What was I to do?" she wept.

"Surrender yourself to your creditors, for the collar," he said.

"No, no!" she wept. "I fled worlds!"

"You continued to live your profligate existence," he said, "doubtless trading on the dwindling and ever more precarious credit of the Calasalii."

"Yes," she said, "until it was denied to me."

"I regard you at my feet," he said.

"Mercy!" she said.

"Where now are your robes, your gowns, your jewels?" he asked.

"Mercy, please," she begged.

"What are you now?" he asked.

"Be merciful," she said.

"I see at my feet, now," he said, "only a naked, neck-ringed slave."

"What is to be done with me?" she asked.

"I have a disposition in mind for you," he said, "one you richly deserve."

"I am to be sold?" she said.

"Perhaps, eventually," he said.

"I shall try to perform well on the block," she said, "to see that you make good coin on me."

"You would perform well on the block, in any event, as other slaves," he said. "The auctioneer's whip would see to it."

"I have knelt before men," she said. "I have experienced incredible sensations, the indescribable, suffusing thrills of what it might be to be owned, dominated, and mastered."

"Of course," he said. "You are a human female. Such beasts are bred for the collar. They are never content until it is on them."

As she lay on her side, her fingers seized at the chain on her neck.

"But you are petty and deceitful," he said. "You lay in wait, armed. You pretended longing. You would have put me off my guard, you tried to kill me. Do you think I would bestow upon you so simply the warmth, reassurance, and joys of bondage?"

"Do not throw me on the wire," she said.

"I do not intend to have you thrown on the wire," he said.

"Am I not to be kept a slave?" she asked.

"You are a slave," he said, "and you will remain a slave, but there are slaveries, and slaveries."

"I do not understand," she said.

"But first," he said, "there are details to which we will attend."

"Master?" she asked.

"I will teach you a little of your collar," he said.

"I do not understand," she said.

"Go to all fours," he said. "Crawl to the foot of the couch. Put your head up, over the couch, you may climb a bit, and grasp the whip in your teeth, do not touch it with your hands, and then draw back off the couch, and, on all fours again, crawl back to me, and lift your head, the whip between your teeth."

He watched the slave fetch the whip. Such simple exercises are useful in apprising a slave of her bondage.

She looked up at him, from all fours, her head lifted, her eyes frightened, the staff of the whip between her teeth.

"Keep the whip as it is," he said. "Do not release it. You are now going to be bound, hand and foot."

He then put her to her belly, crossed her wrists behind her back, and, with a slender leather thong, tied them together. He then similarly served her ankles. He then turned her to her back.

"The whip," he said.

She opened her mouth, releasing the whip.

She looked up at him, frightened.

He, standing over her, shook out the coils of the whip.

"As I recall," he said, "you petitioned me to correct your behavior, you wished to be improved. You petitioned a beating. You wished to be informed that you were a slave. You did not wish to be left in doubt. Indeed, you begged to have the free woman lashed out of you."

"No, no, Master," she said. "It was not my intention that such remarks be taken seriously. It was a ruse on my part, a mere ruse, to distract you, to have you turn away, to gather in the whip, and then I, your back turned, your attention elsewhere, was to strike you."

"You did not mean such things?" he said.

"Certainly not," she said.

"It seems your ruse failed of its effect," he said.

"Clearly," she said. "I can still feel your grasp on my wrist."

"You do not wish to be beaten?" he said.

"No," she said. "Certainly not."

"Why not?" he asked.

"I fear the whip," she said. "Its sight terrifies me. It would hurt. I do not wish to be hurt. I can scarcely conjecture what it might feel like on my body. I do not want to be whipped! I will try to be a good slave! Please do not whip me, Master!"

"I understand you were switched on the *Narcona*," he said.

"Yes," she said.

"But you have never been put under the whip," he said.

"No," she said.

"Why?" he asked.

"I think," she said, "because I am too beautiful to whip."

"No slave," he said, "if she is in the least bit displeasing, is too beautiful to whip."

"I will try to be pleasing, Master!" she wept.

"Wholly pleasing?"

"Yes, Master!"

"I think I will lash the free woman out of you," he said.

"I fear, Master," she said, "there is little of the free woman left in me."

"It is usually unnecessary and pointless to hurt a slave," he said.

"Do not hurt me, Master," she said, eyeing the whip.

"But I think it would be well for you to feel a few strokes," he said, "a few strokes for your instruction, not so much to hurt you, as to inform you."

"Please, no!" she said.

"Few things," he said, "so convince a woman that she is a slave, more than feeling the lash."

"Please, no, Master," she said.

"She can no longer then maintain the pretenses of freedom," he said. "She can no longer lie to herself. Once she has felt the lash she knows that she is truly a slave. She is convinced. She knows it in her deepest heart. All other options are precluded. She knows what she now is, a slave, only a slave, and is zealous to obey, that she not again be whipped."

"Please, no, Master!" she cried.

As she twisted, and turned, crying out, helpless in her bonds, weeping, ten strokes of the lash were put upon her.

He then cast the whip aside, and bent to her ankles, freeing them, and then cast her bodily, she gasping and startled, on her back, upon the deep furs which covered the surface of the couch.

"Behold," he said, "how you are honored, with the very surface of the couch."

She scrambled to her knees, amidst the furs.

He removed his garments, and joined her upon the couch.

She moved back, away from him, as she could, terrified, on her knees. She pulled futilely at her thonged wrists, fastened behind her.

He motioned that she should make her way toward him, bound, over the soft sea of furs.

She could not move.

He then reached out, and seized the chain locked about her throat, and pulled her to him, across the furs, on her knees. The links of the chain struck against one another. The metal disk on the chain, with its message in three languages, including its pictograph, danced beside his fist.

Then, holding her in place by the left hand, grasped tightly on the chain, he cuffed her four times, palm, back of hand, palm, back of hand.

"A slave is to obey instantly, and unquestioningly," he informed her.

He then thrust her down, back on the furs.

She looked up at him, frightened, wildly.

He seized her ankles.

"No!" she wept.

Then the slave found herself, for the first time, and as a slave, put to a man's pleasure.

Later he rebound the ankles of the slave and placed her on the floor, at the foot of the couch. He then fetched a chain from the chest at the side of the chamber, and, with two heavy, metallic snaps, fastened her, by the neck, to the ring fixed in the bottom of the couch.

"In the morning," he said, "you will be branded."

"Do not brand me," she said.

"You are a slave," he said. "All slaves should be marked. You will be marked."

"No," she begged.

"Collars might be removed, or changed," he said. "I am thinking of the slave rose. It is small, tasteful, and lovely, clear, unmistakable."

"But all would then know me as a slave," she said.

"Do you not know you are a slave?" he asked.

"I well know I am a slave," she said. "It has been taught to me. I have felt the whip."

"But perhaps you would hope to conceal your slavery?"

Her lip trembled, but she dared not speak.

"Speak," he said.

"Might not my slavery be a kept a private matter," she said, "something hidden, a secret?"

"Perhaps," said he, "on a world which denies the rightfulness of slavery for slaves, even if they need and seek bondage, if there is such a narrow, dismal world, but on better worlds, more open worlds, more tolerant worlds, more honest worlds, it should be proclaimed."

"But, marked, despite what I might wish, apart from my desires, all would then know me as a slave," she said.

"Yes," he said, "all would then know you as a slave."

"My bondage would be fixed on me," she said. "It would be what I was, openly, publicly, legally. It would be nonrepudiable!"

"Precisely," he said.

"I would be property, and goods, forever," she said.

"Yes," he said. "You would be known so on all the habitable worlds, the mightiest and smallest, the warmest and the coldest, on the most sophisticated and civilized, on the most savage and barbarous, on habitable worlds anywhere, throughout the galaxies."

"I fear the brand," she said.

"Appropriately," he said.

"I do not wish to be branded," she said.

"It is quite possible that cattle do not wish to be branded either," he said.

The slave, helpless in her bonds, her neck fastened by a chain to the ring on a free man's couch, moaned.

"Many slaves," he said, "are proud of their bondage. They do not wish to be free women. They pity and despise free women, for the emptiness, the aimlessness, the boredom, the banality, the worthlessness of their lives, for their lack of identity, purpose, and meaning, for their lack of a Master. They welcome and desire the brand. They realize that it is a mark of distinction, that it is an inflicted badge of quality, of specialness, of desirability and beauty. It proclaims them wanted, so wanted that they are owned by men. They are proud of their brands. They have been found worthy of being owned, of being branded."

"I fear I might be such a woman," she said.

"Some desire and seek bondage," he said. "They desire to submit, to be owned, to belong, to love, and serve. They desire to put themselves helplessly at the feet of a man, to be done with as he might please. They are not whole, nor content, until they are at a man's feet."

"May I speak, Master?" she said.

"Certainly," he said.

"Surely you will sell me," she said.

"In no way that you might expect," he said.

"I do not understand," she said.

"A slave need not understand," he said, "no more than another beast."

"Please!" she said.

"Recall that you have been a willing tool of cunning, duplicitous Iaachus, collaborating in schemes of deceit and treachery, that you would have killed me, that you, though a slave, were found less than wholly pleasing."

"What is to be done with me?" she asked.

"I told you," he said. "I have a special disposition in mind for you."

"What?" she begged.

"Perhaps," he said, "you will have preferred to have had your throat cut, or to have been put out for wolves, or to have been cast upon the wire."

"What, what, Master?" she begged.

"You will see," he said.

CHAPTER TEN

"Great Lady," said Iaachus.

"Loyal servitor," said Atalana, empress mother.

"It seems," said he, "that the throne is safe, if but for a time."

"The schemes of the plotter and pretender, Julian, he of the despicable Aureliani, he with wicked designs upon the throne, have been foiled?"

"One may hope so," said Iaachus, "at least for the time."

The empress mother, her frail body tiny amidst the cushions of the throne in her private audience chamber, leaned forward, fixing her small eyes on the lean, narrow-visaged, sable-attired courtier. "Recount to me, dear Iaachus," said she, "the manner of the falling out of these matters."

"Some months ago," said Iaachus, "on a summer world, you will remember that the secret traitor, Julian, approached the throne, petitioning a commission for the barbarian, Ottonius. We deemed it dubious policy at the time to deny so seemingly innocent and trivial a request by one of his importance, one kin even to the mighty emperor. A refusal might have generated curiosity amongst the worlds. Too, such a refusal might have signaled to the schemer that his machinations had been sounded, with the consequence that he might have become even subtler, and more on his guard. Too, he is known amongst the worlds, and respected. To refuse, let alone topple, so popular a figure might engage speculations, even repercussions, inimical to the throne. Accordingly, we granted the commission, pretending not to discern its more remote import, and its place in his plans. We arranged that the commission for the barbarian would be delivered, as though in good faith, to him at his villa on Vellmer, where the barbarian was his guest. We planned carefully, if unsuccessfully. We assigned an agent, Tuvo Ausonius, a civil servant, from Miton, to seemingly transmit the document, it putatively enclosed in a latched case, to be opened by dialing a combination. The case, of course, actually housed an explosive device, which would fire shortly after the dialing of the combination. Julian and the barbarian, Ottonius, would presumably open the case. It was made clear to the agent that it was to be opened only in their presence. We also dispatched an imperial delegation to Vellmer, suitably and officially, that all would be in order, bearing the actual document bestowing the commission. The delegation was to arrive after the detonation of the explosive device, and would then, in seeming surprise, sorrow, and disappointment, return with the then-meaningless document. We anticipated the possibility, of course, that the agent, or the device, might fail us. Accordingly, the delegation, well armed and trained, was to assault the villa and destroy it. Indeed, upon the detonation of the device, the matter was to be assured by an air strike. As it turned out the device, though detonated, failed of its objective, its intended victims having withdrawn in time. Similarly, the air strike failed, given the shielding of the villa, and its weaponry. As planned, given the contingency, the delegation attacked the villa, which attack was withstood. Indeed, not one member of the delegation survived."

"I am apprised of these matters, dear counselor," said the empress mother.

"It is germane that I recount them," said Iaachus, "that you may the better appreciate certain events which ensued, events consequent upon plans so secret that I did little more than allude to them in your presence."

"Who is to be more in your confidence than I?" she asked, sharply.

"None surely, great lady," he said, bowing, "but private audiences prompt speculation, and I hesitated to speak openly, even in the presence of the emperor himself."

"He is in his quarters, playing with his blocks and soldiers," said the empress mother.

"Or before his beloved sisters, the exalted, beauteous princesses, Viviana and Alacida," he said.

"That was wise of you," she said. "Both are vain, frivolous, shallow creatures. They concern themselves with jewels and clothes, entertainments and amusements. They could no more hold a secret than a sieve water. Would they had been men, stern of thought, wise in counsel, tenacious and far-seeing, with metal in their blood, to defend and expand the borders of the empire!"

"There is the emperor," said Iaachus.

"Yes," said the empress mother, "there is the emperor."

"I fear," said Iaachus, "that the conspirator, Julian, hopes to wed the fair Viviana or Alacida, that he might one day be positioned for the throne."

"The emperor is young," said the empress mother.

"At his age," said Iaachus, "some have led armies, and commanded fleets."

"The emperor amuses himself with other toys," she said.

"Few emperors have died in battle," said Iaachus. "Most have met their ends within the walls of palaces."

"Tasters are employed," said the empress mother. "Physicians are in attendance."

"A rush in the darkness, a knife to the heart," said Iaachus, "renders useless the precautions of the subtlest taster, the ministrations of the most devoted physician."

"Who can I trust but you, noble Iaachus?" said the empress mother, wearily.

"Would that either Viviana or Alacida had the brilliance, the shrewdness, the iron, the courage of Atalana!" exclaimed Iaachus.

"But they do not," said the empress mother. "Would that I had been a man!"

"There would have been an emperor!" said Iaachus.

"Do not flatter a weak, tired, old woman," said Atalana.

"I but speak the patent truth," said Iaachus.

"Is there no cure for the emperor?" said Atalana.

"The emperor is beloved throughout the thousand worlds," said Iaachus. "Glory to him!"

"Yes, glory to the emperor," said the empress mother, wearily, "while the empire totters."

"Despite your possible reservations with respect to the nature and character of your daughters, the beauteous Viviana and Alacida, who share much of your own beauty," said Iaachus, "you must recognize their enormous political importance. A marriage to either would much abet the ambitions of treasonous Julian."

"Or the ambitions of any other," said Atalana.

"I spoke, of course, of our foe, Julian," said Iaachus.

"I would have them strangled first," said the empress mother.

"I see," said the Arbiter of Protocol.

"You are valuable in your place," said the empress mother. "See that you keep it."

"Think not ill of me, great lady," said Iaachus. "Do not misunderstand me. I meant nothing. I do not aspire to heights. My only ambition is to serve you, humbly, and to the best of my poor ability."

"Forgive an old woman," said Atalana. "How suspicious and ungrateful she is! What stouter defense of the throne has she than noble Iaachus?"

Iaachus bowed.

"Do you truly think I am beautiful?" she asked. She

inadvertently touched her cheek, opening a tiny crack in the powder caked there.

"From whence, otherwise," asked Iaachus, "could fair Viviana and Alacida have derived their remarkable beauty, so close to, and yet so far from, yours?"

"You are a scoundrel, counselor," smiled Atalana.

"I but speak the patent truth," he said.

"You set plans in motion without my consent," she said.

"But to achieve ends congruent with your hopes," he said.

"I know only that you feared some alliance of Julian with barbarous forces and hoped, by some secret measures, to preclude their success."

"The empire is stable, safe, and eternal," said Iaachus, "but walls crumble, forces dwindle, fuel grows short, ammunition low, outposts are raided, borders are threatened, worlds with hostile intent loom."

"You failed once to foil Julian," said Atalana, "on Vellmer. Have you failed, again?"

"Others failed there, not I," said Iaachus.

"Have others again failed?" asked the empress mother.

"No," said Iaachus. "We have been successful. Julian sent his minion, the barbarian, Ottonius, to Tangara, to recruit dangerous tribesmen by means of which to prosecute his plans. One man might gather ten, and ten a hundred, and a hundred a thousand, and a thousand untold numbers."

The empress mother shuddered.

"Julian intends to either ascend the throne," said Iaachus, "or destroy the empire."

"He must be stopped!" cried the empress mother. "Have him killed!"

"He is known, and important, and respected," said Iaachus. "That would be dangerous. Few know him as do we. Most deem him a patriot. Many would hope he would ascend the throne."

"Kill him," said Atalana.

"We must be careful," said Iaachus.

"You tried to kill him on Vellmer," said the empress mother.

"Yes," said Iaachus, "on far Vellmer, in a remote villa, not in the midst of troops."

"What is to be done?"

"Nothing must be obvious," said Iaachus. "His murder might precipitate riots, an uprising, a revolution on some worlds. It might serve even as a pretext for secession."

"Let him be exposed to a lethal infection," said the empress mother. "Let a contagion be devised, which might rack planets. Let plagues be engineered. He perishes then, one victim amongst countless others, provoking no suspicion."

"Plagues might do to punish troublesome worlds," said Iaachus, "but there is little point in expending an ocean of poison when but a single drop is needed."

"But a single drop might provoke suspicion?" said Atalana.

"I fear so," said Iaachus.

"Let an accident be arranged," said the empress mother.

"I have arranged things differently," said the Arbiter of Protocol. "An indirect blow, which does not seem a blow, may strike most deeply. An unarmed man amongst armed men is little to be feared."

"I do not understand," said the empress mother.

"We remove the means from Julian and Julian is without means."

"Dear Iaachus?" said the empress mother.

"Julian's plans clearly involve the enlistment of barbarians, preferably in large, expanding numbers, and this enlistment, as he envisions it, begins with, and is contingent on, the services of the barbarian, Ottonius."

"I see now," said the empress mother, "why you have requested this unusual private audience."

"To report, of course, great lady," said Iaachus, "now that the thing is done and the utmost secrecy is no longer required."

"You have slain the barbarian captain, Ottonius," she said.

"In a way most natural, and most unlikely to provoke suspicion, in a venue far from civilization, and by means of an instrument most subtle and suitable, a poisoned blade in the privacy of a chamber, wielded by an agent most unlikely to be suspected, a free woman posing as a mere female slave."

"He reaches out, the lusting brute, and discovers that he has in his arms not a warm, quivering, yielding, moaning, meaningless vessel of pleasure, but death."

"Yes," said Iaachus.

"Where could a free woman be found to risk this?" she asked.

"One was found," he said.

"Some baggage of the *humiliori*?" she said.

"No," he said, "a fallen patrician, even of the senatorial class."

"Interesting," said the empress mother.

"Doubtless she expected to be extracted safely and richly rewarded," she said.

"Certainly," said Iaachus.

"You must beware," she said. "Such a woman would know much. Under fearsome interrogation, she might incriminate others. She might, too, for greater treasure, threaten betrayal, threaten exposure."

"Fear not," said Iaachus. "It was never intended that she be extracted safely, nor intended that she be rewarded, in the least."

"You left her to her fate?"

"Of course."

"You are a cunning rascal," she said. "But I am troubled."

"How so, great lady?" asked the Arbiter of Protocol.

"It seems a shame to use a free woman where a slave would do."

"She thought herself free, to be sure," said the Arbiter of Protocol, "but, unbeknownst to herself, she had been enslaved."

"Excellent," said the empress mother, "the stupid little fool, a slave and not knowing it!"

"Many women," said Iaachus, "for example, by imperial

listings, enslavement proscriptions, personal edicts, and such, have been made slaves without their knowledge. They go about their lives as usual, suspecting nothing, until they are seized, and find the collar on their necks."

"You are sure this delicate matter has been accomplished successfully?" asked the empress mother.

"Yes," said Iaachus, Arbiter of Protocol. "Captain Phidias, captain of the *Narcona*, which bore the barbarian to Tangara, and his two colleagues, two of his officers, officers Lysis and Corelius, have assured me on the matter."

"Excellent," said the empress mother.

CHAPTER ELEVEN

In order to clarify certain events, soon to be recounted, it seems to me germane to deal briefly with certain issues, scientific, historical, and institutional.

There is no doubt that the Telnarian empire existed, or exists. Which is not clear. Is it still with us, somewhere? Much depends on the rooms of space and the mansions of time. Surely evidence abounds in its many dimensions, archaic words, place names, linguistic affinities, customs, day names and month names, holidays, folk tales, legends, a thousand annals, and chronicles, coins, artifacts, the remains of fountains, now run dry for centuries, fallen statues, perhaps of unknown heroes or gods, half-effaced inscriptions, perhaps recounting glories, scraped into unintelligibility by zealots, the watchers or guardians, crumbled walls, damp, worn, overgrown with moss, the ruins of aqueducts, such things. One does not know if the Telnarian empire was founded here, or if it intersected with our world for a time, perhaps in some form of transit. Perhaps it was here, while it passed through. It is hard to know about these things. Are there worlds, and tangled histories of worlds, diverse lines of reality, which might, for a time, touch one another, and intertwine, however briefly? Could it disappear, and reemerge? Is there a circuit in such things, as some believe, as in the routes of comets?

Sometimes one fears the sky, dark with ships.

The orthodoxy on this point is clear, an orthodoxy which I, of course, celebrate and unhesitantly affirm. Make no mistake in this. I, as all good and wise men, subscribe to the correct view. Who would be so unwise as to do otherwise? The countless forms of evidence, so abundant, so seemingly incontrovertible, of so many kinds, scattered over its thousands of latimeasures, is fraudulent, primarily contrived, however inexplicably, or pointlessly, by heretics. Perhaps there was, for a time, a Telnarian empire, but it was a small, untoward sort of thing, a matter of villages, or isolated towns, at best a temporary step, soon left behind, on the path to our contemporary world of simplicity and pastoral perfection. One need only go to the casement, to see the peasants contentedly toiling with their hoes in the field, see the smoke emerging from the chimneys of the tiny, happy cottages in the distance, hear the hourly, monitory chimes of the bells in the watch tower.

We know the stories told of the Telnarian empire, of its galactic tentacles, its thousands of worlds, and such, must then, at least for the most part, be mythical. What a strange way they had of thinking about the pleasant lamps in the sky! It is quite possible they did not even grasp the fact that the universe was created for us, a fact which becomes clear when it is recognized that our world is the single, only world, and that it lies at the exact center of the universe, where there is room for only one world, of course, just one, ours, this indisputably demonstrating our special and privileged position in the cosmos.

How fortunate for our vanity!

How humble we must be, finding ourselves so situated, despite our unworthiness, our lacks and faults, at the very pinnacle and center of all time, truth, and reality!

So reads the orthodoxy.

Who can believe such nonsense?

Almost all who have been so instructed.

Fruitful and abundant are the comforting joys of abject ignorance!

Why bleed on the blade of truth?

I shall pause for a time.

The watcher has been announced.

I do not think I need fear him, at least overmuch.

He is a good man, and, happily, cannot read. I shall reiterate the declarations which he requires, and share some *kana* with him. He looks forward to that. I must not disappoint him. There is some protection, of course, in being a recluse, an eccentric inquirer into obscure things, presumably innocent, antique things. Too, my needs are simple, and I have little to do with others. I have little to fear. I am harmless. I threaten no one. I am safe.

What is an empire, what is an institution?

An empire, clearly, though it may extend in space and endure through time, is not a thing in any usual sense; for example, it is not like a tree or rock. Some empires may perish before a tree might bear its fruit and others might challenge the longevity of a rock. But they are not rocks and trees. One can see soldiers and ships, and walls and roads, but one cannot see an empire. Standards and flags, perhaps, but not empires. Yet not all empires wear the garments of power openly; as did, or does, the Telnarian empire; not all march with legions, and ship with fleets. Institutions, in their various sorts, are invisible, but sometimes real with a terribleness which would trivialize the splittings of worlds and the explosions of stars. Institutions differ. Some redeem and profit a species; others sink poisoned fangs into the mind; some transform and ennoble lives; others sicken quadrants, infecting them with the most virulent of plagues, those which prey on the innocence and vulnerability of the soul, particularly that of the young. How cunningly, cruelly,

and arrogantly they groom the young to do their bidding and
carry their burdens!

Science has become a secret thing, a thing of stealth and
sorcerers. I have known men who believed that light was not
simply there or not there, but that it moved, even as a horse
or dog, and very rapidly. I suspect this is true. I have known
men, too, who believed that the lights in the sky were not lamps,
but distant orbs of flaming gas, some far away. Others, you see,
besides myself, have read old books, sometimes hidden books,
sometimes encoded long ago. Our science is the last word in all
science, and the correct word, of course, for science is ended in
our time, as we know all there is to know, or, at least, all that is
worth knowing, but I know, too, there are a thousand sciences
which differ from ours, doubtless therefore being incorrect, but
I wonder sometimes if our science is correct, and I wonder, too,
sometimes, if all these thousand sciences might not be incorrect.
The world, even a small world, may be a difficult thing to understand. Fixed worlds, like tables, and borne lamps, are easier to
fathom. We know about tables, and lamps, and candles. The
annals hint at untold worlds, separated by almost inconceivable
distances, of systems, and a galaxy, and of galaxies beyond galaxies. They suggest, too, routes, openings, crevices, passages,
foldings, involutions, tunnels, and such, which, in some cases,
would make far worlds neighbors. Two points on a map might
be a yard from one another, but, if the map were folded in a
certain manner, the yard might prove an illusion, and the width
of a ribbon, two juxtaposed surfaces of the same map, pressed
together, might bespeak reality.

I insist on my orthodoxy. What sane man would not? But
in the inside, in the secret place, where there are no frames and
ropes, and burning irons, one wonders. I do not fear thought,
secret thought. It does not frighten me. It neither threatens nor
jeopardizes my prestige, my position in society, my wealth, my
power, or my livelihood.

So what is one to make of the Telnarian empire?

I think it existed, or exists.

Once my sleeve, long ago, briefly, brushed a golden column.

The watcher is gone.

I shall return to the accounts.

CHAPTER TWELVE

"They learn quickly," said Julian.

"They are intelligent, highly so," said Otto.

"Barbarians are to be feared," said Julian.

"I am a barbarian," said Otto.

"I fear you," said Julian.

"Abrogate the project," suggested Otto.

"It is the only hope for the empire," said Julian. "The common citizens care only for their ease and comfort, their pleasures and entertainments, and will have others feed them, support them, and defend them."

"Not all, surely," said Otto.

"No," said Julian, "but many are beaten down, and disheartened, crippled by prolonged labor, particularly by the forced labor of *munera*, in lieu of taxation. Many are mired, too, in the legal bindings, now widely spread, where one must follow one's father's calling, craft, or profession, this intelligently instituted to stabilize the tax base, and others are landless tenants, *coloni*, and others are serfs who, as with the legal bindings, are bound to the soil, who must live and die on the same plot of land. Such folk have little in common but their misery and want, and their hatred for any better off than themselves, for landowners, clerks, officials, overseers, even for the empire itself, which they see as their foe and oppressor. And, too, there are the ambitious, who seek gain, and power, and would pursue their own fortune at the expense of the empire."

"Such, of course," said Otto, "are useful to predators, in equipping and funding incursions."

"True," said Julian.

"My people," said Otto, "lack the skills, the expertise, the tools, the resources, the industrial base to design and build fearsome weaponry and ships."

"Others will do so," said Julian, "others who remain unnoted, on far worlds, who fear to press a trigger, or grasp a helm, who wait to creep forward and feed on the kills of lions."

"I am dismayed," said Otto.

"Be not so, my friend," said Julian.

"I know something of the forging of a blade of steel," said Otto. "I know nothing of the forging of a blade of fire."

"You need not," said Julian. "It is one thing to manufacture a rifle or pistol, and another to use it effectively."

"I do not care for such weapons," said Otto.

"You like to be close to your kills," said Julian.

"One knows then what one is doing," said Otto. "One sees the blood, and may consider how far to go."

"Uneasy restless worlds, several with diminishing, but yet-unexhausted resources, back invaders," said Julian.

"And you would arm such men to resist such men?" said Otto.

"Yes," said Julian.

"It is an unwise shepherd who brings in wolves to guard sheep," said Otto.

"Sheep cannot guard themselves," said Julian.

"Or will not do so," said Otto.

"The perimeter is penetrated," said Julian. "Worlds are lost, or fall away."

"Permit them to do so," said Otto.

"Never!" said Julian.

"The palace will have them abandoned," said Otto.

"It must not!" said Julian.

"Perhaps the empire has grasped beyond its reach," said Otto.

"Never!" said Julian.

"Perhaps it will draw back," said Otto.

"To what?" asked Julian.

"To the inner worlds," said Otto.

"The least retreat," said Julian, "will be understood as a sign of weakness; it will arm enemies, and inspirit defiance. The first rock removed from a wall makes the second easier to dislodge."

"Surely the inner worlds are more secure," said Otto. "Will the palace not have it so?"

"The emperor is a boy, with the mind of a child, coveting toys and fearing insects," said Julian. "He counts for nothing. His sisters are scarce worth a collar. Power is vested in the empress mother, a vain, timid old woman under the baleful influence of a courtier, one who fears me, and a new order in the palace, one intent to keep things as they are, one intent to protect himself, his position, and his power at all costs, though the empire crumbles."

"Perhaps he merely sees the empire differently," said Otto.

"The situation is desperate," said Julian.

"So desperate that you would arm barbarians," said Otto.

"Who else would have the courage and will to face foes so fearful, so dangerous and determined?" asked Julian.

"Hereditary enmities exist amongst tribes," said Otto, "which you would seek to exploit."

"One seizes what weapons lie at hand," said Julian.

Here we may suppose that Julian had in mind, in particular, the hostilities between the tribes of the Vandals, amongst which was that of the Otungs, or Otungen, and those of the Alemanni, whose largest tribe was the Drisriaks.

"I respect the empire," said Otto, "as I might respect the

seasons or the stars, the vi-cat or the *arn* bear, but I do not esteem it. I do not love it."

"Therein we differ, dear friend," said Julian. "Understand it. See in it *civilitas*, the hope of a thousand species."

"*Civilitas*, under the sword," said Otto.

"*Civilitas* cannot survive without the sword," said Julian.

"You are my friend," said Otto.

"*Barbaritas*?" smiled Julian.

"Yes," said Otto.

"So simply?" said Julian.

"So simply," said Otto.

"Is it not much like the bond of the *comitatus*?" asked Julian.

"I think so," said Otto.

"One would die for one's friend," said Julian.

"*Barbaritas*," said Otto.

"*Barbaritas*," said Julian.

"You pause, you muse?" said Otto.

"I sometimes fear the future is yours, my friend," said Julian, "where the blood is hot and fresh, and flows strongly, like a scalding, rushing stream in the veins."

"The empire has always been," said Otto.

"Not always," said Julian. "Once there was no empire. Once there were only nine villages along a river, on a small, unimportant world."

"Long ago?" said Otto.

"Very long ago," said Julian.

"It is said the empire is eternal," said Otto.

"Let it be so," said Julian.

"Yet I fear for your empire," said Otto.

"And well you might," said Julian.

"No longer," said Otto, "are its standards borne bravely."

"The thousand suns must flash again on them," said Julian.

"You weep," said Otto, puzzled.

"Men no longer seek adventure and conquest," said Julian. "They now seek comfort and protection. Even a fortress of iron may be eaten away by the rust of neglect, and, when its walls collapse, the vermin within will be prey for the vi-cat and *arn* bear, or die of hunger and cold."

"Perhaps they will merely change Masters," said Otto.

"And their new Masters," said Julian, "will be the lions of the future."

"You fear for the empire," said Otto.

"Yes," said Julian. "I fear it is no longer loved."

"Surely a thousand worlds will stand for the empire," said Otto.

"On many worlds," said Julian, "there is the loss of soil, soil drained of nutrients, borne away by the wind; there is erosion, widespread desiccation, a scarcity of water, and its contamination; there are seas enfilthed with pollution; there are swamps one cannot approach without protective gear; there is the destruction of forests; there is the abandonment of mines, the exhaustion of mineral resources, cavernous shafts emptied of ore and metals; there is the debasing of currency, famine, disease, chaos, banditry."

"It is so, and yet the empire sleeps?" said Otto.

"It must awaken," said Julian.

"To some nightmare," said Otto.

"No," said Julian. "But to a new dawn."

"A new dawn," said Otto, "but of whose day?"

"Let it be that of Telnaria," said Julian.

"Resources are finite," said Otto. "They diminish. The time will come when few will be able to step amongst stars. Engines will be cold. Radios will be silent. Worlds will be alone. The theaters and stadiums will be empty, the altars untended. The vi-cat and the *arn* bear will reclaim their ranges. The time will come when the forging of the steel blade will become more common than the forging of the blade of fire."

"Let the empire be eternal," said Julian.

"As you will," said Otto.

"The empire is eternal," said Julian.

"How so?" asked Otto.

"I will have it so," said Julian.

CHAPTER THIRTEEN

The month of Igon was now long past. The snows had melted long ago from the flats of Tung, or, if you prefer, the plains of Barrionuevo. The lush cattle grass had sprung, thick and green from the black, moist soil in the spring, and the Herul herds, as was the seasonal indulgence of their herdsmen, had drifted south, wading to their knees in the long, wide river of grass flowing between the foothills of the heights of Barrionuevo on the east, and the winding Lothar River on the west. One could still see, however, even now, in the summer, from the wagons of the Herul camp, snow on the distant heights of the Barrionuevo range, amongst which, far to the east and south, might be found the allegedly schismatic *festung* of Sim Giadini. One could hear the lowing of cattle, the play of children, and the occasional rattle of a slave bell. The Herul wagons, in the ancient fashion, were circled, that a wall of sorts might be formed, to discourage the entry of cattle, and to give pause to nocturnal, prowling vi-cats, and any other intruders which might be so unwise as to attempt an unwelcomed entry into the camp. Now, however, during the long summer days, before nightfall, two wagons, to the Lothar side, were drawn back, affording between them, one on each side, a portal into the camp, through which an occasional rider, his watch done, might enter, or a peddler with his pack or cart, or a trader with his wagon, were he willing to risk his wagon in such a camp, such visitors usually from the provincial capital, Venitzia, or Ifeng, as the Heruls would have it, for Tangara, of course, had been claimed long ago by the empire. Many years ago the camp portal would have remained sealed, even in the daylight hours, but there was little to fear now, as the Otungen were now no longer mounted, and were no longer in a position to dispute the lush grasslands of the flats of Tung. Years ago the lance-bearing Otungen, with their heavy swords and ponderous steeds, had been defeated by the fleet, swiftly encircling, attacking and withdrawing enhorsed archers of the Herul nations, and driven west of the Lothar into the abutting forests. Heruls seldom entered the forests for they were unfamiliar, thick, dark, and dangerous, a milieu so dense that horses could scarcely penetrate, let alone maneuver or race, where branches might sweep an unwary rider from the saddle, and death might lurk undetected in the shadows at one's stirrup. Indeed, in such places the empire, on various worlds, had lost legions. In these days, of course, a truce, or standing-off, of sorts existed between the grassland-roving Heruls and the forest-dwelling Otungs.

As is often the case with splendid enemies, the Heruls and the Otungs, or Otungen, for the most part, respected one another. Each, for the most part, with the sensitivity likely to accompany presently sheathed blades, accorded the other the respect it is common amongst warriors to accord a valuable and worthy foe. Only against the finest stone can one's blade be best sharpened. To be sure, it remained dangerous for a Herul to enter the forest and for an Otung to cross the Lothar. Trade, and converse, amongst these two species, which sometimes occurred, usually took place on the shores of the Lothar, or on trade islands, which, here and there, divided the river. It was rumored in the camps of the Heruls that the Otungs had, within the past year, despite the injunction of the Herul council of chieftains, elected a king, not a year king, emerging from the bloody conflict of clans, which so divided the Otungen, but a king whose authority and leadership did not end with the killings following the winter solstice. This development, assuming it had actually taken place, was not likely to improve the somewhat delicate relations between the two nations.

Cornhair crouched between the wheels of one of the wagons. Her fingers held to the clapper in the bell hung about her neck. To be sure, that was forbidden, as much so as stuffing the bell with grass. It was to be free to swing, and sound, as a slave bell must. This was a large, heavy, dull, plain bell, tapering and rectangular, nothing like the tiered, locked or tied, slave bells with their charming, stimulating jangle, which might be fastened about a slave's ankles, wrists, or neck, bells the jangle of which proclaimed the presence to all within earshot of a helpless, vulnerable pleasure object, bells designed to arouse male interest and passion, and bells cunningly designed to stir the belly of the slave herself, as well, bringing her to a state of readiness and need, a state in which she will kneel and beg for a slave's relief, hoping to be granted the lengthy and exquisite raping which, with fortune, may be accorded to one such as she, a slave, a purchasable animal and property.

Cornhair muchly feared Borchu and her switch.

So she stayed between the wheels, hiding, holding the clapper of the bell, crouching down. She did not dare, of course, leave the wagons without being accompanied or having been ordered to do so, say, to gather *hineen* for the common kettles. For such a lapse a slave might be hamstrung or fed to the dogs. One of the other camp slaves, White Ankles, had told her Borchu was searching for her. She had not yet, however, been seen by Borchu nor had Borchu called her name, at least within her hearing. Cornhair trembled, and clutched the clapper of the bell even more tightly. Where was Borchu? Was Borchu really seeking her, or was it a cruel joke played on her by the other slave, for Cornhair knew she was not popular with the other girls. Perhaps because she was so obviously superior to them?

Should she have sought out Borchu? Would that have been safer, and meant fewer strokes of the switch? She did not know. Borchu, too, seemed to hate her, so much, even more than the other slaves. She did not know why that should be. Perhaps it was because of her hair color, or eye color, which were unusual, even amongst humans? Surely it could not have to do with her character or personality, such as they were. These would have been of no more interest or concern for a Herul than the character or personality of a pig. Perhaps it had to do, then, with her carriage, attitude, or bearing, for it seems possible that, at that time, some trace of her former station and quality, its haughtiness and insolence, the recollection of the arrogant height of her birth, perhaps hinted at now or then in a gesture or expression, might have lingered in Cornhair's demeanor.

Perhaps at that time she did not fully understand the transformation effected in a woman by the affixing of the collar. Perhaps at that time she thought herself a slave only in a legal, or nominal, sense. Perhaps she had not yet realized her collar, had not yet learned it. The time would come when she, as other slaves, would understand that no bit of her was free, that no particle of her was free, that every cell in her body was a cell in the body of a slave. One morning the slave awakens, and realizes she is a slave, helplessly and irremediably, and should be a slave, that this condition is hers, and rightfully and perfectly so, and then she has changed forever. She kneels, and is transformed; the war is done, and may not be renewed; she is ecstatic in the defeat for which she has longed; she experiences the liberation of submission; she has freed her deepest self. She embraces her bondage humbly, gratefully, and joyfully. She has then come home to her being and sex. She is then content at her Master's feet. But, of course, it was common enough for Herul women to hate slaves. In this, Borchu was not unusual. This may have had to do with some Herul men, some of whom found soft, fair skins of interest, as an oddity, if nothing else; surely they were

different, at any rate, from the shimmering, tinted scales of their
women, resistant to the scratching of brush, thorns, and knife
grass. She had cut the calf of her left leg on such grass, and
was now alert to avoid its yellow, innocent-appearing patches.
Accordingly, not only Borchu, but many of the Herul women,
as well, hated the small, soft-skinned beasts about whose neck
was chained the slave bell. Too many men, perhaps, seized and
sported with such stock, and used it liberally for their pleasure,
even as the inclination of the moment might move them. Did the
Herul women not note slaves being dragged up the steps of wagons or being put to the dirt between the wheels? In any event,
by the Herul women, the smooth-skinned wearers of the slave
bell were commonly despised even more than the tiny, raiding
filchen which would try to gnaw through the sacks of *hineen*.
And, unfortunately for the slaves, they found themselves generally under the supervision of the Herul women, for the men, in
general, paid them little attention, save when they were moved
to do so. Now, usually, Borchu was diligent and tenacious, but
there had been the incident, and that had apparently distracted
her, that is, if she had been looking for her at all.

Cornhair did not fully understand the incident, even though
the Heruls spoke a dialect of Telnarian, or something which
seemed part Telnarian, and part something else, something low-
pitched and sibilant. Indeed, Cornhair, to her grief, had had
difficulty understanding the Heruls at first, and had not immediately grasped that they were speaking Telnarian, or something
like Telnarian. Other camp slaves, at first, had translated for
her, and, later, helped her to recognize and expect the phone-
mic substitutions which brought the Herul stream of sound into
something recognizably Telnarian. Happily for her, the Heruls
found her Telnarian intelligible, possibly because her phonemes
were sounds with which the Heruls were familiar, from prisoners, slaves, tradesmen, administrators and officials at Venitzia,
and such. Cornhair had never thanked the other slaves for their

assistance in her linguistic acclimatization, which is understandable, as they had been clearly of the *humiliori*, at best, and she had been not only of the *honestori*, but of the patricians, and even of the senatorial class. Indeed, two of her uncles had served in the senate itself. Shortly after she had made it clear that they were owed nothing, as they had merely, appropriately, served their better, one who had been of a much higher station than theirs, they had withdrawn from her. She did not have anything further to do with them. They were inferior. Too, she did not need them any longer.

It was extremely important, of course, for a slave to understand the language of her Masters. She is to be docile and submissive. She is to obey instantly and unquestioningly. Masters tend not to be patient with stupid or ignorant slaves. Even a claim of noncomprehension, however justified, or a pathetic plea for clarification, or repetition, might bring the lash, or worse. The slave struggles with all her intelligence and application to learn the language of her Masters, and to learn it quickly, and well. She is a slave.

Her first sense of the incident was when a fellow went to the steps of a wagon, followed by several other fellows, and called out to a putatively unseen occupant. Others had soon gathered about, too, amongst them women, and children.

"Hunlaki is old," she had heard.

She did recognize Hunlaki, now and then in the camp. He was one of the few male Heruls in the camp who seemed old. He did seem clear-eyed, and strong, and agile, but, it was true, he was old, or, at least, older than most of the males in the camp. There were several middle-aged and old women amongst the Heruls, and many children, of both sexes, but very few old men. She had speculated that Herul males were not long-lived, at least on the whole. In a sense, she was correct. We, at our distance, and with our familiarity with the annals, are in a much better position to understand what occurred than the slave, Cornhair.

"The wagon is mine!" had called the fellow, at the foot of the stairs leading up to the wagon. "Emerge from my wagon! It is mine, by claim!"

"Blood!" had cried an old woman, to others, as she hurried toward the wagon, soon joined by others, and swarming children.

Indeed, there were one or two Telnarian traders, from Venitzia, as well, in that small crowd.

"Hunlaki is done," announced a short, thickly bodied fellow, his horse tied to a nearby wagon.

"Let us watch, and see if he dies well," said another.

"He will," said another. "He is Hunlaki."

"The dogs have not fed in two days," said another.

"They will feed tonight," said another.

"Excellent," said another, "or they would soon drag down a steer."

"Come out, decrepit one!" called the fellow, in helmet and fur, at the foot of the stairs to the wagon.

But the door to the wagon did not open.

"Come out, old one!" cried the fellow at the foot of the stairs. "The dogs are hungry!"

"Hunlaki was a great warrior," said a man.

"Long ago," said another.

"Depart from my wagon, old one!" demanded the fellow at the foot of the stairs. "I have a throat to cut!" And, indeed, he had in his hand a Herul knife, with its blade from Venitzia, and its handle of yellow bone.

The reason that, to the puzzlement of Cornhair, there were few old men in the Herul camp was that the Heruls, as certain other species, tend to eliminate the old and weak, particularly older and weaker males. There seem to be several strands of consideration which feed into this particular practice, cultural, and, possibly, biological. First, there is an examination of newly hatched offspring. Those deemed unsuitable are thrown to the dogs. Second, there is competition amongst the wagons, for wagons, particularly fine wagons, rather like that in some species for territory. And, as territory is acquired, in many species, so, too, as a consequence, are females. Amongst the Heruls, the possession of a wagon, particularly a fine wagon, confers position and status, and the possessor of a large, strong, well-built wagon is likely to have a choice amongst young females. There are also, of course, as in many species, competitions for dominance, with its usual concomitant of access to females. Sometimes conflicts occur amongst males, with females as, so to speak, the prize. Many Herul females are pleased to mate with a male who has killed to possess her. Even old women, nursing precious memories, proudly tell their grandchildren of such things. One then adds to such things the fact that, throughout much of their tribal histories, the Heruls have faced the natural selections of hunger, disease, and war, and in primitive war, war in which intelligence, keen senses, and physical skill are likely to make the difference between life and death, natural selections take place, selections which, in their way, strengthen certain bloodlines conducive to group survival. As with various peoples, all males are expected to be warriors and face enemies, aggressors, invaders, and such. It is not the case with the Heruls, as it is with more civilized folk, that the healthy, intelligent, adept, and strong are sent forth to die whilst the sickly, stupid, clumsy, stunted, and weak remain at home, in safety, to propagate their kind. In any event, nature, with its blind, unplanned wisdom, the fruit of millennia of harsh selections, for better or for worse, has produced certain animals, such as the vi-cat and *arn* bear, and certain peoples, such as the Heruls.

"Come out, old one!" cried the fellow at the foot of the stairs leading up to the wagon of Hunlaki. "You have lived long enough! Come out! I have a throat to cut!"

Scarcely had these words left his throat when a hand, from behind, seeming to emerge from the crowd, closed over his mouth, tightly, and pulled his head up and back, exposing the throat, and the knife, with a swift, clean draw, cut back to the base of the spine.

"I am out," said Hunlaki. "And it is you who have lived long enough."

The fellow twisted in the dirt and blood at Hunlaki's boots.

"I, too, had a throat to cut," said Hunlaki.

"He did not see you," said a fellow.

"It was not my intention that he should," said Hunlaki.

"You are cunning," said a man.

"I keep my saddle," said Hunlaki. "I keep my wagon."

"Excellent, dear friend," said one whom Cornhair had heard called Mujiin.

Mujiin, it was said, had long ridden with Hunlaki, even from the time of the last, great battle with the Otungen, following which the Plains of Barrionuevo had become the Flats of Tung.

Mujiin seemed much pleased.

He had not, of course, interfered in the business at hand. It was not the Herul way.

"Strip this," said Hunlaki, gesturing to the gasping, choking figure at his feet, its hands clutched about its throat, the blood running between the tentaclelike digits. "The dogs are hungry."

"Tonight they will be fed," said a fellow.

"We will gamble for his helmet, his furs, and horses," said a man.

Mujiin had ascended the steps of Hunlaki's wagon. He carved a deep notch in the right doorpost of the wagon. It was one of six such notches.

The figure at Hunlaki's feet was now inert.

Its helmet, furs, and boots were being stripped away.

"It seems you still live, old warrior, old Hunlaki," said a man.

"As of now," said Hunlaki.

"I thought he would kill you," said a man. "But he did not."

"And you lost a silver *darin*?" said Hunlaki.

"Two," said the man.

"I hope to die in battle," said Hunlaki, "and hope to be killed by a greater one than he."

"Who?" asked a man.

"A greater one than he," said Hunlaki.

He watched the stripped body of the Herul being dragged toward the gate. There was a line of blood marking the furrow of its passage. Outside the gate, one could hear the howling of the dogs, doubtless excited by the smell of blood, a scent which their keen nostrils can detect, even in the summer, at a range of several hundred yards.

Hunlaki wiped his blade on his fur boot.

A Herul youth, perhaps no more than five years of age, looked up at Hunlaki.

"Learn from this, young warrior," said Hunlaki. "Be not boastful, be not vainglorious, do not preen like the bright-tailed sunbird. Do not stand out. Do not be easy to see. Be one with the grass and trees. Do not stand upright on high ground. Be always on your guard. Look about yourself frequently. When one faces north, expect the vi-cat to attack from the south. When one faces south, expect it from the north."

"I will, old warrior," said the child.

"I must to my watch," called Mujiin, pleased, from the high step of the stairs to the wagon of Hunlaki.

"I shall accompany you," said Hunlaki.

The incident had occurred in the neighborhood of noon.

The fortresslike Herul camp was a large one, though many are larger. It consisted of some fifty wagons. The camps are larger in the spring and summer when there is ample grazing for the cattle. That is also a time for trading, converse, courtship, riding contests, martial games, the chanting of histories, and such. In the fall and winter the camps are smaller and, naturally, more numerous. This distributes the herds in such a way as to take advantage of the seasonally reduced pasturage. In the fall the herds begin to grow their winter coats. It is said that the cattle then resemble lumbering, shaggy hillocks, and, when it snows, seem like small, white, living mountains, the air above them steaming with the smoke of breath, crowding together in large circles. The Tangaran winter is often a difficult time for the herds and, in the fall, perhaps anticipating losses, the Heruls thin the herds for meat, hide, and bone, which, in the spring, may be used in trade, usually with the merchants of Venitzia. Fodder is also cut and dried in the summer, by women and slaves, and stored in earthen burrows. This is usually reserved for prime animals, and cows. Many of the steers wax fat in the summer and fall, and live off this fat in the winter. It is common, too, for them to chop and paw through the snow, for grass, lichens, and herbs.

In late Igon, Cornhair, nude, but wrapped head to foot in thick furs, the furs fastened tightly about her with several coils of rope, had been brought to a trade island in the Lothar. There she was flung, from the man-drawn sled, so helpless and wrapped, upon the stony beach of the island, on its eastern side, nearest the Flats of Tung, with other trade goods, for there were several such sleds. Helpless in her wrappings of bound fur she understood little of what was transpiring. After a time she heard the approach of horses, or what we have, for convenience, termed horses, snarling and snorting, apparently breasting the chill stream, several of them, and then she heard their paws breaking the edge of ice, near the shore, and then heard their scratching on the cold, stony beach. Boots struck the beach as riders dismounted. Something, too, or several things, seemed to be dragged over the cold gravel of the beach. She then heard Telnarian, and something else, which she did not at that time recognize. She heard also the cackling of domestic fowl, the squealing of pigs. After a time, she sensed something close to her, and then something was undoing the furs about her head. They were suddenly pulled back and she shut her eyes against the painful, ensuing blast of light, with its concomitant of bitter, piercing cold. She opened her eyes, screamed, and lost consciousness. She had seen her first Herul, the large eyes, the scaled skin, the seemingly earless head. Almost immediately she was returned to consciousness, awakened, slapped again and again, for stockmen, slavers, and Masters tend not to be patient, let alone indulgent, with their beasts, no matter how slight, soft, and fair they may be. "No, no!" she cried. And then, wide-eyed and horrified, she was silent, as a clawlike tentacle was pressed across her lips. She felt the hardness of the monitory digit and realized she was not to speak. Too, in a moment, she felt one of those digits press against the side of her neck. She did not understand this, but, within the digit, then unsheathed at the Herul's will, was a soft membrane which, even in its momentary contact with her skin, registered her unique biological identity, leaving a trace which, in the Herul's memory, was uniquely hers, much as a Herul dog might remember her smell, a slaver might take her measurements, and her finger and toe prints, or an imperial warden obtain and file away a record of her hereditary uniqueness, that borne unmistakably in each of her cells, which no disguise or falseness could alter or conceal. Later, when she would be tied naked to the learning post in the Herul camp, many other Heruls, considering her, would make a similar determination.

Cornhair, to her consternation, and misery, in the cold, was relieved of the ropes and furs, and, by two Otungs, dragged to her feet, and, arms held, exhibited to the Heruls. In that instant, shivering, moaning with cold, she realized she was the only female amongst the trade goods. The other women, nineteen of them, who had been brought to Tangara with her on the *Narcona* had been branded and distributed amongst the Otungs, two by outright gifting, Nissimi and Rabbit, to men named Ulrich and Vandar, and the remainder by lot. The brand, the lovely slave rose, of course, as it had been with the others, had been burned

into the thigh of Cornhair. Indeed, the mighty barbarian, the
imperial officer, Otto, had personally supervised her marking.

The Otungs released Cornhair and she fell to her knees.
Surely now that she had been exhibited, and as a slave is exhibited, openly, fully, and without compromise, she would be
again permitted the warming shelter of the furs, but the boot
of a Herul was upon them. She put down her head, shivering.
She dared not speak, nor, at the moment, reach for the furs. She
wisely sensed that such boldness would not be permitted to a
slave. Along the beach there were several sleds, which, raftlike,
presumably poled or drawn, had been brought to the island
from the forest side, with several Otungs. On the river side of
the beach, nearest the plains beyond, were a number of Heruls,
and a cluster of horses. There were also several light, wheel-
less platforms of poles, to which some of the horses had been
harnessed. Between the sleds and the platforms were heaped
or stacked goods of various kinds. On the forest side were such
things as bundles of pelts, sacks of dried meat, hard-shelled
winter fruit, vessels of honey, canisters of salt, mainly from
brine springs, and quantities of wood, some cut and smoothed
into boards. The salt and wood was of particular importance to
the Heruls, as both wood and salt were rare on the Flats of Tung.
The wood served mainly for the repair and construction of wagons, and the salt for lick blocks, accessible to the herds. Salt,
too, it might be mentioned, might be traded for by the Heruls
with the Telnarians of Venitzia, but that tended to be expensive as it was imported. Pelts obtained from the Otungs might
be traded, in turn, with merchants, usually those of Venitzia,
for any number of manufactured articles. The Heruls, for their
part, had with them such things as crates of domestic fowl,
pigs crowded into small wooden cages, and, from Venitzia, axe
heads, knife blades, beer and *kana*, and a great number of bolts
of cloth, of diverse qualities. The thicker, finer, and more ornate
cloths were favored by the higher women of the Otungen, and

the coarser fabrics were allotted to the lesser women and slaves. Cornhair, head down, her knees half in the sand and grit of the cold beach, shivering, clutched her arms about herself. She listened to the voices. She knew she was being bargained for. She heard the tiny sound of coins, surely not *darins*, but pennies. She saw four cast down on the furs beside her. They were kicked back, and the Herul, hissing, snatched them up again. One of the Otungs pulled her head up and back, and, with his free hand, lifted and spread her hair. Her hair color she had learned, in the hall to which she had been led, bound and leashed, from the Telnarian wilderness camp, through the forest, was not that unusual amongst Otung women. But then Otung women were seldom slaves. It was more common that they owned slaves. Such slaves, as those brought with her to Tangara, were more likely, like most slaves, to be dark haired and dark-eyed. Certainly a hair and eye color such as hers, blue-eyed and blond-haired, was not unknown in the markets, but, too, it was not that common in most markets, particularly in those of the colonial worlds.

After her branding, she had been knelt, nude, hands tied behind her, her ankles linked but some inches apart in thong shackles, her thigh still afire with pain, before the barbarian captain, Otto.

"I am branded," she said.

"As were the others," he said.

"I gather then," she said, "that I am not to be immediately slain."

"Perhaps," he had said, "you were branded merely that you might be slain as a marked slave."

"I think not," she said.

"Where are you?" he asked.

"On my knees," she said, "before a free man."

"You will grow familiar with such a posture, before the free," he said.

"I am not to be immediately killed," she said.

"No," he said. "Even a slave such as you, as worthless as you, might have her uses, putting herself, for example, instantly, at a snapping of fingers, at the disposal of the free, wholly and helplessly surrendered, as a slave is wholly and helplessly surrendered, hoping that lengthy and inordinate pleasures may be derived from her body, that Masters might then feed her and permit her to live. A dead slave is good for little but food for the dogs."

"I see," she said.

"Surely when you were free, you must have wondered what it would be, to kneel as you are now, naked, helpless, bound, a slave, before a free man."

She was silent.

"You will be trade goods," he said.

"I?" she said. "I? Trade goods? Trade goods! I am not to be kept?"

"No," he said.

"You are a king!" she cried. "Am I not to be a king's slave?"

"No," he said.

"I am not trade goods!" she said. "I cannot be traded! I was the Lady Publennia Calasalia, of the Larial Calasalii!"

"We will see what we can get for you," he said. "But, if nothing, then we will give you away, or leave you bound naked on the beach, for animals, or to die of exposure."

"You cannot do this to me!" she cried.

"Put her with the other goods," he said, turning away.

She tried to spring to her feet, but, as she was tied, her ankles fastened but some six inches apart, that she might be well apprised of her bondage, she fell, to her left shoulder. She looked after him, wildly. Hands were then put upon her, and the stock tender, Qualius, had lifted her in his arms, and carried her to a storage area.

She remained kneeling on the beach, shivering with cold, her head down, her arms held about herself.

"Sell me, sell me!" she thought.

Her captors wanted a *darin* for her.

One of the Heruls snorted, explosively. She would later understand that noise as a Herul laugh.

Attention then seemed diverted from her.

She recalled the words of the barbarian, that, if she were not sold, she would be given away, or left helpless on the beach, perhaps for the nibblings of *filchen*, if not of larger beasts, or left to die of exposure.

Surely they would not tell the Heruls that!

The Heruls must suppose her captors might hold her dear, hold for at least a *darin*.

"A *darin*!" she thought. "I should sell for a thousand *darins*, for ten thousand *darins*!"

"I am freezing," she thought. "Sell me soon, for a penny, for the peeling of a fruit, for a crust of bread, for anything, but sell me, sell me soon!"

The tradings were taking place, offers and counteroffers, bargainings and negotiations, these strung out for better than fifty yards along the beach.

The slave necklace was no longer on her neck, with its metal pendant.

Suitably clothed, the brand covered, might she not pass as free, somewhere, somehow?

She thought of trying to rise and run, but where, and to what? Too, she doubted that her legs would hold her. She feared, even, she could not move her legs, that they were too cold to serve her.

"If escape were possible for me," she thought, "it would be here, in the wilderness, into the forest! This would be my chance, here, not in civilization, where I, marked, would be clothed as a slave, where I would be known, recognized, and identified as a slave, where I would be collared, but, alas, even here, there is no escape for me. I could run only into darkness, cold, and death. I would be eaten. I would starve!"

Then she put aside the foolishness of even contemplating flight.

She did not think she could even rise to her feet.

No, she realized, there was no escape for the female slave, not in the cities, not in the forests, not in the fields, nowhere. She had known that when she was free, that was understood, and it had amused her, but, then, she had never thought that she would be a female slave, and that there would never be any escape for her.

"At least I am not in a collar," she thought. "My throat is bare!"

No one seemed to be about.

Her hand reached out, just a little, slowly, to clutch the furs, and, almost at the same time, the knout fell on her body, and then again and again, and she put her head down, covering it with her hands. "Forgive me, Master!" she cried. "Forgive me, Master!"

"Are you cold?" asked he who then was to her as keeper and captor.

"Yes, Master!" she cried.

"Do you wish to speak?" he asked.

"Yes, yes, Master!" she cried.

"Speak," he said.

"I am cold, Master!" she wept. "I freeze! Please let me cover myself with the furs!"

"Do you petition permission to enclose yourself in the furs?" he asked.

"Yes, yes, Master!" she said.

"You reached out for the furs," he said.

"Yes, Master," she said.

"Without permission," he said.

"Yes, Master," she said. "Forgive me, Master."

"Your petition is denied," he said.

Shuddering, Cornhair kept her head down.

She should not, of course, have reached for the furs. Such things, as should have been understood, are not permitted to a slave.

Cornhair was not merely a beautiful woman, but a highly intelligent woman. Yet she had much to learn about her new status, that of the female slave. Given her intelligence, of course, she should learn very quickly.

The barterings and exchanges now seemed less. Indeed, more than one sled, with new burdens, had been drawn back into the forest, and more than one spread platform of poles, heaped with goods, drawn by its horse, slid over the edge ice and splashed into the chill waters of the Lothar, to ascend shortly the far bank, bordering the now-snowy plains beyond.

Cornhair heard the squealing of a pig and looked up, startled. A fellow was walking back to a sled, the pig under his arm. Also, at almost the same time, a heap of cloth was cast before her by a squat Herul. How fine such fellows looked, how at ease, mounted, as they left the island, some alone, some, mounted, tending the platform-drawing horses beginning to cross the river, and how ungainly afoot.

"Dress," said an Otung.

Cornhair seized up the garments and eagerly, gratefully, drew them on. How precious they were to her. Had she ever worn anything so warm? She was familiar, in her way, of course, with such garments, as they were such as the Otung women wore, and such as she had often donned and worn in and about the hall of the Otungs. To be sure, these were plain, and shabby, worn, and such, but they were long, and thick, and layered. She also drew on the thick woolen hose. Although she, and the other slaves brought from Inez IV to Tangara on the *Narcona*, had become familiar with such garments, she and the others slaves had not always been so sedately and concealingly clad. At the evening suppers and feasts in the hall, the Otung women dining apart, in the woman's hall, a long shed adjoining the greater hall, she, and the others, had served the men naked, hurrying to and fro, responding to their cries, hastening to bring them meat and drink, in particular, spiced and honeyed *bror*, brewed from golden *lee*. That slaves should serve so, stripped, and commonly collared, is, incidentally, a not unfamiliar custom amongst not only barbarians, with their rude ways, but is popular, too, amongst many refined gentlemen of the empire. Men, civilized and barbarous, being men, enjoy being served by naked slaves. It is one of the pleasures of ownership, and the Mastery, and few things, it might be added, given the contrasts involved, clothed and unclothed, serving and being served, and such, better impress upon a slave her femaleness and its meaning.

A tentacled appendage seized the now-dressed Cornhair by the back of the neck, and forced her down, to her knees, her head down.

She whimpered, frightened.

She heard a surprising sound, the striking, the clanking, of a clapper within metal, and sensed something under her neck. There was another such sound, and a chain was drawn up about her neck, and behind her neck, closely, and she heard the snap of a lock behind the back of her neck.

It was the first she had known of, or heard of, the Herul slave bell.

The point of the bell was not, in particular, to designate its wearer a slave, for all human females in a Herul camp were slaves. Rather it was, first, to remind the slave that she was a slave, and a beast, for such bells were sometimes hung about the necks of cows in the herds, and, second, to mark her movements. Interestingly, even in civilized areas, slaves are occasionally belled, though seldom so simply and crudely. The jangle of bells fastened about a girl's ankle, wrist, or neck well impresses upon her that she is not like other women, that she is not free, but a slave. Too, it is not unusual that a new slave, one who is not yet sexually subdued, one not yet sexually owned, one who has not yet fully learned her collar, might be belled. This not only helps her to keep in mind, with each jangle, that she is a slave, but is useful for a variety of other reasons, in particular, those associated with location and tracking. How can she conceal her presence when each of her movements is betrayed by the bells put upon her by Masters; and how could she contemplate escape, however absurd such a musing, however foolish such a fancy, where each step would be clearly marked, bright with the informing music of her bondage? Too, as suggested earlier, bells have their effect upon the passions, both those of slaves and Masters. A belled slave, gasping and begging, brought cruelly to the incomparable ecstasies of the slave orgasm, is pleasant to listen to, wild-eyed and gasping, as she bucks and writhes in her chains.

Cornhair, now clothed, on her knees again, as free men were present, straightened her body, and the bell sounded. She then held it, with two hands, though it was cold, that it not sound. "Master!" she begged. "May I speak?"

"Yes," said the fellow.

"I have been sold?" she asked.

"Yes," he said. "You now belong to Heruls."

"How many *darins* did I bring?" she asked, clutching the bell.

"Vain slut," he said.

"Please," she said, "Master."

"You went for a pig," he said, "which is more than you are worth."

The tentacled appendage of a Herul then fastened itself in her hair, and, as she cried out, she was dragged to her feet, and, bent over, her head at his hip, her hands on his wrist, the bell clanking, was conducted to the shore of the island. There, she was thrown to all fours before one of the platforms of spread poles, on which were some empty crates, or coops, which had housed domestic fowl, *vardas*, in this area, and a long, low, narrow, stout, wood-barred structure, also now empty, one of several in which pigs had been brought to the island.

A gesture from a Herul's claw indicated that she should crawl upon the spread platform, then not harnessed to a horse, and enter the wood-barred structure. She hastened within. The bell clanked. She moaned. She clutched it. The smell of the structure's former denizens assailed her. She heard, behind her, the closing of the structure's gate. It took but a moment to thong it shut. The Herul then, his hand in its mane, or neck hair, positioned the horse between the draw poles and adjusted its harnessing. Cornhair could turn about only with difficulty. Kneeling, grasping the wooden bars, she saw Otung sleds, laden, being thrust into the water. Some men stood upon them, waiting, with poles. Some sleds, having crossed from the island, now again being drawn, were already vanishing into the forest.

"Return!" thought Cornhair, clutching the wooden bars. "Come back! Save me! Rescue me! Do not let this be done to me! I acknowledge myself a slave! I have long known it in my heart! I now confess it openly! I will kneel docilely, head down, at the foot of your couch! I will hasten to serve! I will strive to please, as the least of slaves! Keep me! Keep me! I beg it! Keep me!"

Cornhair was half thrown from her knees in the cage, as the platform on which it was fastened jerked forward. Only her hands on the bars prevented her from falling. She heard the paws of the horse break through the ice at the edge of the island, and then, a moment later, its broad chest was cleaving the chill waters. The boots of the rider were high in the stirrups. Water surged about the beast. Cornhair moaned, as water emerged between the close-set poles of the platform, and, in a moment, as the platform departed further from the bank, it washed over the platform, and through the cage. Her knees and hose were soaked. The wind rose. A large, flat piece of ice, broken loose from the shore upstream, struck, grating, against the platform, and then, as the platform continued its progress, spun slowly away. She could see snow being lifted and blown about on the bank being approached. Then, after a time, the paws of the horse, the rider's mount, broke ice at the farther shore and the platform, unevenly, was being drawn across stones and sand, and, shortly thereafter, it had ascended the higher bank, and lurched into the seemingly endless, broad stretches of wind-carved snow.

Cornhair had arrived at the Flats of Tung.

"You now belong to Heruls," had said the Otung.

She clutched the bell, to keep it from clanking.

Cornhair remained, crouching, between the wheels of one of the wagons. Her fingers held to the clapper in the bell hung about her neck. To be sure, that was forbidden, as much so as stuffing the bell with grass. It was to be free to swing, and sound, as a slave bell must.

Cornhair was miserable, hiding beneath the wagon.

To be sure, she had not been summoned, at least not personally, not explicitly, to her knowledge, and certainly she could not be accused of, and had not dared, an unauthorized departure from the camp. That was forbidden. Too, there were hungry dogs about, little better, if at all, than wolves.

She had been told that Borchu was looking for her. On the other hand, that might not be true. Cornhair was not popular with the other girls. Was it a joke, so cruel a joke? Did they want her to seek out Borchu, and present herself, unbidden, to Borchu's switch? That would surely give Borchu a pretext to vent her feelings on a human female, not that she had ever needed a pretext, and, indeed, a human female against whom, for whatever reason, she seemed to bear a particular animus. But what if Borchu was indeed looking for her, and the other slave, White Ankles, should inform her that the message of her summons had been duly transmitted, and yet that Cornhair had not fled to her feet, begging, as was required, to do her bidding?

Cornhair remained where she was, trembling.

It was now an hour or so past noon.

Whereas some female slaves in a Herul camp are owned by particular Masters, and wear appropriate identifying disks fastened to the chain of their slave bells, most slaves are what is known as "camp slaves." For example, Cornhair was a camp slave. Camp slaves, rather as many of the dogs, are the common property of the camp. It is much more prestigious to be a private slave. A particular advantage of being owned by a particular Master is that one is more likely to be fed. It is easy to see why camp slaves look up to, and envy, private slaves. A camp slave, who has no specific owner, must beg, and give pleasure, of one sort or another, before she is fed. That is required. Camp slaves, also, as they are not privately owned, may be disposed of by anyone in the camp, rather as anyone might slay and eat a dog that is not privately owned. It is easy to see why camp slaves are particularly zealous to please Masters, which, in their case, is any free Herul, even a child. They prostrate themselves eagerly. On their belly they hope not to be beaten, and to be spared.

Most worlds in the Telnarian empire, saving some "same worlds," in which, interestingly, men and women are supposedly identical, and other worlds, beyond the current borders of the empire, which wax and wane with political and military fortunes, accept, favor, and celebrate, the institution of slavery, with all its personal and public benefits, economic, social, biological, psychological, and so on. For example, it well serves the woman who can be fulfilled only if she finds herself at the feet of a man, his, owned and mastered, and it well serves the man who, in the proud might of his lust and health, chooses to be himself, and own and master his female, rather than be a stranger to his blood and heart. On the other hand, the Master/slave relationship, with its terrors and pains, its pleasures and fears, its values, rewards, and joys, commonly obtains, as seems appropriate, given the selections of nature, within a single species. It is there that the woman finds the man, her Master, and the man finds the woman, his slave. That would not be the case with the humans and Heruls, of course. Each of these species is alien to the other. The complementarities which, in the habits of nature, have been selected for within a single species are seldom selected for between species. Accordingly, within the Herul camp, Cornhair's loveliness, now, to be sure, somewhat disheveled and sullied, had little relevance to her fate or treatment. Herul males, on the whole, saw little point in protecting her from the excesses of Herul females, no more than a pig, and Herul females, in turn, on the whole, needed not concern themselves with the possible intervention of the camp's males, short of, perhaps, her killing or maiming. She had, after all, some value. She had cost a pig at the trade island.

The relation of female to female within a single species is interesting, human female to human female, Herul female to Herul female, with respect to intraspecific competitions, for example, with respect to attractiveness, prestige, status, appeal to males, mate acquisition, and such. Along these lines, within the human species, the free woman commonly resents, and, I fear, is jealous of, the interest of the males of her species in female slaves, whom they may buy, own, and use for their pleasure, and, I suspect, resents, and, I fear, is jealous of, the fulfillments and joys of the owned, mastered slave, she lovingly, content, wholly surrendered and submitted, at her Master's feet. Then, when dealing with the possible interactions of females of diverse species, not those without commonalities, as, say, those of female pigs and female *filchen*, but those where some commonalities are involved, for example, speech, rationality, sexual dimorphism, paired appendages, and such, as in the case of humans and Heruls, the natural contempt which, say, a Herul female might feel for a human female can be exacerbated, as was the case with Borchu, by a recognition that Herul males occasionally find the small, soft, well-curved, smooth-skinned bodies of their human female slaves, however surprisingly or peculiarly, of sexual interest. Thus, in such a case, the natural contempt of the Herul female for the human female, which she regards as a despicably inferior sort of thing, rather as she might regard a pig as a despicably inferior sort of thing, is upon occasion, as it was with Borchu, somewhat intensified, if not multiplied exponentially.

From her position, Cornhair could look to her right, and see the wide, dusty expanse about which the wagons were arranged. Somewhere, she knew, at least one wagon was moved aside, to leave an opening. This arrangement, a wagon gate, makes it possible for armed men to issue forth from any part of the camp, perhaps unnoted from a given direction. It also makes it possible, if several wagons are moved simultaneously, for a large number of men to pour suddenly, perhaps unexpectedly, into the field, an advantage not obtaining with fixed walls and a gate or gates which might be kept under surveillance. There were women and children in sight, some six horses, tethered, a slave, yoked, carrying water to a trough, in two metal pails, doubtless from Venitzia; and another slave tending to a large, camp kettle, of which several could be seen, slung on their iron racks. It took four men to lift some of the camp kettles. Most slaves would be out, somewhere, under the supervision of free women, picking *hineen*, using their lifted skirts as baskets. In two places Herul men were sitting, cross-legged, facing one another, playing with marked bones, these cast on a blanket between them. Herul men did not attend to camp matters, save for such things as the repair and decoration of the large, colorful, enclosed wagons, like houses on wheels. They tended cattle and horses; taught boys riding and weapons, primarily the bow and lance; hunted, and, as the occasion arose, did war. Occasionally they raided other Herul camps, for horses and women. Beyond the wagons to her right, to the east, she could see, in the far distance, some of the snow-capped heights of the Barrionuevo Range. She looked to her left; somewhere to her left, far off, would be the Lothar River. To the north and south, bending in the wind, were seemingly endless waves of grass. She drew back, further, under the wagon. One of the large, maned dogs was watching her. She would not reach toward it, lest her hand be snapped off. Heruls use dogs to herd cattle, horses, prisoners, and slaves. The dog growled and moved away.

Cornhair was hungry.

She was often hungry in the Herul camp.

She had crawled to Borchu yesterday evening, begging to be put to work, that she might be fed, but Borchu, the Herul female into whose care she had been placed, had declined to offer her work. White Ankles, her arms in the wooden washing pail submerged to her elbows, had smiled, washing Borchu's hose. She had begged Borchu to cast her even a scrap of garbage, but Borchu, instead, had switched her, reminding her that one such as she, a worthless camp slave, was not to be fed for nothing. One such as she must earn her food. She had then hung about the camp kettles, until she, with some dogs, had been driven away by the Herul women. She had fled, weeping. The supple branch had muchly stung. The life of she who had once been the rich and spoiled Lady Publennia Calasalia, of the Larial Calasalii, of the *honestori*, of the patricians, even of the senatorial class, had muchly changed. She who had squandered property was now herself property; her silks had been exchanged for coarse cloth, her jewels for a slave bell locked on her neck. Most devastatingly, she had been marked; on her left thigh, high, under the hip, fixed in place, burned in, was the small, lovely slave rose. She well knew its meaning, and so would others, within the empire, and elsewhere. She was goods, a slave.

The men were mostly out with the herds. Many left early in the morning, to return at dusk, passing others who were then leaving the camp, who, in turn, would return to the wagons near dawn.

A slave such as Cornhair, a camp slave, was more likely to be fed by the Herul men than the Herul women. One might always beg to braid a rope, which might be used to bind them; to smooth out the fur of a fellow's boots with teeth and tongue, to rub down saddles, to polish accouterments, and such. And sometimes they had made her remove her clothes, and perform the "pleading dance" of the female slave. In the empire, there were many "pleading dances," pleadings to be spared, to be permitted to live, sometimes permitted to female captives, pleadings to be forgiven, pleadings not to be whipped, pleadings to be retained by a Master considering her sale, pleadings to be fed, pleadings for sexual attention and sexual gratification, and such. Among the Heruls, the pleading dances of human females were usually pleadings to be fed. Needless to say, it is one thing for a human female to perform a pleading dance before Heruls who, for the most part, regard her as an alien life form, and quite another to perform such a dance before free males of her own species. The common outcome of such a dance before males of her own species is that she will be dragged away from the fire, into the darkness, usually by the hair, and reminded of what it is to be a slave in the arms of a Master. Such dances are often performed on the slave block, to intensify bids. Many slave houses, naturally, provide instruction in such dances, and several others, and woe to the slave who does not learn them well. In such dance, she is to transform herself into an unabashed, shameless, lascivious object of desire. Such dance well impresses upon her that she is a slave, and only that. Too, such dance has its effect not only upon Masters, but upon the slave herself, such that she is now likely to beg for their touch, that they may relieve her inevitably aroused needs. A trained slave, too, of course, is likely to bring more on the block. So, as would be expected, dance, slave dance, of course, constitutes an integral portion of a slave's curriculum. This is natural, as it is the very *raison d'être*, the very reason for being, of the slave to serve men, and provide them with great pleasure. That is what she is for. Sometimes the Heruls would have the human female slaves remove their clothing, and roll about, twisting, and squirming, on the ground. The point of this, for the Heruls, at least commonly, seems to have little or nothing to do with the girls, for they are, after all, slaves, but seems rather to have more to do with some sort of satisfaction they derive from having the women of the enemy at their feet, obedient and prostrate. On the other hand, from their point of view, the exhibition of diverse forms of plunder, say, gold and silver vessels, marble statuary, jewels, paintings, rich, well-woven carpets, and such, would serve much the same purpose, an exhibition of acquired goods, preferably taken from enemies. A visiting Otung, for example, a merchant, ambassador, or such, treated by Heruls to such an exhibition, is less likely to be humiliated or insulted, as to be pleased, as the women are slaves. Indeed he may appreciate the matter as a spectacle thoughtfully presented for his entertainment. On the other hand, should this behavior be inflicted on a free woman, blood might be shed. Lesser things have initiated raids, even wars.

Cornhair, crouching under the wagon, pondered approaching the men who were intent on their gambling. They might not wish to be interrupted. But she was very hungry.

"See! See!" cried White Ankles. "There, hiding under the wagon!"

"Come out, Cornhair!" screamed Borchu.

Miserable, and trembling, Cornhair crawled out from under the wagon, the slave bell clanking, and put herself to her belly before Borchu.

"I told her you wanted to see her!" said White Ankles. "She did not rush to the wagon! She dallied! She hid herself!"

"No, no, Noble Mistress," said Cornhair. "I knew nothing of your pleasure!"

"Liar, liar!" cried White Ankles.

"No!" wept Cornhair.

"Which of you is lying?" asked Borchu.

"Cornhair!" cried White Ankles.

"White Ankles!" cried Cornhair.

"You are both filthy pigs, both liars!" said Borchu.

"No!" said White Ankles.

"No!" said Cornhair.

"Kneel up, look at me!" said Borchu, and Cornhair rose to her knees, but feared to look into that narrow, long, scaled face. The eyes were round and bright. The head was smooth, oval, and elongated, the nostrils no more than a pair of holes in the face. No ears were visible, but there were two holes, listening holes, one on each side of the head. The eyesight of Heruls was much akin to that of humans. Their hearing and sense of smell seems to have been more acute.

Borchu adjusted Cornhair's head with her switch, so that it was lifted and looking up at her.

Cornhair's neck hurt.

"How ugly humans are," said Borchu.

Why, one wonders, would this have been of interest to Borchu?

Notions of beauty, one supposes, would tend to vary from species to species, naturally enough, as most humans would not bid avidly for most female Heruls, nor would most Heruls risk a dozen hides for most human females, but, one supposes, attractiveness and beauty are not always a matter of idiosyncratic species preference. For example, both Heruls and humans might respond to the glory of grass, to the ruggedness of mountains, to the force of rushing streams, to the turbulence of clouds, to the rhapsody of a sunset, to the unsheathing of the cold knife of dawn. Do not Heruls and humans both see beauty in the dog and wolf, in the bull and horse, in the vi-cat and hawk? And certainly, as we have noted, some Herul males have viewed certain of their human properties with interests transcending those of a purely utilitarian nature.

Borchu, it must be confessed, had not been much sought for by male Heruls, with seeding in mind.

"Get your clothes off, pig," said Borchu to Cornhair.

"Please do not beat me!" said Cornhair.

"Now, pig!" said Borchu.

White Ankles laughed.

Cornhair now wore but her slave bell.

"White Ankles," snapped Borchu, "remove your waist cord, and bind the wrists of Cornhair together, and then take her to the wagon wheel, put her on her knees, and tie her wrists to a spoke."

"Please, no, Mistress!" said Cornhair.

"Yes, Mistress," said White Ankles, untying her waist cord, and hurrying to Cornhair.

Shortly thereafter Cornhair faced the wagon wheel, on her knees, her wrists tied to a spoke.

She looked behind her, terrified, but saw no hint of mercy in the visage of her custodian.

"May I beat her?" inquired White Ankles.

"Perhaps it is you who are the liar," said Borchu.

"No, Noble Mistress!" said White Ankles.

"Fetch me the waist cord from the dress of Cornhair," said Borchu.

Swiftly, White Ankles complied.

The waist cord on the dress of a slave is such that, by intention, the slave may be bound with it. Commonly it encircles the waist twice, snugly, and is tied at the left hip, as most Masters are right-handed. This is a common feature of many slave garments, on many worlds. There seems to be three aspects to this practice; first, as a utilitarian measure, the slave may be conveniently rendered helpless, bound, hand and foot; second, carrying her bond about her body, knotted, reminds the slave of her helplessness, her vulnerability, and bondage; and, thirdly, as her figure is emphasized, attention is called to the fact that she is a sexual creature, no longer secretly and shamefully, but now openly and unapologetically, essentially and radically. Let free women pretend what they wish and deny what they will; such privileges are theirs; they are not permitted to the most female of all women, the female slave. Let them not deny their sexuality; that would be farcical in the case of a slave; it is that for which they are purchased. The slave quickly learns the meaning of her collar, which, to her joy and gratitude, frees her to be herself. Perhaps it is little wonder that free women so hate and envy them.

"Mistress?" said White Ankles.

"Remove your clothing, pig," said Borchu. "Kneel before me, your head down, your arms lifted, your wrists crossed!"

"Please, no, Noble Mistress!" wept White Ankles, but she hastened to obey. In moments, head down, she could see only the dirt before her. She also felt her small wrists tied together, closely.

Moments later White Ankles was on her knees, beside Cornhair, the large, painted hub of the wheel between them, the wrists of each bound to a spoke.

"Confess!" begged White Ankles. "Tell the noble Mistress I told you she wished to see you!"

"You told me nothing!" said Cornhair.

"She is lying Noble Mistress," cried White Ankles over her shoulder.

"Who is lying?" inquired Borchu.

"Cornhair!" cried White Ankles.

"White Ankles!" cried Cornhair.

"I will beat both," said Borchu. "I am thus assured the guilty one is punished."

"I will tear out your hair! I will scratch your eyes out!" cried White Ankles to Cornhair, pulling at her wrists.

"The Noble Masters and Mistresses would not be pleased," hissed Cornhair.

White Ankles turned white, sobbed, and pulled again at her tethered wrists.

"I will throw dirt into the pan of your food, dirt into the pan of your water," said White Ankles.

"And I into yours!" said Cornhair.

"I am larger than you," said White Ankles. "I will beat you, and beat you!"

Tears sprang into the eyes of Cornhair, and she jerked helplessly at the cords that held her bound to the spoke. Her knees ground into the dust at the side of the wheel. She knew she was no match for White Ankles.

And then the switch began to fall on the both of them.

"Pigs, pigs!" said Borchu, gasping with her efforts.

"Mercy, Noble Mistress!" begged White Ankles.

"Mercy, Noble Mistress!" wept Cornhair.

"Admit that you are pigs!" cried Borchu.

"We are pigs!" cried White Ankles and Cornhair, their wrists bound to a spoke, their heads down between the spokes.

"Admit that you are less than pigs!" screamed Borchu.

"I am less than a pig!" cried White Ankles.

"I am less than a pig!" cried Cornhair. "Please stop, Noble Mistress!"

"You were purchased for a pig!" said Borchu. "A fool purchased you for a pig. He was cheated. You are not worth so much! You are worth less than a pig!"

"Yes, Noble Mistress!" wept Cornhair. "I am worth less than a pig! Please beat me no more!"

"You, White Ankles," cried Borchu, "were purchased for three pigs!"

"Yes, Noble Mistress!" said White Ankles.

Sobbing, Cornhair jerked at her bonds. Could it be that Heruls had paid three pigs for White Ankles, and only one pig for herself? Was she so poor a slave, that even Heruls would pay so little for her?

She suddenly realized that she was inferior to White Ankles. Free women are entitled, in their vanity, to regard themselves as superior to all other women, but slaves are beasts and commodities, and their value is determined objectively, by what men will pay for them.

"And you, too," snarled Borchu, "are worth less than a pig!"

"Yes, Noble Mistress!" said White Ankles.

"The Otung robbers, the Otung bandits, the Otung scoundrels!" cried Borchu. "You are both worth less than pigs!"

"Yes, Noble Mistress!" cried White Ankles and Cornhair.

Then, mercifully, the blows ceased.

"I am tired," said Borchu. "The day is hot."

Cornhair gasped, and shuddered. The slave bell hung about her neck clanked. Her back and body were afire. Borchu knew something of the beating of slaves. Cornhair put her head down, against the spoke. Yes, she thought, acquiescing, I am less than a pig, for I am a slave. Is there not a sense in which all slaves are worth less than pigs, as they are slaves? You would not even beat a pig. She knew, of course, that Borchu's assessments were spiteful. Yet, too, she knew, with wars, and such, slaves on many worlds were cheap. But, too, she knew that even a low slave might bring several *darins*. And some slaves, she knew, sold for many *darins*, and some even for a dozen rifles, with a thousand cartridges, even a hoverer. But here, she thought, I am worth only a pig, or less! The barbarian, and Qualius, and Ronisius, she thought, have well had their vengeance. She could not expect to be saved by Iaachus, the Arbiter of Protocol. His minions, Phidias, the captain of the *Narcona*, and the others, Corelius, and Lysis, had abandoned her, and doubtless had reported the assassination done, and would have supposed her to have been killed shortly thereafter, presumably slowly and unpleasantly. Too, what had she to hope, should she find herself before dour Iaachus, in his dark robes, for she had not only failed in her task but knew his complicity in the affair, which knowledge rendered her a threat to him, one who was not likely to be tolerant of unresolved threats.

Borchu freed White Ankles and Cornhair of the spokes, but kept their hands tied, before their bodies.

"Stand," said Borchu.

Both could stand only with difficulty.

"Precede me," said Borchu, pointing toward the center of the camp.

Cornhair and White Ankles preceded her for several yards, until she called for them to stop, near the center of the camp, near the large cooking kettles.

Men in the vicinity scarcely noted them.

A child ran by, pursuing a ball of fur, casting it into the air before him, and then hastening to catch it.

"I am not finished with you," said Borchu.

"Cornhair was the liar!" said White Ankles.

"White Ankles!" said Cornhair.

"Kneel," said Borchu.

Swiftly Cornhair and White Ankles assumed the prescribed position.

"Bakaar!" called Borchu, "here! Assist me!"

Bakaar, like many of the Heruls, a short, thickly bodied male, shuffled to Borchu's side. On horseback Heruls seemed at ease, as we have noted, even graceful, in a menacing way, but afoot, they often seemed ungainly.

"Tie their ankles," said Borchu.

This was promptly done, with narrow thongs.

"Now," said Borchu, "fasten their wrists, behind the back of their necks."

"Noble Mistress?" said White Ankles, as her bound wrists were pulled up, jerked over her head, and then down, back, behind her neck, where they were fastened.

The same was done with Cornhair.

Both slaves then knelt, their ankles crossed and tied behind them, and their hands, bound, behind the back of their necks.

With a common key, Borchu unlocked the slave bells from the girls' necks, and cast them to the side.

"Noble Mistress?" said Cornhair, questioningly, plaintively.

"Heat two kettles!" called Borchu to a slave, who scurried to obey.

"No, please, no, Noble Mistress!" cried White Ankles.

Cornhair screamed with misery.

At a gesture from Borchu, the Herul, Bakaar, lifted White Ankles first, and then Cornhair, placing each in one of the kettles, where the water swirled about their throats. As their ankles were tied, they could not rise to their feet.

Smoke curled upward, about the sides of the kettles, where the turf grass, the sticks, and dried dung sprang into flame.

"Mercy, Noble Mistress!" screamed White Ankles!

"Spare us, beloved Noble Mistress!" wept Cornhair. "We will be better slaves, the best of slaves, beloved Mistress!"

Some Heruls gathered about, amongst them some women, and children.

"Boil White Ankles! Cook her! Not me!" wept Cornhair.

"No, no!" cried White Ankles. "Cornhair! Not White Ankles!"

"No!" screamed Cornhair, her eyes wild, thrashing about, unable to rise.

"Be silent, Pigs," scolded Borchu. Then she turned to the slave who had lit the fires. "Bring tallow," she said, "rags, and brushes."

"Mistress?" begged White Ankles.

"You are filthy, both of you," said Borchu. Then she called to two other slaves. "Wash the dirt from their hair, from their bodies, comb them, scrub them!"

"Yes, Noble Mistress!" cried the two slaves.

Bakaar then, by the hair, thrust the head of White Ankles under the water, and shook it, painfully, and then served Cornhair similarly. Both girls raised their heads from the water, half blinded, gasping for breath.

"Stupid pigs," said Borchu. "If you were to be cooked, your hands would have been bound behind your back, that you might boil more uniformly."

"Oh!" cried Cornhair, recoiling from the bristles of a stout brush on her body. In moments, she shut her eyes, from the yanking at her hair of a horn comb. To her left she heard White Ankles, sobbing.

Herul men drew the slaves to their feet, and held them in place. The water was then to their waist.

Cornhair had not washed since the wilderness camp.

"Be gentle!" begged White Ankles.

In a few moments the two Heruls released their hold, and White Ankles and Cornhair, unable to stand, fell to their knees in the kettles, putting their heads back, that they not be submerged.

"Are they ready?" asked a voice.

The voice was not that of a Herul. It was a human, male voice.

"Yes," said Borchu. "Bakaar, hold that pig upright. You, Odai, hold up the other one."

Both girls were then, again, held upright, the water in the kettles now, again, about their waist.

The human was a large man, muscular, in a sleeveless leather jacket. A knife sheath, at his waist, was empty. Heruls seldom allowed armed humans in their camps. Each large wrist was bound with leather.

Held, Cornhair tried to lift her feet from the bottom of the kettle, as it was becoming uncomfortably hot. A growl from the Herul caused her to remain unmoving.

"I see you have them in an exhibition tie," said the human.

Suddenly, then, Cornhair flushed with embarrassment. Not only was the behind-the-neck tie an attractive tie, and one of superb slave security, but it lifted the breasts in such a way as to flatter and accentuate the figure.

"We have washed them for you, even in warm water," said

Borchu. "That is better for removing filth, all the dust, the dirt
and dung."

The muscular fellow approached the kettles.

Seldom had Cornhair felt examined, as she then was.

"Mouth open, head back," said the man.

"Good teeth," said Borchu.

Cornhair felt her body slapped, variously.

How dare the brute?

She was furious.

Had she not been bound, she would have been tempted to
cry out, even to strike at the fellow. At that time, you see, Cornhair was not yet fully aware of what it was to be a slave. She
knew the dreadful slavery of being a human female in a Herul
camp, but the Heruls were not of her species. In the camp, most
Heruls viewed her as they might have viewed a pig, or a dog,
something that had little personal meaning to them, and was not
of great interest. But then, examined as an animal by a man of
her own species, and being considered as an animal by a member of her own species, she suddenly realized, to her terror, that
among such, amongst members of her own species, she would
be a thousand times more a slave than she had been in the Herul
camp. Amongst the Heruls she had been, for the most part, a
simple animal, such as a dog or pig, but amongst humans she
would be not merely an animal, such as a dog or pig, but a very
special sort of animal, an unusually attractive and exciting form
of animal, the female slave. The members of her species would
understand her bondage and its meaning, only too well, as it was
meant to be understood. She would be an object and a commodity, vulnerable to, and helpless before, the free. Men might lust
for her, and have their will with her, as they might please. And
women would hate her.

The muscular fellow then, to Cornhair's satisfaction, subjected White Ankles, whom he had saved for last, for some reason, to a similar, thorough, explicit examination.

He then stepped back.

"See, sound," said Borchu.

"Lift them from the kettles," said the fellow.

Bakaar and Odai lifted the wet, dripping bodies of White Ankles and Cornhair from the kettles.

Cornhair and White Ankles were then knelt before the muscular fellow. Neither dared to meet his eyes.

Water slipped from their heated bodies, dampening the ground. The soles of their feet were sore and reddened, from the metal of the kettles. Their hair was wet, and coarsely combed. There was water about their knees.

The muscular fellow walked about the pair. "They have been beaten," he said.

"They are slaves," said Borchu.

"What do you want for them?" he asked.

"Consider their ankles, their flanks," said Borchu. "Would they not be of interest to a human?"

"Perhaps," said the fellow.

"Twenty *darins* for each," said Borchu.

"Ten, for the pair," he said.

"Too little!" cried Borchu.

"Keep them, eat them," said the fellow, and turned away.

"Pig, human!" said Borchu.

"Take it," said Bakaar. "Ten *darins* will buy eight to ten pigs."

Borchu wavered a moment, her body seething with anger. Then she called out, "Sir! Sir!"

The fellow turned about, perhaps as he had expected to do.

"Agreed!" said Borchu. "But that only for good will, for good will with the dealers of Venitzia!"

"Take them to my wagon," said the fellow, unslinging the purse from about his shoulder."

Bakaar undid the thongs on Cornhair and White Ankles. He then put a hand in the hair of each, and, holding them bent over, their heads at his hips, Cornhair on his left, White Ankles on his right, took his way toward the current portal to the camp, where two wagons had been drawn to the side, one to the left, one to the right, this opening the wagon wall, broadly, outside of which waited the dealer's wagon, drawn by two horses.

"Kneel here," said Bakaar, releasing them behind the dealer's wagon and then returning to the interior of the wagon camp.

"We are out of the camp!" said White Ankles, elatedly. "We have been sold! We have been sold!"

"I cannot be sold!" said Cornhair.

"You have been sold," said White Ankles, "as have I!"

"I can not be sold, not truly," said Cornhair, "for I am a free woman."

"Are you mad?" said White Ankles.

"I am the Lady Publennia Calasalia," said Cornhair, "of the Larial Calasalii!"

"You are whoever Masters choose to name you," said White Ankles.

"The dealer is from Venitzia," said Cornhair. "It is a provincial capital. If he knows the empire, he will know of the Calasalii!"

"Once perhaps you were of the Calasalii, whoever they are," said White Ankles. "But now you are no more than a slave, as am I."

"No," said Cornhair.

"They would not want you back," said White Ankles, "you are now no more than an embarrassment, an insult and a scorn to them. The collar spoils a woman for freedom. Once collared, she can no longer be free. She is then a slave, and knows herself a slave."

"Not I!" said Cornhair. "I am not a slave!"

"Your left thigh bears the rose, printed in as deeply, and as unmistakably, as mine!" said White Ankles.

"Garmented," said Cornhair, "no one will know we are marked!"

"And perhaps you will simply ask for the garments of a free woman, perhaps one of quality?" said White Ankles.

"We are not collared!" said Cornhair.

"That is true," said White Ankles, tensely.

"I need only make myself known," said Cornhair, "and I will be freed."

"Then you admit you are not free now?"

"No," said Cornhair.

"Then you admit you are now a slave?"

"Yes, now," said Cornhair, "but only until I speak my name and station."

"Your former name and station," said White Ankles.

"Yes, if you will," said Cornhair.

"Will you not speak for me, as well?" asked White Ankles.

"No," said Cornhair. "You are a natural slave, and should be a slave, and will remain a slave! You are the sort of girl who should crawl about the ankles of a Master, and lick and kiss them!"

"So are you!" said White Ankles.

"I am not one of those neck-ringed sluts who melts in a man's arms, and lives only to please him!"

"Have I not heard you weep in your sleep for a Master?"

"When I am free, and rich," said Cornhair, "I will buy you, and then you will see how pleasant your life will be!"

"I fear the dealer will soon approach," whispered White Ankles, looking about.

"Perhaps we should have fled," said Cornhair, looking about, as well. "We might have reached Venitzia, on foot!"

Cornhair, on a wild impulse, leaped to her feet, but, warned by a fearsome growl, not feet away, she fell immediately, again, to her knees.

"Do not move, the dogs," said White Ankles.

Cornhair then realized why the Herul, Bakaar, had simply left them, as he had. Herul dogs, as many others, were often used to control, herd, and monitor slaves. Cornhair and White Ankles had been put on their knees. The dogs, then, would see that they remained in place, pending the arrival of some suitable authority, one who might alter the situation.

"Are we such poor stuff?" asked Cornhair, angry, on her knees. "We brought only ten *darins*!"

"They must have been divided," said White Ankles. "Perhaps eight for me, two for you."

"Nine for me, one for you," said Cornhair, "if any."

"I sold for three pigs, you for one," said White Ankles.

"*Filch*!" said Cornhair.

"The dealer!" whispered White Ankles.

Both slaves put down their heads.

In the presence of free persons, slaves commonly will not speak without permission.

The dealer went forward, about the horses, checking harnessing, or such. He then came back, about the wagon, and, reaching over the side of the wagon, busied himself with something toward the rear of the wagon. Cornhair heard some sounds of metal.

Then the fellow was near them.

"May I speak?" asked Cornhair.

"'Master'?" asked the man.

"May I speak, Master?" asked Cornhair.

As I have suggested, Cornhair was not yet fully apprised of the depth and perfection of her bondage, that appropriate for a female such as she.

"No," he said. "Get on all fours, both of you, heads down."

Both slaves complied, instantly.

Dalliance is not permitted to female slaves.

That was well understood, even by Cornhair.

"Master!" said Cornhair.

"Keep your head down," he said.

"What are you going to do?" asked Cornhair.

"Get collars on you," he said.

"It will not be necessary to collar me, Master," said Cornhair.

"You are not a bad-looking little *filch*," he said.

"Please do not collar me, Master!" begged Cornhair.

"You have been complimented," said the dealer.

"Thank you, Master," said Cornhair. "Please do not collar me. I do not look well in a collar."

"All women look well in a collar," he said. "A slave collar much enhances the beauty of any woman."

"Please, Master!" begged Cornhair.

"If you speak again without permission," he said, "you may expect to be whipped."

"Yes, Master," said Cornhair.

She then felt a circlet of metal placed about her neck, and snapped shut.

How helpless Cornhair felt, on all fours, her head down, now so unmistakably designated!

A tiny moan of dismay, of misery, of utter helplessness, escaped her soft, fair lips.

One might conceal a brand. How could one conceal a collar? Almost any garment might conceal a brand. Who would know what insignia might bedeck the thigh of a woman clothed as free? Who would know in what secret locales might bloom the flower of bondage? The rose of servitude need not bloom publicly. But the collar was another matter. It cannot be hidden. It is visible, prominent, and secure; it is lovely, unslippable, and fastened; it is the ideal symbol of bondage. Brand her, yes, by all means, but see that she is in her collar. There is no mistaking the woman who wears a collar. She is a slave.

Cornhair heard another click.

White Ankles, too, was now collared.

Cornhair, lifting her head a little, a very little, noted that the muscular fellow's previously emptied sheath now bore a blade. He must have retrieved this from the wagon, doubtless when he was fetching the collars. Heruls, as we recall, did not care to admit armed strangers within the circle of the wagons.

"May I speak, Master?" asked Cornhair.

"Yes," he said.

"In the camp," she said, "we were dressed. Our dresses were removed. They must be about, in the camp. We understand that men might wish to buy us naked, that they might the better examine us, perhaps for blemishes, but we have now been bought. Might they not now be fetched? A child might do so."

"One can hardly see a slave in such sacks," said the man.

"But they are clothing," said Cornhair.

"I do not want you in the unchanged, stinking rags of Herul slave girls," said the man. "That is disgusting."

"But perhaps something similar," said Cornhair.

"Slaves will be clad as slaves," said the man.

"Master!" protested Cornhair.

"—if clad," he added.

"I hope that I may be granted a fetching tunic, Master," said White Ankles. "I wear the garments appropriate for me well."

"Surely I will be given more than a tunic," said Cornhair, "a gown, slippers!"

"Master is strong, and handsome," said White Ankles. "Perhaps he may keep me for himself."

"You are not without interest as a slave," said the dealer. "Do you crawl well to a man's feet?"

"Yes, Master!" said White Ankles.

"Slave!" hissed Cornhair.

"She is Cornhair," said White Ankles. "I am White Ankles, but you will name us both, as you please."

"Slave, slave!" said Cornhair.

"Do not mind her, Master," said White Ankles. "She does not know how to crawl to a man's feet. She is nothing, just suet, cold and uninteresting meat, stale bread, tepid porridge."

"White Ankles!" protested Cornhair.

"Do you deny it?" asked White Ankles. "Are you hot in your collar, do your thighs heat?"

"Slave!" said Cornhair.

"I know I am a slave," said White Ankles. "That is better than being a slave and not knowing one is a slave! I love men, and want to belong to one of them!"

"I hate you!" said Cornhair.

"Perhaps I made a mistake in purchasing this one," said the dealer. "Perhaps I should have left her in the kettle."

"No, no, dear Master," said White Ankles. "She is just ignorant, and stupid. She does not understand herself. She tries to deny herself to herself. I have heard her weep in her sleep for a Master."

"Liar!" said Cornhair.

"It is true, stupid little fool," said White Ankles.

"No!" cried Cornhair.

"Despite what might appear to be the case, Master," said White Ankles, "she is a female, and needs her Master, and can never be fulfilled without one."

"No!" cried Cornhair.

"She needs to be owned, wholly and without compromise," said White Ankles.

"No, no!" protested Cornhair.

"She can never be herself, save at a man's feet," said White Ankles.

"It does not matter, one way or another," said the dealer, "as long as her neck is in a collar."

"Master!" protested Cornhair.

"Keep your head down," he said. "Stare at the dirt."

"Yes, Master," said Cornhair.

"May I inquire, Master," asked White Ankles, "in what sort of collars we have been placed?"

"Market collars, selling collars," he said.

"We are to take our place on some block in Venitzia?" she asked.

"I will probably ship you elsewhere," he said.

"To some other provincial world?" she asked.

"Probably," he said. "Do you think you will be sold on Tel-naria itself?"

"No, Master," she said.

"Why did you ask?"

"I thought that perhaps Master would consider placing me in his own collar," said White Ankles.

"You are a forward *filch*," he said.

"In a collar," she said, "a girl can only hope that she will be found pleasing."

"The whip will see to such things," he said.

"Master has strong arms, and his hands are tanned and large."

"Do you know how to please a man?" he asked.

"In your arms," she said, "I could not help myself, even should I wish to do so."

"Can you cook?" he asked.

"Yes," she said.

"You, with flaxen hair," he said, "do you know how to please a man?"

"No," said Cornhair, on all fours, head down, staring at the dirt.

"Can you cook?" he asked.

"Certainly not," she said.

"Can you sew?" he asked.

"Certainly not," she said.

"What of you, Dark Hair," asked the dealer. "Can you sew?"

"Of course, Master," she said.

"Dark Hair, White Ankles, for now," said the dealer, "you may rise."

"Thank you, Master!" said White Ankles, springing to her feet.

"May I lift my head?" asked Cornhair.

"If you wish," he said, "but remain on all fours."

Cornhair glared at White Ankles.

"Master," said White Ankles, "may I sit beside you, on the wagon bench?"

"You may kneel beside me, on the floor of the wagon box," he said.

"Chained?" she said.

"That will not be necessary," he said. "You are in a collar."

"I would hope," she said, "that Master might one day fasten his chains on me."

"Perhaps," he said.

"I want to wear Master's chains," said White Ankles.

"Slave!" said Cornhair.

The dealer reached over the edge of the wagon, into one of the boxes there, removed something, and cast it to White Ankles.

She cried out, with surprise, and delight.

Cornhair heard a brief rustle of cloth.

"See!" said White Ankles to Cornhair. "I am tunicked!"

"It is a slave tunic," said Cornhair. "In it, you are more naked than without it!"

"Thank you, Master!" said White Ankles.

"It is indeed a garment appropriate for you," hissed Cornhair. "The meaningful, degrading garment of a slave!"

"I love it!" said White Ankles.

"It well displays my property," said the dealer, "and as the property she is."

"Yes, Master," said White Ankles, delightedly.

"Turn about," he said. "I am going to tie your hands together, behind your back."

Apparently this was soon done.

"I do not trust Heruls, Master," said White Ankles, pulling a bit at her wrists. "Let us be on our way, and put much distance between ourselves and the camp."

The dealer then looked about, and to the opened gate between the wagons. Might not four or five riders emerge from that portal, later, after dark, riders which he might encounter later, in less than pleasant circumstances?

"I am known," said the dealer to White Ankles. "I think I

have little to fear, but, it is true, it would not hurt to be on our way."

"No, Master," said White Ankles.

"I am now going to lift you into the wagon," said the dealer, "and put you on the floor of the wagon box, where you will kneel."

"Yes, Master," said White Ankles, delighted.

"Slave, slave!" said Cornhair.

One gathers that White Ankles was soon ensconced, kneeling, bound, beside the driver's bench, for the dealer had returned to the back of the wagon, where Cornhair waited, on all fours, her head down, rather toward the right-rear wheel of the wagon.

"What of me?" asked Cornhair.

"What of you?" said the dealer.

"Am I not, too, to be clothed?" asked Cornhair.

"Do you wear a tunic well?" he asked.

"It is my hope that I would be more amply concealed," she said.

"Do you wear a tunic well?" he asked.

"Doubtless as well as any other woman," she said.

"As well as a slave?" he asked.

"Doubtless," she said.

"And appropriately?" he asked.

"Surely not appropriately," said Cornhair.

"You have a slave body," he said.

"Master!" protested Cornhair.

"You may thank me," he said. "You have been complimented."

"'Complimented'?" she said.

"Yes," he said. "Slave bodies are the loveliest, the most exciting, and desirable of female bodies. Those with such bodies should be slaves, and, obviously, in the way of nature, have been bred for bondage."

"I?" she said. "Bred for bondage?"

"Yes," he said, "externally, and internally."

Cornhair, of course, from the tale of a thousand mirrors, was well aware of her lineaments. She was well aware that they might bring coin off a slave block. Indeed, had it not been for such, she supposed she would not have been recruited as a tool for shaping deeds to the ends of Iaachus, he, Arbiter of Protocol in the court of the emperor, Aesilesius. Surely her beauty, such as it was, had been germane to his projects, a beauty which, as it seems, had not been marred, but, rather, considerably enhanced by being fastened in a collar. But, what of internality? Could she, in virtue of the simple realities of her sex, emotionally, profoundly, psychologically, and needfully, have been bred for bondage? It would be a strange nature, indeed, which would content itself with façades, and leave unattended, neglected, and unfurnished the rooms within, the chambers and housings of the heart and mind. Nigh overwhelming her, there rushed upon her a thousand memories and desires, and readinesses, tremblings, and hopings, feelings which she had tried to cry out against, against which she had tried to levy and lodge a thousand prescribed, acculturated denials, only to be once more afflicted by the persistent, intrusive whispers of a prohibited nature.

"You may thank me," said the dealer.

"Thank you, Master," said Cornhair.

She struggled to reject the thought that her body was suffused with warmth when she uttered her response.

Then she clung again, desperately, to the mockery and deceit, the veil, behind which she dared not look, for fear of what might be found.

"In time, you will learn yourself," said the dealer.

"I now know myself," she said.

"I think not," he said, "not yet."

"Master," she said.

"Yes?" he said.

"I am not yet clothed," she said.

"Clearly," he said. "Keep your head down."

"And," she said, "it seems, a mere slave has been given pre-
cedence over me, placed forward, near the reins of the horses, at
the side of the wagon bench."

"So?" inquired the dealer.

"Why she?" asked Cornhair.

"It pleased me," he said.

"I beg permission to speak to Master," she said.

"You may do so," he said.

"Master does not understand who I am," she said.

"You are a slave," he said. "What else is there to know?"

"I am not a common slave," she said.

"I see you as common, indeed, as more common than most,"
he said.

"Master," she said, "is apparently unaware of my antecedents."

"I do not understand," he said.

"May I kneel before Master, and look up at him?" asked
Cornhair.

"Very well," he said, puzzled.

"I have awaited the opportunity to identify myself," she said.
"It is now at hand."

"I do not understand," he said.

"Master is Telnarian?" she said.

"Yes," he said.

"Master is then well aware of many of the high families of the
empire, families which brought about the glories, the victories,
the achievements and conquests, of the empire, the thousand
families which, in their way, are the historical foundation on
which the empire rests, which constitute the entwining, genea-
logical fibers which bind worlds together, which dignify, ennoble, and enhance the *imperium* itself."

"I am aware," he said, "of the rapacious, high *honestori*,
which seizes land and covets resources, which loots peasant-
ries and buys palaces, which renders land sterile, poisons seas,
and, with fumes and noxious vapors, clouds and darkens skies,

which manages and ruins worlds, which takes all and gives nothing."

"No!" said Cornhair. "I speak of the finest and the best, of the true nobility of the empire, of the highest and most glorious of the ancestral lines, such as that of the Larial Calasalii!"

"The worst!" snorted the dealer.

"You have heard of the Larial Calasalii?" she said.

"Yes," he said.

"Regardless of what you may think of them," she said, "they are powerful. Their wealth could buy worlds!"

"You think so?" he said.

"Yes!" she said.

"What has this to do with you, a naked little slave, at my feet, in your collar?"

"I am the Lady Publennia Calasalia, of the Larial Calasalii!"

"You tell me," he asked, "I have such a person before me, kneeling in the dirt, not yards from a Herul camp, collared?"

"I am she!" said Cornhair.

"Your thigh," said he, "wears, tiny and unmistakable, the rose, your neck the circlet of bondage."

"Very well," she said, "if you wish, I was the Lady Publennia Calasalia, of the Larial Calasalii!"

In imparting this information it seems that Cornhair failed to mention that she had been cast from the family, in effect, put aside and disowned.

"Very impressive," said he.

"So, now," she said, "have me rise, remove this dreadful, degrading object which encircles my neck, and bring me, as soon as possible, suitable clothing, garmenture fit for a lady of quality."

"Why?" he asked.

"That I may be restored to my rightful dignity."

"Ransomed, perhaps?" he asked.

"Of course," she said.

"Or bought?" he said.

"If you wish," she said.

"By your family?" he asked.

"Of course," she said.

"What would they pay?" he asked.

"They will pay any price," she said.

"Thousands of *darins*?" he asked.

"Of course," she said.

"I have seen your sort," he said, "on many selling platforms, at crossroads, at fairs, at provincial markets, on holidays. You would bring between fifteen and twenty *darins*."

From her position forward, in the wagon box, kneeling at the side of the wagon bench, the voice of White Ankles trilled with laugher.

"I do not understand?" said Cornhair.

"On your belly," said the dealer. "Cross your ankles, and cross your wrists, behind you."

Dismayed, Cornhair put herself to her belly, and assumed the prescribed position. Shortly thereafter, her crossed ankles were bound together, and her wrists, behind her, as well.

She was then lifted up, over the side of the wagon bed, and deposited on the boards.

"Do not do this to me, Master," she protested. "I am—I was!—the Lady Publennia Calasalia, of the Larial Calasalii!"

"You know little now of the Larial Calasalii," said the dealer.

"We are of the exalted *honestori*, of the high patricians, of the senatorial class!" she said.

"No more," he said. "It began as a clash of private armies, between the Larial Calasalii and the Larial Farnichi."

Perhaps it might be noted that private armies were not rare in Telnarian times. There were many reasons for this, given the frequent absences of enforceable imperial authority, the precariousness of life, the lack of, or fragility of, communication, the exhaustion of land, the paucity of goods, the desire to protect and control dwindling resources, the desire to suppress banditry and piracy, the desire to rule and wield power, and such. Indeed, as the empire became ever more expanded and unwieldy its effective power, so attenuated, diminished. And while lawlessness prowled perimeters, and displaced populations fled to cities, to form restless, dangerous, idle, hungry crowds, requiring pacification, if not a velvet suppression, supplied by doles of grain, and plentiful, lavish amusements, spectacles, pageants, plays, races, and games, strong men, here and there, sometimes in barren provinces, took to the saddle and imposed order. Indeed, it is speculated that at the founding of honored kingdoms, if one should seek far enough, one might find something surprisingly inauspicious, a renegade soldier, a local tyrant, an ambitious leader of a handful of armed men, what, at the time, might have been denominated a brigand or rogue.

"Four campaigns were waged," he said, "on three worlds. Much blood was shed, much gold expended. Then, allegedly to keep the peace, but at the invitation of the Farnichi, an invitation weighted with gold, the empire intervened, intervened on behalf of the Farnichi. The forces of the Farnichi then, now abetted by the striking hammer of the empire, shattered your vaunted Larial Calasalii. Its surviving forces were disbanded. Its goods were confiscated by the state, and distributed, half to the empire, half to the Farnichi. The family was stripped of its titles and privileges. It, reduced to poverty, was demoted to the *humiliori*. Then, at the request of the Farnichi, it was secretly outlawed, an outlawry which became public, only on the morning after its men were arrested and imprisoned, many to be sentenced to the mines and quarries. Its thousand women were collared and sold at auction, most to be house slaves, and scullery slaves, many to serve in the houses of the Farnichi, and others became field slaves, many then to labor in the fields, orchards, and vineyards of the Farnichi. Many, to be sure, became pleasure slaves, and many of these, doubtless, eventually found themselves chained at the foot of the couches of Farnichi Masters."

"No, no, no!" cried Cornhair, twisting, writhing, tied, on the boards of the wagon bed.

White Ankles laughed, merrily.

"We must be on our way, slave girl," said the dealer.

"What is to be done with me?" wept Cornhair, struggling.

"You are going to be marketed," he said.

In a bit, with a jolt, the wagon lurched forward.

In a few minutes, the wagon was making its way through the grass.

"We leave the Herul camp behind!" said White Ankles, joyfully.

"You are a pretty slave," said the dealer.

"I am more than pretty, Master!" said White Ankles.

"Stop that!" laughed the dealer.

"I would please my Master," said White Ankles.

"You are an appetitious little brute," he said.

"I am a slave, Master!" said White Ankles.

"Stop it!" laughed the dealer.

"Let me please you, Master!" said White Ankles.

"Slave! Slave!" cried Cornhair.

"Later, later!" laughed the dealer.

"As Master wishes," said White Ankles.

Cornhair thrashed on the floor of the wagon bed. She pulled, futilely, at her bonds.

"Stop twisting about," called the dealer, from the wagon bench. "You must not abrade your body. We want it to look smooth and pretty on the sales block."

"Yes, Master," wept Cornhair.

"You cannot free yourself," said the dealer. "You are a tied slave. Do you know what it is to be a tied slave?"

Cornhair pulled a little at her bonds, futilely.

"Yes, Master," she said, sobbing. "I know what it is to be a tied slave."

NOTES, PRIOR TO CHAPTER FOURTEEN

Our principal source for reconstructing these accounts is the manuscript, or, possibly, the manuscripts, given certain subtleties in the text, discovered several years ago in the ducal library of Valens, one of the lesser duchies in the confederation of Talois. The ducal librarians cataloged the text, or texts, as 122B Valens, and it, or they, have, on the whole, remained identified under this designation, despite certain disruptions in the confederation, mostly consequent on schisms. The swords of faith are not uncommonly bright with the blood of zealotry. In any event, as I once made clear, long ago, the Valens manuscript, while not unique in this particular, is unusual amongst Telnarian, or allegedly Telnarian, manuscripts, as the narrative is relatively personal, and deals, on the whole, with individuals, rather than institutions, with personal lives, rather than the broad, tumultuous storms and tides of history. I think there is some point in this, not only for its own interest, for we, as human beings, have an interest in human beings, but, beyond that, we discover our species, and thus ourselves, in the lives of others. Have we not lived, then, at the edge of icy seas, not met the lances of foes on distant fields, not trekked beside wagons seeking new lands? Have we not waited at dawn for the attack of Heruls, not noticed the dim horizon dotted with advancing horsemen, not noted, to our unease, the tracks of the vi-cat near our camp? Love, fear, sorrow, rage, joy, curiosity, suspicion, betrayal, friendship, treason, trust, are these not our name, and that of our brothers? In glimpsing other lives we live our own more deeply, more keenly, more richly. We understand the nature of our species in the record of its deeds. How could it be otherwise? What is the vi-cat without claws, the keen-sighted hawk without its wings? It is less than itself. Let our desert be enriched with the greenery of kinship. Meadows laid waste may again bloom. What are these great movements and institutions, these migrations and dislocations, these inventions and discoveries, these wars and recoveries, but the outcomes of human action? Let far rain refresh our aridity. A mariner resides in the heart of man. Is it wrong for caged wolves to howl and recall the forest? Might they not, somehow, slip between the bars? All is not as we find it in our own chambers. The mountains of history consist of human particles. Let us observe the mountain, but remember that it consists of human particles, and one learns of the mountain, in a way, by learning of those particles, those which contribute to its grandeur and might, its terror and fearsomeness, those without which it would not have existed. In short, other times are our times, as well. In learning of others we learn of ourselves. How can one learn the meaning of borne standards, without understanding who bears them, and why?

Although we are concerned in this work primarily with individuals, and less with herds and flocks, environments and weathers, as most histories, it seems clear that certain developments in our narrative, shortly to be recounted, might appear somewhat out of joint, or somewhat surprising and anomalous, if treated bluntly. Accordingly, to render our accounts more intelligible, it seems judicious, if not imperative, to devote some attention, in however cursory a manner, to a number of events which were simultaneously occurring in the empire, events which have been only tangentially noted, if at all, to this point in the Valens manuscript.

For purposes of simplicity these events might be denominated political and religious, which semantic differentiation, however, is misleading, for they were often closely intertwined, and, upon occasion, seemingly fused.

Early in our chronicle, even before certain events transpired in a Terennian arena, the Floonian phenomenon was noted. At that time, attention was paid to the nature of the phenomenon, its founder, his teachings, its doctrinal controversies, its development, its relationship to the empire, and other matters. It would be repetitious, and, I think, unnecessary, to delineate these particularities once more. Let us say, rather, simply, and looking forward, that the Floonian phenomenon had undergone significant changes since its inauspicious and local beginnings as a tiny, eccentric, ridiculed, despised sect on the reptilian world of Zirus. Floon himself was a rational salamander or, perhaps better, a salamanderlike creature. Later, of course, Floon was represented under the likeness of a thousand species, on a thousand worlds. His teachings, for example, that rational creatures possessed an invisible, undetectable *koos*, which was their real self and eternal; that Karch, the chief god, and later supposedly the sole god, endorsed Floon's teachings, and was somehow identical with Floon, but not really as they were different, too; and that Karch, as Floon taught, was particularly partial to the unhappy, ignored, belittled, envious, resentful, and unsuccessful, who were, as one might expect, numerous, tended to be understandably popular. To these latter folk, the unhappy, ignored, and so on, was promised, for a temporary investment of behaving in a certain way, an eternity of wealth, palaces, gold dishes, good food, happiness, and such. As might be expected, Floon ran afoul of an establishment rather fond of its own notions of a rightly ordered universe, and was executed, being burned alive on an electric rack. This did not prove to be the end of the Floonian phenomenon, however, as Floon was reported to have appeared, though briefly, thereafter, in good

health and none the worse for his tragic demise, on a large number of worlds, possibly in a large number of forms. To the skeptic
two problems, at least, lingered: first, did this remarkable event
occur, and, second, if it occurred, what was its logical relationship, if any, to the Floonian phenomenon? For example, what if
a minor god liked Floon and reassembled his charred remains
from the grid. Would that somehow be relevant to Floon's teachings, teachings for which the minor god might be willing to forgive Floon, in the light of Floon's exemplary, if strange, life? In
any event, in the earlier period of the Floonian phenomenon,
Floonians were largely societal outsiders, concerned with little
but denouncing the world in which they tended to be unsuccessful, and caring for, and nurturing, their *koos*. The empire,
as was its policy, tolerated thousands of gods and thousands of
faiths. It had enough trouble on its hands without gratuitously
meddling in matters which were largely immaterial to its own
security and prospects. On the other hand, as the Floonian phenomenon developed, its relationship to the empire proved more
problematic. For one thing Floonians tended to be reluctant to
serve a state they found to be, at best, irrelevant to the *koos*,
and, at worst, inimical to its welfare. The state, it seems, was
unnecessary and, possibly, opprobrious. For example, it wanted
taxes, in the form of money or service; it wanted servitors and
soldiers; it wanted respect; it wanted loyalty. The empire, naturally, particularly as Floonianism began to spread, was not eager
to see the supposed fibers of its security and power, of its very
existence, unraveled, or cut. Also, one might note, whereas the
empire tended to be permissive and tolerant, these virtues, or
faults, were not shared by the Floonians, or at least by their leaders, exploiting an unexpected source of power, who tended to
be dogmatic and intolerant. The developing competitive hierar-
chies within Floonianism, sometimes by majority votes in councils, sometimes by assassinations, sometimes by riots, sometimes
by burning and looting districts, including consecrated edifices,

began to develop an impressive maze of unintelligible doctrine which it was important to get just right, even if it was incomprehensible; for example, in some of the clearer announcements, it was discovered that Karch was the sole god, after all, and, by lucky chance, was their god. Further, as noted, Karch and Floon were identical, except different, too, which was a mystery, and all the more awesome for that. In any event, in the hands of various prophets, ministers, patriarchs, deacons, bishops, and such, the gentle, loving teachings of Floon tended to be replaced, as suggested, with dogmatism and intolerance. Also, if the Floonians were correct, their particular faith, in one or another of its several forms, must be the one, true faith, with the result that the thousands of other one, true faiths were not simply mistaken, but wicked, and suitably, justifiably, extirpatable. It was, moreover, alleged that individuals who benightedly failed to profess certain prescribed unintelligibilities would experience a less than pleasant afterlife, very much so, which was not welcome news to large, uneasy, diverse populations. In any event, whether in virtue of intimidation, threats, terrorism, coercion, the burning brand, or whatever, or in virtue of the splendid example of their ideal and blameless lives, Floonianism was spreading throughout the empire. And, as suggested, it was not clear that it was in the best interests of the empire, even that it was compatible with the empire. For example, Floonians kept much to themselves, formed their own societies, declined military service, and so on. A trivial illustration of the increasing friction between this faith and the state, but one that came to assume significant symbolic import, was the matter of professing allegiance to the empire. For example, annually, commonly on the emperor's birthday, but sometimes on other holidays, it was thought appropriate that an expression of loyalty be vouchsafed to the empire, for example, that a sprig of laurel, a flower, a pinch of incense, a handful of grain, or such, might be placed on the altar of the *genius*, or spirit, of the empire. This trivial act, so trivial that most citizens did not even bother with it, nor did the state much care, was publicly repudiated by some Floonians, which action forced the state to take notice. As I have suggested, the general policy of the empire toward religious belief was tolerance, and, for the most part, it was as tolerant of Floonianism as it was of the thousands of other faiths within its borders. It did, however, rarely, and sporadically, as it felt threatened, persecute certain Floonians at certain times and in certain places, perhaps to supply the larger populace with monitory examples. On the whole, however, officials found Floonians, wisely or not, quaint and harmless. On the other hand, Floonianism, as time passed, was becoming a force to be reckoned with. It was either, then, to be challenged and fought, or, perhaps more wisely, put to one's own purposes.

While these religious, or ideological, developments were unfolding, the empire, as was not unusual, given its history, was subject to familiar stresses of a more secular, or political, nature. These stresses, in the current era, however, seemed particularly acute, ranging from those encountered at uncertain and disputed borders, invasions, raids, illicit migrations, failed punitive expeditions, and such, to those erupting within the core of the empire itself, unchecked crime, widespread corruption, and civic disturbances. To these more visible and explicit difficulties were added less dramatic, but similarly serious, difficulties, such as mineral and soil exhaustion and the contamination of air and water. As poverty became more widespread, famine and pestilence became more common. An epidemic, with the crowding and imperfect sanitation, could wipe out more than half of a city's population in a matter of weeks. The state had become, even in previous centuries, overcentralized, unwieldy, and ill-governing, but remained vainly jealous of clinging to even minor worlds, worlds with which, in many cases, it was only in tenuous touch. Many worlds remained little more than nominal members of the empire. Others, still listed on the rolls of the imperial bureaucracy, had long ago repudiated the absent empire altogether, and instituted their own modes of governance.

In the face of dwindling resources the empire must exercise restraint and care in the applications of its still considerable power, judiciously applying it, on the whole, only to critical points at crucial times, and only to the measure deemed suitable to a given situation. Accordingly, to speak figuratively, while the farmer might go forth bravely to confront the wolf or *arn* bear, a thousand *filchen* might be free to nibble in his granaries.

We have already mentioned elsewhere, the cheapening of citizenship. No longer was it something of considerable value which, for many, must be earned, but it was now a gift bestowed in virtue of the accident of birth. Few respect that which costs nothing; it is taken for granted, and not prized. As the ecology of life deteriorated, the empire sought remedies. In the hope of improving the economy, the coinage was debased, with the natural consequence that, after the semblance of a brief recovery, money became less valuable, would buy less, and the situation, instead of being improved, grew worse, which lapse initiated a further debasement, with similar results, and so on. Later, the state would seek out those who might still be in a position to pay taxes, and attempt to save itself at their expense. But confiscatory taxes tended to be resisted by the prosperous who, expectedly, would reduce the output of their enterprises, transfer resources to new locales, conceal resources, and so on. To be sure, many of the prosperous were punished for such unconscionable behavior, and, accordingly, as they were methodically and systematically ruined, and reduced to the *humiliori*, the tax base declined proportionately. And finally, of late, on many worlds, to stabilize the tax base, the bindings had been emplaced, which forbade changing locales and occupations. For example the son of a farmer must be a farmer, the son of a physician a physician, the son of an artist or actor must be an artist or actor, and so on. On many worlds, associated with the decline of the influence of the empire, this would lead, particularly in agriculture, to a "binding to the soil," or serfdom, as strong men with armed followers would come to take the place of a larger, more civilized state.

Lastly one might note that the remaining wealth of the distraught empire, its gold, its women, and such, particularly given the attenuation and deterioration of imperial power, constituted no small temptation to the eyes and appetites of the ambitious, strident, and covetous. Many "barbarian nations" existed within and without the empire, and several of these nations, so to speak, despite certain rude customs, traditions, and values, were technologically adept in their own right, and others might be armed and trained by jealous or rebel worlds who bore no love to the imperial court. The successful attack of the Ortungen, a secessionist movement within the Drisriaks, on the imperial cruise ship, the *Alaria*, might be recalled.

Prominent amongst the barbarian leaders was a man known as Abrogastes, the Far-Grasper.

We apologize for these historical remarks, but I felt they might render certain aspects of the succeeding accounts more readily comprehensible.

CHAPTER FOURTEEN

"Elena," said Iaachus, Arbiter of Protocol, "you may withdraw."

"I have brought *kana*," she said. "Am I not to serve it?"

"No," he said.

"But who, then, will serve it?" she asked.

"Leave it on the table," said Iaachus.

"Surely I have not offended you?" she said.

"Not at all," Iaachus assured her.

"I do not understand," she said.

"Do not concern yourself," he said.

"You are to entertain a secret guest?" she said.

"Not at all," he said.

"I hope I am not in disfavor," said Elena.

"No," said Iaachus.

"I fear I have offended you," she said.

"No," said Iaachus. "I fear you might offend another."

"Ah!" she said. "Your guest is a free woman!"

"Perhaps," he said.

"I am fully clothed," she said, "and well, if simply, gowned."

"You are barefoot," he said, "and neck-ringed."

"Of course," she said.

"Nonetheless," he said.

"I see," she smiled.

"What free woman would not detest you?" asked Iaachus. "You are beautiful, quite so, your brown hair, your gray eyes, your exciting limbs and latitudes, the turns within your plain gown, that permitted you, your only garment, your body which, suitably exhibited, would fetch good coin off a girl block."

"It is my hope," she said, "that Master has no intention to sell me."

"Not at present," he said.

"I love Master," she said. "I love his chains! I love the feel of his hands on my body. Long ago he made me his! I was banded and branded, and then, later, he caressed me into the understanding of what I truly was, one appropriately submitted to a Master, which I had only suspected when a free woman."

"It was pleasant for me to do so," he said.

"Doubtless there are many pleasantries attendant on the Mastery," she said.

"Of course," he said.

"But there are pleasures, too," she said, "I wonder if you understand them, on the part of the owned, on the part of those who find themselves subjected helplessly and without recourse to a welcome, coveted, enforced servitude."

"The feelings of a beast," he said, "need not be considered. It exists for the service and pleasure of its Master."

"Master made me what I most desired, in my deepest heart, to be," she said, "a slave."

"You had no choice," he said. "It was done to you."

"As it should have been!" she said. "How I longed to have it done to me! It prospered in my most secret dreams! How I longed to be one who is owned and must obey, one who must yield all and serve choicelessly, one who would find herself, kneeling, collared, head down, wholly subject to another."

"I see," he said.

"The conflicts, the wars, were done," she said. "I was subdued, as I had desired, I was chained, made helpless, as I had hoped. In losing, reduced and tethered, I won, as I had dreamed, and wished. My victory was in my defeat."

"Do not concern yourself," said Iaachus. "These things are neither here nor there. You are a slave."

"The unhappinesses, the uncertainties, the troublings, the ambivalences, the anxieties, the confusions were done," she said. "I would belong! So let it be confirmed! Let the collar be locked on my neck!"

"It was done," he said.

"A beast is grateful," she said.

"What free woman would not see you as a reproach? What excitement and fear you might inspire in her! She need only look at you, gowned, and banded, to see herself similarly reduced and owned. What recognitions, and uneasinesses, what fears and desires, you would stir in her body!"

"I shall withdraw," she whispered.

"Do so," said Iaachus, "but the guest is not a free woman."

"No?" said Elena.

"No," said the Arbiter of Protocol, "but I fear the guest is one who might be as much, if not more, offended, at your presence."

"I withdraw," said Elena.

"Hasten," said the Arbiter of Protocol.

"Yes, Master," said Elena, and slipped from the chamber.

Shortly thereafter the guest was announced.

CHAPTER FIFTEEN

"How gracious of you to accept my invitation," said Iaachus.

"I have long anticipated receiving it," said the guest. "You may kneel, and kiss my ring."

"I think not," said Iaachus.

"As you will," said the guest.

"Be seated," said Iaachus. "*Kana*?"

"Is the Arbiter of Protocol to pour?" inquired the guest. "Is there no servitor?"

"I thought privacy might free our tongues," said Iaachus, "even more than *kana*."

"I have not yet been granted an audience with the emperor and the empress mother," said the guest.

"Nor have thousands of others," said Iaachus.

"I am not as others," said the guest.

"That is why I have sought this exchange," said Iaachus.

"We no longer meet in caves, in abandoned buildings, in private homes," said the guest.

"Indeed," said Iaachus. "You have four temples here in Telnar alone, imperial city of Telnaria."

"Only three," said the guest. "One is a false temple."

"Even so," said Iaachus, "three temples here, in imperial Telnar, Telnar, the seat of the empire, the august and famed meeting place of the senate itself."

"The senate is meaningless," said the guest.

"Surely not," exclaimed Iaachus.

"If it does not enact the imperial will," said the guest, "it will be dissolved, and replaced, it being a trivial matter to appoint a more acquiescent membership."

"I fear you know little of the power of the senate," said Iaachus.

"It lacks fleets and armies," said the guest.

"Even so," said Iaachus.

"I think it must be unpleasant to be cast to serpents or boiled in the blood and fat of lizards," said the guest.

"I do not understand," said Iaachus.

"I think you do," said the guest.

"I fear not," said Iaachus.

"More benignly," said the guest, "many a time a senator or fellow of deeds and wealth has been invited to revise his will in favor of the empire, following which, caring for his family and name, he has been found lifeless in a scarlet bath, his veins parted."

"No more," said Iaachus. "Such dreadful doings, if they existed at all, would characterize more primitive times, more savage days, times and days lacking *civilitas*."

"Men are satellites," said the guest. "They orbit various suns of power."

"The emperor would not hear of such a thing, nor the empress mother," said Iaachus.

"I suspect they would not hear of such a thing," said the guest. "I suspect they would not be told."

"Speak with care," advised Iaachus.

"The emperor is a boy," said the guest, "and the empress mother a timid, irascible, vain old woman."

"Beware," said Iaachus.

"Arrest me," said the guest, "and Telnar will erupt in flame."

"You must be fatigued from your journey," said Iaachus. "I understand you have recently arrived from Zirus."

"From the Holy World of Zirus," said the guest.

"Of course," said Iaachus.

"In whose marshes once swam and waded the Redemptor," said the guest.

"I understand," said Iaachus.

"Telnar," said the guest, "is not merely the seat of the senate, as you remark, but it is also the seat of the imperial court."

"In season," said Iaachus.

"That season is now," said the guest.

"It is not easy to obtain an audience," said Iaachus. "There are many others."

"Not such as I," said the guest.

He fingered the device slung about his neck, over his voluminous purple robes. It, and the chain from which it was suspended, appeared to be of gold. The device itself appeared to be a small replica of a rack, or grid.

"The empire prides itself on its fairness, its tolerance and impartiality," said Iaachus.

"Faults, not virtues," said the guest. "Falsity deserves no fairness. Surely you cannot think so. Iniquity deserves no toleration. Who could entertain such a thought? Wickedness is not to be viewed with impartiality. Is that not itself the greatest of wickednesses?"

"*Kana*?" said Iaachus.

"Please," said the guest.

"I am curious as to these movements within the empire," said Iaachus.

"Movement," said the guest. "Truth is one."

"The individual in question, as I understand it," said Iaachus, "died long ago."

"Not so long ago," said the guest.

"Generations ago," said Iaachus.

"If you like," said the guest.

"And left no written records, or writings."

"No," said the guest.

"Written accounts dealing with these matters date from long after the individual's demise."

"Not so long," said the guest.

"Generations," said Iaachus.

"If you like," said the guest.

"Doubtless there was a prior oral tradition."

"Of course," said the guest.

"Some doubt that the individual existed," said Iaachus, "for example, the unusual accounts, the surprising occurrences, the similarities with other prophets, teachers, gods, and such."

"To deny truth is blasphemy," said the guest.

"I have no objection to supposing the individual, or such individuals, perhaps conflated into one, existed," said Iaachus.

"The Arbiter of Protocol is generous," said the guest.

"His, or their, nature, doings, lives, views, teachings, and such, seem obscure."

"Not at all," said the guest. "Truth is one."

"There are many differing versions and accounts of the teachings in question," said Iaachus.

"But truth is one," said the guest.

"It must be difficult to know which version or account is true," said Iaachus.

"Not at all," said the guest.

"If any one of them," said Iaachus.

"One is true, truth is one," said the guest.

"Surely others cling as tenaciously to their own accounts and versions, as you to yours," said Iaachus.

"Persistence in error is execrable," said the guest.

"The Redemptor, as I understand it," said Iaachus, "is identical with Karch."

"Yes," said the guest, "but different, as well."

"That is hard to understand," said Iaachus.

"Of course," said the guest.

"Your doctrines, in their abundance and complexity, seem to far exceed the simple words ascribed to your Redemptor."

"But are entailed by them, by irrefragable logic."

"Many seem unintelligible," said Iaachus.

"They transcend reason," said the guest.

"That is a virtue?" asked Iaachus.

"Of course," said the guest.

"You take much of this on faith?" asked Iaachus.

"Yes," said the guest.

"Why?" asked Iaachus.

"Because our faith is based on truth."

"Truth is hard to find," said Iaachus.

"Not when seen through the eyes of faith," said the guest.

"Which faith?" asked Iaachus.

"Mine," said the guest.

"I see," said Iaachus.

"I hoped you would," said the guest.

"Your doctrines, and those of other temples, all claiming to be the one, true temple of the Redemptor, seem to differ."

"Heresy is rampant," said the guest.

"Perhaps the empire might be of assistance?" said Iaachus.

"If properly guided," said the guest.

"Perhaps that has something to do with your desire to meet with the emperor and the empress mother?" said Iaachus.

"Perhaps you can arrange such an audience," said the guest.

"As I understand it," said Iaachus, "differing temples, and sets of temples, define themselves in terms of beliefs, or creedal commitments. For example, your temple, or your temples, commit themselves to, say, propositions one, two, and three."

"Proceed," said the guest.

"But, as these propositions appear to be unintelligible—"

"Such as exceed the grasp of reason," said the guest.

"—they can be neither proved nor disproved."

"They are beyond proof," said the guest.

"And they cannot be disproven," said Iaachus.

"That is their strength," said the guest. "They are irrefutable."

"But," said Iaachus, "these differing temples, or sets of temples, have their own propositions, say, one, four, and five, similarly irrelevant to the world, similarly compatible with any situation whatsoever, more propositions which in no way could be shown to be either true or false, propositions to which evidence is immaterial, propositions similarly immune to refutation."

"What is your point?" inquired the guest.

"And yet the adherents of your Redemptor, who spoke of peace, sweetness, gentleness, love, patience, resignation, and such, are willing to burn and kill one another over these competitive gibberishes."

"Perhaps you can arrange an audience with the emperor, or the empress mother," said the guest.

"Do you truly believe," asked Iaachus, "that your mighty Karch, invisible and mighty, unseen and vast, sculptor of universes, designer of the cobra's fangs and the vi-cat's claws, the germ that can fell a *torodont*, stars which can engulf worlds, cares whether or not some street sweeper believes in propositions one, two, and three, or one, four, and five?"

"The audience?" politely inquired the guest.

"You are a highly intelligent man," said Iaachus. "You cannot convince me that you take these things seriously."

"I think that you can arrange such an audience," said the guest.

"Permit me to speculate," said Iaachus, "on the practical relevance of creedal commitment, and on the importance of the singularity claim, as well, both of which, viewed simply, appear so implausible, anomalous, and absurd. What lurks behind the contrived veil of nonsense, so objectively pointless, on the other hand, is mighty with meaning. Behind the fog of appeal and distraction lies something quite real, quite comprehensible.

Concealed in the night of nonsense is something quite different. In the darkness, the beast is afoot, alert, eager, and ravenous. How ironic that simple, loving teachings should be turned to the familiar ends of ambition and greed, of power. How wise to claim sole proprietorship of the keys that lead to golden worlds. What prestige redounds to the humble! How paradoxical to cast oneself down to be exalted over one's brothers. Consider the self-image, the self-esteem, the community image of the self-less servitors of so innocent and benign a creed! Celebrate them! Contemplate the public's acceptance and approval so lavishly awarded, so justifiably deserved, so humbly acknowledged, the garnered livelihood so easily acquired, the economic support bestowed by the faithful. Who would be willing to divide the spoils of such a possible victory? Who will contest a hut of reeds on Zirus? But many might do much for a golden palace."

"Men are satellites," said the guest. "They orbit various suns of power."

"And there are a hundred suns," said Iaachus.

"A thousand," smiled the guest, "and even more." He then sipped his *kana*.

"I shall arrange the audience," said Iaachus.

"I thought you might," said the guest.

CHAPTER SIXTEEN

"I cannot see it!" cried Otto, reining the horse up suddenly, it squealing, the clawed forefeet raking at the sky.

"Steady!" cried Julian.

The horse was spun about, jerked forward again, reins taut, mouth bloody at the bit, eyes wide and wild, the clawed feet tearing at the turf.

"Steady, steady!" said Julian.

"Why have you brought me here?" demanded Otto, standing in the stirrups.

"That you might know," said Julian.

"Where is it?" demanded Otto.

"Gone," said Julian.

"No!" said Otto. "It is there, somehow, as the mountain itself!"

"No longer," said Julian.

"From the beginning of the world!" said Otto.

"Those are stories," said Julian.

"For a thousand years!" said Otto.

"Perhaps," said Julian. "I do not know."

"I cannot see it!" said Otto. "I cannot see it!"

"It is gone, dear friend," said Julian. "Like the village, remembered only by rubble and charred shambles."

"See!" cried Otto, pointing. "There should be path guards, trail watchers!"

"They no longer stand their posts, no longer keep their rounds," said Julian.

"They are remiss," said Otto. "They must be reprimanded. Let them be nailed to boards!"

"Things are no longer as they were," said Julian.

"Discipline!" said Otto.

"It does no good to reprimand the dead," said Julian. "The dead are done with discipline."

"Dead?" said Otto.

"It seems, all," said Julian. "Hold! What is your intention?"

"It is to ascend," said Otto.

"I encourage you to remain here, at the foot," said Julian. "There is less here to stir fearful rage."

"I shall ascend," said Otto.

"Better not, dear friend," said Julian.

"Do not fear," said Otto. "It is day. The invisible eyes will not be open, the fences will not be alive, the lightnings will not strike."

"Even were it night," said Julian, "even if beasts were to prowl, or Heruls to intrude, the defenses are inert."

"I ride!" snarled Otto, and struck heels into the startled mount, and the great beast leapt forward.

Julian, astride his own mount, hurried in the wake of his friend, beginning the long, steep, winding climb to the summit.

In less than an hour they dismounted their driven, gasping, trembling, unsteady, chest-heaving, worn beasts.

The boots of Otto and Julian ground into the cold gravel of the path.

They sucked the thin, cold air into their lungs. If they had turned, they might have seen the green, summery expanse of the Plains of Barrionuevo, of the Flats of Tung, far below, stretching even to the Lothar.

"The gate was here!" said Otto.

"No longer," said Julian.

A light coating of snow covered the area, common here throughout the year.

This imparted to the scene, despite its jumbled, jagged outlines, an appearance of passivity and serenity.

"It is lovely here," said Julian.

"This place was chosen for it remoteness, its stillness, and beauty," said Otto.

"A fit place for the prayers, the contemplations, the meditations of the brothers," said Julian.

"What is it that the snow so innocently, so gently, veils?" said Otto.

"Let us return to the plain," said Julian.

Otto drew back, and struck the snow from his damp hand on his jacket. "The stonage is black," he said. It seemed a scar lay on the snow.

"From the blast," said Julian. "Within, it is worse, toward the center, where rock melted. One can still see where it flowed, where it cooled, like the spines of snakes."

Otto scraped his boot in the snow, and the side of his boot was rimmed with brittle crystals and chill ash.

"Serviceable timber, even half-burned, was salvaged," said Julian, "by peasants, and Heruls."

Wood, as one might have surmised, was a precious commodity in the area.

There was a stirring, and scratching, to the side.

"The horses are uneasy," said Otto.

"Yes," said Julian.

The men regarded their mounts.

One of the beasts lifted its head, its nostrils distended. There was a susurrating, uneasy rumble in its throat, answered by a similar sound from its fellow.

"They smell death," said Otto.

"No, dear friend," said Julian. "It has been too long. What could be found of death was borne away, long ago, by peasants."

"What could be found?" said Otto.

"Not a great deal," said Julian. "The leavings of birds, the discards of *filchen*."

"I am angry," said Otto.

"I encouraged you to remain below," said Julian.

The heads of the horses turned about, uneasily, nostrils distended. They stirred in place. There was mud about their paws, where snow, trampled, had melted.

"They are restless," said Otto.

"Not from death," said Julian.

"A vi-cat then?" said Otto.

"Probably," said Julian.

"The beasts return," said Otto.

"They always will," said Julian.

Otto and Julian mounted.

Julian turned his horse toward the backtrail. "Let us descend," he said.

But Otto, asaddle, continued to regard the calm, terrible scene before him. The broad reins were enclosed in massive, clenched fists.

Julian turned his mount once more, and drew his beast up, beside, but a bit behind, that of his friend.

"What happened here?" said Otto, speaking quietly, as softly as the darkening of a sky in the north.

"The wars," said Julian.

"I cannot understand this," said Otto. "It is pointless, there is nothing to be gained here. This is incomprehensible carnage, inexplicable, wanton devastation."

"Explicable in terms you might not understand," said Julian.

"Why would Abrogastes attack this remote, isolated place, of no political or military significance? Why would he, or Ingeld or Hrothgar, or Ortog, or a hundred other chieftains, kings, and commanders, waste resources here?"

"They would not," said Julian.

"I do not understand," said Otto.

"This was done by no barbarian fleet," said Julian.

"I do not understand," said Otto.

"It was done by imperial cruisers," said Julian.

"By the empire?" said Otto.

"By imperial forces," said Julian.

"You said 'the wars'," said Otto.

"Faith Wars," said Julian.

"Civil war?" said Otto.

"Of a sort," said Julian.

"I do not understand," said Otto.

"There are numerous sects and cults, some larger, some smaller, each purporting to be the one, true institution founded by the Ogg, Floon."

"But Floon did not found an institution," said Otto. "He was outside institutions, even opposed to institutions. He appealed to individuals as individuals, urging them to look into their own hearts and live their own lives well. He was opposed to artificiality, to artifice, to convention, to government, law, taxes, marriage, family, money, many things. Such things were denounced as unnatural. Many conceived of him as posing a threat to rules, to order, to civilization itself. Thus, it seems, he was brought to his miserable end. Certainly he would have been opposed to any institution which would presume to interpose itself between the individual, an Ogg or not, and the face and blessings of the god, Karch, who may or may not have been an Ogg, or any other god."

"Nonetheless," said Julian.

"It is hard to understand," said Otto. "Are they unfamiliar with the teachings of Floon?"

"Perhaps only unfamiliar with the meanings," said Julian.

"Or do not care to be familiar with them," said Otto.

"Perhaps," said Julian.

"It would not be convenient?" said Otto.

"Presumably not," said Julian.

"It is all very strange," said Otto.

"There are many views," said Julian. "Perhaps the most benign is that Floon was a sweet, pleasant, compassionate, benevolent, normal Ogg, sincere and concerned, who wanted to help people live better, happier lives, and he made the mistake of going ahead and attempting to do so. The difficulties arose, as I understand it, in trying to understand what relationship might obtain between Floon and Karch. Was Floon an ordinary, normal Ogg who would speak for Karch, who seemed unwilling to speak for himself? And, if this was the case, did he speak on his own prerogative for Karch, or was he directed to speak by Karch. Or was there some more mysterious relationship involved? For example, was Floon related to Karch, as a nephew, or brother, or cousin might be related, though in some unusual sense, not well specified? Perhaps Floon was an attribute or property of Karch? Or, if Floon was Karch, or a part of Karch, and Karch was perfect, might not the seeming Floon have been an illusion, as Karch, or his progeny or relations, or such, would presumably not be allowed to feel pain? Too, why would Karch allow himself, or such, or his emissary or representative, or such, to feel pain, at all? Then there is the Emanationist theory which is that Floon was an emanation of Karch."

"The brothers were Emanationists," said Otto, "whatever that might mean, or however it might be understood, if at all."

"That is accounted a heresy, one of several," said Julian, "and heresies are accounted dangerous to the welfare of the *koos*."

"I have heard of a *koos*," said Otto. "But I do not understand it."

"No one does," said Julian. "The notion is unintelligible."

"What is a heresy?" asked Otto.

"It is a departure from orthodoxy," said Julian.

"And what is an orthodoxy?" asked Otto.

"A heresy from someone else's point of view," said Julian.

"I understand little of this," said Otto.

"It is all nonsense," said Julian. "It is only necessary that one learn to manipulate the terminologies, to utter certain words in certain sequences, approved sequences, of course, that is important."

"Words that merely float about, and never touch earth?"

"They are safer that way," said Julian.

"How is it that folk can hate one another, and burn and kill one another, over such sillinesses?"

"It is apparently easy," said Julian. "And there is nothing silly about being burned alive."

"But Floon preached peace and love," said Otto.

"Forget about Floon," said Julian. "He has nothing to do with it. You do understand, I take it, how men might fight and hate, and burn and kill, for gold, power, prestige, and influence?"

"Yes," said Otto.

"Well," said Julian, "there are many roads leading to such things, some more obvious, others more subtle, and it is tempting to follow such a road, particularly for some, if you can draft others to clear the way for you, to accept the risks of removing obstacles from your path, to bloody their hands while yours remain sanctimoniously clean."

"What occurred here," said Otto, surveying the gentle snow, which so softened the contours of what lay beneath, "wants righting."

"In any event," said Julian, "the more important theories, depending on the rulings or the councils, creating truth by decree, or majority vote, seem to maintain that Karch and Floon, in one way or another, are identical, except that they are different, as well. These views seem to be the orthodox views, orthodoxy indexed to numbers, position, wealth, power, or influence."

"Why did you not inform me of these things?" asked Otto.

"What good would it have done?" asked Julian.

"Abrogastes, and others, had no hand in this?"

"No," said Julian.

"Then my enemy," said Otto, "is the empire."

"No," said Julian.

"Its ships have done this," said Otto, sweeping a hand forth, a gesture that hinted not so much of the brushing aside of a cloak of snow which, with its chill covering, might conceal memories best left neglected, as of the darkening of stars and the striking of worlds from their orbits.

"Direct not your rage unwisely, dear friend," said Julian.

"How many ships can you command?" asked Otto.

"The empire has made tools of others," said Julian. "Now others make tools of the empire."

"A hundred ships, two hundred?" asked Otto.

"Dissidence racks the empire," said Julian. "Worlds secede, barbarous fleets arm themselves. Citizens turn away from ancient altars. Want roams barren fields. Faiths spring at one another's throats. Vultures wait with patience. Weakness and rottenness festers at the core of power."

"May the empire fall," said Otto. "And may I strike the blow of its death!"

"Rather let the empire be cleansed, and live," said Julian.

"Give the Otungen ten ships and they will hurl themselves against a thousand."

"And fruitlessly scatter their bones in the airless fields of space."

"You council patience," said Otto.

"That of the lion waiting in the shadows, by the watering hole."

"You have been here, have you not, before?" asked Otto.

"Once," said Julian. "To learn of you."

"One here, Brother Benjamin, was as a father to me," said Otto.

"I met him," said Julian. "You were brought to this place as an infant, nearly newborn, by a Herul, one named Hunlaki, in the month of the god, Igon, in the year 1103, of the Imperial Claiming Stone, set at Venitzia."

"I know some of this," said Otto, "but not much. I was not told much. I did not know the name of the Herul. I gather it was not deemed necessary to tell me much."

"One gathers so," said Julian. "It was probably just as well. One must be careful of what one speaks, and to whom one speaks. Princes seldom sow grain. Few kings remain at the handles of the plow. How foolish it would be for one to seek vanquished and vanished worlds, to seek thrones which no longer exist. Is it not best to remain ignorant of glories which are unattainable, from which one is barred? Let the peasant be content in his hovel. Let him not glimpse far-off golden walls."

"You speak strangely," said Otto.

"There was a medallion and chain, deeply cut, profoundly formed, weighty and gold, with the babe, the found infant," said Julian. "I saw it. Brother Benjamin had held it for years. It is the symbol of office of the King of the Vandal Nations."

As I may have mentioned, the most likely origin of the word 'Vandal' is from "Vanland," or "woodland," or "forest land." The Vandals, thus, would be the "woodland folk" or the "forest people," or such. Later semantic accretions to the term should not be allowed to reflect on the etiology involved. Such accretions have more to do with historically acquired associations.

"The Wolfungs, of whom I am chief, and the Otungs, of whom I am King, are Vandal nations," said Otto.

"Yes," said Julian, "and so, too, are the Darisi, the Haakons, and Basungs."

"True," said Otto.

"And there are other nations, too," said Julian, "who are related to the Vandals, or look up to the Vandals."

"Perhaps," said Otto.

"The greatest threat to the empire," said Julian, "is the threat of the Aatii, as they are referred to in the imperial records. You know them as the Alemanni, a nation which consists of eleven tribes, though I fear it influences and enleagues others, as well.

As you are well aware, the largest, the mightiest, and most fierce of the Alemanni tribes is the Drisriaks."

"The Vandals and the Alemanni are traditional enemies," said Otto.

"That is known to me," said Julian.

"You would use me for your purposes," said Otto.

"For our purposes," said Julian.

"But, perhaps, trained and armed, we will turn on you," said Otto.

"Do you think the Alemanni would share worlds with the Vandals?" asked Julian.

"No," said Otto, "nor with the empire."

"The empire is sick with a thousand poisons," said Julian. "Men do not love her. They hope to thrive in her body as parasites. They suck blood they refuse to replenish. Virtue is mocked; honor derided, trust forsworn. Weapons rust; barracks are empty. Patriotism is jeered, loyalty scorned. Incense no longer perfumes our temples; the smoke of burnt offerings no longer rises to the sky; ancient altars are bereft of gifts."

"The empire is done," said Otto, "even if it should take a thousand years to die."

"No!" said Julian.

"Small men," said Otto, "will not do the work of giants. They will concern themselves with small things."

"The empire was the work of giants," said Julian.

"The giants are no more," said Otto.

"A miserable fate, that the heritage of lions must be bequeathed to *filchen*."

"There are few lions, many *filchen*," said Otto.

"I fear the sky will become dark with the coming of ships."

"What is that to me?" said Otto.

"The loss of *civilitas*, the beginnings of chaos and tramplings, the rise of a thousand tyrannies," said Julian.

"You would pit Vandals against Alemanni," said Otto, "your

enemies against one another. Let them erode and exhaust themselves, and then, wounded and weak, drained of blood, succumb to the mace of the empire. It is an old trick, one remembered in the tents and halls."

"Rather," said Julian, "let fresh blood enliven the empire, let forceful, clean winds sweep rot away. Let new giants be enlisted in noble, antique causes, let new swords be forged."

"Where is the medallion and chain?" asked Otto.

"You are interested?" said Julian.

"Where is it?" asked Otto.

"You could use it for your own ends, but I would that it be used for the needs of worlds, for the promotion of *civilitas*, for the cleansing and rebirth of the empire."

"The empire," said Otto, gesturing to the cool, white, quiet, desolate expanse before him, "did this."

"Forces within the empire," said Julian, "which must be thwarted and overcome."

"Let the empire perish," said Otto.

"And with her the walls beyond which hungry beasts lurk, walls which for ten thousand years have kept the thoughtless, encroaching, teeming forest, and its creatures, at bay?"

"Where is the medallion and chain?" said Otto.

"I do not know," said Julian. "I have had it much searched for. Officers have combed the ruins, moved stones, sorted rubble, pried up tiles, raked and sifted ash, all to no avail."

"Then there is nothing to be done," said Otto. "Without it the Vandals cannot be gathered. The empire must deal with the Alemanni, and its allies, as best it can."

"It must exist," said Julian. "I saw it. It would not be destroyed."

"It must be concealed, perhaps in the ruins," said Otto.

"It was not hidden. Brother Benjamin kept it in a box, a leather case, in his cell. I saw it there. The attack was not anticipated. It was sudden and unexpected, fierce and thorough.

There would have been no reason, nor time, to hurry it into hiding, to take special precautions on its behalf."

"Then it was destroyed in the attack," said Otto, "the blast, the heat."

"The search was thorough," said Julian. "Not even a droplet of gold, not even a bead, was found in the ruins."

"It was stolen?" said Otto.

"I fear so," said Julian.

"By a brother?"

"Unlikely," said Julian.

"After the attack, by peasants, by Heruls?"

"Perhaps," said Julian. "But there is no reason to believe so. Inquiries have been made, rewards offered. Nothing has materialized."

"Then by whom?"

"A visitor, a spy," said Julian.

"It matters not," said Otto.

"It matters much," said Julian. "He who possesses the artifact might rally the Vandals to any cause."

"Not the Wolfungs, not the Otungs," said Otto.

"Perhaps even they," said Julian. "You do not know the portent of the medallion and chain."

"I knew not that it existed," said Otto.

"If nothing else," said Julian, "its loss might well prevent another from rousing the Vandals."

"Such as Otto, King of the Otungs?" said Otto.

"Yes," said Julian.

"Look before you," said Otto. "See white snow. It covers blackened stone. Where there stood a mighty edifice now reposes a bleak summit. The wind here is cold and the clouds bright. A hawk soars overhead."

"I am sorry, dear Ottonius," said Julian.

"Do you think the empire can be conquered so easily?" said Otto.

"Not easily conquered," said Julian, "but easily seized."

And then the two men turned their mounts to the backtrail, leading down, far below, to the Plains of Barrionuevo, or the Flats of Tung, leaving behind them the ruins of a great house, the *festung* of Sim Giadini.

CHAPTER SEVENTEEN

Cornhair fought the close-fitting metal circlets on her wrists, pulling against the three short links that fastened them together.

"Free me!" she cried. "I do not belong here! It is a mistake! I am a free woman! Clothe me!"

Her hands were braceleted before her so that she, as the others, could reach into the gruel bowl to feed herself, when it was available.

Her hands, now, were clenched on the coffle chain before her, at her neck. The chain ran from the coffle collar to the back ring of the collar of the girl before her, rather as, from the back ring of her own coffle collar, the chain ran back to the front ring on the girl's collar who followed her. Her position in the coffle, which consisted of forty girls, was rather toward the center, as the coffle was arranged in terms of height, the tallest girls first.

"I am a free woman!" she cried.

But her thigh, as we noted earlier, bore the small, lovely, delicate slave rose.

To be sure, she wore no personal collar, and certainly not the clumsy chain collar of the Heruls, with the bulky, attached slave bell, obviously suggested by the cattle bell, or herd bell, by means of which Heruls were occasionally wont to mark out particular beasts, as of one kind or another. The bell might also, upon occasion, obviously, assist in locating the animal, following it, keeping track of it, and so on. Too, in the case of certain animals, the bell, as would a normal collar, serves to keep the animal in mind of what it is, and only is, an owned animal. She had been placed, as the reader might recall, in a market collar outside the Herul camp. And while White Ankles had been knelt, bound, delightedly at the knee of the wagon driver, the dealer, Cornhair had endured the trip to Venitzia, bound and foot, prone or supine, or on her side, as she might turn, on the rough planks of the wagon bed. Things were not much better at the overnight camps, for there Cornhair had been freed of her ropes but had been close-shackled, and put about gathering grass for bedding for the dealer and White Ankles, drawing water from a nearby stream, and bringing in wood for the supper fire, and, later, the watch fire. White Ankles cooked the food, and was permitted to feed as soon as the dealer had taken the first bite. How privileged she was, though yet in a mere market collar, like Cornhair. Had she won the heart of the dealer? Surely his hands were often on her. Did she dare hope he would lock his private collar, his personal collar, on her neck? But Cornhair must wait until the dealer and White Ankles had finished, and then, when she herself had finished, she must attend to the simple pots, bowls, and utensils, after which she must prepare the bedding for the dealer and White Ankles, after which her shackles were removed and she was chained by the left ankle to a tree. Hearing the gasping, delighted cries of White Ankles, thrashing about in the blankets with the dealer, did not further render her more fond of White Ankles, not that she had been that fond of her ever, even in the Herul camp. As White Ankles had not been bound, Cornhair wondered why she had not run away. Did a stronger chain than one of iron fasten her heart to the dealer's foot? Early in the night, Cornhair was certain that, should she herself be freed of bonds, she would have run away. But then, sometime in the middle of the night, seeing a pair of bright, baleful eyes, bright in the darkness, just beyond the watch fire, she revised

her view. At Venitzia Cornhair was sold, having been placed
on a table and assessed. To her astonishment, and chagrin, she
had brought only fifteen *darins*. She had then been placed in
a house collar, and put in a storeroom with other girls. White
Ankles, she noted, was kept by the dealer. She looked well at his
feet. Cornhair, feigning congeniality, a ruse she had thought it
wise to adopt following her unfortunate experiences with other
girls in the Herul camp, was soon apprised of an abundance of
information. Most particularly, she learned that she, with several others, was to be freighted to Point North, which is in the
vicinity of the city of Lisle, on Inez IV. She was owned by a company known as Bondage Flowers, which had assets on several
worlds. Many companies dealing with a particular form of merchandise used the expression "Flowers" in their company name,
for example, "Hermione's Flowers," "Love Flowers," "Pleasure
Flowers," "Flowers of Gathrol," "Desire's Flowers," and "Flowers
of the Six Yellow Stars," and so on. To be sure, most companies
dealing with goods of the sort in question took pains to eschew
allusions so common and obvious, such as "Sendex's" and "The
House of Worlds." The "House of Worlds," for example, licensed
on more than a hundred worlds, processes tens of thousands of
girls, of diverse species, annually, indexing the year to the orbit
of Telnaria. Its hunters and slavers, with their purchase coins,
and ropes and cages, are familiar on a thousand worlds within
and outside the empire. In the wake of war, harvestings are particularly plentiful. Many young females who might otherwise
have been summarily slain are now kept for sale. It might be
noted that Bondage Flowers was neither the smallest nor the largest, neither the least known nor the best known, neither the
cheapest nor the dearest, of such enterprises. Its reputation,
with respect to resources, quality of merchandise, and volume
of business, would have placed it, we suppose, a bit above the
center in most rankings pertinent to such matters. In the days
awaiting her shipment, Cornhair, discreetly to be sure, learned

much from the banter and idle chatter of her uninhibited sisters, particularly when sitting at the margin of one group or another of young slaves hanging on the words of one perhaps no older than themselves, but one whose neck was no stranger to the collar. Many a time she thought to withdraw in indignation, even to flee away in dismay, scandalized, given the nature of such alarming discourses, but she, perhaps with misgivings, but with rapt fascination, as well, could not be moved from her place. She learned a thousand little things, secrets of the collar, of hair, cosmetics, and perfumes, of the turning of a hip, the extension of a foot, the draping of a tunic, of prostrations, beggings, tiny gestures, movements, smiles, timidities, boldnesses, of caresses of small hands, of lips, tongue, body, and hair, of the bathing of men and the combing of their hair, of dressing them and tying their sandals, of licking their thighs and whimpering, of how to move in chains and a hundred other things, of how to please a Master in a thousand modalities, and how, perforce, submitted and will-less, choiceless and grateful, to open oneself, yielding and enraptured, to a thousand ecstasies a thousand times beyond those a free woman could know, and which a free woman could only dare to suspect. Could it be true, Cornhair wondered, that there could be such a life, one so real, one of being owned, one of submission, service, and love. "No, no, no!" thought Cornhair, her fingers on the band at her throat. "It cannot be!" she thought. "It cannot be!"

"Someone is coming!" said a girl.

Cornhair remembered, only too vividly, the dealer's account of the alleged downfall of the Larial Calasalii, but surely he had lied, if only to discomfit her. She did recall, from long ago, from a conversation with a high official, one Iaachus, the Arbiter of Protocol in the Imperial Court, that all might not be well with her family. She had heard, for example, of the burning of the piers at Governor's Landing, the loss of the cargo contract between Archus and Miton, and such things, but such reverses, or lapses, would be negligible to the wealth of one of the greatest of houses in the empire, surely nothing like the loss of a war, the seizure of assets, its outlawing, and such. "No," thought Cornhair, "it cannot be true! And even if there were something to it, much must remain!"

And no one need know that she had been put aside by the house. And few, in any case, would know that!

Surely, with wit, she might win her freedom!

Clearly the two bolts on the heavy door to the storeroom were thrust aside.

"Down," whispered a girl, and Cornhair, and her sisters, knelt, facing the door, their heads to the floor, the palms of their hands flat on the floor beside their head.

"It is too early for the supper gruel," thought Cornhair.

"Kneel up," said a man's voice. Cornhair recognized the voice. She and the others straightened up. It was that of a stocky fellow, with close-cropped hair, who was their keeper. He wore the livery of the company, red, with a chain-encircled flower on the left sleeve. "In the morning," he said, "you will gather up your straw, you will sweep up your sawdust. You will fill bins. You will be given brushes and water. The boards will be scrubbed. No mark, no stain, no stink, will remain. Everything will be fresh, and clean. Tonight you will have a piece of meat in your gruel. Tomorrow morning you will be ankleted, and your house collars will be removed."

He then turned about and left. Cornhair heard the two bolts thrust into place.

"What does this mean?" asked Cornhair.

"It is good news," said one of the girls. "We are not to be sold in Venitzia."

"I knew we would not be," said another, "when we were purchased by the company and kept here. We are to be shipped elsewhere."

"Where?" asked a girl.

"Masters know, not we," said another.

"Meat in the gruel would tell you something is afoot," said another.

"Too, he did not speak of changing the straw, or such," said another.

"Fresh straw, fresh beasts," said another.

"I am not a beast," said Cornhair.

"You are a beast," said a girl, "only a mediocre one, as you sold for only fifteen *darins*."

"A—a—thousand!" said Cornhair. "No, ten thousand!"

"The slave, White Ankles, was present, with her Master, and heard," said a girl. "She told the gruel-bringer, and the gruel-bringer told me."

"White Ankles is a liar," said Cornhair.

"What is your name?" asked the girl.

"Publennia, Lady Publennia, of the Larial Calasalii!" said Cornhair.

"We have a great lady amongst us," laughed a girl.

"Your name is 'Liar'," said the first girl.

"You may call me Filene, if you wish," said Cornhair.

"'Liar'!" said several of the girls.

"Then, 'Cornhair'!" said Cornhair, tears in her eyes.

"'Liar', 'Liar'!" chanted several of the girls.

"No one here," said the first girl, "sold for more than one hundred *darins*."

One of the girls gasped in astonishment. "So much?" she said.

"How many sold for as little as fifteen *darins*?" asked the first girl.

"I did," said a girl.

"I sold for only eleven," said another girl.

"Only three then, of us all," said the first girl, "sold for fifteen *darins* or less."

"How many did you sell for!" demanded Cornhair.

"Forty," said the first girl.

"Now you see, great lady," said one of the girls to Cornhair, laughing, "what you are worth, aside from robes and pretenses, and jewels, and embroidered purses, weighty with gold, and the artifices of society, if you were ever truly a great lady, what you are worth, as a female."

Cornhair clenched her fists in frustration.

Tears ran down her cheeks.

"Understand yourself for what you are, Publennia, or Filene, or Cornhair," said the first girl. "You are a beast. Only a beast. You, as we, can be bought and sold, and will, as we, be bought and sold, and you, as we, as what we are, as neck-ringed, branded beasts."

"And you, Liar, are a cheap one!" laughed a girl.

"I do not like house collars," said a girl. "I will be glad to have it off my neck."

"They need them for the next girls," said a girl.

"I want a good collar, a private collar," said the girl who had spoken of house collars. "It need not be fine, it need not be belled, or plated with gold, or set with jewels. I just want a nice collar, light, simple, and plain, locked on me by a kind, strong Master, who will well master the slave in me!"

"Our ankleting will take place before our collars are removed," said a girl.

"Of course," said another.

"Why ankleting?" asked a girl.

"Shipping anklets," said a girl.

"Why not shipping collars?" asked another.

"Do not fear," laughed a girl. "Your neck will not be naked long."

"I do not understand," said a girl.

"It will wear a coffle collar," said a girl. "We are to be coffled."

"Please do not call me 'Liar'," said Cornhair.

"On your knees, and beg," said the first girl.

Cornhair went to her knees. "Please do not call me 'Liar'," she said.

"Yes?" said the first girl.

"Please do not call me 'Liar', *Mistress*," said Cornhair.

"What would you be called?" asked the first girl.

"You will be called whatever men name you!" said a girl.

"'Publennia'," said Cornhair.

"'Cornhair' will do," said the first girl.

"Thank you, Mistress," said Cornhair.

Cornhair fought the close-fitting metal circlets on her wrists, pulling against the three short links that fastened them together.

"Free me!" she cried. "I do not belong here! It is a mistake! I am a free woman! Clothe me!"

Her hands were braceleted before her so that she, as the others, could reach into the gruel bowl to feed herself, when it was available.

Her hands, now, were clenched on the coffle chain before her, at her neck. The chain ran from the coffle collar to the back ring of the collar of the girl before her, rather as, from the back ring of her own coffle collar, the chain ran back to the front ring on the girl's collar who followed her. Her position in the coffle, which consisted of forty girls, was rather toward the center, as the coffle was arranged in terms of height, the tallest girls first.

"I am a free woman!" she cried.

"Be silent!" said the girl before her, turning back. "They will lash us all!"

"I will buy and sell you all!" screamed Cornhair. "I will put you in the fields to draw water for laborers, in pens to swill with pigs, in stables to shovel dung, shackle you in public sculleries, have you fed on garbage and beaten every morning and evening!"

"Be quiet," said the girl, "or we will all be beaten!"

"What is going on here?" asked a docksman.

"Nothing, Master," said the girl before Cornhair.

She put her head down, humbly, and Cornhair did so, as well. What might be hoped for, from a simple docksman?

He was soon about his business, and Cornhair raised her head.

It was warm on the loading pier, and, to her left, the immense, vertical hull of the freighter towered above her, gray against the blue sky and white clouds. At its side, open and gantry-like, was a vertical frame, its loading platform now at the pier level.

The sky was bright and the air clear. The world's star, Inez, was near its zenith. Docksmen called to one another. An official, with his white uniform, was some fifty feet away, turning papers in a ringed tablet. One could hear the trundling of wheeled carts on the pier. Some minutes before, some two hundred yards away, there had been a roar and a geyser of smoke; the pier had shaken, and a blast of heat had swept the pier, and, trailing flame and smoke, a ship, gradually at first, like a thoughtful arrow, and then, as though resolved, ever more quickly, sped away, disappearing in the sky, as though hungry for some unseen, but intended, target.

Cornhair lifted her head.

Somewhere meat was roasting, probably in the pan of a pier vender. She could detect the scent of baled spices, and the scents, too, of a hundred forms of flowering plants, exotic perennials in their potting troughs, for Inez IV, from her noted flower markets, famed throughout the galaxy, exported such things to many worlds, often barren worlds, where guests and neighbors, informed, might come from miles about to look upon a flower, and too, of course, now and again, one might scent, sharp, acerbic, and repelling, the acrid remembrance of combustion.

Beneath her bared feet Cornhair could feel the roughness of the thick planks of the pier. She pulled a little at the circlets of steel confining her wrists. She tossed her head, feeling the coffle collar on her neck, its weight, and how it, moved, returned to its place, and noted the rattle of the attached chain. A slight breeze played on her skin. As a free woman she had traversed life muchly unaware of the bright wealths of sensation about her, of sight, touch, sound, taste, and smell, each so different and precious, each so lavishly bestowed, each so little noted. As a free woman, shod and robed, the natural world, of rain and sunlight, of grass and wind, had been of little interest or importance to her. Muchly she had managed to shut it away, to overlook it. She had scarcely attended to the world in which she found herself. How easy it is to shelter and protect oneself from the world which has given one birth. It is easy to walk inertly, to hear without listening, to see without noticing. It is easy to be a stranger in one's own world. Cornhair was not trained, of course, or not well trained, but she had learned, in the storeroom, something of the thousand elements involved in a girl's training, and one was sensitivity to one's environment or surroundings, to a bit of moisture on a stone, to the cordlike knap on a carpet, to the smoothness of a tile, to the feel of rope on one's body, to the hands of a Master on one's skin, and such. To be sure, one can be blinded and dazzled, distracted and overwhelmed, by sensation, but one should be aware that it is always there, even when wisely banished. But surely one can open the door a little, now and then, from time to time.

Cornhair shuddered, feeling the wind on her body, the clasp of the bracelets, the tiny sound of their linkage, the weight of the chain.

It is said that the body of a slave girl is the most alive of all female bodies.

Certainly Cornhair had heard that, in the prison of the storeroom, while she and the others had awaited their shipment.

"But I am not a slave girl!" she cried out to herself.

Yet she knew that on her thigh, tiny, clear, unmistakable, lovely, was a mark, one recognized throughout galaxies, the slave rose.

Cornhair knew, of course, that she was, however often or strenuously, or irrationally, she might seek to deny it, in all the profundities of legality, in all the exactness of indisputable law, a female slave.

But what she more feared was that she was, beyond all the explicit obduracies of legality, beyond the clear implacabilities of the law, as inflexible and mighty as they might be, in her deepest heart and nature, fittingly and suitably, a female slave.

She feared she was such as are born for the collar, and cannot be themselves without it.

"No, no!" she cried to herself.

Surely one can deny oneself to oneself. Do not many do so?

Indeed, are there not societies which recommend, if not require, that one deny oneself to oneself?

Could such societies exist without their hypocrisy and lies?

But might not one, even in such a society, kneel, bow one's head, and beg the collar, without which one cannot be oneself?

Surely not!

Never!

But what if, in some society, in the midst of one's confusions, protests, and denials, one should be simply seized, and put in the collar, routinely, in a businesslike fashion, by indifferent, efficient, callous brutes who cared nothing for one's denials, to whom one's feelings and protests, whether sincere or fraudulent, were not merely unavailing, but of no interest, brutes whose simple interests were merely those of owning you, or making a profit on you, selling you for others to own?

What could one do?

One could do nothing. One would be on one's knees, collared.

She then understood how a woman, voluntarily, of her own free will, might prostrate herself, and petition the degradation of the collar, the liberating, fulfilling, joy-bringing gift of the neck-band.

If one is a slave, how can one be happy if not a slave?

Let slaves be slaves; let others be what they wish.

"No, No!" she thought. "I dare not entertain such thoughts! I must not think them! I will banish such thoughts! I will not permit myself to think them! They must be denied! I am not a slave! I am not a slave!"

She put her braceleted hands on the coffle chain, angrily.

Tears ran down her cheeks.

Many men were now on the pier, near noon, coming and going, loitering, passing.

Any one of them, she supposed, might buy her.

Who could not afford fifteen *darins*?

But surely in such a crowd there might be one, a gentleman, a noble citizen, one sensitive to her fate, one touched by compassion, who might discern her plight, and rescue her!

"Help! Help!" she cried, suddenly. "Rescue me! Save me! I am not a slave! I am a free woman! I should not be here! I should not be here, confined and helpless, as you see me! I should not be naked! I should not be chained! I am a free woman. Help! Help!"

"Be silent!" said the girl before her, frightened.

"Stop! Stop!" said she behind her. "You will get us all punished!"

"What noisy beast is that?" said a man in the crowd about.

"That one," said a fellow.

"A pretty beast," said another.

"A curvy beast," laughed another.

"Perhaps twenty *darins*," said a fellow.

"Please!" called Cornhair. "Please!"

"Guardsmen!" said one of the girls in the coffle, tensely.

"What is going on here?" said a gruff voice.

"I am a free woman, officer!" said Cornhair.

"You have the curves of a slave," said the voice.

"I am a free woman!" said Cornhair. "I am the Lady Publennia Calasalia, of the Larial Calasalii!"

"Is there trouble here?" asked a man, in the red livery of the company, Bondage Flowers, the patch on his left sleeve, with its chain-encircled flower. He carried a whip, useful in the control of slaves.

"This pig," said the guardsmen, "claims not to be a pig."

"Turn your left thigh to me," said the second guardsman. "Do you dare to meet my eyes?"

"Forgive me, Master," said Cornhair, looking away. "I mean, 'Forgive me, sir'!"

"The rose," said the first guardsman.

"I was marked!" said Cornhair.

"Slaves are often marked," said the second guardsman.

"But not always," said the first.

"What is the slave's name?" asked the first guardsman of the attendant.

"I am Publennia Calasalia, of the Larial Calasalii!" said Cornhair. "I am not a slave!"

"Call her whatever you wish," said the attendant. "She is a slave."

"She wears a shipping anklet," said the first guardsman.

"Of course," said the attendant. "They all do."

"Then she is a slave," said the first guardsman.

"No!" said Cornhair.

"Of course," said the attendant. "The papers of all of them are in order. Check with the pier officer."

A whistle indicated that departure was imminent.

"Free me of this hideous impediment!" said Cornhair, shaking the coffle chain with her braceleted hands.

The girl before her put her head down, and shuddered.

The official, he earlier remarked, with the white uniform and the ringed tablet, now approached.

"We have a schedule to meet," he said.

"You are the loading officer?" asked the first guardsman.

"Yes," he said.

Almost at the same time another officer, in a blue uniform, that of the pier administration, approached.

The two guardsmen apparently recognized him, for both deferred to him, stepping back.

"What is going on here?" asked the newcomer.

"I gather the slave is disruptive," said the first guardsman. "She claims not to be a slave."

"Unfortunate," said the man in the blue uniform.

"For the slave," said one of the guardsmen.

"The papers on this lot are all in order," said the fellow from Bondage Flowers. "They have been reviewed, and certified."

"I have the certification confirmation here," said the fellow in the white uniform.

"Then all is in order," said the fellow in the blue uniform.

"Certainly," said the loading officer.

"I am not a slave!" said Cornhair.

"Check with the pier officer," suggested the fellow from Bondage Flowers.

There were then two blasts on the departure whistle.

"Hurry!" said the loading officer, anxiously.

"I am the pier officer," said the fellow in the blue uniform.

"Sir!" begged Cornhair.

The pier officer then fixed his gaze on Cornhair.

"Sir?" she said, putting her head down.

"Are you aware," he asked, "of the penalties for a slave impersonating a free person?"

"No, sir," she whispered.

"It is a capital offense," he said.

Cornhair was silent, shivering, her head down.

"I am sure," said the pier officer, "you are intelligent, as well as beautiful. I am sure, too, you know the law, and what you are. I am now going to ask you a clear, simple question, and I require a clear, simple answer. Do you understand?"

"Yes, sir," said Cornhair.

"Think carefully," he said. "And answer with the absolute truth."

"Yes, sir," said Cornhair, not daring to raise her head.

"Are you a slave?"

"—Yes, Master," said Cornhair.

The fellow in the blue uniform then turned away.

"You should be punished," said the man from Bondage Flowers to Cornhair.

"Forgive me, Master," she said.

"A slave," he said, "is not a free woman. A slave should be invariably pleasing, and perfectly so."

"Forgive me, Master," she said.

"You called attention to yourself," he said. "You were disruptive. You dallied, you made a nuisance of yourself, you inconvenienced free men, you delayed our departure. You told a lie, claiming to be free, when you knew better."

"Please, forgive me, Master," she said.

"Do you know why you are all front braceleted," he asked, "though coffled?"

"No, Master," she said.

"It further reminds you that you are slaves," he said.

"Yes, Master," she said.

She felt the key thrust into the right-hand cuff lock, and her wrist freed. "Left hand back, behind the small of your back," said the man. With a jangle of chain Cornhair complied, and felt the opened right cuff strike against her back. A moment later, her freed right wrist was whipped behind her and locked into the dangling cuff. Her hands were then fastened behind her.

"How will I feed, Master?" she asked.

"You should all be whipped," he said.

"Please, no, Master!" said more than one of the girls.

"Punish Cornhair, not us!" said another.

"She it was who displeased Masters!" said another.

"Leave her to us," said a girl.

"We will attend to it," said another.

The fellow from Bondage Flowers raised his whip.

Several of the girls tensed.

"Load, board!" pleaded the fellow in the white uniform.

The fellow from Bondage Towers looked about, and then he lowered the whip.

Time was short, the weather hot.

"Stand as slaves," he said. "Stand beautifully. Stand as what you are, the most beautiful, exciting and desirable of women, women accepted for bondage, women found suitable for servitude, women found worthy of chains, women found fit for the great privilege and honor of wearing a Master's collar!"

There was a rustle of chain, down the line, from the linkages, and the braceleting.

"Ah!" said more than one man about.

"May we speak, Master?" asked a slave.

"Yes," said the fellow from Bondage Flowers.

"Are we to be coffled on the ship?"

"No," he said.

"But braceleted?" she asked.

"Yes," he said.

"How are we to be kept, Master?" asked a girl.

"Will we have cells, or stalls, Master?" asked a girl.

"You will occupy a common slave bin," he said.

"No!" cried more than one slave, in dismay.

"Do not fear," said the man. "It will be washed down with a hose, once each ship day."

"Whither are we bound?" asked a girl.

"You will learn in time," he said. "Pigs need not be informed of where they will be marketed. Do you understand?"

"Yes, Master," she said. "Thank you, Master."

"How will I feed, Master?" begged Cornhair, pulling at the light, but stern circlets which now confined her hands behind her back.

"If at all, as the pig you are," said the man from Bondage Flowers.

"Board! Hurry!" called the loading officer, from some yards away, near the gantry.

"Move, move!" said the fellow from Bondage Flowers. "Onto the loading platform!"

Some of the lower hatchways had already slid shut. One remained open, at the seventh level.

The forty ankleted, coffled slaves were crowded onto the metal platform. The man from Bondage Flowers flung shut the gate.

There seemed something significant and decisive about that closure, rather as a new slave might find something significant and decisive in the snapping shut of the first collar on her neck.

There was a whirr of machinery, and the platform beneath their bared feet vibrated.

Cornhair, miserable, pulled again, futilely, frustratedly, at the close-linked metal circlets by means of which her small hands, captured, were held behind her back. These circlets, light and tasteful, even attractive, were designed for women. They are designed to be comfortable and lovely, and to enhance a woman's beauty, rather as bracelets, anklets, armlets, necklaces, and such. They have one additional property, of course. That is to guarantee that their occupant will find herself helplessly and wholly at the mercy and disposal of others.

"Sisters!" pleaded Cornhair.

But she saw no sympathy or pity in the eyes of her fellow slaves. Perhaps they might have all been lashed, with the possible exception of herself, for her indiscretion. Had there been more time, perhaps the leather might have addressed itself in abundant, stinging admonitions to their defenseless softness. It is not unusual to punish a group of slaves for the fault of one. This keeps surprisingly good order in the pens and bins.

Sometimes the one whose indiscretion has resulted in the punishment of the group, say, its switching or lashing, is not herself punished. That is left to her sisters.

"We are not pleased with you, Cornhair," said a girl.

"Forgive me, dear sisters," said Cornhair.

"You may lie on your belly on the plates," said a girl, "and wait for your superiors to finish, to see if you will be fed."

"Have mercy," said Cornhair, pulling helplessly at her confined wrists. "I am back-braceleted!"

"You can kneel and feed like a dog," said a girl.

"Perhaps we will let you lick the pan, when we are finished. Perhaps there will be some gruel left. You may hope so, Cornhair," said a girl.

"The trip may be long, and you may become quite hungry," said another.

"It will not hurt you to lose three or four pounds," said another. "You may then be trimmer on the block."

"Some men prefer a trimmer slave," said a girl.

"Others prefer a more generous, ampler buy," said another.

"It depends on the taste of the Master," said another.

"Please be kind to me, Mistresses," begged Cornhair.

"You will have a pleasant trip to the market," said another.

The platform shook a little beneath their feet, and it began to slowly rise. Many of the slaves now crowded more closely together, toward the center of the platform.

The man from Bondage Flowers had informed her that the front-braceleting was to assist in reminding them that they were slaves. What then would be indicated by the disciplining of back-braceleting? Surely she was not a new slave, who might be back-braceleted, shackled, and even belled. Let her now, then, assess her status, not only as a slave, but as a slave amongst slaves.

"No," she thought to herself, in misery, "he would not punish all, here or on the ship, but, instead, in the unchallengeable wisdom of Masters, as he chose, would use all to punish me! He has seen to my punishment, and, indeed, excellently well!"

"How foolish I was," she thought. "Do I not understand what I now am? I am now only a slave!"

The platform was now rising. There was the feel of the corrugated, sun-warmed metal beneath her feet.

The hull of the freighter seemed to be sinking behind her.

The pier was far below, and the men and carts on it, seemingly small. She could see the roofs, with red tiles, of the warehouses.

Looking out over Point North, she could see Lisle in the distance, and roads, some bearing vehicular traffic, and a small lake.

The roar of departing ships, though, she thought, would carry even to distant Lisle.

The platform then stopped.

"Here, here!" called a voice from within the freighter.

Cornhair turned about, and looked within, to a dimly lit steel corridor. There were two men there, brawny fellows, with bare arms. Clearly, they were not members of the ship's crew. They were keepers, stock keepers. They carried whips.

"A pretty bouquet of roses, slave roses," said one of the men.

"Weeds," said the other.

"Forward," said the first, gesturing down the hall.

The lead girl, the tallest in the coffle, though small compared to the keepers, hastened forward. There was a rattle of chains as the others followed.

Suddenly there was a snap of a whip, sharp, unmistakable. Several of the girls cried out in fear, but Cornhair did not believe that anyone had been struck. The cry of a struck woman is quite different from that of a merely frightened woman. But the message of the whip was quite clear.

The coffle hurried down the hall.

A bit behind them, Cornhair heard the smooth sound of the hatch's closing.

Cornhair did not know it, of course, nor did the others, but they were on their way to Telnaria, and, indeed, even to Telnar itself, the capital itself, the seat of the empire, for the holiday sales associated with that world's spring equinox.

CHAPTER EIGHTEEN

"Excellent," said Sidonicus, Exarch of Telnar, fingering the tiny, golden replica of a metal-ribbed torture rack slung about his neck, over the purple robes, standing behind a railing, circling the golden domelike roof of the high temple of Telnar, observing the smoke rising in the distance across the city.

"It is the judgment of Karch," said a robed figure at his side.

"Karch provides," said Sidonicus, devoutly.

"It is so," said others about, pale, thin men, standing back, also robed, but in white.

"Let us sing a hymn of thanks, of praise," said the fellow at the side of Sidonicus. He, as Sidonicus, wore purple, but of a lighter shade. Already gradations of the ministry were instituted, and a hierarchy emplaced. This did not, however, compromise the teachings of holy Floon, who had denounced such things.

"None will be allowed to escape, I trust," said Sidonicus.

"No," said the fellow at his side. "Orders were strict."

"It is a miracle," said one of the white-robed fellows in the background.

"Yes," said another, "the false temple sprang spontaneously into flame."

"At the very moment of its high services," said another.

"A judgment," said one of the men.

"Yes," said another.

"Thus Karch speaks," said a man.

"But would not many die?" asked a man, nervously.

"Heretics," said another man.

"Let us hope the fire does not spread," said a man. "Then more might die, many more, even those of the true faith."

"Do not concern yourself," said Sidonicus. "That very hour they will feast at the table of Karch."

"True," said the fellow at his side, in the lighter purple.

"It is so," said more than one man on the roof.

"How is it that the temple was so suddenly and fully enfired?" asked a man wonderingly.

"It is miraculous," said a man.

"It is so," said several.

"One does not question the doings of Karch," said another.

Sidonicus turned about.

"I did not mean to question such things!" said the fellow who had asked the question, frightened. "One does not question the doings of Karch!"

"Heresy is everywhere," said Sidonicus.

"But not so much as before," said a man.

There was a ripple of mirth, but it was soon silenced.

Sidonicus returned his attention to the smoke in the distance.

There was then a sighted lapse, a caving inward, of the distant, spired roof, then fallen, no longer pointing skyward, followed by a burst of flame, and more billowing smoke, and, a moment later, the sound of a distant crashing came to the ears of the observers.

"I heard cries, far off!" said a man. "Screams of agony."

"It is your imagination," said Sidonicus. "It is too far off."

"Many would be trapped, choking, crushed, crying out, beneath the flaming timbers," said a white-robed man.

"Heretics," said Sidonicus.

"It would be a terrible way to die," said one of the white-robed men.

"Heresy must be rooted out," said Sidonicus.

"If necessary," said the fellow in the lighter purple, "by fire and sword."

"Those who thrust the brand of fire and cleave with the sword in the name of Karch do his holy work and are thrice blessed," said one of the white-robed figures.

"It is so," said another.

"Better," said the fellow in the lighter purple, "that ten thousand should die such a death, or worse, than that one *koos* be led astray, even briefly."

"It is so," said a man.

"Your Excellency," said a white-robed figure, one but now emerged onto the roof, "one below would speak to you, in your chambers."

Sidonicus nodded.

"One who was expected?" said the man in lighter purple.

"Doubtless," said Sidonicus, Exarch of Telnar.

He then looked again, into the distance, where smoke still stained the sky.

"May a hymn of praise be now raised?" inquired the fellow in the lighter purple.

"Yes," said Sidonicus.

"This is a day of glory," said his fellow, he in the lighter purple, to those about, behind the railing, on the roof. "Let us now raise a hymn of gladness, of joy, of thanksgiving! Let us sing praise, and glory, to Karch!"

"Let it be," said Sidonicus, "'I shall trust in the tenderness, love, and mercy of mighty Karch, who protects and shelters me, and destroys my enemies.'"

"It is so," said the man in lighter purple, and nodded, at which signal the others on the roof began to intone the strains of the hymn, a solemn but joyous, swelling hymn, purportedly one of the most pleasing to Karch.

Sidonicus cast one last look at the distant smoke, and then went back, away from the railing, to the height of the narrow stairway leading down, into the precincts of the temple complex, through the vestry, past the chancel, to his private chambers, followed by the man in lighter purple.

"Your Excellency," said the man in lighter purple.

"Yes, dear Fulvius?" said the exarch.

"He will want his gold," said Fulvius.

"And he shall have it," said the exarch.

"It seems ironic, if not deplorable," said Fulvius, "that one should want pay for doing the work of Karch."

"Nonetheless, he shall be paid," said the exarch. "It is well known that the obligations of the servitors of Karch are inevitably and impeccably discharged."

"I fear he knows too much," said Fulvius.

"Perhaps," said the exarch, "he will think the better of the matter, and be moved to restore the gold to the coffers of the temple."

"I fear he may not be so benevolently disposed," said Fulvius.

"The gold will be recovered," said the exarch. "Arrangements are already in place."

"And what of him?" asked Fulvius.

"He will be sent to the table of Karch," said the exarch.

"Excellent," said Fulvius.

"He knows too much," said the exarch.

"What of the others," asked Fulvius, "those who closed the street, cordoned off the area, guarded the exits, and slew any who might have tried to flee?"

"They know nothing," said the exarch.

"They will miss their pay," said Fulvius.

"They will be unable to find their paymaster," said the exarch.

"Perhaps he has fled from the city," said Fulvius.

"Perhaps," said the exarch.

"This is a good day," said Fulvius.

"Any day is a good day, on which is done the work of Karch," said the exarch.

"It is so," said Fulvius, humbly.

"I have a bottle of *kana*, a century old, brought from the highlands of the holy world itself, at great expense," said the exarch. "I would be pleased if you would share a cup with me."

"I would be honored, your Excellency," said Fulvius.

"Let us descend," said the exarch.

"After you," said Fulvius.

The two men then left the roof of the temple.

Behind them, as they took their way downward, they could hear, for a time, the strains of the hymn.

In the distance, from the roof, more smoke could be seen, this suggesting that the fire might have spread.

CHAPTER NINETEEN

The Annals are often laconic.

Consider the terse entry, "The sky was dark with the coming of ships." Much, we suppose, lies behind so curt an entry.

One can gather, of course, that there were a great many ships. Something may be gathered, as well, from the apparent fact that reports and notices from various worlds, usually toward the perimeters of the empire, seem to have lapsed at much the same time. This does not, of course, entail that such worlds were destroyed. That seems unlikely for various reasons, for example, first, the prohibitive expenditure of resources which would be necessary for shattering a world and spinning its fragments into its star, or even to scorch its surface and destroy the great majority of, if not the entirety of, its life forms, and secondly, the pointless stupidity of destroying coveted objects. It would be a strange thief who would risk destroying what he intends to steal. This is not to deny that more than one world, by the empire, or others, was destroyed, or sterilized, to avenge a perceived insult or to set into public view an example of the foolishness of rebellion or dissent. On the other hand, a shattered world, or a scarred, and burned, world, would be a dismal, sorry prize for victory, a guerdon scarcely worth seeking in the expensive, dangerous, arduous games of ambitious men. One seeks productive populations, salubrious climates, and rich mines, established industries, green expanses and teeming seas, not ashes and cinders. Accordingly we may suppose that after the clash of fleets and the hammering and extermination of resistances, things might be much the same. Perhaps new ceremonies might be instituted and new oaths required. Indeed, in some cases, the same individuals might be doing much the same thing, only in different liveries and uniforms, under new flags. To be sure, once the mighty web of the empire, with its organization, its massive civil service, its networks of communication, its facilities of enforcement, its report lines leading ultimately to Telnar, built up over millennia, was torn, a thousand worlds would go their thousand ways. Indeed, on many worlds conquerors would come and go, taking worlds, losing worlds, abandoning worlds, seeking new worlds, their engines and ships remembered only in the stories of old men. And on such worlds districts, provinces, towns, and manors multiplied, and order and law would become diversified and local, often anchored to keeps and strongholds, often extending only as far as men could ride, only as far as swords could reach.

Nonetheless it is easy to understand, as it must have begun, the terror of the darkening sky, the ships, so many of them, the fire from the sky, the flames, the sounds and roars, the whines and crashings, the collapsing buildings, the leveling of entire areas, the screaming and running, the loosed, startled animals, the frightened, swarming *filchen*, birds, blackened, burned, falling to earth, the disruption of commerce, the lack of order, the loss of shelter and heat, the contamination of water, the cessation of traffic on the roads, save for refugees, the guttings and emptying of stores, the lootings, the banditry, the fear of anyone not known, and that of some known.

The storm that was rising over the empire had been long in its brewing. For centuries there had been, here and there, a flash of lightning, far off, a squall, a hint of the rising of wind, a crash of thunder in the distance. These signs were evident, but, we suppose, were commonly ignored. Is that not the way of men? Small objects, a plate, a chair, a table, before one, seem larger than the mountain, so tiny, so far away. A *torodont*, in the distance, seems smaller than the *filch* crouching under the table. But the mountain is large, and the *torodont* is mighty, even far away.

Clearly the empire was threatened. It was under siege. Walls were weakened, and crumbling. Borders were crossed. Strange ships plied familiar skies.

But the vi-cat and the *arn* bear are dangerous, quite dangerous. One enters their lair only at one's peril.

This was well known to Abrogastes, the Far-Grasper. He was no more willing, in an era of diminishing resources, where a woman might be exchanged for a cartridge, and a town for a rifle, to risk his Lion Ships than the empire was to risk the imperial cruisers.

Two parameters might be mentioned, one which favored Abrogastes and his sort, and one which did not. First, dissatisfaction with the empire, fear of its power, resentment of its oppression and tyranny, hatred of its taxes and exactions, were resented on many worlds. Indeed, some had seceded long ago from the empire, secessions often ignored by the empire, given the costs of an attempted reclamation, particularly on worlds regarded as less important. Indeed, alien forces were, on many worlds, welcomed as liberators, until the nature of the new chains became clear. This parameter worked out well for Abrogastes, and many like him, for it enabled him to woo and subvert worlds. Indeed, the industrial complexes of various worlds, some surreptitiously and others more openly, armed, supplied, and trained foes of the empire. On such worlds, Abrogastes, and his sort, could move and recruit, particularly amongst barbarian peoples, with impunity. The second parameter, however, worked muchly in favor of the empire. The empire, at least until the Faith Wars, was largely united, whereas those who would threaten, attack, and despoil it, were often foes of one another, as well as of the empire. No core of *civilitas*, no shared loyalties or traditions, bound them together as allies in a common cause. Indeed, the longevity of the empire was often understood as having been best explained by its skill in pitting its foes against one another.

Many were the entangled strands, political, tribal, economic, social, and ideological, which constituted the restless, tumultuous skein of the times in question. Briefly, to facilitate the understanding of what follows, accept that the threat to the empire posed by Abrogastes, and such kings, was perceived as formidable and perilous. No longer was it a matter of subduing sporadic, localized banditry on the frontiers. Certain individuals, some of royal blood, realized the empire was in danger. One such was Julian, of the Aureliani; another was Iaachus, Arbiter of Protocol, in the court of the boy emperor, Aesilesius; another, in his way, was Sidonicus, Exarch of Telnar, whose particular interests seem to have been more his own than those of either the empire or its foes, from both of whom it seemed he might, by judicious arrangements, advance his own ends.

CHAPTER TWENTY

"This is Telnar!" said a girl.

The vehicle, a carrier, rumbled down the street, on its treads. Fuel was more plentiful on Telnaria than in many other sectors of the empire.

A shadow raced on the street, cast by a passing hoverer.

"What has happened here?" said another girl.

Cornhair hooked her small fingers into the chain-link webbing.

"Fire," said a girl.

There lingered, even days later, a smell of smoke.

Fire, incidentally, was always a hazard in the large cities of the empire, given widely spread poverty, squalor, and crowding. Certain districts, of course, would be more at risk than others. Many streets were too narrow to admit a wagon, scarcely allowing the passage of a sedan chair, should any choose to dare such streets. In some places, leaning forward, a lamp could be handed from a window on one side of the street to a window on the other side of the street. In many areas, there was no running water except in local fountains. Many availed themselves of public latrines. Wastes were often disposed of in the streets. Construction in such areas was often inferior. Buildings were often torn down and rebuilt. A wall, or a floor, might collapse. Repairs were endemic. Interior furnishings, stairs, walls, and such, and roofs, were usually of wood. Most heating was in the form of fire, contained in bowls or braziers. Most individuals lived in apartments, generally small, of a single room, and most windowless, many without smoke holes, on upper floors. The higher the apartment the less the rent. More well-to-do tenants in these buildings lived on the first floor, or that directly above the numerous open-fronted shops which lined many streets. In this way, they could avoid climbing dark, narrow stairwells, where brigands might lurk, and, in the case of fire, had a more immediate access to the street. Many times a building was afire, flames quickly spreading, climbing and raging, through rickety construction, before those on the upper floors became aware of the situation.

In any event, it seems there had not been so destructive a fire in the capital city in four hundred years. As the annals have it, between a tenth and a fifteenth of the city was destroyed. To be sure, in distant millennia, greater portions of the city, from time to time, had been ravaged by flames. Certainly fire was not unprecedented in Telnar. As the records have it, the fire began in one of the Floonian temples, an Illusionist temple, which doctrine, it seems, was to the effect that Karch, in his benevolence and perfection, in speaking to diverse species, would not have permitted grievous harm, or, indeed, any harm or pain whatsoever, to come to an actual, feeling, living individual doing his will, bearing his message, and such, whether an Ogg, a Vorite, or whatever. That would be unworthy of the goodness of Karch. Accordingly, he had chosen to communicate his word to the many worlds not by an actual person, but, rather, by means of a seeming person, a simulacrum, an image, or illusion. Anything else would be unthinkable, casting discredit on the moral character of Karch.

In any event, as might be expected, the Illusionists were blamed for the fire. Had it not begun in their temple? What better evidence of the bitter fruits of heresy? Naturally, there

were numerous, spontaneous demonstrations against the Illusionists. Many were hunted down by gangs and either beaten
or slain. In the senate there were claims that the Illusionists
constituted a danger to the state, and should be sought out and
sacrificed to one god or another, or be exiled to barren worlds.
Nothing came of this, however, first, perhaps, largely, because
there was no reason to believe that the traditional gods and
goddesses, Orak, Umba, and so on, would welcome such sacri-
fices, seeming to prefer, at least according to tradition, those of
cattle, and small animals and birds, and, second, because most
Telnarians were unclear on the doctrinal differences amongst
the many sects of Floonians. It is suspected they could not, for
example, tell the difference between an Illusionist and an Emanationist. In such a case, any retaliation, state-sanctioned or
not, as was pointed out by Sidonicus, Exarch of Telnar, in both
public pronouncements and private interviews, might affect
not only Illusionists, but, tragically, Floonians in general. In
any event, the Exarch of Telnar pleaded for mercy, at least for
reformed heretics, and implored their conversion to the true
faith, which, it seems, was his own. His prayers, it seems, were
answered, for the fire, and its consequences, broke the back of
the Illusionist doctrine, now generally understood to be mistaken, if not pernicious, and many fled to the more orthodox,
or more general, view, the identical-but-different view, so to
speak. Some, of course, remained unrepentant, proclaiming
their innocence, as one would expect.

"Smoke," said one of the girls.

It is true that the smell of smoke lingers. Indeed, if one were
to prod about in the rubble, one might, here and there, even
now, have stirred some embers alive, uncovering a dully scarlet
residue, a subtle recollection of falling walls and flaming timbers.

"See the buildings," said another.

"It is a whole district," said another.

The carrier rumbled on, and soon the blackened rubble, the

projecting, half burned ribs of buildings, the trash, and debris, were left behind.

To be sure, the stink of the fire, given the direction of the wind, would continue to be evident, here and there, for days.

"What will become of me?" wondered Cornhair, on her knees, unclothed, collared, continuing to cling to the linkage of the chainlike mesh.

The Telnarians were not noted for their consideration of slaves.

CHAPTER TWENTY-ONE

"Shall I withdraw, Master?" inquired Elena.

Iaachus, Arbiter of Protocol, looked up, angrily, from his notes. He cast the notes on the table before him. He turned his curved chair toward the girl.

"Is Master angry?" asked Elena.

"Approach," said Iaachus, irritatedly. "Kneel down, here, before me. Put your head down. Press your lips to my feet. Kiss and lick them, tenderly, and at length. Press your cheek against them. Let your hair fall about them."

The girl knelt before him, and put her head down.

"I must think," he said.

"I trust Master is not angry," whispered the girl.

"I am angry," he said.

"I trust not with Elena," she said.

"No," he said. "Continue."

"Yes, Master," she said, head down.

"It is restful to have a woman at one's feet," he said.

"It is where we belong," she said.

"Continue," he said, idly.

"Yes, Master," she said.

"Very restful," he said.

"A slave hopes to please her Master," said Elena.

"Enough," he said.

She lifted her head.

"I would think," he said.

He turned a bit away from her.

"I shall withdraw," she said.

"No," he said. "Stay here, as you are, kneeling here, beside me, at my knee."

The slave complied.

"Let us speak together," he said.

"You would speak with me?"

"Yes," he said.

"I am only a slave," she said.

"You are an extremely intelligent woman," he said.

"I am a mere slave," she said.

"Do you think the locking of a collar on your neck makes you less intelligent?"

"No, Master," she said.

"Intelligent women make by far the best slaves," he said.

"Perhaps," she said, "we are more in touch with our own feelings and needs, more ready to accept ourselves, more sensitive to our desires and depths, more open to, and more ready to acknowledge, what we want, what will fulfill our truest and most profound nature."

She pressed the side of her face down, against his knee.

"Do not dare to love," he said.

"It captures one," she said. "It is stronger than chains."

"How far you are from the glory of a free woman," he said.

"I do not envy them their freedom," she said. "Let them not envy me my servitude."

"Would you not fear to be seen so, as you are, by a free woman?" he asked.

"No, Master," she said, "for I am a slave."

"What if a free woman should enter?" he asked.

"Many free women own slaves, of either sex," she said.

"Perhaps she might enjoy seeing a slave humbled, one of her sex collared, owned, and prostrated before her."

"The contrast might much exalt her own freedom, and superiority," said Iaachus, Arbiter of Protocol.

"Doubtless," said the girl.

"And humiliate you a thousand times," he said.

"No, Master," she said.

"'No'?"

"No."

"Do you know some free women have themselves accompanied by leashed slaves, as by apes and monkeys, that their own raiment and beauty, by contrast, will seem all the more dazzling?"

"Of course, Master," said Elena. "But I fear this stratagem may be ill-considered, as the attention of men is often the more directed to the ape or monkey."

"Do you know that all women are rivals?" asked Iaachus.

"Of course, Master," she said. "Collared, I need no longer deny it."

"Doubtless there is some gratification for a free woman in finding a rival so helpless, so reduced and vulnerable."

"I suspect so, Master," she said.

"Particularly," said he, "if a personal rival, and perhaps one now personally owned."

"I would think so, Master," said Elena.

"I am angry," he said.

"Not with Elena?"

"No."

"Master is tired," she said.

"Perhaps," he said.

"May I serve Master *kana*?" asked Elena.

"No," he said.

"Master has worked hard," she said. "He is weary."

"The weight of the empire is heavy," he said.

"It need not be borne alone," she said. "There is the emperor, the empress mother, the ministers, the generals, the admirals, a thousand servants, ten thousand functionaries, on Telnaria alone."

"Is the empire eternal?" he asked.

"Surely, Master," she said.

"I wonder," he said.

Once again, the girl put her lips to his knee, gently.

"How precious you are," he said.

"I am Master's slave," said Elena.

Again she bent her head to his knee.

"Cease!" he suddenly cried.

She drew back, frightened.

"It is a contagion, a superstition, a plague," he said, angrily, "an infection. It spreads through the empire like a pestilence!"

"Master?" said the slave.

"What do you know of Karch?" he asked.

"He is one of the many gods," said Elena.

"And who speaks for him?" asked Iaachus.

"Who would dare speak for a god?" she asked. "And what god would be unable to speak for himself?"

"Are there not a billion gods?" he asked.

"I have heard, a great many," she said.

"I know a hundred sects, with a hundred different gods," he said, "each of which claims their god is the only god."

"How would they know?" she asked. "And if there are so few, perhaps there are none. If most do not exist, perhaps none exist."

"And do you know which god is the only god? In each case it is their god."

"I am not surprised," she said.

"Can you conceive of such colossal arrogance?" he said.

"It seems a breach of good manners," she said, "if not of mutual respect and common civility."

"What do you know of a prophet, Floon?" he asked.

"Are there not ten thousand prophets?" she said.

"Of one called 'Floon'," he said.

"As others, little or nothing," she said. "An Ogg, from Zirus. I have heard he preached to all living things, to people, to trees, to insects and dogs. He seems clearly to have been insane."

"He preached to the lowliest," said Iaachus, "to the lazy, stupid, ignorant, and incompetent, to the penurious, to the miserable and failed, to the unsuccessful, to the unhappy, the frustrated, the jealous, resentful, and envious, to the secret haters, to the outsiders, to those who want prosperity by magic, without effort, who feel they are entitled to the fruits of others' labors, who feel they are entitled to share in what they have not produced, to those who castigate not themselves, but others, for their own miseries, lacks, failures, and shortcomings, men who, having nothing, claim to have been robbed of riches they never possessed, enemies of the better, enemies of the superior, and strong."

"Surely not, Master," she said.

"He may have been executed on Zirus," said Iaachus.

"But surely he was innocent, wholly inoffensive, if unusual, or strange," she said.

"Apparently more dangerous than you realize," said Iaachus. "He called out to the lowly, to the unhappy and dissatisfied, preaching not so much a radical reorganization of society, as, essentially, its abolition, a doing away with duty, rank, discipline, order, obligation, form, and stability. All convention is to be eschewed, as rulers and ruled, as taxes, as money, as law, as family, as marriage."

"He is said to have been a sweet and kindly creature," she said.

"Do you not see the volcanoes into which such ideas may tap?"

"But men need such things, discipline, institutions, law, stability," she said.

"And they will soon have them again," he said, "even if they are called by new, lying names."

"I do not understand," she said.

"There are many ways to turn the wheel of power," he said. "Thrones will not long be empty. He who would abolish one throne intends to occupy another. He who would reform one society intends to rule another."

"Surely not the gentle Floon," she said.

"No," he said, "but those who would pervert his doctrine and turn it to their own advantage."

"I trust not," she said.

"I am thought wise," said Iaachus, "but I am a fool. I understand the turning of one man against another, the balancing of ambition against ambition, of jealousy against jealousy, the steel edge of honed, prepared weapons, the discharge of a rifle, the death concealed in a grenade, the destructive power of an imperial cruiser, the chemistry of poisons, but I know little of the darker poisons, the poisoning of the minds of men, the craftsmanship that can produce dupes, martyrs, and murderers, the sanctimonious technology of shaping the minds of men into a self-serving means of suppression and governance."

"I think Master would not care to master such arts," she said.

"True, sweet slave," he said. "Such things would turn the stomach of even feared, dreaded Iaachus."

"Yes, Master," she said.

"Why is the temple superior to the palace?" asked Iaachus.

"Is it?" asked the slave.

"No," he said. "The palace is real, like mortar, bricks, and wood, like steel and stone; the temple is an invention, ruling through the minds of men."

"Surely it need not then be feared," she said.

"It is much to be feared," he said, "for it can mobilize mobs, set a torch to cities with impunity."

"Surely not," she said.

"It would be a shadow empire," said Iaachus, "claiming the right to guide and rule the real empire, or disrupt and destroy it."

"It would use the force and might of others to promote its own policies and achieve its own ends?"

"That is its ambition," said Iaachus.

"It seems a lying, terrible thing," she said.

"Have you heard of a *koos*?" asked Iaachus.

"No, Master," said Elena.

"That is just as well," said Iaachus, "for women do not possess a *koos*."

"There are many things I do not possess, Master," said Elena. "Indeed, I possess nothing, for I am a slave. I own nothing. It is I who am owned."

"Supposedly only men possess a *koos*," said Iaachus.

"What is a *koos*?" asked Elena.

"It is supposedly the true person, the real person," said Iaachus, "temporarily attached to the body, but somehow not in space."

"How can that be?" asked Elena.

"It cannot," said Iaachus. "Supposedly the body, and its senses, are irrelevant and unnecessary."

"Why then do they exist?" asked the girl.

"I do not know," said Iaachus. "I suppose it is another one of many mysteries."

"A mystery?" asked Elena. "What does that explain?"

"Nothing," said Iaachus. "It is a substitute for an explanation."

"This is hard to understand," said Elena.

"One does not understand the incomprehensible," he said. "One can only understand that it is incomprehensible, and cannot be understood."

"How could anyone take such things seriously?"

"Many do not," he said, "but the verbiage is easy to flourish.

It is necessary only to say something confidently and frequently, and many will suppose it must be true, though they have no idea what it might mean, if it means anything. Essentially it is not even a belief or a lie, for something must be comprehensible to be either a belief or a lie."

"But people take such things seriously?"

"There are a dozen or more sects amongst the Floonians alone," said Iaachus, "whose adherents are willing to kill, or die, for competitive gibberishes."

"This is all hard to understand," said Elena.

"It apparently goes far beyond the conflicting accounts of the teachings of Floon," said Iaachus. "In some of the accounts, now rejected as untrustworthy, he did not even speak of a *koos*. He seems to have been more interested in how men should live this life. In one account, now denounced as a false scripture, he seems to have suggested that the table of Karch, at whose board one is to feast, is set on this world, or, in his case, on Zirus."

"It is unfortunate that Floon is not about today," said Elena. "He could then explain more clearly what he meant."

"He would not have the opportunity," said Iaachus. "He would count as a false Floon, an impostor, a heretic, and be sent once more to the burning rack."

"I still do not understand the *koos*," said Elena.

"Do not concern yourself," said Iaachus. "Women have no *koos*."

"Women do not have a *koos*?" she asked.

"That is the orthodox doctrine," said Iaachus.

"Only men have a *koos*?" she asked.

"Supposedly," said Iaachus.

"What of animals?" she asked. "It seems they see things, hear things, feel things, taste things, smell things, and such."

"It seems so," said Iaachus.

"And they manage without a *koos*?"

"It seems so," said Iaachus.

"As do women?"

"Apparently."

"Why do women not have a *koos*?" she asked.

"I do not know," he said.

"If women have no *koos*," she said, "why should men have a *koos*?"

"Do not concern yourself," he said. "Insofar as the notion is at all intelligible, which seems to be not at all, there is no such thing as a *koos*, so you are no better or worse off than men. Neither has a *koos*."

"But why," she asked, "should women not have a *koos*?"

"I do not know," said Iaachus, "but I suspect because Floonians are not too fond of women. Women are regarded as dangerous, as seductive, as temptresses, as alluring beasts whose charms might divert men from the life of the *koos*, which would lead them astray from the paths of righteousness, and such."

"Then, Master," she said, "these faiths will all be extinct in a single generation."

"No," said Iaachus. "Not all adherents of Floon are as perfect, and stalwart, in the faith as others."

"I see," she said.

"But they have their uses, for they regularly contribute their pennies, and *darins*, to the temple's coffers."

"What benefit do they receive for this?" asked Elena.

"Two, it seems," said Iaachus, "first, the assuagement of instilled guilt, guilt inflicted upon them, guilt for their numerous, inevitable lapses and imperfections, for perfection, as you will understand, is difficult to attain. Indeed, the goal is designed to be unreachable. There is always more that could be sacrificed, more that could be done. Second, they are assured, though the matter is always quite uncertain and precarious, that their *koos* will eventually dine on golden dishes at the table of Karch himself."

"It is all mysterious," she said.

"I fear," said Iaachus, "the empire may eventually find itself embroiled in the feuds of warring dogmatisms."

"It cannot, Master," said Elena.

"Already blood has stained a world," said Iaachus.

"Tolerance is the invariable way of the empire," said Elena. "The empire has always assiduously avoided the squabbles of faiths, ever maintaining its neutrality in such sensitive matters, always insisting on tolerance."

"Save when the empire felt itself threatened," said Iaachus. "Brief, minor, isolated persecutions, on one world or another, have occasionally taken place when some members of one sect or another, Floonians or otherwise, would renounce their loyalty to the state, would publicly and prominently refuse to perform, say, even a token sacrifice of allegiance."

"I have not even heard of such things," she said.

"The empire never had its heart in such things," said Iaachus. "It is not the way of the empire. Such actions, occasional, intermittent and selective, were always founded on a concept of secular expedience, never on zealotry. It would never occur to the empire to systematically, over generations, hunt down and exterminate entire populations. The empire does not even understand such single-mindedness, such radical, fundamental commitment, such devotion, such dedication, such a willingness to despoil, torture, and murder, such unending and uncompromising fanaticism."

"Why do you speak of these things, Master?" said Elena.

"Sidonicus, Exarch of Telnar," said Iaachus, "wants the sword of the empire to be unsheathed in the name of Floon, his Floon. He wants the secular sword to seek out and exterminate heretics, namely, those who do not accept the doctrinal supremacy of his particular temple, or temples."

"He is mad," said Elena.

"Dangerous," said Iaachus.

"Fortunately, he is weak, he has no power," said Elena.

"The empire has power," said Iaachus. "He wants the empire."

"Surely he shall not have it," said Elena.

"Do you realize the horror," he asked, "should the empire endorse one such faith, one such dogmatism, so obsessive and immoderate, so radical, so extreme, so bigoted?"

"It would be insane to do so," said Elena.

"Have you ever heard, sweet Elena," asked Iaachus, "of the *festung* of Sim Giadini?"

"No," she said.

"It was on Tangara," he said. "It was a fortress, and holy place, maintained by holy creatures, the brotherhood of Sim Giadini, a Floonian brotherhood."

"'Was'?"

"Yes."

"I know nothing of it," she said.

"Sim Giadini, or Saint Giadini," said Iaachus, "was an Emanationist."

"What is that?" she asked.

"The Emanationist doctrine is that Floon was an emanation of Karch."

"How could an Ogg be an emanation, and not an Ogg?" she asked.

"I do not claim the doctrine is intelligible, no more than a dozen others," said Iaachus, "but what is important is that it is not the orthodox doctrine as the Exarch of Telnar understands orthodoxy."

"And how does he understand orthodoxy?"

"A great coincidence is involved," said Iaachus.

"It is his own doctrine," said Elena.

"Yes," said Iaachus. "In any event, briefly, the Exarch of Telnar, with his smooth manners, his flattery and honeyed words, has the ear of the empress mother. He has informed her of the joys of Floon. I fear he has begun her instruction. He has undoubtedly informed her of the dangers of diversity, how frightful it would be if all did not think the one, true thought, his thought, of the threat which heresy poses to the empire, to the throne, and to her son, the emperor."

"Did he not inform her that she has no *koos*?" asked Elena.

"I suspect it did not occur to him to do so," said Iaachus.

"What of the *festung* of Sim Giadini?" asked Elena.

"Its destruction was ordered," said Iaachus.

"Surely not by the emperor," said Elena. "The emperor is simple. He cannot even write his own name."

"By another," said Iaachus.

"The imperial signet ring is in the keeping of the empress mother," said Elena.

"Of course," said Iaachus.

"Then it begins," said Elena, "the intervention of the state on behalf of a particular sect."

"It is not so simple," said Iaachus. "Why an imperial attack on the *festung* of Sim Giadini, and not on a hundred other *festungen*, many of more portentous heterodoxy, many of which would be within easier range?"

"I do not understand it, Master," she said.

"Nor do I," said Iaachus. "But there must be a reason."

"Master is tired," she said.

"No," he said, "I do not think so, not tired, not really, rather, troubled, puzzled, concerned."

"Shall I go to your chamber?" she asked.

"Yes," he said.

"Shall I lay out chains and a whip," she asked, "and then kneel at the foot of your couch, my head down?"

"Naked, of course," he said.

"Of course, Master," she said.

"And hope that you will be found pleasing?"

"Most certainly, Master."

"Elena," said he.

"Master?" she said.

"You are subject to the whip," he said.

"Yes, Master," she said, "for I am a slave."

"What is it like, to know yourself subject to the whip?" he asked.

"It is to know oneself a slave," she said.

"You fear the whip?"

"Very much."

"Interesting," he said.

"But it thrills me, too, to be subject to it," she said.

"Speak," he said.

"I wanted to be such that I would be owned, and must obey, and would be punished if I were not pleasing."

"You wanted to be a slave?" he said.

"I wanted to be true to myself," she said, "for I am a slave."

"Do you like the feel of the whip on your body?" he asked.

"Very seldom its stroke," she said, "for that hurts, and terribly. I would do much to avoid it."

"I see," he said.

"But I like to feel it against my body, its touch, its motion, and caress, for I well know what it could do to me, and in its touch I am well reminded that I am what I most want to be, a slave."

"'Very seldom'?" he said.

"Must I speak the truth?" she asked.

"You are a slave," he said.

"Naturally I know that I will be punished, if I am not displeasing," she said.

"Of course," he said.

"But there are rare times," she said, "when I relish its stroke, if but briefly, for it confirms my bondage upon me, my beloved, precious bondage."

"You may precede me to my chambers," he said.

"Thank you, Master," she said.

He watched her rise, back away, and then turn, and exit from the room. He could see the stairwell behind the briefly opened door.

"Why," muttered Iaachus, Arbiter of Protocol, to himself, "why the *festung* of Sim Giadini? It is not that important, it is too far away, it is too remote from the centers of empire. Why? There must be a reason."

He waited for a few minutes, and then he, too, left the room.

CHAPTER TWENTY-TWO

"Stand straight, with the others," he said.

"Yes, Master," said Cornhair.

She stood straight, on the platform, not meeting the eyes of any in the crowd, some loitering, some passing, in the street. About her neck, suspended by two cords, hung a small, rectangular, wooden placard, about six inches in width, some four inches in height. On it was inscribed a legend as to her origin, age, physical condition, accomplishments, and defects, information which might be of interest to a possible buyer. Cornhair, in the way of accomplishments, had no notable skills. For example, she could not cook, was not a seamstress, could not play a musical instrument, or such. She could, however, read and write Telnarian, which many slaves, brought from far worlds, could not. With respect to defects, which were few, unless, say, one would prefer a larger, stronger woman, one more fit for heavy labors, one less vulnerably or helplessly feminine, or, say, one of a different color or figure, buyers were merely apprised of her newness to bondage and her lack of training. A buyer, accordingly, must be prepared to supply these lacks, and improve his purchase, which is easy enough to do, of course, by the switch or whip.

Above the placard, and within the cords, as one might expect, she wore a market collar. Naturally, too, she, as all the others, all women, for this was a woman market, was stripped.

That is the way beasts are sold.

Too, it is natural for buyers to wish to well apprise themselves of an item prior to its purchase.

She became aware of a figure near her, robed, masculine. She dared not turn her head, nor meet his eyes.

How keenly then was Cornhair aware of her bondage, her slightness, and bared beauty, the large, looming, fully clothed body near her.

She was naked, and, at her side, was a male, fully clothed.

It is quite meaningful for a woman to be unclothed in the presence of a fully clothed male.

She is then, in such a contrast, well apprised of what she is, of her startling and marvelous difference from the male, of her radical femaleness.

In no way can she then conceal or diminish her dramatic difference from the male.

Too, to be unclothed before the clothed, how could the contrast between forms of life, between free and slave, between owner and owned, be more clearly drawn?

She then realized that her nudity was not a mere convenience, having to do with the exhibition of merchandise.

Far more was involved.

It was a way of making clear what she was, and was not, that she was not free, but a slave.

Are there not a thousand symbolisms involved? Are there not a thousand ways of drawing the most telling, and salient, of distinctions between forms of life, between the free and the slave, between the noble, worthy citizen and the meaningless beast? The free may clothe themselves as they choose; the slave may not. Let her hope to be granted clothing. Its extent and nature, if it is permitted, will be determined by the free. And men, commonly, if permitting the slave clothing, will enjoy dressing the slave for their own pleasure, and in such a way that it is clear to herself and others that she is a slave. Many are the symbolisms, and realities, involved. The free command, the slave obeys. The free stand; the slave kneels. The free speak as, and when, they wish. The slave may speak only upon the sufferance of the free, and her speech must be suitable, soft, gentle, respectful, and deferent, and its diction must be clear. She dare not raise her voice to a free person; she is not to speak stridently or shrilly; she is not to speak shortly, sharply, or impatiently. Such lapses will bring punishment, commonly the whip. Slovenliness of speech, or, indeed, of appearance or movement, is not permitted the slave. She is to be well spoken when permitted to speak, and is to be attractive and graceful. She is not free. The free are to be pleased, the slave is to please. The free is as he chooses to be. The slave is marked, and collared. The free behave as they please. The slave kneels and requests permission. The slave may be blindfolded, gagged, braceleted, thonged, chained and roped; she may be kenneled and caged, bought and sold.

She must fear her Master's displeasure.

She must fear the whip, and switch.

She is a slave.

It is hard for a woman to keep her pride or to pretend to status or worth when she is stripped and collared, and kneeling, head down, before her Master.

So Cornhair stood naked, wearing her placard, beside a fully clothed male.

That was not an unusual juxtaposition, of course, for a slave being marketed.

"Straighten up, slave," said the man. "Draw in your gut. Put your shoulders back. Lift your head."

"Yes, Master," wept Cornhair.

She felt the placard about her neck adjusted, so that it hung more straightly.

"Smile," he said. "We are trying to sell you!"

Tears ran down her cheeks.

"Catch the eye of a fellow in the crowd," he said. "Smile at him. Make him want you! You are for sale!"

He then descended the two steps from the selling ledge to the street level, turned, and looked up at the display.

He drew on the sleeve of a passing fellow, and, with a broad, generous motion, a sweep of his hand, gestured to the selling ledge.

Was he calling attention to her?

No, it was another!

She half fainted.

She felt the sun on her body, the cement wall behind her. It was near noon. She felt the warm, granulated surface of the ledge beneath her bared feet. She moved a little, sensing the small, wooden placard on her body. She was not chained. She felt an untoward, bizarre impulse to flee from the platform. How absurd that would be! She was naked. Even if she had been clad, she would have been clad as a slave. And there was a market collar on her neck, which would assure her prompt return to the market. And on her left thigh, high, under the hip, tasteful, lovely, and unmistakable, was the slave rose. And if, somehow, she might slip away, into the crowd, obtain garments forbidden to her, what could she do, where could she go, who would she be, how would she fit into society? Such as she had no place, save at the feet of a Master.

"Oh!" she cried, startled.

A form had leapt to the ledge beside her, and two large, strong hands, held her head, and forced it back.

"Open your mouth," she was told, "widely."

She complied, frightened, her eyes shut, her mouth widely open. She felt fingers forced into her mouth and it was stretched open even more, painfully so.

She kept her hands at her side, as she knew she must do. One is not to interfere with the hands of Masters. The body of a beast being vended is public to potential buyers.

It may be touched, and explored, tested for soundness, and responsiveness.

"See?" called the merchant from the street. "It is as I said. Her skin has not been altered, by the knife, or by rinses of chemicals. Her skin is fresh, and unblemished, as you see it. She is twenty-two years old. She is originally Telnarian, probably a debtress. If you are not Telnarian, would you not enjoy owning a former Telnarian, a former free woman of the empire, now a humbled, meaningless slave, now yours to do with as you please?"

"Oh!" said Cornhair.

"Yes," called the merchant from the street, "the hair color is natural. We would not dare to deceive a customer in such a matter. Buy her. Forty *darins*!"

"Too much," said the fellow, his hands now clasping Cornhair at the waist. His hands made her uneasy, terribly so. She knew she was a slave, and was well aware of what, in the eyes of men, slaves were for.

"Make an offer!" suggested the merchant.

"I shall look for a better," he said.

He then departed from the platform.

A moment later the merchant, in a temper, ascended the ledge, took Cornhair's hair in his left hand, and then, with the palm of his right hand, slapped her face twice, sharply, stingingly.

"Master?" she wept.

"Did I not tell you to smile?" he asked. "Attract him, but subtly. This is a middle market, not a low market. Trust that you will not be sent to a low market. You need not be blatant. But excite him! You have all the wiles and tricks of a free woman at your disposal, the smiles, the turnings, the movements, the glances, the hints, the veiled promises, and you have, besides, an inestimable advantage over her, that you are, as well, the most desirable of all women, the woman who is collared, who can be owned, the female slave. He was a male! He was within an arm's reach, and you did nothing!"

"I was afraid, Master," she wept.

"Then tremble," he said, "pull your arms back, pull back your shoulders, lifting your breasts, cross your wrists, as though tied, behind you, lift your head, exposing your throat, that he may imagine it fastened in his collar."

"I fear I am a poor slave," she said.

Indeed, she knew she was largely worthless, save for the interests which her body might stir in the loins of men.

Still, that might be considerable.

"He put his hands on you," he said. "Did you feel nothing?"

"I fear I am unattractive," she said.

"You would not have been bought on Tangara, had you not been of interest."

"I was once thought," she said, "to have been very beautiful."

"Among free women," he said.

"And others," she said.

"You are still beautiful," he said.

"Thank you, Master," she said.

"Very beautiful."

"Thank you, Master."

"But stiff, like wood," he said.

"Forgive me, Master," she said.

"His hands were on you," he said. "Did you feel nothing?"

"I could not help myself," she said.

"Nor should you," he said. "You are a slave."

"I am uncertain," she said. "I am confused."

"You are not a free woman," he said. "You need not wrestle with yourself. You need not deny your body; you need not forswear your heart. You need not languish in the traps of convention, need not fear the words and frowns of the ignorant, stupid, and frustrated. It is not wrong to be yourself. If your heart is the heart of a slave, rejoice, kneel, and be the slave you are. The collar frees you; the slave, collared, is a thousand times more free than the free woman."

"No, no, no!" she said.

"Do not fear," he said. "It is only that your belly has not yet been enflamed."

"It will not be!" she said.

"You will have no choice in the matter," he said. "It will be done to you. You are a slave."

"I want to feel heat," she said. "I want to be piteous, open, and begging! I want to blaze with passion, and need!"

"You will," he said.

"No, no!" she said. "I must not!"

"You will," he said.

"I will struggle not to feel," she said.

"Why?" he asked.

"I do not know," she said.

"Your struggle will be unsuccessful," he said.

"I fear so," she wept.

"You sense it?" he said.

"I fear there is a slave in me," she said.

"There is one in every woman," he said.

"We must resist our slave," she said.

"Why?" he asked.

"I do not know," she said.

"Resistance," he said, "is for the free woman. It is permissible for her. It is forbidden to the slave."

"I have heard women cry out in need," she said.

"Slaves," he said.

"Can a woman be such?" she asked.

"Certainly," he said.

"I would not be so pathetic, so miserable, and weak," she said.

"They are not pathetic, miserable, and weak," he said. "They are alive, very alive."

"I fear I could be so," she said.

"You will be so," he said. "You will be unable to help yourself. Fuel ignited burns; moons stir oceans; worlds turn; journeys are made; blood courses in its thousand channels; hands reach out; desire, in its torrents, like raging rivers, sweeps aside the debris of vacillation, hesitation, and artifice; one senses the coming of storms, the beating of drums."

"I am afraid," she said.

"And well you should be," he said, "for you are a slave."

She trembled, despite the warmth of the ledge.

"If we cannot dispose of you here," he said, "in the open, for a decent price, in this market, a middle market, we will put you in a low house, a cheap house, one patronized by a motley rabble, for auctioning."

"I have heard of such places," she said. "Let it not be so!"

"In such a place," he said, "beware of not being sold. Such fellows are not patient. You may be thrown to dogs."

"I do not understand," she said.

"For feed," he said.

"What am I to do, Master?" she said.

"Stand straight," he said. "Smile."

He then adjusted the small placard hung on its two cords about her neck.

"There," he said.

He then turned away.

CHAPTER TWENTY-THREE

Huta stirred at the foot of the high seat, her hands on the neck chain fastened to the ring set in the planks to her right.

Ingeld, seated in the high seat, of his own hall, awaiting his guest, pressed his boot against her thigh.

"Oh, yes, Master," she whispered, and leaned toward him, to press her lips, swiftly, to his knee.

"Back," he said, and she whimpered, but quickly drew back. The lash is not pleasant.

Ingeld smiled to himself.

How different she was, from months ago, from the time when she had, as the proud, aloof, lofty, white-gowned high priestess of the Timbri, claimedly the servant of the ten thousand gods, by means of prophecies and false signs, abetted the ambitions of Ortog, first son of Abrogastes, or, as some would have it, led him astray into treason. Ortog had been popular, a lusty, laughing, hardy fellow, a natural leader of men, one born to rally followers, one from whom men would gladly accept rings. It seems, too, he was not only the first son of Abrogastes, but his favorite son, as well. But Ortog, it seems, was too like his father, a man of large appetites, a warrior of vaulting ambition, of sovereign interests, one not honed by nature to follow in the tracks of others, one who would be the lord of new, fresh countries. He would govern his own fleets, command his own armies, found his own nation. And so, as it happened, he had withdrawn his allegiance from his father, Abrogastes, the Far-Grasper, lord of the Drisriaks, the major tribe of the Alemanni nation, commonly known in the imperial records by the Telnarian name, the Aatii. He, Ortog, had founded the secessionist tribe to be known, from his name, as the Ortungen. And thus a prince of the Drisriaks had become a king. His venture had, however, not been long-lived, as, mere months following the secession, his forces had been defeated and scattered by the pursuing, implacable Abrogastes. He himself, Ortog, with several followers, unaware of the recent fate of his cohorts, had been surprised and apprehended on a meeting world, a neutral world, at a place called, in Alemanni, Tenguthaxichai, which, it seems, might be brought into Telnarian as, say, Tengutha's Camp, or the Camp, or Lair, of Tengutha. The justice, or vengeance, of the betrayed Abrogastes had been violent and bloody, leaving few survivors. Abrogastes himself had dealt an apparently lethal blow to Ortog, his rebellious son. But Otto, a chieftain of the Wolfungs present, had cast a robe over the body, as it was to be borne from the meeting tent on blanket-wrapped spears. In this way it was concealed that the body borne away on the spears yet lived, at least at the time. It had been speculated that Abrogastes, no stranger to the killing of foes, had directed his stroke in such a manner as to convey to his followers the semblance of justice, while simultaneously permitting his son at least a tenuous possibility of life. The ties of blood are strong, and fast. It was generally understood amongst the Alemanni and their allies that Ortog had perished at Tenguthaxichai. Ingeld and Hrothgar, two other sons also, as we understand it, believed Ortog dead; on the other hand, Abrogastes himself, if we are correct, after dealing his grievous blow, would have remained unaware of his first son's fate, being ignorant of either his demise or recovery.

Abrogastes, as the records have it, had several sons, doubtless by various wives. On the other hand, only three are dealt with by more than brief references in the Annals. Indeed, we know of some only by name. The three we encounter more sub-stantially in the Annals are Ortog, the first son, Ingeld, the second son, and Hrothgar, who may have been the third or fourth son. Hrothgar seems to have been a straightforward, uncompli-cated, congenial, cheerful, boorish fellow, one disinterested in politics and power, one surely more fond of the pleasures of the feasting board than of the intricacies of councils or the ardors of windswept, muddy fields; it is suggested, as well, that he was fond of drink, horses, falcons, and women. Ingeld, the second son of Abrogastes, on the other hand, seemed composed of a darker, less tangible, subtler stuff. He was apparently hard to know, hard to fathom. Perhaps none knew him; perhaps none fathomed him. Surely he kept his own counsel. He spoke lit-tle. It seems he was an unlikely giver of rings. Few sought his hall. Men were often uneasy in his presence. He was never seen drunk. Abrogastes feared Ingeld.

Ingeld, on the high seat in his hall, watched the large double-doors at the far end of the hall.

An unusual visitor had sued for an audience.

"Why not," Ingeld wondered, "with my father, in his hall?"

Huta whimpered, again.

"Silence, pig," said Ingeld.

But he was not displeased to hear her tiny signal of need.

It had been done to her.

"How helpless they are, and needful," he thought, "once it is done to them, once Masters ignite their bellies, once they know themselves in collars."

Yes, men had done it, clearly, transforming her, casually, routinely, giving the matter, though she had been a priestess, no more thought than would have been bestowed upon the least of block girls. She, as they, had been dragged down a path of reality and comprehension from which there was no return.

"How pleasant it is," he thought, "to have them at your feet, as piteous, begging, kneeling beasts."

He looked down on the former priestess, the white skin, the long black hair, now unbound, the chain on her neck.

"Good," he thought. "Excellent," he thought.

She, Huta, the former priestess, was no longer a person, no longer the Mistress of her own body. She was now a beast, and her body was the body of a beast, an owned beast, a lovely, owned beast. She who had once prided herself on her superiority to sex, on her disdaining of biology, on her denial of nature, on her repudiation of her deepest self, on her immunity to need, on her frigidity and inertness, now found herself, originally to her shock and dismay, brought home to the fact that she was, and would be henceforth, profoundly, radically, helplessly, and needfully, a sexual creature. She was now, as others, the victim of her own needs, liberated and aroused, released and stimulated; she, as others, was now helplessly subject to the incendiary tortures of desire. She who had held men in contempt for their insatiable, brutish nature now found in herself the response to, and the complement of, whether she willed it or not, such gross, signal appetites. Not only that, but she found now that her responsiveness to the very presence of men, let alone to their touch, was weakness, helplessness, a readiness for yielding, and a hoping, and even a plea, to be wanted, and, given the touch of even a hand or tongue, this responsiveness could become uncontrollably explosive, even violent. It was difficult, moaning, crying out, whimpering, and thrashing, to even comprehend what she had become. Yet the answer was simple. She had become a slave.

"Is your body your own?" asked Ingeld.

"No, Master," she said.

"Is anything your own?" he asked.

"No, Master," she said.

"What of your least thought, or feeling?" he asked.

"They, too, are owned," she said.

"Who owns you?" he asked.

"Men," she said.

"But who, in particular?" he asked.

"Your father," she said. "I am afraid to be here. Does he know I am here?"

"No," said Ingeld.

"I am afraid," she said.

"Why should you be afraid?" he said. "You are chained to a ring."

"I fear Master wants Huta," she said.

"Perhaps," he said. "Would you object?"

"Master is young and handsome," she said. "And I am only a slave."

"You look much better now," he said, "than when you were a priestess. Nudity and a chain become you."

"I belong to your father," she said.

"As of now," he said.

"Your father," she said, "is possessive, a man of great power, a man of temper, of wrath, of mighty fury."

"As of now," he said.

"Might we not both be slain?" she asked.

"I am heir apparent to the high seat in the great hall," he said.

"So, too, was Ortog," she said.

"Ortog did not plan well," he said. "He managed his business badly."

"There is your brother, Hrothgar," she whispered.

"Hrothgar is a fool," he said. "He is often in his cups. He would rather have a falcon on his wrist than a scepter in his hand."

"I am afraid," she said. "I fear your words, I fear your voice, your eyes."

"Why?" he asked.

"Behind your eyes," she whispered, "I think there are secret thoughts."

"Nonsense," said Ingeld, "I am merely another simple, pleasant fellow."

"Subtle, ambitious thoughts," she said.

"Of treason?" he asked.

"Yes," she said.

"I speak no treason," he said.

"Who would be so unwise as to do so?" she said.

"Why are you afraid?" he asked.

"In the presence of treachery, or treason, who would not be afraid?"

"Only the free need be afraid," he said. "Beasts, dogs, horses, slaves, need not be afraid."

"Even the beast of a traitor, his dog or horse, might be slaughtered," she said.

"True," he said. "Once loosed, it is sometimes difficult to restrain the sword of anger and vengeance."

"Too," she said, "I am your father's property. He does not know I am here. I do not belong here."

"But you like the touch of a boot on your thigh, do you not?" he asked.

"Master Abrogastes, my Master," she said, "hates me, and suspects it was I who seduced Ortog into the paths of secession."

"Was it not?" asked Ingeld.

"One such as Ortog does not follow well, or long," she said. "He wanted signs, and prophecies. Assurances of success. I supplied such things."

"Hastening defection," said Ingeld.

"I fear so," she said.

"And hoped to gain concessions thereby, recognitions, status, and profits for your fraudulent rites and claims."

"Yes, Master," she said, "but now I am naked, on a chain."

"If you were to be found here," said Ingeld, "it is possible that Abrogastes would hold you accountable, suspecting that you hoped to ply your wiles once more, hoping to seduce yet

another of his sons into the paths of secession, into the country
of deceit and treachery."

"It is not true, Master!" she said.

"You and I know that," he said, "but my father does not."

"Master?" she said.

"He might not be pleased to learn of your new stratagem,"
said Ingeld.

"I have no stratagem," she said. "I am a slave!"

"But perhaps a sly slave," said Ingeld. "I need only hint such
a thing to my father."

"You would not do so!" she said.

Ingeld smiled.

"Have mercy on me, Master," she said. "I am now only a girl,
marked, and fastened to a ring at your feet."

"You are afraid, are you not?" he asked.

"Yes, Master," she said.

"Do you know why you have been brought here?"

"No, Master!"

"Surely you suspect," he said.

"No, Master!" she said.

"Are you not a slave?" he asked.

"I belong to your father!" she said.

"As of now," he said.

"I beg to be sent back to my cage!"

"Perhaps I shall have you on the planks at the foot of the
high seat," he said.

"What if the shriek of my ecstasy should carry to the ears of
Abrogastes?" she said.

"Surely, as a slave," he said, "you are familiar with gags."

"Have mercy on me, Master," she wept. "Beat me, if you
wish, but return me to my cage!"

"When I touched you," he said, "you responded."

"Forgive me, Master," she said.

"Do not fear," he said. "I will have you in my arms, and as

the slave you are, when I wish. But I have not brought you here for such a purpose."

"Master?"

"I am expecting a guest," he said. "And when he is admitted, and welcomed, I want you at my feet."

"As I am?" she asked.

"Yes," he said, "exactly as you are."

At this point, there were three loud knocks on the left side of the double door, as one would face it from within, from the high seat, what would be the right side of the door, from the outside. These sounds were the result of the measured striking of a spear butt three times against the heavy wood. The Drisriaks, as many other peoples, even in a day of hoverers, rifles, and sky ships, were fond of traditions and antique usages. For example, the vaulted ceiling of the hall was of timbers, and its floor was of earth, strewn, in the ancient fashion, with rushes.

"Enter," called Ingeld.

CHAPTER TWENTY-FOUR

The whip snapped.

Some men looked up, from the house, to the platform.

"Lot two hundred and twenty-seven," said a voice.

Cornhair winced, bent over, a keeper's hand tight in her hair.

Again the whip snapped, and Cornhair was yanked upright, and then, her hair released, thrust forward, stumbling, she climbed the seven steps to the height of the broad, rounded surface, seven steps as there are seven letters in the most common Telnarian word for a female slave.

Cornhair, brightly illuminated, centered in a pool of light, unable to see well into the darkened house, was turned about, before the crowd.

She heard her attributes, in detail, her hair and eye color, her height and weight, her lovely measurements, pleasant to behold, proclaimed to the men. This was done by a clerk, he who had read her lot number, at a table near the foot of the block, on its right side, as one would face the house.

Then, small drums pounded, and two double flutes came alive.

There were four musicians, who were, as the clerk, near the foot of the block, but they were more to the left side, as one might look toward the house.

The melody was sensuous, suitable for its purpose, to

enhance the exhibition of a slave. It swayed in the house like a snake of sound.

Not all markets employ musicians.

Interestingly it was more often done in the lower houses, where, one supposes, lower-level merchandise would be more likely to be offered.

Supposedly it stirs the crowds, makes men more willing to part with their coins.

Too, one supposes it might compensate to a degree for, or distract attention to a degree from, the quality of merchandise being offered in a lower house.

To be sure, sometimes a genuine bargain may be obtained in such a place.

"Can you dance?" he asked.

"Stately dances, if suitably partnered, dances appropriate to my former station," she whispered.

"Are you stupid?" he asked.

"No, Master," she said. "I do not think so, Master."

"You hear the music," he said. "Can you dance, the dances of what you are, the dances of slaves?"

"No, Master," she said.

"Dance," he said.

Again the whip snapped.

Cornhair cried out in fear and misery, but the leather had not touched her.

"Put your hands over your head," he said. "Bend your knees, hear the music, use your hips! You are for sale!"

So Cornhair, in her terror and misery, tried to dance.

But we fear she was too frightened to do well. Or, perhaps there was a subtle unwillingness or resistance in her, an inhibition owing to her former status and station in life. Could she be truly a slave? Could it be she, truly, on this smooth, rounded block, barefoot, in the sawdust, in the pool of light, being exhibited before men?

Could she be truly for sale?

Was this not incomprehensible, unthinkable?

What woman could even imagine herself being sold?

Was this not some fantastic aberration, or illusion, some untoward nightmare?

No.

But how then did she do so poorly?

Did she not yet realize, in her emotions, and thoughts, and belly, that she was a slave?

It was now what she was.

Was the knowledge of her bondage as yet a mere matter of intellectual acknowledgement, little more than an acquiescence of sorts, little more than some abstract recognition of an indisputable fact of law?

To be sure, perhaps her belly had not yet been suitably enflamed; or perhaps she had not yet come to the treasured point where her entire being would become one with the understanding of, and the joy of, bondage, the point where her entire nature would be suffused with what she was, the point at which she would kneel instantly, naturally, and gladly, waiting to be commanded, wishing to be found pleasing by her Master, the point at which she would know the ecstasy of being owned, the point at which she would choose no other life for herself than one of submission, slavery, and love.

"Call out," he demanded.

"Please buy me!" she wept. "I beg to be purchased!"

There was laughter from the crowd.

Clearly the fellow beside her, with his whip, was not pleased.

Cornhair even heard, here and there, in the house, muchly dark before her, the faces hard to see, the laughter of two or three women. What were they doing here, in such a place, a vending place for low slaves? Did they think to find some trained woman's slave here, some mistress of the care of hair and skin, the possessors of subtle cosmetic secrets, one wise in the matching and folding of garments, in the arrangements of jewelries, a confidant from whom seductive insights, likely to be known only to a slave, might be garnered, a discreet and reliable messenger capable of arranging assignations?

So Cornhair, despite being a woman, and one of admittedly comely and delectable attributes, found herself, to her chagrin and humiliation, an object of ridicule and scorn.

How strange this was, as any woman, even if untrained, has it in her body, like the beating of her heart and the circulation of her blood, like the chemistry of her glands, the disposition and readiness, the primed latency, to move as a supplicatory female before men, if only in kneeling, and lowering herself gracefully to the ground, if only in prostrating herself, if only in extending and withdrawing limbs, in calling attention to charms, in smiling, pleading, in moving, rolling, turning about, on back or belly. Surely they realize, somehow, what desirable objects they are, what alluring, luscious objects they are, must sense, if not realize, how men might see them, with such possessive excitement, how men might want them, literally to the rope, collar, and manacle. Have such things not been selected for, over millennia, at the mouths of caves, in forest glades, in capture camps, on streets amidst burning buildings. By such behaviors have not thousands saved themselves from the ax and sword though at the expense of the collar and chain?

"Very well," he said, abruptly.

He indicated that the music should cease.

"Thank you, Master," said Cornhair, relieved.

He snapped the whip, smartly, and she, inadvertently, cried out.

"If you cannot dance," he said. "At least, I trust, you can move."

"Master?" she said.

"Now," he said, "move! Writhe! Twist about! Extend your hands! Crouch! Rise! Display yourself! Plead! Beg! You are merchandise! Show it! Why do you think you are where you are? What do you think your belly and hips are for? Please buyers! Beg to be purchased! Whimper for the chains of a Master! Have no fear, they will be locked on you! Sell cheap and you will live in dirt and work hard. Sell dear and you need fear little more than being displeasing."

A moment or two later Cornhair sank to her knees on the block, shuddering, only to have her head pulled up, by the hair, by the man's left hand.

One gathers the bids were desultory.

Also, there was apparently a minimum bid of twenty *darins*, which sum, however modest, was apparently not reached.

In disgust the fellow thrust Cornhair from the block, into the arms of a keeper, to the left, waiting on the fifth stair.

"Noble sirs," he called to the crowd, "what a flower you have allowed to escape your grasp!"

There was laughter from the house.

"But, woe," said the man. "The sale has been long, the weather warm, the hour late. But be patient! We shall do better now! Much better!" Then, at his nod, the clerk, near the foot of the block, called out, "Lot two hundred and twenty-eight!"

The auctioneer glanced to his left, where the keeper, now on the fourth step, preparing to descend, had Cornhair, bent over, his hand locked in her hair, in custody.

"Lash her," said the auctioneer.

"It will be done," said the keeper.

"Please, no, Master!" wept Cornhair.

"There are other dispositions for such as you," he said. "Take her away, and see that she is well lashed."

"It will be so," said the keeper.

In the tiers, Lady Delia Cotina, of the Telnar Farnacii, turned to her companion, Lady Virginia Serena, she of the lesser Serenii, also of Telnar.

"I think she will do very nicely," she said.

"I think so, too," said Lady Virginia.

"Certainly she will be cheap," said Lady Delia.

"That is nice, as well," said Lady Virginia.

CHAPTER TWENTY-FIVE

"Do not cover yourself," said Ingeld sternly.

"But, Master!" she protested. "See his robes!"

"Hands down, knees wide, head up, back straight, palms of hands on your thighs," said Ingeld. "Kneel proudly. You are a slave of Drisriaks."

"Yes, Master," she said.

"Displayed goods," he said.

"Yes, Master," she said.

The figure in light purple had scarcely been admitted, and was picking his way carefully amongst the damp earth and rushes toward the high seat, when he cried out with dismay, and threw his arm up, before his eyes.

"Please, great Lord," he cried, his eyes covered, "what is that beside your chair?"

"It is a naked slave," said Ingeld, "a girl with a chain on her neck, fastened in place, kneeling before you, in an appropriate posture, one of submission. Would you prefer that she have her head to the planks, the palms of her hands down on the boards, beside her head, or perhaps be fully prostrated, on her belly, her hands clasped behind her?"

"Horrifying!" he cried. "Cover it, throw a blanket over it, so that it may be hidden from my sight!"

"She is a pretty little beast," said Ingeld, "and quite pretty on her chain. You need not look upon her if she offends you."

"It is a female, is it not?" asked the visitor, not removing his arm from before his eyes.

"Yes," said Ingeld, "and one who might bring good coin in a market. She is nicely formed, soft to the touch, and, if I am not mistaken, though she might not care to be so, excellently responsive. Would you like to have her tonight?"

Huta shuddered.

"Take her away, or cover her, great Lord," said the figure. "I fear I might faint, or become ill."

"I fail to understand the source of your distress," said Ingeld.

"It is a female!" said the visitor. "Surely that is enough, even if it were faraway, enclosed in a room, swathed in clothing. It is a snare, a temptation, a dangerous, beguiling enticement. It exists to test our faith, to see if we are worthy of the table of Karch, to see if we can be led from the path of righteousness. It is not permitted to sit at the table of Karch. It has no *koos*!"

"I see," said Ingeld, "that it is true that you are sick."

"Yes, Milord," said the visitor.

"I made some inquiry into your beliefs, or into some of them," said Ingeld, "though I gather there are different views on such things, amongst different versions of your faith."

"There is only one true faith," said the visitor.

"Yours?" said Ingeld.

"As it happens," said the visitor.

"What is the teaching of your, as I understand it, redemptor, Floon, on this matter?" asked Ingeld.

"Precisely that to which the true faith adheres," said the visitor.

"I have heard," said Ingeld, "that Floon was silent on this matter. Indeed, Floon, as I understand it, was an Ogg, and most Oggs are neuters, as many members of certain species of insects. If that is the case, the views of Floon, as of many Oggs, would most likely be quite neutral on the matter, they having no interest in such things, saving, perhaps, making some provision for the reproductives to see to the survival of the species."

"Floon never mentioned females," said the visitor.

"Nor," said Ingeld, "as far as I can understand it, did he mention males. He seemed to do his preaching in a rather broadcast fashion, addressing it to many things, trees, rocks, dogs, birds, horses, clouds, Oggs, Vorites, humans, and whatever forms of life, or reality, he encountered."

"His love was universal," said the visitor.

"There is nothing in the extant books, as it is explained to me," said Ingeld, "which distinguishes between men and women, or, for that matter, between trees and Oggs."

"There is oral tradition," said the visitor.

"Were you there?" asked Ingeld.

"The oral tradition was there," said the visitor.

"In some of the books, the *koos*, whatever it might be, if it is anything, is not even mentioned," said Ingeld.

"It need not be mentioned in every book," said the visitor. "Nine of the fifty is sufficient."

"In some books," said Ingeld, "it seems the 'table of Karch' is set on this world, or in this reality, if not on Zirus alone, and not somewhere else."

"That is a metaphor for somewhere else," said the visitor.

"There seems little in the simple teachings of Floon having to do with obscure matters of doctrine," said Ingeld.

"It is there implicitly, all of it," said the visitor. "It has been worked out carefully, after studying the holy texts, separated from the many false and corrupt texts, of course, and after much prayer and meditation. Karch would not permit his true faith to be mistaken in such matters."

"Your faith," said Ingeld.

"Yes," said the visitor.

"As I understand it," said Ingeld, "Floon loved all nature, seeing it as rich, beautiful, and living, even worlds and suns."

"That is the Pervasiveness Heresy," said the visitor.

"Human beings have a nature," said Ingeld.

"Alas, yes," said the visitor, "that is their fundamental culpability, their fault and challenge. Nature must be met, fought, and overcome."

"Why?" asked Ingeld.

"So that one can live the life of the *koos*, and eventually sit at the table of Karch."

"What if there is no *koos*?" asked Ingeld. "What if Karch, if he exists, approves of the world and nature, which does exist, in the way it exists, rather than its repudiation and denial?"

"It would be my hope to bring you to see the light, and convert you to the true faith," said the visitor.

"And what am I to get for this?" asked Ingeld.

"The life of the *koos*, and, perhaps, if you live well, obey, and do not question, though much is uncertain, a place at the table of Karch."

The arm of the visitor was still before his eyes.

"Perhaps you can do better than that," said Ingeld.

"Gold, and power," said the visitor.

"Speak," said Ingeld.

CHAPTER TWENTY-SIX

Cornhair, kneeling in the darkness, and dampness, chained to the wall ring, her hands high, by her forehead, sobbed. Her back still burned, from the lash.

She heard the key turn in the heavy lock of the door, behind her.

She turned her head about, as she could.

The door creaked open, slowly. She could see the light, from a small lamp, being borne by someone, presumably a man, a keeper. In its light, she could see the dampness glistening on the wall before her. She cried out, frightened, as a small *filch* scampered over her left calf, presumably disturbed by the opening of the door and the bit of light. She knew that she shared her quarters with such small, furtive forms of life, for she had heard them scratch about, but they had not bothered her. This was the first time one had touched her. Her cell was not a pleasant one, and she had little doubt but what it served as a suitable holding place for recalcitrant prisoners, or slaves who had failed to be found fully pleasing. Indeed, the building, as she had learned, served as a prison, as well as a slave house. Although the conditions of her incarceration were far from ideal, Cornhair had been relieved not to have been killed, and there is a security, of course, in being chained, for one knows then that one is still being kept, at least for a time.

The tiny light was still behind her, and not moving. She could not make out what was in the room with her. She turned about, again, as she could. She sensed there were at least two men present, one back in the hall, and perhaps others.

"Please do not whip me further, Masters," she said. "I will be good. I will call out well. I will smile. I will try to please you. I will try to bring you coin!"

Cornhair had now learned what it is to be a whipped slave, and she was prepared to go to great lengths to avoid any further encounters with the hissing lash. No longer was it a mystery to her why slave girls were so eager to be found pleasing. They knew their softness and beauty was subject to the leather, and that they must expect to be punished for any infractions of rules or lapses of discipline. Even a careless word, a clumsy movement, a tardy response to a command, might bring the sting of a switch. Most Masters are kind, but they expect beauty, grace, and obedience in a slave, and will have it so.

There was no response to her protestations.

"Masters?" she said, uneasily.

She pulled a little, at the manacles.

"Is this the one?" asked a male voice.

"Hold the light closer, higher," said a woman's voice.

"This was lot number two hundred and twenty-seven," said a male voice, from back in the hall.

"Yes," said the woman's voice, "this is the one."

"Five *darins*," said the man.

Cornhair heard the coins being counted out.

"You have been sold, 227," said a man's voice.

"Yes, Master," said Cornhair. "To a woman, Master?" she asked.

"Yes, dear," said a woman's voice.

"We have something special in mind for you," said the voice of another woman.

"Hood her," said the first woman. "Then unchain her and tie her hands behind her back. I have a leash."

CHAPTER TWENTY-SEVEN

"Gold, and power?" said Ingeld.

"Much gold, and much power," said the visitor.

"How can that be?" asked Ingeld. "It is well known that such as you are sworn to simplicity and poverty, that you abhor luxury and shun wealth, that you are professionally destitute. How many pennies do you collect in your temples?"

"I do not speak of pennies," said the visitor, "even of mountains of pennies, gathered on a hundred worlds, but of armies, and ships."

"Take down your arm from before your eyes," said Ingeld.

"But the creature beside you," said the visitor. "Be so kind as to conceal her. Have her crawl behind your chair, if nothing else."

"Remain where you are, as you are," said Ingeld.

"Yes, Master," said Huta.

"Spare me this distress," said the visitor. "We are a pure, holy, ascetic faith, a spiritual faith, a *koosian* faith."

"Spare me your hypocrisy," said Ingeld. "It wearies me. Save it for the cattle you slaughter, skin, and milk. I know of your public meals, and services, with your dram of water and your bit of bread, and the secret banquets in hidden chambers. Your plumpness is not the product of pans of water and crusts of bread, designed to bring you closer to the mysteries of the *koos.* And your exarch, a pompous, sanctimonious, clever scoundrel, has enough blubber to be the envy of aquatic mammals traversing polar seas. And I know about the plate in the temples, the golden vessels, the secret storerooms, the credits in a thousand banks, the treaties with kings, the bribings of tyrants, the suborning of officials."

"You mistake us, great Lord," said the visitor.

"Coarse cloth lined with rich fur," said Ingeld.

"No, Milord," said the visitor.

"Perhaps you would like a repast at my table," said Ingeld, "though it be a humble one and of this world, a repast with scarlet wine, from the terraces of Chiba, the Wine World, or honeyed *bror*, from Cirax, with juicy, steaming, roasted meat, from cattle fattened on the plains of Tangara, with candies, custards, cakes, and fruits?"

"A swallow of water, and a crust of bread, would be more than ample, Milord," said the visitor.

"Save your posturing and platitudes for your stricken, guilt-ridden, moaning, whining believers, who take such things seriously," said Ingeld.

"You mistake the joys of Floon," said the visitor.

"You rule through flattery, lies, and guilt," said Ingeld. "You capitalize on loneliness, disappointment, failure, and fear. You teach your followers that they are esteemed and special, unique and inestimably precious, far above others, if not in this world, in another world, one conveniently invisible; you twist the powers and joys of organic nature, for your purposes, into sources of humiliation, doubt, suspicion, misery, and terror; you will have your benighted followers understand their most normal and natural impulses, things as inevitable as the surging of tides and the rotation of worlds, as things of which they should be afraid, of things to be eschewed, things of which they should be ashamed, things for which they should feel guilty, and then you dare to palliate for a price, for your support and enrichment, the effects of the poisons which you yourselves have brewed; you make aberrations and illnesses of what is fine, beautiful, robust, healthy, and inevitable, and then charge for the cure of these tragic diseases which you yourselves have wrought. It is a marvelous fraud, worthy of brilliant and unscrupulous minds, minds skilled in the architecture of control and torture, or minds originally sick, pathetically intent on spreading their own infections to others."

"You mistake us, Milord," said the visitor.

"What is most brilliantly insidious in this cultural malaise," said Ingeld, "is that you inflict this pathological madness on the young and innocent, on the unquestioning, trusting, and gullible, who will believe whatever is taught to them, and do whatever is told to them. It is a sowing of seeds from which to harvest future crops. From such dismal gardens one will reap gold."

"Surely you do not see such a pure and holy faith as contrived and mercenary?"

"Its effects belie it," said Ingeld.

"We have thousands of ministrants," said the visitor. "Surely you do not suspect they serve Karch with duplicity and calculation."

"I am sure many do not," said Ingeld. "Worlds are filled with the innocent and trusting, the well intentioned and ignorant, products of the same disease which they then mindlessly propagate, and would fear not to do so."

"It was not to discuss or defend the truths of the one true faith that I have sought this audience, great Lord," said the visitor.

"The joys which you denounce and dread," said Ingeld, "in many faiths are understood as nothing to be feared or doubted, as nothing to be ashamed of; rather, they are understood as, welcomed as, and treasured as, the gifts of the gods themselves who, in their generosity and bounty, would bestow such happiness, such delights, and riches on all rational creatures."

"False gods, of course," said the visitor. "Perhaps next you will commend sacral prostitution, the solicitations of priestesses in public thoroughfares, exchanging embraces for coins, the public intoning of hymns to vulgar goddesses, the garish clash of cymbals and tambourines in caves and groves, the scandalous movements of temple dancers."

"I am sure it is true," said Ingeld, "that you did not approach the high seat to discuss or defend the doctrines of your faith."

"No, great Lord," said the visitor.

"You still avert your eyes from the slave at my side," said Ingeld.

"Might she not be covered, or withdrawn?" asked the visitor.

"Perhaps you should regard her," said Ingeld. "It might do you good."

"Please, great Lord," said the visitor.

"Face me," said Ingeld. "When you speak, I would see your eyes, your expressions. Much may be read from such small things."

"I would rather not, Milord," said the visitor.

"You would prefer to be a martyr to Floon?" asked Ingeld.

"Milord?"

"The limbs are tied to four horses," said Ingeld. "The horses are then, in four directions, driven apart."

"I would be pleased to gaze on the gracious countenance of the great Lord, Ingeld, of the Drisriaks," said the visitor.

"Do so," said Ingeld.

The visitor complied, while, at the same time, averting his eyes from the lithe, splendid animal kneeling to the right of Ingeld, he, the second son of Abrogastes.

"Abrogastes, your father," said the visitor, "refused to see me."

"Why?" said Ingeld.

"The great Abrogastes," said the visitor, "is older, and, I fear, more rigid, less practical, than his noble son."

"He is trammeled with honor," said Ingeld.

"The war of the empire and the Aatii, and their numerous allies, waxes fiercely," said the visitor. "Fleets clash. Planets are riven. Worlds are broken from the chain of their star. Systems hesitate to declare themselves. Who would not prefer to wait, to see how the die falls? Yet neutrality is not easily purchased. The empire, its resources strained, trembles. It fears a looming dawn, implacable, of unstayed *barbaritas*. Much fighting has been done, much munition expended. Indeed, the war now, so many resources exhausted, resources of many worlds, on both sides, may be fought in narrow corridors, and hang on small battles. Two great weights, largely inert, depress the scale. A penny or a bullet might tip the scale and plunge one weight to the earth, the other to the sky. It could be a small thing, a skirmish leading to a thousand reactions; even a surrender in Telnar, a mistake or defection, a palace coup, could decide matters. It is difficult to see, at this point, the future."

"Men are fond of their empire," said Ingeld. "My father does not intend to destroy it. He intends to own it, in one way or another."

"The empire is unwieldy, and vast," said the visitor. "It will break apart."

"It will be held together, by the sword," said Ingeld.

"But by whose sword?" asked the visitor.

"By that of the Alemanni," said Ingeld.

"I can guarantee that," said the visitor.

"That is the purpose of your visit?"

"Of course."

"How can it be guaranteed?" asked Ingeld.

"You are aware that a Telnarian, Julian, of the Aureliani, a pretender to the throne, recruits *comitates* amongst barbarians, in particular, the Vandals, and has already entered into understandings with two of the Vandal tribes, the Otungs, and a lesser tribe, the Wolfungs."

"The People of the Van Land, the Forest People," said Ingeld, "are hereditary enemies of the Alemanni."

"It is his intention to employ such allies in the defense of the empire," said the visitor. "Already, on a dozen worlds, they have made their landings, navigated rivers, seized strategic points, entered cities. The empire, with such allies, stiffens, takes heart, senses renewed hope, is reinforced."

"The Vandals," said Ingeld, smiling, "will prove a dangerous ally. They will not be immune, no more than the Alemanni, to the lure of worlds, of arable lands, of gold, and women. As well, as the saying is, bring in vi-cats to guard *vardas*."

"But," said the visitor, "they, leagued with the empire, may counter the incursions of your father, great Abrogastes, check his ambitions, even drive him back, to far worlds."

"It would be unwise for either the Alemanni or the Vandals to exhaust their resources on one another," said Ingeld. "Indeed, if they sufficiently weakened one another, a preserved empire might then turn on the remnants of both, with ensuing destruction or, as before, with enforced relocation and exile."

"Precisely, Milord," said the visitor.

"The Alemanni and the Vandals must be wary of one another, and both of the Empire."

"Certainly, Milord," said the visitor.

"And how would you resolve this most problematical situation, beloved ministrant?"

"By means of a league, a confederation," said the visitor, "an alliance."

"I do not understand," said Ingeld.

"A joining," said the visitor, "to destroy the empire, a joining of the Alemanni and Vandals."

For a moment, Ingeld gazed upon the visitor with incredulity, and then, seizing the arms of the high seat, threw back his head and laughed. "Monstrous fool," he said. "Seldom have I encountered one so abundantly endowed with idiocy."

"Milord?" said the visitor.

"Oil and water," he said. "Alemanni and Vandals? Better, put *arn* bears and vi-cats in the same field."

"Crush the empire," said the visitor. "Then divide the spoils."

"I think I shall call for the ropes, and have the horses brought to the killing yard," said Ingeld.

"Allow me to tell you a story, Milord," said the visitor. "Long ago, on a world called Tangara, you know the world, Milord, there was one of many wars, one between Otungs and Heruls, which culminated in a bitter winter campaign. This took place in the Year 1103, from the Setting of the Imperial Claiming Stone on Tangara. The Otungs were bested. A great king of the Otungs, high tribe in the Vandal nation, was slain. His wife, a captive amongst herded prisoners, gave birth, beside the trail, in the cold and snow, to an infant. She died of exposure. The child, a son, was brought by a Herul warrior, a man named Hunlaki, to a schismatic *festung*, one espousing the despicable Emanationist heresy, on the heights of the Barrionuevo Range, the *festung* of the false saint, Sim Giadini, Saint Giadini. The child, originally given into the keeping of a Floonian brother, Brother Benjamin, a salamanderine, was subsequently raised in the *festung* village located at the foot of the pass, leading upward to the *festung*."

"What has this to do with anything?" inquired Ingeld.

"With the child," said the visitor, "was found an artifact, weighty and of gold, a medallion and chain."

Ingeld leaned forward. "It does not exist," he said.

"It exists," said the visitor.

"It was lost," said Ingeld.

"It has been found," said the visitor.

"The symbol, the talisman, of the unified Vandal peoples," said Ingeld.

"It was entrusted to the Floonian brother, Brother Benjamin," said the visitor. "For years it reposed, encased, in his cell, its presence known only to certain members of the Brotherhood, creatures pledged to harmony and peace. The hated Julian, he of the Aureliani, pretender to the throne, seeking information as to the obscure origins of his colleague, Ottonius, seemingly an Otung, pursued the matter, met with Brother Benjamin, and ascertained the existence of the object. An Otung, Urta, a former King Namer, similarly inquiring into the origins of the new, mysterious king of the Otungs, Otto, or Ottonius, whom he resented and feared, also discovered the existence of the artifact."

"And then?" said Ingeld.

"This Urta, once a King Namer of Otungs," said the visitor, "anxious to recover lost prestige and power, dreaded that this object should come into the possession of the new Otung king, Otto, or Ottonius, for he might then hold sway over the entire Vandal nation."

"The Vandals, the nation," said Ingeld, "must not side with the empire!"

"They will follow he who holds the medallion and chain," said the visitor. "It is sworn. The matter surpasses the will of kings and chieftains. If they do not submit themselves to the holder of the medallion and chain, declaring adherence to his banner, pledging themselves his loyal vassals, then their subjects and followers will desert them."

"I listen," said Ingeld, leaning forward, "speak further, and clearly, not in vague hints and obscure allusions."

"It was clearly important to this fellow, Urta, consumed with envy and resentment, that the medallion and chain not come into the possession of Ottonius, new king of the Otungs, whom he despised, and because of whom he had lost his office as King Namer. He wished then, somehow, to obtain or destroy the artifact. But how might this be managed? He knew little or nothing, of course, of the joys of Floon, nor of ugly schisms, or dire heresies. He could not even, incredibly enough, distinguish between

Illusionists and Emanationists, let alone between them and the
one true faith. Many are the false prophets who, and many are
the wayward cults which, arrogantly profess to proclaim the
true messages and meanings of the Redemptor, Holy Floon."

"I am sure of it," said Ingeld.

"This Urta, then, fearing an inauspicious disposition of
the medallion and chain, and covetous of its power, wished
to either obtain or destroy it. But he knew not how to do so.
How could he, an Otung, one who knew nothing of Karch,
and his prophet, Floon, obtain the freedom of the halls of the
festung in such a way that he might manage, sooner or later,
to steal or destroy the Vandal talisman? Surely he would need
a better leverage than that of a mere wayfarer or needy sup-
plicant, in the guise of which he had conducted his original
inquiries. Indeed, at this point it is not clear that he had even
seen the talisman. He decided to seek the counsel of ministrants of Floon, naturally enough in Venitzia, the provincial
capital on Tangara. And here we see the hand of mighty Karch
at work, and his mysterious and wondrous workings, for, in
Venitzia, who should Urta encounter but ministrants of the
one true faith?"

"It is not so surprising," said Ingeld, "for other versions of
your faith in Venitzia, where not exterminated, had, following
arson, looting, murders, and riots, been driven from the city. It
does not seem to be an accident, for example, that the *festung* of
Sim Giadini, a fortress as much as a holy place, was located in the
remote heights of the Barrionuevo Range."

"Urta proceeded as advised," said the visitor. "He, the matter
justified in terms of the end to be obtained, presented himself in
the guise of a proselyte to the false faith of Emanationism, suing
for admission into the Brotherhood. Accepted as a neophyte, he
played his role well, earning the trust and respect of the brothers. In particular, he cultivated Brother Benjamin, whom he
chose as his mentor. Needless to say, by means of visits to the

festung village at the foot of the pass, he remained in contact with agents of the true faith in Venitzia. All was then in order. Brother Benjamin was drugged in his cell, and Urta seized the medallion and chain, and made his way down the long pass to the *festung* village, where our agents awaited him. In moments he and his prize, borne in a hoverer, were on their way to Venitzia, and the coded signal was transmitted to Venitzia, to the readied imperial cruisers, which then took flight, to attack and destroy the loathed citadel of Emanationist iniquity. In this way, the medallion and chain were acquired, and a villainous den of heresy, offensive to the true faith, was eradicated."

"Where is the medallion and chain?" asked Ingeld.

"In a safe place," said the visitor.

"Brands burn brightly," said Ingeld. "They warm and loosen tongues. Pincers clutch and twist; knives cut; the spiked wheel turns unpleasantly; *filchen* flock to shed blood. Ropes and horses are far stronger than pale, bloated flesh."

"I do not know its location, of course," said the visitor. "I assure you I could not begin to withstand afflictions of the sort to which you allude. I suspect few could. On the other hand, I cannot reveal a secret which has not been entrusted to me. Surely you do not believe that I would be put before the high seat of the noble son of Abrogastes if I possessed such information. The ministrants of Floon are not naive; they are not unaware of the nature of the world they despise and repudiate."

"You cannot use the medallion and chain," said Ingeld.

"We have no intention of doing so," said the visitor, "not directly."

"To whom is it to be entrusted?" said Ingeld.

"To a suitable recipient," said the visitor.

"I wonder if you understand its power," said Ingeld.

"I think we do," said the visitor.

"If the Alemanni possessed the talisman," said Ingeld, "the Vandal nation must pledge itself our vassals."

"And the empire would be doomed," said the visitor, "and the Vandals could not in honor attack their lords."

"What do you want?" asked Ingeld.

"The conversion of the Alemanni and the Vandals," said the visitor, "and then that of the conquered empire."

"I see," said Ingeld.

"It is little enough to ask," said the visitor.

"We would promote your faith with the sword," said Ingeld.

"It is appropriate that the true faith be promoted," said the visitor, "whatever might be the means at hand."

"We would risk our treasure and blood in your behalf, fight your battles, suppress your enemies, extirpate your supposed heresies, burn books, cleanse libraries, close uncongenial schools, impose your views and values, abet your policies of shaping the young, gather and guard your wealth, drive the skeptical, reluctant, and indifferent to your temples, silence recalcitrants, enforce your collections."

"You might put it so," said the visitor.

"Yours is the wisdom of the hypocrite and coward," said Ingeld. "Risk nothing, do nothing, and reap much."

"The secular arm," said the visitor, "is to be subservient to the *koos*, as the body to the mind. Its noblest mission is to serve the *koos*."

"I see," said Ingeld.

"And the work of the sword, you must understand, however necessary, is not the appropriate province of men such as I, men of the holy cloth, men of peace who dwell in holiness, devoting themselves humbly, exclusively, to matters of the *koos*."

"Certainly not," said Ingeld.

"Hopefully, by the second or third generation," said the visitor, "the reddened sword may be cleaned, wiped dry, and sheathed."

"By then no divergent options will be available," said Ingeld. "Concepts will be rooted out. Language will be purified. Dangerous words will not exist."

"The channels will have been prepared," said the visitor. "Thought will then flow in them, as it must."

"Minds will be unable to frame unwelcome thoughts. Men will know nothing else."

"For their own good," said the visitor. "Sheep need their shepherd, pigs their sty tender."

"I fear," said Ingeld, "you underestimate the curiosity, the inventiveness, the independence, the astuteness of men."

"I do not think so," said the visitor. "Men herd nicely. They are born to follow, and ask only to be led. Thus they are spared the uneasiness, even the torment, of thought. And dissidents may be done away with."

"But they will rise," said Ingeld. "And sow the seeds of thought."

"When necessary," said the visitor, "the secular sword, summoned forth, may once more depart its sheath."

"I know little of gods," said Ingeld.

"You need not be converted," said the visitor, "only your peoples."

"I see," said Ingeld.

"We possess the medallion and chain," said the visitor.

"And to whom are they to be delivered?" asked Ingeld.

"To a suitable recipient," said the visitor.

"Have you chosen such a recipient?" asked Ingeld.

"Yes," said the visitor, "one we believe most suitable."

"Who?" asked Ingeld.

"You need not seek him out, and kill him," said the visitor. "You would have no need to do so, and you would have little interest in doing so."

"Who?" said Ingeld.

"Ingeld, son Abrogastes, of course," said the visitor.

"Deliver it," said Ingeld.

"Can I trust the great Lord?" asked the visitor.

"As I can trust you," said Ingeld.

"The medallion and chain," said the visitor, "will be yours within twenty days."

"Apparently it reposes then in Telnar," said Ingeld, "in the very seat of empire."

"Perhaps," said the visitor. "I would not know."

"Kneel straighter, slave," said Ingeld.

"Yes, Master," said Huta.

"Behold this slave, comely and helpless, on her chain," said Ingeld. "She was once Huta, high priestess of the Timbri, supposed servant of the supposed ten thousand gods."

"False gods," said the visitor.

"She is now the slave of Drisriaks," said Ingeld, "owned as might be a pig or dog, a boot or shoe."

"Excellent," said the visitor. "Would that such a fate befell all priestesses, sacral courtesans, temple dancers, and such. Let them all be sold in public markets. Let them all tremble on the chains of Masters."

"She fell afoul of Drisriaks," said Ingeld. "Had she been less stimulating, stripped in a collar, or had she writhed less well, naked, for her life, embracing, caressing, and doing a slave's homage to the mighty Spear of Oathing, she would have been slain."

"Milord?" said the visitor.

"Such opportunities would not have been accorded a male," said Ingeld.

"I do not understand," said the visitor.

"It would not be well to fall afoul of Drisriaks," said Ingeld. "Do you understand?"

"Yes, Milord," said the visitor.

"Clearly?"

"Yes, Milord."

"Are we not all friends?" asked Ingeld.

"Most certainly, Milord," said the visitor.

"Perhaps," said Ingeld, "we may then prevail upon you to share our celebratory feast."

"I would be honored," said the visitor.

"Afterwards," said Ingeld, "shall I have this slave at my feet sent to your quarters?"

"Please, no, Master!" begged Huta, and then put down her head, quickly, cringing, fearing to be struck, for she had spoken without permission.

"For what purpose, pray?" said the visitor.

"For the purpose of serving you, as the slave she is," said Ingeld.

"I see," said the visitor.

"Shall I have her delivered to you, naked and chained?"

"That would be thoughtful," said the visitor.

"But woe," said Ingeld, "I may not do so, for she belongs to my father."

"Thank you, Master," whispered Huta.

The visitor turned away.

"Hold," said Ingeld.

The visitor turned about, to face the high seat.

"Within twenty days," said Ingeld.

"As agreed," said the visitor.

"You will, of course, attend the celebratory feast," said Ingeld.

"Of course," said the visitor.

"I shall arrange that, in your place, you will find a dram of water and a crust of bread," said Ingeld.

The visitor then turned about and left the chamber.

With a rustle of chain Huta put down her head and pressed her lips softly to the dark leather boot of Ingeld. "Thank you, Master," she whispered.

CHAPTER TWENTY-EIGHT

The sand was warm, even uncomfortably so, beneath the bared feet of Cornhair.

She could not see for the hood, covering her entire head, snugly buckled about her neck.

"Mistresses?" she begged.

But she was not answered.

She did not know to whom she belonged.

"This way," she heard, a woman's voice, "here, before the box of honor, housing the throne of the hostess."

Cornhair felt the tug of the leash, and she followed on its strap, a few feet across the warm sand.

In the tunnel she had not been hooded.

She did not think the structure was a large one.

Two days ago she had been purchased from the slave house in Telnar, for five *darins*.

She did not know where she was.

She had been taken from the slave house, hooded, bound, and leashed. On the street outside the slave house, she had gathered, from sounds, and words spoken, that two palanquins had been waiting, with their bearers, or attendants. The two women, one of whom it seemed had purchased her, took their places in the two conveyances, which were then put to the shoulders of the bearers. Her leash was fastened to the rear of the first palanquin, which she must follow, on foot. She was still naked, from the slave house, even in the street, but naked slaves, though not common in the public streets of Telnar, were not unknown. For example, the citizens of Telnar were not unfamiliar with chains of nude girls, captives not yet put under the iron, and marked slaves, sometimes from far worlds, being conducted from port pens to markets. Also, as a discipline, or punishment, Masters might send their girls about the city, on errands, and such, clad only in their collars. Slaves are well aware that a tunic may be awarded, withheld, or removed, at the discretion of the Master. The control of clothing, like food, blindfolding, gagging, whipping, binding, and such, are at the prerogative of the Master. Girls are well aware of this, and it is nothing likely to be forgotten more than once. Some Masters keep their slaves nude indoors, but almost all will have them clothed in public, though clothed as what they are, as slaves. Cornhair, on her leash, was grateful for the hood. In its way, it granted her a certain welcome anonymity. What would it matter if she should walk as a slave, if no one knew it was she? Had she not, as a woman, at least after she had been embonded, been often tempted to do so, to walk as a slave is expected to walk, so naturally, so gracefully, so beautifully? Might it not be thrilling to do so, to walk as other girls, so excitingly, so desirably, women who were well aware they were slaves, women who were delightedly slaves, women grateful to be slaves, women proud of specialness, vain of the collars on their necks? Certainly she was a woman and much more aware of her womanhood, and its power, in a collar than she had ever been as a free woman. As a free woman she would have been afraid to walk unabashedly as a woman. As a slave she need have no such inhibitions. Indeed she might be lashed if she tried to conceal or deny the loveliness, vulnerability, and fullness of her sex. It was no wonder free women so hated slaves, for in the chains of their freedom they were denied the freedom of their sex. As she followed the first palanquin she could not but be aware of the vulgar sounds, comments, compliments, and reactions which greeted her passage. Indeed, she started several times, crying out in the hood, in response to pinches and good-natured, sharp, stinging slaps. It was natural then, in her vanity, that she walk as a slave. Who would know?

"She is a nasty little slave, Delia," called out the woman in the second palanquin. "She will do very nicely!"

"Excellent!" was the response from the first palanquin.

"They are pleased," thought Cornhair. "They must have bought me for a man, perhaps for a friend, a husband, a son, or nephew."

Whereas it was unusual for a wife to buy a female slave for her husband, it was not unusual for a husband to buy himself a female slave, for his couch ring. To be sure, this liberty was not reciprocated. If a wife desired extramarital male attention she would be well advised to proceed with caution, to arrange judicious assignations, or, incognito, visit male brothels.

Perhaps it was the anonymity of the hood, or knowing herself leashed, or being unable to part her hands, bound behind her, but Cornhair had seldom felt herself so much alive as now, when she was so fully and helplessly in the power of others. Could it be that she was a natural slave, living to be owned? Too, the sensations of the unexpected attentions, a pinch, a slap, had been acute, keenly enlivening, not really painful, but assuredly stimulating. And were they not, in their way, flattering, as well? And surely the feel of a pinch, the sting of a slap, lingered in her body. To be sure, such things were far less troubling, or disturbing, or significant, she was sure, than would have been a kiss, put on her as a slave, a caress or a grasp, a handling of her as a slave. There was no mistaking such things. Why should she fear certain sensations, she wondered, if she were hooded? Who would see the parting of her lips, the sudden, astonished widening of her eyes? Who would even be close enough to sense the tiny changes in her breathing, its quickening, who so close that they might hear the tiny inadvertent noises which might escape her, scarcely audible beyond the layers of closely woven canvas?

Cornhair had the uneasy sense that she might become needful, as a slave is needful.

How helpless would she then be!

Could she resist being enflamed? What if men should do it to her?

What would it be to feel a man's hands on her, to know herself truly his slave?

She must then hope to please him.

She had felt the lash in the slave house.

"I am afraid of the whip," she thought. "How is it that I should fear the whip? Only slave girls fear the whip. I fear the whip. What can that mean? Is its meaning not clear? I am a slave girl!"

Cornhair was well aware of the responses from the crowd, the noises, the comments, assessing her, as a beast may be assessed.

"Thirty *darins*," she heard. "Thirty-five," she heard.

And then Cornhair walked, as might have a thirty-five-*darin* girl.

She heard the women in the palanquin behind her call out to her companion in the lead palanquin, that to which her leash was attached. "She is the sort that men like," she heard.

"Excellent," she heard, from the lead palanquin. "She will do very nicely."

But Cornhair was puzzled. It was a woman who had bought her. But, why? Surely to give her to a male. But what woman would buy a girl for a man? Was there not a war between the free woman and the slave?

Cornhair followed on her tether, for better than an hour, through various streets, some perhaps, from the sounds, and from the smoothness of the footing, boulevards, others less favored, more cobbled, streets of a more common sort, and, occasionally, it seemed, from the adjustments of the bearers, from the dampness and spillage, from the coolness, from the absence of sunlight on her body, from the sense of compressed, narrowly channeled wind brushing her, streets less streets than dismal alleys or secluded walkways, some little more than muddy trails, crevicelike, between walls. Then, later, the passage of the palanquins once more grew linear and their progress proceeded apace. Why, Cornhair wondered, had a seeming detour, through narrow, poorly paved, even sodden, streets, been effected? Were the grand ladies, for already Cornhair had begun to think of the free in terms quite different from those in which she thought of herself, reluctant to be recognized in this part of the journey? Did they wish to conceal their approach to a particular destination, by recourse to a less public, more circuitous route? Had she not thought she had heard the drawing of the curtains on two palanquins?

What is becoming of me, wondered Cornhair.

What are these strange feelings I am beginning to have? Surely they are not appropriate for one of the *honestori*, for one, even, of the patricians, even of the senatorial class! But I am no longer of the *honestori*, no longer of the patricians, no longer of the senatorial class!

I am becoming different. I cannot help myself!

Are these two women so truly grand, so different from me?

Would I not have despised them, even mocked them, in my freedom?

Why do I now fear them as so far above me, so far beyond me?

Why do I tremble before them? Why do I fear to meet their eyes?

Why should I stand in awe of them? Why should I hurry to kneel before them, and feel it right that I should do so?

Would they not be the same as me if their thighs were marked, if they were stripped, if their necks were clasped in the close-fitting, locked band of servitude!

No, they would not then be different.

But now they are!

So different!

I am changing, she thought. I cannot help myself. I am beginning to see the world as what I now am, as a slave, as one who is owned. I am beginning to think as a slave, move as a slave, speak as a slave. I am beginning to feel my body as the body of a slave, my mind as the mind of a slave, my feelings as the feelings of a slave.

And I want it so!

No, no, no, I must not want it so!

After something more than an hour, the small procession had halted, and the two palanquins had been set down.

To Cornhair's surprise the bearers, or their leader, were paid. The palanquins, then, had been rented.

The ladies then, if they owned palanquins, had elected not to use them. Would private palanquins have been recognized, or noted?

Also, almost at the same time, Cornhair heard the warming of an engine, and the familiar hum of a hoverer.

Too, one may have landed nearby.

It seemed another was being readied.

Someone undid her leash from the back of what had been the lead palanquin. From the feel of the leash on the leash ring Cornhair conjectured it was in someone's hand. A slave grows quite aware of such things. Did they truly fear she might dart away, hooded, her small wrists tied behind her back? Did they truly think that a bound slave was heedless or unmindful of the futility of eluding her restraints? Did they not realize how helpless, disoriented and dependent, a woman is, blindfolded, or hooded?

She felt herself lifted in strong, masculine arms and placed over the rail of the hoverer. A moment or two later, she was knelt on the floor grating of the hoverer; her ankles were crossed; her head was forced down to the grating; the leash was taken back between her legs, it was then pulled back tightly, tautly, and used to fasten her crossed ankles together.

Her head was then held down.

She could not raise it, in the leash collar.

Her hands moved a little in the cords that held them fastened behind her back.

"Satisfactory?" asked the male voice.

"Quite," said a woman's voice.

"A compact, fetching little slave bundle," said the male voice.

Cornhair supposed that a woman did look well, so tied, so displayed, so helpless. She could scarcely move.

"Do you think men would find her attractive?" asked another woman.

"She would do for a use or two," said the man.

"Do you think she could do for a brothel slut?" asked the first woman.

"Certainly," said the man.

"She is the sort?" he was asked.

"Eminently," said the man.

"I do not want to be sold to a brothel!" thought Cornhair. "Do not sell me to a brothel, Mistresses!"

Cornhair had hitherto, for no good reason, taken it for granted that she would be sold to a private Master. It had never occurred to her that she might be sold to a business, an organization, a household, or such. Suddenly, to her astonishment, as she had not really thought of it before, she realized that, as a slave, she hoped very much for, and, for some reason, as though it made any difference, desperately wanted, a private Master. She hoped to be owned by a man, by one man, by only one man, whom she might then strive to serve and please, and, interestingly, she wanted to be his only slave. She suddenly realized, too, to her surprise, that she would hope to be a good slave, and would try, with all her intelligence and her emotional being, to be a good slave, indeed, the best slave she could be. And she sensed more might be involved in such a matter than merely being frightened of the whip. To be sure, the whip would be there, for she would be a slave.

"So," said the man, "you are going to sell her to a brothel?"

"No!" thought Cornhair.

"No," said the voice of the first woman.

In her bonds, Cornhair rejoiced.

The fellow then, apparently, left the hoverer, though she was not altogether sure of that, and, shortly thereafter, she felt the vibration of the grating, the hum of the engine, and, a moment later, the sweep of wind on her back, as the small, circular vessel rose swiftly, smoothly, into the air.

"Stand here," said a woman's voice.

"Yes, Mistress," said Cornhair, her feet in the warm sand to the ankles.

"Is this a market, of some sort?" she wondered. "It does not seem likely. There is sand. Perhaps I am to be run for boys, with ropes, to be awarded to the winner in a game? I have heard of such things. Perhaps they will have nets, and be on horseback? But I do not want to be won by boys. I would want to be owned by a man. If I am hooded, I would be helpless to favor a given contestant. I hope they will unhood me."

She considered the assailing of her lips with a Master's claiming kiss.

This made her uneasy, but she knew she would yield, as a slave.

She sensed she would press against him, begging.

Could this be me, she wondered?

Cornhair had no idea, for a time, where she was, but she, of course, had some familiarity with Telnar, and, given her time in the hoverer, she assumed she must be a hundred miles or so from the capital. She was reasonably sure she was somewhere in the countryside, perhaps in the vicinity of a villa, or set of villas, from which one might commute to Telnar.

She heard birds. Perhaps there were trees about.

Once the hoverer had landed, her ankles had been freed and she had been stood upright, though with some unsteadiness and awkwardness, on the grating. She had then heard the rail gate of the hoverer opened, and she had been led from the vessel down the gate ramp, for the gate, when unlocked and opened, swings out, and lowers, to form the ramp. Exiting the hoverer, to her pleasure, she descended to a surface of short, soft grass, this constituting a most welcome change following her earlier trek through the streets of Telnar.

She heard no men about.

Perhaps a male had piloted the hoverer, but she did not know. Perhaps it had even been the fellow who had lifted her over the rail in Telnar. He might have returned to the small ship, or not really have left it. She did not know. There was the hood. In any event, shortly after landing, and the disembarking of the passengers, including at least the two women whose voices she was familiar with, it had departed.

She was led across the grass and into some structure, and down a passage. At the end of a short journey over a smooth, tiled surface, her journey was arrested.

The hood was unbuckled and pulled from her head, and she knelt instantly, naturally, as became her status as beast and slave. She shook her head, freeing her hair, and blinked her eyes. There were several women about, perhaps seven or eight, richly clad in Telnarian regalia. Clearly they were women of station and, doubtless, of means. And she heard the voices of others from somewhere, doubtless in another room. Several of the women present had laughed when she had shaken her head, freeing her hair. "See?" said one to another. "Yes," laughed the other. But surely it had been a natural enough gesture for a woman, any woman? "Let them sweat blindly in a canvas hood," she thought. "See if they would not be grateful, when it is pulled away. See if they would not struggle to accustom themselves to the light, and try to see through wet, matted hair!"

"Mistresses?" she said.

"What is your name?" asked the woman who seemed first amongst them, whom she would learn was the Lady Delia Cotina, of the Telnar Farnacii.

"Publennia," said Cornhair.

"Oh!" cried Cornhair, struck with a switch.

"What is your name?" asked Lady Delia.

"Filene!" cried Cornhair, frightened. Then she winced, and sobbed, as the switch struck her again.

"What is your name?" asked Lady Delia.

"Cornhair!" cried Cornhair, and then she recoiled twice more, from two fresh blows of the switch.

"Mistresses?" she begged.

"A slave has no name, no more than any other beast, unless the Masters or Mistresses please," said the woman. "She is named whatever Masters or Mistresses please."

"Yes, Mistress," said Cornhair. "Forgive me, Mistress."

"What is your name?" asked Lady Delia.

"Whatever Mistresses please," said Cornhair.

"She is indeed a poor slave," said another woman, she whose voice Cornhair recalled from the cell in the slave house, and the palanquins, the woman who was Lady Virginia Serena, of the lesser Serenii. She was also, as one recalls, of Telnar. "I first saw her," said the woman, "standing on a slave shelf in one of the Woman Markets, one supplied by Bondage Flowers. I had a fellow read her placard. She is new to bondage."

"It does not matter," said Lady Delia, "for our purposes."

"Certainly not," said another woman.

"She will do as well as another," said another woman.

"They are all the same," said another.

"Yes," said another.

"You were a pretty little thing," said the Lady Virginia, "standing there, the placard hanging about your neck."

"Thank you, Mistress," murmured Cornhair.

"I would think men would find you a tempting morsel," she said.

Several of the women laughed.

"Thank you, Mistress," whispered Cornhair.

"That makes you ideal for our purposes," said another woman.

There was more laughter.

"In the slave house," said Lady Delia, "they referred to you as 'Cornhair'."

"Yes, Mistress," said Cornhair.

"You are Cornhair," said Lady Delia, naming the slave. "Who are you?"

"'Cornhair', Mistress," said Cornhair.

"You are going to be put in a temporary collar," said Lady Delia.

"'Temporary', Mistress?" said Cornhair.

"Yes," she said. "And then you will be unleashed and unbound."

"Yes, Mistress," said Cornhair.

"You will also be conducted to a bath," she said. "You will be given oils and tools, towels, brushes and combs. You are to clean and groom yourself, and well. We want you to be as fresh, clean, and lovely as though you were being sent to the couch of a Master."

"Yes, Mistress," said Cornhair.

"Also," said Lady Delia, "though we recognize that your lineaments are such that they might attract and excite men, we have little interest in them. You will be clothed."

"Thank you, Mistress," said Cornhair, gratefully.

"Appropriately, of course," said Lady Delia, "in the scanty, degrading tunic of a slave."

"Yes, Mistress," said Cornhair. "Thank you, Mistress."

"Afterwards," said Lady Delia, "you will be fed amply, and given drink. Even a bit of wine. You may then rest. Later, this evening, you, with some others, will serve our table."

"Yes, Mistress," said Cornhair. "Mistress is kind."

"We will get on nicely, will we not?" asked Lady Delia.

"Yes, Mistress," said Cornhair. "May I speak?"

"Surely, dear," said Lady Delia.

"Who is my Mistress, who owns me?" asked Cornhair.

"I am Lady Delia Cotina, of the Telnar Farnacii," said Lady Delia. "I suppose I own you, as it was I who purchased you. But, in a sense, you belong to all of us. You need not know the rest of us. To be sure, you are doubtless familiar, to some extent, with my friend, Lady Virginia Serena, of the lesser Serenii."

"Yes, Mistress," said Cornhair. "But, I do not understand. In some sense, I belong to all of you?"

"Yes, in a sense," said Lady Delia. "At least we all have an interest in you. Perhaps that is the best way to put it."

"I hear others, elsewhere," said Cornhair.

"In the auditorium and about," said Lady Delia. "There are better than seventy-five of us here, for our meeting."

"Where are the men, Mistress?" asked Cornhair.

Lady Delia frowned, and Cornhair shrank down, fearing another stroke of the switch. But then Lady Delia smiled. "There are no men here," said Lady Delia. "We are all women here."

"A sisterhood?" asked Cornhair.

"Of sorts," said Lady Delia. "Surely we all have something in common, something which we find rather significant, something which binds us together, in a sort of sisterhood."

"A meeting?" said Cornhair.

"Yes," said Lady Virginia. "We are met here, well met, in congenial surroundings, equipped with suitable amenities. We are met to exchange stories, to share experiences, to enjoy collations and share decanters of *kana*, met for, in a sense, conviviality,

for sport, and amusement, following which, after three or four
festive days, we will return to our various, scattered domiciles,
many in Telnar itself."

"May I know the nature of this sisterhood, what binds you
together, what is the point of your meeting, why you are gathered here, without men?"

"It will all be explained to you, in good time," said Lady
Delia. "Now we must put a nice collar on you, free you of this
dreadful leash, and rid you of these nasty, slender, yellow cords,
which, in their snug loops, make you so delightfully, so absolutely, helpless. Then you must hie to your bath."

"Yes, Mistress," said Cornhair. "Thank you, Mistress."

Cornhair stood where she had been told, in the warm sand.

In the dark tunnellike passage, her hands had been taken
behind her and tied together. Through a small aperture in the
door, at the end of the passage, some yards away, she could see a
small rectangle of light, little else. It was probably early afternoon.
A leash had then been put about her throat. A moment later a
hood, quite possibly the same one she had worn in her trek from
the prison and slave house to the hoverer port, had been drawn
over her head and buckled about her neck. "Come along, dear,"
said a woman's voice, but not that of Lady Delia or Lady Virginia.
She did not know where they were. She followed, on her tether,
heard the door opened, and, in a moment, felt the sand about her
ankles and the warmth of the sun on her arms and thighs. She was
tunicked. The tunic, of course, was a slave tunic. It would not do
at all for free women and slaves to be clothed similarly. The clothing of a free woman must make it clear that she is a free woman.
The clothing of a slave must make it clear that she is a slave. And
Cornhair's tunic made that quite clear.

Outside, here, in this area, she heard the raucous cry of what
she took to be river fowl. It was possible, then, she was in the
vicinity of the Turning Serpent. Telnar, long before men had

conceived of silver standards, thrones, and law, long before there had been an empire, had been a gathering and trading place, in effect, a trading station on a great river, what men now called the Turning Serpent.

There had once been eleven major ports at the far edge of the delta of the Turning Serpent, presumably far from here, given the brevity of the hoverer's flight, where it, in its dozens of channels, poured its fresh water miles into the sea. Now, however, particularly in its lower courses, untended, poorly dredged, twisting, and treacherous, the Turning Serpent, now muchly forgotten, now muchly superseded by other transportation systems, was no longer the mighty thoroughfare of commerce it had once been. It now bore no more than a lonely vestige of its once abundant traffic; on the other hand, almost like a memory of the past, it was still plied by keel boats, some masted, and, downstream, by rafts, barges, and flatboats. In some areas, portage areas, boats were disassembled and carried overland, from one branch of the Turning Serpent to another, thence to be reassembled after reaching clear water. In other areas, particularly in the late summer, boats must be towed from the banks, this done by men or cattle. There were even, in some such places, tracks along the banks, prepared for such a purpose. Too, as one might suppose, given the neglect of the route by the empire, its lapse from economic preferment, the withdrawal of imperial supervision, and such, certain atavistic features of its historical past had reemerged, in particular, the spawning, in places, of a raw, lusty river culture, one of vain, proud, short-tempered, harddrinking men, one in which claims as to prowess, or disputes as to taste, say, as to the quality of drinks or the beauty of slaves, and such, were likely to be adjudicated promptly, often by fist and boot, and sometimes by club and knife. It was rumored, too, that lonely stretches of the river, between villages, were not always immune to piracy. Certain areas along the river, of course, were far lovelier, and less troubled than others. We may assume

that our current locale, then, is one such or, at least, was taken
to be such. Indeed, the river did not become dangerous, supposedly, until one reached courses more than two or three hundred
miles from Telnar. Certainly the shield of the *imperium* would
be satisfactorily emplaced locally. There would be nothing to
fear, surely, so close to Telnar. Accordingly, the area in question
might be commended on two counts, first, it was close enough,
presumably, to Telnar to be quite safe, and it was far enough
away, it seemed, to prove a comfortable ambit of privacy and
seclusion, which seems to have been desired by the Ladies Delia
and Virginia, and their friends, or guests.

In the villa, or domicile, if one wishes, Cornhair had been
well treated, at least for a slave. She had been well rested, and,
for a slave, well fed. The last two evenings she, with others,
also slaves, all quite lovely, doubtless selected with this in
mind, had served the long tables in the dining hall. Each was
barefoot and each was clad in a single garment, a slave tunic.
These tunics, serving tunics, however, were discreet, at least
for a slave tunic. The hems fell only slightly above the knees
of the slaves. Perhaps that was because the supper was one
for free women, and a certain properness or decorum was in
order. A dinner for males might have been rather different.
It was not unusual for a convivial gathering of males to be
served by naked slaves, bared save for their collars. In some
cases the slaves are shackled and their serving is supervised
by a "Dinner Master" with his switch. Too, it is not unusual
for entertainment slaves to be rented, who are musicians and
dancers. The use of such slaves is often gambled for and the
won slave, claimed, is chained at the winner's place whilst the
guests converse, whence she will be conducted, at the close
of the evening, to his room. Men, it might be noted, at least
on the whole, do not object to being served by naked slaves.
It seems appropriate. And, interestingly, it seems appropriate
to the slaves, as well. After all, they are slaves. It is hard to

mistake the demure contentment of the female who finds herself in the place in which she senses she belongs, that of a Master's collared slave.

At the suppers, Cornhair was one of the girls who served *kana*. She served humbly, keeping her head, for the most part, down. She felt it would not be well to meet the eyes of one of these women, women so different from herself, free women. She did not wish to invite the lash. The girls who served were not allowed to speak to one another. Cornhair had not even realized that there were other slaves about until the evening of her first day in the house, when she was brought forth from her cell to assist in the serving. The serving slaves, Cornhair felt, like herself, were uneasy. Timid, questioning glances had been exchanged. They might not speak, of course. "They know little more than I of these things," Cornhair thought to herself. "They do not know, no more than I, why they are here. There are no men here. What, then, is our purpose here? I wonder if they are separated from one another when not serving. Are they, as I, put in cells, alone?" One thing that made Cornhair even more uneasy was that she sensed, from time to time, the eyes of one or another of the free women on her. She saw some smile. There was a comment. Had it had anything to do with her? She heard a tiny bit of laughter more than once, of which she feared she might be the subject.

She put her hand lightly to the collar on her neck. It had been referred to as a temporary collar. She was not sure what that might mean. Certainly it was fastened on her neck quite as effectively as any other collar. "Perhaps," she thought, "it is temporary because I am to be given to some man, perhaps an uncle or brother, who will then put me in his own collar."

As Cornhair had ruminated on these matters, her original curiosity as to the purpose of this gathering or meeting returned. Why had it been convened? What was its purpose? Too, in serving, even at the first supper, she had noted something else which seemed puzzling to her, perhaps an odd coincidence, or at least, surely, something unexpected. There seemed no older women in the household, at least none amongst those she had seen. The several free women in the household, or, at least, those she had seen, were all rather young.

"Cornhair!"

Cornhair looked up, frightened.

"Put down your decanter, Cornhair," called Lady Delia, "and come here, dear, and stand before the table of favor."

That would be the table behind which sat Lady Delia, Lady Virginia, and several others, several of whom Cornhair had first seen when her hood had been removed. It had a place of honor, at the head of the room. Cornhair supposed that the individuals at that table might have some special status. Perhaps they were officers, of a sort, ones who stood high in this gathering, this organization, or sisterhood, whatever might be its purpose.

"Shame on you, Cornhair," laughed Lady Delia. "Do not disappoint us! You are a slave. Stand as a slave! Tall, soft, at ease, gracefully, desirably, proudly! Be attractive. Do not be ashamed of your sex! Be proud of it, love it, want it! Be excruciatingly, unapologetically female."

"Please, Mistress!" wept Cornhair.

"It is permissible, you are a slave," said Lady Delia.

"Please, Mistress," begged Cornhair.

"Do you know you are in a collar?" asked Lady Delia.

"Yes, Mistress!" said Cornhair.

She now knew that only too well.

"Must you be lashed before you show us you know it?" asked Lady Delia.

"No, Mistress!" cried Cornhair.

"Suppose we were men and you wanted us to buy you!"

"Yes, Mistress," wept Cornhair.

"That is why she did not sell from the shelf, or from the

block," said Lady Virginia. "That is why we had her for only five *darins*."

"I see," said a woman, "a slave, but a poor slave."

"Yes," said Lady Virginia.

"But she is pretty," said a woman.

"Yes," said another.

"Do you hear me, Cornhair?" asked Lady Delia.

"Yes, Mistress," said Cornhair.

"You are a slave," said Lady Delia. "It is what you are! Do not be ashamed of it. Be proud! How could you be more female? Feel your bondage, feel it in every fiber of your lovely, desirable body. Feel your need, let it suffuse you, let it heat you; let it torture you; feel it in every particle of your body, in every drop of your blood. You need to be owned, and to serve. You need to be handled, and mastered. You are a helpless, worthless slave, only that! Now, pathetic, delicious, worthless slave, let your body beg to be bought!"

Several of the women about the tables gasped, and others cried out in rage.

"Turn, turn slowly, slave!" said Lady Delia. Then she cried out, "Will she do?"

"Yes, yes," cried several of the women, eagerly. A circuit of polite applause rippled about the room. Some women struck their utensils, or knuckles, on the table, in a gentle, refined tattoo of approval.

"You may return to your serving, Cornhair," said Lady Delia.

"Yes, Mistress," said Cornhair. "Thank you, Mistress."

Things then muchly returned to normal.

But Cornhair was troubled.

"I fear I am becoming a slave," thought Cornhair. "What am I? I know there is a collar on my neck. Am I a slave? But this goes far beyond the collar! What is the collar but a symbol, a confirmation? I fear I am becoming a slave, a true slave."

*   *   *

Cornhair, in the warmth, standing in the sand, where she had been told to stand, felt someone close to her.

She heard, overhead, or about, the snapping of canvas, almost as though a banner, or flag, might be torn by the wind.

"That is odd," she thought. "I hear wind, but I do not feel it. Surely on my arms, or legs, I should feel it, but I do not."

"Steady, dear," said a voice, a woman's voice.

She felt the leash and the leash collar removed. Then she felt her hands being untied.

"Keep your hands at your sides," she was told.

The leash and the leash collar, and the cords, were apparently handed to someone. There were at least two then on the sand near her.

"Hold still, dear," she was told.

To her amazement, she felt the collar grasped and a small key thrust into the lock at the back of her neck. She felt the back of the collar press against the back of her neck, and the key turn in the lock. Then the collar was opened, and removed.

"Why," she wondered, "had another collar not been locked on her before the first was removed?"

"Mistress?" she asked.

She had the sense then that the collar had been given to the second person. She waited, expecting a new collar. She was, after all, a slave.

"What, dear?" asked the female voice.

"I have no collar," whispered Cornhair.

"That frightens you, does it not?" asked the voice.

"I am a slave," said Cornhair. She was surprised that she had said this as simply, as naturally, as she had.

"Do not concern yourself," said the voice.

"Am I to be freed?" asked Cornhair.

"No," said the woman. "And if I were to lift the hem of your bit of cloth, here, on the left side, your brand would be clearly visible. Have no fear, my dear, you are nicely marked."

"I do not understand," said Cornhair, frightened in the hood, her hands at her sides.

"For what is to be done to you," said the woman, "it is important that you be a slave. You must be a slave."

"I do not understand," said Cornhair.

"You will understand, shortly," said the woman.

"What is to be done to me?" asked Cornhair.

"It will be clear, shortly," said the first woman. The other person, also a woman, laughed.

"Your hood is going to be removed," said the first woman. "You are to keep your hands at your sides, until you are given permission to move them."

Cornhair then felt the hood being unbuckled. It was spread a bit, and loosened, and then it was jerked from her head.

There were cries of pleasure from several women, cries which seemed to come from above her, and about her.

Cornhair blinked, half blinded by the light, and the glare from the sand. For a moment she could barely keep her eyes open.

There had been two women with her, who now withdrew, taking with them, as was shortly clear, the leash and leash collar, the cord with which her hands had been bound, the collar which had encircled her neck, and the hood which had covered her head.

"There is one!" cried a woman's voice.

"See her!" cried another.

"See the slave!" she heard cry.

"Good, good!" cried another.

Cornhair looked up, bewildered, frightened.

"Slave!" she heard cry.

She heard screams of derision. She saw faces contorted with hate.

"Mistresses!" she cried, plaintively.

There was laughter.

She now understood why she had felt no breeze, for she stood within a walled enclosure. The walls did not seem unusually high, perhaps only seven or so feet in height, surmounted by what seemed to be a railing of large, white, wooden cylinders. There were tiered seats, circling above and behind these cylinders. In these seats, there might have been a hundred, even a hundred and fifty, women, ringing her. Looking up, Cornhair could see, stretched on poles, shading the stands, yellow-and-red striped, silken awnings. It was these she had heard snap in the wind. Where she stood, for the time of day, in the early afternoon, there was no shade from the walls. The sun was fierce, the glare cruel, the sand hot. Cornhair looked wildly about herself. She stood, alone and trembling, in a small arena, some fifteen yards in diameter.

Cornhair looked up.

She still stood where she had been told, her arms at her sides. She was standing below, and before, what seemed to be a small, boxed area just behind one of the railings.

A woman stood up, elegantly robed, and, with a gesture, silenced the small crowd. This was the Lady Delia.

"Mistress!" called Cornhair.

Lady Delia had been kind to her.

"Approach, female slave," said Lady Delia.

Cornhair hurried forward, her arms at her sides, as she had been told to keep them, to stand closer to the wall, behind and above which was situated Lady Delia's box. Lady Virginia was with Lady Delia, on her left, and Cornhair recognized some of the other women in the box, as well. They had been present when she had been unhooded after her arrival in the domicile. Cornhair put her head back that she might the more easily look up.

"You are a pretty thing," said Lady Delia.

There was some laughter in the stands.

"Thank you, Mistress," said Cornhair.

"How are you clothed?" called the Lady Delia.

"In a tunic, Mistress," said Cornhair, puzzled.

"What sort of tunic?"

"A slave tunic, Mistress," said Cornhair.

"Why?"

"Because I am a slave, Mistress."

"It is rather short, is it not?"

"We are clothed, if clothed, as our Masters or Mistresses please," said Cornhair.

"You are well displayed," said Lady Delia. "It leaves little of your body to conjecture."

"It is a slave tunic," said Cornhair.

"Unfortunately," said Lady Delia, "there are no men here."

"Mistress?" said Cornhair.

"No men here, to want you," she said.

"I do not understand," said Cornhair. "May I speak?"

"Certainly," she heard.

"May I move my arms?" asked Cornhair.

"Certainly," said Lady Delia, "you may move your arms, your body, move as you wish. That will make things more interesting."

"I do not understand," said Cornhair.

"Be patient," she was counseled.

Cornhair put her hands to her throat. "My collar was taken," she said.

"You feel naked without it, do you not?"

"I am afraid not to be collared," said Cornhair.

"I can understand that," said Lady Delia. "A slave who impersonates a free woman is to be put to a terrible death."

"I beg to be collared," said Cornhair.

There was more laughter in the stands.

"Why?" asked Lady Delia.

"Because I am a slave, Mistress," said Cornhair.

"You acknowledge that you are a slave, wholly a slave, and only a slave?" asked Lady Delia.

"Yes, Mistress!" said Cornhair.

"To be sure," said Lady Delia, "not all slaves are collared, at least publicly. Some seem to be free women, moving about, conducting their business, and such, but, when they return to their Master's domicile and the door closes behind them, they kneel, and await their commands, as the slaves they are. They may then be stripped, collared, tunicked, bound, whipped, whatever the Master pleases."

"Yes, Mistress," said Cornhair, wonderingly.

"But such slaves are not impersonating free women, in the legal sense," said Lady Delia.

"No, Mistress," said Cornhair.

"But slavery should be public, and manifest," said Lady Delia.

"Yes, Mistress," said Cornhair.

"It would be quite embarrassing, and annoying, even an outrage," said Lady Delia, "to discover that one whom you took to be free, one with whom you may have actually conversed, thought of as an equal, and such, was naught but a slave, who should have been kneeling, collared, ill-clad, and trembling, at your feet."

"Yes, Mistress," said Cornhair. Cornhair realized how mortified, and furious, she would have been, had she, as a free person, been the victim of such an imposture. But, too, she wondered if she might have been the victim of such an imposture, and more than once. How would she have known? One could not expect every woman one met to bare her left thigh. No, it was better, as Lady Delia thought, for slavery to be public, and manifest. It would not do, at all, to confuse free women and slaves. It would not do, at all, to confuse citizens with beasts, persons with objects, with properties.

"It is my impression," said Lady Delia, "that slaves like their collars."

"Mistress?" said Cornhair.

"That, in a sense, they like having their necks encircled with the band of servitude."

Cornhair was silent. She feared to think such thoughts.

"It warms and heats them, it frees them, to become the most female of women, the most complete and perfect of women, the owned, submitted complement to masculine power," said Lady Delia.

"How can it be, Mistress," asked Cornhair, "for they are slaves?"

"As, in their heart, they wish to be," said Lady Delia.

"Slaves!" cried a woman in the stands, "meaningless, worthless slaves!"

"Yes," said Lady Delia, fiercely, "they have been found worthy of the collar! They are content, and reassured, in their collars! Not every woman is collared! Only those men want, the most exciting, the most desirable! So the sluts know how special the collar makes them! They have been selected not for their standing in society, their connections, the advantages they can provide, their wealth, but merely for their femaleness, which men will own, dominate, exploit, and master!"

"Have mercy, Mistress!" cried Cornhair, lifting her hands to Lady Delia.

"The sluts are proud of the bands on their necks," said Lady Delia. "How unique, and special, that makes them! How superior to free women!"

Women in the stands cried out with rage.

"No, no, Mistress!" cried Cornhair. "They are only slaves!"

"Do they not see how men look upon their faces, their limbs, their figures, look so frankly, so appraisingly, so approvingly, knowing that such delights could be theirs, in exactly the same sense that they might purchase a pig or dog?"

"Be kind, dear Mistress!" wept Cornhair.

"Perhaps, slave," said Lady Delia, "you are curious as to why your collar was removed."

"Yes, Mistress," said Cornhair.

"We would not want it soiled," said Lady Delia.

There was laughter in the stands.

"Mistress?" said Cornhair.

"Nor," said Lady Delia, "would we wish it to injure the jaws of fine beasts."

"I do not understand, lovely Mistress," cried Cornhair. "Be kind to me!"

"You were curious as to the nature of our gathering, of our sisterhood, so to speak."

"Yes, Mistress," said Cornhair.

"You may have wondered as to its purpose."

"Yes, Mistress," said Cornhair.

"We all have something in common," said Lady Delia.

"Mistress?" said Cornhair.

"We all hate slaves," said Lady Delia.

"Yes, Mistress," said Cornhair. This made Cornhair decidedly uneasy, but she understood it well enough. Certainly it was common enough that free women resented, if not hated, slaves, for their attractions, for their appeal to men. Where men were concerned there was a natural rivalry between the free woman and the slave. Why should a man prefer a lovely, needful, collared beast on his chain to the inestimable privilege of relating to a free woman? Was that not incomprehensible? Who could understand it? Cornhair, as a free woman, had not hated slaves so much as despising them, and holding them in an utter contempt, for the meaningless animals they were. One can well imagine then her feelings at her own reversal of fortune, when she found herself in a collar. Still, even as a free woman, she had often wondered what it might be, to find herself owned, and helpless, at a Master's feet.

"But," said Lady Delia, "our feelings go much beyond simple hatred. No. Much more is involved. Each of us has a personal interest in these matters. Though we are free women, each with the status and resources of free women, each of us, at one time or another, has been put aside or neglected, even abandoned, for a worthless slave. How foolish and stupid are men! Each of us, each a free woman, in all our glory, at one time or another, sustained this unspeakable indignity. Realize the outrage of being superseded by, or discarded in favor of, a meaningless, curvaceous beast, a slave, something we ourselves could have bought for a handful of coins!"

"It is not our fault, Mistress!" said Cornhair. "We are taken in war, chained, seized, abducted. It is done to us by men!"

"I have seen you, such as you," said Lady Delia, "content, lips parted, half naked, pressing your lips to a man's thigh!"

"Have mercy, Mistress!" said Cornhair.

"You, such as you, belong chained at a man's feet," said Lady Delia.

"Mercy, please, Mistress!" said Cornhair.

"We are met here for vengeance on such as you," said Lady Delia.

"Hateful slave!" screamed a woman from the stands.

"I have done nothing, Mistress!" cried Cornhair.

"We know your sort," cried Lady Virginia, from the side of Lady Delia. "You are all seductive sluts. You will all beg, all lick and kiss, all crawl for the caress of a Master!"

"How can a free woman compete with a slave?" cried a woman from the stands.

"Mercy, Mistresses!" cried Cornhair. "Have their bellies never been enflamed," she asked herself, "as the bellies of slaves? Do they know what it is to wear a collar and be owned? Have they never felt the lash?"

"Slave! She is a slave!?" cried a woman.

"I have done nothing!" cried Cornhair.

"You, and others, will stand proxy!" said Lady Delia.

"Others?" said Cornhair.

"Those who served with you," said Lady Delia. "They will be given knives and set on one another in the arena."

Several of the women in the stands clapped their hands, and laughed.

"It will be amusing to see them set on one another," said Lady Virginia, "screaming, weeping, crying for mercy, cutting and hacking, bleeding in the sand, slave girls set on slave girls!"

"Have mercy!" begged Cornhair.

"A different fate is in store for you," said Lady Delia.

"The dogs, killing dogs, will be set on you," said Lady Virginia.

"We will see you torn to pieces, before us," said Lady Delia.

Cornhair looked wildly about, and ran across the sand to the heavy door which she had seen from within, from the far end of the tunnel, before she had been hooded and led to the sand. It was through this door that the two women who had accompanied her to the sand had recently withdrawn.

Cornhair yanked, again and again, with all her strength, on the handle. It was of iron. The door was of heavy timbers. It scarcely moved.

She looked about, again, and saw another door, to the side. She hurried, gasping, sand about her legs, halfway up her calves, to that door. Then she stopped. There was no handle on that door. It was such that it could only be opened and shut vertically, as it would be lifted and lowered, probably by means of balanced weights.

Then, from behind the door, she heard snarling and growling, and the movement of excited, massive bodies.

She threw her hand before her face, and cried out in misery, and then turned and ran to the sand before the box of Lady Delia and her friends, and fell to her knees, and extended her hands upward, piteously. She could now hear, from across the arena, the agitation of beasts from behind the vertical door, beasts now disturbed, now alerted, doubtless now anticipating their release and feeding.

"Do not release the dogs, kind, lovely Mistress!" cried Cornhair. "I am only a slave!"

"Slave! Slave!" cried several of the women in the tiers.

"Do not despair, Cornhair," said Lady Delia, kindly. "Would you like a chance for your life?"

"Yes, yes, Mistress!" cried Cornhair, tears streaming down her cheeks.

"Note the walls, and the railings," said Lady Delia. "They are not too high. Might you not leap up and seize the railing and draw yourself up to safety?"

"I would be permitted to do so?" asked Cornhair.

"Yes," said Lady Delia. "And, if you succeed, we will see that you are conveyed to Telnar and sold in some nice market."

"Mistress?" said Cornhair.

"You have my word on it," said Lady Delia, "freely and publicly given, the unimpeachable, sacred word of a free woman of the empire."

"Thank you, Mistress!" cried Cornhair. It would require effort, surely, serious effort, for it was not an easy leap for a woman, or a normal woman, but Cornhair was desperate, and terrified, and she felt convinced she could reach the railing, grasp it, and then pull herself up, and over it, and thus reach the lowest level of the seats.

"You do not have a great deal of time, dear," said Lady Delia. "I am preparing to give the signal, letting this lifted scarf fall, following which the dog gate will be opened."

"Hurry, slave," called a woman.

"It is fortunate that you are clad as you are," said a woman.

"Decent robing would be an encumbrance," said another woman.

There was laughter.

It may be recalled that the railings about the height of the wall were in the form of large, white, wooden cylinders.

Cornhair backed away, grateful, determined, secured good footing in the sand, hesitated, and then raced toward the nearest railing. A few feet away she was sure that she had been right, that she would be able to reach, and clutch, the railing.

She did so!

Her hands were on it.

To be sure, given its size, it could not be embraced, but she need only pull herself, inch by inch, up, inch by inch, over its painted, solid, immobile, dry curvature.

Then she cried out, a small cry of misery.

The cylinder was solid, indeed, but it was not immobile!

It turned!

She pulled herself up an inch or two.

The cylinder then, like an elongated wheel, like a heavy bar, rotated on its axis, toward the arena, some two or three inches.

There was laughter in the stands.

She drew herself up another inch, desperately.

The heavy bar turned again, slowly, four or five inches.

Cornhair's own efforts forced it to turn.

Then Cornhair slipped from the cylinder, and fell to the sand.

She heard cries of mirth.

She ran about the arena, and tried, again and again, at different points, to scramble to safety.

Each time the railing, like a smoothed log, spun slowly, reacting to her desperate grasp.

Her nails dug into the wood.

The railing again turned, and, again, she fell to the sand.

She stood up, and looked to the box.

She realized then that the railings had been designed to prevent escape from the arena, by animals, and, it seemed, slaves.

"No!" she cried. "No, please, no, Mistress!"

But even as she cried out, she saw the scarf flutter from the hand of Lady Delia.

CHAPTER TWENTY-NINE

There are many varieties of dogs, or what we have, for convenience, tended to speak of as dogs, from various worlds, rather as we have spoken of "horses," "pigs," and such.

Cornhair, then, did not know, really, what lay behind the vertical door.

She was familiar, of course, with the savage, or half-trained, "dogs" from the Herul camp. She knew she might be torn to pieces if she left the camp, but there was not much to fear when one remained within the assigned perimeter, usually within the circle of wagons, and the dogs had been fed within the week. Indeed, even Heruls would be in jeopardy if such creatures grew lean and impatient. Sometimes she knew that prisoners were run naked for the dogs.

She watched the dog gate, waiting for it to lift.

"Just one dog, at first, Cornhair," called Lady Delia. "We do not want it to feel challenged, that it must act in haste. We want to see it circle you, and frighten you, and harry you. If you run, it will pursue you and bring you down, instantly. So do not run, not right away. To be sure, you will run soon enough, if you have the opportunity. Then you will be dragged down. Then, when the dog has you, we will release the other dogs and watch them fight over you."

Cornhair, of course, knew enough not to run, not immediately, unless shelter might be reached. Even the Herul dogs were not likely to attack an immobile target, not immediately. Too, if one did not move, one might have somewhat longer to live. Stillness can confer invisibility, of a sort. Visual predators are particularly sensitive to movement, but may fail to notice the rabbit, paralyzed with fear. This behavior seems to have been favored, at least in the case of the rabbit. To be sure, if detected, it flees, instantly, darting away, with its sudden, difficult-to-predict changes of direction, and such. A Serian oolun can starve to death before a plate of dead crawlers, but, if one should move, the oolun strikes. The dog sees but not with the acuity of the hawk. It hears well, but not as well as the vi-cat. It does inhabit a world rich with scent, and may locate prey which the hawk does not see and the vi-cat does not hear.

Cornhair stood very quietly, in the sand, rather to one side of the arena.

The vertical door had lifted only a foot, when a snarling shape, eager, squirming, impatient, on its belly, thrusting up on the bottom of the door with its shoulders, scratched its way onto the sand. Its fur was flattened back, where it had scrambled under the door.

A small sound of fear, and dismay, escaped Cornhair, quite inadvertently.

Across the sand she saw the head of the beast instantly turn toward her, and the large, pointed ears rise, and turn toward her, like eyes.

It was similar to the Herul dogs, as large, as quick and agile, but it was more heavily furred, particularly about the head.

About its neck was a heavy leather collar, probably to protect it against competitive feeders, should the division of the prize be contested.

Dogs are trained for many purposes, war, herding, tracking, guarding, game location, game retrieval, pit fighting, *torodont* baiting, warning, message bearing, and such. These animals, or their sort, Cornhair had gathered had been bred for, and trained for, the hunting and killing of men.

The stands were quiet, and expectant. Many of the women leaned forward.

The beast padded toward Cornhair, some yards across the sand.

Cornhair knew she must not run, but it is one thing to know that, and another not to run.

The beast stopped, and looked about itself.

It was alone, save for Cornhair.

Doubtless it welcomed this intelligence.

It padded softly toward her, another three or four yards.

"She is afraid," said a voice in the stands.

"See her tremble," said another.

"She cannot run, even if she wished," said another voice. "She is too frightened."

"She is pretty, is she not?" said a voice.

"Just wait," said another voice.

There was laughter.

"You may move, if you wish," called a woman.

There was more laughter.

Cornhair's collar had been removed. She recalled that it was not to have been soiled, and that one would not wish to risk injuring the jaws of a fine animal.

Cornhair lifted her hand, timidly, to her throat.

The beast growled, and padded a step closer.

It had not circled Cornhair.

It had not feinted toward her, snapped, bitten and drawn back, to bite again.

Perhaps Lady Delia was not really used to such dogs. Perhaps she did not know their training, their dispositions. Perhaps this was the first time she had purchased, or rented, such beasts. Perhaps a smaller animal might have circled, circumspectly, considering the prey, assessing it, or harried it, testing its reflexes,

seeing if it would threaten or strike back, perhaps trying to
stimulate it to flight, when the leaping, the seizing and claw-
ing, the bite through the back of the neck, would be facilitated,
but this animal, crouching down, only watched Cornhair, who
backed away a yard or so, which interval the beast closed immediately, crawling forward its yard or so.

It was not clear why the dog, which was a large, trained
animal, weighing perhaps three or four times what Cornhair
weighed, did not rush upon her, knocking her from her feet,
sprawling her to the sand, and then seizing an arm or leg, shaking her, dragging her about, and then, having tasted blood,
working its way, grip by shifting grip, to the throat. Certainly it
would have been hungry enough. Its keepers would have seen
to that. Our speculation is that it was unaccustomed to prey of
the sort constituted by such as Cornhair. It had been trained on,
and was habituated to, larger, stronger, more fearsome prey, prey
which might resist, and fight, prey on which more than one dog
at a time would be likely to be loosed, prisoners of war, crimi-
nals, and such, uniformly, men. Cornhair, on the other hand,
was much different. Her entire form and demeanor was unfamiliar. She was slight, slender, small, and soft.

The eyes of the beast were on Cornhair.

They blinked, and then they were on her, again.

Slave girls seldom figured in arena sports, save as prizes to be
bestowed on victors. Whereas free women might be slain, slave
girls, as they were domestic animals, were no more likely to be
slain than other domestic animals. They had value. They would
merely change hands. Too, of course, there were better things
to do with slave girls than feed them to dogs. That option, of
course, was always at a Master's disposal, should a girl prove a
poor slave.

The beast had not yet attacked. But it was, of course, quite
hungry. That, as we noticed earlier, had been seen to.

Had there been more than one dog on the sand, say, two or

three, this delay, most likely, would not have taken place. Each beast would have been apprehensive that the other might first seize the prey, and then stand over it, to defend it. Too, it was not as though several had attacked at once and a frenzy had ensued, in which each, with tearing, bloody jaws, must fight for its share of the common spoils.

"Why does it not attack?" queried a woman in the stands.

The beast growled. Cornhair could see fangs at the side of its mouth. Some saliva dropped to the sand, dampening it.

Cornhair's body tensed to run.

She wanted to stay still.

She wanted to run.

She knew she must not move.

She knew she would move.

She knew she must not run.

She knew she was going to run.

Perhaps she could reach a railing and clamber to safety.

"We paid good money for these beasts," said Lady Virginia.

"Be patient," said Lady Delia.

"Are you afraid, female slave?" called a woman.

Cornhair dared not respond, for she feared the slightest sound, or movement, might tip a precious, invisible balance, precipitating the beast's charge.

"Open the gate!" cried a woman in the stands.

"Loose the dogs!" cried another.

Then Cornhair noted a subtle change in the demeanor of the beast, difficult to place, but indisputable. The fur rippled, almost unnoticeably. Muscles were moving, tensing. She saw the hind legs move a little deeper into the sand. The head of the beast lowered some inches, but the eyes remained fixed on her.

"It is going to charge," thought Cornhair.

"Run, Cornhair!" cried Lady Delia. "Run!"

"She wants me to run," thought Cornhair. "I must not run. It is going to charge. I am close. I see it. I must run!"

"Run!" cried Lady Delia.

Cornhair, in misery, crying out, terrified, turned and ran.

She heard the shriek of the crowd, the sudden, scrambling scratching of paws in the sand behind her, the great beast speeding forward.

She sensed the great body in flight, as she threw herself to the sand, was conscious of a sharp, hissing sound, the shadow of the beast above her, wild, hawklike, then its furred weight half on her, half beside her, her tunic and body spattered with blood.

She heard cries of alarm and dismay from the stands.

She struggled to free herself from the weight of the dog, half on her. She pulled herself free, and stood, unsteadily, bewildered, in the sand, beside the beast. It was half torn apart. She could see bones, half of its head. The sand was drenched with blood. She looked to the box of the hostess, the box where Lady Delia had presided over the sport. A man stood there, large, roughly clad, bearded, behind the railing, in his arms a rare Telnarian rifle, a weapon seldom found these days except in the possession of members of the imperial guard and certain elite forces.

The free women were on their feet, and were being thrust, and herded, at gunpoint, toward one of the exits from the stands, except one, the Lady Delia, who was held in place, standing alone, in the box of the hostess.

There were perhaps twenty or thirty men about, in shabby garments, in the caps of boatmen, variously armed.

Perhaps there were others, elsewhere.

Cornhair saw the last of the free women, saving the Lady Delia, disappear through one of the exits of the stands.

"Slave!" called the fellow with the rifle, perhaps the leader of the strangers.

"Master!" responded Cornhair, and ran quickly to the sand before the box, and fell to her knees. How natural, and right, that now seemed to her.

The fellow with the rifle gestured to a confederate, and he unlooped a rope at his belt and flung its loose end over the railing to the sand.

"Hold to it!" he called, and Cornhair seized the rope and was soon pulled up to, and over, the railing. She instantly knelt and put her head down before the man with the rifle, and pressed her lips to his boots.

"Stinking slave," hissed Lady Delia.

"Thank you, Master," whispered Cornhair.

"You are sweaty, filthy, covered with blood," said the man with the rifle. "Do you know where you can wash, and clean yourself?"

"Yes, Master," said Cornhair. She recalled the room of the bath. To be sure, it was little more than a cistern, a bath for slaves. Doubtless, in the domicile, there were facilities fit for free women.

"Do so," said he, "and then return here, naked."

"Yes, Master," said Cornhair.

"Doubtless," said Lady Delia, bitterly, fixing her contemptuous gaze on the man with the rifle, "you like to look on the bodies of slaves."

"Yes," he said.

"You have done well, for robbers and pirates," said Lady Delia. "We here, your captives, are not merely free women, but each of us, each one, is a woman of station and means."

"That is known to us, fine lady," said the man.

"We may be exchanged for handsome ransoms," she said.

"Doubtless," said the man.

"You seem strange fellows, for river men," said Lady Delia.

"We are not river men," said the man.

Cornhair then rose, and hurried to the room of the slave bath.

On her way she passed several cells. Many were empty. In one cell, now crowded together, frightened, were the twenty or so slaves who had served with her at the suppers. They were still in serving tunics. The eyes of one, wildly, regarded her. Clearly none, Cornhair realized, understood what had transpired, nor, really, did she. They saw her bloody, in a brief, bloodied tunic, hurrying by, feet and legs covered with clinging sand. They would not know she had been in an arena. Probably they did not even know there was an arena. Nor, Cornhair supposed, would they realize what the free women had held in store for them, that they would be given knives and set on one another. They did not speak, nor, in her uneasiness, did Cornhair. They had not been given permission to do so. Speaking without permission, as slaves were well aware, could bring the whip. A bit later, on her route to the bath, Cornhair passed several cells crowded with free women, still in their abundant, expensive finery. So closely were they packed into the small cells, that they could scarcely move. Several, bodies pressed against the bars, cried out to her.

"Free us, slave!"

"On the wall, across the way, see, keys! Take them! Undo the locks! Free us!"

"Open the cells!"

"Now!"

"Obey!"

"Obey!"

Cornhair hurried past, frightened. Free men had turned the keys in those locks! How could she, a slave, dare to undo their work?

Soon Cornhair had finished her bath, and, with a few hasty strokes, had brushed and combed her hair.

As she was hurrying back, making her way through the domicile, to ascend the internal stairs leading up to the stands, several of the strangers, certainly looking much like rough river fellows, passed her, apparently on their way to the cells below, that of the slaves, those of the free women.

Cornhair kept her eyes down. It is not always wise to meet the eyes of a free man.

"Thirty *darins*," said a fellow.

"Thirty-five," said another.

"Perhaps forty," said another.

Cornhair, who had last sold for five *darins*, was quite ready, perhaps in her vanity, to welcome such enlarged, unsolicited assessments of her likely block value. Whereas free women quite commonly compare themselves to one another with respect to beauty, and have very clear views on the matter, most such estimations remain speculative. The value of the slave, on the other hand, is what men will pay for her.

In a moment, Cornhair had made her way up the stairs, and emerged amongst the tiers of the small arena.

The man with the rifle was still in the box of the hostess. He was with four or five of his fellows. The Lady Delia was also in the box, standing, proudly, disdainfully, looking across the arena, over the sand, to the now-empty tiers on the opposite side.

At a gesture from the man with the rifle, Cornhair hurried to him, and knelt before him, humbly, head down.

"I note that the stinking slave has returned," said Lady Delia.

"Not stinking, Lady," said the man with the rifle. "She is now cleaner than you."

"Doubtless," said Lady Delia.

"A free woman may be careless in such matters, even slovenly," said the man, "but a slave may not. A slave is to keep herself fresh, clean, and well-groomed, that she may be the more pleasing to her Master."

"Yet," said Lady Delia, "I have seen them sweaty and filthy, naked, chained by the neck, in coffles, being herded through the streets. I have seen them stinking on slave shelves, standing, in rags, their wrists bound before them, or behind them, placards hung on their necks. I have seen them filthy, too, standing on such shelves, displayed, not even in rags, but naked, not even bound, held in place simply by the Master's will, their placards hanging about their necks."

"Perhaps, too," said the man with the rifle, "you have seen them laboring under burdens, pulling plows in the fields, carrying water, tending pigs, cleaning stables."

"They are slaves, despicable slaves," said Lady Delia.

"Slave," said the man with the rifle to Cornhair, kneeling before him, "are you a despicable slave?"

"Yes, Master," said Cornhair.

Lady Delia laughed merrily.

Were not all slaves despicable? But why, then, would men buy them, and prize them? Of course, because they might then be lovely, domestic animals.

"Perhaps the slave would be less offensive," said the man, "if she were clothed?"

"Perhaps," said Lady Delia.

"You are richly robed," said the man.

"I patronize only the finest shops in Telnar," said Lady Delia.

The man gestured, curtly, to one of his fellows. "A length," he said.

"Yes, Lord," said the man.

"Stop!" cried Lady Delia. "What are you doing?"

The fellow's knife, moving swiftly, removed a swath of cloth from the outer, silken, summer robe of Lady Delia.

He threw the fruit of his work to the floor, before Cornhair.

"Slave," said the man with the rifle, "twisting, tearing, and tying, fashion for yourself from that material the semblance of a tunic."

"Do not!" screamed Lady Delia.

"I must, Mistress," moaned Cornhair.

"Make it short," he said, "*slave* short."

"Yes, Master," said Cornhair.

"Despicable slave!" said Lady Delia.

"Yes, Mistress," said Cornhair.

"What is your name, slave?" inquired the man with a rifle.

Cornhair, kneeling, grasping the light, silken cloth cut from Lady Delia's outer summer robe in two hands, instantly put her head down. "Whatever Masters or Mistresses please," she said.

"She is Cornhair," said Lady Delia.

"That will do," said the man. "You are Cornhair."

"She is already named," said Lady Delia.

"I have renamed her," said the man. "What is your name, slave?"

"'Cornhair', Master," said Cornhair.

"Contrive your garment, slave," said the man.

"Yes, Master," said Cornhair, stretching the cloth out.

"If I think it is too long," he said, "you will be lashed."

"Yes, Master," whispered Cornhair.

"Clothe them in revealing, degrading brevity," said Lady Delia.

"If they are to be clothed, at all," said the man.

"Doubtless," said Lady Delia, coldly.

"I have seen no men here," said the man.

"There are none," said Lady Delia.

"That scarcely seems wise," said the man.

"Two keepers of dogs will return for their animals tomorrow. The day after, pilots, with hoverers, will arrive, to return my party to Telnar."

"Still," said the man.

"We are no more than a hundred miles from Telnar," said Lady Delia. "We deemed ourselves safe."

"Still," said the man.

"We are here on woman's business," she said, "the business of free women."

"What sort of business?" he asked.

"Vengeance," she said, "vengeance on slaves."

"May I speak, Master?" asked Cornhair.

"Yes," he said.

Cornhair rose to her feet, and smoothed down the ragged

hem of her improvised tunic. "Is Master pleased?" she asked. "I can make it shorter."

"You have lovely legs, pleasant flanks," said the man.

"For a slave," said Lady Delia.

"Surely, for any woman," said the man.

"Thank you, Master," said Cornhair.

"Perhaps," said Lady Delia. "I understand men buy them with such things in mind."

"So you gathered here for vengeance on slaves?" said the man.

"Yes," said Lady Delia, angrily.

"And how were you injured by slaves?" asked the man.

"It is a personal matter," she said.

"But on its nature it is not difficult to speculate," said the man.

"Perhaps," she said.

"The women here, in your party," he said, "seem uniformly young, and rather attractive."

"We are a sisterhood, of sorts," she said.

"You have much in common?" he said.

"Yes," she said.

"And perhaps you share a grievance?"

"Perhaps," she said.

"The members of your party seem of an age, and such, where they might be interested in contracting useful alliances, fortunate and profitable relationships, with males of prominence, means, and station."

"Perhaps," she said.

"And so, in the way of women, you thought to dangle your charm and body before men, to improve your prospects, and win treasure."

"Do not be vulgar," she said.

"But, in each case," he said, "your intended conquest brought home something in a collar, to crawl about his feet, to fear his whip, and beg to please him."

"Perhaps," she said.

"This frustrated your mercenary intentions," he said.

"Perhaps," she said.

"And what is your name, fine Lady?" asked the man of Lady Delia.

"'Delia Cotina'," she said, "of the Telnar Farnacii."

"So you are she?" he said.

"Yes," she said. "You know of me?"

"By reputation," he said.

"Strange that you should know that, unusual intelligence for a river pirate," she said.

"I am not a river pirate," he said.

"I assume you are in touch with, or can soon be in touch with, certain parties in Telnar, through whom ransoms can be arranged."

"Possibly," he said.

"I shall give you specifics on the matter," she said, "as will other members of my party, on their own behalf. I am sure we will all wish this matter to be concluded as expeditiously as possible."

"I expect it will be," he said.

"I am curious," she said. "What had you heard of me?"

"I had heard that you were one of the most beautiful women in Telnar," he said.

"I see," she said, pleased.

"And, it seems," he said, "that the other members of your party were also noted beauties in the society of the city."

"Perhaps," she said.

"Otherwise how could they have hoped to trap such fine game?"

"I object," she said, "to the crudeness of your discourse."

"It is surprising, is it not," he asked, "given your beauty, and that of your friends, that the males whom you sought to interest and entice, from whom you hoped to win position

and treasure, failed to succumb and languish, failed to surrender to your charms, failed to lift you to the heights you
hoped to reach, failed to fall prey to your plots?"

Lady Delia turned away, angrily.

"How could it be?" he asked.

Lady Delia spun about, in fury. "Slaves!" she cried. "Meaningless, worthless, buyable, stinking slaves!"

She then flung herself on Cornhair, her small fists flying,
striking her, again, and again, pounding on her, until two of the
men pulled her away.

"Steady, steady, fine lady," said the man with the rifle.

Cornhair, her head down, almost to the floor, her hands held
over her head, cringed in fear.

"Forgive me, Mistress!" she begged.

"And so," said the man with a rifle, "you and your friends
gathered together, and would have your vengeance on slaves."

"They are only slaves," said Lady Delia. "Now let us discuss
terms of ransom."

"Gundlicht," said the man with a rifle, "you may now have
the slaves brought up to the tiers. See that they are neck-roped.
They will not object. They are slaves. And it would not do, of
course, to have one wander off, carelessly. Hendrix, you may
have the free women put in the arena."

"The arena?" said Lady Delia.

Two of the rough fellows left the tiers. They departed by
means of the same exit which had been used earlier by Cornhair.

"Yes," said the man with the rifle. "Now the slaves will sit in
the tiers."

"I do not understand," said Lady Delia, apprehensively.

"You will, shortly," he said.

"You are not a boat man," she said, "not a river pirate!"

"No," he said.

"What are you?" she said. "Who are you?"

"You are beautiful," he said, eyeing the Lady Delia.

"Oh?" she said.

"For a free woman."

"'For a free woman'?" she said.

"Yes," he said. "Surely you know that the most beautiful women are taken for slaves. Men will have it so."

"How could the beauty of a slave compare with that of a free woman?" she said.

"Quite favorably," he said. "Where do you think slaves come from?"

"I do not understand," she said.

"To be sure," he said, "in a collar, given the nature of things, a woman becomes far more beautiful."

"Why are members of my party to be conducted to the arena?" she asked. "What has that to do with ransoms?"

"Nothing," he said.

"I do not understand," she said.

He turned to the men about.

"Strip her," he said. "And use that scarf to tie her hands behind her back."

"No!" cried Lady Delia, as rude hands tore the clothes from her body. A moment later her hands were confined behind her back, wrapped in folds of her scarf, that she had used to give the signal to open the dog gate. One of the men thrust her to her knees, and forced her head down to the floor.

"Remain as you are, female," said the man with the rifle.

Cornhair realized that, as Lady Delia had been positioned, she could not be seen from the sand below, onto which, even now, the members of her party, in consternation, were filing.

"What of ransoms, noble sir?" said Lady Delia, frightened, kneeling, her head down to the floor.

"How many are in your party?" asked the man.

"One hundred and fifty-two," she said, "including myself."

"Free men," he said, "do not approve of the killing of slaves."

"They are only slaves," said Lady Delia.

Meanwhile the several slaves who had assisted at the suppers with Cornhair, each on the same long rope, a section of which would be looped and knotted about the neck of one, and then taken forward and looped and knotted about the neck of the next, and so on, had been positioned in the front row of the tiers.

They had been brought up to the level of the tiers by the man who had been addressed as "Gundlicht."

"What of ransoms, noble sir!" beseeched the Lady Delia, more urgently.

"Not all men are stupid," said the man. "And very few are stupid who are rich, powerful, and significantly situated, the sort you and your friends chose for your victims, your dupes, and quarries."

"I do not understand," she said.

"Yet," he said, "being men, being strong men, they doubtless recognized that you and your party had certain attributes of interest, lovely features, intelligence, possibly stimulatory curves."

"What are you saying?"

"And such men," he said, "might be willing to pool certain resources to perpetrate a joke, one worth the telling, and retelling."

"I do not understand," she said.

"I have already been paid," he said.

"What of the ransoms!" she cried.

"One does not ransom slaves," he said.

"We are not slaves!" she cried.

"One sells them," he said.

"We are free women!" she said.

"Then you have nothing to fear," he said. He then turned to the fellow he had addressed as "Hendrix." "Hendrix," said he, "are the free women now in the arena?"

"Yes, Lord," said the man. "All, and the arena exit portal is locked."

The man with the rifle then went to the railing before the box of the hostess, and surveyed the women in the arena.

"Ladies!" he called down to them.

"Release us!" he heard. "Let us go!" "*Filch*! Pirate, boor!" Some of the women shook their fists upward. "Beware!" cried others.

He extended a hand, in a gesture for silence.

"Thank you, ladies," he said.

The women looked uneasily to one another.

"Slaves, though worthless, though meaningless, though mere commodities," he said, "are the most female, the most perfect, the most luscious and desirable of women."

"No! No!" several cried.

"That is why men buy them," he said.

"Release us!" cried a woman.

"Yet," he said, "you would waste such pleasant beasts, such silken, curvaceous objects, of such interest to men, in the arena."

"Let us go!" cried a woman.

"It is not enough that you, in your hatred, would own, terrify, and beat them, but you would destroy them, even cast them to beasts."

"They are slaves," cried a woman.

"Gundlicht," said the man with the rifle. "Exhibit Lady Delia to the free women below."

"Oh!" cried Lady Delia, as Gundlicht yanked her to her feet by the hair, thrust her rudely to the railing, and then held her there, his right hand in her hair, holding her head up, and steadying her with his left hand, it grasping her bound, upper left arm.

Cries of dismay escaped the many women on the sand.

"My dear Lady Delia," said the man with the rifle, softly, the words not audible beyond the box of the hostess, "it is my intention to throw you now, as you are, naked and bound, to the sand below, and release the dogs. There are four left.

Doubtless they will attack you first. This should be instructive to the other women in the arena."

"Do not do so, great and noble sir," wept Lady Delia. "I am
helpless."

"Cast her to the sand," said the man with the rifle to Gundlicht, who then swept the Lady Delia up easily into his arms, and
readied himself to cast her over the railing.

"No, no, Master!" wept Lady Delia.

"'Master'?" said the man with the rifle.

"Yes, yes!" wept Lady Delia.

The man with the rifle indicated that Gundlicht should stand
the Lady Delia behind the railing.

"Publicly, and loudly, slut," said the man with the rifle, "so
that all may hear."

"I am a slave!" she cried. "I beg to be made a slave! Make me
a slave! I beg the collar! Keep me, Masters!"

Many were the cries of dismay, and outrage, from the sand
below. "No, no!" cried Lady Virginia, and others. "Treason!"
cried others. "You betrayed us!" cried a woman. "Contemptible
baggage!" cried another.

Gundlicht, at a sign from the man with the rifle, pulled the
former Lady Delia back and flung her to her knees behind the
railing. "Untie her hands," he said to Gundlicht, who did so,
promptly.

"Go to all fours here, beside me," said the man with the rifle,
"and await your collar."

"Yes, Master," said the slave.

"Bring two," said the man with the rifle, to another fellow,
glancing at Cornhair, who instantly, too, unbidden, went to all
fours, which is a common position in which a slave is collared.

"Now, dear ladies," called the man to the women on the sand,
"I am going to release the dogs."

"No!" cried many. "No! No!"

"No, no, our ransoms! Our ransoms!" cried more than one.

"I have been well paid," said the man with the rifle. "But not to hold you for ransoms. And you have not been pleasing. I shall now release the dogs!"

"No, no!" cried many of the women.

"Let us be pleasing!" cried a woman.

"Yes, yes," cried others. "Let us be pleasing!"

"Pleasing, *as women*?" asked the man with the rifle.

"Yes, yes!" cried several.

"But you are free women!" said the man with the rifle.

Several of the women had fallen to their knees in the sand. Did they not realize that that was undignified, and might sully or injure their garments?

"Yes, yes," cried several of the women. "We beg to be pleasing, *as women, as women*!"

"Remove your garments, every stitch," called the man with the rifle from the box of the hostess. "Then, go to all fours, and, in line, crawl slowly to the exit portal from the arena. There, one by one, you will be collared, and chained."

"Good," said Gundlicht, after a bit, looking over the railing. "They are block naked," he said.

"We have clothing!" cried one of the neck-roped slaves down to the sand.

"Lash her," said the man with the rifle. "She did not request permission to speak."

"It will be done," said a man.

The slave who had called out, loudly, derisively, to the women below, so triumphantly, moaned in dismay. She had not requested permission to speak. She would be lashed.

"We shall proceed as planned?" asked Gundlicht.

"Yes," said the man with a rifle. "We will take them down-river, through the delta, in a covered barge. Then, as we have arranged, they will be distributed, and sold."

At this point the fellow whom the man with the rifle had sent for the two collars had returned to the tiers.

"Collar them," said the man with the rifle.

"Hold still," said the man.

"Yes, Master," whispered the former Lady Delia.

There was a click and the new slave was collared. She put her head down.

"Hold still," said the man, again.

"Yes, Master," said Cornhair. She closed her eyes, briefly. She felt the metal being placed about her neck, and adjusted. She waited. Then she heard the click, and she, too, was collared. She opened her eyes, on all fours, her neck once again encircled with the badge of bondage.

"I am now, again, in a collar," she thought. "I am pleased. How can I be pleased? I am collared. Why do I not mind this?"

"You are Delia," said the man with the rifle to the former Lady Delia.

"Yes, Master," she said.

"How fitting it is," Cornhair thought to herself, "that we are collared. We are so different from free women. Who could mistake a girl in a collar? It is so clear, what she is. I would not want to be mistaken for a free woman, for I am not a free woman. I am so different. I am a slave."

"What is your name?" the man with the rifle asked the former Lady Delia.

"'Delia', Master," she said.

"Strange," thought Cornhair to herself, "I welcome the collar. I am happy that I have been put in it. I am choiceless. I want it that way. What has become of me? I am a slave. I know that now."

She heard the snap of the silken canopy over her head. Part of the arena was now in the shade.

"I love it that men are strong, and will do with me, as they will," she thought. "I do not mind being sold. I hope to have a good Master. But I will have whatever Master buys me. I am a slave."

Onc of thc mcn was now leading the string of tunickcd, neck-roped slaves down from the tiers.

She was not sure they would be mixed with the new slaves. Perhaps they would be sold in Telnar. That was apparently not to be the case with the new slaves.

"What will be done with me," wondered Cornhair. "I will be given away, or sold."

It occurred to her quite naturally now that she would be given away or sold. She had stood on a slave shelf, bared, with a placard on her neck. She had been exhibited, stripped, on a sales block, displayed as goods. There was now no doubt that she might be given away or sold. She now understood herself, wholly and deeply, as what she was, a slave. Her hopes and fears were now those of a slave. Her consciousness was now the consciousness of a slave

She now wished to be a slave, and to belong, and obey, and serve.

"I am a slave," she thought. "It is what I am. It is what I want to be. Let others have their freedom. I have experienced that. Now I want to be owned, to belong. I want to be handled, dominated, exploited, and ravished. I want to be vulnerable and helpless. I want a Master. I need a Master."

"May I speak, Master?" asked the slave, Delia, of the man with the rifle.

"Yes," he said.

"What is to be done with us, with myself, and those who were with me?"

"For the most part," he said, "you will be scattered amongst a hundred markets on a hundred worlds."

"I have gathered you are not a boat man, not a river man, not even a river pirate," she said.

"No," he said.

"The names 'Gundlicht' and 'Hendrix'," she said, "are not Telnarian names."

"No," he said.

"May I inquire as to the nature of my Master?" she asked.

"I am Alemanni," he said, "or, as you will have it, of the Aatii."

"No!" she cried.

"It is so, pretty animal," he said.

"A barbarian owns me!" she cried in misery. "I am the property of a barbarian!"

"Amongst the Alemanni," he said, "my tribe was the Drisriaks. I was high amongst them. I broke away, to form a new tribe, the Ortungen. We fared badly, muchly struck down by the forces of Abrogastes."

"Abrogastes," she said, "the great barbarian lord whose fleets and armies attack and plunder worlds, which threaten the empire itself, Abrogastes, he called the Far-Grasper? His very name is scarcely dared spoken in Telnar!"

"He is my father," said the man with the rifle. "I am Ortog, his son, no longer in his favor."

"Woe," she wept, "I am not only fallen into the hands of a barbarian, but into the hands of the son of the dreaded Abrogastes himself."

"As a woman of the empire," he said, "it makes little difference as to what barbarian you might fall. We all know what to do with women of the empire."

"Please sell me, Master," she said. "Please sell me soon, to someone of civilization."

"Perhaps," he said. "But barbarians enjoy owning women of the empire, particularly former high women. They look well in rags, or less, tending pigs, and such."

"Have mercy," she pleaded, on all fours, head down, collared.

"I may keep you," he said.

"Please, do not, Master," she begged.

"Who, slave," asked Ortog, "was second to you, when you were free?"

"Lady Virginia Serena," said Delia, "of the lesser Serenii, of Telnar."

"Then I may keep both of you," he said, "that you may compete for my favor."

"Have mercy, Master," she said.

"It is pleasant to own slaves," he said. "Who do you think would be my favorite, amongst you two?"

"Doubtless we would both try to be pleasing to our Master."

"The whip will see to it," he said. "And then, later, when you are aroused, aroused as slaves, the whip of your needs."

"Surely not!" she said.

"It will be pleasant, to see you naked on your belly, begging for a caress."

"How could such a thing be?" she said.

"Wait until you are longer in a collar," he said.

She put her head down, trembling.

"Why is it," she whispered, "that one who was once high amongst the Drisriaks, a captain or chieftain, even a king perhaps, stooped to raid a small compound on the Turning Serpent?"

"Even a man of great wealth," he said, "may pick up a coin found on the street, and I am not of great wealth. The Ortungen have fallen far. I have men to feed, and ships to fuel. Remnants of scattered followers are to be regathered. The banner of the Ortungen must be once more unfurled."

"And gold is needed," said Delia.

"Of course," he said, "and even copper, and silver."

"I see," she said.

"But the costless acquisition of one hundred and fifty two slaves, Telnarian slaves," he said, "young and lovely slaves, formerly of significant station, is scarcely a negligible coin to be picked up on the street. I am paid to acquire them and, once they are acquired, I may distribute and sell them as I please."

"Treating us as properties," she said, "as loot, and plunder!"

"Women are properties," he said, "loot, and plunder. It is the way of nature. They belong to men, kneeling, collared, their lips to our boots. Surely you have suspected this."

"Yes, Master," she whispered.

"It is true," thought Cornhair. "We are slaves."

"May I speak?" asked Cornhair.

"Yes," said Ortog.

"When I was put into the arena," said Cornhair, "the noble free women, in their cruelty, promised that if I could climb from the arena, I would be spared and sold in some nice market in Telnar."

"So?" said Ortog.

"May I not then be sold in such a market," asked Cornhair, "a nice market, one which might be frequented by men of modest means, in the capital, in Telnar?"

"You will be sold when, where, and how I wish," said Ortog.

"Yes, Master," said Cornhair.

"How helplessly female I am," she thought. "How helplessly female are slaves! Yet I would not have it otherwise, for I am a slave. How disturbed and outraged, and bewildered, and frightened, I was, as a free woman, when such thoughts, so frequent, telling, and persistent, intruded into my thoughts and dreams! But now I am collared, and content."

"Master," said Delia.

"Yes?" he said.

"What is it to be a slave?"

"Tonight, in your chains," he said, "you will learn."

"Yes, Master," she said.

CHAPTER THIRTY

"These are the darkest of days," said Tuvo Ausonius. "The empire is doomed."

"I will not have it so," said Julian, striking his fist on the rude plank table, in the training camp.

"The fleets of Abrogastes loom," said Tuvo Ausonius. "The ships of the empire, what few with scarce fuel remain, are inert in their steel concealments. Worlds prepare to welcome barbarian lords."

"Telnaria stands," said Julian.

"And muchly alone," said Tuvo. "What say you, dear Ottonius?"

"I know little of what is going on," said Otto. "I know the sword, the bow, the noble, declared foe. I know little of politics, or secret wars."

"The *comitates* have withdrawn," said Tuvo.

"Some remain," said Otto.

"I remain, my king," said young Vandar, who had been the first, long ago, in a simple hall, to accept meat, meat cut from the hero's portion by a giant, blond stranger, one who had brought the pelt of a white vi-cat to a hall of Otungs.

"I, too," said two others, Ulrich, who had conducted the stranger to the hall, and Citherix, who had been bold enough to challenge a king.

"We, as well," said Astubux and Axel, who had known Otto since Varna, where he had ascended to the chieftainship of the Wolfungs.

"The tents are empty, the camps abandoned," said Tuvo Ausonius.

"I feared it would be so," muttered Julian.

"How could men withdraw from kings in honor?" asked Otto.

"In the name of a higher honor," said Julian.

"It is the medallion and chain, once held by Genserix," said Vandar. "It is the talisman of the Vandal Nation, what unifies the Vandal Nation, what unifies the Otungs, the Darisi, the Haakons, the Basungs, and the Wolfungs. It is tradition that the tribes will follow he who holds the talisman."

"Why then," asked Otto, "have you, my friends, not also departed?"

"Once," said Astubux, "there was no tradition."

"If a pig wore the medallion and chain, if it were slung about his neck," said Citherix, "I would not then follow a pig."

"Many would," said Tuvo Ausonius.

"One follows men," said Axel, "not workages of crafted metal."

"I feared this would occur," said Julian. "Long ago, in investigating the antecedents of dear Ottonius, I journeyed to a remote *festung* high amongst the crags of the Barrionuevo Range, the *festung* of Sim Giadini."

"I was raised in the *festung* village," said Otto.

"There I learned that an infant, retrieved from the mud and snow, from the debris of a march of prisoners, one suckled by a dog, had been entrusted to the brothers of Sim Giadini, in particular, to a salamanderine, Brother Benjamin. With that infant had been found the medallion and chain."

"We may conjecture then," said Ulrich, "that after the death of Genserix, the medallion and chain, if it is the true medallion and chain, was concealed, probably by his queen, Elsa, who was said to be near the time of giving birth. We may further conjecture that she, a prisoner, gave birth during the march, in which she, as many others, perished."

"The child, as I had it from Brother Benjamin, was brought to the *festung* by a Herul warrior, named Hunlaki," said Julian.

"Why," asked Otto, "would a Herul warrior have any interest in a human child?"

"I do not know," said Julian. "But Heruls seldom act without reason. In any event, Brother Benjamin guarded the medallion and chain for many years."

"The *festung* was destroyed by imperial ships," said Otto, bitterly.

"But the medallion and chain, the talisman, was not found," said Julian.

"It may have been destroyed," said Otto.

"Possibly," said Julian, "but it, it seems, or some surrogate, was delivered to Drisriaks."

"Perhaps there is no such thing," said Axel.

"I saw it, in the cell of Brother Benjamin," said Julian.

"The medallion and chain is a Vandal thing," said Ulrich. "Why should it have been delivered to the Alemanni, to Drisriaks?"

"No Otung would do that," said Vandar.

"No loyal Otung," said Citherix.

"The point," said Julian, "is to join the barbarian nations for a common onslaught against the empire."

"One which could not be withstood," said Otto.

"One which must be withstood," said Julian, angrily.

"And so perished your plan, noble friend," said Tuvo to Julian, "of enlisting barbarians to defend the empire against barbarians."

"This outcome might have been envisaged," said Otto. "Barbarians have more in common with one another than with men of the empire."

"Not Vandals and Alemanni," said Ulrich. "They are blood enemies."

"Many have doubted the wisdom, friends," said Tuvo, "of settling barbarians on imperial worlds, of arming them, of training them in the arts of war."

"There was no alternative," said Julian.

"Surely they would think soon of gold and worlds, rather than acres and a mercenary's fee," said Otto.

"There was no alternative," said Julian.

"In any event," said Citherix, "given the medallion and chain, Vandals and Alemanni now enleague themselves."

"And the empire trembles," said Axel, "doomed, happily, to be felled by the sword of *barbaritas*."

"No," said Julian. "Telnaria stands."

"For how long?" asked Axel.

"I do not think Abrogastes is much mixed in this brew," said Otto. "I read him as proud and powerful, a true king of the Drisriaks. His way is the ax and challenge, not tricks, not poison, not whispers."

"Who, then?" said Julian.

"Another, I think," said Otto.

"But Drisriak," said Julian. "The medallion and chain is in the counting house of the Drisriaks."

"One high," said Otto, "perhaps Ingeld, perhaps Hrothgar."

"This business is independent of Abrogastes?" asked Julian.

"I think so," said Otto.

"I still do not understand," said Ulrich, "how Vandals and Alemanni could sit at the same table. They are blood enemies."

"To feast on the riches of the empire," said Tuvo.

"Two can lift a weight which might not be borne by one," said Axel.

"And what," asked Otto, "when the feast is done, when the weight need no longer be borne?"

"Then," said Ulrich, "knives will be once more unsheathed."

"I know little or nothing of the medallion and chain," said Otto, "though I now understand its importance. Perhaps this was understood, as well, even long ago, by Brother Benjamin. Why, then, would he, a creature of peace, a gentle creature, a seeker of holiness, relinquish the talisman, and its power, to either warlike Vandals or Alemanni?"

"I do not think he did," said Julian. "I think it was stolen, and the *festung* soon destroyed, to conceal the matter."

"The matter had naught to do with heresy?" said Otto.

"Very little, I suspect," said Julian. "The first project is power, the controlling of worlds. Heresy may then be extirpated at one's leisure."

"I did not even know it existed," said Otto.

"It had become much a thing of legend," said Julian.

"But now," said Tuvo, "it appears, as if from nowhere, and in the hands of Drisriaks."

"It is not just the Drisriaks and the Vandals," said Julian. "Tribes, peoples, and worlds are affected, as well. Many look with envy on the empire, and, seeing the Vandals and the Drisriaks joined, will flock to surprising standards, that they, too, may hurry to so golden a trough."

"And, in the light of the talisman," said Tuvo, "the empire is lost."

"No," said Julian.

"How, no?" asked Tuvo.

"I have seen the talisman," said Julian.

"So, dear friend?" said Tuvo.

"I have a plan," said Julian.

CHAPTER THIRTY-ONE

"How kind of you to visit me in my humble quarters," purred Sidonicus, Exarch of Telnar.

"I thought it unwise to decline your invitation," said Iaachus, Arbiter of Protocol.

"You may kneel, and kiss my ring," said Sidonicus.

"I think not," said Iaachus.

"As you wish," said Sidonicus. "You were somewhat late. Did you have difficulty negotiating the streets?"

"They are dangerous," said Iaachus. "The riots."

"Civil disturbances are most regrettable," said the exarch.

"Perhaps you might resist the temptation of fomenting them," said the Arbiter of Protocol.

"I assure you," said Sidonicus, "I know nothing of them."

"The temple of Orak, father of the gods, has been burned," said Iaachus.

"A false god, of course," said Sidonicus.

"A large and beautiful building," said Iaachus. "Similarly, shrines, temples, and chapels have been rifled, offerings stolen, images defaced; devotees beaten; scroll houses have been forced, and scrolls torn apart, taken outside, and burned."

"What is needful," said Sidonicus, "is contained in the scrolls of Floon, in the holy books of Floon, in the canon. If what is in such scroll houses duplicates what is in the canon it is superfluous; if it contradicts what is in the canon, it is pernicious, and should be destroyed."

"Statues have been pulled down, broken, and defiled," said Iaachus, "those of Umba, Andrak, Foebus, and many others, even that of Kragon, the god of war."

"We of the conversion of Floon," said Sidonicus, "are gentle folk, lovers of peace, and holiness."

"Two priests of Orak were killed in the streets," said Iaachus, "torn apart, cut to pieces."

"Better they had been converted," said Sidonicus.

"What do you want?" asked Iaachus.

"Peace and holiness," said Sidonicus.

"Worlds have fallen," said Iaachus.

"Would you care for *kana*?" asked Sidonicus.

"We have called men to arms," said Iaachus. "Old men, boys, beg for weapons. But many men decline service. They despair. They wait. Cowardice is hailed as patriotism, treason as service to the empire. Generals are threatened. Admirals have no ships. Aristocrats wallow in their luxuries, commoners hide, foundering in their comforts. Thousands of your Floonians not in the streets gather to sing hymns, will not touch a weapon."

"Do not be surprised," said Sidonicus. "Floon was a prophet of peace, of holy substance, indeed, identical with that of Karch, but different."

"What do you want?" asked Iaachus, again.

"What we will have," said Sidonicus. "The empire."

"I think your private quarters," said Iaachus, "are less humble than one would suppose for a ministrant, the drapes, the silken hangings, the silver and gold vessels, the golden candelabra, the paintings, the objects of art, the rich carpets, from Beyira II, if I am not mistaken, the giant replica, in gold, it seems, of a torture rack, covering a wall."

"I pay no attention to such things personally," said Sidonicus, "but I find them useful in impressing secular visitors."

"Of a given station?" asked Iaachus.

"Certainly," said Sidonicus, "lesser men expect simpler arrangements."

"I am impressed," said Iaachus.

"I expected you would be," said the exarch.

"I see there is no tortured figure of Floon, portrayed in gold, on that rack on the wall," said Iaachus. "I gather that is because when the current was turned on there would soon be little left but scraps of flesh clinging to the heated metal."

"No," said Sidonicus. "It has to do with the many species."

"Floon was an Ogg," said Iaachus.

"Strictly, in a sense," said Sidonicus, "but we must remember that he was identical with Karch, as well as different. Thus, we think it best for every species to think of Floon as being of their own species. In this way it is easier to spread his holy teachings."

"You are astute," said Iaachus.

"The faith is astute," said Sidonicus.

"You want the empire?" said Iaachus.

"And will have it," said Sidonicus.

"You know my reputation?" said Iaachus.

"Of course," said Sidonicus. "A master of intrigue, a subtle and unscrupulous monster of duplicity, an almost invisible mover of men and shaper of policies, such things."

"And yet," said Iaachus, "I could not even bring myself to think in your terms, let alone act in them, to lie, to trap minds, to promulgate superstition, to incite cruelty and violence, masquerading as right and justice."

"Where the *koos* is concerned," said Sidonicus, "one must not vacillate or compromise."

"There is nothing in the teachings of Floon to condone or legitimize what you are doing," said Iaachus. "He eschewed institutions. He preached simplicity. He seemed to love all things, rational creatures, irrational creatures, stars, moons, pebbles, weeds, all things, living and dead."

"His teachings must be properly understood, of course," said Sidonicus. "Also, there is unfolding revelation."

"And who unfolds it?" asked Iaachus.

"Qualified ministrants," said Sidonicus, "after prayer and fasting."

"And who qualifies these qualified ministrants?"

"Other qualified ministrants."

"And who qualifies them?" asked Iaachus.

"Surely you do not think this has anything to do with Floon," said Sidonicus.

"No?" said Iaachus.

"No," said Sidonicus, "Floon has nothing to do with this."

"I see," said Iaachus.

"I thought you would, eventually," said Sidonicus.

"You shall not have the empire," said Iaachus.

"I understand that your influence with the empress mother is waning," said Sidonicus.

"Call back your people," said Iaachus. "Free the streets."

"Dogs, once unleashed," said Sidonicus, "are often difficult to restrain."

"I will have troops fire on them," said Iaachus.

"And create a thousand martyrs?" asked the exarch.

"They are arsonists, looters, murderers," said Iaachus.

"Floonians welcome martyrdom," said the exarch. "It assures one a place at the table of Karch."

"Perhaps you could become one such," said Iaachus.

"As a humble man," said the exarch, "I dare not aspire to so exalted a fate, so noble an end."

"Even so," said Iaachus.

"Touch me," said the exarch, "and not only Telnar will burn, but the empire."

"And how will you have the empire?" asked Iaachus.

"How would you like a million Floonians, on a hundred worlds, to take up arms on behalf of the empire?"

"I do not understand," said Iaachus, "Floonians, as gentle, loving Floon, repudiate weaponry. They will die rather than bear arms. It is against their faith. They reject matters of the world. They live as parasites within walls built by, and defended by, others. They will not even look upon a standard or flag. They decline civic responsibility. They will not even participate in the councils of villages. They live for the *koos*, whatever that may be. They repudiate the gods of the empire, the ways of the empire. They have no love for the empire, no loyalty to the empire. They will not even burn a pinch of incense on the altar of the emperor."

"A million Floonians on a hundred worlds," smiled the exarch.

"You could do this?" asked Iaachus.

"Surely," said the exarch. "Unfolding revelation."

"I do not understand," said Iaachus.

"You cannot expect Floonians to die for your empire," said the exarch, "but, properly enlightened, suitably guided, they will die obediently, gladly, and unquestioningly for theirs."

"For yours," said Iaachus.

"If you wish," said the exarch.

"Men will believe anything," said Iaachus.

"Most," said the exarch.

"The empire is to declare for Floon?" said Iaachus.

"The true faith," said the exarch, "is to be the only faith. False faiths are to be banished."

"Your views are to be spread by fire and sword?" asked Iaachus.

"Only where recalcitrance is met," said the exarch.

"I see," said Iaachus.

"It is a great wrong to spread a false faith by fire and sword, by the garrote and burning rack," said the exarch, "but right to do so for the true faith. One must not risk men being misled. Superstition is pernicious. It places the *koos* in jeopardy. One must not, in so far as possible, risk the loss of a single *koos*."

"And what is the relation of the state to the true faith in these matters?" asked Iaachus.

"It exists to do the work of the faith," said the exarch. "The civil sword is to be unsheathed on behalf of the *koos*."

"Soldiers are to gather faggots and ignite fires," said Iaachus, "to hunt men like *filchen*, to redden blades you are too holy to touch."

"You cannot expect ministrants of Floon to shed blood," said the exarch.

"Only to have others do so, as they will have it done," said Iaachus.

"There must be an order in things, a hierarchy," said the exarch. "One must be first; one must be second. Accordingly, as the *koos* is highest, most holy, and supreme, it is to be first, and the state second. The secular sword is to be subordinate to the *koosian* sword."

"There is no *koos*," said Iaachus.

"It does not really matter, does it?" asked the exarch.

"I suppose not," said Iaachus.

"Then go forth and conquer in the name of Floon," said the exarch. "Go forth bravely, slaughtering and burning, singing hymns, doing righteous destruction on a thousand worlds."

"And if we decline to accept this madness?"

"There are others who will," said the exarch.

"Barbarians?" asked Iaachus.

"Possibly," said the exarch.

"You will have the empire, even if it falls?" said Iaachus.

"Yes," said the exarch. "Either way."

"I shall return to the palace," said Iaachus.

"Be careful in the streets," said the exarch.

"I shall," said the Arbiter of Protocol.

"Before you leave," said Sidonicus, "you may kiss my ring."

"I think not," said Iaachus.

"Perhaps later," said the exarch.

"I think not," said Iaachus.

"As you wish," said the exarch.

CHAPTER THIRTY-TWO

"It is so, Lord," said Farrix.

"Does my father know?" inquired Ingeld.

"I think not, Lord," said Farrix.

"I do not understand!" cried Ingeld. "Things were moving well. Pledges were made. Calendars were agreed upon. I had prepared rings to give. Now confusion reigns. The wretched Vandals are divided. Otungs will not move. Haakons and Darisi draw back. Basungs denounce us. Wolfungs will not rendezvous with our fleet."

"Others hesitate, as well," said Farrix. "Unaligned tribes now decline commitment. Neutral worlds refuse contact. Advance orders for thousands of Telnarian slaves are canceled. Consternation inhabits high offices. Curfews are established, roads patrolled, bridges closed. Administrations watch, and will not stir. And a thousand claimants to the medallion and chain struggle to summon troops, to lead movements."

"A thousand claimants?" said Ingeld.

"Yes, Lord," said Farrix.

He, Farrix, standing before the high seat of Ingeld, second son of Abrogastes, the Far Grasper, was a chieftain of the Teragar, or Long-River, Borkons. The Borkons were the third largest of the eleven tribes of the Alemanni nation, the second largest being the Dangars. There were several branches of the Borkons, the largest being the Lidanian, or Coastal, Borkons.

"And none will follow?"

"He who would follow one leader cannot follow a thousand."

"I do not understand," said Ingeld.

"Are you sure you possess the authentic talisman, the authentic medallion and chain?" asked Farrix.

"How can you ask that?" said Ingeld, angrily.

"I cast no aspersions, I perform no treason," said Farrix. "But, as a chieftain of the Borkons, of the Teragar, I do ask it. Are you sure you possess the authentic talisman, the authentic medallion and chain?"

"Yes!" said Ingeld. "It was stolen from the *festung* of Sim Giadini by an Otung, Urta, after which the *festung* was destroyed, that the manner of its acquisition be concealed. It was then delivered to the Exarch of Telnar, one named Sidonicus. One of his subordinates, a legate and plenipotentiary, a ministrant named Fulvius, contacted me. Agreements were reached. Arrangements were made. The talisman was delivered here, to this hall, less than a month ago."

"Here, Lord," said Farrix, reaching within his cloak, and drawing forth a handful of dangling metal, "are two such medallions and chains."

"They are false!" cried Ingeld.

"Undoubtedly, Lord," said Farrix, "but these, and a thousand others, or more, on a hundred worlds, are proclaimed to be the one and only talisman of the Vandal nation. It is little wonder then that confusion abounds, that the Drisriaks are denounced, derided, and mocked. Who, who know little of these things, is in a position to know the authentic talisman? Vandals, wary of the Alemanni, were reluctant to begin with, to follow a Drisriak. And now, confronted with a thousand or more alleged talismans, in a thousand or more pairs of hands, what are they to do? Surely they will not call their fellows forth from the forests, will not march, will not man their ships. Vandals are no more willing to be deceived than we of the

Alemanni, and they are certainly unwilling, in particular, to be our dupes. They speak of deceit, of trickery. Let us fear that the dreaded Vandals do not now plunge themselves into the arms of our enemies."

"It is I who have been tricked," said Ingeld.

"I have no doubt you possess the authentic talisman," said Farrix, "but it is not difficult to understand doubt on the part of others."

"It is not wise to trick Ingeld, of the Drisriaks," said Ingeld.

"It seems, Lord," said Farrix, "that it was not you alone who was treated so shabbily, so disgracefully, but others, as well, this Sidonicus, of Telnar, this Fulvius, of Telnar, and doubtless other members of their party."

"I shall have this Urta, a renegade Otung, this Fulvius, a pompous ministrant, torn apart, by horses, by wild horses."

"It is not you alone who were duped, Lord," said Farrix.

"I, Ingeld, of the Drisriaks, of the Alemanni, duped?" said Ingeld.

"Forgive me, Lord," said Farrix. "I spoke carelessly. You were not duped, but betrayed."

"Men now mock the Drisriaks?" asked Ingeld.

"I fear so, Lord," said Farrix.

"Does my father know of this?" asked Ingeld.

"I do not think so, Lord," said Farrix.

"Good," said Ingeld.

"How proceed things with my beloved father?" asked Ingeld.

"His forces are well deployed," said Farrix. "In effect, Telnaria is blockaded. It is dangerous at this time to move more quickly. Lord Abrogastes awaits reinforcements. His agents are active in Telnaria. They celebrate Abrogastes as a liberator. Many prepare to welcome him, with garlands and flowers. I think he is readying himself for a landing."

"Surely there are imperial forces about," said Ingeld.

"They are scattered, many are posted on far worlds."

"My father is in the vicinity of Telnaria itself?"

"He forced a passage," said Farrix. "He penetrated defenses. I think few expected him to avoid engagements, and move decisively to Telnaria itself."

"He is a fool," said Ingeld. "The war was to be fought on a thousand fields. No foe was to be left behind us. It was for this we needed the Vandals and our allies. He has put himself in a trap."

"He has moved boldly," said Farrix.

"How will this destroy the empire?" asked Ingeld.

"I fear, Lord," said Farrix, "mighty Abrogastes does not wish to destroy the empire, but to possess it."

"By seizing Telnaria?" said Ingeld.

"By seizing Telnar, the capital, by seizing the throne," said Farrix.

"He must be mad," said Ingeld.

"If he seizes the throne," said Farrix, "he seizes the capital, if he seizes the capital, he seizes Telnaria, if he seizes Telnaria, he seizes the empire."

"He embarks upon a dangerous course," said Ingeld.

"He is Abrogastes," said Farrix.

"If he fails?" asked Ingeld.

"What then?" asked Farrix.

"Ingeld is first amongst the Drisriaks," said Ingeld.

"Precisely, Lord," said Farrix.

"Perhaps mighty Abrogastes will fail," said Ingeld.

"It is possible, Lord," said Farrix.

"Perhaps it can be arranged," said Ingeld.

"It is possible, Lord," said Farrix.

"I shall not forget my faithful servitors, my liegemen," said Ingeld.

CHAPTER THIRTY-THREE

"Move!" said the river man.

The whip cracked.

Cornhair, and the others, twenty-one others, feet on the wet, graveled path, cried out in misery, and thrust their slight weight against their hempen harnessing, the towing lines stretching back to cleats on the keel boat, some five of six yard from shore. On the boat itself, on each side, men leaned on poles; these poles, thrusting against the river bottom, serve to propel the craft; they also serve to thrust away debris, to push the craft from sand bars, and to keep the banks of the river at bay. The sweep of such a pole, too, may discourage boarders; they can crush skulls and break ribs; and, jabbing, tear their way into an abdomen. The boat had a single mast, with a single yard, but its square-rigged sail, a fifteen-foot square of woven reeds, hung slack. The keel boat, as opposed to the flatboat, is designed to be used more than once, designed to sustain a passage both upstream and downstream. They are then, as one would expect, more sturdily crafted and better kept, than the flatboat, which is put together to make a single trip. The keel boats, also, are likely to be more ornamented and, as they are commonly painted, more colorful than flatboats. The paint, also, serves to protect the timbers of the keel boat, an important consideration as one hopes to utilize them for several years. Some keel boats even boast a deck cabin. Cargo, on both keel boats and flatboats, is stored on the single, open deck, and is commonly, boxes and barrels, lashed in place to prevent its dislodgement or loss should the craft spin or tip in rapids. A loose barrel, rolling and tumbling, descending a forty-five degree slope, can crash gunwales and break arms and legs. In addition to the roping and strapping of cargo in place, it is also commonly covered with canvas. This protects it from the weather, and also conceals it, should curious eyes, from trees on the bank, or in passing boats, notice it, and find it of interest, with perhaps unwelcome consequences. Too, keel boats, as flatboats, will usually have a rigged arrangement of canvas and stanchions to protect the crew from rain and hail, and the sun, which, in its heat, combined with the glare on the water, can produce a number of undesirable effects, ranging from disorientation and heat stroke to discomfort and the impairment of vision.

The whip cracked, again, and, again, the twenty-two slaves, those who had served at the suppers in the villa of Lady Delia Cotina, including Cornhair, leaned into the traces. Each had fixed, on her right shoulder, under the hempen harness, a cushioning cloth, to prevent the rope from burning into their bodies. Rope burns, scars, and such, can reduce a girl's likely block price. These slaves were not draft slaves, but slaves of the sort which had been so resented and loathed by the free women of the party of Lady Delia, slaves of the sort which free men are likely to buy, presumably having in mind the incredible pleasures derivable from such purchases.

The whip, though its report was startling, and menacing enough, had not struck the slaves. It would not do so unless one of the slaves proved a laggard, or cheater, shirking her share in the common effort, letting it be borne by her collar sisters. The occasional, unexpected snap, it seems, in itself provided the slaves with sufficient motivation. This was doubtless because, presumably, there was not one slave in the harnessing, struggling along the path beside the river, who had not, at one time or another, felt the stroke of such a device.

Cornhair, as the others, struggled forward, thrusting against the harnessing, moving west, upstream, toward Telnar.

She was pleased, that she was to be sold in Telnar. Was that not the dream of many slaves in the galaxy?

Interestingly, Cornhair did not much mind the rope harness, the dirt, the heat, and sweating, the strain of the labor, not that she liked it, you understand, but, rather, that she did not mind it as a free woman might have minded it. She did not find it outrageous, unconscionable, inappropriate, humiliating, or such. She found it quite natural that she, and the others, would be put to such work. They were not free women, but slaves. Was it not natural that the free woman should stand and the slave kneel? Was it not natural that the free woman should command and the slave obey? Was it not natural that the slave, on her hands and knees, naked, should scrub the tiles while the free woman supervises her work, switch in hand? Was it not natural that the free woman, inert, haughty, and calculating, finding herself observed by a free man, might ponder what profit might be derived from his attention, whereas the slave, finding herself observed by a free man, might tremble, and kneel, hoping not to be beaten, but rather to be caressed, and as a slave is caressed? Certainly, Cornhair now had a very different relationship to men than any she had had as a free woman. This was natural. The slave sees men very differently from the way a free woman sees them. The slave sees them as Masters. She knows that this one, or that one, might buy her. She is likely to belong to one. Too, the slave, given her cultural realities, is very much alive, and rich with feeling; her garb, if she is permitted garb, is special, and symbolically significant, as well as unencumbering, aesthetic, and sexually simulating. It is slave garb, designating her as a slave. Too, she has doubtless been marked. Similarly, who could mistake the collar on her fair neck? The slave is a profoundly biological organism, a natural, sexual creature. It is natural then that she, a lovely, purchasable animal, is seen in terms of the pleasure she might provide, and that she sees the free man as a Master she must please, and one who may do with her as he wishes. It is little wonder then that she fears his whip, and hopes, in her service, that he, her Master, may consent, if only for his own amusement or pleasure, to subject her to those unspeakable ecstasies which may be inflicted on a slave, ecstasies for which she lives, ecstasies a thousand times beyond what a free woman can know. Is this not one of the secrets between Masters and slaves, which free women can only suspect? And what of other joys, such as those of kneeling, of serving, of yielding, and of pleasing? There are men and women, and, in a natural order, Masters and slaves.

She had not done well in Telnar before, on the selling shelf, or on the block, but she now looked forward to her sale, to belonging, hopefully, to a private Master, whom she must then strive to please. Even as a free woman, long ago, when she had despised slaves, she had had recurrent, uneasy fears that her own throat might be suitably encircled with the bondage ring. How such thoughts had distressed, and fascinated, her. How she had forced such thoughts away, and then waited, hopefully, for their return. In her confidence and pride, in her days of station and wealth, it had never occurred to her that the collar might one day be locked on her own neck, and that she would find herself on her knees before free persons. Then, after the social debacle of her waywardness and debts, her de-facto abandonment by her family, her trying to scratch out a pitiful existence on the pittance of an allowance, limited to only one slave, the girl, Nika, she had been recruited by Iaachus, the Arbiter of Protocol, in the court of the emperor, Aesilesius, to assassinate a barbarian mercenary, Ottonius, a captain in the auxiliary forces, this having largely to do with frustrating the plans of Julian, of the Aureliani, regarded by Iaachus as a threat to the throne and empire. As we recall, she was to be so situated, in the guise of a female slave, that she might, by means of a poisoned dagger, complete this task, following which she was to be richly rewarded. As we recall, prior to her thwarted attack, she had actually been enslaved, but without her awareness. After her failure to kill the barbarian captain, Ottonius, and having been abandoned by her supposed confederates, she found herself in the hands of Otungs. Instead of having her tortured and executed, she had been branded and sold to Heruls. She sold for one pig. Eventually, purchased from Heruls by a dealer, she had been sold in Venitzia, the provincial capital on Tangara, to the company, Bondage Flowers, which had an office in Venitzia, after which she had been shipped with other slaves, first to Inez IV, and thence to Telnaria, eventfully finding herself in Telnar. We remind ourselves of these perhaps familiar matters, because they, in their way, remind us of moments in a slave's journey. Too, she had certainly begun to learn herself on a dock at Inez IV, in the hold of a freighter, on a shelf in Telnar, on a block in Telnar, in a dining hall in a remote villa, where she had served at a woman's supper, in an arena at that villa, and then, later, being conveyed downstream in one of four covered barges, to some village port whose name she did not even know, in the delta of the Turning Serpent.

If only there had been a wind from the east, she thought, swelling the wide, matted sail!

"Ah!" had said the man at the village port. "Excellent!"

"There are two sets," had said Ortog, "a larger set of one hundred and fifty-two, and a smaller set of twenty-two. The larger set, with the exception of two whom I will keep for my own pleasure, we will ship to far worlds, Omar II, Vellmer, Tangara, Inez IV, Varna, and a dozen others."

"Some of those are rude worlds," said the man.

"There are towns, and trading stations," said Ortog.

"I suppose so," said the man. "But you are unlikely to do much shipping for a time."

"Why?" asked Ortog. "I have four Lion Ships, fueled, waiting in their sheds."

"The blockade," said the man. "It was not anticipated. Lightning from a clear, blue sky. The barbarian commander is in place."

"The war is not to be fought so," said Ortog. "Much must transpire first."

"Troops, ships, are at far-flung borders," said the man. "They man walls, but the wall has been over leapt."

"A bold stroke," said Ortog.

"A perilous stroke," said the man. "Even now border cruisers must be hurrying to Telnaria. The siege will be broken and lifted. The barbarian commander has erred grievously. He will be caught and destroyed."

"How long does he have?" asked Ortog.

"It is estimated only a few days," said the man.

"If what you call the wall is deserted," said Ortog, "barbarians will flow in."

"The barbarian commander must be mad," said the man. "What can he do? The great explosives, which could split worlds and thrust planets from their orbits, have been expended."

"Some may yet exist," said Ortog.

"But surely not in the hands of barbarians," said the man.

"I suppose not," said Ortog.

"You should be able to leave in a few days," said the man. "Slave gruel is cheap."

"Who is the barbarian commander?" asked Ortog.

"A man named Abrogastes," said the man. "Have you heard of him?"

"Yes," said Ortog. "I have heard of him."

"He must be mad, to isolate himself so, to place himself in such jeopardy."

"Perhaps," said Ortog, "this Abrogastes is not mad. Perhaps he hopes to conclude the wars with a single blow. Why should one scratch at the skin of the empire when one might strike at its heart?"

"Telnaria's defenses are not weak," said the man. "If the blockading cruisers should come within firing range, the planetary batteries will burn them from the sky. Telnaria's only fear then will be the rain of molten debris."

"Surely this commander, Abrogastes, must be aware of that," said Ortog.

"The blockade is annoying, but pointless," said the man. "You cannot starve a planet into submission. So, my friend, what if a few aristocrats must do without their favored wines, or imported eels, for a few days?"

"I do not think this Abrogastes is a fool," said Ortog.

"You know him?" asked the man.

"I have heard of him," said Ortog.

The village fellow then cast his glance on the one hundred and fifty-two slaves standing on the river wharf, chained together by the neck, naked, as is common with women in coffle.

"A nice lot," he said. "Where did you get them?"

"I picked them up, a bit to the west," said Ortog.

"You raided a slave caravan," said the man, "and stole their goods."

"Something like that," said Ortog.

"We are tolerant of thieves here," said the man. "What of this smaller lot?"

This smaller lot consisted of Cornhair, and the twenty-one other slaves who had served at the suppers of the free women in the remote villa.

"Why are they clothed?" asked the man.

Cornhair's group was chained together by the ankle, the left ankle.

"That the larger set may the more acutely be aware that they are not clothed."

"I have not noted one of them speaking," said the man.

"They dare not," said Ortog. "They are under discipline."

"The other group, the smaller group, sits together, pleasantly, looking about, chatting," said the man.

"Let the larger group notice that," said Ortog.

"The smaller group sits, the larger group stands," said the man.

"Discipline," said Ortog.

"Excellent," said the man.

"The larger group," said the man, "seemed reluctant to go to all fours, and eat their slave gruel from pans, not using their hands."

"We did not, by design, command it," said Ortog.

"I see," said the man.

"When they are sufficiently hungry," said Ortog, "they will not merely do so, but beg to be permitted to do so."

"Excellent," said the man. "What disposition have you in mind for the smaller lot?"

"They are lovely sluts, are they not?" asked Ortog.

"Very much so," said the man.

Cornhair rejoiced to hear this assessment. As a free woman she had been beautiful and, now, she hoped to be even more beautiful, beautiful as a slave is beautiful.

"I shall rent a boat," said Ortog, "one capable of plying the river west."

"A keel boat," said the man.

"And then I hope to sell them in Telnar," said Ortog.

"You should have no difficulty," said the man.

Cornhair was pleased to hear this.

"Good," said Ortog.

"But I place you as a barbarian," said the man.

"Perhaps," said Ortog.

"So beware of Telnar," said the man. "There are few river men and few barbarians in Telnar."

"Perhaps, eventually," said Ortog, "there will be more."

"I have a friend, Orik," said the man, "who has recently disembarked cargo, loaded more, and would welcome additional
coin for an upstream voyage."

"He would not object to carrying twenty-two slaves?"

"Not at all," said the man. "They might take two or three
days off the length of the voyage."

"How so?" asked Ortog.

"They will do very nicely as tow beasts."

"These are not draft slaves," had said Ortog.

"But they are slaves," had said the man.

"True," had said Ortog. "Please be gracious enough to conduct me to your friend, Orik."

"This way," had said the man.

Cornhair, with the others, in the line, on the narrow trail, her
feet sometimes slipping in the mud and gravel, pressed her body
again against the hempen harness.

If only there had been a wind from the east, she thought,
swelling the wide, matted sail!

"Rest!" called Orik, captain of the keel boat, from its deck,
behind its blunt prow.

He had his right hand raised, shading his eyes, looking to the
side, over the trees. There would be perhaps two more hours of
daylight.

"Rest!" called the Harness Master.

Two men from the keel boat lowered themselves over the side
and waded to shore, the water to their thighs, and tethered lines
to two half-submerged, adjacent trees. The vessel pulled against
these lines, turning slightly. The keel boat is seldom beached.
This is less a matter of practicality and convenience, given its
structure, weight, and size, than one of judicious precaution.
The beached vessel is immobile and requires time to be thrust
back into the water. It takes but a moment to cut mooring lines
and free the vessel to the current. Similarly, it is seldom tethered
snugly to shore. In this way a sudden rush of men would have

difficulty in effecting a boarding, having to wade to the hull and then clamber over the gunwales, a most unpleasant prospect if men above them, behind the gunwales, should be moved to deny them entry.

Cornhair, with the others, still harnessed, crept to the side, and lay down in the shaded grass.

She lay on her belly, and dug her fingers into the grass.

She was covered with sweat, her legs were filthy. Her body ached, her feet and shoulders were sore.

She clutched at the grass.

She, as the others, in the lines, was naked. That was natural, and practical, given the heat, and misery and torment, of the work. Too, they were slaves. Too, nudity is, in a way, like the slave tunic, a bond. Not all slaves are naked, but one who is naked in public is likely to be a slave.

She was not chained.

That was commonly done at night, on the deck of the keel boat, or in one of the shore camps.

In the business at hand, chaining would have impaired the efficiency of the operation.

Chains keep women together. One whip, its leather admonitions poised, can master an entire chain. Many think of chains as being utilized to prevent escape. That is certainly true, of course, for they prevent escape with perfection; a chained slave knows herself helpless; but, too, there is another reason for chaining which is less commonly recognized, and that is to prevent theft. It is as difficult to steal a slave chained to a ring as it is, say, to steal any other property so secured. Similarly, where one might steal one shackled woman, carrying her away, gagged and struggling, into the night, it is not easy, at all, to steal a string of fifteen or twenty women shackled together. Surely that is a much greater challenge. Too, might that not call for several men, and bloodshed? Too, of course, it is easier to track a chain of twenty shackled properties than to pursue and recover one such property, just as it is easier to track a string of twenty horses or a herd of twenty pigs than a single horse or pig.

There are, of course, many aspects of chains which transcend simple matters of management, for example, matters mnemonic, aesthetic, stimulatory, psychological, and so on. Chains, as cords, ropes, straps, thongs, and such, have their effects on the female slave.

In any event, the slaves were not chained.

Cornhair was aware that she might slip the rope harness, but she, no more than the others, would not do so.

It was not, interestingly, simply that there was no escape for them, given their lack of garmenture, their marks, their collars, the enclosing society, the lack of anywhere to escape to, and such, but that they now, or at least Cornhair, understood themselves as quite other than free women. They now understood themselves as something radically, fundamentally different, as properties which might be bought and sold, as slaves.

Cornhair closed her eyes, put her head down, and felt the grass against her cheek.

She and the others, obviously, were not draft slaves. One would be a fool to buy such as they for haulage. Clearly such as they would be purchased for other purposes.

Yet, they, the twenty-two of them, had been put to haulage.

Did this not seem madness? How had Gundlicht, lieutenant to Ortog, with several others, delegated to dispose of the slaves in Telnar markets, permitted this? Would he bring fresh, rested slaves, hoping to be well purchased, to the shelves and blocks, or exhausted, strained, worn, sore, and weary slaves, pathetic beasts unlikely to be sought after otherwise than as bargains, purchased with an eye to the future?

What Cornhair, in her misery, did not realize was the attention and solicitude with which she and the others were being handled and treated. The Masters realized full well they were

dealing with prize stock and had no intention of diminishing
its value. They had not been driven and hastened as hauling
slaves are often driven and hastened. They were well fed and
frequently watered. The rope harness was cushioned at the
shoulder. Their towing time was less than six hours per day. Rest
periods were frequent. Men assisted at the poles. The whip had
scarcely touched them. In Telnar, with a day or two's rest, they
would be put up for sale in a condition calculated to display
them to their vender's best advantage.

Cornhair opened her eyes, and looked back to the keel boat,
a few feet from shore, on its mooring lines, and looked back, aft,
to the deck cabin.

Who, she wondered, were the strangers who remained so
much in that cabin.

Certainly they were not the two fellows who had had unpleasant, if not altogether untypical, experiences in the delta village,
not the one who had returned bloody from a brawl, a handful of
tavern cup dice in his grasp, nor the fellow severally slashed in
some dispute about the charms of a slave. Men speculated that
the luck of the first fellow might now change. Orik had advised
him not to gamble with his crew mates. The second fellow had,
at least, on foot, made it back to the keel boat. His antagonist,
it was said, was likely to recover, as the blade had missed the
heart.

In the delta village, on the evening the keel boat, hired by
the barbarian, Ortog, was readied for the river, cargo lashed in
place, to depart at dawn, one of the girls on the wharf, not yet
boarded, had cried out and pointed to a streak in the sky. It
seemed, at first, to be one of those familiar meteorological phenomena which some understood as the fiery passage of the vessel of Orak, king and father of the gods, or the cast, burning
spear of Kragon, god of war, but others, doubtless more sophisticated, as merely the dislodgment and plummeting of a star.
To be sure, those in the imperial navy, and, we suspect, some

barbarians, would be likely to understand such things differently, as marking the flight of sky stones, often partly metal, which might occasionally, and sometimes, like a fierce rain, imperil ships, the far-ranging ships, those traversing the airless, lonely, nigh-vacant deserts between worlds. The passage of such stones through atmospheres, abraded by friction, would be marked by a debris of flaming particles. Indeed, occasionally, despite so tortuous a passage, the residue of such a stone would impact a surface.

But, in this case, such interpretations would have proved erroneous.

Several of the girls screamed and covered their ears, and shrank down in their chains, and large, rough men, startled, cried out in alarm.

It seemed a roaring projectile was now hurtling toward them, from over the sea, beyond the delta, and then it was passing overhead, taking its way past the village, northwest. The dusk was blasted with the sudden light of its brief, linear passage, and the air tore at them, affrighted with noise and heat, and then the object disappeared, descending into the marshes.

Cornhair lay in the darkness, her two hands on the chain, padlocked about her neck, which fastened her to the others.

Some yards away there was a small fire, and some boatmen, four or five, gathered about it, drinking.

From where she lay, she could hear the soft sounds of the river, the flowing, the rippling and stirring, the pressing amongst the reeds, the eddying about trees, lower trunks under the water. Interestingly, she had never noticed such sounds during the day. But at night, it was different. There was, too, the smell of rich, rotting detritus at its borders.

There was, too, the sound of some insects.

She suddenly became aware of a movement in the darkness, near her. It was a small party of men, three men, apparently those who had boarded the keel boat four days ago, before dawn, at the delta village. Shortly after their arrival the keel boat's matted sail was raised, and the boat was poled from the wharf, to essay the long journey upstream to Telnar. She had not really seen the newcomers as she, with the other slaves, now chained to one another by the neck, were forward, behind a leaning canvas sheet fixed on poles, which might, if it were wished, be raised, and adjusted, to shield the girls from the sun, or, if it were thought judicious to conceal cargo, be drawn over them. Doubtless one of the main motivations for this arrangement, having the girls forward and behind the canvas wall, was to conceal the slaves from the sight of the crew. River men, no matter how unruly and rowdy they might be ashore, are commonly reliable and disciplined while doing the business of the boat. On the other hand, Orik, the captain of the keel boat, presumably saw little point in subjecting discipline, at least unnecessarily, to what might prove to be excessive stress.

Cornhair lay very quietly.

She again felt the chain on her neck. It would hold her well in place, as it did the others. The chain had been taken about a large tree, and then closed. The girls were thus held to one another by the chain, and, by the chain, to the tree itself.

"How helpless we are," thought Cornhair to herself. "They do with us what they want." She twisted a little in the grass. "But why not?" she asked herself. "It is fitting; we are their animals, the animals of men. I am a slave. I want a Master. I need a Master! How free I am, that I am now a slave. I am now free to belong to a Master, to be owned. I hope that I am beautiful enough to be pleasing to a Master. I do not want to be whipped."

The three men were now close to her.

They had avoided the fire.

They spoke softly.

It seemed clear they did not wish to be overheard.

They had remained muchly in the deck cabin, during the day.

Then, suddenly, they ceased speaking.

A lantern was approaching, from the side of the river, moving inshore.

"Greetings," said a voice, that of Gundlicht, to the three men. Gundlicht, and several others, of the men of Ortog, were accompanying the slaves west. Ortog himself, Cornhair gathered, had remained behind in the village with the larger set of slaves, presumably waiting until the blockade might be lifted, and he, with his ships, some four, she gathered, might make their departure. Indeed, for all Cornhair knew, the blockade might have been lifted already, and Ortog might have taken his leave. Indeed, perhaps even now the ships of the barbarian, Abrogastes, had been destroyed, or had fled, fearing the arrival of imperial fleets.

"Greetings," said one of the three men to Gundlicht.

Cornhair feared, suddenly, she had heard the voice before.

"Do not lift your lantern to our faces," said another.

"It matters not," said Gundlicht, "I do not know you."

"You might remember us," said another voice.

"Very well," said Gundlicht, turning away with the lantern. "I am doing slave check."

He then began to make his way about the chain.

"Have I heard that voice before?" Cornhair asked herself. "Perhaps long ago, perhaps when I was free. If only he would speak more, so that I might rid myself of this apprehension, that I might recognize the foolishness of my uneasiness. I could not have heard that voice before. It is impossible."

The lantern was then beside Cornhair, who turned her face away, frightened, away from the light.

She did not wish any of the three men, there in the darkness, to see her features. What if one of them was he whom she feared it might be?

"Oh!" she sobbed, for Gundlicht had seized her head by the

hair, and turned it toward him, holding it helplessly before him, its features exposed, in the full illumination of the lantern.

"A slave is to be looked upon as men please," said Gundlicht, holding her head still, in the light.

"Yes, Master," whispered Cornhair. "Forgive me, Master!"

Then Gundlicht released her, and she put her head down, away from the light.

The lantern moved away.

The three men, in converse to one side, seemed preoccupied. It was not likely they had noticed the discomfiture and fear of a slave.

Too, what would it matter? Slaves are unimportant.

Supposedly Telnar was to be reached tomorrow, in the afternoon. She and the others would then, she supposed, be housed ashore and, within two or three days, sold, individually or as a lot.

Until this night, Cornhair, wisely or not, had had only the fears common to a slave, who would buy her, to what sort of Master would she belong, would she be able to please him, would he permit her to use her hands to feed herself, would she be permitted clothing, would he keep her on all fours and refuse her speech, would she be whip-trained to his pleasure, and such? But now, given that wisp of a word heard in the darkness, matters seemed far more problematical.

We recall that, long ago, at least in part because of her beauty, she had been recruited for a sensitive, clandestine mission by no less a personage than Iaachus, the Arbiter of Protocol in the emperor's court. She had failed, utterly, in this mission, though she had little doubt that a mistaken account of her success had been transmitted to the Arbiter. Those who had misreported the outcome of her mission would presumably now be zealous to protect themselves, at her expense, for her discovery would prove the error of their report. Indeed, they had doubtless assumed her successful, and had fled Tangara, to leave her to her fate. But she had not been slain, following lengthy tortures, by the Otungen, but, rather, perhaps because of the failure of her mission, had been sold to Heruls, to be a "pig slave," a cattle bell chained on her neck. And what would she have to hope for should she come, too, to the attention of the Arbiter himself, for surely she knew far too much, having been privy to his original plot, the secret arranging of an assassination, and would constitute a threat to his security and power.

Hitherto she had assumed that she, now a nondescript, unimportant property, just another slave, more beautiful than some, less beautiful than others, in the business of worlds had nothing to fear.

Was not being on a chain the most perfect of concealments? How could one better hide than by being just another animal in a cage, not sought, not noticed, not important, not expected? Who would look for the former Lady Publennia Calasalia, of the Larial Calasalii, in a slave house? Who would see her in a string of slaves? Who would see her as a commodity on a slave shelf, a placard hung about her neck? Who would see her in a naked, nameless slave being vended under torches in a cheap market? Who would see her as a tender of pigs, a carrier of water in the fields, a server of *kana* in a tavern, a cheap girl in a poor man's hut, a house girl in the palace of a merchant prince?

"Yes," thought Cornhair, "there is invisibility, protection, security, on a chain or in a cage, but, if one is seen, there is no escape from the chain; if one is noted, there is no escape from the cage; it has bars.

But she feared she had recognized the voice in the darkness.

Down by the river, she heard one of the boatmen, keeping a guard between the camp and the river. "Away, beast!" he said, and apparently, with a pole, shoved something back into the water, a river thing we suppose, which we will call a "crocodile," rather as we have spoken of horses, pigs, dogs, and such. The general configurations involved, the ecological niches occupied, and such, would seem to excuse, if not justify, such liberties.

Cornhair strained her hearing.

But the three men spoke in low tones. Had she recognized a voice, from a clue so slight? Of course not; it would have been impossible.

"Why," Cornhair wondered, "had the crocodile emerged from the river, so near the keel boat, at the edge of the camp? Surely this was unusual. It prefers to make its kills in the water. Even should it seize something on land, or in shallow water, say, an animal come to the river to drink, it drags it back into the water to drown it, before feeding. It seldom attacks at night. Usually it would leave the water only to lay its eggs or sun itself. Yet it had come out of the water, in the vicinity of a keel boat which would surely be unfamiliar to it, and a visible fire, which would presumably constitute another anomaly, likely to be aversive to its form of life. It was not a curious, mammalian land creature, not a dog, a wolf, a vi-cat, or such.

Then Cornhair dismissed the matter.

Had she recognized the voice? Presumably not.

But she was aware, almost a moment later, of a change which had taken place in the attitudes and dispositions of the three men whose presence she had earlier noted. They seemed tensely alert, and had separated themselves. She heard the unmistakable sound of a blade being withdrawn from a sheath. She also heard a small click, which she failed to understand. This was the disengagement of a Telnarian pistol's trigger lock.

Almost at the same time some dull, blunt sounds, like logs scraping against, or striking against, a hull, came from the far side of the keel boat, and there was the sound of men scrambling over the gunwales of the boat, from small boats which had been brought alongside the keel boat. Cries of alarm instantly arose. Some of the keel boat's crew, who had been sleeping on the deck, sprang to their feet. Most of the crew was ashore, a few about the fire, most away from the light, in sleeping bags or wrapped in blankets. Weapons were seized. The fellows about the fire kicked it apart. Some of the fellows who had been on the deck of the keel boat, those who could, leaped into the water and waded to shore. At the same time bodies were rushing through the darkness toward the river from the shore side. Men turned to face them. Slaves awakened, screaming. Bodies were grappling in the darkness. "Take these!" said a voice. There was an angry rattle of chain. "They are chained!" said another voice. "Herd them away!" he was ordered. "The chain is fastened about the tree!" said the second man. "Cut it, break it!" he was told. Slaves crouched down. Cornhair covered her head. Then other men were about. Bodies moved in the darkness, there were cries of pain. "A swordsman!" cried a fellow, alarmed. "Who is captain?" demanded a great voice, and Cornhair feared she knew that voice. When no answer was received to this inquiry, a sword must have moved with great swiftness. Men were mixed in the darkness. "Who is captain?" cried the great voice, again and again, exultantly. And when no answer was received, the blade apparently moved again, and again. "More!" cried the great voice, laughing, "more, my blade is thirsty!" "Run!" cried a man in the darkness, and it seemed the interlopers who had come from behind the camp turned and fled. "I know the voice," thought Cornhair in misery, though she had never heard it so before, so pleased, so claimant, so fierce, so darkly bright, so exultant, so terrible. "Men are monsters," thought Cornhair, "and they are our Masters!" The three men whom Cornhair had marked before, still little more than shapes in the night, one very large, now turned toward the shore, where fighting ensued, half in the mud, half in the water. The weapons of river men, friend and foe, were few, and simple, but such as served their purposes, weapons of the taverns and alleys, of mud streets, of reddened wharves and decks, the knife and ax, rocks, fists and teeth, boots and clubs, for river men will fight and kill, and

gouge, and maim, and penetrate, and bite, and strike and stran-
gle as they can, sometimes in earnest, sometimes in the mere
ebullience of high spirits.

There was a sudden hiss and a cord of fire briefly illuminated
the terrain away from the river. The backs of fleeing, stumbling
men were seen. Also, briefly noted, were several crumpled
shapes, sprawled in the foreground. Apparently there was little
to be feared from that quarter at present. "Shall we pursue?"
asked a voice. "Not in the darkness," said another, that voice
which Cornhair feared she knew.

Almost at the same time as the shot was fired into the darkness, away from the river, the melee at the river, at the bank, in
the water, ceased. "A firearm!" someone cried. "A pistol!" cried
another. "A rifle!" cried another, from the deck of the keel boat.

The immediate, startled silence which followed the firing
of the pistol, the cessation of action, was the product of astonishment, on the part of both attackers and defenders, as such
weaponry was almost unknown on the river. This is not surprising. We earlier noted the widespread diminution of many finite
resources in the empire. There were worlds in which a town or
city might be given for a rifle, one or more women for a cartridge. To one who holds lightning in one's hand, even a bolt or
two, little is to be denied. Such things have not unoften paved
the path to thrones. He who carries a rifle, as the saying has it,
carries a scepter. In any event, the empire collects and hordes
such things, fuels, explosives, and such, zealously, as it can,
and, comparably, they are as avidly sought by barbarian nations.
Presumably it had not occurred to the raiders that they might
encounter such a weapon on the river. Its display and activa-
tion, from their point of view, would come as a most unwelcome
surprise. A fox entering a *varda* coop does not expect to find a
vi-cat in residence.

"Axes!" cried a voice, from the deck of the keel boat. "Cut
the lines!"

At the same time, a second charge was loosed from the weapon which streamed overhead, past the keel boat, and ended in a blast of fire, with a tree raging like a torch, on the opposite shore. The charge had been expended, one supposes, to inform the raiders of their jeopardy, and to illuminate, however briefly, the terrain.

Cornhair saw bodies, as though frozen, in the water, on the bank, on the deck of the keel boat, illuminated faces, startled, bright cloths, painted timbers, then darkness, again.

"Cut the lines!" cried the voice, again, from the deck of the keel boat.

Cornhair heard men splashing through the water, toward the hull of the boat. She supposed some raiders, others, members of the crew. Some were surely cut down before they could climb to the deck. She heard the chopping of axes at the boat's rail, doubtless striking at the mooring ropes, that the boat might be freed to the current. She also heard a hideous cry which suggested that the men were not alone in the water.

"Torches!" cried Orik. "Let us see what we kill!"

No torches were lit on the deck of the keel boat, but two were soon flaming on the bank, and they cast their weird, frantic light out to the keel boat and yards behind it, to the dark, shimmering river. Some small dugouts were drawing away from the keel boat. Other men were swimming to them. One disappeared, screaming, beneath the surface. The keel boat, freed, began to turn in the current, moving from the bank. There was a cry of exultation from some raiders on its deck. And then Cornhair, standing, looking to the river, saw, in the light of the torches, a mighty figure, half again the size of a large man, wade into the water and seize the rudder, holding it, and turning it, and then beginning, foot by foot, to thrust the great form back toward the bank. Other men rushed into the water, with lines, to secure it to the shore. Those on the deck of the keel boat then, with cries of dismay and rage, leapt into the water, swimming after the dugouts moving downstream.

The giant waded to the bank, where he, by extended hands, under torchlight, was helped to ascend to the level of the towing path.

"The cargo is safe," said Orik, captain of the keel boat.

"You did well," said a crewman to the giant.

"It is long since I have laughed with steel," said the giant.

"A better watch should have been kept," said one of the companions of the giant, holstering a pistol, it now less two charges.

"How is it you have such a weapon?" asked one of the river men.

"That I have it is important," said the man, "nothing else. Inquire no further."

"We are near Telnar," said Orik. "Raiders never come this far west."

"Some did," said the man with the pistol.

"We feared only the beasts of the river, that they might crawl ashore," said Orik.

"One did," said a man.

"You might easily have lost your boat and cargo," said the man with the pistol.

"This is safe country," said Orik.

"Not so safe for pirates," laughed a crewman.

"You should carry professional guards," said another man, who was the third of the three Cornhair had noted in the darkness, those who had been conversing quietly amongst themselves. He was unarmed. "Spearmen, bowmen, crossbowmen," he added.

"Who can afford them?" asked a man.

"What good are they?" asked another. "They are not rudder men, not even docksmen. They do not pole. They do not handle the lines or sail. They do not pull from the bank. They sleep, they eat. They are passengers one must pay."

"Still," said the third fellow.

"Only greater boats hire such," said Orik.

"This part of the Serpent is safe, or supposedly so?" said the man with the pistol.

"Always," said Orik. "I do not understand."

"We do not always carry such passengers," said a man, indicating the giant and his two companions.

"What is their business, in Telnar?" asked a man.

"Our business in Telnar," said the man with the pistol, "is ours, not yours. It may seem mysterious to you. Let it be so. But our presence here is unlikely to have been known. I think you must search further for your explanation."

"If," said the third man, he who had been with the giant and his companion, "the explanation is not to be well given in terms of our presence, or of the captain, or of the crew, or of the cargo, or such, one must seek elsewhere."

"Where?" said the man with the pistol.

"In Telnar," said the third man. "Something is different in Telnar."

"What?" asked the man with the pistol.

"I do not know," said the third man.

"This may affect our plans," said the man with the pistol.

"I fear so," said the third man.

Cornhair saw the lantern again approaching.

"Kneel, pretty pigs, heads up," said Gundlicht, moving about the tree, the lantern lifted.

Cornhair, despite her misgivings, obeyed. Masters are not tolerant of disobedience, or dalliance, in slaves.

Happily none of the men at the shore took note of Gundlicht's inspection. Still, Cornhair was grateful to find herself once again in the darkness.

"What of the slaves?" inquired Orik.

"Frightened," said Gundlicht, returned to the shore. "None injured, none buffeted, none cut."

"All is tidy on the chain?" said a man.

"Yes," said Gundlicht.

"Extinguish the torches," said Orik. "We shall rest now, and return to the river at dawn."

"Set a firm and dutiful watch," said the man with the pistol.

"We shall," said Orik.

"On the river," said the man with the pistol, "my companions and I will remain in the cabin."

"As you wish," said Orik.

"Our arrival in Telnar will be as anticipated?" asked the man with the pistol.

"I think so," said Orik. "We should wharf in the afternoon, the late afternoon."

"My companions and I will remain in the cabin until after dark," said the man with the pistol. "We shall then disembark."

"As you wish," said Orik.

"You know nothing of us," said the man with the pistol. "You have not seen us."

"I know nothing of you," said Orik. "I have not seen you."

"You were fortunate to survive the crash of your ship in the marshes," said a man.

"Few have pierced the blockade," said a man, "and even fewer without cost."

"The penalties of detection are commonly weighty," said a man.

"Do you know anything of a ship, my friends?" asked the man with the pistol.

"No," said Orik. "We know nothing of a ship."

"Good," said the man with a pistol.

"But mayhap, of a purse of gold," said one of the crew.

"Silence may be as easily purchased with steel as gold," said the man with the pistol.

"We are silent," said Orik.

"We owe you our lives," said a crewman.

"I am weary," said the giant. "I think that I shall sleep."

"After what you have done?" asked one of the crew.

"My sword has fed," said the giant.

"You are not Telnarian," said a man.

"You are not of civilization," said another.

"There are many civilizations," said the man with the pistol.

The giant then turned away, to return to his blankets.

"What of the fallen," asked the man with the pistol, "ours and theirs? Are they to be buried, or burned?"

"They will be returned to the river," said Orik.

"I see," said the man with the pistol. "There are many civilizations."

A watch was then set, and men returned to their places of rest, some near where the fire had been, some back, away from the fire, and some on the deck of the keel boat itself.

Cornhair lay on her side, her head on her elbow, the chain running beneath her elbow and neck.

"They do not know I am here," she thought. "So far then, I am safe. In daylight they will remain sequestered in the deck cabin. They would not know of my presence. Even should they emerge, doubtless the canvas shelter will be set, and they could not see me, or the others, unless intending to do so, which is unlikely. They will wish to remain unseen. I think there are things on their mind quite other than eye feasts. So I, as the others, will be concealed from them. And they will not emerge at Telnar until after dark. By that time I, and the other slaves, will be well disembarked. I do not know their business in Telnar, but doubtless it has naught to do with buying slaves. Larger, darker matters, I suspect, are afoot. I have escaped their notice. Soon I should be purchased, and be safe, as safe as any slave can be safe, and I am beautiful, so I, even if harshly punished, should be more safe than many others."

It had been a difficult night for Cornhair, and her collar sisters. There had been the raid, and the fighting. They might have been carried off, or herded away, as the sort of stock, or cattle, they were, one form of loot amongst others. But the raid had been beaten off, and things were now muchly returned to normal. There was little to be concerned with now other than the prices they might bring off the shelves or blocks, and the new Masters before whom they must kneel.

To be sure, Cornhair's apprehension had exceeded that of her collar sisters in certain ways.

There had been no mistaking, in the light of the torches, the three strangers near the shore. She had seen the three before, on Tangara, in an imperial camp, on a dark cold night, a cloudy winter night, long ago, a remote camp set in the snow, ringed with its defensive wire, a camp at the edge of a deep forest into which few would intrude, in which it was said that Otungs roamed.

She had failed in her attempt to kill the giant, whom she had been commissioned to assassinate with a poisoned knife.

He was Otto, the king of a Vandal tribe, the Otungs, or, perhaps better, Ottonius, a captain of auxiliaries. The other two, who had hurried to the camp to warn the giant of his danger, had arrived at the camp shortly after her failed attempt to complete her projected work. One was Julian, of the Aureliani, of high family, cousin even to the emperor, an officer in the imperial navy, he whom she knew was feared by Iaachus as a possible pretender to the throne, and the other was an agent and colleague of the scion of the Aureliani, a Tuvo Ausonius.

CHAPTER THIRTY-FOUR

"Aside! Aside!" cried the driver.

Cornhair, chained under the canvas, hand and foot, on the shallow, flat-topped wagon, with four others, jolted and bruised, wept.

She could smell smoke. She heard shouting. She had the sense men were running about. She could see nothing.

The horses squealed, and the whip cracked.

The large wooden wheels of the wagon trundled over the stones. The wagon dipped. The flatbed lurched.

The slaves cried out, frightened.

Something cut at the canvas, a long slash, as the wagon sped on its way.

"Aside!" cried the driver.

The whip cracked again, and there was a cry of pain, of rage.

"Aside, I said!" the driver shouted. And then he addressed the horses. "On! On!" he cried, the whip cracking. "On! On!"

This was not a common wagon, or dray wagon, with mountable sides, to enclose a wagon bed, not even a rustic slave wagon, with its rings for girl chains.

Surely it was a far cry from the treaded carrier with the linked steel mesh in which Cornhair and others were first transported through the streets of Telnar, to be delivered to a slave house, and thence, soon, to a street market, a woman's shelf market.

She had heard no hoverers, or motorized vehicles, since she had been disembarked from the keel boat two days ago. The wharves had been little frequented.

"It is uneasy in Telnar," Gundlicht had been told, shortly after the wharfing of the keel boat. "The city is unruly. Lawlessness reigns in the streets."

"Many have left the city," said another fellow.

"Those who could," said another.

Whatever Gundlicht and his fellows had been told, it had apparently convinced them to return quickly to the delta, to rejoin their lord, the barbarian, Ortog.

"These are fine slaves," Gundlicht had told the wharf dealers, those few whose houses were not yet barred shut, their stock removed from the city.

"Acceptable merchandise," he was told, "but fit for better times. Take them east. Return in six months."

"Coin now," had said Gundlicht.

"I make you out a barbarian, friend," had said a dealer. "Your life, and that of your companions, would be worth little in Telnar at any time, and now, I fear, even less. Surely you know of the blockade. A landing is feared. A beard, a strange accent, a garment of hide, a trim of fur, could loose the arrows of guardsmen, the clubs and knives of the beasts who now prowl the streets."

"Coin now," said Gundlicht.

"Two hundred for the lot," said the dealer.

"That is less than ten per slave, is it not?" said Gundlicht.

"As it happens," said the dealer.

"That is not enough," said Gundlicht.

"It is my offer," said the dealer.

"I will sell you the lot," said Gundlicht, "for five hundred *darins*."

"That is an excellent wholesale price," said a man, a bystander.

"Two hundred," said the dealer.

"Most houses seem closed," said Gundlicht.

"They hope for better times," said the dealer.

"Your house is open," said Gundlicht.

"And I risk much by keeping it so," said the dealer.

"Why have you not fled, as many others?" asked Gundlicht.

"There is still a market for slaves," said the dealer. "There is always a market for slaves."

"Five hundred *darins*," said Gundlicht.

"Times are hard," said the dealer.

"Five hundred *darins*," said Gundlicht.

"Times are hard," said the dealer. "Two hundred."

"No," said Gundlicht.

"Times are unsettled," said the dealer. "Prices are depressed. Pirates range westward."

"Five hundred," said Gundlicht.

"One hundred and fifty," said the dealer.

"The wharves are muchly deserted," said Gundlicht. "Few guardsmen are about."

"They have been called to the city, to contain a confused, stirring populace," said the dealer.

"Thus, they are not here," said Gundlicht.

"So?" said the dealer, uneasily.

"Five hundred," said Gundlicht, "and I will throw in your business."

"I do not understand," said the dealer.

"Light torches," had said Gundlicht, to his fellows.

"Hold," had said the dealer. "I will give you five hundred."

"Six hundred," had said Gundlicht.

"Very well," had said the dealer, "six hundred."

"That is not a bad price," had said a bystander.

Cornhair cried out in misery as the wagon jolted.

The wagon, a common flatbed, was not designed for the transportation of slaves. It was designed for the convenient loading and unloading of heavy materials, such as lumber, sewerage piping, and blocks of stone. Certainly more suitable conveyances were in short supply in the vicinity of the wharves, but exigency was not the explanation for the selection of this particular vehicle.

"Deliver these to the House of Worlds, on Varl," the driver had been ordered. The House of Worlds was a major, well-known company, with outlets on several worlds.

"Today?" had asked the driver.

"Have this receipt signed," said the dealer.

Much business in Telnar, incidentally, as in many economies, was conducted in terms of notes of various sorts, exchanged amongst parties. Such notes were not generally negotiable. Few would prove of interest, or value, to a common thief. Considerable sums, as one would expect, might be transferred amongst businesses, and even amongst worlds, without a physical *darin* being moved.

"Better tomorrow, next week," said the driver.

"You will proceed easily, and in safety," said the dealer. "No one will know your cargo. We are not chaining them to the back of the wagon, where they must follow on neck chains. They will be covered with a canvas. From the nature of this wagon, none will suspect the nature of your delivery."

"Tomorrow," said the driver.

"Days have passed," said the dealer. "Why should tomorrow, or the next day, be better? I am going to close the house. I depart from the city. There may be a landing in Telnar."

"Surely not," said the driver. "Surface batteries would incinerate any intruder within range."

"Keep the receipt," said the dealer. "Bring it to my villa."

Cornhair and her four collar sisters were the last of the twenty-two slaves recently purchased from Gundlicht. Each was in a market collar, identifying them as having been sold to the House of Worlds. The market collars had been affixed by an agent of the House of Worlds after the sale had been arranged. Each was naked and ankle-shackled. The hands of each were chained behind their back.

Cornhair was not much pleased that she was in the last group of girls disposed of by the dealer, before he would leave the city.

Surely she and the other four were not poor stuff.

Cornhair knew little of what was transpiring in the city, but she had gathered, from a hundred things said and not said, from a hundred hesitations, and glances, that something, as Tuvo Ausonius had said earlier, near the shore of the river, was now different in Telnar.

Were she a free woman, perhaps she would have fled the city. But she, as horses and dogs, would remain, or depart, as Masters wished.

"Oh," she said, as she was lifted, the fourth of the five, by the driver onto the boards of the wagon.

"Lie on your bellies," said the driver, "and keep silent. I have a whip, and it may be used on you as easily as on the horses."

The whip then lightly touched each on the back.

"Yes, Master," said each, as she felt, in turn, the touch of the whip.

The canvas was then drawn over them.

"May good fortune attend you," said the dealer.

"And you," said the driver.

And then the reins were shaken, the whip cracked, and the wagon lurched forward.

"Hold!" demanded a voice.

Cornhair was thrown forward on the boards. She heard the protesting squeals of the horses.

"Stand aside!" said the driver.

"We allow no wagons here!" said a voice.

"A pity," said the driver. "Rioters must then carry their loot on their backs. Remove the bar!"

"The road is raw," said the voice.

"How so?" said the driver.

"The road has been trenched, to withstand guardsmen, to impede transports," said the man. "Stones have been pulled free, for hurling, for building barricades."

"This district was pacified," said the driver.

"Two days ago," said the voice. "Not now."

"You are no guardsman," said the driver. "Move aside the bar. Stand aside!"

"I am guardsman enough," said the fellow. "This is our orchard now."

"Where you pick gold," said the driver.

"What have you there, beneath that canvas?" said the voice.

"Rock," said the driver, "for street work, for fillage on Varl."

"Varl is quiet," said the man.

"Good," said the driver.

"Lion Ships prowl the sky," said the voice. "Mobs unbridled roam streets. Guardsmen are few. Districts burn."

"*Civilitas* is fragile, and easily cast aside," said the driver.

"And you, in these times, are carrying stone, for street work?" said the voice.

"Stand aside," said the driver.

"We shall see," said the voice.

"Ho!" cried the driver. "On!" The whip cracked, the horses plunged forward, there was a breakage of wood, a cry of anger, and the wagon, half tipping, rumbled forward.

Cornhair heard men shouting.

"Stop! Stop!" she heard.

Someone must have clutched at the canvas, and lost his grip, for it jerked on the bodies of the slaves, but was not much disarranged.

The wagon rolled on for several minutes, lurching, the whip cracking, the clawed paws of the horses scratching at the stones of the street.

Then the wagon, lifting half off two wheels on the left, turned a corner, and sped forward, even more swiftly.

"Hold!" Cornhair heard cry, more than once. There was a sharp sound of steel interacting with wood, as some implement struck at the passing wagon. A bit later, from the sound, a blow and cry, one of the horses must have buffeted aside someone on foot.

Suddenly Cornhair cried out with fear for an arrow, perhaps fired from a high window or rooftop, piercing the canvas, was in the planking at her shoulder.

"Steeds, on, steeds, on!" cried the driver.

"Stop!" she heard, again. "Stop! Stop!"

There must have been men about, for cries came from all sides.

Men must have fled from the path of the rushing, hurtling vehicle, as it sped amongst them.

A short time later, the wagon slowed, and then stopped.

The canvas was drawn aside.

"Off, off," said the driver.

The five slaves were put on their feet, in a line. Cornhair was placed third in line, as the two girls before her were taller than she, the tallest girl first, and the two behind her were shorter than she, the shortest last. It is common to arrange slaves aesthetically.

Cornhair looked wildly about herself.

"We are safe," said the driver. "We have reached the barricade."

"Master?" said one of the girls.

"Men have sealed off this district from the looters," said the driver. "Any who try to cross this border are killed."

On this side of the barricade, which was several feet high, and formed of a miscellany of objects, as carts and wagons, boards, timber, cratage, bags of sand and dirt, furniture, and blocks of paving stone, there were, as is common in Telnar, several street level shops. These were empty and dark, abandoned. The boards of their wooden closing screens were missing or strewn on the street; the rods and chains which would have held them in place, when they had been fitted into their receiving slots, in floor and ceiling, lay about. Some bolt rings had been pried from the wall. Here and there, broken, massive padlocks dangled. Some of these shops were black from the residue of burning. The smell of smoke lingered, infecting the air, clinging to surfaces. In none of these shops, even those free of fire, could Cornhair see aught but vacancy and ruin, tables with broken legs, chairs fallen, and awry, debris scattered on floors, empty shelves, some broken from the sides of the shop.

"Bring your goods through here," said a man, high on the barricade.

He indicated a narrow opening below him and to his right, where two other men had swung back a makeshift gate of planks, with projecting spikes.

"Move," said the driver.

The slaves, in line, proceeded.

"They are nicely shackled, close shackled," said a man.

"They will not rush quickly away, so impeded," said a fellow.

"I think they will stay muchly where we want them," said another.

Within the barricade Cornhair saw there were several more men, variously armed, most with clubs.

"The ankles of women look well in shackles," said a fellow.

"Consider their hands, chained behind their backs," said another, approvingly.

"Excellent," said another.

"Women look well, stripped and in chains," said a man.

"Would that we had our free women so," said a man.

Slaves may be discussed so, for they are not free women.

The fellow at the height of the barricade, who seemed to be first amongst these men, called out, apparently to some

fellows beyond the barricade, in the vicinity of the looted
shops.

"Stay away!" he called out. "If you come here we will club
out your brains, if you have any!"

"Keep moving," said the driver. "It is not far now."

To her surprise, Cornhair heard music, coming from a tavern.
Within there were lights. Men loitered about.

Too, here, behind the barricade, some shops were open, and
men were about, though she saw no women. Cornhair did not
realize it but there were parts of Telnar to which the general
unrest in the city had not much penetrated, or, perhaps better,
had not been permitted to much penetrate. Many of the windows in the walls above the shops did remain shuttered. Fear,
she supposed, hid behind shutters. Strange, she thought, how
life might differ, from one side of a wall to another, how *civilitas* and the jungle might exist within yards of one another. In
parts of Telnar, musicians and street dancers performed, recitals
and plays were presented; poets sang their work to the music of
flute and lyre; in other parts, streets were unlit and doors were
bolted, blood flowed and men roamed the streets like wolves.

"We are here," said the driver. "Stand here. I will deliver
you. I must have a receipt."

He strode to a heavy double door, and swung the knocking
ring thrice against its bolted metal plate.

He turned back to the slaves.

"You are to be sold tonight," he said.

He was then admitted.

The slaves, naturally, remained in place. Should the Masters
return, and find them elsewhere, even slightly, or differently
ordered, it might mean the lash.

In a few moments two men emerged from the double door,
the driver and another, from within.

He from within carried a switch.

Slaves view such things with apprehension.

How different it is from being a free woman!

The driver folded a paper, and thrust it into his tunic, presumably the receipt. "I must gather my horses," he said. "I abandon the wagon. It is an impediment. It has been noted. Perhaps, with good fortune, in better days, it can be reclaimed."

"Return by some circuitous route," suggested the man from within.

"I return not now at all," said the driver. "I am under a different instruction."

"The wharf house is closed, I take it," said the man.

"Things there are not safe," said the driver.

"Things are not safe here, either," said the man from within.

"I fear a landing," said the driver.

"The palace and senate have proclaimed such a thing impossible," said the man from within.

"Let us hope that dreaded Abrogastes is listening," said the driver.

"There are the batteries," said the man from within.

"That is true," said the driver.

"Farewell," said the man from within.

"Farewell," said the driver.

The driver then turned about to unharness his horses, and the man from within, with his switch, approached the slaves, and regarded them, not speaking.

"Lift your heads," he said.

The slaves stood, and stood well, not wishing to be cuffed, or switched.

Inspected, they refrained from meeting his eyes.

Slaves are accustomed to being looked upon by men.

It is part of being a slave.

"Average goods," he said.

He then tapped the first girl lightly with the switch indicating she should proceed within.

"You, too," he said to the second girl.

With a rustle of her shackling, she followed the first girl.

He paused at the side of Cornhair, but then, to her uneasiness, moved beyond her.

Why was that?

And could it be true, that they were "average goods"?

"I like red hair," he said to the girl behind Cornhair. "I think you will bring your share of *darins*. Why were you not, I wonder, in an earlier lot?"

She then moved forward, making her way through the double doors. Cornhair could see lamp light within.

Why was I not in an earlier lot, wondered Cornhair. I have been accounted beautiful. Surely, when I was a free woman, I was thought beautiful, very beautiful. And, indeed, was beauty not germane to the plans of Iaachus, Arbiter of Protocol, when he sought to recruit an agent for a clandestine mission of great import, an arbitration of delicate political matters by means of a poisoned dagger? Well do I remember when I, to my indignation, to my mortification, to my outrage and humiliation, was ordered to strip myself, I, the Lady Publennia Calasalia, of the Larial Calasalii, before him, as though I might be a captive, even a slave! But I was found beautiful, even beautiful enough to wear a collar! And thus the poisoned dagger would be delivered to me, and not to another! And as a slave, too, surely men have found me beautiful. Surely it is not difficult to comprehend their appraising regard, their assessment of the likelihood that I might look well on my belly before them, my lips pressed to their boots.

"You, Slave Five," said the man, "have a nice width, would be a cuddly package in a Master's grasp."

Cornhair heard a rustle of chain, but the slave did not respond.

"You came from the delta, by keel boat," he said.

"Yes, Master," she said.

"Proceed," he said. "Inside, your chains will be removed, and before you are put in your cage, you will be washed and fed."

"Yes, Master," she said. "Thank you, Master."

Cornhair, understandably, was uneasy, at her apparent neglect.

She felt the switch under her chin, and she lifted her head more.

"You tremble," he said. "Are you afraid?"

"Yes, Master," she whispered.

"You are rather slight," he said.

"Forgive me, Master," she said.

"But such as you look well, stripped, on your hands and knees, in a cage."

Cornhair was silent.

"But all women do," he said.

Cornhair started.

"Yes," he said, "all women."

He then walked about Cornhair, and paused when he was again on her left.

"Blond hair, blue eyes," he said.

"May I speak?" asked Cornhair.

"Certainly," he said.

"Why does Master concern himself with me?" she asked. "Should I not be within, to be relieved of my impediments, as the others, to be cleaned and fed, before my caging?"

"Yes," he said, "you are the same one. I am sure of it."

"Master?" said Cornhair.

"You were on a sales shelf in Harmony Street," he said, "with others, the placard on your neck. And you failed of a sale in the market of Horace, in Endymion's Way."

"I was soon sold from the house," she said.

"After having entertained the leather, I suspect," he said.

"Yes, Master," she said, wincing, recalling the generous application of the torch of leather to her back, her hands tied over her head, to a ring.

"But you seem different now," he said.

"Different, Master?" she said.

"Let us see," he said.

"Oh!" she said.

"Ah," he said, "the little beast is now ready for a Master."

Cornhair trembled, not speaking.

"What are you?" he asked.

"A slave, Master," she said.

"For what do you exist?"

"To give pleasure to Masters," she said.

"You are going to be pretty on the slave block, are you not?" she was asked.

"I will try, Master," she said.

"You are going to be such on the slave block," said the man, "so desirable, so exciting, and pathetically needful, that every man in the house will want to own you, that every man in the house will want his collar on your neck, that every man in the house will want to throw you in chains to his feet."

"I will try, Master," she said.

"You want to be in a collar, and in chains at a Master's feet," he said.

"Master?" she said.

"You want to be in a collar, and in chains at a Master's feet," he said, again.

"Yes, Master," she said, startled. "I want to be in a collar, and in chains at a Master's feet."

"Yes," thought Cornhair, shaken, and trembling, "I want to be in a collar, and in chains at a Master's feet. I am a slave!"

"Enter," said the man, indicating the portal of the double door, the lamp somewhere within. "Enter, the House of Worlds."

CHAPTER THIRTY-FIVE

"I would feel easier," said Otto, "if I carried the long sword."

"So mighty a blade would speak of barbarism," said Julian. "We need not cleave open the timbers of gates, shatter posts, cut off the heads of horses. Be content with your captain's blade."

"Why could I not wear freer garments?" asked Otto.

"Be content with the uniform of your office," said Julian.

Otto, or Ottonius, it might be recalled, had been commissioned to recruit *comitates* amongst Otungs, to supplement the auxiliary forces of the empire, this in support of the project of Julian of the Aureliani, to stiffen resistance to barbarian influxes of a hostile nature, to shore up threatened borders, to enact selected missions, to enlist barbarians on behalf of a flagging empire, corrupt and degenerating, unwilling or unable to unilaterally mount and sustain its own defenses. Might not the empire be refreshed and invigorated with new blood? Let barbarians see the standards of the empire as their own, to be fought for, even died for, rather than as those of a foe. Sidonicus, Exarch of Telnar, had managed to acquire an artifact, a medallion and chain, high symbol of the Vandal nation, on Tangara, and have it delivered to Ingeld, a Drisriak, the second son of Abrogastes, the Far-Grasper. By means of this artifact, Ingeld hoped to bring together the Alemanni and the Vandals in a coalition which might doom the empire. The reward of Sidonicus, for the bestowal of the medallion and chain on a Drisriak, was to be the conversion of united barbarian nations to a particular faith, not surprisingly his own, which they would then impose on the empire. Interestingly, he was simultaneously negotiating, much to the same end, with the empire, with the end in view that his faith be decreed the official faith of the empire, whilst all other faiths, as false faiths, dangerous to the *koos*, or such, were to be rooted out and destroyed. The empire's reward in this would be that Sidonicus, breaking with Floonian tradition, let alone the teachings of Floon, as nearly as they could be determined, would then release his followers, in their millions, to support and defend the empire, to observe its laws, to pay its taxes, to pledge it allegiance, to take up arms in its behalf, to fight for it, even unto death. In either case, obviously, his faith would be triumphant, whether advanced by the rude insignias of barbarism or by the silver standards of Telnaria itself. The one plot, however, that of the medallion and chain, as we have learned, was subverted when Julian, who was familiar with the original artifact, from the cell of an Emanationist brother in the *festung* of Sim Giadini on Tangara, produced a great many copies of the artifact, which were distributed widely, to the dismay and consternation of Ingeld's projected allies. As a consequence the Alemanni, or the Aatii, as they appear in the imperial accounts, remained the major threat to the empire, and other barbarian nations, in particular, the Vandals, remained to one side, like wolves in the darkness, curious, patient, watching a fire, hostile to the Alemanni, but bearing no love to the empire.

"Why needed my beard be shaved, my hair be cut?" growled Otto.

"Your scrub of a beard was not much of a beard," said Julian.

"Short, it is harder to seize in combat," said Otto.

"Cease complaining, my friend," said Julian, walking briskly forward.

"My hair," grumbled Otto. "What would they say in the hall?"

"You are not in the hall now," said Julian. "In Telnar men do not wear their hair like the mane of a Herul dog."

"How many charges have you left?" asked Otto.

"Four," said Julian. "Two were lost at the river."

"You could buy others," said Otto.

"The empire controls such things," said Julian. "The populace is to be defenseless."

"Like cattle," said Otto.

"It is the empire's way," said Julian.

"In the streets, in the dark, narrow streets?" said Otto.

"I doubt you can find them there now," said Julian. "Months ago, one charge might cost five to ten thousand *darins*, even here, in Telnar. Have you five to ten thousand *darins*?"

"No," said Otto.

"I have concealed the pistol," said Julian. "If it was known we had such a weapon, we might be killed for it."

"*Civilitas*," said Otto, scornfully.

"*Civilitas*," said Julian, "is more frequently praised than practiced."

"Men stare at me," grumbled Otto.

"And they might stare at a *torodont*, were it walking here, on Palace Street," said Julian. "You are large, your stride, your coloring, are not typically Telnarian."

"Good," said Otto.

"At least you are not clad in skins, with a necklace of claws," said Julian. "Remember your troubles on the Summer World."

This remark pertained to an occurrence which had taken place several months ago.

"There is the senate," said Julian. "See the columns, the dome."

"Is this wise, to approach the palace?" asked Otto. "Surely Iaachus, and others, perhaps even the empress mother, have little love for the Aureliani, and any enleagued with them. Indeed, we established on Tangara, from the blond slave, that it was he,

Iaachus, who hoped to strike at you, and your plans, by means of my assassination."

"By the way," said Julian, "you slew the slave, after lengthy tortures, did you not?"

"No," said Otto. "We marked her, and sold her to Heruls. She sold for one pig."

"Excellent," said Julian. "There are better things to do with a woman than kill her. Their necks look well in collars. Collars keep them nicely in their place."

"Others escaped," said Otto, "Phidias, captain of the *Narcona*, and two others, lesser officers, a Lysis and a Corelius."

"I have no doubt they reported the work well done to Iaachus," said Julian.

"And yet," said Otto, "we approach the palace?"

"Surely Iaachus will not slay us before the throne," said Julian. "Too, I think things may have changed. Iaachus is a devious fellow, but he is not irrational, no more than a knife or pistol. I think that he, in his way, is as concerned for the empire as we, though doubtless only in so far as it advances his own interests."

"You will crave an audience?" asked Otto.

"It cannot be refused," said Julian. "I am cousin to the emperor."

"If we can make it to the gate of the palace grounds," said Otto, looking about himself.

"I think we shall," said Julian. "There are guardsmen about. There is peace here, guaranteed by the drawing of bows, the leveling of spears."

"Not so elsewhere," said Otto.

"No, I think not," said Julian. "I gather that much of the city is in chaos."

"Somewhere, above the blue sky," said Otto, "lurk the Lion Ships of Abrogastes."

"I do not think he can long maintain the blockade," said Julian. "I would give him no more than four days."

Otto walked beside Julian, quietly.

"I do not understand the blockade," said Julian. "Why would it be mounted? What is it to accomplish?"

"Perhaps," said Otto, "it is not a blockade."

CHAPTER THIRTY-SIX

"Who has purchased me, Master?" begged Cornhair. "I could not see. The house was dark. I was illuminated by torchlight."

Cornhair had been sold last night.

She was still, the following morning, in the selling house, that maintained on Varl by the House of Worlds.

The slaver's man held a bit of cloth in his hand.

"One who saw you first in the slave bath," he said, "with the others."

"We were alone," said Cornhair.

"You, and the others," he said, "were seen through the grid, high, in the wall. Did you expect privacy?"

"I thought we were alone," said Cornhair.

"Why do you think the bath chamber was so well lit?" he said. "Why do you think that the bathing pool was only six inches in depth?"

"I see, Master," said Cornhair.

She and the others, able to do little more than sit or stand in it, crouching down, bending down, splashing water on the body, applying the oils, and utilizing the concave, wooden scrapers, had not known about the grid.

Afterwards they had been well fed, for slaves, permitted even to use their hands to feed themselves. Was there not, even, some fruit, some meat, some nuts, mixed with the gruel?

And they had been given a draught of warm *kana* before being put in their small, individual cages.

"He inspected you through the grid," said the slaver's man. "Then he bid on you, while you were being put through slave display."

"I went for forty *darins*," she said.

"You are not a bad looking slave," he said. "But I would have thought, in last night's selling, twenty-five or thirty *darins*."

"What is he like?" asked Cornhair. "Is he handsome, strong, rich?"

"He must be well-fixed," said the man. "He bought you for forty *darins*, yesterday, with the situation in the city as it is."

Cornhair's market collar had been removed.

She was not now collared.

"If he is well-fixed," she said, lightly, "doubtless he will have several slaves, and I will have less work."

"And be less favored, and have less attention, and be less caressed," said the man.

Tears came to Cornhair's eyes.

"You meretricious little baggages," said the slaver's man, "cannot fool me. You are slaves. You all want to be the single slave of a private Master. You want to be his sole slave, the only slave in his house. You wish to be the one who brings him his sandals in your mouth, on all fours. You want to be the only one feeding from the pan at his feet. You want his whip to be his whip for you, and only you. You want to be the only slave helpless in his chains. You wish to be the only vessel upon which he will vent his lust."

"He may have wanted me, very much," said Cornhair.

"Perhaps," said the slaver's man.

"Am I to be picked up, soon?" asked Cornhair.

"Shortly," said the man.

"Master holds a tunic, does he not?" asked Cornhair.

"Yes," he said.

"Should I stand?"

"Remain on your knees," said the man.

"Yes, Master," said Cornhair.

"Do you know what I saw on the block?" asked the man.

"No, Master," said Cornhair.

"A slave," he said.

"I trust so," said Cornhair, softly.

"Are you a bred slave?" he asked.

"Yes, Master," she said, "for I am a woman." She could remember her feelings, even long before the collar had been locked on her neck, even long before the tiny rose had been burned into her thigh.

"Stand," he said.

Cornhair rose to her feet. She felt small before him. She was small before him.

She was frightened of men. There were at least two reasons for this. First, she was a woman, and most women, unless they are unusually dull, realize what men might do with them, if they wished, and, second, she was a female slave, and thus she was one such who realized that men would do with her as they wished.

"Put it on," said the man, tossing her the scrap of cloth.

Swiftly Cornhair pulled the small tunic over her head, and down, about her thighs.

"There is unrest in the city," said the man. "You should be clothed."

"Yes, Master," said Cornhair.

The concept of being clothed is interesting. The same garment which Cornhair received readily and gladly, scarcely more than a scrap of cloth, might have reduced a free woman to rage and tears.

Cornhair tugged down, at the sides of the garment.

"What is wrong?" asked the slaver's man.

"It is too short, is it not?" she asked.

"Would you prefer to be naked?" he asked.

"No, Master," she said.

"It is a slave tunic," he said.

"Yes, Master," she said.

To be sure, there is little to choose from, between being naked and being put in a slave tunic.

Free women wish slaves to be so degraded. Free men wish them to be so exhibited. To be sure, the slave tunic, in a sense, is a badge of female excellence. Its occupant is so attractive that men have made her a slave.

"You may now place your hands behind your back, your wrists crossed," said the slaver's man. "And face the wall."

Cornhair felt her wrists tied behind her, with a short length of leather thong. "It is interesting," she thought, "how with so little, so quickly, a woman can be made so helpless."

"My Master is soon to pick me up?" she said.

"Oh?" she said, surprised, for a slave hood had been drawn over her head, from behind, and, in a moment, it was buckled shut, behind the back of her neck.

"I do not understand," she said.

"Your Master is not picking you up," said the slaver's man. "He is sending two agents."

There was then a sturdy knocking at the door of the chamber.

"Do not kneel," said the slaver's man.

Cornhair heard the door of the chamber swung open, and she gathered that two men, at least two men, had entered.

"This is the slave?" said a voice.

"Yes," said the slaver's man.

Cornhair felt her upper left arm seized in a strong grip, and she was turned about, facing the door.

"Am I to be taken to my Master?" she asked.

Her only response was an ugly laugh.

She was then conducted from the chamber.

CHAPTER THIRTY-SEVEN

"It cannot be!" cried Iaachus, to the startled courtier.

"Lord?" asked the courtier.

"Ambitious Julian, dog of the Aureliani, who would seize the throne, yes," said Iaachus, "but the oaf, Ottonius, his minion, his guard dog, he of the peasants, of the hunting games, the killing games, in a hundred arenas, no! No!"

"It is a captain," said the courtier, "uniformed and emblemed, insignias in order, Ottonius, officer in the Auxiliaries."

"You are sure?" asked Iaachus.

"Yes, Lord," said the courtier, half drawing back. Never had he seen the Arbiter of Protocol so.

"It cannot be," muttered Iaachus.

"I do not understand," said the courtier.

"It is nothing," said Iaachus.

"Is noble Iaachus well?" said the courtier.

"How dare they come here?" asked the Arbiter.

"Lord?" said the courtier, uncertainly.

"Yes, I am well," said Iaachus. "I am very well."

"They crave audience," said the courtier. "Borders succumb. Clubs and torches are brandished in the streets. Rioters rule. Mobs rove with impunity. Guardsmen cower, arrows enquivered, not daring to fire on looters. Lion Ships, unseen, guard corridors. The city burns, the empire totters."

"Who," asked Iaachus, "could deny audience, in such a time, or, indeed, at any time, to the august Julian, he of the Aureliani, cousin to the emperor?"

"Indeed, Lord," said the courtier.

"I shall have the royal family notified," said Iaachus, "the empress mother in her chambers, the royal daughters, and the emperor, too, who must be summoned, however unwillingly, I fear, from his toys."

"You do not understand, Lord," said the courtier. "They crave audience with you, only you, with the Arbiter of Protocol, and in private."

"I see," said Iaachus.

"I do not know the reason for the audience," said the courtier.

"I think I do," said Iaachus.

"Lord?"

"Have guards about," said the Arbiter of Protocol. "Then, admit my guests."

"Yes, Lord," said the courtier.

The Arbiter then went to a side cabinet, and removed, from its satin sheathing, a Telnarian pistol. It was much like that which Julian bore, for both were imperial issue. It contained six charges. One would seldom consider firing such a weapon indoors, for the charge, as normally fired, its beam focused, might take out a wall. Iaachus, studying the weapon, for he was not familiar with its use, adjusted the beam lens, that effecting the distribution of the charge, that a broader, more fanlike emission might be produced. There is an inverse correlation involved in such things, a narrow beam providing a greater range and a more severe, more localized strike, and a wider beam, in which an impact is much reduced but a much larger area is affected. As the weapon was now set, there would be a sudden, flat oval of fire, some ten feet in width at close range, perhaps, say, across a desk, or, as the impact area expanded, some twenty or twenty-five feet in width, at a target some yards away, say, across a room.

Iaachus slipped the pistol into the center drawer of his desk, which he left partly open. He then seated himself in his chair, behind the desk.

CHAPTER THIRTY-EIGHT

Cornhair, hooded, her hands tied behind her, her upper left arm bruised in that powerful grip, was hurried along, half dragged.

Her feet burned from the hot ground. Her ankles had been cut by coarse grass.

She feared she was no longer within the city's walls.

"This is a lonely, vacant place," said the first man, he in whose grip was Cornhair.

"It is not far from the city," said the second man.

"Where are you taking me, Masters?" she said. "Who has purchased me?"

She coughed within the hood, she felt sick, she feared she might vomit.

The sun was hot on her bared arms and legs.

The air was thick, still, oppressive. It reeked with filth and decay. There was an overwhelming atmosphere of spoilage and waste, of urine and excrement, of rotting organic debris, of fish, hide, and flesh. She heard a raucous cry of some form of birds.

"The stench," said one of the men, half choking. "I cannot stand it. Let us go no further. Let it be done quickly."

He, Cornhair surmised, was the second of the two men.

"Masters!" wept Cornhair. "Where are we?"

"They are all about," said the other, he whom Cornhair took to be first, the leader of the two. "Beware of your step. A false step and you might sink within, and die, a most unpleasant demise."

"And the gold would then be yours," said the second.

"Yes," said the first man.

"There is nothing here but snakes, birds, and *filchen*," grumbled the second.

"They do not mind," said the first, "why should you?"

"How can they exist here?" asked the second man.

"Men set tables," said the first. "Guests invite themselves. They feast."

"Let us be done with it," urged the second man.

"After a century they cover them," said the other man, "and excavate new ones. Some opened, even after a thousand years, cannot be approached. Few can stand them. Few will enter their vicinity. Who would do so willingly? Even animals balk. Men are overcome, and faint. They must be dragged away. These things poison the earth."

Cornhair heard a wagon roll nearby, and stop.

"Release the load," called someone, "quickly!"

Cornhair heard a heavy, sliding noise, and, a moment later, a sound, as of weights of debris plunging into mud or quicksand.

"See how it sinks," said the first man, he in whose charge was Cornhair.

"This one, use this one!" said the second man.

"Further, further from the city," said the first man. "You know the orders. There must be no trace."

"He will not know," said the other. "And there will be no trace."

"Done, then!" said the first.

"Masters!" cried Cornhair.

One of the men, the second, then unbuckled Cornhair's hood and drew it away, and Cornhair threw back her head and wailed in misery.

They stood at the edge of one of the giant, circular garbage pits of the city of Telnar, its diameter some twenty yards or so. From where she stood she could see more pits, others, stretching away. There were few men about, at least on foot, but there were some wagons about, one approaching a pit, and the other withdrawing, leaving the vicinity of another pit. She could also see another, far off, returning to the city, whose walls she could see in the distance, perhaps a mile away.

Cornhair looked down into the pit before her. She knew these pits were often a hundred or more feet deep. This pit might have been three-fourths full. She could see the surface below her. It seemed a sea of filth. It was primarily brown, with streaks of black, like oil. There was little that was clearly identifiable in that viscous, semisolid morass but she saw shards of pottery, still held on the surface, and the leg and paw of a horse.

Both men, she saw, had wrapped cloth, like bandages, about their mouth and nose.

The second man picked up a stone and tossed it into the pit and Cornhair, sick, watched it slowly disappear.

"Why have I been brought here, Masters?" she said, scarcely hearing herself speak.

"Why do you think, little slave?" asked the first man.

"I do not know, Master," she said.

"These pits are noxious and noisome, even dangerous," said the first man, "in spreading disease, in breeding parasites, but they have their purposes. For example, they provide a place in which to dispose of the refuse and garbage, the offal, of a city, rotted fruit, the entrails of butchered animals, dead horses, unwanted relatives, enemies, whom one wishes to have disappear, displeasing slaves, and such."

"I would strive to be pleasing, Masters!" Cornhair cried.

"Of course, you are a slave," said the first man.

"What if my Master learns of this?" said Cornhair.

"It is on his orders we act," said the first man.

"Surely not!" said Cornhair.

"It is true," said the first man.

"I do not understand," said Cornhair. "I cost forty *darins*, only forty *darins*, and yet you have been paid in gold to discharge this commission?"

"Six gold *darins*," said the first man.

"Three for each," said the second man.

"And you will do so?" she asked.

"Throw her in, and be done with it," said the second man.

"Who is my Master?" wept Cornhair.

"He gave no name," said the first man.

"Is he of the Larial Farnichi?" said Cornhair.

It may be recalled that the Larial Calasalii and the Larial Farnichi were two great families ill disposed toward one another. Cornhair, when free, and before being disowned, had belonged to the Larial Calasalii. The altercation betwixt these two families had begun as a clash of private armies, but, later, given the intervention of the empire, it had ended with the outlawing and ruination of the Larial Calasalii.

"I do not know," said the first man. "He gave no name, no account of his background or origin."

"He had gold," said the second man. "Who needed to know more?"

"I cost forty *darins*," she said. "Surely that is a fair price for my face, my figure, the pleasure I would do my best to bring a Master. You would cast aside forty *darins* so lightly?"

"Not we," said the first man, "he who bought you, for this."

"Keep me," she begged. "Keep me, for yourself!"

"We would have the gold, and the slave," said the second man.

"Yes, yes, Masters!" said Cornhair.

"It is too dangerous," said the first man.

"This place offends my nostrils, my eyes sting, the sun is hot, my flesh crawls, dispose of her, here, now," said the second man.

"No, no, Masters!" wept Cornhair. She pulled away, wildly, from the first man's grip, spun about, and tried to run, but, in a moment, was caught by the second man, who thrust her back, she struggling, weeping, to the edge of the pit.

Cornhair cast about, wildly, and screamed, "Help! Help! Help a slave, a poor slave, Masters!"

"There is no one to hear you," said the first man.

The nearest wagon, with its driver, and his assistant, was now far away.

"Tie her ankles together," said the first man.

"Why?" asked the second.

"She will sink more rapidly," said the first. "The business will be consummated more expeditiously."

"One cannot swim in this muck," said the second man. "It sucks one down, like quicksand."

"If her legs are not tied, she might be able to keep her head above the surface for two or three minutes."

"No one is about, what does it matter?" asked the second man.

"Do it," said the first, angrily, and put Cornhair to her back, at his feet.

The second man, angrily, whipped a cord from his belt and crouched down beside Cornhair, to loop the cord about her ankles.

Cornhair screamed, for she saw, as the fellow bent over her did not, the knife. He did not even have time to raise his head, for the knife was driven into the base of his skull, into the back of his neck, severing the vertebrae. It took the second man only a minute to die. The first man then wiped his knife on his thigh and returned it to its sheath. He then rifled the purse of the second man, and withdrew from it three gold *darins*, a silver *darin*, and a handful of pennies. These he added to his own purse.

He then looked down at Cornhair.

"Keep me," she whispered, "Master!"

"It would not be wise," he said. "Slaves speak."

"No," she said. "No!"

"A loquacious slave is more dangerous than the three-banded viper," he said.

"I will not speak," she wept.

"It would be too dangerous," he said.

"Mercy!" she said.

"I will not tie your legs," he said. "Thus you can struggle for a time, perhaps one or two minutes, until your head is sucked beneath the surface."

"I am only a poor slave," she wept. "I beg mercy, Master!"

"It should be amusing to see you thrash about for a time," he said. "Then you will disappear from sight, and it will be as though you never were."

"Please, no, Master!" she wept.

He bent down, and she was lifted from the grass. Her weight was as nothing to him. One arm was behind her back, the other behind the back of her knees. She could see only his eyes, hard, above the bandages he had wrapped about his mouth and nose, to fend away the locale's miasma.

Suddenly the bright glare of the sun was gone.

The man, holding the slave, looked up, startled, his face in shadow. It seemed as though some object, surely a cloud, had interposed itself between the sun and the foul, heated earth. But this was a broad cloud, and one of steel and flame, and one of several such clouds.

"Aatii!" he cried, casting the slave to the turf, turning, and running, stumbling, toward the distant walls of Telnar.

There were six such clouds of steel which lowered themselves gently on feet of fire to the earth. No sooner had these great forms, like platforms resting on legs of metal, come to rest than several ports in the hulls slid open and ramps protruded, descending to the earth. Down these ramps rumbled strings of armored vehicles, some on treads, while, from other ports, open hoverers with mounted weaponry emerged, like hornets streaming from a nest.

Cornhair struggled to her feet, frightened, but laughing hysterically with joy, elated to be alive.

Then she winced for she saw the running figure of the man who had held her, several yards away, burst into flame, and vanish in smoke, and a hoverer, low, only a dozen feet in the air, continuing on its way toward the walls of Telnar.

Vehicles, skirting the refuse pits, roared about Cornhair, who dared not move. Hoverers, like dark plates, dotted the sky.

There could be no landing, she had heard. The ensconced batteries might incinerate anything within range.

But here, in this place of stench and horror, in this lonely, vacant, avoided place, the walls of Telnar in the distance, before her very eyes, the air still hot and stirred from their descent, were ships, the fabled Lion Ships, six such ships, of the Aatii.

Cornhair screamed, and twisted away, nearly struck by a hurtling vehicle.

She stood upright, that the pilots of those armed, racing ground ships might see her, that she might not be caught in treads or crushed into the earth by broad, heavy tires.

Though she was not collared she was alone in this terrible place, and her hands were tied behind her, and she was tunicked, tunicked as was thought fit for a slave. Her slim, well-turned lineaments were well exposed, as would be unthinkable for a free woman. Surely there could be no doubt as to her status. If so, it might be instantly confirmed, by tearing aside the hem of her skirt, on the left side, revealing the slave rose.

Bondage has its terrors and its joys.

So much depends on the Master!

What slave does not wish to be owned by a severe, but kindly Master, one who has some sense of what it is to be a woman, some sense of what a woman wants and needs, one who will subject her to the domination without which she cannot be her true self, a female at the feet of a male, one by whom she, as she wishes, will be owned and mastered? How joyful to be subject to the whip and know that one will be punished if one is not pleasing, and then not feel the whip, because one is pleasing, and one finds one's joy in serving, in loving, and being pleasing.

One advantage, of course, in being a property, is that, as one is a property, one can be owned. Properties have value, lesser or greater value. A slave is a property, one of greater or lesser value. Thus, she is in little danger of being killed, no more than any other domestic animal, of greater or lesser value. She, as other domestic animals, may be purchased, sold, gifted, stolen, seized, appropriated, and such, but she is likely to have little to fear where her life is concerned. Where a free man or a free woman might be summarily slain a slave is likely to be merely acquired. Where a free woman might have her throat cut a slave would be more likely to have a ring put in her nose and then, by means of a cord attached to that ring, her hands bound behind her, be hurried after a new Master.

Cornhair had little doubt that if she had been a free male, or perhaps even a free female, and certainly, if she had run, or resisted, she would have been burned to a burst of ashes, as the fellow who had fled from her side, leaving her at the edge of the vast, foul pit.

These men about now, in the vehicles, and the hoverers, passing about her, and over her, moving toward the city, were clearly of barbarian stock.

Although she was filled with trepidation, she had no immediate apprehension of grievous danger. She was more stirred, more excited and thrilled, than terrified.

These men were barbarians.

They had uses for women, she knew, particularly beautiful women.

Too, she was alive!

She knew that the blockade of Abrogastes could not have been emplaced and managed without a great many ships.

Here were only six ships.

This must be a small part of what must be a large, impressive force.

Clearly then this was not an invasion, but something very different, a raid, of sorts.

How was it that the batteries had been silent?

The swarm of land vehicles and hoverers which had issued from the hulls of the six great ships had now muchly abated, having apparently reached and entered the city.

Indeed, no hoverers were now in sight. On the other hand, at intervals, one or more of the smaller vehicles, treaded or wheeled, rolled down the corrugated steel ramps, and moved, though in a leisurely way, toward Telnar. Their purposes, we may suppose, were various, but, at a minimum, it seems likely that some were intended to establish and maintain a defensive perimeter within which the six ships might be relatively secure, should a sortie emerge from Telnar; others to maintain some physical communications between the preceding wave of attackers and the ships, for example, carrying personnel back and forth; others to safeguard exit routes and prevent attackers from being cut off from the ships, and so on.

Suddenly one of these small vehicles swerved toward Cornhair.

"Take her!" she heard.

The small vehicle, tearing up turf, ground to a stop beside her.

"Masters!" cried Cornhair.

She had no time to kneel, for a hand reached out, seized her by the bound arm, and drew her into the vehicle.

"I have her," said the fellow in whose grasp, tied as she was, Cornhair was helpless.

The vehicle then continued on its way.

Cornhair was thrust to her knees on the steel flooring, at the feet of two or three men, who stood behind a raised, slitted, shieldlike projection, through which they could peer.

A hand thrust her head down, almost to the floor.

"What are you doing out here, tied like a pig?" asked a man.

"I am as a pig, Master," she said. "I am a slave!" Cornhair wished it to be immediately clear, if it were not already clear enough, that she was not a free woman, and was thus, hopefully, immune from the hazards which might accompany that state.

"These are unlikely lakes in which to go swimming," said a man.

"Yes, Master," said Cornhair.

"What were you doing here?" asked the first man.

"I do not know," said Cornhair.

"She was brought here to be disposed of," said one of the men.

"I fear so," said Cornhair.

"Doubtless deservedly," said another.

"No, Master!" said Cornhair, her head down, her eyes on the steel flooring.

"She's a pretty one," said one of the men.

"You are not wearing much," said a man.

"I am a slave," she said.

"At least we need not rip silks from her body," said a man.

"Still, it is pleasant to do that," said another.

"Are there more like you, in Telnar?" asked a man.

"Yes, Master," said Cornhair. "Thousands, and free women, too!"

"Are the free women good looking?" asked a man.

"I do not know," said Cornhair.

"It is easy enough to find out," said a man.

There was laughter.

"Spoils," said a man.

"Booty," said another.

"Loot!" said another.

"What do you think, little slave?" asked one of the men.

"We are women," said Cornhair. "We belong to those strong enough to take us and make us slaves."

"That is a slave's answer," said a man.

"I am a slave," said Cornhair.

"You have no collar," said a man.

"It was taken away," said Cornhair. "I assure you I am a slave. Examine my thigh! You will discover that I am well and clearly marked, nicely marked."

"Every slave should be in a collar," said a man.

"Yes, Master," said Cornhair.

"Collars are lovely on a woman," said a man.

"Yes, Master," said Cornhair. There was little doubt in her mind but what a collar muchly enhanced a woman's attractiveness, and not merely aesthetically. Much had to do with its meaning. It said much about the woman who wore it.

Cornhair, looking up, as the vehicle rumbled on, saw above her the arch of a gate. They were now in the city.

"May I speak, Masters?" asked Cornhair.

"Yes," said a fellow, considering windows and rooftops. The street seemed deserted. Doubtless the main attacking force had plied this street, and perhaps others, like it.

"Telnar is large," said Cornhair. "It is the capital. Millions reside here. Surely you cannot reduce Telnar with the forces at your disposal."

"We have briefer business here," said a man.

"We shall not be long," said another.

"The assault will have gathered by now," said a man. "The strike is imminent."

"Within the hour," said another of the men.

"What is our destination, Masters?" asked Cornhair.

"The palace, the imperial palace," said a man.

"No!" cried Cornhair, and sprang to her feet, only to have her hair seized and held, and she was then cuffed, back and forth, four blows, left cheek, right cheek, left cheek, right cheek, and then, subdued, miserable, lips bleeding, she sank again to her knees.

"What is wrong, little slave?" asked a man.

"Let me go!" she begged. "You need not untie me. Just let me go! Put me from the vehicle! Cast me to the pavement, but do not take me to the palace!"

"You fear the palace?" said a man.

"Yes, yes," she said. "Please do not take me there! Please, Masters!"

"It is our destination," said the fellow at the controls of the vehicle.

CHAPTER THIRTY-NINE

"Ah," said Iaachus, "my noble friend, Julian! How wonderful to see you again, dear fellow, and, too, cousin to our beloved emperor! How often I have thought of you!"

"My dear friend, sweet Arbiter, prop of the empire, defender of the throne," said Julian, "I, too, have often thought of you."

"You will forgive me, I trust," said Iaachus, "if I do not rise to greet you. There is a certain tightness in my knee, a fall."

"Certainly," said Julian.

"And, if I am not mistaken," said Iaachus, "you are accompanied by the noble Ottonius, captain in our esteemed Auxiliaries."

Otto did not speak, but looked about the room.

"And king of Otungs," said Julian.

"I trust not a tribe of the Aatii," said Iaachus.

"No, of the Vandal peoples," said Julian, "a confederation commonly hostile to the Aatii."

"There are so many of these barbarian nations," said Iaachus. "It is very confusing."

"The chamber, outside, is heavily guarded," said Julian.

"Yes," said Iaachus. "Times are trying."

"Doubtless," said Julian.

"It is my understanding," said Iaachus, "that you wished to see me, privately."

"Yes, dear friend," said Julian, "privately."

"I see," said the Arbiter.

"We are not alone," said Otto.

"I left my pistol outside," said Julian. "You may close your center desk drawer."

"Tyrus, Arsus," said the Arbiter, "you might go and see if our friend's pistol is safe."

Two men stepped from behind drapes and went, briefly, to the chamber portal. "It is secure, Lord," said one of the men.

"Excellent," said Iaachus. "You may now leave, both of you."

"Yes, Lord," said one of the men, and they both exited.

"The drawer," suggested Julian.

"Of course," said Iaachus. He then slid shut the drawer.

"Perhaps you are surprised to see my friend, Captain Ottonius," said Julian.

"Pleasantly, of course," said Iaachus. "I had thought him engaged on Tangara, recruiting allies."

"And I?" asked Julian.

"At your villa, I supposed, on Vellmer."

"I, too, was on Tangara," said Julian.

"Interesting," said Iaachus.

"Abrogastes, king of the Drisriaks, of the Alemanni, the Aatii, blockades Telnaria," said Julian.

"Briefly," said Iaachus. "Even now imperial cruisers rush nigh, from a hundred worlds."

"And leave a hundred borders undefended," said Julian. "Through abandoned gates stream unwelcome guests."

"Telnaria comes first," said Iaachus. "It is the seat of the senate and empire."

"Surely," said Julian, "you do not think these developments unrelated."

"How do barbarians think?" asked Iaachus. "Perhaps we should ask one, our friend, noble Ottonius."

"Noble Lord," said Otto, "let us conjecture that Abrogastes, called the Far-Grasper, though a barbarian, is not a fool. Clearly his blockade cannot win him an empire, even bring a world to its knees. Therefore, it has another purpose, or other purposes. It is not a blockade, truly, or at least not a blockade for its own sake, even something as negligible as demonstrating the possibility of intrusion or the performing of a trivial, superficial act of annoyance, but rather a tactic, one already successfully executed. The empire is like the egg of a *varda*, a hard shell, and, within, a soft center. Now the shell is shattered and the center at risk."

"At less risk, noble Ottonius, than you imagine," said Iaachus. "Telnaria has conserved mighty weaponry, which may be employed in its defense."

"The batteries," said Julian.

"Of course," said Iaachus.

"Which may not fire," said Otto.

"I do not understand," said Iaachus.

"In many districts of the city," said Julian, "there is unrest, civil disorder, rioting, looting and burning."

"Unfortunately," said Iaachus.

"The blockade?" said Julian.

"That is the pretext," said Iaachus. "More is concealed."

"Guardsmen are few," said Julian. "They do not interfere."

"They have been forbidden to interfere, save to defend their own safety," said Iaachus.

"What madness is this?" said Julian.

"Much has transpired since Tangara," said Iaachus. "New games are afoot, and new players move unfamiliar pieces."

"I shall tell you what I have learned," said Julian, "and you may tell me what you know."

"Proceed, dear friend," said Iaachus.

"Recruitment amongst Vandals, once promising, is imperiled," said Julian. "Loyalties are uncertain and confusion reigns. By tradition, Vandals, in all their tribes, will follow the wearer of a given medallion and chain, a war lord's emblem of office.

Drisriaks, a tribe of the Aatii, or Alemanni, by custom hereditary enemies of Vandals, obtained that token, and threatened
plausibly to use it to unite the Alemanni and Vandal nations in
an alliance which would portend doom to the empire. But many
such medallions and chains were smithed and distributed, this
casting doubt on the authenticity of any such device."

"Excellent!" said Iaachus.

"Now," said Julian, "that alliance is forestalled, but Vandals,
even Otungs, hesitate to declare for the silver standards."

"There is much here," said Otto, "which I do not understand.
I do not see in this matter the thinking of Drisriaks. There is a
subtlety and an astuteness here, a narrow slyness and cunning,
which seems unlikely to have sprung from camps and halls.
What is here speaks rather to me of cities, of sheltered colon-
nades and sealed chambers."

"Let us suppose," said Julian, "as my colleague suspects, that
machinations are herein involved, and machinations originating
in, or supported by, forces within Telnaria itself."

"Yes," said Iaachus, "let us suppose that."

"Then what I cannot understand is the possible motivation for
such an act. What could be gained? Why would one tear down
walls? Why would one open gates in the presence of an enemy?"

"Clearly there would be something to be gained," said
Iaachus.

"Surely nothing in the interest of the throne," said Julian.

"No," said Iaachus.

"Then, what?" demanded Julian.

"I fear I know," said Iaachus.

"What?" said Julian.

"You have noted the unrest in the city, the rioting, the looting," said Iaachus.

"Yes," said Julian.

"What you are unlikely to have noted, or understood," said
Iaachus, "is that the temples of the gods, and the temples of

Floonians, save for one such cult, have been attacked, despoiled, and burned, by zealots, supposedly in the holy cause of propagating a particular faith, one of the several supposedly one true faiths, only the other one true faiths, at least to date, have refrained from promoting their views by destruction, arson, murder, robbery, and such."

"Surely the city is in turmoil," said Julian. "There is general looting and burning. Many districts are unsafe, some devastated."

"Some of this is spillage," said Iaachus. "Fire spreads. One object of value appropriated leads to another. Who can resist the temptation to seize unprotected treasure? Is there no elation in stealing, burning, and killing? In a crowd small men are large, weak men are strong. The unhappy, envious, and resentful are liberated within the concealment of anonymity. Once the beast with many heads has tasted blood it longs for more. In what other country than the mob can hatred and violence, theft and greed, be unleashed with impunity? But there is more, as well, and intention, and calculation."

"I do not understand," said Julian.

"These riots are fomented with a purpose," said Iaachus, "and the purpose is the acquisition of power."

"I have been long from Telnaria," said Julian.

"Do you know of Floonianism?" asked Iaachus.

"Very little," said Julian.

"It is a demand of a particular Floonian leader, the leader of one of the several Floonian faiths, a man named Sidonicus, entitled 'Exarch of Telnar'," said Iaachus, "that the empire adopt his version of Floonianism as the official faith of the Telnarian empire, and that the empire should then use its power to supplant and exterminate all other faiths, of whatever sort."

"Tolerance is the way of Telnaria," said Julian, "even from the time of the village kings, even before the institution of the senate, even before the empire."

"Sidonicus demands intolerance," said Iaachus, "on behalf of his own views, of course."

"He is insane," said Julian.

"Perhaps, rather," said Iaachus, "brilliant and unscrupulous."

"Surely the empire will do nothing so cruel, heinous, and divisive," said Julian.

"Rewards would attend this concession," said Iaachus. "Floonians, in their millions, on many worlds, as you probably know, have largely existed as inactive, benign parasites, living within the shelter of the empire they refuse to support and defend. They ignore state authority, flout law, eschew taxes, decline *munera*, refuse to bear arms, and so on. They are, I gather, primarily concerned with the welfare of their own *koos*, whatever that is."

"Interesting," said Julian.

"But," said Iaachus, "in exchange for declaring Floonianism the official faith of the empire, and extirpating all other faiths, Sidonicus will bring his flocks into the fold of the empire, supposedly then a reformed, redeemed empire."

"As committed, participating citizens, to support, defend it, and so on," said Julian.

"Precisely," said Iaachus. "You can see the potential value to the empire of additional millions of zealous patriots now defending an empire they regard as their own."

"And what of our other citizens?" asked Julian.

"Over one or two centuries," said Iaachus, "there may be no other citizens. The confused and hesitant, the opportunistic, can be converted, the recalcitrant killed, or, if any should survive, exiled, deported, forced into wastelands, driven into wilderness worlds, to eke out what livelihood they can in scattered, despised enclaves."

"And if the empire does not so declare, as the exarch wishes?"

"Opposition, disruption," said Iaachus. "Treason, inertness, treachery, betrayal of the empire. You have seen the streets."

"Clear them," said Julian.

"We dare not," said Iaachus. "One would do no more than produce martyrs."

"And thus the quiescence of guardsmen?" said Julian.

"What, in any event, would be a hundred guardsmen, or two hundred, against an avalanche of ten thousand?"

"What will the empire do?" asked Julian.

"I urge resistance," said Iaachus.

"Because of the threat to your own power?" asked Julian.

"If you wish," said Iaachus.

"What of the emperor?"

"He plays with his toys."

"The empress mother?"

"She is receiving instruction in Floonianism," said Iaachus.

"Your power in the palace wanes," said Julian.

"Another has her ear," said Iaachus, "Sidonicus, Exarch of Telnar."

"The princesses, Viviana and Alacida?"

"They care for little but their jewels and gowns, and the flattery of spineless courtiers."

"Surrender to Sidonicus," said Julian, "and the empire survives?"

"In an unconscionable, unrecognizable form," said Iaachus, "as an outrage to its former self, as a tyranny which far exceeds that of the sword, a prison of the mind, a citadel of oppression."

"I would miss the openness and glory of the empire, its vastness and complexity, even with its faults," said Julian.

"The empire has been shrewd," said Iaachus, "it has calculated, plotted, and done war, but it has never flown the flag of fanaticism."

"We spoke earlier," said Julian, "of the matter of the medallion and chain, and the threat of uniting barbarian peoples under the aegis of that artifact, a threat, we trust, now muchly reduced in portent by a plentitude of competitive devices."

"Nothing of this had reached the palace," said Iaachus.

"I am not surprised," said Julian. "But a puzzle lingers. If the scheme of the artifact originated in, or was supported by, forces in Telnar, what could be the motivation for such an anomaly? Who would multiply enemies? Would it not be a matter of throwing oneself on one's own sword, before the battle had even begun? I am without an explanation. You said, as I recall, you feared you knew."

"In this," said Iaachus, "I see the hand of Sidonicus, Exarch of Telnar."

"How so?" said Julian.

"Think, dear friend," said Iaachus. "Barbarians desire the defeat of, or the possession of, the empire. Now they are approached by someone who will place in their hands the means for realizing that ambition. To be sure, such a gift is not bestowed without the expectation of receiving something of comparable value in return."

"Surely not," said Julian. "But, what?"

"I suspect," said Iaachus, "the conversion of the victorious barbarian peoples, this another road to a familiar end, the imposition of a particular faith on countless worlds."

"If the empire were seized?"

"Yes," said Iaachus.

"But what," said Julian, "if the empire was collapsed, broken in battle, communication lost, cities emptied, men divided, the state vanished, save for local law enforced by bandits?"

"Still," said Iaachus, "the faith would be everywhere, and perhaps the more precious and stronger for the uncertainty and precariousness of life."

"Woe," said Julian.

"Perhaps the future belongs to those such as your friend," said Iaachus. He slid the center drawer of his desk partly open. "And perhaps to those who are their friends," he added.

"I do not understand," said Julian.

"It might be politic for successful barbarians, if they wish to preserve the empire, to place a tool upon the throne, one which might preserve the illusion of continuity and stability."

"One of high family, such as the Aureliani?" said Julian.

"Such things are not unknown in statecraft," said Iaachus.

"In the forest," said Otto, "such an insult would call for knives, and entry into the circle of death, from which only one contestant might leave alive."

"My dear Ottonius," said Iaachus, "I fear, in any such contest, I would be ill matched even with dear Julian, let alone with one such as yourself. In any event, we are not in the forest, but in the imperial palace in Telnar, with several guards within easy summoning distance, and, even if we were in the forest, I think I would prefer not a knife but a pistol, much as the one I now draw from the desk."

"I came here in good faith," said Julian, "that I might inform and be informed, and that we might engage in consultation. I assume that we both, in our ways, care for the empire."

"I, at least," said Iaachus.

"I, as well," said Julian.

"You are spies," said Iaachus, "testing resolve, assessing defenses, scouting for Abrogastes."

"No," said Julian.

"Clearly you are in league with him," said Iaachus. "That is made evident by your presence here. No ship has penetrated his blockade."

"One did, mine," said Julian. "We were fired on in our passage, and disabled. We crashed in the delta of the Turning Serpent. We came west on a keel boat."

Otto tensed.

"Do not move," said Julian.

"I place you under arrest," said Iaachus, "as enemies of the throne. As for your lord and ally, Abrogastes, he will be shortly destroyed, or in custody, as imperial cruisers approach from all quadrants."

"Abrogastes is not our lord and ally but our common enemy," said Julian. "If you were more familiar with barbarians you would know they are complex and diverse. Do not expect them to run about in skins and drink *bror*. Some speak several languages. Some design weapon systems. Some are at home on the bridges of Lion Ships. Abrogastes is the king of the Drisriaks, a tribe of the Aatii, or, as they know themselves, the Alemanni; Ottonius is the king of Otungs, a tribe of the Vandal peoples, and the Alemanni and the Vandals are hereditary enemies."

"Where did you conceal your ship?" asked Iaachus.

"In the courtyard of the palace," said Julian. "In the emperor's play garden. In the wardrobes of the imperial princesses. In the private quarters of the empress mother."

"Come now," said Iaachus.

"Look for it in the marshes of the delta, where it crashed," said Julian.

"As you will, dear traitors," said Iaachus. "Quarters will be arranged for you. I trust they will be to your liking. I shall now summon guards."

At this moment there was, far off, a series of explosions.

"Do not move!" said Iaachus.

There was a heavy, frenzied pounding on the door of the chamber, and then it was thrown open, and a courtier, distraught and wild-eyed, was framed in the portal. "Exalted Lord," he cried, "barbarians are in the streets, they approach. Guardsmen, poorly armed, flee. Rioters and looters, in their crowds, at first at ease, noncognizant, and complacent, fearing nothing, then startled, terrified, running, are fired on. Hundreds lie bloody in the streets."

"Resistance?" cried Iaachus, standing, dazed, lowering the pistol.

"Little or none," said the courtier. "What are bows and blades against the rumbling engines of war?"

"It cannot be!" said Iaachus. "The batteries!"

"The city batteries did not fire!" said the courtier.

Iaachus looked wildly at Julian and Otto.

"We know nothing of this," said Julian.

"One can hire loyalty," said Otto, "one can hire disloyalty."

"Put away your pistol," said Julian. "See to the safety of the emperor, the royal family."

Iaachus raised the pistol, leveled it at Julian and Otto, and then lowered it.

"Hurry!" urged Julian.

There was another explosion, this one much closer.

"Hurry! Hurry!" said Julian.

"They are at the gate!" cried the courtier.

CHAPTER FORTY

Cornhair lay on her left shoulder, on the steel flooring of the motorized vehicle. Her wrists were still tied behind her but now, looped within a thrice-circled cord, her ankles were fastened together.

"We cannot have you wandering about," had said one of the vehicle's crew.

"No," Cornhair thought, "you have seen to that. I will remain where you have put me, helpless." Slaves, of all women, are most aware of their sex, for the sex of both men and women is defined most clearly by the relation of each to the other, the larger and stronger to the smaller and weaker, the taker to the taken, the captor to the captive, and so on. These relationships are, of course, much accentuated and intensified in the institution of bondage. As Master the man is most male, and, as slave, the woman is most female. Slavery permits the woman no lies or pretenses, no falsifications of her nature. She is at a man's feet, where she belongs.

Although Cornhair had initially been quite distressed at the thought of approaching the palace, where she might encounter those who had known her as the Lady Publennia, particularly Iaachus, the Arbiter of Protocol, whom she had failed so signally in her attempt to assassinate a barbarian captain of auxiliaries, she was now far less concerned, as it seemed unlikely that such a harrowing encounter would take place. Who but barbarians would note her as she was, a mere tethered prize in a vehicle? And even if Telnarians, common citizens and such, should gaze upon her, they would see no more than what she now was, a common slave.

Cornhair lay quietly amongst the booted feet of the barbarians.

"That is the palace," said one, pointing, standing on the level which permitted him to look over the slitted metal visor half circling the vehicle.

"It will be pleasant to own the empire," said another.

"Rather, destroy it," said another. "Burn it. Break it, world by world! Tear it down, stone by stone."

"See the palace," said another, impressed, "the portico, its columns, the steps, the pediment, the great portal, the sculptures."

"There are many buildings about the great court," said another.

"Fountains spraying colored water," said another.

"Scented water," said a man.

"So where are our noble Telnarians, so brave with their sticks and torches?"

"Fled, or resting in the streets, flooded with their blood," said another.

A fellow laughed.

"What building is that?" asked one of the men.

"How should I know?" said another.

"Oh!" said Cornhair, the side of a boot striking on her thigh.

"Do you know Telnar?" asked the fellow whose boot was still at her thigh.

"She will know nothing," said one of the men. "She is an outworlder, probably from Varna or Tesis II. She is stupid, too; they were going to garbage her outside the city."

"A little, Master," said Cornhair.

She was caught under the arms and lifted up, tied as she was, by the fellow whose boot had honored her with the attention of a free person. He then placed her on his shoulder, steadying her with one hand. In this fashion, she was held high, well over the slitted metal visor. Doubtless she would have preferred a less conspicuous ensconcement.

"There," said the fellow, facing a building, pointing with his left hand.

"The senate house," she said, "the supreme power in Telnaria."

"Does it launch fleets, does it march armies?" asked a man.

"No, Master," said Cornhair.

There was laughter.

"Beyond that, Master," said Cornhair, "are houses of documents, of deeds and wills, the house of administration, that of law, the housings of the high courts."

"What blackened shell of a building is that?" asked another, pointing.

"It was the temple of Orak Triumphant," she said. "Emperors sacrificed there. Offerings were burned at the foot of the steps, that the temple not be stained, a hundred white bulls with gilded horns, the incense and smoke detectible for miles about."

"It is now a hollow, burned shell," said a man.

"It fell upon bad times," said Cornhair.

"Look!" said a fellow, pointing back, beyond the broad court.

"Conceal the slave," said another.

Cornhair was lowered to the floor of the vehicle. She drew up her legs.

"Lie still," said one of the men.

"Yes, Master," she said.

Cornhair heard cheers, cries of pleasure.

A large vehicle rumbled past. Turning about, she saw little more than a pennon atop a supple, swaying, metal rod.

"Hail, Abrogastes!" men cried.

"Behold," said a man, "he has with him, lying at his feet, the slave, Huta."

"I fear, and hate her," said a man.

"She is nicely chained," said a man.

"Why would he bring her?" asked a man.

"She is well curved," said another.

"She makes a suitable display slave," said a man.

"I have heard that Ingeld has noted her flanks," said a man.

"Let Abrogastes not discover that," laughed a fellow.

"She is dangerous," said the fellow who had spoken before. "I fear her, and loathe her."

"Once she was dangerous," said a man. "But no longer. She is now a slave. Abrogastes has aroused her, caressed her into submission, into need and pleading, enflamed her belly. She now lies in chains, begging to be touched."

Again the fellow's boot brushed Cornhair's thigh. "What of you, blond slut?" he asked.

"I am a slave, Master," whispered Cornhair.

"I do not wish to dally here overlong," said a man, uneasily.

"No," said another, looking about.

"Enemy fleets approach," said a man.

"Surely," said another.

"If we are caught here," said a man, "we will be stomped on, crushed like a ten-legged crawler under the hoof of an angry *torodont*."

"There is time," said another.

"Not enough," said a man.

"Enough," said another.

"Let the king be about his business quickly," said a man.

"What is his business?" asked a man.

"I do not know," said another. "He did not consult with me."

This remark was followed by laughter.

Cornhair heard a woman's scream.

"Ho," said one of the fellows, "we are not the only ones with a bauble."

"There are two there," said a man, "stripped, hands tied behind them, with rings in their noses, being led on their cords."

"And four there," said another, turning about, "slaves, tunicked, not bound, save for a common neck rope."

"The two must be free women," said a man.

"They have not yet earned a rag," said a man.

"I wonder if they are worth branding," said a man.

"They had best hope so," said another.

"They will soon grow accustomed to having their necks encircled with the badge of servitude," said another.

"What shall we do with our little piece of sleek, well-turned garbage?" said a fellow.

"We can cast lots for her," said a man.

"She will probably be put in a common bin," said a man.

"We may leave them behind," said a man. "We can always pick them up later, with other millions, when the empire is ours."

Cornhair again felt the boot, the toe nudging her.

"Master?" she said.

"You are a slave, are you not?" she was asked.

"Yes, Master," she said.

"You want a Master, do you not?" she was asked.

"Must I speak?" she asked.

"Yes," he said.

"Yes," she said, "I want a Master."

"Why?" he asked.

"I am a slave," she said.

"You do not even have a collar," he said.

"It was taken away," she said.

"But you will soon have another, will you not?" she was asked.

"Doubtless, Master," she said. "I am a slave. I should be collared."

"You want the collar?"

"Yes, Master."

"Why?"

"Because I am a slave," she said.

CHAPTER FORTY-ONE

"Ho!" cried Abrogastes, seated on the throne of the emperor, "where is the sniveling child, Aesilesius, majestic ruler of worlds, where is the empress mother?"

"They are in the emperor's play room," said a trembling courtier, "under guard, the emperor frightened, weeping in his mother's arms, she holding him closely, sheltering him, trying to comfort him. He is inconsolable, deprived of his playthings."

"Give him toys," said Abrogastes.

"Is he not to be brought forth, Lord," asked a Drisriak officer, "to consign to you the empire, or be slain?"

"Such an act," said Iaachus, boldly stepping forward, "would be an act performed under duress and thus nonbinding. Similarly, there are rules of succession. If the emperor should perish, Orak forbid, another would step forth, and another, and then another."

"Who is this fellow?" asked Abrogastes, interested.

"I am Iaachus, Arbiter of Protocol," said Iaachus. "In the absence of the emperor or empress mother I presume to speak for the throne."

"And perhaps," said Abrogastes, lifting a Telnarian pistol, "you and your robes may vanish in a burst of fire."

"I but speak the law," said Iaachus.

"And you speak it well," said Abrogastes. "I like you."

There were several people in the throne room, both Telnarians and barbarians. Julian, Otto, and Iaachus stood to one side, before a number of cowering courtiers. All were disarmed. Weapons were trained on them. No slaves were present, save one, Huta, tunicked and chained, kneeling at Abrogastes' left. Most of those of the palace, servitors, slaves, and such, and high officials, and generals, marshals, admirals, and such, were confined elsewhere. There were perhaps a hundred men in the room, some thirty of the palace, and the rest intruders.

"I think I know you," said Abrogastes, eyes glinting, pistol on his knee, regarding Julian and Otto, from the throne.

"We know you, Drisriak," said Julian.

"Tenguthaxichai!" said Abrogastes.

This barbarous expression can be variously translated. 'Tengutha' is a common male name amongst several barbarian peoples. The expression, as a whole, would seem to signify "the place of Tengutha." It is most often translated as "Tengutha's Camp," "Tengutha's Lair," or such.

"Yes," said Julian.

"You have risen in the world," laughed Abrogastes. "You were in rags, a prisoner, a tender of pigs, and now you are a neat, well-groomed, well-dressed, clean-shaven fellow, clad along military lines, it seems."

"I am a lieutenant in the imperial navy," said Julian.

"How is it I find one of so lowly a rank in so august a milieu?" asked Abrogastes.

"Perhaps you remember me, as well," said Otto, standing better than a head above the others, his arms folded across his mighty chest.

"He speaks insolently," said a barbarian, a Dangar. The Dangars were the second largest of the tribes constituting the Alemanni nation. Abrogastes' party, thus, was not limited to Drisriaks.

Several weapons were focused on Otto. As soon as he had

spoken, they had turned toward him, quickly, like beasts of steel, noticing beasts, responsive to an unexpected sound.

"Chieftain of the Wolfungs," said Abrogastes.

"Chieftain of the Wolfungs," said Otto, "and king of the Otungs."

"When the empire is on its knees, or prostrate, awash in its own blood," said Abrogastes, "we will have time for Otungs."

"Beware!" said Julian.

"And we for you," said Otto.

"Little slave," said Abrogastes, "with your white skin, dark hair, high cheek bones, and your eyes like black and burning velvet, perhaps you remember our friends, from Tenguthaxichai?"

"Yes, Master," she said.

"And we remember you, as well, false and scheming priestess," said Julian.

"I am no longer a priestess," said Huta.

"You look well in chains," said Julian.

"Thank you, Master," she said.

"What woman does not?" asked a Borkon.

"True," said several about.

"I trust you have been marked," said Julian.

"My thigh has been well marked," she said.

"You are obviously well subdued," said Julian. "Are you also mastered?"

"Yes, Master," she said. "I am mastered, well mastered."

Abrogastes turned and held the barrel of his pistol to her lips, and she, trembling, licked and kissed the barrel.

"Master," she whispered.

"Later," he said, pulling the pistol away.

She knelt back on her heels, tears in her eyes, her small fists clenched in the chains she wore.

"How is it, noble Abrogastes," asked Otto, "that you bespeak hostility to Otungs and, at the same time, sue for their support in war?"

"I do not understand," said Abrogastes.

"The medallion and chain," said Otto, "your intent to enlist Otungs, indeed, all Vandals, behind your banners."

"I know nothing of a medallion and chain," said Abrogastes. "Vandals and Alemanni are enemies, to the knife. Who would be so mad as to expose his throat to a treacherous and vile Otung?"

"Forgive me," said Otto.

"Do you suggest there is treason amongst the Alemanni?" asked Abrogastes.

"He does not, noble Abrogastes," said Julian.

"In high places?" asked Abrogastes.

"Certainly not," said Julian.

"Perhaps, Lord," said a Borkon, a Ledanian, or Coastal, Borkon, "the slave, Huta, is apprised of such a rumor."

Uneasiness stirred amongst several of the barbarians in the chamber.

"Slave?" asked Abrogastes.

Huta turned white. "I know nothing of such things, Master," she said.

"Do you think I cannot read the body I know so well?" he asked.

Huta put down her head and clutched her small arms tightly about her body.

"It seems you must be lashed," said Abrogastes. "Fortunately for you, your flanks are still of interest. Else I might have you cut to pieces and fed to pigs."

"My friend, Ottonius," said Julian, "meant nothing."

"Sometimes," said Abrogastes, "those who mean nothing say much."

"Surely," said Julian. "You know that imperial cruisers hasten even now to Telnaria."

"Hrothgar," said Abrogastes, "is a good-hearted, jovial, much-laughing, loyal, hard-fighting, hard-drinking fool; he keeps his heart in his gut and his brains in his scabbard. He would die for me between the courses of a banquet, but not until a certain dish was served. Ingeld is clever and prone to dark thoughts. I am not well served in my sons."

"You were well served in Ortog, my Lord," said a Drisriak.

"Ortog was a traitor," said Abrogastes.

"A secessionist," said a man.

"He is gone now," said Abrogastes.

"We could use his sword," said a man.

"He is gone," said Abrogastes.

"As my young friend, he in the uniform of the imperial navy, has pointed out," said Iaachus, "you and your men are in jeopardy each hour you remain on Telnaria, or, indeed, in its vicinity. Imperial war ships approach with great speed. It is certain your forces, trapped in our space, would be grievously dealt with, quite possibly exterminated, to a man, to a ship."

"You can accomplish little of serious effect here," said Julian. "You might burn Telnar as a symbolic gesture, but I doubt that one of your perspicacity would see any point in doing so. You might destroy one city, but a hundred thousand would remain. And surely Telnar itself would be of more value as a prize than as a dozen districts of ashes. Too, as the Arbiter has pointed out, an act enforced on the emperor would be unavailing, and the murder of one emperor would mean nothing more than the succession of another, and then another, and so on."

"I am aware of all this, young counselor," said Abrogastes.

"And yet you are here," said Julian.

"So, why?" said Abrogastes.

"Yes, why?" said Julian.

"I am patient," said Abrogastes. "Succession proceeds immediately through the imperial line, does it not?"

"Yes," said Iaachus.

"I think we may disregard the senate," said Abrogastes.

"Possibly," said Iaachus.

"The empress mother is weary, vain, malicious, unfit, old," said Abrogastes.

"The emperor is young," said Iaachus.

"He lives for his toys, but the empire is not a toy. He might surrender the empire, if permitted, for an attractive toy, one he would enjoy."

"He would not be permitted to do so," said Iaachus.

"Who knows under what conditions an emperor might abdicate," said Abrogastes.

"Or die?" said Julian.

"Perhaps," said Abrogastes.

"This is madness," said Iaachus.

"Not at all," said Abrogastes.

"I do not understand," said Iaachus.

"Have the princesses, Viviana and Alacida, brought into our presence," said Abrogastes.

CHAPTER FORTY-TWO

"Release me!" said blond Viviana, princess of Telnaria, perhaps in her early twenties.

And Alacida, younger, perhaps by a year or two, a brunette, pulled against the grip on her arm, which she could not break.

They were released, with a swirl of their robes, before the throne, on which reposed Abrogastes, king of the Drisriaks.

"How dare you, barbarous ape," cried Viviana, "sit upon the throne of my glorious brother, Aesilesius?"

"Your glorious brother," said Abrogastes, "is content, playing with his toys."

"Depart," said Viviana.

"Thrones are made to be sat upon, Princess," said Abrogastes. "The only question is who shall sit upon them."

"I command you," cried Viviana. "Go!"

"Commands without power are at best requests," said Abrogastes.

"Then, noble king," said Iaachus, "with all gentleness and courtesy, I bid you pay heed to the request of Princess Viviana."

"I do not request!" cried Viviana. "I command. Go. Depart!"

"We shall depart shortly, Princess," said Abrogastes.

"Good!" she said, stamping her small, slippered foot.

"May I inquire," asked Iaachus, "for what purpose the princesses have been brought forth?"

"To inform them of their good fortune," said Abrogastes.

"I do not understand," said Iaachus.

"We are standing, you are seated," said Viviana to Abrogastes, angrily. "This is insupportable. We are regal, of the blood royal, you are base. My sister and I will now ascend the dais and take our proper places, on the princess thrones. And they should be, even if they are not, on a level well above you!"

There were only four seats in the throne room, by design. There was the throne of the emperor, which was broad-armed and splendid, and draped with purple, and, beside it, on the right, but slightly behind it, the throne of the empress mother, similarly splendid. The two princess thrones, somewhat simpler, were to the left of the imperial throne, and set one level beneath it. Such arrangements, levels, the limitation of chairs, and such, are not unusual in situations where rank, distance, and hierarchy are deemed significant. For example, who would dare to sit, unbidden, in, say, the presence of a king?

"Remain standing," said Abrogastes.

Viviana and Alacida arrested their approach to the thrones. This action was doubtless influenced by the menacing attitudes of the several barbarians who placed themselves between the princesses and their projected destination.

"There," said Abrogastes, who, with the barrel of his pistol, indicated where they were to stand, on the ground level, so to speak, to his left.

"We will not stand near that despicable beast," said Viviana, "a chained, unclothed slave."

"She is not unclothed," said Abrogastes. "She is tunicked."

"Unclothed," said Viviana.

"Forgive us, great king," said Iaachus, "but slaves in the palace, though commonly bare-armed and barefoot, that their worthlessness and meaninglessness be made clear, are commonly modestly gowned, in ankle-length garments of white wool, white silk, white *corton*, or such."

"Slaves should be clad as slaves, as men like to see them," said Abrogastes.

"It is not the way of the palace," said Iaachus.

"Remain where you are," said Abrogastes to the princesses.

"Very well," said Viviana, tossing her head, looking away.

"Dear Princess," said Iaachus, "your boldness well befits a princess, or a fool, but be apprised of the nature of our situation. We are defenseless, we are in the power of these men; our fortunes, our lives, are in their hands."

"Until our soldiers come," said Viviana, "until our ships fill the skies!"

"Doubtless," said Iaachus, "but our soldiers have not yet come, nor do our ships yet fill the skies."

"I think the princesses need to be instructed," said Abrogastes.

"Surely not!" exclaimed Iaachus.

Julian moved forward, but was stayed by the hand of Otto, king of the Otungs.

"Do not be concerned," said Abrogastes. "I do not mean instructed as a slave is instructed, with the switch and whip, with tight ropes, with close chains, with the bit, and such, but as free women of refinement, of gentleness and station, might be instructed."

"I encourage you to withdraw, great king," said Iaachus, "time is short."

"Go forth, into the city," said Abrogastes, with a gesture of his pistol. "Fetch forth a handful of slaves!"

"There are few easily about, Lord," said a Borkon. "Our presence in the city is well known. Within the city, men hide; they crouch in cellars; they inhabit sewers; they remain indoors, with bolted portals and shutters; they secrete coins beneath the floors and in the walls; they conceal slaves; outside the city, roads are crowded with refugees, fleeing, laden with goods."

"Four or five will do," said Abrogastes, "tunicked."

Several men rushed from the tiled, high-vaulted throne room.

"Great king," said Iaachus.

"I hear you, he who would speak for the throne," said Abrogastes.

"How," asked Iaachus, "were the two batteries, both well supplied, both potent and lethal, to which the security of Telnar was entrusted, disabled?"

"They should have burned anything out of the sky which came within ten thousand miles of the city," said Julian, angrily. "How did you obtain the signals, the passwords?"

"Or how did you smuggle dire explosives into the firing enclaves undetected?" asked Iaachus.

"The batteries were not disabled," said Abrogastes, "though they are now disabled, and repairs, I assure you, will not be speedily or easily accomplished. And we needed know nothing of signals and passwords."

"Subversion, then," said Otto, "not sabotage."

"The battery coordinator was picked by me," said Iaachus, bitterly, "and the captain of each battery, as well, men I trusted, who performed secret deeds, attending even to a private commission on a far world, men who, through me, received the thanks and rewards of a grateful state."

"The subtle, yellow whispers of gold are often persuasive," said Otto.

Iaachus suddenly turned to Otto.

"I understand," he said. "It is all now clear."

"Gold?" said Otto.

"Fear," said Iaachus.

"Arbiter?" asked Julian.

"I should have realized the danger," said Iaachus.

"When?" asked Julian.

"As soon as I glimpsed Ottonius, captain of auxiliaries, chieftain of Wolfungs, king of Otungs."

"I do not understand," said Julian.

"He was recognized, on Tangara," said Iaachus.

"I do not understand," said Julian.

"Ho!" called Abrogastes, heartily. "You have been successful."

Two of his men approached, emerging from amongst several others. One, the free end of the rope in his possession, led forward a coffle of four neck-roped, tunicked slaves. The other conducted forward a single slave, also tunicked, holding her by the left, upper arm. Her hands were tied behind her. She was blond. All the slaves seemed filled with trepidation. Surely such as they, common slaves, would never expect to be brought into a palace. And they were doubtless, too, well aware of how they now found themselves, slaves in the keeping of barbarians. Who could conceive of the terror of having a barbarian Master? Were they not aware of how barbarians might see, and treat, slaves, particularly slaves of the empire? They were knelt in a row, these five, four on the neck rope, one separate, on the tiles before the throne. One, a blonde, she who was separate, threw her hair forward, and down, as she could, about her features, and kept her head down, almost as though she might be unwilling to let her features be seen.

"Behold," said Abrogastes, to Viviana and Alacida, standing below, like commoners, on the tiles, on his left, "women, as they should be."

"Slaves!" said Viviana, scornfully.

"Yes, slaves," said Abrogastes.

"And what instruction are we supposed to receive from this exhibition?" asked Viviana.

"You, pretty Alacida," said Abrogastes, "you do not speak."

"I am afraid to speak, Lord," she said.

"It seems you are wiser than your sister," said Abrogastes.

"Do not call him 'Lord'," said Viviana.

"He is a lord," she said, "amongst barbarians."

"Look upon these slaves," said Abrogastes, "and be instructed."

"And what am I to learn from half-naked slaves?" asked Viviana.

"Behold how generously they are clad," said Abrogastes.

"In scarce a scrap of cloth," she said.

"Still," said Abrogastes.

"I do not understand," said Viviana.

"Many women of the empire," said Abrogastes, "serve naked in our halls, in locked collars, barefoot, in the dirt and rushes, hurrying about our tables, serving meat and *bror*, hoping not to be switched. Many, naked, neck-ringed, tend our huts, serve in our fields, care for our pigs, weave in the women's quarters, are slept at our feet."

"What has this to do with us?" asked Viviana.

Otto, unable to restrain himself, burst out in a great laugh.

"Ho, Otung," said Abrogastes. "I see you have considered these supposedly noble creatures as what they are, mere females."

"Yes, Lord," said Otto. "And even, long ago, in a summer palace. Even then I wondered, doubtless as have many others, what they might look like, stripped and collared, kneeling, bent down, their lips pressed to a Master's feet."

"Beast! Beast!" cried Viviana.

"Viviana," said Abrogastes.

"Do not presume to use my name, barbarian," said Viviana. "Address me as 'Princess'."

"Viviana," said Abrogastes, "say 'I, Viviana, princess of Telnaria, am the captive of Abrogastes, the Drisriak. I understand that he can do with me as he wishes.'"

"Never!" said Viviana.

"Very well," said Abrogastes, "strip her, and whip her."

"No, no!" said Viviana. "I, Viviana, princess of Telnaria, am the captive of Abrogastes, the Drisriak. I understand that he can do with me as he wishes."

"And you, pretty Alacida?" asked Abrogastes.

"I," she said, "Alacida, princess of Telnaria, am the captive of

Abrogastes, the Drisriak. I understand that he can do with me as he wishes."

"I think, now," said Abrogastes, "we understand one another."

"Imperial fleets close," said Julian. "I do not understand why you linger."

"Perhaps," said Iaachus, "we should do our best to delay your departure."

"I do not linger," said Abrogastes. "I conduct my business with dispatch."

"May I inquire," said Iaachus, "what is the king's business?"

"Why," said Abrogastes, "to inform the princesses of their good fortune."

"I see no good fortune in this," said Viviana, "lest it be to observe your immediate departure."

"In Telnaria, as I understand it," said Abrogastes, "it is the custom, in triumphs, to parade captive queens through the streets in chains of gold."

"It has been done," said Iaachus.

"In what you call barbarian worlds," said Abrogastes, "it is customary to place them in chains of iron and teach them to juice at a man's glance."

"Despicable beast!" said Viviana.

"Have the engines warmed!" called Abrogastes. "We depart!"

A susurration of satisfaction coursed amongst the intruders. Who knew if the timing of captains was inerrant? It takes a finite amount of time for a string-sprung arrow, a fired charge, a falling bomb to reach its point of impact. It is not well, obviously, to misjudge the interval.

Several men rushed from the room.

"Go!" cried Viviana, pointing to the great portal of the throne room. "Go!"

"Gather up the princesses," said Abrogastes, "put them in the carts, outside."

Rude hands were placed upon the royal bodies.

"Unhand us!" cried Viviana.

"You are coming with us, princesses," said Abrogastes.

"No!" cried Viviana.

Alacida wept, struggling in the grasp of a barbarian.

"I now inform you of your good fortune," said Abrogastes. "You will be brides for my sons."

CHAPTER FORTY-THREE

"No, no, never!" cried Viviana.

Telnarians surged forward, but stopped, short, menaced by leveled rifles. They clenched their fists, helpless.

"Brides for my sons," laughed Abrogastes, slapping the arm of the throne with his left hand.

"No, never!" cried Viviana. "My sister and I will never consent! You cannot enforce such an outrage upon us!"

"Then I will have you sold as sluts on a mud world," said Abrogastes.

Viviana threw her hand before her face, in horror, as though some physical, monstrous thing had intruded itself upon her sight. Alacida was limp, lapsed unconscious within the grasp of the warrior who held her.

"Put them in the carts," said Abrogastes, "and hie to the ships, with all speed."

Viviana was dragged screaming from the throne room, and Alacida, unconscious, was borne away in the arms of her keeper.

"Great king," cried Iaachus, "no priest, no ministrant, no judge, no official, no captain of a vessel, not of sea or air, or space, would officiate at such a marriage!"

"Thousands would do so," said Abrogastes.

"The empire would not recognize it," said Iaachus. "It would not be sanctioned by the senate!"

"The senate will sanction whatever it is told to sanction," said Abrogastes.

"Such a marriage would be spurious," said Iaachus.

"Not if done at the behest of the princesses," said Abrogastes.

Abrogastes then stood, holstering the pistol. He then adjusted the purple draping on the throne, regarded it for a moment, and then turned and descended to the level of the tiles. He paused to glance at the five kneeling, tunicked slaves, four on a neck rope, and one with her head down and her hands bound behind her back.

"What shall we do with these, Lord?" asked a Drisriak.

"Leave them," said Abrogastes. "They have served their purpose."

He then strode from the room.

A barbarian, a Dangar, lifted up Huta, in her chains, and carried her, following Abrogastes. Most of the barbarians then left the chamber. Those who held Iaachus, Julian, Otto, and the others at bay backed away a few feet, and then turned, and, too, left the chamber. One could already hear the readying of engines from beyond the great portal.

"What can be done?" asked Julian.

"Little, at present," said Iaachus.

"Surely the plan of Abrogastes is mad," said Julian.

"Not at all, my noble friend," said Iaachus. "I fear he has researched the matter with care. He is doubtless better informed of the rules of dynastic succession than many jurists. The princesses may not sit upon the throne, but, if they bore male issue, their issue would be next in line to the throne. If Emperor Aesilesius should abdicate, or, Orak forbid, in some way meet his end, perhaps as did his father, and his grandfather, the son of either Viviana or Alacida, whichever was first born, would be emperor."

"And the regent then, governing in the emperor's minority, would be Abrogastes," said Julian.

"Or one of his sons," said Iaachus.

"Confusion would be rampant," said Julian. "Incipient revolution would be abetted, secession would be invited, invasion welcomed."

"The empire might be divided a dozen ways," said Iaachus.

"Civil war would ensue," said Otto.

"The empire, divided against itself," said Julian, "would do work on which a dozen armed barbarian nations could not improve."

"And then," said Otto, "the Lion Ships return."

"And," said Iaachus, "the empire becomes, in essence, barbarian."

"Alemanni," said Otto.

"Beasts, unrestrained, befouling temples, swarming in sacred precincts," said Julian.

"Already," said Iaachus, "this is the fate of more than one world."

"Imperial fleets should arrive shortly," said Julian.

"And find no trace of Abrogastes, save in Telnar," said Otto.

"The game is not done," said Julian.

"No, it is not yet done," said Otto.

"Remove those slaves," said Iaachus. "Filthy, tunicked sluts have no place here, where emperors receive ambassadors and hold court."

"Yes, Lord," said a courtier.

"Wait!" said Iaachus. "Why does that slave conceal her features?"

Cornhair, her hair about her face, put her head down, to the tiles.

"Get her head up, where I may see her!" said Iaachus.

The courtier put his hand in her hair, and yanked her head up, and held it back, tightly, far back.

Iaachus rushed forward, and stopped.

"You!" said Iaachus.

"Forgive me, Master!" said Cornhair.

"Obviously she failed," said Julian, "to assassinate my friend."

"It seems you know a great deal, friend Julian," said Iaachus.

"Enough, Arbiter," said Julian.

"I think you would find it difficult to expose me and have me executed," said Iaachus.

"Certainly," said Julian. "Evidence is muchly lacking. And what exists would be challenged, or discounted. Too, I have little doubt that your plan, if disclosed, would have been supported by certain elements in high places, as judicious, warranted statecraft."

"Covert actions are sometimes in order," said Iaachus.

"Doubtless," said Julian.

"Perhaps you will now attempt to arrange another assassination," said Iaachus, "one which might prove more successful."

"One in your position is always in danger," said Julian.

"And perhaps one in yours," said Iaachus.

"I would prefer you as an ally, not as an enemy," said Julian.

"That may not be wise," said Iaachus.

"Perhaps not," said Julian.

"You came here to kill me," said Iaachus.

"No," said Julian. "I came here in good faith, as I said, and, as I said, to inform and be informed. I hoped that we might consult together, perhaps enleaguing ourselves, to the benefit of the empire."

"You have designs upon the throne," said Iaachus.

"If so," said Julian, "only to save the empire. The emperor is a mindless child."

"Was he always so?" asked Otto.

"That is a strange question," said Iaachus.

"I ask it," said Otto.

"From an early age, surely," said Iaachus.

"Who governs?" asked Otto.

"Essentially the empress mother," said Iaachus.

"But you advised, you had her ear," said Julian.

"Once," said Iaachus. "I fear not now."

"She now attends to the Exarch of Telnar?" said Julian.

"I fear so," said Iaachus.

Iaachus then turned to the slaves. "Take those four away, those on the neck rope," he said. "They have collars. It should be easy to return them to their Masters. If there is any difficulty, sell them."

"Yes, Lord," said a courtier, and led the small coffle away.

Iaachus then turned to Cornhair.

"Release her hair," he said.

The courtier removed his hand from Cornhair's hair, and she thrust her head to the tiles at Iaachus' feet.

"Lady Publennia," said Iaachus.

"I am not Lady Publennia, Master," she said. "I am a slave."

"What is your name, slave?" he asked.

"Whatever Masters wish," she said.

"What were you most recently called?" he asked.

"'Cornhair', Master," she said.

"That is a good name for you," he said, "given the particular shade of your blond hair."

"Thank you, Master," she said.

"You seem considerably different from when I last saw you," he said.

"I am a slave, Master," she said.

"Are you marked?"

"Yes, Master," she said.

He then bent down and pulled up the brief tunic, at her left side.

"Nicely marked," he said. "Tastefully."

"Thank you, Master."

"Unmistakably."

"Yes, Master."

"You have no collar," he said.

"It was taken," she said.

"I was told," he said, "that your colleagues were unable to extricate you from the imperial camp on Tangara."

"They made no effort to do so," she said.

"They left you to the mercy of Otungs," he said.

"Yes, Master."

"I was informed you were successful in your mission," he said.

"I failed, Master," she said. "Those who abandoned me, whom you call my colleagues, doubtless presumed I had succeeded, or would succeed, in my task."

"They fled."

"Yes, Master."

"I am surprised you were not tortured and slain," said Iaachus.

"I owe my life to Captain Ottonius," she said. "I was spared, to be sold. I was sold for a pig to Heruls."

"I did not know you failed until this afternoon," said Iaachus.

"Others doubtless knew, Arbiter," said Julian. "Captain Ottonius was actively engaged in recruiting, and training, allies. There was, too, doubtless communication between Tangara and Telnaria, probably through the Floonian enclave in Venitzia, the provincial capital on Tangara. I can well understand the dismay on the part of those you call her colleagues when they realized that Captain Ottonius lived, particularly following, I suppose, their assurances to you that the deed had been successfully completed."

"Much was kept from me," said Iaachus.

"They must live in terror," said Julian, "knowing that the truth, which is publicly known, which is widely known, must, sooner or later, come to your attention."

"Today it has," said Iaachus, "and much else has become clear, as well."

"What shall we do with this slave, Lord?" asked the courtier who stood near Cornhair, he who had held her head up, that her features might be exposed to the inspection of the Arbiter.

"What shall be done with you, slave?" inquired Iaachus.

"It will be done with me as Masters please," she whispered.

"You tremble," said Iaachus.

"Forgive me, Master," she said.

"You are well tied, are you not?" he asked.

"Yes, Master," she said. "I am helpless."

"Then," said he, "get up, run, flee, hasten, go, out into the city."

"Master?" she said.

"Have no fear," he said. "You will not be mistaken for a free woman."

Cornhair bent down and thrust her lips to the Arbiter's shoes, kissed them, several times, weeping, half hysterical with gratitude, and then sprang up and ran from the chamber.

"The Arbiter is merciful," said Julian.

"It is not important," said Iaachus. "She is only a slave."

"How did the father of the emperor die?" asked Otto.

"What does it matter?" asked Julian.

"I am curious," said Otto.

"Poison," said Iaachus. "And his father, the grandfather of Aesilesius, by assassination."

"Such things in the empire," said Julian, "are not unusual. The corridors in which power walks are often dark."

"I think," said Otto, "I will visit the emperor."

"Why?" asked Julian.

"To pay my respects," said Otto.

"On what grounds?" asked Iaachus.

"As king of the Otungs," said Otto.

"Take a toy," said Julian.

"I do not think so," said Otto.

"I do not understand," said Julian.

"A king does not bring a toy to an emperor," said Otto.

He then turned away.

"Hold, dear Ottonius," said Julian.

Otto paused.

"I have a question for the Arbiter," said Julian. "I would like for you to listen."

"I listen," said Otto.

Julian then turned to Iaachus. "Who, dear friend," said he, "is in charge of the city batteries?"

"There is a coordinator of batteries," said Iaachus, "and two captains, one in charge of each battery. The coordinator's and the captain's names will be, I am sure, familiar to at least our friend, Captain Ottonius. The coordinator's name is 'Phidias'. The two captains are named 'Lysis' and 'Corelius'."

"Yes," said Otto. "The names are familiar."

CHAPTER FORTY-FOUR

Cornhair, standing, alone, frightened, in the deserted street, Palace Street, several hundred yards from the palace, did not know which way to turn. She stood, uncertain, on the paving.

By the time she had been ordered to leave the palace, the many vehicles which had crowded the courtyard had withdrawn, doubtless to rendezvous with the waiting ships, outside the walls, in the large, much-avoided area of the noisome pits.

She had fled through the great portal, now unguarded, and had made her way down the several broad steps, more than fifty, to the level of the courtyard, then deserted.

Several fountains still sprayed their cascading rainbows of perfumed water. In the general silence one could hear the soft falling of water into water.

Then her small, lonely figure, had sped away, down Palace Street.

Now, out of breath, she stood in the street, far from doors on each side. Who knew what might issue forth from a door?

She pulled at the thongs which held her wrists behind her back. She was helpless. It is not even easy to run when so bound.

But she was alive!

But she wore no collar.

This made her decidedly uneasy.

Slaves are to be in collars. Free persons are clear on that. An uncollared slave could be in considerable jeopardy. Who is it who owns her? It is much safer for a slave to be in her collar. Too, of course, there is much security in the collar. It makes her status perfectly clear and it identifies her Master. Slaves know they must belong and the collar makes it clear they do belong, and to whom they belong. It says, in effect, this is not a stray. It tells us she has a home, that there is a pan from which she eats, a ring to which she is chained, a Master at whose feet she will warmly and happily curl.

To be in her Master's collar is reassuring to a slave.

It makes clear the nature of the proprietorship to which she is subject, that she is her Master's property.

Let free women scorn the slave, despise her, and beat her, but they do not know the joys of the slave, who lives to be owned and to submit to her Master. They do not know the wholeness of a submitted femininity, the rewards accruing to the female who is her Master's slave. She rejoices, knowing that she is owned, wholly, as a dog or shoe is owned; that she must obey and will be punished if she is not pleasing. She has a perfect identity, sanctioned by culture and grounded in nature.

In the collar, choiceless, owned, serving, she finds her fulfillment.

No woman can be truly happy who is not collared.

But, as we recall, Cornhair was not collared.

To be sure, she, barefoot, lovely, marked, half naked, her hands tied behind her, was in no danger of being mistaken for a free woman. Iaachus had assured her of that.

She started, hearing the creak of a hinge, on a door, to her left.

"Have they gone?" inquired a free man, through a crack in the doorway.

Addressed, she went to her knees. "Yes, Master," she said. "I think so, Master."

He emerged a yard or so into the street, and looked to the left and right. He then withdrew into the domicile. Cornhair had glimpsed a woman behind him, and a child. The door was narrow, and stout. There were no windows on the street level, but there were windows on the second level, the third, and fourth level. One was unshuttered, as she knelt.

She sensed a door opening some yards away, on her right. There would probably be others, shortly.

She sensed no one was now concerned with her. She leapt up, and hurried farther along Palace Street. As suggested earlier, she had no destination in mind, other than, perhaps, to put the palace, and its terrors, far behind her. She did not know what to do. Certainly she would not wish to return to the outlet of the House of Worlds, on Varl Street, as she had been sold from that house, and might be returned to the very Master who had planned to dispose of her in a particularly hideous and efficient manner. Indeed, it would have been as though she had never been. His two agents, of course, were dead, one killed by his companion and the other, the murderer, incinerated in his attempt to reach the city.

"Who owns me, or owned me," she wondered. Surely not even a madman would buy a slave simply to dispose of her. And the agents had been paid in gold, which betokens someone of affluence. Who would profit from her disappearance? She had mostly feared Iaachus, of course. He knew much, he had resources. The knowledge she bore, she had feared, if injudiciously broadcast, might put his role, his power, even his person, at risk. Yet now, from her experience in the palace, she no longer feared Iaachus. He had dismissed her. She was no longer important. Too, Julian, of the Aureliani, and his mighty friend, the barbarian, were clearly aware of his schemes, but, apparently, intended no prosecution or vengeance for several reasons, not simply for lack of evidence, and for recognition that his work would be likely to have been approved at higher levels, but, most significantly,

because of their desire to recruit the Arbiter and what influence
he might retain in some common cause. This left the three who
had been given the charge of abetting the projected assassination, those who had brought her, on the freighter, *Narcona*, to
Venitzia on Tangara, who had placed her in the remote camp
in the wilderness near the Otung forest, who had supplied the
poisoned dagger, those who had abandoned her, those who had
doubtless given assurances to the Arbiter that the barbarian,
Captain Ottonius, was no more, thus precluding the success of
the plan of Julian, scion of the Aureliani, to recruit barbarians,
and perhaps personal liegemen, in the imperial forces. These
would be Phidias, who had been captain of the *Narcona*, and
two of his officers, Lysis and Corelius. Surely these would have
much to fear from Iaachus and his power, if he learned of their
presumed incompetence, and, surely, of their duplicity. Indeed,
she had learned in the palace that these three had been rewarded
for a service they had failed to perform, and one whose failure
they had concealed. It would be, then, she was sure, that one or
more of these three had discovered her in Telnar and arranged
for her disposal. Too, it seemed that these three, either for gold,
or for fear of exposure, had betrayed their posts, permitting the
safe landing of the six Lion Ships of Abrogastes. She did not
know for certain, of course, of the present whereabouts of these
three. As their lives would be forfeit in Telnar following their
treachery, it seemed likely that they would have withdrawn
from Telnaria with Abrogastes in the Lion Ships. This supposition, as it turned out, though she could not have been sure of it
at the time, was correct. One may despise traitors; one may deny
them trust; but one is well advised to reward them well and
see to their security and welfare. Else it may prove difficult to
recruit others in the future.

Cornhair was reasonably sure that no one in Telnar bore her
ill will, at least to the extent of seeing fit to cast her into one
of the vast refuse pits outside the city. One who is dissatisfied

with a slave commonly beats her and sells her. After all, she is a commodity and, like any other domestic animal, has some value, however negligible. Iaachus had had her in his power, and released her. And Phidias, Lysis, and Corelius were presumably no longer in Telnar, or even on Telnaria.

She was now making her way, uncertainly, confused, anxiously, bound, down Palace Street, presumably because she had no idea what else to do. She was very much afraid she would be stopped. Frighteningly, there was no collar. Too, if the name of her Master was demanded, what could she do, or say? She did not know who had bought her. And who would believe that? Presumably it had been one or more of three traitors who had facilitated the raid of Abrogastes, but she could not know that for certain.

Various individuals were now emerging from the buildings. Shortly it would be generally known that the Lion Ships had departed.

She wondered if the abduction of the princesses, Viviana and Alacida, would be made public. She guessed not. Not immediately. But it would surely be difficult to conceal their absence.

The intruders had behaved with purpose and dispatch. They had not burned the city. They had done little, if any, looting. Speculation would be rampant as to their motivation, torrential with respect to what they had done, what they had taken, if anything.

Yes, it would be difficult to conceal, overlong, the absence of the princesses.

Cornhair now kept to the side of the street, hurrying along, not meeting the eyes of free persons. She kept her head down. Her hair, she hoped, would conceal to some extent her lack of a collar. The fact that she was bound did not excite much attention. Some Masters will keep a slave bound in the streets, sometimes as a punishment or a discipline, or merely to help her keep in mind that she is a slave. Naturally, being bound muchly increases a slave's sense of vulnerability. A slave is the most vulnerable of all women, and a bound slave, roped, thonged, chained or such, is the most vulnerable of slaves. Interesting, as well, is the fact that vulnerability in a slave muchly increases her sexual sensitivity, her readiness for the attentions of a Master. Many a bound slave writhes at the Master's feet, begging for the assuagement of her needs. Too, of course, many errands on which a slave may be dispatched do not require the use of her hands, for example, the communication of a message on behalf of her Master. It has also been suggested that a slave whose hands are tied behind her back is less likely to help herself to, say, a fruit from a vender's cart, the vender's attention being elsewhere directed. A small fruit, of course, might be seized in the teeth. A girl caught in such a peccadillo, of course, bound or unbound, is likely to be well switched. Even worse, her indiscretion might be recorded in an ink or grease marking on her body to be read by her Master on her return, quite possibly with unpleasant consequences.

More men and women were now about in the streets. Sometimes they picked their way amongst bodies.

As suggested earlier, in many districts of Telnar, there had been unrest, arson, looting, and such. The individuals, sometimes crowds, engaged in such activities had been largely, and deliberately, ignored by guardsmen, under orders from the palace. The consequences of the destruction of businesses and the burning of buildings, of general looting and widespread violence, were thought to be less politically grievous than would be firing on citizens. It also seems clear that such unruly activities may have been encouraged in certain quarters, in order to further some agenda. Certainly some of the looters, arsonists, and such, left graffiti about which suggested their actions were in accord with a variety of moral and religious principles, justice, restitution, and such. Somewhat paradoxically, an act which in one instance is accounted a crime and its perpetrator heinous is, in another instance, accounted a noble deed and its agent praiseworthy. We leave these mysterious matters to the ponderings of the reader. In any event, the intruders, in their approach to the palace, doubtless unfortunately, did not suffer from the same compunction, or orders, as the Telnar guardsmen, and did not hesitate to clear the streets, which put an instant end to a variety of miscellaneous civil disturbances.

Cornhair saw a body, most of a body, being dragged away.

Perhaps things would soon return to normal.

A shopkeeper was unchaining his guard planks, removing them from their grooves in the ceiling and floor of his shop.

Some of the planks had been struck by axes.

The shopkeeper glanced at Cornhair, and she hurried on.

She passed a two-wheeled hay cart being drawn by a single horse. Four bodies were heaped in the cart.

A small boy was casting a ball against a wall, and catching it as it rebounded. "Twenty-seven!" he said to a sandaled, robed fellow passing by.

Cornhair put down her head, being scrutinized by a free woman, leaning on the sill of a second story window, the shutters flung back.

There had been no mistaking the hostility in that glance.

Cornhair saw two guardsmen approaching, with bows.

Would they see that she was uncollared?

She moved to the other side of the street, keeping her head down.

They were making their way toward the palace, which was now well behind Cornhair. Had she turned, she could have seen it, small in the distance.

"Hold, slave!" said a sharp female voice, clearly that of one who knew she was Mistress.

Cornhair immediately knelt, her head down.

Cornhair knew that tone of voice. Often she had used it herself, when free, doubtless to the terror of frightened, instantly kneeling, small, exquisite, red-headed Nika, the single slave to which she had been reduced in her time of nigh destitution, abandoned by the Larial Calasalii, save for a pittance. That tone of voice was normally a prelude to a switching or whipping.

The hatred of the free woman for the female slave is well known. The cruelty of the Mistress to the female slave is legendary. All women are, in a sense, competitors for the attentions of men. Even women who claim, however hysterically, to hate men wish, it seems, to be found attractive by them. Surely that is of interest. And does not each woman hope to be found more beautiful, and more desirable, than the other? Take then this natural rivalry of woman and woman, and see it as it is manifested in the relationship of Mistress to slave. Here, the Mistress has all power and the slave none. Her rival is subordinate to her; her rival is at her mercy; she owns her rival. Exacerbate this relationship then with the understanding that the most desirable men, powerful, virile, intelligent, ambitious, possessive, aggressive men, are not immune to the charms of slaves. They want them, and can have them. They can buy them, and work them, and do what they want with them, exacting inordinate pleasures from their lovely bodies. Indeed, not every woman is collared; the collar is usually a badge, a certification, of female desirability. Indeed, many a free woman must face the annoying fact that men may find her slave not only her superior in beauty and desirability, doubtless much to the fear of the slave, whose skin may suffer for this, but may also find her more desirable simply in being a slave, the men understanding all that is involved in that lowly status.

One courts the free woman, commonly for gain; one buys the slave, invariably for pleasure.

Too, of course, if one should entertain an interest in female responsiveness, attention to the slave may be commended. In the slave, orgasms are easily elicited, often irrepressible, successive, and profound. Indeed, being a slave is to be in a state of incipient, global, sexual readiness; she is a needful, sexual creature. One supposes all this has something to do with the collar, with being subject to the whip, with the condition of being a slave in itself, with being owned, with having a Master.

"Hold, slave!" had said the woman.

How often had Cornhair used that tone of voice to Nika!

That had been a bitter, frustrating time for Cornhair, before her recruitment by Iaachus, Arbiter of Protocol, her credit blasted, her jewelries and possessions muchly sold, little more than a handful of pennies in her purse at any one time, forced to wear the same gown over and over, unable to buy new slippers, ignored by former acquaintances, tended by only one slave. Cornhair would have been a demanding, difficult Mistress even in her days of plenty, of station and affluence, but, in the miseries of her ostracization and penury, her normally arrogant, acerbic temper had considerably worsened.

She had not seen Nika since Tangara, when Nika, accompanied by Julian of the Aureliani and his colleague, Tuvo Ausonius, had been forced to identify her as her former Mistress. Where was Nika now? Cornhair had no idea. Slaves are commodities, and can be traded about, sold and so on, as other commodities. Doubtless Nika was still in a collar. Men kept beauties like Nika in collars. They wanted them that way. She also suspected that Nika wanted to be in a collar, though, she supposed, she would have preferred to pick the man whose collar she wore. But, of course, the slave is in no position to do that.

Cornhair was aware of a purple-hemmed robe before her, and small, golden slippers.

"You changed your position on the street," said the woman, "doubtless to evade the guardsmen. Why?"

"Oh, no, Mistress!" said Cornhair. "I search for an address."

"What address?" said the woman.

"Forgive me, Mistress," whispered Cornhair.

"I thought so," she said.

"May I proceed, Mistress?" asked Cornhair.

"Ah! I see!" said the woman. "Your collar! Where is it?"

"It was taken, Mistress," said Cornhair. "The barbarians!"

"They took it, and not you?" she asked.

"Yes, Mistress," said Cornhair.

"Liar!" she said. "It is the same with all you sluts. The less clothing you wear the more you lie!"

"Forgive me, Mistress," said Cornhair. Actually, of course, the penalties for lying in a slave are grievous, whereas in a free woman they are nonexistent or negligible. Cornhair, sensing herself in severe straits, dared not speak the truth.

"Why are you tied?" asked the woman.

"Masters were pleased to have it so," she said.

"Who is your Master?" asked the woman.

"Forgive me," said Cornhair. "I do not know, Mistress."

"Absurd," said the woman. "Have you had a fall? Are you drugged? Are you a runaway?"

"I am bound, Mistress," said Cornhair, weakly.

"Speak up," she said, "who is your Master?"

"I do not know, Mistress," said Cornhair.

"I see you are a slave," she said. "Need I examine your thigh?"

"No, Mistress," said Cornhair. "I am a slave."

"But you are uncollared."

"Yes, Mistress," said Cornhair.

"That is a serious matter," said the woman. "I shall summon a guardsman."

"No, please, do not, Mistress!" begged Cornhair.

"You are at my mercy, wholly," said the woman.

"Yes, Mistress," said Cornhair, in misery.

"Your Master!" demanded the woman.

"I think, Mistress," said Cornhair, "I was purchased by an unknown traitor, who fled with the barbarians."

"That is a rich story," she said.

"I think it is true, Mistress," said Cornhair.

"I pronounce you a loose, unclaimed slave," said the woman.

"Mistress?" said Cornhair.

"I claim you," she said.

"Mistress?" said Cornhair.

"Get your head up, slave," she snapped, "and look at me!"

Cornhair raised her head.

"I thought so!" said the woman. "Excellent!"

"Mistress?" said Cornhair, bewildered.

"You are claimed, and owned," she said. "Like a loose dog."

Cornhair looked about, wildly, from her knees.

"You do not recognize me, do you?" asked the woman.

"No, Mistress," said Cornhair.

"What have your Masters called you, worthless slut?" she asked.

"'Cornhair'," said Cornhair.

"Excellent," said the woman, "an excellent slave name for you, a name based on a physical characteristic, as in many animals. I like it much better than 'Publennia'."

Cornhair groaned.

"Yes," she said, "I knew you well, though from afar, when you were so proud, so superior and beautiful in your gowns and jewels, sparkling at the races and gambling tables, witty in the galleries and salons, esteemed at banquets, applauded in the streets, beleaguered by suitors, celebrated by sycophants, the jewel of the society of a dozen worlds, until the crash of your fortunes, the Larial Calasalii's loss of patience with your profligacy, and now you have come to this, a trembling, marked, tunicked slave kneeling on the pavement in Telnar."

"Be merciful, Mistress," said Cornhair.

"You still do not know me, do you?" said the woman.

"No, Mistress,'" said Cornhair.

"Even in the days of your triumphs and glory," said the woman, "I saw through the finery and show to the worthless slut beneath, who deserved no better than a collar, and a minute or two on a cheap slave block."

"Forgive me, Mistress," said Cornhair. "I do not remember you."

"I remember you well enough," she said. "You declined my overtures of friendship. Though I extended you invitations you would not respond in kind. I might not attend your salons, nor would you attend mine. You mocked my state, you would not greet me, you ignored me in public. I, though of the *honestori*, was too small for you, of the noble patricians, even of the senatorial class! What pleasure you must have taken in humiliating me! How pleased I was at the reversal of your fortunes, and now, what a triumph, to have you on your knees before me, a meaningless slave."

"Please, Mistress," said Cornhair. "Be kind!"

"To a slave?" she laughed.

Cornhair moaned.

"I now own you, slave," she cried.

Some men, and two women, had gathered about.

"Behold my slave!" said the woman to the small crowd. She then returned her attention to Cornhair. "Bend down, slave," she snapped, "head to the pavement, and cover my slippers with kisses."

Cornhair, miserable, terrified, bent down, and, again and again, desperately, pressed her lips, kissing, to the golden slippers of the Lady Gia Alexia.

"Whose property are you?" demanded the Lady Gia Alexia.

"I do not know," wept Cornhair. "I do not remember you."

"Stupid slave!" said the woman.

"Yes, Mistress," said Cornhair.

"I am the Lady Gia Alexia, of the Darsai, of Telnar!" said the woman.

"Oh, yes, yes!" cried Cornhair, in misery.

"You remember?"

"Yes, Mistress," wept Cornhair.

"There were doubtless many such as I," said Lady Gia Alexia.

"Forgive me, Mistress," said Cornhair.

"So, speak!" demanded the Lady Gia Alexia. "Whose property are you?"

"I am the property of the Lady Gia Alexia, of the Darsai!" wept Cornhair, her lips barely lifted from the slippers of her Mistress.

"Of Telnar!" demanded the woman.

"Of Telnar!" said Cornhair.

"Minister again, to my slippers," said the woman.

"Yes, Mistress," said Cornhair.

"She is not collared," observed one of the men.

"On the way home," said the Lady Gia Alexia, "I will purchase a collar, and a whip."

The small crowd then dissipated.

"On your feet, slave," said the Lady Gia Alexia.

Cornhair struggled to her feet.

"Get your head up," said the Lady Gia Alexia.

"Yes, Mistress," said Cornhair.

"Good," said the Lady Gia Alexia.

"What are you going to do with me?" begged Cornhair.

"Treat you as the slave you are," said the woman. "And then I shall sell you and make some coin on you. In this way, you will be good for something, perhaps for the first time in your life, if not much."

"Yes, Mistress," said Cornhair.

"We will now go to my domicile," said the Lady Gia Alexia.

"Yes, Mistress," said Cornhair.

"But, first," she said, "we will stop by a shop I know, and buy a collar and a whip."

"Yes, Mistress," said Cornhair.

"That way, move," said the Lady Gia Alexia, gesturing.

"Yes, Mistress," said Cornhair.

CHAPTER FORTY-FIVE

"So," said Iaachus, "it is the Day of a Thousand Martyrs."

"It seems Sidonicus, the noble Exarch of Telnar, will have it so," said Julian.

"Will he not send his mindless minions into the streets again?" said Otto.

"I do not think so," said Iaachus. "A thousand martyrs will do for now."

"At least," said Julian, "he will be unable to blame the blood in the streets on the empire."

"Not at all," said Iaachus. "It will depend on what he sees as judicious at the time. He may well, he being skilled in conspiracies, see conspiracy here. For example, the city batteries did not fire. Thus, perhaps the empire, colluding with barbarians, arranged for the raid, a small raid, that civil disturbances might be ended, but seemingly by a third party. Thus, the empire is at fault. And thus allegiance to the empire may be foresworn."

"But the princesses were abducted," said Julian.

"How would one know?" asked Iaachus. "Perhaps the supposed abduction was merely a clever way of lending a smell of authenticity to the conspiracy. Perhaps they were not abducted, but merely hidden away, to be produced later, when appropriate."

"What is the exarch to gain," asked Otto, "by lawlessness, by trespass, by arson and theft?"

"Power," said Iaachus. "He wishes to use his adherents, his converts, and such, to bring about a new society, one in which such as he will be sovereign. He who wishes to rule, and cannot rule in the world as it is, wishes to change the world in such a way that he will rule. It is not an unusual situation. It requires little more than the unscrupulous readiness to lie, and the willingness to destroy and kill. The dilemma presented to us is patent. Either surrender the empire or lose it."

"I do not understand," said Otto.

"If the empire does not declare for his faith," said Iaachus, "the riots will continue, or may begin again, destroying the empire from within, or, alternatively, at the very least, Floonians, in their growing numbers, will remain quiescent while the empire perishes. If, on the other hand, the empire does declare for his faith, as he wishes, and promotes it with imperial resources, by means of the burning rack, the sword, and such, he will see to it that his herds and flocks support the empire, the new, revised empire, the empire as he wishes it to be. Thus, the empire as we know it is to be either lost or surrendered, either to perish or change, either to be destroyed or transformed into an eccentric, hideous tyranny, a prison house of the mind and body, with Sidonicus and his sort, with their riches, ensconced as jailers and guards."

"I have known Floonians," said Otto, "when I was on Tangara, some, brothers of the *festung* of Sim Giadini, and others, as well. They were good, kind people. Many were devout, unworldly, humble, sincere in their strange faith."

"These are the cattle on which the herdsmen batten," said Iaachus. "And I have little doubt of the honesty, the devotion, and sincerity of many of the ministrants of Floon, as well. Indeed, where would Sidonicus and his sort be were it not for the services of simple, unquestioning men?"

"Most men will believe whatever they are told," said Julian. "It is only necessary to tell it to them repeatedly and with confidence. Who would dare to suppose that what is heard so often and uttered with such assurance might, nonetheless, be a lie, or simply false, or, more likely, merely meaningless? Who asks for evidence? Is that not in poor taste, or even dangerous? Thought, like pain, can be unpleasant. When the body does not move less pain is felt. Many men would rather die than think, and some who can think would rather die than act."

"We know," said Otto, "from the business of the medallion and chain, that the Exarch of Telnar, or his agents, have contacted barbarians."

"The strategy, as I now realize," said Iaachus, "and had not realized before, is not only devious, but multifaceted. Sidonicus will accept the empire either from the throne or from the bloody swords of barbarians. Consider the possibility that Sidonicus enrolls his Floonians under the banners of barbarians. Instructed, they would do war for the empire or its foes, either one. Or, indeed, otherwise instructed, do no war, at all. Indeed, it would be more in accord with the purer, more primitive teachings of Floon, as I understand it, that no resistance is to be offered to enemies."

"Yes," said Julian, "and on some worlds entire populations of such obliging Floonians were summarily exterminated, their worlds then effortlessly acquired by the scions of more business-like nations and species."

"I could conceive of Floonians welcoming invaders as liberators," said Iaachus.

"I, as well," said Otto.

"The empress mother has left the palace, to attend the obsequies of the Thousand Martyrs," said Iaachus.

"She would prove a mighty ally to Sidonicus," said Julian.

"But a more dangerous ally than he might think," said Iaachus.

"How is that?" asked Julian.

"There is one thing in the Floonian phenomenon," said

Iaachus, "a subtle political flaw, which I hope will never be remedied, which gives me hope."

"What is that?" asked Otto.

"It may be nothing," said Iaachus. "We may speak of it later."

"The empress mother, as I understand it," said Julian, "is receiving instruction in Floonianism from the exarch himself."

"That is true," said Iaachus.

"Suppose she is converted, smudged with the holy oil," said Julian. "Consider her influence over the emperor."

"I fear it," said Iaachus.

"I, too," said Julian. "Very much."

"As I understand it," said Iaachus, "our friend and colleague, Captain Ottonius, has recently had an interview with the emperor."

"Yes," said Otto. "That is true."

"It is unfortunate," said Iaachus, "particularly in these perilous times, that the emperor is only a boy, a retarded simpleton who cares for little but toys, and can barely sign his own name."

"Yes," said Otto, smiling, "it is unfortunate."

"Why do you smile, friend Ottonius?" asked the Arbiter of Protocol.

"We may speak of it later," said Otto.

CHAPTER FORTY-SIX

Cornhair shook her head a little, rustling the loop of chain wound about her neck, padlocked behind the back of her neck, fastening her to the others.

"Lift your head, stand straight," said the slaver's man.

Cornhair lifted her head, and straightened her body.

The long chain passed through rings, fastened to the wall behind the slaves. Every four or five feet, or so, it was wound about a slave's neck and, as with Cornhair, two of its links were fastened together, behind the girl's neck, with a padlock. In this fashion a girl may be easily added to the chain, or removed from it. The slave shelf on which the slaves stood was some one hundred feet in length and some four feet in depth. It was about three feet in height, from the street. The hands of each slave were manacled behind her back. The height of the shelf makes for easy viewing from the street, and the surface of the shelf, reached by four steps, entirely along its front, is wide enough to allow a prospective customer to ascend to its surface and more closely examine a slave, to test her limbs and body for soundness, to examine her skin for blemishes, her teeth for regularity, and so on. The prospective buyer may also test the slave for responsiveness, as that is extremely important in a slave. She is not a free woman. It might also be mentioned that most female slaves are extremely, helplessly responsive. That seems to be an accompanying characteristic of the condition, and the collar. Also, they do not wish to be whipped. The market, as one would suppose, was one of Telnar's woman markets. There were several such markets in Telnar. This particular market was known as Tenrik's Woman Market. It was in one of Telnar's more shabby districts. It had seen its share of looting and arson. Indeed, from where Cornhair stood, her back to the wall, one of some twenty to twenty five or so slaves, she could see two burned-out shops. Some debris had been gathered together and placed to one side. Aside from this, things had returned muchly to normal here, and elsewhere, in Telnar. The guard planks of shops, with their rods and slung chains, which would be run through plank rings, were again stored to the side. Once more guardsmen, in their pairs, or larger numbers, made their rounds. Shutters were opened at higher levels. In two windows Cornhair could see plants. From another window, a pole was extended, on which washing hung. Men and women were about, passing by, conversing, shopping. A tunicked slave hurried by. Occasionally a man or woman paused to look at the slaves on the shelf. Cornhair could hear the tapping of a smith's hammer somewhere. Within the last hour a redhead had been sold from the chain.

Across the street, some fifty feet or so away, and to the left of Cornhair, as she was chained, there was a small restaurant, catering mostly to workmen, little more than a room, a kitchen, and a counter. Within there were four tables, and outside, two tables on the street. In such a place one might get some bread, olives, and cheese, which one might wash down with beer or a cheap, pale *kana*. Soup, if one wished it, could be ladled out from a lidded receptacle within the counter itself. Many took their orders with them, wrapped in folds of brown, waxed paper.

Cornhair felt the tip of the slaver's man's switch at the side of her neck. Frightened, she straightened her body more.

"I have seldom seen a slave so switched," said the slaver's man, examining Cornhair's tortured skin.

"My Mistress found me displeasing," said Cornhair.

"Women do not know how to handle women," said the man.

"They handle them as they wish," said Cornhair.

"Pray to Dira," he said, "that a man buys you."

Dira, the goddess of love and beauty in the Telnarian pan-theon, herself a slave girl, the slave girl of the gods, was the god-dess of slave girls.

"I shall surely hope that a man buys me, Master," she said.

This hope was common amongst female slaves. The natural subordination of the female is to the male. There you have the perfect complementarity of owner and owned, of Master and slave. Men may own, dominate, and master their slaves without compromise, but they are also quite likely, having what they want, to be satisfied with them, and happy with them. Indeed, many men, at least to other men, boast of the quality of their rope sluts and chain bitches. Too, as every slave girl knows, men are easy to please. When a man has what he wants, he is content. Why should he not be? Most men are kind to their slaves and treat them well, as they would any other beast they own. Indeed, it is rumored some men, unwisely perhaps, actually grow fond of their meaningless, luscious chattels. Indeed, the female slave is very special amongst the beasts a man might own. In his slave the man has all the intelligence, beauty, needs, depth, emotions, and feelings of the human female, all her excitement, desirabil-ity, sensitivity, helplessness, and vulnerability, and it is all his, all safe in his collar.

Too, the intervention of the free male is often the only thing the slave girl can hope for, to protect her from the hatred, jeal-ousy, and cruelty of the free woman. The free male is often the only thing standing between the slave and the free woman, reso-lute and unconstrained, driven by vindictiveness and malice.

"Tenrik will soon be about, himself," said the slaver's man, "to hang your placard about your neck."

"What will it say, Master?" asked Cornhair.

"I do not know," said the slaver's man.

"Should we not be permitted clothing, Master?" asked Cornhair.

"Not on Tenrik's shelf," said the man. "Do you think you are a free woman?"

"No, Master," she said.

"Men like to see what they are buying," he said.

"Yes, Master," said Cornhair.

The fellow then seized one of Cornhair's wrists, behind her, it manacled, chained to the other, by three links. He shook the wrist, with a rustle of linkage.

"You are well held," he said, releasing her wrist.

"Yes, Master," she said.

"Tenrik will be along presently," he said.

"Yes, Master," she said.

It had now been six days since the raid of Abrogastes on the capital, leading to the encounters in the palace, and the abduction of the two royal princesses, Viviana and Alacida. As nearly as Cornhair could gather, the abduction was not generally known.

The last few days had surely been amongst the worst in Cornhair's life. In the lofty behaviors of her days of freedom, long ago, she had given little attention to the men and women she had routinely dismissed and slighted. They were not even enemies. They were too far beneath her. They were little more, from her point of view, than *humiliori*, save for their pretensions. Sometimes she mocked them, more often she ignored them, patently. Whereas she had frequently received the gratifications attendant on the superior person's license to despise and humiliate inferiors, she had failed to realize, in her naïveté, that these others, however mistakenly, might take themselves as seriously as she took herself, and that slights, and such, unavenged, not replied to, might rankle, and fester, for years. How pleased then would so many have been, had they discovered the downfall of that haughty, thought-less patrician, even of the senatorial class, the Lady Publennia, of the Larial Calasalii, who had been the source of so many of their most keenly felt humiliations. Cornhair, in the mat-ter of the Lady Gia Alexia of the Telnar Darsai, had fallen into the clutches of an enemy whom she had wholly forgotten, and even earlier, when aware of her, would never have accorded the dignity of being regarded as a rival, let alone an enemy.

"There!" had cried the Lady Gia Alexia, as she had snapped the collar on Cornhair's neck. And then had come the first of Cornhair's many switchings. The Lady Gia Alexia, almost beside herself with fury, had laid the switch liberally on the body of her slave, until scarcely an inch of Cornhair had not felt its stroke. She was even struck across the face, and she feared she might be blinded. She put her head down. She was struck even on the back and sides of the neck, and on the calves and ankles, as well as on her back and belly, sides, and arms and legs. "Please stop, Mistress! Please, stop, Mistress!" had begged Cornhair.

"There you are," laughed the Lady Gia Alexia, lowering the switch, her arm weary, "once the rich, arrogant Publennia, scion of the Larial Calasalii, now a blubbering, beaten slave! Is it not true?"

"Yes, yes, Mistress," wept Cornhair. "Please do not beat me more!"

"Can you cook, slave?" asked the Lady Gia Alexia. "Can you sew?"

"No, Mistress," wept Cornhair, her body a shuddering ter-rain of stinging fire.

"Can you do hair? Can you draw baths? Can you mix cosmet-ics, perfumes, use the pencils and brushes?"

"No, Mistress," wept Cornhair. "Such things were done for me."

"Useless slave!" said the Lady Gia Alexia.

"Yes, Mistress," said Cornhair.

"Perhaps you can launder, scrub floors, and carry a market basket behind your Mistress?"

"Yes, Mistress," wept Cornhair.

"And carry notes for me, to my male friends?" she said.

"Yes, Mistress," wept Cornhair.

"I have chains in my domicile, left over from a former tenant," she said. "I am sure they will fit you nicely."

"Yes, Mistress," said Cornhair. "Thank you, Mistress."

"You are familiar with slave gruel, are you not?"

"Yes, Mistress," said Cornhair.

"We will find a pan for you," she said. "In the domicile, as you are a beast, you will, of course, not use your hands to feed yourself. Too, as you are a beast, you are not to stand upright. You may, of course, sit on the floor, kneel, lie down, be on your belly, be on all fours, or such. Too, you are not to use human speech unless permitted. If you wish to speak, you must approach me on all fours and whimper, for permission."

"Yes, Mistress," said Cornhair.

Such strictures, of course, impractical on the street, were limited to the domicile.

As mentioned earlier, the last few days had been amongst the worst in Cornhair's life. She was confined to lowly domestic labors, primarily the scrubbing of floors, naked and shackled, and, in this task, was loaned out, for a pittance, to several neighbors. She was also used for laundering, polishing leather, polishing silver, and such. Occasionally, she accompanied her Mistress to the market, bearing her basket, some steps behind her. Once, on the street, encountering some of her friends, the Lady Gia Alexia had turned to Cornhair, and had held out her switch to her. "Take it, if you wish," she said. "I give you permission to strike me with it." "No, no, Mistress!" had cried Cornhair, terrified, and fell to her knees, and put down her head, and piteously, in her terror, kissed, again and again, the Lady Gia Alexia's slippers. One of her friends had laughed.

"Now," she said, "dear Gia, you need not cut off her ears and nose." Cornhair, of course, from her days of freedom, was fully cognizant of the penalties which might attend such things, perceived imperfections in a slave's deportment or service, things, for example, such as failing to speak deferentially to a free person, let alone such things as raising one's hand to a free person, or striking a free person.

Nights were unpleasant for Cornhair, for the Lady Gia Alexia kept her in close chains, and chained by the neck, closely, to a ring in the foot of her couch. The morning and bedtime switchings, brief as they were, were also unpleasant.

Cornhair, in her days of freedom, with her slaves, and, later, after her reduction in wealth and status, consequent upon the Larial Calasalii's loss of patience with her profligacy, with her single slave, Nika, had never considered that she herself might one day find herself in her present position, herself a slave at the mercy of a free woman.

The free woman hates the slave; the slave lives in terror of the free woman. And Cornhair was now a slave.

Aside from her various tasks, scrubbing, laundering, and such, Cornhair had also been utilized, as is not unknown for a free woman's slave, to convey messages on behalf of her Mistress.

Naturally it is much preferable to use one's own slave for such a purpose, particularly in certain instances, than to rely on the slave of a friend, a friend who has friends, with whom she is accustomed to exchange pleasantries.

The free woman's slave, as she is inconspicuous, generally not known, and such, is, accordingly, a frequently relied upon instrument in her Mistress' adventures. She constitutes an invaluable go-between in situations where a visible presence of the Mistress would be perilous, if not unthinkable. Indeed, the intrigues and assignations of a free woman would scarcely be conceivable were it not for the mediation of the free woman's slave. By means of the slave, of course, bearing the relevant notes back and forth, assignations, trysts, secret meetings, and such, may be conveniently and discreetly arranged.

Four times, and twice in one day, Cornhair had borne a note from her Mistress to a gentleman in the Lycon district, an attorney and rhetor, Titus Gelinus, prominent in the courts. Indeed, his cross-examinations, summations, and perorations were commonly greeted with applause by auditors, many of whom, it seems, had crowded into the galleries to hear him speak. This was particularly impressive because, apparently, this applause was not previously arranged for, and paid for, as was rumored to be the case in many trials. Sitting in on trials, and following interesting cases, and such, was a favorite pastime of many citizens of Telnar, at least those who, apparently, had little else to do.

Cornhair knew little of the law. She did know, even from her days of freedom, that the testimony of slaves was taken under torture.

"There are many welts on your body," had said Titus Gelinus, when first Cornhair had knelt before him, head down, and held up, in two hands, she small, scented note she was to deliver.

"My Mistress was not pleased with me, Master," had said Cornhair.

"I suspect she is seldom pleased with anyone," said Titus Gelinus.

Cornhair remained silent.

"Are you a good slave?" asked Titus Gelinus.

"I am a slave," said Cornhair. "I try to be a good slave."

"Look up," said the rhetor.

Cornhair looked up, but avoided meeting the rhetor's eyes.

"I have seen many such as you on the rack," he said.

Cornhair, again, was silent. She did shudder.

Titus Gelinus then took the note, held it briefly to his nose, smelled it, and then opened it, and glanced at it, following which, with an annoyed gesture, he put it on a silver dish, on a marble-topped table to the side.

The rhetor had then returned his attention to Cornhair. "You are new," he said.

"I have only recently had the honor of being put in Mistress' collar," said Cornhair.

"You are well-curved," he said.

"Thank you, Master," said Cornhair.

"You should be a man's slave," he said.

Cornhair put down her head, and dared not respond. Cornhair realized that he, no more than anyone else, had questioned that she should be a slave, only that she would be more suitably owned by a male. And Cornhair herself, as we have gathered, had come to the realization, from her deepest thoughts, fought against for so long, in stark contrast to all that she had been taught, and her former life of arrogance and affluence, that she was appropriately a slave. That former life had been a lie. She belonged in a collar, at a man's feet. She could not be herself otherwise; she could not be whole otherwise.

"Do you know the contents of this note?" asked Titus Gelinus.

"No, Master," said Cornhair.

"Can you read?"

"Yes, Master, but I did not read the note."

"Your Mistress wishes a tryst in a secret place," he said.

"She is a free woman," said Cornhair.

"Doubtless she fears for her reputation," he said.

"Doubtless, Master," said Cornhair.

"I am tempted to oblige her," he said.

"I am sure she would be delighted, Master," said Cornhair.

"You are pretty," he said. "Perhaps you are worth a roll on the rug at the foot of my couch."

"Please, no, Master!" said Cornhair. "I am a woman's slave!"

"You are to be denied the touch of men?"

"Yes, Master," said Cornhair. "Please do not put me to your pleasure, lest I be maimed, mutilated, or slain by my Mistress!"

"She would know?"

"I fear so, Master," said Cornhair.

"I grow weary of your Mistress, and the others, their kind," he said. "I would, if I could, bar them from the galleries. Let them keep to the theaters, let them adore actors who portray heroes; let them applaud and acclaim poets, singers, gladiators, wrestlers, muleteers, drivers of four-horse and two-horse teams, athletes, vegetable growers, whoever, whatever, and refrain from wasting my time."

"Is there a response to the note, Master?" asked Cornhair. "My Mistress will be waiting."

"Tell your Mistress," he said, "I have never received a more remarkable note."

"I am sure she will be pleased," said Cornhair.

"I am a man of influence and power," he said.

"That is my understanding," said Cornhair.

"Times are uncertain, and trying," he said.

"Yes, Master," said Cornhair.

"Would your Mistress' ankles look well in shackles?" he asked.

"I do not know, Master," said Cornhair, uneasily. "I have never thought of it. But perhaps, Master, she is a woman."

"Good," said Titus Gelinus, attorney and rhetor. "Leave through the kitchen. Ask for food, and a draught of *kana*."

"Yes, Master!" said Cornhair, gratefully.

"You will take such things on your knees," he said.

"Yes, Master!" said Cornhair.

Two days ago the Lady Gia Alexia had been returning from the market, and Cornhair had been following her, four paces behind, with the shopping basket.

The Lady Gia Alexia was, if possible, in a less favorable mood than usual. Certainly she had bargained in the market in a most demanding and abusive manner, which modality of discourse seemed, however, to have had little, if any, influence on the quantity, quality, or cost of her purchases. The underlying disgruntlement on the part of the Lady Gia Alexia, which had spilled over into the unpleasantries in the market, had to do, as the reader may already suppose, with Titus Gelinus. As yet, despite the Lady Gia Alexia's zeal and importunities, no private meeting had been arranged with the rhetor.

Understandably, given the dispositions and personality of the Lady Gia Alexia, this lack of progress was conjectured to have, quite possibly, something to do with the bearer of her notes.

Cornhair was still in the tunic in which she had been turned over to the two agents of her mysterious buyer, that given to her in the outlet of House of Worlds on Varl Street, here in Telnar. It had been laundered several times, of course, in the interval between the House of Worlds and this current trip to the market, several days later. It was a light garment, and certainly not substantial, either in its length or weaving. Given the washings, its normal wear, and, we fear, the attentions of the lady Gia Alexia's switch, often applied to its miserable occupant, it had become a bit parted, here and there, and, here and there, somewhat tattered, even ragged. As a result, certain aspects of Cornhair's appearance were accentuated, if possible, even more so than is commonly the case with such a garment, designed, it seems, as much to reveal as conceal. It seems probable that the Lady Gia Alexia's intention in the matter of her slave's clothing was, at least in her view, to debase and degrade the slave. Had Cornhair been a free woman doubtless she would have been appropriately debased and degraded, but, of course, she was not a free woman. As a slave she took such a slight garmenture for granted. It was cultural for such as she, even as the collar. Too, slaves are commonly content with their bodies, indeed, happy with them. It seldom occurs to them, as it often occurs with free women, to be ashamed of their bodies. They rejoice in their naturalness, in their health and beauty; enjoying the same entitlements in this regard as would be accorded to any other lovely domestic animal. Too, it must be noted that slave garmenture is quite comfortable, and permits a considerable freedom of movement, two features not always found in the garments of the free woman, more constrained by convention and the dictates of propriety. Lastly, women wish to appeal to men. What woman does not wish to be found attractive? What woman does not wish to be found stimulating? What woman objects to being found exciting? Surely it is flattering and reassuring to a woman to know that she is desirable, that men want her, that men would like to have her in their collar. And what woman, then, finds herself the most wanted, and desired, of all women? The woman on the slave block, the one chained at his feet, the one in his collar.

Do you think the slave does not know how she is seen by men? Do you think she does not know how they turn to regard her in the street, how they assess her, how they speculate on what it would be to own her?

She is the most female, and desirable, of all women, the female slave.

"Oh!" cried Cornhair, almost spilling produce from the basket.

Had the Lady Gia Alexia not been so determined to enact her vengeances on the former Lady Publennia, of the Larial Calasalii, she might have provided her with a garment more suitable to a woman's slave, one longer, more opaque, and such.

The Lady Gia Alexia spun about, angrily, switch in hand. "What is wrong?" she demanded.

"I was touched, Mistress!" wept Cornhair.

It was crowded, near the market. It was not clear who might have accosted the slave, in passing.

"Shameless, provocative slut!" said the Lady Gia Alexia, striking Cornhair across the upper left arm with her switch.

Cornhair knelt, head down, clutching the basket to her. She was then struck thrice more, once on the left side of the neck, once on the right side of the neck, and then, again, on the left side of the neck.

"Forgive me, Mistress," said Cornhair. "I cannot help that I have the body I have, that I am in a collar!"

The Lady Gia Alexia backed away a pace.

"I do not see what men see in slaves," she said. "Their beauty cannot begin to compare with that of a free woman."

Cornhair kept her head down.

"Are you attractive?" she asked Cornhair.

"Some men have found me so, I think, Mistress," whispered Cornhair, hoping not to be again struck. Her arm and neck still stung. "Do you think Titus Gelinus might find you more attractive than I?" asked the Lady Gia Alexia.

"Surely not, Mistress," said Cornhair, shuddering.

The switch moved near her, but did not strike her. Cornhair could see its shadow.

"I cannot risk that," said the Lady Gia Alexia. "Men are so stupid."

"Forgive me, if I have been displeasing," said Cornhair.

"I shall borrow, or rent, a plainer slave," said the Lady Gia Alexia.

"Mistress?" said Cornhair, looking up.

"I have had enough of you," said the Lady Gia Alexia. "Tomorrow morning I will see what I can get for you."

"Mistress is going to sell me?" asked Cornhair.

"Yes," said the Lady Gia Alexia, "and I trust you will not be so fortunate as to be purchased by a woman. That would be too good for you. Men are stupid, lustful beasts, gross brutes. Therefore, it is my hope that you will find yourself at the mercy of one."

"Yes, Mistress," whispered Cornhair.

"Indeed, that is almost certain," she said.

"Yes, Mistress," said Cornhair.

"Weep, lament, and cry 'woe'," she laughed.

"Yes, Mistress," said Cornhair.

"And I will make sure of something in your sale which will make a difference," she said, "something which some may find of interest."

"I do not understand, Mistress," said Cornhair.

"You will see," she said.

"Yes, Mistress," said Cornhair.

The slaver's man had now left Cornhair in her position on the shelf, with the others, the long chain running through its rings from the girl to her left, looped and padlocked about her throat, and then continuing on through the rings to the girl on her right, who was similarly secured, and so on.

Cornhair's hands were manacled behind her. She was unclothed. Men, it seemed, liked to see what they were buying.

Men occasionally inspected the slaves. Sometimes they climbed to the height of the shelf, to inspect them more closely, to handle them, and such.

Cornhair could see the small restaurant across the street, to her left. A girl, a slave, was ladling out soup from the pot recessed in the counter. Another slave, briefly tunicked, was waiting on one of the interior tables. Such establishments commonly buy attractive female slaves, which is good for business. There is a turnover amongst such slaves, as men occasionally wish to take one home. Indeed, in its way, two girl markets faced one another across the street, the slave shelf and the restaurant, whose waitresses might be purchased. The waitresses had an advantage over the shelf girls, as they might move about before the Masters, chat with them, flirt with them, and such. Within the restaurant, on its right side, as one looked inward, was a narrow stairway, which led up, Cornhair supposed, to some rooms or apartments on a higher floor. There were few private homes in Telnar. Most of the buildings were four to six stories in height. The building across the street was four stories in height. The slaves would not be housed upstairs, as they were slaves. Presumably they would be housed in the back of the restaurant, or in its cellar.

Cornhair had been assured that Tenrik, owner of Tenrik's Woman Market, where she was exhibited, would soon be about, to hang her placard about her neck.

It was warm on the shelf.

The intruders, the raiders, had not taken her with them. So easily she might have been the slave of barbarians! So easy it is to carry a woman away in ropes or chains! That still might occur, of course. Many girls had changed hands a number of times, and had worn their collars on several worlds, barbarian, imperial, primitive, and so on. The slave rose was known on agricultural worlds, industrial worlds, jungle worlds, desert worlds, sophisticated worlds, provincial worlds.

Cornhair was aware of being approached.

She straightened her body, and lifted her head.

She felt a placard, on its cords, being hung about her neck.

"May I speak, Master?" she asked.

"Yes," she was told.

"I thank Master for the soothing balm," she said. It had been applied by a slaver's man before she was brought to the shelf and added to the chain. She knew it need not have been applied.

"The welting will subside in time," he said.

"Master," she said.

"Yes," he said.

"May I inquire what I was sold for?"

"Vain bitch," he said.

"Yes, Master," she said.

"Twenty-five *darins*," he said.

"That seems very little," said Cornhair, puzzled. Had she not recently sold for forty *darins*?

"Your Mistress let you go cheaply," he said.

"That I might know myself worth so little," she said.

"Doubtless," he said. "But she specified certain conditions."

"Master?"

"That certain entries be included on your placard."

"What, Master?" asked Cornhair, frightened.

"You were a poor slave, I gather," he said.

"I tried to be a good slave," she said.

He adjusted the placard.

"The first entry," he said, "is 'See that this slave is treated as she deserves'. That should encourage your new Master or Mistress to be ready with the whip, to punish you richly for the least flaw or dalliance, the least imperfection, in your service."

"Yes," said Cornhair, in misery.

"The second entry," said Tenrik, "is that you were once the Lady Publennia Calasalia, of the Larial Calasalii."

"No, no, Master!" begged Cornhair. "Scrape it away. Rub it out! Do not let that be known! The Larial Calasalii were hated. They were ruined! That is behind me! That is far away! Please, Master! I am now only a poor slave! Remove it from the placard. Men would hate me! I would be treated badly! I would live under the lash! I might be tortured, and slain!"

"It was a condition of your sale," said Tenrik.

"Please, no, Master!" begged Cornhair.

Tenrik turned away, and left the shelf.

Cornhair pulled futilely at her wrists, manacled behind her. She struggled, shaking the chain looped about her neck. She sobbed.

Then she stood still, head down, the placard dangling about her neck.

She recalled the words of her former Mistress, that she would make sure of something in her sale, which would make a difference, something which some might find of interest.

"Perhaps I will not be sold," she thought. "Perhaps no one will want me. Perhaps I will be auctioned somewhere, in a different market, as before. Perhaps he who buys me will have no interest in the placard. Perhaps he will be unable to read, or unable to read Telnarian. Perhaps he will know nothing of the Larial Calasalii. Perhaps he will have no interest in such things. This is a small market. Telnar is a large city. I have little to fear."

It was now late in the afternoon.

The street was more crowded.

"Make way!" she heard. "Make way!"

Cornhair first saw two soldiers, or two whom she took to be soldiers, from the uniforms and accouterments, but the uniforms were none she recognized. Certainly they were not those of familiar contingents in the imperial forces, or those of guardsmen. These two soldiers, for they were soldiers of a sort, each carried a staff, some four feet in length, some two inches in width, with which they pressed aside men and women, cleaving a passage through the crowd. These two men were followed by another man, a large, proud-walking, darkly bearded man of fierce aspect. He, too, was uniformed, but differently. Cornhair understood him to be an officer, or official, of sorts, in any event, a person of some importance and authority. Behind him, armed with swords and bows, were four men, following in twos. This small entourage, then, consisted of an officer, or official, and six men, two to clear the way, and four in support.

The officer, as we shall speak of him, stopped, and viewed the shelf. Presumably there would be little of interest here to one of such apparent degree. The slaves were lovely, but, then, that is common with slaves. Presumably not one of the commodities which Tenrik hoped to vend were high slaves, exquisitely and lengthily trained slaves, unusually gifted slaves, familiar, say, with the songs of Tenabar IV and Sybaris, mistresses of the lyre, lute, and giron, knowledgeable in the literary classics of antique Telnaria, skilled in the dances of the desert world, Beyira II.

Cornhair did not know what such men might be doing in Telnar, or, particularly, in this rather shabby district. Surely they should be about some business in the vicinity of the palace, in, say, the administrative halls or courts.

The officer then turned away from regarding the goods on the shelf, and spoke to one of his subordinates, who then turned and, to the amazement of Cornhair, entered the restaurant across the way, and ascended the narrow stairway within it, on its right side, as one would look inward, which would lead up, doubtless, to various rooms or apartments. Some such rooms may be rented for the hour, or the night. In this way, they may serve the purposes of the less affluent in much the same way as more elegant and more discreet surroundings may serve the purposes of the better fixed and more discerning.

A short while later the subordinate descended the stairs followed by, to Cornhair's dismay, the Lady Gia Alexia.

The Lady Gia Alexia then, with great deference, and servile awe, approached the officer. They conferred briefly. The Lady Gia Alexia then pointed to Cornhair, and the officer said something to his subordinate, the man who had fetched the Lady Gia Alexia, and he approached the shelf, and ascended to its surface.

Cornhair shrank back against the wall.

The subordinate lifted the placard on its cords away from Cornhair's neck, descended from the shelf, and, in a moment, presented it to the officer, who perused it briefly, and returned it to him. The subordinate then returned to the shelf, ascended again to its surface, and hung the placard again about Cornhair's neck. These proceedings had not escaped the notice of Tenrik, who now appeared beside Cornhair.

"Perhaps Master, or his principal," he said, glancing toward the officer below, "is interested in a slave?"

"This slave," said the subordinate, indicating Cornhair.

"Fifty *darins*," said Tenrik, to begin the bargaining.

"One *darin*," said the subordinate.

"Surely Master jests," said Tenrik. "Consider the eyes, blue as the velvet of the skies of Corydon, the hair as golden as the shimmering crops of the Corn World, in the third planting, the exquisiteness of her features, so exquisitely, so helplessly, so vulnerably feminine, the delights of her bosom, the narrowness of her waist, the sweet width of her hips, the softness of the shoulders, the sweetness of her thighs and calves, the slimness of her ankles. Cheap at fifty *darins*."

"One *darin*," said the subordinate, "but you will receive this gold *darin*, should you sell her for a single *darin*."

Tenrik grasped the gold piece. "She is yours, for a single *darin*!" he said.

"Master!" wept Cornhair, in protest, and Tenrik seized her by the hair, turned her head toward him, and cuffed her twice. Tenrik was not ill disposed toward her. Indeed, he had just made a considerable profit on her. But she should have known better.

The subordinate placed a single copper *darin* in Tenrik's palm. He then drew a small, folded sheet of paper from his purse, unfolded it, and gave it to the merchant. "Deliver her to this address," he said.

"Ah!" said the merchant, his eyes widening, regarding the opened bit of paper.

Cornhair dared not speak.

The subordinate then withdrew from the shelf, and rejoined the officer and the others.

Cornhair saw that the officer then handed something to the Lady Gia Alexia, on which her small fist closed instantly, greedily.

The small group then turned about, and, remarshaling themselves, withdrew, returning in the direction from which they had come.

"Make way!" called the two soldiers, now, again, in the lead, brandishing their pressing, crowd-cleaving staffs. "Make way!"

The Lady Gia Alexia thrust her way through the crowd, to the foot of the shelf, and, looking about herself, and holding the object so that few were likely to see it, she opened her palm to Cornhair, who saw within it a golden *darin*. "Farewell, slave," she said, laughed, and then turned away, and hurried through the crowd. She had been successful, it seems, in finding a suitable buyer for Cornhair. A golden *darin*, of course, would purchase several slaves of the normal market value of Cornhair.

"May I speak, Master?" begged Cornhair.

"Certainly," said Tenrik.

"Those men who bought me," said Cornhair. "I do not recognize the uniforms, the emblems, and badges."

"There is no reason you should," said Tenrik. "The forces in which they serve are private forces. They have no official position within the empire. Their army is a private army, to be sure, one of the largest and most dangerous in the empire. It is the first time I have dealt with them."

As indicated earlier, certain men, and families, have retainers, armed or otherwise. Just as a man might have a bodyguard, he might have ten bodyguards, or a hundred, and so on. A band may become a company, and a company a small army, and a small army a larger army. It was not unusual in the empire, particularly on more remote worlds where the authority and power of the empire was limited, or absent, for powerful men to form such groups. In our accounts we have already met one such, that of the wealthy merchant, Pulendius, of Terennia. Captain Ottonius, long ago known as the peasant, Dog, had trained in his gladiatorial school. And, needless to say, such armies, being the instruments of their commanders, and occasionally the tools of ambition and greed, do not always restrict their activities to enforcing the law and keeping the peace. Similarly, it is not always wise, or safe, to inquire into the antecedents of dynasties. Brigands and bandits not unoften lie at the roots of kingdoms.

"Ho!" called Tenrik to his man, the slaver's man. "Behold!"

The slaver's man joined Tenrik on the shelf and looked at the paper in Tenrik's hand, that given to Tenrik by the subordinate, that on which was inscribed the address to which Cornhair was to be delivered.

"By the sky," said the slaver's man, "I know the place, the great villa northeast of the city, overlooking the river, with the walls, the barracks, with the guards, the unleashed, prowling vi-cats."

"I have never been there," said Tenrik.

"Nor I," said the slaver's man. "It is not to be approached."

"They will be expecting the slave," said Tenrik.

"Master," said Cornhair. "May I know who bought me, may I know who owns me?"

"It is on the paper," said Tenrik.

"Master!" begged Cornhair.

"Take her from the shelf," said Tenrik, to his man. "Wash her, and feed and water her. And then kennel her, stoutly. In the morning, we will put her in the wagon and deliver her."

"Very good," said the slaver's man.

"And have her chained," said Tenrik, "heavy chains."

"But she is a woman," said the man.

"Nonetheless," said Tenrik, "put heavy chains on her."

The padlock was removed from the two links of the common chain it bound, that looped about Cornhair's neck, which chain, then freed, was opened and lifted away, over her head, which freed her from the common chain. She was not freed from the manacles which fastened her hands behind her. One key, incidentally, as is often the case, was matched to all the shelf padlocks and all the manacles used to hold the shelf stock. This constitutes a considerable convenience for the merchants and their staffs.

As she was in the presence of free men Cornhair immediately knelt.

"Master," she said to Tenrik.

"Slave?" he responded.

"May I inquire," she said, "to whom I belong, who owns me?"

"Keep her on her knees, your hand in her hair," said Tenrik to his man.

Cornhair was then on her knees, her hands manacled behind her, the slaver's man's hand fastened in her hair, looking up at Tenrik.

"Master?" she begged.

Tenrik glanced, again, at the paper. "Rurik," he said, "Rurik, Tenth Consul of Larial VII, Rurik, of the Larial Farnichi."

CHAPTER FORTY-SEVEN

"This," said Julian, "is our colleague, Tuvo Ausonius, of Miton, once an executive in the finance division of the first provincial quadrant. He came with us from Tangara to Telnaria."

"The noble Ausonius is not unknown to me," said Iaachus. "We have had dealings."

"More than one of your dealings has not turned out well," said Julian.

"One tries to do what is in the best interests of the empire," said Iaachus.

"As you see it," said Julian.

"Of course," said Iaachus.

The force of the explosive device had been evaded; the attack of the ship had been thwarted; the raid of the bearers of the imperial commission had been countered. These events had occurred at Julian's villa on Vellmer, when Otto had been in residence, awaiting the documentation pertinent to his commission in the auxiliaries.

"How nice to see you again," said Iaachus to Tuvo Ausonius.

"And you," said Ausonius, bowing.

"On Vellmer," said Julian, "Ausonius learned manhood and honor."

"Such things," said Iaachus, "may complicate, even impede, statecraft."

"Tuvo Ausonius is our eyes and ears on the street," said Julian. "I am known, Captain Ottonius is conspicuous."

"I have my sources of information, as well," said Iaachus.

"A hundred spies," said Julian.

"In Telnar alone," said Iaachus. "The empire is large and information is precious. Without it one gambles."

"And with it, as well," said Julian.

"True," said Iaachus.

"And you will gamble on us?" said Julian.

"I have little choice," said Iaachus.

"You need us," said Julian.

"I, and the empire," said Iaachus. "Unfortunately one must sometimes trust those whom one does not trust."

"We, as well," said Julian.

"There are demands in the street, for the public appearance of the princesses," said Iaachus.

"Few know the princesses by sight," said Otto. "Substitute actresses, or slaves in gaudy finery."

"But some know," said Iaachus, "and large, vulnerable secrets are the least well kept."

"Too," said Tuvo Ausonius, "word is spread about, that the princesses vacation abroad, venturing to scenic places, light-heartedly touring on a dozen worlds."

"In this, see the hand of Sidonicus," said Iaachus.

"Obviously you know more than we," said Julian.

"In his way," said Iaachus, "Sidonicus poses a greater threat to the empire than Abrogastes."

"How so?" said Julian.

"He wants the empire, the galaxy, the galaxies, either from the throne or from its enemies. He preaches the superiority of the *koos* to the state. The *koos* is to rule, which, of course, he speaks for, and the state is to obey. He wants to crown emperors, and have it that no one can be emperor who is not crowned by him."

"He would then select emperors," said Otto.

"And would-be emperors would hasten to do his will," said Iaachus.

"And without risk he would rule worlds," said Otto.

"At his word," said Iaachus, "he might declare an emperor unfit, false, or illegitimate, unfavored by Karch, and his subjects thereby relieved of all allegiance and duties to their sovereign."

"Madness," said Otto.

"Weapons, even in the hands of the insane, have edges and weight. A knife in the hand of a lunatic is still sharp. It obeys the hand that wields it."

"Surely men can see through this sort of thing, understand its purposes, the motivations involved," said Otto.

"Some men," said Iaachus. "Not others. And many men who understand the absurdity, the sickness, and the madness refrain from speaking, reluctant to perish at the hands of homicidal zealots."

"There are rumors, too," said Tuvo Ausonius, "of miracles."

"Of course," said Iaachus, "why not? Do they not, supposedly, abound in the pantheon of Orak and Umba, and in the lore of a thousand other faiths, sometimes weird and minor faiths, on ten thousand worlds?"

"What is a miracle?" asked Otto.

"Words are easily multiplied," said Iaachus. "Facile verbalism produces in simple minds the illusion of understanding. In reality the concept is unintelligible."

"Let us suppose," said Julian, "that Orak supposedly does something which violates the laws of nature."

"How would one know it violated the laws of nature?" asked Otto.

"One would not," said Julian.

"What if there were no laws of nature?" asked Otto.

"Even granted iron laws of nature, which seems unlikely," said Iaachus, "many unusual and surprising things still take place, things we do not understand and cannot now explain."

"Miracles?" asked Otto.

"There seems little point in calling them that, but I suppose one could do so, if one wished," said Julian. "Most, of course, have no relationship whatsoever to one faith or another."

"Perhaps such things could be staged, faked, and such," said Otto. "Tricks, such as magicians perform, dazzling us."

"Or more likely, simply alleged to have occurred," said Iaachus. "Lies are less costly than tricks, which often require a context, an apparatus, confederates, and such."

"What is the point of miracles?" asked Otto.

"They are supposed to attest the soundness of claims and doctrine," said Iaachus. "They cannot do so, of course, for a variety of reasons. For example, logical relations obtain amongst propositions, formulas, and such, whereas things, occurrences, and phenomena do not entail anything, no more than, say, waterfalls, trees, and rocks. Surprising events, for example, are cognitively independent of their interpretation. Any event might be interpreted variously. Let us suppose that I maintained that the star of Telnaria orbited Telnaria, rather than Telnaria orbiting its star, and produced an unusual event. That would not prove that our star spun about our world. Similarly, suppose I claimed to be a prophet of Karch and something surprising took place. That would not prove I was a prophet of Karch, or even that there was such a thing as Karch. The point may be even more easily made. Let us suppose we have three individuals making incompatible claims, only one of which could be true, if any, and each of these individuals produced exactly the same miracle, or unusual phenomenon. What is one then to suppose, that the three logically incompatible claims are all true? Rather, it is clear that surprising occurrences and truth are logically independent."

"When I was a boy, tending pigs in the *festung* village of Sim Giadini," said Otto, "I wondered why faiths did not begin earlier, why they waited for thousands of years to appear. If Orak or Karch, or some other god or gods, made the world, if it was made, should they not have made their faith at the same time? For example, many must have died, tragically deprived, before this or that faith was even known."

"It had not been invented yet," said Iaachus.

"Many of the brothers in the *festung*," said Otto, "claimed to have had visions of Floon."

"And doubtless many did," said Iaachus. "Experience is internal to the organism. It commonly has both internal and external causes. There is doubtless a tree outside your body but your seeing of the tree is within you, an aspect of your consciousness. It could not be otherwise. All experience is internal to the organism, but some experiences may lack external causes. They may have only internal causes. The most common instance of this is the dream. The dream tree is internally generated. It is rooted only in dream soil, and shimmers only in dream light."

"Men sometimes see what they hope to see, what they want to see," said Julian.

"Certainly thousands have had visions of Orak and Umba, and thousands of other gods," said Iaachus.

"What of signs in the sky, as claimed on several worlds?" said Otto.

"It is easy to see figures in the clouds," said Iaachus, "particularly if one wishes to see them, is eager to see them, and so on. Furthermore, some such claims seem to have been simply fabricated, as they are not reported in other sources in the same locale at the same time. Too, not everyone inspecting the sky sees such things, even at the same time others are claiming to do so. Remember the internality of experience. And, who knows how many claim to see such things who do not see such things, for one reason or another, perhaps wishing to conform, perhaps wishing to be approved, perhaps wishing to gain attention, perhaps wishing to seem important, perhaps wishing to avoid discrimination or persecution."

"It is hard to know what to think," said Otto.

"Things which do not move, too," said Iaachus, "may seem to move. This has to do with movements in the eye itself."

"What of those on whose bodies appear the marks of the torture rack?" said Otto.

"The mind," said Iaachus, "can do strange things with the body."

"It is hard to know what to think," said Otto.

"Perhaps it is not all that hard, dear friend," said Julian.

"The trust which human beings have is surely one of their most endearing characteristics," said Iaachus. "Without it the enterprises of the charlatan and fraud would be far more difficult and perilous."

"Why should Sidonicus, if he has, spread rumors of the princesses being on holiday?" said Julian. "Surely he knows the truth, if only from the empress mother."

"May I speculate?" said Tuvo Ausonius.

"Surely, noble Ausonius," said Iaachus.

"The Floonian ministrants wish to stand between humans, and other rational species, and Karch. They wish to control access to the table of Karch. Accordingly, they have the business of the smudging with oil, the approved prayers, the demanded exercises and required services, reserving to themselves the exclusive alleviation of the miseries and guilts which they themselves have produced, and so on."

"Continue," said Iaachus.

"Compatible with this program of managing and controlling the lives of others, whose economic resources they command, and on which they rely, they wish to regulate and supervise matings, to approve or disapprove of marriages, to perform or dissolve marriages."

"That is known to me," said Iaachus.

"Suppose, then," said Tuvo Ausonius, "the princesses, in their alleged holiday, encountered, and allegedly fell in love

with, as the reports might have it, unexpected and magnifi-
cent swains, young, handsome princes of mighty barbarian
nations."

"I see," said Iaachus.

"New blood for the empire," said Julian.

"The empire totters," said Otto. "Fear bestrides the times. In
what quadrant might dawn the sun of hope? Foreign blood and
might, conjoined with sophistication and civilization, might
undo a thousand years of diffidence, subsidence, and retreat."

"It will never be," said Iaachus.

"And who might arrange, and sanctify, and with what in
mind, such unions?" asked Tuvo Ausonius.

"Sidonicus, obviously," said Iaachus.

"One must not allow the dark, ugly hand of these madmen to
cheapen, soil, and pervert life," said Julian.

"Many will welcome such things," said Iaachus, "provided
it is done in the name of right, of goodness, of justice, of love,
and such."

"What a meretricious pursuit of power," said Julian.

"Better the fist and blade," said Otto.

"They, at least, are honest," said Iaachus.

"But in the world there are many mysteries," said Otto.

"True," said Iaachus. "Many things are mysterious. I fear the
world does not speak our language, or have us much in mind."

"If Sidonicus performs the marriages of the Princesses Viviana and Alacida to the sons of Abrogastes, and they have male
issue, which, in time, seems likely," said Tuvo Ausonius, "blood
right to the throne will have been established."

"Too," said Iaachus, "such an act would much increase and
enhance the prestige and power of the exarch, the high ministrant. He is so mighty that he may preside over the marriages of,
so to speak, kings and queens. The next claim would surely be
that ministrants alone have the right to ratify unions."

"Quite possibly," said Julian.

"And the hand of the exarch is laid ever more heavily on the empire," said Iaachus.

"The sons of Abrogastes," said Julian, "will further his schemes, as he has theirs. The exarch gives credence and legitimacy to their pretensions, and they, in turn, would lend him the support, and sword, of the state."

"Would that we had an emperor!" said Iaachus.

"We do," said Otto.

"A drooling, mindless child," said Iaachus, "enamored of toys and terrified of insects."

Otto was silent.

"What is to be done?" asked Tuvo Ausonius.

"The projected marriages must not take place," said Julian. "We must recover the princesses."

"We do not even know where they are," said Iaachus. "They could be on any one of a thousand worlds."

"Surely on a barbarian world," said Julian, "one not too far, not too close, a world familiar to the Alemanni and their allies."

"There may be dozens such," said Iaachus.

"There are," said Otto.

"There is little time," said Julian.

"Let us suppose," said Otto, "there is a likely world. How would one proceed?"

"Any attempt to extricate the princesses from their predicament," said Iaachus, "would have to proceed with great delicacy and in great secrecy. This militates against a massive effort, which would be easily detectable and the bungling or clumsiness of which might result in the removal and concealment of the princesses, or, even, worse, Orak forbid, in their loss. This is work for the surgeon's blade, not the woodsman's ax. Too, it would seem to me unwise to invest imperial forces in this enterprise. Questions would arise; security might be breached."

"Mercenaries, then?" said Julian.

"Surely," said Iaachus. "Mercenaries, trustworthy, fresh from bloody wars, who owe the state much."

"You have such men in mind?" said Julian.

"Yes," said Iaachus, "but it avails naught, for we do not even know where to seek the princesses."

"You will be dealing with barbarians," said Otto. "I will command."

"I will accompany you," said Julian.

"And I," said Tuvo Ausonius.

"I do not understand," said Iaachus, Arbiter of Protocol. "We do not even know where to look."

"True," said Otto. "But there is a likely world, a barbarian world, one not too far, not too close, one known to the Alemanni and their allies, a crossroads world, an assembly world, a rendezvous world, a meeting world."

"What world is that?" asked Iaachus.

"Tenguthaxichai!" said Julian.

"Yes," said Otto, "Tenguthaxichai."

CHAPTER FORTY-EIGHT

Cornhair lay curled at the feet of her Master, Rurik, in the Farnichi enclave, overlooking the Turning Serpent, somewhat northeast of Telnar. A silver chain ran from the ring on her silver overcollar to the ring set in the floor to the left of his thronelike chair, in which he received visitors. Beneath the overcollar she wore a simple close-fitting collar bearing the Farnichi emblem, the five petaled Pin Flower, native to Larial VII. She was not clothed. This was partly, doubtless, because she was lovely, and her Master enjoyed seeing her naked, and partly because she had once been a scion of the Larial Calasalii.

"We await guests," said Rurik.

"Yes, Master," she said.

"I am curious as to their business," he said. "It is interesting. They come incognito."

"Master may have me removed," she said, "or he may unchain me, and I shall hurry to my cage, and crawl within."

"You will remain," he said. "I enjoy displaying you, a pretty slave, once a woman of the Calasalii."

"As Master wills," she said. "I am his slave."

Some days ago Cornhair had been laden with heavy chains and put naked into a wagon. A few hours later the wagon had been admitted behind the first gate of a high-walled enclave.

When the gate had been closed behind the wagon, Cornhair was relieved of her chains, and placed, kneeling, on the paving stones between the first and second gate. The officer in charge of the gate guard, which consisted of four men, made his mark on the delivery receipt and the wagon was turned about, and, the gate opened, took its departure. Cornhair heard the gate close behind her, but did not look, as she had been knelt facing the second gate. She saw a small door open in the second gate, which door would permit the passage of only one person at a time. Through this door emerged a fellow clad in normal Telnarian garb, perhaps a constable or bailiff. Dangling from his left hand was an opened collar.

He approached Cornhair and stood before her, and she lowered her head.

"Look up," he said.

Cornhair looked up.

The collar was held before her.

"Do you know this design?" she was asked.

"It is the five-petaled Pin Flower," she said.

"It is the mark of what great family?" he said.

"It is the mark of the Farnichi," she said.

"So it is a Farnichi collar," he said.

"Yes, Master," said Cornhair.

"And you are going to wear it, are you not?"

"If Masters please," she said.

"Assume the posture of a bitch," he said, "slut of the Calasalii."

Cornhair went to all fours, her head down.

The collar was then snapped about her neck.

"You are one of the few sluts of the Calasalii who have long avoided the collar," he said.

"Yes, Master," said Cornhair.

"But now you are in it, where you belong," he said.

"Yes, Master," said Cornhair.

"Wait here," he said, "as you are."

"Yes, Master," said Cornhair.

He then exited through the small door in the larger gate.

As the reader may recall, the Calasalii and the Farnichi, both originally native to Larial VII, maintained private armies, devoted to their interests on more than one world, interests which were occasionally incompatible. These private armies, on more than one world, met in the fierce adjudications of war. Eventually the empire saw fit to intervene, an intervention apparently, at least partly, in response to an invitation of the Farnichi, which saw little profit to be reaped from a continuance of hostilities, hostilities which seemed likely to be indefinitely prolonged, with the obvious diminution of resources on both sides and an ever-mounting toll of burned and gutted cities and towns, and planetwide widths of barren, untilled fields. This invitation to imperial forces, it was rumored, this repast of harmony and conciliation, was sweetened by substantial condiments of Farnichi gold. Surely it was more in the interests of the empire, to restore order, to side with one foe or another, thereby increasing the power and leverage of the favored faction, rather than try to impose its will on two intransigent parties, each of which might, particularly on certain worlds, more than overmatch any imperial cohorts likely to be applied in the appropriate sectors. In any event, abetted by the empire, the Farnichi brought the war to a brief and bloody close. Calasalii forces were disbanded. Calasalii property was confiscated by the state, and divided between the empire and the Farnichi. In this way each of the original Farnichi gold pieces was multiplied several times, an outcome more than justifying the original investment. After the war the Calasalii family was stripped of rank, and the associated perquisites of rank. The family was reduced to the *humiliori*. Later, as we earlier noted, presumably at the instigation of the Farnichi, who may have had long memories and apprehensions concerning the future, the

Calasalii were outlawed, an outlawry kept secret until its consequences were enacted without warning. Men and women of the Calasalii were seized by the state. The men were largely consigned to the mines and quarries, the women to the collar.

A short while after the exit of the attendant, perhaps the enclave constable or bailiff, a tunicked slave came through the small door in the gate.

Cornhair noted, to her apprehension, that the slave carried a switch.

"You are the new girl," said the slave.

"Yes, Mistress," said Cornhair.

"As I understand it," she said, "you are a bitch of the Calasalii."

"I was once of the Calasalii," said Cornhair. "I am now a slave, only a slave."

"Like the other bitches in your family," she said.

"I do not know," said Cornhair.

"What are you here for," she asked, "for the kitchen, for the fields?"

"I do not know," said Cornhair.

"Kneel," said the slave. "Get your head up."

Cornhair knelt. She wanted to touch her collar, but did not dare do so.

"Back on your heels, straighten your back, keep your head up, your hands, palms down, on your thighs!"

Cornhair complied.

"You are pretty," said the slave, "in a cheap way."

"I was of the Calasalii," said Cornhair, "of the *honestori*, the patricians, even of the senatorial class!"

"Yes," said the slave, "you are pretty, in a cheap way. Remain as you are."

"Yes, Mistress," said Cornhair.

Even had she been a free woman, she would have felt herself a slave, kneeling so.

"What would it be like," she wondered, "to be a man and see a woman kneeling before him so, and knowing she was a slave?"

She suspected then, something of the heat of the male.

"And what would it be like, to kneel so before a man, one who is your Master?" she wondered.

"And can the man," she wondered, "suspect something of the heat of the slave?"

How it excited a slave to be a slave!

Dare men know that?

"Split your knees," said the slave.

"Surely not!" exclaimed Cornhair.

The switch was lifted.

"Good," said the slave.

The switch was lowered, to Cornhair's relief.

"I do not see you for the kitchen, or the fields," said the slave. "I see you, Calasalii bitch, as a Thong Girl, a Couch-Ring Girl, a Split-Knees Girl. Rejoice, or despair, as the notion strikes you."

"Yes, Mistress," said Cornhair.

"Do you think you can please a man?" she asked.

"I do not know, Mistress," said Cornhair. "I am a slave. I will try to be found pleasing. I do not wish to be beaten, or tortured."

"I know your type," she said. "You need not fear being beaten or tortured. You will fear only that he may not touch you."

Cornhair tasted a drop of blood on her lip. She had bitten herself.

"Follow me," said the slave, turning about.

Cornhair leapt up, and followed the slave. As she sped forward, she felt, touching it, the collar on her neck, the lock at the back of the neck. It was a light, close-fitting collar, and was comfortable, as most slave collars. The point of the collar is to identify its occupant as a slave and, commonly, her owner. It also, to be sure, enhances the beauty of its occupant. It is designed, in part, with that in mind. The common slave collar is so light and comfortable that one would often forget that it was there. But it would be there.

The slave, at the small door fixed in the large second gate, turned, and faced Cornhair.

"Adjust your collar," she said.

Cornhair did so, carefully. She knew that she was so slave, and so vain, that she would wear her collar well. Slave girls are entitled to their vanity as well as free women.

"It is a Farnichi collar," said the slave. "You are now a Farnichi girl. Do you understand?"

"Yes, Mistress," said Cornhair.

"I do not envy you, Calasalii bitch," she said.

"Mistress?" said Cornhair.

"Follow me," she said, turning. "We must clean you up and feed you, and make you presentable."

"Your tunic is lovely," said Cornhair. "May I hope to be so clothed?"

"You will probably be kept naked," said the slave.

"Why, Mistress?" asked Cornhair.

"Because you were Calasalii," she said. "The Farnichi enjoy owning the women of their enemies."

The slave then exited through the small door in the large, second gate, and Cornhair followed her.

Cornhair stood behind the large, double doors leading to the audience chamber, waiting to be formally presented to her Master, and selected retainers. She had been washed, and brushed and combed, and well fed, on fresh, hot bread and warm slave gruel. There are many forms of, and recipes for, slave gruel, as one would expect, and the mixtures and consistencies vary considerably, ranging from little more than thickened water to rich, weighty porridges. Whereas some slave gruels, usually weak, with inferior ingredients, may be fed to prisoners and slaves under discipline, most, as one would expect, are substantial and nourishing.

Certainly a husbandman will normally take care to see that his stock is well cared for. Most slave gruels, the primary ingredients for which, grains, are commonly sold in bulk, in large sacks, are intended to constitute a portion of a carefully supervised, controlled diet with the end in view of the stock's vigor, health, and general wellbeing. Accordingly, the quantity and quality of provender supplied to the slave is regulated, as is the case with other domestic animals. An enslaved free woman commonly finds her figure, whether she wishes it or not, is becoming slave lovely, of greater interest to Masters, and the slave finds she is in little danger of losing a figure which would sell well off the block. Masters see to such things. There is little to be surprised at, that the average slave is trim, healthy, energetic, and appetitious. The average slave's diet, of course, as that of her Master, is likely to be varied and delicious. Indeed, most private slaves eat substantially the same meals as their Master, if only because they are likely to have prepared those meals. Mealtime differences are usually independent of the food. For example, the first bite is to be taken by the Master, the slave may feed on her knees, the seat of a chair serving as her table, and so on. Slave gruels do tend to have one thing in common. They are bland. They may be seasoned of course, if the Master permits it. Too, meat, fruit, and vegetables may be mixed with the gruel. Indeed, a slave's diet often contains generous amounts of fruits, nuts, and vegetables. A slave's zeal to obtain occasional treats and rewards, such as a candy from her Master's hand, may be attributed, one supposes, at least in part to the frequent plainness of her diet, and, in part, one supposes, to the fact that she is a slave.

"They make me wait," said Cornhair, standing before the heavy, varnished, paneled double door leading to the audience chamber.

"Do not complain, do not be in a hurry," said the slave with the switch, she in the lovely tunic. "Inside, you may be whipped."

"What are they doing inside?" asked Cornhair.

"Business, discussion, a meeting, conferring," said the slave. "Who knows what the Masters do. When they are finished with the work of men, that will be time for you."

"What shall I do?" asked Cornhair.

"We are slaves," she said. "We will kneel, and wait."

Cornhair and the slave then went to their knees, to the side of the door.

Cornhair stood alone, small, forlorn, nude, collared, in the portal, at the end of the long carpet leading toward the thronelike chair at the far end of the audience chamber, the large, double doors now closed behind her.

"The slave," said he whom, earlier, between the two outer gates, Cornhair had conjectured to be the enclave's constable or bailiff. It was he who had put her in her new collar.

"Approach your Master," said he whom we shall now refer to as the constable, "on all fours, naked and collared, as befits a woman once of the Calasalii, before one of the Farnichi."

Cornhair went to all fours. She raised her head to look to the far end of the room. There, on a dais, was a large, thronelike chair. On this chair, though now in informal robes, simple house robes, not a uniform, was the officer she remembered from Tenrik's market, he whose subordinate, on his behalf, had dealt with Tenrik. Flanking the thronelike chair were several men, some in uniform, some in house robes, as well. Of these men, some were to the right of the chair, others to the left of the chair, some on the dais, others on the floor. She was the only woman in the room.

"Head down," said the constable.

So, head down, on all fours, Cornhair began the long journey down the long carpet to the foot of the dais.

The constable accompanied her.

"Stop," he said.

Cornhair could see the first step of the dais before her, the robes and sandals of the constable to her left. She kept her head down.

"A bitch, once of the Calasalii, naked and collared, fittingly so, before her Masters, the Farnichi," said the constable.

"Speak your former status, slave," said the figure on the thronelike chair.

"I was once the Lady Publennia Calasalia, of the Larial Calasalii," said Cornhair, "of the *honestori*, of the patricians, of the senatorial class."

"How is that?" he asked.

"Master?" she said.

"You were not on the rolls of the Calasalii," said the officer.

"I fear not," said Cornhair.

"We utilized these rolls to prepare the Morning of the Great Apprehension, that morning on which, on three worlds, every identifiable, locatable scion of the Calasalii, male, female, and child, was taken into custody."

"I was removed from the rolls," she said, "for profligacy, for irresponsibility, for scandal, for bringing disgrace, discredit, on the family. I would no longer be recognized or received. I was allotted a pittance, and denied all contact with the family."

"Unfortunately," said the officer, "we did not seize you on the Morning of Apprehension, in the full glory of your freedom. It would have pleased us to strip and brand you, and then fasten your neck in its first collar."

"I fear," she said, "I was already marked and collared before what you call the Morning of Apprehension."

"How came you to the collar?" he said.

"I was party to a political intrigue," she said, "in which I thought myself, in judicious masquerade, to play the part of a slave girl, but I later discovered that the legalities inflicted on me were authentic, and I had been truly enslaved."

"Where did this take place?"

"On Inez IV," she said.

"Continue," he said.

"I first discovered myself truly a slave," she said, "on Tangara, when the plot of the intrigue was foiled. I was then marked. I was sold to Heruls, a dreadful, fearful form of life, who later sold me to a dealer from Venitzia, the provincial capital of Tangara. In Venitzia I was sold to an agent, or agents, of Bondage Flowers. I and others were shipped to Telnar. I subsequently found myself in various collars. Most recently, as Master is aware, I was purchased from the sales shelf of Tenrik's Woman Market, in Telnar."

"We will want a name for you," he said. "What were you most recently called?"

"Cornhair, Master," she said.

"It will do," he said. "What is your name?"

"'Cornhair', Master," she said.

"The highest women of the Calasalii," he said, "are worthless tarts and belong in collars, at the feet of Masters. Their noblest and finest deserve no better than to be the degraded slaves of the Farnichi."

"I fear, Master," said Cornhair, "that I am not amongst their noblest and finest. Indeed, I have been removed from the rolls of the Calasalii."

"But once?" he said.

"Yes," she said, "once."

"Do you know what this is?" he asked, lifting an object which had been reposing on the right arm of his chair.

"Yes, Master," she said, "it is a slave switch." Surely there was no mistaking the nature of the artifact. Any Telnarian would be familiar with such things. And surely she knew it well from her miserable days in the collar of the Lady Gia Alexia of the Telnar Darsai.

The officer then cast the switch to the side. "Fetch," he said, "and bring it to me, in your teeth."

Cornhair crawled to the artifact, put down her head, and picked up the object in her teeth. She held it crosswise between her teeth, evenly, and aesthetically, as is expected, when a slave is put to this simple task.

"See the Calasalii bitch," laughed a man.

Cornhair, the switch between her teeth, crawled to the dais, and climbed upon it, and, when she was before her Master, at his knees, she lifted her head, proffering him the implement, which he took, and put across his knees.

"You may now beg to be beaten," he said.

"I beg to be beaten," she said, "Master."

"Do you truly wish to be beaten?" he asked.

"No, no, Master!" she said. "Please do not beat me."

Men about the thronelike chair laughed.

"But you are a slave," said the officer.

"Even so, Master!" said Cornhair.

"Why do you wish not to be beaten?" he asked.

"Because it hurts," she said. "Because it hurts, terribly, Master."

"Back off the dais," he said. "Go down, to the floor, some feet before the dais, where we can all see you, and well."

Cornhair, shuddering, complied.

"On your belly," he said.

Cornhair then lay prone before her Master.

"A fitting posture of a Calasalii woman before one of the Farnichi," said a man.

"You are unclothed," said the officer.

"I have not been given clothing, Master," said Cornhair.

"On your back," he said.

Cornhair could now see the vaulted ceiling above her. She felt very vulnerable, lying so.

"You, and you," said the officer, addressing himself to two of the men in uniform. "Fetch each of you a slave whip, and position yourselves a few feet from the slave, one on each side."

A minute or so later, perhaps following some sign given by the officer on the thronelike chair, which chair Cornhair could not see, both whips were suddenly unexpectedly, snapped.

Cornhair, startled, cried out in misery. She had not been touched.

"You do not wish to be beaten?" he said.

"No, Master!" said Cornhair.

"We shall see," he said. "Are you willing to try not to be beaten, and try in the way of the slave?"

"Yes, Master! Yes, Master!" said Cornhair.

"You are not to rise to your feet," he said.

"Yes, Master," said Cornhair.

"Begin," he said.

A few minutes later, the officer said, "Stop," and Cornhair lay on the carpet before the dais, on her belly, gasping for breath, drenched with sweat. She realized, half failing to understand it, that the leather had not touched her once. She also tried to grasp what had occurred, and what might be its import. She knew she had never felt more female than she had before these men, unclothed, and collared, writhing, begging, rolling, kneeling, extending limbs for scrutiny, casting glances, engaging in the display behaviors of the female slave. How thrilled she was to be so free, to exhibit herself as the purchasable object she was. How devastatingly was she then aware of her sex, and its fundamental, radical difference from that of the male. How could it not be so, as she was naked and collared, vulnerable and helpless, commanded, under the will of Masters. She was not exploited. She was owned, and must obey. Never before had she been so aware of her sex, its nature, and its meaning. She was satisfied with herself, and lay there gasping, and sweating, joyful to be a woman and a slave, rejoicing that she wore a man's collar.

It was so much what she wanted, and it was on her neck, and, owned, she could not remove it.

"You have been trained," said the officer.

"No," said Cornhair, gasping, "no, Master."

"You belong in a collar," he said.

"Yes, Master," whispered Cornhair, "I belong in a collar."

The officer turned to a subordinate. "Take her away," he said, "and see that she is cleaned, rested, and fed. Then, tonight, at the tenth hour, bring her to my chambers. There, on her knees, this woman, naked and collared, once of the Larial Calasalii, will serve me *kana*."

Several men laughed.

"And then," said a man, "have a pleasant time with her, Rurik."

"I will," said the officer.

So Cornhair lay curled at the feet of her Master, Rurik, in the Farnichi enclave, overlooking the Turning Serpent, somewhat northeast of Telnar. A silver chain, as we recall, ran from the ring on her silver overcollar to the ring set in the floor to the left of his thronelike chair, in which he received visitors. Beneath the overcollar she wore a simple close-fitting collar bearing the Farnichi emblem, the five petaled Pin Flower, native to Larial VII. She was not clothed, quite possibly for reasons we earlier suggested.

"We await guests," had said Rurik.

"Yes, Master," she said.

"I am curious as to their business," he said. "It is interesting. They come incognito."

"Master may have me removed," she said, "or he may unchain me, and I shall hurry to my cage, and crawl within."

"You will remain," he had said. "I enjoy displaying you, a pretty slave, once a woman of the Calasalii."

At that point a staff, presumably that of the constable, or some other official, smote thrice, in a measured fashion, on the outside of the large, double door leading into the audience chamber.

"Enter," called Rurik.

The two doors swung open, and three men approached, in nondescript garb; the first was blond, handsome, and well-formed, whose bearing, despite his garmenture, suggested that of the military; the second was a very large man, with bold, coarse features which suggested barbarian blood; the third was the slightest of the three and seemed more suited to accounts and records than traversing the possibly dangerous precincts of a Farnichi enclave in the vicinity of Telnar.

"We are gown-and-jewel merchants from Tinos," announced the young man with military bearing.

Behind them, at the end of the long carpet, the double doors closed.

"Scarcely," said Rurik.

"Sir?" said the young man.

"We are alone," said Rurik. "You may speak openly."

"I gather we are expected," said the young man. "Our credentials have been transmitted?"

"Yes," said Rurik, "but not the purport of your call."

"I am Julian, of the Aureliani," said the young man, "cousin to the emperor, now embarked on imperial business of the greatest moment." He then indicated the large form to his right. "This," he said, "is Ottonius, captain in the imperial auxiliaries, and this," and here he indicated the third of the visitors, "is Tuvo Ausonius, formerly of the imperial civil service."

"I am Rurik," said the host, "Tenth Consul of Larial VII, Rurik, of the Larial Farnichi."

"Forgive me, sir," said Julian, "but I find it strange that the Tenth Consul of Larial VII should be on Telnaria."

"And perhaps also," said Rurik, "that a foreign enclave this redoubtable should be located so close to the imperial palace and senate?"

"Doubtless there is a purpose," said Julian.

"There is," said Rurik, "but I suspect that it is only now that the purpose will become clear."

In the exchange of introductions, Cornhair, a slave, was no more to be introduced than a dog lying at his Master's feet.

Needless to say, Cornhair was much disturbed to see Otto and Julian, whom she had not seen since the palace, and Tuvo Ausonius, whom she had not seen since the trouble in Orik's camp, on the shore of the Turning Serpent. She kept her head down, and lay very still, hoping not to be noticed. To be sure, the beautiful curves of a chained slave are not likely to escape notice.

"We have been referred to you," said Julian, "by a high personage, close to the throne."

"Iaachus, Arbiter of Protocol," said Rurik.

"Possibly," said Julian.

"It is interesting," said Rurik. "One would suppose that an arbiter of protocol would be a minor officiant, little more than an authority on the etiquette of receiving and announcing visitors, a determiner of seating arrangements at state banquets, and such."

"The title of an office and its power are not always congruent," said Julian. "Sometimes an office or role is instituted which, over time, in the hands of the bold and ambitious, arrogates to itself functions and powers never envisaged by its founders, indeed, functions and powers which would be likely to have dismayed its founders."

"Let us suppose your principal is Iaachus, the Arbiter of Protocol," said Rurik.

"There seems no harm in the supposition," said Julian.

"Proceed," said Rurik.

"You are aware, of course," said Julian, "that a raid, brief and fierce, took place recently in Telnar."

"Batteries failed," said Rurik.

"By intent," said Julian.

"The point of the raid was to assassinate the emperor?" said Rurik.

"Better for the enemies of the empire that the emperor should thrive," said Julian, "given his weakness and simplicity, his gibbering inanity."

"The emperor is well?" asked Rurik.

"Yes," said Julian.

"What, then, could be the point of the raid?" asked Rurik. "Merely an endeavor to inform the empire of its vulnerability?"

"Bold dynastic pretensions," said Julian. "The princesses, Viviana and Alacida, have been abducted, to be wedded to the sons of Abrogastes, king of the Drisriaks, high tribe of the Aatii."

"Surely this is not known," said Rurik, leaning forward.

"It is not generally known," said Julian.

"Surely such a matter cannot be long concealed," said Rurik.

"We fear not," said Julian.

"I begin to suspect the point of your presence here," said Rurik, leaning back.

"As I understand it," said Julian, "Larial VII and certain worlds were ravaged by internal strife, the clash of large, well-equipped, private armies."

"Those of the Larial Calasalii and the Larial Farnichi," said Rurik.

"Strife appears to have been costly, and indecisive," said Julian.

"Worlds were in flames," said Rurik. "It was madness."

"Truce would seem to have been in order," said Julian, "some sensible demarcation of territories, some rational division of authority, some acceptable allotment of spoils."

"Certainly," said Rurik. "To a neutral observer, outside the bloody compass of war, to one who has not been in the field, who has not suffered, some such solution appears obvious, even necessitated. But you do not know the Calasalii and the Farnichi, the bad blood, the history of animosity, the century of strife, the hatred, the tradition, how they view one another."

"The empire intervened," said Julian.

"Yes," said Rurik.

"At the invitation of the Farnichi," said Julian.

"As it happens," said Rurik.

"It is rumored," said Julian, "that Farnichi gold was involved."

"I have heard that rumor," said Rurik.

"And you know, I assume," said Julian, "that it is true?"

"Who knows?" said Rurik. "It is difficult to say about rumors."

"And it seems that more than gold was involved," said Julian.

"Oh?" said Rurik.

"Your enclave is located near Telnar," said Julian.

"Consider it an embassy," said Rurik.

"Abetted by the empire," said Julian, "you crushed the Calasalii."

"The contribution of the imperial forces were, of course, welcome," said Rurik.

"But, later," said Julian, "there was a surreptitious outlawry of the Calasalii, subsequently, suddenly, made public, complete with pervasive seizures and arrests."

"It was time their outlawry, practiced for a century, was legally recognized and acted on," said Rurik.

"There would seem, in the view of many, in such a respect," said Julian, "little to choose from, amongst the Calasalii and the Farnichi."

"All are entitled to their opinion," said Rurik.

"Men to mines and quarries," said Julian, "women to the slave block, the chain and collar."

"A condign resolution to the inequities of the Calasalii," said Rurik.

"You have a well-curved slave at your feet," said Otto.

Cornhair, her legs drawn up, kept her head down, hoping not to be recognized. She had shaken her hair a bit about her face.

Rurik nudged her with the side of his foot, and she whimpered a little, but kept her head down.

Rurik bent down and brushed the hair away from the back of her neck. In this way the silver overcollar was more clearly seen.

"This is a woman once of the Calasalii," he said.

"I cannot see her well," said Julian, "but I assume her features are delicate, feminine, and exquisite, slave-acceptable."

"I find them so," said Rurik. "Large, gross, plain, masculine women, if collared at all, which is presumably a mistake, for who would want them, are best put in the fields, the kitchens, and laundries."

"Surely," said Julian. "The collar is for the most desirable of women."

"Yes," said Rurik, "for true women, fit slaves."

"They need only acknowledge to themselves that they are slaves, fit slaves," said Julian, "and they will learn themselves, find themselves, and be happy."

Cornhair, trying to hide her face, trying to keep her body small, trembled.

"She seems frightened," said Otto.

"She is a slave,"' said Rurik.

"The outlawry seems to go beyond the simple matter of alliances and the outcomes of battles," said Julian.

"Perhaps," said Rurik.

"More gold exchanged hands?" asked Julian.

"Who would know?" asked Rurik.

"I suspect an independent consideration was involved," said Julian.

"What would lead you to suppose that?" asked Rurik.

"An armed enclave of the Farnichi on Telnaria," said Julian, "under the command of the Tenth Consul of Larial VII."

"Proceed, conjecture," said Rurik, pleasantly.

"I suspect that in exchange for imperial help against the

Calasalii, and perhaps, in particular, afterwards, for the outlawry of the Calasalii, more was involved than Farnichi gold."

"A favor, or favors, perhaps," suggested Rurik.

"Iaachus, the Arbiter of Protocol, should he be involved in
this," said Julian, "is an extremely clever and, I fear, unscrupulous man."

"One hears various things," said Rurik.

"Statecraft is subtle, and occasionally dark," said Julian,
"and sometimes unseen. It is not all broadcast negotiation, open
meetings, public bargainings, flags, banners, proclamations,
decrees, and such.

Sometimes one acts when there is no appearance of action."

"And sometimes," said Otto, regarding Cornhair, "it resides
on the point of a knife."

Cornhair shuddered, her head down. Had she been
recognized?

"I am sure," said Rurik, "my esteemed guests have something
in mind."

"Which doubtless you suspect," said Julian.

"Surely you do not expect me to respond to what has not
been spoken," said Rurik.

"As the empire abetted the Farnichi, so, too, might the Farnichi be expected to abet the empire," said Julian.

"Speak," said Rurik.

"Why are you here?" said Julian. "The motivation is clear.
Events precipitate specifics. Iaachus has brought you here
to have a tool at readiness, a weapon which might be used in
various ways at various times, to have at his disposal a private
army, one outside of official channels, one unrelated to familiar
resources."

"Perhaps," said Rurik.

"The princesses must be recovered," said Julian.

"I understand," said Rurik.

CHAPTER FORTY-NINE

"Which one do you want?" asked Ingeld.

"Neither," said Hrothgar.

"Release us!" said Viviana. She spun about, robes whirling, on the rush-strewn, dirt floor of Ingeld's hall. "Return us to Telnaria!"

Ingeld's hall, on this world, incidentally, had once been the hall of Ortog, a secessionist Drisriak prince.

"Be patient, Princess," said Ingeld.

"We are of the royal blood," said Viviana. "We will never espouse commoners, let alone barbarians. It is unthinkable. Release us!"

"Shall I have their clothing removed?" inquired Farrix, he of the Teragar Borkons, the Long-River Borkons.

"Stay away!" cried Viviana.

"It might make it easier to decide," said Farrix.

"Neither would bring much on a block," said Hrothgar.

"We are beautiful, I, in particular," cried Viviana.

"Sister!" protested Alacida.

"I am going to the stables," said Hrothgar. "I must tend my horses."

"Clear your mind, dear brother," said Ingeld, "of horses, hot *bror*, falcons, and slaves. We talk here of important things, of power, of worlds."

"Have your power, and your worlds," said Hrothgar. "I want a blue sky, a fine morning, fields of green grass, a good horse beneath me, a falcon on my wrist, and game afoot. Then, at the end of the day, give me *bror* in my cup and a slave in my arms."

"Barbarian!" said Viviana.

"You know the will of our father, the king," said Ingeld. "For my part, I would be pleased to give you a hundred horses and a hundred falcons, a barrel of *bror*, and a hundred slaves. I cannot, in Telnarian law, marry both princesses."

"You shall marry neither!" said Viviana. "Even now imperial ships rush to rescue us!"

"Our information," said Ingeld, "is that ships remain in their housings, why should they not, they do not know where to go, and your disappearance is denied. They can do nothing. They are helpless. They must wait for us to contact them."

"They seek us! They search! They speed to our rescue," insisted Viviana.

"Your head must be as empty as one of your brother's rattles," said Ingeld. "Resources are limited, few, and precious. Surely you are aware of the rationing of resources. In places, a town might be exchanged for a pistol, a city for a rifle and ten charges. Do you think this is a hundred thousand years in the past? Finding you would be more difficult than locating a single grain of sand on a beach a thousand miles in length."

"Liar! Liar!" said Viviana.

"As far as I am concerned, dear brother," said Ingeld, "you need not marry a princess. I am perfectly ready to marry one of the princesses, either one. I cannot marry both. If you marry neither I need only marry one, and make certain the other never returns to Telnaria, where she might marry a Telnarian and bear a son, indeed, better, that she remain unmated."

"That is easily enough arranged, Lord," said Farrix, "a simple motion of the knife."

"I do not want either of them," said Hrothgar.

"And you are not wanted!" said Viviana, angrily.

"Hrothgar is a strong, handsome fellow," said Farrix. "I am sure he could make you kick, and buck."

"Do not be vulgar," said Viviana.

Alacida began to weep.

"Stop blubbering, female," said Ingeld.

"'Female'?" said Alacida.

"Yes," said Ingeld, "even a princess, even a queen, is a female."

"I loathe men," said Viviana. "I will have no feelings toward them. They are either brutes or fops. I cultivate frigidity. I pride myself on my inertness. I know nothing of sex, and will know nothing of sex. I am of the royal blood. I am a princess. I am superior to sex."

"Let us get her clothes off, put her in a collar, and give her a taste of the whip," said Farrix.

"Beat him, cast him out!" demanded Viviana.

"It is my understanding," said Ingeld, "that many free women of civilization, of the empire, think themselves superior to sex."

"They are different, once they are sold off the block," said Farrix.

"And you, pretty Alacida," said Ingeld, "are you superior to sex?"

"I fear not," whispered Alacida.

"Good," said Farrix, "strip her and get her in wrist-to-ankle shackles. It is easy to learn womanhood in chains."

"It is easy to make a woman moan, and beg," said Hrothgar.

"Please, let us desist in such vulgarity," said Ingeld. "Consider the feelings of our guests."

"Females," said Hrothgar.

"Women of station, of refinement and sensibility, of education and breeding," said Ingeld, "indeed, even princesses, not half naked, collared slaves."

"I want neither," said Hrothgar.

"And you will have neither!" exclaimed Viviana.

"I trust, dear brother," said Ingeld, "you will reconsider your position on this issue."

"No," said Hrothgar.

"It is the wish of the king, our father," said Ingeld.

"It is not my wish," said Hrothgar.

"Then," said Ingeld, "explain your reluctance to our father. Proceed, displease him! And remember Ortog!"

"Very well," growled Hrothgar. "I will marry one or the other. What do such things matter?"

"Viviana is the eldest, and doubtless the most prestigious to wed, but Alacida, I speculate, would most likely be the first to bear a son."

"You gentlemen, in making your plans," said Viviana, coldly, "forget one thing. Neither my sister nor myself will consent to such an infamy. We are adamant. We would as soon espouse *filchen* as such as you, rude, gross barbarian lords."

At that moment, the door of the hall swung open.

"The king," was heard, from the door herald.

In the portal stood Abrogastes, looking about himself, then regarding the princesses, and his sons, near the high seat.

"It is raining outside," he said, shaking his cloak, from which water fled, handing it then to an armsman. "It storms. The wind rages. It is cold. The night is dark."

Ingeld and Hrothgar slipped to one knee, heads bowed. Viviana and Alacida remained standing, to the right of the high seat, as one would face it.

Abrogastes strode forward, and seated himself on the high seat of Ingeld's hall. As soon as Abrogastes had passed them, his sons rose up, and turned to face the high seat.

"Ah," said Abrogastes, straightening his small shoulder cape, with the large, dully glistening golden clasp, "here we have two princes, and two princesses. I trust matters have now been resolved."

"Hrothgar and I, noble king and father," said Ingeld, "as dutiful sons, loyal to the throne, stand ready to obey. As yet, the princesses prove reluctant to abide by your will."

"You have not yet agreed on your brides, nor set a date for joyful nuptials?"

"No, father," said Ingeld.

"By now," said Abrogastes, "arrangements were to have been made."

"I am sorry, father," said Ingeld.

"Princesses?" asked Abrogastes.

"Release us!" said Viviana. "Return us immediately to Telnar!"

"I do not understand," said Abrogastes. "You are princesses. My sons are princes. What, fine ladies, do you wish? I am prepared, against my better judgment, in unprecedented generosity, to permit my sons, of Drisriak blood, of the blood of kings, to mate with you, pale, flawed weaklings of the empire. Are you ignorant of the honor that is paid to you? Why do you not kneel thankfully to me? Why do you not rejoice? Why are your lips not pressed in gratitude to my boots?"

"Let us go!" said Viviana.

"Is that your wish, as well, slight, gentle Alacida?" inquired Abrogastes.

Alacida glanced to her sister, and then turned to face Abrogastes. "Yes!" she said, defiantly.

"Our guests wish to be released," said Abrogastes to Ingeld, Hrothgar, and Farrix.

"It seems so," said Ingeld.

"Well, then," said Abrogastes, "let us release them."

CHAPTER FIFTY

"Where am I?" asked Brother Benjamin. "Surely this is not the table of Karch."

"No," said Hunlaki. "This is the wagon of Hunlaki. You are in a Herul camp, the camp of the Herd of Chuluun, east of the Lothar."

"How came I here?" asked the salamanderine, weakly. His small body took up scarcely a third of the rude couch.

"You were found near the edge of the herd," said Hunlaki, "by my friend, Mujiin, unconscious in the grass. He nearly did not see you. The brown robe might have been cast-aside cloth. You might have been trampled."

"He should have left me," said Brother Benjamin. "I failed the brothers, I failed others."

"You were nearly dead of exposure," said Hunlaki. "For days I was afraid you would die."

"Better I had," said Brother Benjamin.

"You were alone," said Hunlaki. "Mujiin found no others."

"I wandered in the fields, for weeks, perhaps half mad," said Brother Benjamin. "I failed the brothers, I failed others, as well."

"How did you live?" asked Hunlaki.

"I drank from pools of water, I fed on roots, when I could find them," said Brother Benjamin.

"How is it," asked Hunlaki, "that you were found in the Flats of Tung, alone?"

"I failed the brothers," said Brother Benjamin. "I failed others, as well."

"I do not understand," said Hunlaki.

"I am Brother Benjamin, of the *festung* of Sim Giadini," said Brother Benjamin.

"The *festung* is no more," said Hunlaki. "It was attacked and destroyed by imperial cruisers. There remains only ash and rubble, and the black, scarred, burned skin of a mountaintop."

"No!" said Brother Benjamin. "The brothers!"

"They are all dead," said Hunlaki. "You, alone, remain."

"Woe," said Brother Benjamin, weakly, in misery.

"How is it you were not in the *festung* when it was destroyed?" asked Hunlaki.

"There was a recreant novice, an Otung, named Urta, supposedly eager to join the brothers," said Brother Benjamin. "He claimed to have received the calling of Floon, the emanation of Karch, on a windy, starlit night in the Otung forest. He made his way to the *festung*. Barefoot, and ill clothed, he besought admittance for days, outside the gate, waiting in the snow. The gate was opened. How could he be refused? He was accepted. He seemed a model of propriety; he ingratiated himself with everyone; he strove to serve the brothers, all, selflessly and tirelessly; he was zealous in his prayers and dutiful in his devotions; he was popular; all were pleased with him. He honored me, by seeking me out, to be his special guide and mentor. I was flattered. How could he be refused? He was accepted. He learned, as was no secret in the *festung*, that I was the guardian of a Vandal artifact, a medallion and chain. It had been found with a newborn infant in the Month of Igon, on the plains of Barrionuevo, in the year of the Claiming Stone, 1103, and entrusted to me by a Herul warrior."

"He was I," said Hunlaki.

"The Otung, Urta," said Brother Benjamin, "as it turned out, had not come to the *festung* to seek the holiness of Floon, but to steal the artifact."

"I know this Urta," said Hunlaki. "He is a renegade Otung. He served us well. For years he was the Otung King Namer, the reign of a king, as we would have it, limited to a single year. In this office, he did much to thwart Otung unity, inciting competition amongst the clans, dividing them, keeping them at one another's throat."

"As he expressed interest in the artifact," said Brother Benjamin, "I saw no harm in showing it to him. Doubtless, he marked well its housing in my cell. I returned to my cell one morning to find it gone, and Urta vanished from the *festung*. I suspect he knew more of its significance than I. Muchly distraught, for the artifact had been entrusted to me, to be held for another, I set out immediately, in pursuit of the thief, hoping to recover the artifact."

"You would not do so," said Hunlaki. "We conjecture it was soon conveyed to Venitzia, to the Exarch of Venitzia, to be transmitted thence, for some reason, to Telnar. Much seems to have transpired swiftly."

"You said the *festung* is no more," said Brother Benjamin.

"It is no more," said Hunlaki.

"Why?" asked Brother Benjamin. "It is a quiet, holy place, innocent, untroubled, and remote, devoted to peace, prayer, spiritual exercises, the emulation of Floon, the contemplation of Karch. It stood for a thousand years."

"No more," said Hunlaki.

"But why would it be attacked, and why by imperial cruisers?"

"We speculate for two reasons," said Hunlaki, "one political, one religious, both apparently weightier to humans than to Heruls. We think the medallion and chain has great importance to the Vandals and its possessor would have great power amongst them. To be sure we understand very little of this. Politically, the destruction of the *festung* would be designed to cover the theft and remove those who would know of it. Religiously, there are many versions of, and interpretations of, the teachings and traditions pertaining to Floon and Karch, their natures, their relationship to one another, and so on."

"Of course," said Brother Benjamin, "but what difference do such things make? The important thing is to respect one another, to care for one another, and love one another."

"That seems to be less important to some than to others," said Hunlaki.

"I do not understand," said Brother Benjamin.

"It has to do with competitions for power, prestige, importance, and gold," said Hunlaki.

"What have such things to do with Floon?" asked Brother Benjamin.

"Nothing, one supposes," said Hunlaki, "but apparently it has much to do with power, prestige, importance, and gold."

"That is to betray Floon," whispered Brother Benjamin, frightened.

"Yes," said Hunlaki, "profitably."

"But in such competitions," said Brother Benjamin, "would not the most ruthless, the most unscrupulous, the most determined, the least self-critical, the least humble, the farthest from Floon, the most arrogant, the strongest rise to the top?"

"Yes," said Hunlaki, "and, to the extent possible, destroy all others."

Brother Benjamin closed his eyes.

"It is not only the *arn* bear and the vi-cat which are territorial," said Hunlaki.

"But imperial cruisers," said Brother Benjamin. "I do not understand. Why would the empire be involved? The empire does not meddle in such matters. It is tolerant. It has always been. It does not stand between rational creatures and their gods. It does not choose one rational creature's gods and force them, like laws and taxes, on other rational creatures."

"Perhaps," said Hunlaki, "until now."

"Gods exist or not," said Brother Benjamin. "They do not require the state's attention or licensing in either case."

"The existence or nonexistence of gods is not relevant," said

Hunlaki. "What is important is power, prestige, importance, and gold."

"Woe," whispered Brother Benjamin.

"Had the medallion and chain not been stolen, and had you not left the *festung*, hoping to recover them," said Hunlaki, "you would have perished, as the others, in the destruction of the *festung*."

"Better I had," said Brother Benjamin.

"No," said Hunlaki.

"Sir?" asked Brother Benjamin.

"I saw, and handled, the medallion and chain briefly, long ago," said Hunlaki. "Yet I remember it clearly. You received it. You cared for it for years. Doubtless you could recognize it, as well."

"Yes," said Brother Benjamin. "Each tiny flaw and blemish, each link in its order, the proportion of each link to another, wider or narrower, the cuts of blades on links and on the medallion itself, apparently sustained in combat."

"So," said Hunlaki, "it is better you did not perish in the destruction of the *festung*."

"How so?" said Brother Benjamin.

"We know the story of the medallion and chain," said Hunlaki. "We can recognize it."

"So?" said Brother Benjamin.

"I delivered the artifact to you long ago," said Hunlaki. "I am not pleased that it was stolen. I am determined to recover it."

"It is gone," said Brother Benjamin.

"I am old," said Hunlaki. "But I am a Herul. I am a rider, a hunter. I am tenacious."

"Where would you look?" asked Brother Benjamin.

"Given the destruction of the *festung*, putatively a holy place, and what I can gather of the lethal absurdities of religious strifes, pretending the authorizations and endorsements of one god or another, this excusing murder, and such, I suspect the medallion and chain were conveyed to Venitzia, to the Exarch of

Venitzia. If this is so, as the Exarch of Venitzia, a provincial capital, is subordinate, as I understand it, to the Exarch of Telnar,
the imperial capital, I am supposing that, for whatever reason, it
was carried to Telnar, and, presumably, to the Exarch of Telnar.

I am unclear as to what the purpose of all this would be."

"You would venture to Telnar?" said Brother Benjamin.

"We will venture to Telnar," said Hunlaki. "I shall pose as
your servant. The salamanderine is recognized as a rational species. Indeed, your Floon, as I understand it, was of a kindred species. They need not know that the Heruls are a superior species."

"There are no superior species," said Brother Benjamin.

"The *arn* bear is superior to the *filch*," said Hunlaki.

"The arrow which slays the *arn* bear ignores the *filch*," said
Brother Benjamin. "The *filch* passes easily through the meshes of
the net which snares the *arn* bear. The *arn* bear needs much on
which to feed, the *filch* little. Indeed, the *arn* bear starves where
the *filch* thrives. The *arn* bear is little nourished by the *filch*,
but a hundred *filchen* may feed for three days on the carcass of a
single *arn* bear."

"The fleet ones," said Hunlaki, "the pine deer, the antelope,
the *tiernik*, the gazelle, the spotted forest ram, and such, are
swifter than the steers of Tung."

"But one stroke of the horns of a steer of Tung can disembowel a fleet one," said Brother Benjamin.

"Doubtless you frequented the library of the *festung*," said
Hunlaki.

"Yes," said Brother Benjamin, "but some things are generally
known."

"I will speak for you," said Hunlaki.

"I will speak for myself," said Brother Benjamin.

"That is my fear," said Hunlaki.

"Perhaps I may be able to instruct the Exarch of Venitzia,
who, as I understand it, suffers from theological confusions, in
the error of his ways," said Brother Benjamin.

"Allow him to persist in his ignorance," said Hunlaki.

"I would enlighten him, of course, in a kindly, gentle, loving way," said Brother Benjamin.

"And pave the way to the burning rack, for both of us," said Hunlaki.

"Is it not a beautiful thing to die for Floon?" inquired Brother Benjamin.

"Not, really," said Hunlaki. "You will take a vow of silence."

"A vow of silence?" said Brother Benjamin.

"You are not permitted to lie, are you?" asked Hunlaki.

"No," said Brother Benjamin.

"I do not suffer from a similar impediment," said Hunlaki, "except where those of the camp are concerned."

"So I am to take a vow of silence?" said Brother Benjamin.

"Yes, but I will set its terms, conditions, limits, and such," said Hunlaki.

"Would Floon approve of this?" asked Brother Benjamin.

"Wholly," said Hunlaki.

"I see I am not of the camp," said Brother Benjamin.

"Do not concern yourself," said Hunlaki. "A great many are not. Few are so fortunate. I will now fetch you some broth, and you may rest. You must regain your strength."

"What you propose is exceedingly dangerous, is it not?" asked Brother Benjamin.

"Yes," said Hunlaki.

"Then I may yet die for Floon," said Brother Benjamin.

"It is quite possible," said Hunlaki.

"Good," said Brother Benjamin.

"For myself, I would prefer to occupy myself otherwise," said Hunlaki.

"Broth?" asked Brother Benjamin.

"I will fetch it," said Hunlaki.

CHAPTER FIFTY-ONE

"Let us in! Let us in!" screamed Viviana, pounding on the stockade gate, outside the compound of Ingeld on Tenguthaxichai.

"Please! Please!" wept Alacida.

"We are cold!" cried Viviana.

"Give us clothing!" cried Alacida.

"We are hungry!" cried Viviana.

"We fear a beast is about!" cried Alacida.

It may be recalled that it was a dark, cold, stormy, windy night when Abrogastes entered the hall of Ingeld. It may also be recalled that the princesses had made known their disinclination, after what must have been a painful interview, to remain any longer the guests of Drisriaks. "Let us go!" had cried Viviana, to which request Alacida had readily and earnestly assented. To this request, as it may also be recalled, Abrogastes had acceded. "Well, then," he had said, "let us release them."

Shortly thereafter, at the hands of several willing Drisriaks, armsmen of Abrogastes, the clothing of the princesses had been torn from their bodies, and they had been conducted, stumbling, from the hall, bent over, the hair of each in the rude, tight grasp of a Drisriak armsman, their head held close at his right hip, a familiar leading position for slaves, but scarcely for princesses.

At that time it was still pouring, with a chill rain, and the yard was a sea of mud.

The gate in the palisade was opened, and the princesses were thrust outside. Viviana, we fear, fell. But she was soon again on her feet, and, followed by the weeping Alacida, sped into the darkness. The ground around the palisaded compound was cleared for something like a hundred yards on all sides, a military precaution to make a surreptitious approach difficult, and to provide defenders, on the catwalk behind the palisade, with a clear range of fire. In a few moments the girls, panting, and muddied, particularly Viviana, had made their way through the downpour, and reached the trees of the surrounding woods. It was quite dark. There was, at that time, no light at the palisade. There was, however, an occasional flash of lighting, which suddenly illuminated the terrain, the palisade in the distance, the falling rain, until the darkness fell again, accompanied by closer or more distant rumbles of thunder.

In the woods there was some shelter from the rain, but, given the ferocity of the storm, and the time of year, less than might have been desired. Leaves and branches can only sustain certain weights of rain, until they bend or turn, and the water spills to yet lower branches and leaves, and so on. Eventually much of the water, directly or indirectly, reaches the ground. Too, as it was late fall in this latitude of Tenguthaxichai many of the nearby trees were rather denuded of leaves.

"We have escaped!" announced Viviana, holding her arms about herself, shivering.

"To what, dear sister?" moaned Alacida.

"We can hide in the forest, no one will be able to find us," said Viviana.

"They may not want to find us," said Alacida.

"They will not do so," said Viviana. "Rejoice, dear sister, we have escaped."

"We did not escape," said Alacida. "They put us out!"

"We will hide ourselves in the woods, until we are rescued," said Viviana.

"We will not be rescued!" said Alacida. "No one knows where we are. There are thousands of worlds. Supposedly our absence has not even been made publicly known. It seems plausible, as the handsome, barbarian prince said, that ships remain in their housings. Why should they not? Where would they look for us? The empire must wait for word from our captors, issuing demands for ransom, or such. What else can they do? Surely resources essential to the defense of the empire cannot be randomly and extensively expended, perhaps for months, for years. It would be absurd, insane, inconceivable, suicidal. Indeed, some attempt in force to rescue us might result in our end, either in the attack or at the hands of our captors. We must return to the hall, and beg for admittance!"

"Never!" cried Viviana.

"We will die here, of cold and hunger," wept Alacida.

"As princesses then," said Viviana, "as princesses of the royal blood!"

"You think either to be rescued, or that the barbarians will relent," said Alacida.

"We are prized, we are needed," said Viviana, "by the empire, by the barbarians."

"The empire does not need us," said Alacida. "There are others who bear royal blood, as well, a hundred cousins!"

"The empire will seek us out," said Viviana. "They dare not risk our mating with barbarians."

"If we are destroyed," said Alacida, "either in some massive attack by imperial ships or by the barbarians, it need not be concerned in such a matter."

"Surely the barbarians need us," said Viviana, shivering, "to further their vulgar, daring schemes."

"We are no good to the barbarians, if we are not cooperative," said Alacida. "The emperor and the senate would never recognize a forced marriage. If we do not accept these suits, we are useless to the barbarians. Do you not understand? They put us out. They will seek other stratagems. It is nothing to them if we should die in the woods!"

"Surely not," said Viviana, shuddering, holding her arms about herself.

Suddenly branches, scattering chill, drenching water, shook about them, a torrent of wind, from the north, swirling through the crowded, dark trees.

"These are not men of civilization," said Alacida, "sensitive and courteous, attentive and understanding, trained in etiquette, shaped by convention, who would never dare to let a free woman be displeased or uncomfortable. These are not like the men we know, not men as you think men are. These are barbarians, honestly self-seeking men, unapologetic, determined men, men of enterprise and will, men of decision and deeds, men of the hunt, of the battle, of the ax and sword, men who loathe the empire, and would not care if it perished in flames, men who despise such as we, and, if they cannot get from us what they desire, would view with equanimity our perishing in the woods."

"Surely not!" moaned Viviana.

"I am cold!" said Alacida. "I shiver. I am soaked with rain. My eyes sting. My feet hurt, from dried leaves, branches, and stones."

"We must be brave," said Viviana. "We need only wait a moment. The barbarians will come to fetch us, and beg us to return."

"I see no light at the palisade," said Alacida. "I see no opened gate, no lanterns moving through the night, searching for us."

"Be of good cheer, sister," said Viviana. "Take heart. The storm abates. The sky is no longer riven. Lightning has fled. Thunder is faraway."

"The wind is incessant, and cold," said Alacida. "It has claws of ice. They clutch at me. The night is dark. I freeze."

"Hold your arms about yourself," said Viviana.

"I am," said Alacida.

"How am I to know?" asked Viviana. "It is dark."

"I would give all my jewels for a blanket," said Alacida.

"Do not be foolish," said Viviana. "The least of your jewels would buy a hundred blankets."

"I am hungry," said Alacida.

"Certainly you would not have had us consume the simple barbarian provender put before us this noon?" said Viviana.

"You would not let me," said Alacida.

"Served by half-naked barbarian slaves," added Viviana.

"Some, I fear, were women of the empire," said Alacida.

"Surely not," said Viviana.

"They were forbidden to speak," said Alacida.

"Fittingly, as they were slaves," said Viviana.

"It is dark, and I am cold," said Alacida.

"The rain is less," said Viviana.

"I am hungry, terribly hungry," said Alacida.

"When the storm is done, and it is light," said Viviana, "we can search for food."

"When the storm is done," said Alacida, "other things, as well, and it need not be light, may search for food."

"Other things?" said Viviana.

"Yes!" said Alacida, weeping.

"Do you see any light at the palisade, any lanterns?" asked Viviana, anxiously.

"No!" said Alacida.

"Where can they be?" asked Viviana.

"Inside, warm, feasting," said Alacida, bitterly.

"I, too, might part with a jewel, a small one, for a blanket," said Viviana.

"Perhaps we should petition readmittance," said Alacida.

"No," said Viviana. "They will soon emerge, searching for us. And then, after a suitable interval, we may, if it seems proper, and lest they be too distraught, permit ourselves to be found.

They may then conduct us within, contritely, in dignity and honor."

"These are not men of civilization," said Alacida. "Think! These are barbarians, and we are women, only women."

"Royal princesses!" insisted Viviana.

"Women, only women," said Alacida. And sweet, dark-haired Alacida, who had feared she might not be superior to sex, trembled, and pondered the apparent fact, that, whatever might be its import, women were different, very different, from men. Once, when she was very young, only a girl, with her chaperones, in the vicinity of a market, in Telnar, she had heard a man remark that women were property. Later the same day, she had eavesdropped on slaves, she standing in the street, in her girl's robes, outside a street-level, barred window, that of a market dungeon, and listened to the girls within, possibly to be sold that afternoon. She had not heard them lamenting, as one might expect, their degraded status and impending fate, wearing their informative, debasing placards on a slave shelf, but rather, eager and delighted at their impending sale, they clearly welcomed and celebrated their propertyhood; they found fulfillment and reassurance in their status as vendible, meaningless objects; they wanted nothing else; they scorned freedom; they wanted to be what they were, properties, the properties of men; they had experienced the slave's freedom and joy; now they wished nothing else; they wanted to be purchased and owned, by a fine, kind, strong man, one severe and uncompromising, but understanding and nurturing, one who would master them with perfection, wholly, one before whom they would be, and know themselves, slaves.

"The storm is over," said Viviana. "We shall wait here until morning."

"We may be dead by morning," said Alacida.

"Surely not," said Viviana.

"I am stiff with cold," said Alacida. "I can hardly move."

"Perhaps," said Viviana, "as the rain has stopped, we might venture a bit into the clearing, merely to see if we might be hailed, and invited within the palisade."

"It is too dark," said Alacida. "They would not see us."

"There is no light at the palisade?" said Viviana.

"No," said Alacida.

"What shall we do?" asked Viviana.

"Let us approach, and call out, while we have the strength," said Alacida.

"Certainly not," said Viviana. "That would be unthinkable."

"Sister!" cried Alacida.

"What?" said Viviana, startled.

"I heard something, there!" said Alacida.

"I heard nothing," said Viviana, "and, if you are pointing, I cannot see where you are pointing. It is too dark."

"Listen!" said Alacida.

"I hear nothing," said Viviana.

"It is quiet now," said Alacida.

"It is the wind, stirring the leaves," said Viviana.

"Only now?" asked Alacida.

"One supposes so," said Viviana, uneasily.

"The leaves are wet, flat, thick, carpeted," said Alacida.

"So?" said Viviana.

"Something stirred the leaves," said Alacida. "And it was not the wind."

"We are alone," said Viviana.

"I do not think so," said Alacida. "Be silent, please, dear sister."

"It will not be light for hours," said Viviana.

"There!" cried Alacida. "I heard it again, closer!"

The vi-cat, like the princesses, was quite possibly hungry, that it should emerge from its den in such a muddy, half-flooded terrain, particularly as, with its long, rough tongue, it tends to keep its fur dry and groomed. To be sure, we do not know that,

that it was hungry. It may have emerged from its den simply because of curiosity, having detected, with its unusually acute hearing, unusual sounds. The vi-cat does tend to be a curious, investigatory animal.

The vi-cat is a common form of life on several of the Telnarian worlds. It is not known to what world it is native, as that knowledge, if it was ever possessed, at least by Telnarians, was lost long ago. Varna, Tangara, Terennia, have all been suggested, even Telnaria itself. What is known is that, in historical times, the vi-cat was introduced into several worlds, usually to cull flocks and herds, sometimes on game worlds. Too, the interaction of prey and predator obviously favors certain features in both, for example, in a prey animal, alertness, width of peripheral vision, acuity of smell, fleetness, and such, and, in the predatory animal, a binocular focus in vision, teeth, claws, stealth, strength, swiftness, and such. Too, on some worlds the vi-cat was apparently introduced as being an animal worthy of being hunted by emperors, when emperors were concerned with such things. The vi-cat, too, is a favored arena animal. Whereas most vi-cats are found in the wild, some are bred for various purposes by rational species. On the other hand, dogs and wolves are more easily trained. It is not unknown for even a domestic vi-cat, with several generations of domesticity behind it, to turn and attack its Master without warning. The vi-cat has its place in the literature of several worlds, figuring in proverbs, fables, folk tales, and such. Among the Otungs, as we learned earlier, the pelt of the white vi-cat is assigned some symbolic significance, being regarded as appropriate, for example, for the cloak of a king.

At this point, we suppose the vi-cat in the vicinity of the princesses, here in the vicinity of the compound of Ingeld on Tenguthaxichai, was, at least initially, more puzzled than aggressive. Surely encountering two soft-skinned young animals of an unusual species, the human, in the forest after a storm was not a

frequent occurrence within its experience. It might also be noted
that, whereas the vi-cat, if sufficiently hungry, will attack anything, even a *torodont*, its customary prey is what we might call
"the fleet ones," and not the human. Too, perhaps the vi-cat, if
pondering a charge, was somewhat distracted not only by the
unusual nature of the possible prey objects but by there being
two. Which would it first attack? If it attacked one, it would presumably lose the other. An analogy, though one not all that profitable or convincing, would be the value of schooling amongst
certain forms of fish. For example, a single fish may be easily
detected, and easily pursued, and often seized, but if it is flickering about in a shimmering swirl of similar fish, it is much more
elusive. A similar problem seldom occurs, incidentally, with a
land predator, such as the Persian lion, the vi-cat, the Megarian
leaper, or the fanged *ort*. This seems to be for two reasons, first,
the difference between land and marine predation, such as differences in size of the prey group, the type of movement involved,
and the attack dimension, which, for the land predator is simpler,
and more one dimensional; second, differentiation amongst prey
animals. Fish in a school seem much the same, but in a herd or
flock, some animals are likely to be slower, weaker, older, sicker,
more isolated, and such, and, statistically, these will be most at
risk. While the vi-cat was possibly puzzling the matter out, it had
tended to approach the two princesses in the typical fashion of
the vi-cat, low, tail nervously lashing, a quick forward movement,
then stillness, then another quick forward movement, and so on,
until, of course the charge. It seems clear that it was at least two of
these short, quick movements which Alacida had heard.

What decided the princesses to vacate the supposed shelter
of the woods, emanating from a source not feet away from
them, was an unmistakably menacing sound, a rumble or growl
in the darkness. They may not have understood this sound as
the growl of a vi-cat, but there was no mistaking that its source
was large and dangerous. It is not clear whether or not the

vi-cat had given this announcement of its presence intention-
ally or unintentionally. It might have been a simple inadvertent
expression of its curiosity or puzzlement; it may have been
deliberate, to wait for a response, in this problematic situation.
In any event, the princesses did something very understandable, if, possibly, very foolish, which was to cry out and race,
in terror, toward the gate of the palisade.

Whereas the princesses were substantially in the darkness,
and would have had great difficulty in seeing the vi-cat, even
had they turned about and cared to do so, the vi-cat suffered
from no comparable handicap, as it, as many predators, had
excellent night vision.

The princesses fled, screaming, toward the palisade gate.

The vi-cat, presumably still puzzled, padded along, behind
them, remaining some yards in the rear.

"Let us in! Let us in!" had screamed Viviana, pounding
on the stockade gate, outside the compound of Ingeld on
Tenguthaxichai.

"Please! Please!" had wept Alacida.

"We are cold!" had cried Viviana.

"Give us clothing!" had cried Alacida.

"We are hungry!" had cried Viviana.

"We fear a beast is about!" had cried Alacida.

"There is a beast about!" cried Viviana. "I am sure of it! We
heard it! Let us in! We are cold! We are hungry! We are princesses of the empire! We are unclothed! Mercy! Have mercy!"

"Please!" wept Viviana.

After a time, presumably to investigate the commotion at the
gate, a lantern, borne by someone, it could not be clearly seen
who, on the catwalk behind the palisade, appeared, several feet
above the piteous, desperate princesses.

"Let us in! Please! Please!" called the princesses, looking up
toward the light, their faces, and fair forms, illuminated in the
light, they standing in the mud below.

The lantern then disappeared.

The princesses turned about to peer into the darkness. But they could see nothing.

"Is it there?" asked Alacida.

"I do not know!" said Viviana, in misery.

Then, again, Viviana pounded on the gate, weeping.

After a time the lantern again appeared, above them, held over the palisade wall.

Alacida turned about, again, looking back, into the darkness, toward the woods, and screamed.

Viviana, turning, too, screamed in fear.

Reflected in the lantern light, like two burning coals, were the eyes of the vi-cat, only yards away, its body low, almost flat on the ground, its powerful legs gathered under it, like springs.

They heard heavy metal keys thrust into massive locks, and turned, and then a jangling of metal and chain, and, a bit later, two wooden bars being slid free of their metal housings, behind the gate.

The gate opened, some two yards or so, but the princesses, to their dismay, could not enter, for the way was blocked by a number of armed men. Of these men, two carried lanterns, and one a torch. There was no mistaking the massive, stern figure of Abrogastes, foremost amongst these fellows, mostly armsmen and retainers. On either side of Abrogastes were his sons, Ingeld and Hrothgar.

"On your bellies!" said Abrogastes.

The terrified princesses then placed themselves prone, naked, in the mud, before Abrogastes.

Doubtless it was the first time they had been bellied before males.

"Which one do you want?" Abrogastes asked Ingeld, who had priority, as a prior son to a subsequent son. The annals are clear that Ingeld was the second son of Abrogastes. The ranking of Hrothgar is less clear. It is usually supposed he was the third or fourth son of Abrogastes. As noted earlier, some of the sons of Abrogastes are known only by brief references, and some by name only. Too, the names of some may not have figured in the imperial records, at all.

"The blond slut," said Ingeld.

"You," said Abrogastes, to Viviana, "crawl to him on your belly. Cover his boots with kisses, and then speak as follows. 'I, Viviana, princess of the empire, despite my unworthiness, beg on my belly to be permitted to be the bride of Ingeld, prince of the Drisriaks.' You will then kiss again his boots, in further supplication. Following that you are to rise to all fours and, head down, wait to the side. We will tell you then what you are to do."

Shuddering, Viviana complied.

"Next, you," said Abrogastes to Alacida.

Alacida then crawled on her belly, through the mud, to the feet of Hrothgar, and pressed her lovely lips to his boots, ministering to them as though she might have been no more than a slave. "I, Alacida," she said, "princess of the empire, despite my unworthiness, beg on my belly to be permitted to be the bride of Hrothgar, prince of the Drisriaks." She then, as had her sister, again addressed her lips to his boots. Afterwards, she, too, rose to all fours, and, head down, went to wait beside her sister. They were now similar to two docile, obedient quadrupeds.

Both were concerned, though neither spoke of the matter, at the strange feelings which had been precipitated in their bodies.

They now knew that they were different from what they had been before.

"Away! Away!" cried the retainer with the torch, thrusting it in the direction of the vi-cat, which then snarled, but turned about, and padded back to the woods.

The gate was then closed, and secured.

"Dear Princesses," said Abrogastes, turning to the positioned princesses, "we shall consider your petition. If we see fit to accept it, you will sit upon jeweled thrones and be the mothers of emperors. If we do not accept it, you will be collared and sold on far mud worlds, never to be heard of again in the empire. Do you understand?"

"Yes, great Lord," said Viviana.

"Yes, great Lord," said Alacida.

Abrogastes then turned to one of his armsmen. "Herd these two imperial sows back, as they are, on all fours, head down, to the hall, and then place them on their bellies, before the high seat. We will consider whether or not to chain them, naked, later."

"Yes, Lord," said the armsman, and he thrust a whimpering Viviana forward, with the butt of his spear.

When the princesses were out of earshot, Ingeld turned to Abrogastes. "Things may not proceed as easily as envisaged, father," he said.

"Let us suppose," said Abrogastes, "the princesses now understand two things, that they are women, and where their best interests lie."

"Things are not so simple, father," said Ingeld. "Surely one needs more than the mere acquiescence of princesses in this matter. There is the acceptance of such things, by the empire, the throne, the senate. Who would honor, or ratify, a putative union supposedly formed faraway on a foreign world? Is it to be taken seriously? Might it not have been enacted under duress? Is it authentic, genuine, meaningful?"

"I have made arrangements," said Abrogastes. "The marriages will take place in Telnar itself, openly, and publicly. They will be proclaimed broadly, throughout the empire; they will be anticipated eagerly; they will be celebrated with elaborate ceremony, with detailed pomp and pageantry, with formality and complex ritual. All will look forward to this most desired consummation, bearing in its train peace and the union of peoples."

"I find it hard to believe these arrangements would be entered into by the throne," said Ingeld.

"The throne is not the only force in Telnaria," said Abrogastes.

"I do not understand," said Ingeld.

"The marriages will be performed by the Exarch of Telnar himself," said Abrogastes. "He will bestow on them the supposed blessing of a faith. Interestingly, some take such things seriously. In short, he will allegedly, in the foolishness he propagates, solemnize things, sanctify matters, and so on. Advantages obtain in such a procedure. We gain standing and legitimacy, and he gains prestige and power. We serve each other. We play his stupid game and his game, in our playing of it, is confirmed as the game to play."

"I think," said Ingeld, "the exarch has more in mind."

"Why should you think that?" asked Abrogastes.

"It is a thought, I have," said Ingeld, warily.

"You are right," said Abrogastes. "He wants to own the empire. "The *koos*, whatever that is, is to be superior to the fist. The fist is to fight for the *koos*, obey the *koos*, do the work of the *koos*, and so on. In this way the *koos* gets its way and does not have to risk skinning its own knuckles."

"Who knows," asked Ingeld, "what the *koos* wants?"

"That is made clear by the spokesman for the *koos*," said Abrogastes.

"The exarch," said Ingeld.

"Of course," said Abrogastes.

"Surely, if we obtain the empire, by our steel, our ships, our blood, our toil, you would not surrender it to some sleek, cowardly, pernicious fraud," said Ingeld.

"Fortunately for frauds, they are few," said Abrogastes. "Otherwise they could not batten with impunity on the trust of the many. They take advantage of the honesty and decency of the many. A population of frauds would soon have no frauds or be extinct."

"It seems so," said Ingeld. "But surely you would not surrender a won prize to the deceit and contrivance of an ambitious
spectator."

"Perhaps the spectator might make the prize more accessible," said Abrogastes.

"I do not understand," said Ingeld.

"An interesting thing about liars and frauds," said Abrogastes, "is that they do not expect to be lied to, or defrauded.
They assume that those with whom they deal dishonestly will
deal honestly with them."

"And they may not?" said Ingeld.

"I see no harm in betraying the betrayer, in doing treason to
the treasonous, in lying to the liar, in defrauding the fraudulent."

"You would use the exarch for your ends, as he would use
you for his?" said Ingeld.

"Yes," said Abrogastes. "And, if necessary, or if it seems
judicious, he can always be martyred at one's convenience. The
sword of the fist has a clear advantage over that of the *koos*. It
exists. The sword of the *koos* is helpless without the sword of the
fist; the sword of the fist, as it is real, does not need the sword
of the *koos*."

"The princesses are scarcely in a condition to participate in
the splendor of some imperial wedding," said Ingeld.

"They can be washed up, brushed and combed," said Abrogastes. "Too, it would not do to put them muddy in the tiny kennels I have prepared for them."

"We brought them from Telnar with only the clothes on their
backs," said Ingeld, "and those, thanks to the attentions of your
armsmen, are in shreds."

"Do not fear," said Abrogastes. "We will look after our lovely
guests. We will fit them out, appropriately. They will have gowns
and jewels, tiaras, entire wardrobes. They will awe multitudes."

"I think there is little of that sort here," said Ingeld,
"wardrobes, tiaras, and such. This is Tenguthaxichai. This is

a little-known world, rude, simple, unspoiled, little settled, known to few but Alemanni."

"Our agents have been in touch with gown-and-jewel merchants on four worlds, including Telnaria," said Abrogastes. "The merchants contacted will know nothing of princesses. They will think their goods are sought for the daughters of kings."

"How will they find Tenguthaxichai?" asked Ingeld.

"Gold has been bestowed, ships may be hired, coordinates will be supplied," said Abrogastes.

"Surely it will be difficult to keep such things secret," said Ingeld.

"Certainly," said Abrogastes.

"Do you know which merchants our agents have contacted?" asked Ingeld.

"No, but several," said Abrogastes.

"There is then danger," said Ingeld.

"No," said Abrogastes.

"Yes, dear father," said Ingeld. "Unwelcome visitors, agents of the empire, impostors, pirates, raiders, spies."

"Of course," said Abrogastes.

"You expect them?"

"Yes."

"Then you see the danger," said Ingeld.

"No," said Abrogastes. "Those contacted by our agents will have something impostors will not."

"What, father?" asked Ingeld.

"The password," said Abrogastes.

CHAPTER FIFTY-TWO

"Have you seen the daughters of the kings?" inquired Rurik, politely, of a saffron robed, turbaned fellow.

"Yes," he said, "four days ago. Do you wish to sell your slave?"

"No," said Rurik, "not now." Then he turned to the kneeling slave. "Get your head to the floor!" he snapped.

"Yes, Master," said the slave.

"She is nicely tunicked," said the turbaned fellow.

"She is not now chained to my couch," said Rurik.

"You are of the Larial Farnichi, are you not?" asked the turbaned fellow.

"Yes," said Rurik.

Doubtless his interlocutor's supposition was based on the recognition of the emblem, that inscribed in the circular patch sewn into Rurik's jacket, at the left shoulder, that of the five-petaled Pin Flower.

"A great merchant house," said the turbaned fellow.

"We have such interests, amongst others," said Rurik.

"A pretty slave," said the turbaned fellow.

"I am still training her," said Rurik.

"The whip and switch are useful in such training," said the fellow.

"This slave lives in terror of both," said Rurik. "I need only glance at the whip or switch and she strives ever more earnestly to please."

"Is her training going well?" asked the fellow.

"Quite well," said Rurik. "She is extremely intelligent, and well aware of the penalties for being found in the least bit displeasing."

"She bellies, and licks, and kisses well?" said the fellow.

"Of course," said Rurik.

"By now, she has doubtless felt the Master's caress," said the fellow.

"Yes," said Rurik.

"That changes them," said the fellow.

"Of course," said Rurik.

"Women are pleasant in collars," said the fellow.

"They belong in them," said Rurik.

"What else are they good for, but to wear a Master's collar?"

"True," said Rurik.

"It is interesting how the collar brings a woman so alive, and renders them so needfully helpless."

"Iron bands are not the strongest of bonds," said Rurik. "You say you saw the daughters of the kings four days ago?"

"I understand the lamentable disagreements between the Larial Calasalii and the Larial Farnichi have been resolved."

"Quite," said Rurik.

"Larial VII is now a Farnichi world?"

"Within the empire, of course," said Rurik.

"It is said that the Calasalii women now belong to Farnichi Masters."

"Some, many, not all," said Rurik. "But it is true that they were put in collars."

"This slave?" asked the fellow.

"She may have been the last apprehended," said Rurik.

"But she was of the Calasalii?"

"Yes," said Rurik.

"It is always pleasant to enslave the women of the enemy, and enjoy them," said the fellow.

"Yes," said Rurik.

"My house," said the turbaned fellow, "had difficulty dealing with the Calasalii."

"Many did," said Rurik.

"Perhaps the Farnichi might be easier to deal with."

"Perhaps," said Rurik.

"My house," said the fellow, "is interested in an outlet on Larial VII."

"Perhaps such might be arranged," said Rurik. "What of the daughters of the kings?"

"Let us speak to the side," said the fellow.

Rurik, quite willingly, followed the turbaned fellow to the side of the room.

"My delegation has done well here," said the turbaned fellow. "We have sold plentifully and reaped much profit."

"Splendid," said Rurik. "May my house do as well. Tell me of the daughters of kings."

"There are two," said the merchant. "Their names are withheld, and those of the fathers."

"Strange," said Rurik.

"Both are young and beautiful," said the turbaned fellow, "one is blond, and one dark. They were already, when we presented our goods, richly gowned and bejeweled. They seemed discriminating and astute in their judgment of women's finery. Yet, oddly, they scarcely would bargain. Almost, we could name our own prices. Both seemed subdued, even apprehensive."

"You do not understand these things?" asked Rurik.

"No," said the fellow, "and that is why I speak softly, and to the side. Something, I fear, is amiss."

"My curiosity is aroused, fellow merchant," said Rurik. "What were their accents?"

"I make them out to be Telnarian," said the fellow.

"Interesting," said Rurik.

"They are the daughters of rich merchants, I conjecture," said the fellow, "merchants who would barter their daughters' beauty for lucrative trade relations with barbarian nations."

"Quite possibly," said Rurik, "but might they not be what, it seems, they are alleged to be, the daughters of kings, presumably barbarian kings, who wish to form alliances with other barbarian kings."

"The accents?" said the fellow.

"The daughters of many kings are trained in languages, and certainly in imperial Telnarian. It is the common language in Telnaria, and in the provincial worlds, and the common second language in hundreds of border worlds, and many in the high barbarian houses are fluent in the tongue."

"You are doubtless right," said the fellow, "but, still, should the times of readying for marriage not be times of eagerness, of anticipation, and joy?"

"One would suppose so," said Rurik.

"You have not yet been called to present your goods?" asked the fellow.

"It seems we are being held for later," said Rurik.

"And some others, as well," said the fellow.

"It seems so," said Rurik.

"I trust you will make much profit," said the fellow.

"Thank you," said Rurik. "We shall hope so."

"We shall contact Larial VII, to essay a mutually agreeable mercantile arrangement with the house of the Farnichi," said the fellow.

"Do so, by all means," said Rurik.

"One last thing causes me uneasiness, with respect to the daughters of the kings," said the fellow.

"What is that?" asked Rurik.

"It is something I do not understand," said the fellow.

"What?" said Rurik.

"In the reception chamber, there is a large, heavy metal ring, set in the floor."

"So?" said Rurik.

"The daughters of the kings are chained to it," he said, "each, by an ankle."

CHAPTER FIFTY-THREE

"I am uneasy," said Julian. "Why this delay?"

"Others wait, as well," said Otto, looking about.

In the trading hall, where Julian, Otto, and Tuvo Ausonius waited, with their bolts of cloth and flat, lacquered boxes of jewels, were at least eleven other mercantile delegations, these, too, occupying benches arranged around large display tables.

One would be summoned from the trading hall, used for bulk trading, to the private, more exclusive selling chamber, the reception chamber, provided the preliminary ascertainments of abundance and quality, these made by agents, had been deemed satisfactory. This portion of the business had already been concluded satisfactorily, and our friends, and some others, were now waiting for an opportunity to bring their goods to the attention of buyers, presumably, in this case, the daughters of kings, selecting goods for a trousseau.

"Do you think we are taken seriously as gown-and-jewel merchants?" asked Tuvo Ausonius.

"Why not?" asked Julian.

"You would seem more in place on the bridge of an imperial cruiser," said Tuvo, "and friend Ottonius might seem more at home on some leaf-strewn path in a dark forest, a bow in hand."

"Rurik, then," said Julian. "The house of the Farnichi is a great trading house."

"Perhaps," said Tuvo Ausonius.

"He even brought a slave with him," said Julian.

"Doubtless as an accouterment to his disguise," said Tuvo.

"Doubtless," said Julian. "Still, some men are fond of their little beasts, and it is pleasant to have one at one's feet."

"I doubt that he would risk a valued slave in our desperate enterprise," said Tuvo.

"One supposes he would not," said Julian. "He is of the Farnichi, and the slave, as I understand it, was of the Calasalii. If so, she is fortunate not to have been thrown to dogs or wolves."

"I know the slave," said Otto. "Once, when she thought herself free, she tried to kill me."

"Surely you are mistaken," said Julian.

"No," said Otto.

"In any event," said Julian, "there is little point in worrying about that now, she now in a collar, and well at Rurik's feet."

"Do you not remember her, from Tangara?" asked Otto.

"From Tangara?" said Julian.

"From the wilderness camp," said Otto.

"Surely she is not the one!" said Julian.

"You saw her, briefly," said Otto.

"Yes!" said Tuvo Ausonius.

"She was soon marked and sold to Heruls," said Otto.

"She is so different!" said Julian.

"Yes," said Otto. "Now she is not only collared, but now knows herself collared."

"I did not recognize her," said Julian. "She is far more beautiful now."

"Surely," said Otto, "the collar does much for the beauty of a woman, in a thousand dimensions."

"It is more than a collar," said Julian.

"Of course," said Otto. "It is the being of a slave."

"She was the one, the assassin planted by Iaachus amongst slave girls?" said Julian.

"Yes," said Otto.

"There was a knife," said Tuvo Ausonius.

"Yes," said Otto.

"Slaves fear even to touch a knife," said Tuvo, "for fear of having their ears and nose cut off, and their hands."

"At that time," said Otto, "she naively thought herself free, thought to accomplish her act, and be rushed away to safety and wealth. Doubtless she grew disabused of this notion when she found the cattle bell of the Heruls chained about her neck."

"It seems a shame to waste such a slave on Heruls," said Julian.

"Perhaps she would be safer with them than the Farnichi," said Tuvo Ausonius.

"I do not like the delay," said Julian, looking about.

"Other mercantile delegations wait, too," said Otto.

"Surely some have been admitted," said Tuvo Ausonius.

"I am sure of it," said Otto.

"You have wandered much about the compound," said Julian.

"It seemed well to do so," said Otto.

"Did you discover the housing of the princesses?" asked Julian.

"No," said Otto.

"I thought not," said Julian. "The princesses would be concealed, and guarded. Thus, there is little point to such peregrinations."

"Perhaps there is more of interest in the compound than the princesses," said Otto.

"What?" asked Julian.

"Let us not concern ourselves," said Otto. "It is just a thought I have."

"Is the ship ready for departure?" asked Julian.

"Yes," said Otto.

"Somehow," said Julian, "we must contact the princesses."

"I fear there is little prospect of success," said Tuvo Ausonius, "if we must fight our way free."

"Subterfuge is in order," said Julian. "There are slaves about, you have seen them. Drisriaks, like all strong men, are fond of slaves, and will have them. They particularly enjoy enslaving women of the empire. Supposedly they make excellent slaves. I wonder if they, in their silken, golden beds, know that. We will meet with the princesses, I trust privately. We carry with us collars, and tunics. We shall disguise the princesses as slaves, and conduct them to the ship, and make our departure. Of the hundreds of men in this compound, I suspect few would recognize the princesses, and fewer yet, in the guise of slaves."

"It is a bold plan," said Tuvo Ausonius, "but fraught with danger."

"I trust the princesses, in their haughtiness and royal modesty, will approve of our plan," said Otto.

"I have brought along soft cloths," said Julian, "and a potion which, soaked into these cloths, might be applied perforce to the lovely visages of possibly reluctant princesses, producing almost immediately a state of unconsciousness. One need then only strip them and replace their doubtless splendidly concealing attire with a garb more suitable to slaves. We may then carry them, half naked, with collars on their necks, to the ship."

"But we have not yet made contact with the princesses," said Tuvo Ausonius. "And we have been here for days."

"We must be patient," said Julian.

"Surely you are apprehensive," said Otto.

"Of course," said Julian.

"Each of these other delegations were contacted, and invited here, by agents of Drisriaks," said Otto. "I determined this by inquiry."

"It is also clear, or seemingly so," said Julian, "given the need for secrecy, and concealment, there has been little, if any, communication between such agents and Tenguthaxichai. A breaking of radio silence might soon cloud the sky with imperial ships. Thusly we pose as having been invited, a ruse which, if hazardous, appears vindicated, as we have not been challenged or molested. Our stay here has been, thus far, if trying, untroubled."

"Look," said Tuvo Ausonius, "one of the delegations is being summoned."

"Good," said Julian.

"Where is Rurik?" asked Otto.

"I have not seen him today," said Julian.

CHAPTER FIFTY-FOUR

"All other delegations have been summoned," said Julian. "I do not care for this."

"One delegation must be last," said Otto.

"Where is Rurik?" asked Tuvo Ausonius, uneasily.

"He must be soon about," said Julian. "Surely he must be aware of the imminence of the summoning."

"He must be here," said Tuvo Ausonius. "He is taken to be first in our group. He is the only member of the Farnichi family in our delegation. We are seen as agents, at best. He is the only one properly informed of the value of our goods. The rest of us might error in our representations. I, personally, cannot tell a false stone from a true stone, or the silk of Talis IV from that of Talis III. Let him appear swiftly! All may otherwise be undone!"

"We must speak boldly, and appear knowledgeable," said Julian.

"Rurik would not have brought inferior goods," said Otto.

"And what would be the intelligent asking price for a square foot of prime Sorbian slipper leather?" asked Tuvo.

"Surely Rurik will be here presently," said Julian.

"And if he is not?"' asked Tuvo Ausonius.

"In the false bottom of the red jewel case is a pistol with four charges," said Julian.

"Perhaps these concerns will be for naught," said Otto. "We may meet with the princesses privately."

"Let us hope so," said Tuvo.

"Where is Rurik?" asked Julian.

"Woe," said Tuvo Ausonius, "I fear it is too late."

"How so?" said Julian.

"A servitor approaches," whispered Tuvo Ausonius.

"Gentlemen," said the servitor, bowing slightly.

"Sir," said Julian, rising.

"You are the Farnichi delegation," said the servitor.

"Yes," said Julian. "How is that we have not been summoned until now? Do you know with whom you deal? Do you not know the weight of a Farnichi delegation? Are you unfamiliar with suitable priorities?"

"Ten thousand pardons, noble sir," said the servitor. "No slight, but rather great honor, was intended. Is not the king the last to enter the feasting hall? Is not the finest wine the last served, the most exquisite slave the last to dance before the Master's table? The glory of the Farnichi is well known. Whose goods could compare with those of the Farnichi? All else, until now, is naught but preface and prologue."

"Nonetheless, the delay grew tiresome for our leader, the high merchant, Rurik, scion of the high Farnichi," said Julian.

"He must be about," said Tuvo. "I am sure he will soon be present."

"I do not understand," said the servitor. "He is already present. He is in the selling chamber, the reception chamber, awaiting you."

"Of course," said Julian.

"Please be so kind as to gather up your goods," said the servitor.

The goods were gathered up by Julian, Otto, and Tuvo Ausonius. Julian made it a point to carry one of them himself, a red jewel case.

"We are to be conducted into the presence of the daughters of the kings," said Julian.

"How could it be otherwise?" said the servitor. "Please, follow me."

CHAPTER FIFTY-FIVE

"Who are you?" asked Julian. "Where is Rurik? We bring our goods. We would display them. Surely we have not come to lovely Tenguthaxichai in vain. Where are the daughters of kings?"

"Rather," said Farrix, "who are you?"

"Members of the Farnichi delegation," said Julian, "invited to assist in the gowning and bejeweling of the daughters of kings. Where may the fair maidens be?"

"No invitations were issued on Larial VII," said Farrix.

"No," said Julian. "Our invitation was received on Telnaria, delivered to the Farnichi merchant house in Telnar."

"There is no Farnichi merchant house in Telnar," said Farrix.

"Near Telnar, just northeast of the city," said Julian.

"That is a military enclave, whose purpose is obscure," said Farrix.

"The house operates through the enclave," said Julian.

"I did not understand," said Farrix. "Perhaps you will forgive me."

"Surely, noble Lord," said Julian. "In your place, I, too, would have made inquiries. May we now be conducted into the presence of the daughters of kings?"

"You are the leader of the delegation?" asked Farrix.

"No," said Julian. "I speak for him, in his absence. He is Rurik, scion of the Larial VII Farnichi."

"I see," said Farrix. "And where do you think he might be?"

"We were told he was in the reception chamber, awaiting us," said Julian.

"And so he is," said Farrix. "Shall we join him?"

"By all means," said Julian.

"Are you fond of horses?" asked Farrix.

"I ride," said Julian.

"Perhaps you are fond of horses," said Farrix to Otto.

"Yes," said Otto. "But they are quite dangerous."

"Many who are fond of horses," said Farrix, "under certain conditions, grow less fond of them."

"Undoubtedly," said Otto.

"You have the look of an Otung," said Farrix.

"I have been told so," said Otto.

"We have goods to sell," said Julian. "We have waited days. Please conduct us to Lord Rurik, and the daughters of kings. Doubtless he has already discussed our offerings with their highnesses, and they are now ready, their curiosities aroused, their appetites whetted, to at last peruse merchandise worthy of their interest and attention."

"After you, dear sirs," said Farrix. "Beyond this door lies the reception chamber." Then he turned to Otto. "Please do not linger," he suggested.

Two armsmen closed in behind Otto, whose presence he seemed not to notice.

"What is the meaning of this!" cried Julian.

In the center of the audience chamber, on the broad, darkly vanished wooden floor, were two individuals, both gagged, and bound, hand and foot. The larger figure, that of a male, was closely fastened by a neck rope to a large, heavy ring anchored in the floor. The smaller figure, that of a female, was closely fastened, by a neck rope, to the bound feet of the male. Near the ring were two cushioned, regal chairs, both empty.

"How dare you?" said Julian.

"Quite easily," said Farrix.

"By what right?" demanded Julian.

"By the right of the will of the Alemanni," said Farrix.

"Release Lord Rurik, and the slave, as well," demanded Julian.

"Surely there is some dreadful misunderstanding," said Tuvo Ausonius.

"We think not," said Farrix.

"We do not choose to brook this insult," said Julian. "We shall take our goods and return to Telnaria. The daughters of kings must do without our goods."

"They already have," said Farrix.

"Release Lord Rurik and the slave," said Julian. "We depart."

"Of all," said Farrix, "only you were not invited."

"But we were!" said Julian.

"No," said Farrix. "You did not provide us with the password."

"What is the password?" inquired Otto, standing back, by the door, the two armsmen closely behind him.

"'Victory to Abrogastes'," said Farrix.

"Very well," said Julian. "We confess. We were not invited, but we learned of the gathering, and hoped to participate, hoped to do fine merchant work. Do you think such lucrative opportunities are not whispered about? They are. It is not our fault if others lacked the courage to similarly intrude. Surely you are aware of how difficult it is for a merchant not to pursue a possible profit. Boldness often leads to bounty. If you are not interested in our goods, excuse us, and we shall be on our way."

"But we are interested in your goods," said Farrix.

"Good," said Julian. "We are prepared then to overlook this unfortunate incident. Free Lord Rurik and the slave, and conduct us to the daughters of kings."

"But you were not invited," said Farrix.

"So?" said Julian.

"The Alemanni breed draft horses, as well as steeds for war,"
said Farrix. "Their harnesses are stout and massive. They can draw
plows through heavy clay, through Lion grass, through the wooden
fibers of vinous Malik growth, uproot stumps of the Farn tree."

"So?" said Julian.

"And four such horses, suitably harnessed," said Farrix,
"driven in four directions," said Farrix, "may easily tear the
arms and legs from a man."

"Interesting," said Julian.

"It often takes, however, three or four minutes to do so," said
Farrix.

"Interesting, indeed," said Julian.

"And you were not invited," said Farrix.

"Lord Rurik is amongst the high Farnichi," said Julian.

"The Alemanni do not fear the Farnichi," said Farrix. "The
Alemanni is a nation. We are eleven tribes, and have the allegiance of allied tribes. Do you think we would fear a single Telnarian family?"

"I see," said Julian.

"And I doubt that your Lord Rurik is here on Farnichi business. I suspect his presence here is not even known to the Larial
VII Farnichi. I suspect he was embarked on some covert business
for the empire."

"Surely not," said Julian.

"And I doubt that even the enclave near Telnar was aware of
his intentions, or suspects his whereabouts."

"Surely one cannot blame a fellow for seeking a private
profit," said Julian.

"We will spare the slave, of course," said Farrix. "She would
have value, serving our tables, kicking, moaning, and pleading
in our furs."

"You are thinking seriously, I take it," said Julian, "of the
matter of the horses."

"Certainly," said Farrix.

"It is not difficult to perceive your intent," said Julian. "But our goods are of considerable value, and you might consider accepting them in lieu of our lives."

"Under certain conditions, perhaps," said Farrix, "but it seems, under the current set of conditions, we may have both."

"In a sense, yes, in a sense, no," said Julian.

"I listen," said Farrix.

"You may easily acquire our goods," said Julian. "But what are you to do with them? Surely you are not interested in clothing your robust forms with the silk of Talis III. Surely you are not planning on adorning yourselves with a woman's jewelry."

"Beware," said Farrix. "There are deaths other than that of the ropes and horses."

"You, or others, will sell or gift these things," said Julian. "But you do not know their value. Perhaps you cannot even tell a true stone from a false stone, are unable to discriminate between the silk of Talis II and that of Talis III. You might make fools of yourselves, and risk your lives, by requesting too much, or fools of yourselves by requesting too little, and being duped or swindled. We, as merchants, on the other hand, in particular, our colleague, Tuvo Ausonius, here, are knowledgeable, profoundly skilled in the subtle assessments which are particular to our trade. Our colleague, Tuvo Ausonius, here, is especially skilled, as noted. He can calculate the latest market value of a stone to the penny."

"What of you?" asked Farrix.

"I, too," said Julian, humbly, "must grant that I am similarly skilled. For example, consider this red jewel box, which I now open."

Here Julian put back the lid of the box, revealing, displayed on purple velvet, a complex, scintillating array of various stones.

There was a gentle rustle of awe in the room, as the several armsmen in attendance on Farrix, including those behind Otto, beheld the sparkling, marshaled contents of the box.

"And this," said Julian, "is but one of several similar assortments."

"Hand it to me," said Farrix.

"May I not delineate the stones, and their value?" said Julian.

"Give it to me, now," said Farrix.

"Of course," said Julian, not pleased.

"Now," repeated Farrix.

Julian then surrendered the box, reluctantly, to the Teragar Borkon.

Farrix hefted the case two or three times, then looked at Julian, and laughed. "I thought so," he said. "Do you think this a plausible weight for a handful of stones? Rather, a plausible weight for a handful of stones and something else. The box obviously has a false bottom. How is it opened?"

"Permit me to show you," said Julian.

"I will manage," said Farrix. "Think now of horses."

At this point there was the sound of a startled cry, from the back of the room, near the door. Armsmen spun about. Two of their numbers were slumped to the floor. The flash of a robe, like a banner, was seen. "After him!" cried Farrix. There was the sound of a key in a lock. Armsmen pounded on the door. "Break it down!" screamed Farrix. Julian lunged for the jewel box, but was struck unconscious. A knife was at the heart of Tuvo Ausonius. A moment later the door was forced asunder, and several armsmen streamed through, only to be halted at the further door, that leading to the waiting chamber. "Break it down!" screamed Farrix, again, but this was no easy task, for the barbarian, after turning the key in the second lock, securing the door, had thrust, and braced, against floor rings, in case slaves were being assessed in the room, more than one of the heavy trading tables against the door.

Armsmen flung their weight against the door.

"Open it, open it!" cried Farrix, in fury.

"It is blocked!" said a man.

"We need a ram!" cried another.

"Get it open!" cried Farrix.

One of the armsmen staggered back, grimacing in pain. "My shoulder!" he said. His arm hung useless at his side.

"Call out!" cried Farrix. "Some will hear!"

"There is no one to hear," said an armsman. "The trading hall is empty!"

"More men!" said Farrix. "Rouse the two louts who let the prisoner escape!"

An armsman hurried to the two slumped figures, and tried to shake them awake.

"Hurry!" screamed Farrix. "Get them up!"

"I cannot do so, Lord Farrix," said the man, looking up. "Their heads are broken."

Meanwhile Otto, now walking swiftly, purposefully, made his way through the compound to one of the three small, temporary halls earlier reconnoitered, those serving as provisional quarters on Tenguthaxichai for Abrogastes, Ingeld, and Hrothgar.

"Hold!" cried an armsman, blocking Otto's way with a spear.

"Victory to Abrogastes!" said Otto.

"Pass," said the armsman, stepping back.

Otto then strode within the hall of Ingeld.

CHAPTER FIFTY-SIX

Otto looked quickly about.

Ingeld was not present.

He had hoped to get his hands on the throat of Ingeld.

Ingeld, he was sure, had something of value, even if he did not know its value.

The hall was bare, with few furnishings, only the high seat, and some benches. He saw no chests, no strong box.

Yet the hall had been guarded.

Did that not suggest that something of value might be about?

Otto looked carefully about the hall. However simple, primitive, and bare it might be, there must be a place to sleep, a place to store things.

And in such a place, a place to sleep, a place to store things, might there not be something of value?

Liegemen might sleep about, in their blankets and furs, on the floor, but surely not the liegelord himself.

Otto then noticed a small door, almost concealed in the rude, heavy planking of the wall. Such a door, he was sure, must lead to a small room, a storage room, a sleeping chamber.

He strode to this door, and flung it open.

"You!" cried Huta, spinning about in alarm.

She stood next to a couch, presumably the couch of Ingeld. There was a ring in its foot, but she was not chained to this ring.

"On your knees," said Otto, "head to the rushes."

Instantly, the former priestess knelt, thrusting her head, with the long, flowing dark hair cascading about it, to the rude flooring of the small room.

"Do not move," said Otto, looking about.

"Yes, Master," said Huta.

Otto saw no strongbox. Aside from the couch, the small room was not much different from the large chamber without.

Otto turned to regard the former priestess.

"She looks well as a kneeling slave," he thought. "But then what woman does not?"

"Where is Ingeld?" he asked.

"He, Abrogastes, and Hrothgar," she said, head down, "two days ago, took ship to Telnar."

Otto clenched his fists, in frustration.

"With two prisoners?" he asked.

"The Princesses Viviana and Alacida," said Huta.

"Surely it is dangerous for Drisriaks, and high Drisriaks, not agents, to venture to Telnaria," said Otto.

"Not only to Telnaria, Master," she whispered, "but to Telnar itself."

"How can it be?" asked Otto.

"It is arranged through the empress mother and the Exarch of Telnar," sobbed Huta, suddenly.

"To what end?" demanded Otto, wishing to hear the suspected answer from the slave herself.

"To celebrate the nuptials of the sons of Abrogastes to the princesses," sobbed Huta.

"What is it to you, a slave?" asked Otto.

"Nothing, Master," she sobbed. "I am a slave, only a slave."

"You were taken for the collar long ago, here, on Tenguthaxichai," said Otto, "in the time of Ortog, by Abrogastes. What are you doing here, in the hall of Ingeld?"

"I hate the princesses!" wept Huta.

"What are you doing here, in the hall of Ingeld?" said Otto, again.

"He did not take me with him!" sobbed Huta.

"Ingeld?" said Otto.

"Yes!" she said.

"What should that matter to you?" asked Otto.

"I love him!" she said.

"But you are a slave," said Otto.

"Yes," she said. "I am a slave!"

"By what right then?" asked Otto.

"By the right of a slave, to love her Master!" said Huta.

"Slaves have no rights," said Otto.

"But we love, we love!" wept Huta.

"You can be bought and sold, like a pig," said Otto.

"But we love, we do love!" wept Huta.

"You were a priestess," said Otto, "superior to such things."

"A collar was put on my neck," she said. "I learned the weight of chains. I learned to crawl to a man, the switch between my teeth, whimpering for his touch. I learned to love, not as a free woman loves, but as a slave loves, without reservation or quali-fication, without expectations or demands, to love helplessly, completely, and abjectly, as is appropriate for one who is sur-rendered, submitted, and owned."

"As you are here," said Otto, "I take it that Ingeld is your Master."

"Yes, Master," she whispered.

"Oh!" she cried, as her head was yanked up, and bent back.

"I cannot read," said Otto, "but I know the sign of Abro-gastes, and the sign of Ingeld. Your collar bears not the sign of Ingeld, but that of Abrogastes. And, could I read, I suspect that the legend on your collar in Drisriak, and that in Telnarian, attest not to the fact that you are the property of Ingeld, but that you are the property of Abrogastes."

She clutched her collar futilely weeping. "My collar betrays me!" she wept.

"As it would any lying slave," said Otto.

"Do not kill me, Master," she begged, putting herself to her stomach and pressing her lips, again and again, piteously, desperately, to Otto's boots.

Otto stepped back, pulling away from her, and she looked up, frightened, tears in her eyes.

"What are you doing here?" he asked.

"I love Ingeld," she said. "I wanted to be near his couch. I wanted to kiss its slave ring. I wanted to touch its furs. I wanted to lie, humbly, like a dog, at its foot."

"What if you are found here?" asked Otto.

"I must not be found here!" she said.

"How did you get here?" asked Otto.

"I was unnoticed," she said. "When there are several slaves about, who notices slaves, or pigs?"

"A slave such as you would be noticed," said Otto. "You would sell nicely off a block."

"I am only a slave," she said. "I slipped past the guard."

"How do you propose leaving?" asked Otto.

"Similarly," she said. "I have done it before, many times."

"But perhaps," said Otto, "you shall not manage it this time."

"Master?" she said, looking up.

Otto looked about the small, plain room. On one wall was some harnessing, and some loops of thongs.

"Squirm about, as you are, on your belly," said Otto. "Get your head facing away from me. Cross your wrists behind your back. Cross your ankles."

Huta obeyed, promptly. "Master?" she said, frightened.

"There are thongs here, on the wall," said Otto. "Doubtless Ingeld uses you as a Thong Girl."

"He does with me what he wishes," she said.

"Perhaps you enjoy his thongs," said Otto.

There are many ways in which a girl may be thonged.

"In his thongs, I am helpless," she said. "In his thongs I know rapture."

"But you do not know rapture now, do you?" asked Otto.

Huta had now been thonged.

"No, Master!" she said. She squirmed about, on her side, to face him. Her small ankles fought the thongs. Her lovely wrists pulled futilely against them.

"You are well trussed," said Otto, standing, admiring his handiwork.

"Please unbind me, Master!" she whispered. "I cannot free myself."

"It was not my intention that you should be able to do so," said Otto.

"In time, men will search for me, the armsmen of Abrogastes. I must not be found here!"

"Farewell," said Otto, turning away.

"Do not go!" she pleaded. "I will scream."

"Do so," said Otto.

"But someone would hear," she wept. "They would find me here!"

"That is why I did not bother gagging you," said Otto.

"Surely you cannot leave me here, as I am!" she said.

"You are a slave who has been unfaithful to her Master," said Otto. "Farewell."

"No, no, wait, Master!" she wept. "It can be no accident that you are here. You must have a purpose. What do you want? Perhaps I might be of assistance. Is it information you want? I might know something of interest. A slave hears much, knows much! Might I not be of help? Is there nothing I can do?"

"I search for an object," said Otto. "It is a medallion; it is on a chain."

Huta's face went white. "I dare not, Master," she said.

"Very well," said Otto, placing his hand on the latch.

"Do not go!" she wept. "You do not want it! It is worthless! Lord Ingeld told me. It is only one of more than a hundred, perhaps a thousand, similar things. Once it was thought of great value. Now it is meaningless."

"Where is it?" said Otto.

"I do not know," she said.

"I depart," said Otto.

"It is a thing of Lord Ingeld," she said. "I dare not reveal its hiding place."

"If it is worthless, why should it have a hiding place?" asked Otto.

"I do not know," she said.

"It is about," said Otto. "I am sure of it."

Huta struggled, futilely.

"There is no point in struggling," said Otto. "Surely you are familiar with what it is, to be a well-thonged slave."

"I beg mercy," she said.

"Does Lord Ingeld know that you are aware of the location of the object?" asked Otto.

"No," she said. "I discovered it when alone in the hall. Dirt had been turned. I was curious."

"Does anyone know you frequent the hall in the absence of Lord Ingeld?" asked Otto.

"No," she said. "I have never been discovered here."

"Until perhaps an hour from now," said Otto.

"Mercy!" she whispered.

"Where is it?" asked Otto.

"In the hall, buried," she said. "I will show you the place."

"The guard will remember me," said Otto. "It will be understood I have taken the object. Your role in this will be unknown. After I have departed, I advise you to disturb the soil of the hall, in several locations, so it will seem that a search of some sort was conducted."

"Yes, Master," wept Huta.

Otto then bent to undo the thongs on the slave's wrists and ankles.

"Where is the place of the 'Horse Death'?" asked Otto.

"In the yard behind the hall of Abrogastes," she said.

"You will have no difficulty leaving the hall this afternoon," said Otto.

"How is that, Master?" asked Huta.

"The guard will be unconscious," said Otto.

CHAPTER FIFTY-SEVEN

"What is going on here?" demanded Farrix. "Move back!"

"I and my colleagues," said the merchant, "have come for the feast."

"There is no feast," said Farrix. "Beware that you are not trampled."

One of the horses growled, and shied its massive form to the side.

"They are large, are they not?" said the merchant.

"Beware you do not lose an arm," said Farrix.

"To be sure, I am early, but so, too, I see, are others," said the merchant.

"There is no feast here," said Farrix.

"Is this not the yard behind the hall of noble Abrogastes?" asked the merchant.

"It is," said Farrix, angrily.

"Then this is the place," said the merchant.

"What do you need these cumbersome beasts for?" asked another.

"They are half the size of a *torodont*," said another.

"I have seen some as large," said another.

"What are these beasts for?" asked another.

"They are to draw wagons with crates of steaming viands from the kitchens, kegs of *bror* and *kana*," said another.

"Go away," said Farrix.

"We are here for the feast," said another merchant, one in yellow robes.

"There is no feast here," said Farrix.

"You must be mistaken," said a merchant. "The word is all over the compound. The noble Alemanni are entertaining all the delegations with a great feast. It is celebrating the end of the selling, and in anticipation of the joyous unitings of princes and princesses. See? Here come several others, in festive regalia. There is no gainsaying the generosity of the Alemanni."

"There is no feast!" said Farrix.

"Do you mean to say you have not been told?" asked another merchant. He looked about. "Where are the tables, the benches, the tents?"

"There is no feast," said Farrix. "Be careful there! The animals are not used to crowds."

"Here come more guests, at least a hundred," said a merchant.

"Many have brought their domicile slaves," said another merchant.

"And retainers," said another.

"You there," said Farrix. "You, big fellow, you in the hood, you on the other side of the horse. It is dangerous. It could turn and seize you. Get away from it."

As the large fellow did not much move, and seemed inclined, rather, to stroke the beast, perhaps to pacify it, Farrix, angrily, moved about the large form.

"Away!" he said, waving his arm. "There is no feast!"

"There are different sorts of feasts," said the large man in the saffron merchant robes. "There are feasts of blood, of steel, of joy, of vengeance, of war, of peace, of hate, of justice."

"You!" cried Farrix.

A massive hand thrust forth from the saffron sleeve and seized Farrix by the throat, and shook him, and Farrix fell dazed, gasping for breath, at Otto's feet. It took Otto only a moment or two to fasten the ropes on Farrix's half inert, shuddering form, a rope on each limb. He then led the animals in such a way as to tauten the ropes.

"I would lie quietly, friend," said Otto. "A quick word and a few slaps and these four fine beasts will go their separate ways."

"Do not stir the beasts!" said Farrix.

"What is this all about?" asked a merchant, curious.

"Entertainment, for the feast," said Otto.

"How is he to free himself?" asked a merchant.

"You must wait, and see," said Otto.

"You are listening to me, are you not?" Otto inquired of the prostrate Farrix.

"Yes!" said Farrix. "Do not stir the horses. You do not know them. The slightest signal might stampede them."

"This is interesting," said a merchant.

"I think so," said Otto.

"What do you want?" whispered Farrix.

"Your men are about," said Otto, "or will soon be about, with prisoners. They may be here now, somewhere in the crowd. Call out to them. Tell them to come here, unbind the prisoners, and submit themselves for binding with the same ropes."

"Why should I do that?" said Farrix.

"I am prepared to start the horses," said Otto.

"Wait!" said Farrix. "Einar, Eserich! To me!"

Shortly thereafter, though Farrix need call twice, his men, with their bound prisoners, made their way through the crowd to rendezvous with their chief. And a bit after that, Julian, Tuvo Ausonius, and Rurik were freed of their ropes, which were then transferred to the limbs of the two fellows we suppose must have been Einar and Eserich.

Rurik's slave, Cornhair, her wrists bound behind her, and on a leash, it now dangling from her leather leash collar, had been brought along, apparently to witness the proceedings, and absorb a lesson as to what might be the fate of a slave who might prove to be less than fully pleasing. There were bruises on her arms, legs, and face. She now knelt near Rurik, her head down.

"Free me, now," said Farrix. "I have had done what you asked."

One of the horses began to scratch at the turf with its clawed paw.

"It is getting restless," said Otto. "I suspect it is waiting for the signal."

"If one bolts, the others will bolt," said Farrix. "They have been used in this place before!"

"Why is the slave bruised?" asked Otto of Rurik.

"She was reluctant to afflict me with the torture of the lascivious slave girl," said Rurik.

"She would arouse you while you were helpless, for the sport of your captors, that they might jeer you," said Otto.

"Yes," said Rurik.

"Do not stir the horses!" said Farrix.

"She was slow to obey the command of a free man?" said Otto.

"Yes," said Rurik.

"But she saw reason," said Otto.

"Even after being struck, she was reluctant," said Rurik.

"Apparently she thinks little enough of her life," said Otto.

"She obeyed quickly enough when I cast upon her my frown," said Rurik. "Slaves are not to dally or be disobedient. Such is cause for discipline."

"The torture of the lascivious slave girl," said Otto, "is most effective when the slave hates the man, and relishes her control over him, and how she may force him to writhe, yield, and explode at her pleasure, as though it were he in a collar, and not she."

"It is effective only when she has Masters behind her, to support and protect her," said Rurik, "for she is, and remains, only a woman and a slave."

"I would not be the slave who falls into the power of the man whom she so enjoyed abusing," said Otto.

"Cornhair's heart was not in her work," said Rurik.

"Of course not," said Otto. "You are her Master. She knows it is she, and not you, who are to be controlled, grasped, owned, mastered, handled, caressed, and put to pleasure."

"That reminds me," said Rurik. "The slave was slow to obey the command of a free man. That is cause for discipline."

"The horses, the horses," whispered Farrix. "Free me!"

Rurik then seized the hair of the kneeling slave, and yanked up her bowed head. "You were slow to obey the command of a free man," he said.

"Forgive me, Master," she said.

He then cuffed her, sharply, twice.

"Thank you, Master," she said, went to her belly, and pressed her lips to his boot.

"She knows you are pleased with her," said Otto. "She is very pleased."

"I do not understand what is going on," said a merchant. "I understand this is staged, that it is an entertainment, and all, but I do not understand the entertainment. Should this supine gentleman and the others not now free themselves, somehow, of the ropes, or be rescued, or such?"

"I trust the ropes are not truly tied," said another.

"I think there is danger," said another.

"Dismiss the thought," said Otto.

"Horses are dangerous," said another.

"Surely you cannot mean these," said Otto. "Surely you cannot suppose that we might risk these nice fellows. Surely these beasts are as gentle, mild, and sweetly tempered as they are large."

"Of course," said a merchant.

"That is obvious," said another.

"Where is the food?" asked another.

Otto then knelt near Farrix and, with a knife, taken from a guard who would not be likely to miss it for some time, the very fellow dragged within the hall of Ingeld, cut one of the ropes which bound Farrix to the harness of one of the horses.

"Do not speak loudly or quickly," said Farrix.

Otto then severed a second rope.

"You will never escape," said Farrix.

"Perhaps not," said Otto. "But I have seen to it that the ship is in readiness."

"You will never reach the ship," said Farrix.

"The camp guard is uninformed," said Otto. "They know nothing of what has transpired here."

"There is no way in which you can reach the ship," said Farrix.

"Perhaps not," said Otto. "But what if there was a distraction, if a crowd was alarmingly disbanded, if many men, perhaps two hundred, with retainers, domicile slaves, and such, were rushing about, here and there, many in confusion, perhaps in panic."

"But they are not," said Farrix.

Otto then severed the third rope, and stood up.

This left one rope in place, that on the left ankle of Farrix.

"Cut the last rope," said Farrix.

Otto looked down upon him, and smiled.

"No!" cried Farrix.

Otto's sudden cry startled not only the horses but all those about him. The four horses sped away, in the four directions. But they met little or no resistance. It was not as they expected; it was not even like drawing a plow through Lion grass, or tearing a way through the vinelike Malik growth, or drawing the stump of the Farn tree from the earth. There was no exertion, no digging in, and then the tearing, and then the breaking free. Three of the horses, the ropes dangling behind them, raced away, unencumbered, plunging through the crowd, buffeting bodies aside like bundles of robed straw, and the fourth, too, raced way, scarcely less unencumbered, dragging its tethered burden, rolling and tumbling, by an ankle, plowing its own fresh, broad furrow through the surprised, festive thong. There was much crying out, screaming, and protesting. Soon the awareness that loose, hastening, uncontrolled beasts were abroad reached to the very edges of the crowd, which began to scatter.

"To the ships, to the ships!" cried Otto.

The horses themselves were doubtless confused. Two, beyond the crowd, turned about and, to the consternation of many, milling about, proceeded to make their way back to the point of their departure, that to which their harness managers had always returned them. The other two, including that which was conveying Farrix about, once clear of the crowd, unmanaged and undriven, perhaps unnerved or frightened by the many bodies about, the cries, the fluttering robes, began to race about, through the compound.

"Seek safety in the ships!" cried Otto.

Certainly several of those about heeded this recommendation, which was soon, voice by voice, broadcast throughout the compound, rather as Otto had anticipated.

At this point, Otto, Julian, Tuvo Ausonius, and Rurik joined the many merchants, retainers, and domicile slaves bent on reaching the ships, Cornhair, bound, the leash dangling from the leash collar, hurrying behind them.

In the ships there was indeed safety, rather as behind the safety wall in an arena, where bulls and *torodonts* are hunted.

The advice which Otto had offered to the multitude, it seems, had been sound, and, certainly, happily, it had been well received.

Before boarding, from the boarding ladder leading to the second hatchway, Otto paused and looked back.

The compound was now nearly deserted, save for some soldiers and grooms. Three of the horses were quiet, some men about them. One of the horses was being unharnessed. The fourth horse was more unruly, or skittish, perhaps because of its unforeseen impediment, perhaps not fully understood, an object attached to it by a rope. The horse moved about, skittishly. In a bit, three grooms had managed to turn it about, and close with it, and seize its harnessing. They freed it of its burden, which tried to rise to its feet, stood unsteadily for a moment, and then collapsed into the arms of a groom.

Otto then entered the ship, and the hatch was closed behind him.

Shortly thereafter, about the time several of the merchants, and their fellows, the danger, it seems, now past, were preparing to leave their ships and return to the compound, one ship, to the surprise of many, departed, leaving behind it the fields and forests of lovely Tenguthaxichai.

CHAPTER FIFTY-EIGHT

"I had hoped," said Iaachus, "that you might have been successful, that you might have located and, somehow, rescued the princesses."

"Our conjecture," said Julian, "was correct. The princesses were being held on Tenguthaxichai. Unfortunately they were removed before we could make contact with them, let alone attempt their rescue."

"Now all is lost," said Iaachus.

"How so?" asked Julian.

"The exarch planned well," said Iaachus. "It seems that once certain ascertainments were made, rumors were spread that the princesses were on holiday, visiting and sightseeing on various worlds, imperial worlds and some others, others well disposed to the *imperium*. On this holiday it is claimed they met, were wooed by, and succumbed to the charms of, two mighty princes, both Drisriaks, the Drisriaks being a tribe of the Aatii, or, as they will have it, the Alemanni. This event is being heralded as an ostensible fortuity, in which, by more subtle minds, might be seen the hand of the great god, Karch, one fraught with joyous consequences for a future of peace, order, love, justice, and harmony. Currently the princesses and their swains are the guests of the exarch, while preparations are underway to celebrate the forthcoming nuptials."

"Preparations?" said Otto.

"Certainly," said Iaachus. "This is not some simple affair where the bride, clad in scarlet and garlanded, to music and torches, to the intoning of wedding hymns, is led by relatives and friends to the house of the groom. The entire city must be prepared. Avenues must be washed. Buildings on the route of the procession must be repainted. Bunting must be strung, ribbons and banners obtained, and arranged, windows and doors adorned, flowers imported from Inez IV. Musicians must be organized. Ambassadors, officials, and dignitaries must be invited and housed. Consider the catering alone required to feed more than four thousand guests."

"Surely that will take time," said Tuvo Ausonius.

"Certainly," said Iaachus, "but the exarch has that time."

"Let us," said Rurik, "strike, seize the princesses, and return them to the palace."

"That is not practical," said Iaachus. "To transgress the perimeter of holy precincts would be understood as desecration. Who would risk the outrage of hopeful, deluded millions throughout the empire? Even those who are not Floonians would be aghast. Rebellion would be invited, riots, vandalism. Who dares cheat populations of their anticipated spectacles and holidays?"

"We can act, and justify things later," said Rurik. "It is often done. It is common statecraft. Too, one can always promise, and provide, new spectacles and holidays, preferably celebrated at the same time, or nearly so, so that populations need not wait. People are not pleased to be cheated of their holidays."

"Things are not so simple, my noble friend," said Iaachus. "The army is divided. Corruption is rampant. Amongst high officers there flow dark currents of ambition. Indeed, some suspect our dear friend, Julian."

"And perhaps one such is the Arbiter of Protocol?" said Julian.

"Perhaps," said Iaachus.

"Surely our forces are overwhelmingly loyal," said Tuvo Ausonius.

"Yes," said Iaachus, "but to whom? To what leader, to what general, to what minister?"

"There might be a thousand loyalties," said Otto.

"As a barbarian you are well aware of that," said Iaachus.

"Not all barbarians," said Julian, "dress in skins, carry axes, and wear necklaces of pierced claws."

"Intrigues can occur even within the palace," said Iaachus.

"The seeds of ambition grow well in the soil of power," said Julian.

"Who can one trust?" asked Tuvo Ausonius.

"We do not even trust one another," said Iaachus.

"Surely the palace itself is secure," said Tuvo Ausonius.

"Less secure than the farthest outpost," said Iaachus. "Both the father and the grandfather of the emperor were slain within the palace, in one coup, or plot, or another."

"How dreadful for the emperor," said Tuvo Ausonius.

"The emperor is not even aware of it," said Iaachus. "The emperor is aware of very little."

"You, dear Ottonius, have seen the emperor," said Julian. "Surely you have something to say."

"No," said Otto.

"It is madness," said Julian. "The empire is in peril, and on the throne we find a child, a retarded, drooling boy, terrified of insects, enraptured by the simplest of toys."

"The empress mother wields power," said Iaachus.

"A timid, confused, vain old woman," said Julian.

"Beware you do not speak treason," said Iaachus.

"So truth is treason?" said Julian.

"Frequently," said Iaachus.

"I cannot believe the senate will ratify the projected marriages," said Tuvo Ausonius.

"It will ratify what it is told to ratify," said Iaachus. "What senator wishes to be the recipient, by means of the royal post, of an imperial dagger?"

"Might it not take a stand?" said Otto.

"The exarch has planned even for that," said Iaachus. "The senate will be proclaimed to be irrelevant in such matters. It has to do with the alleged superiority of the *koos* to the fist, or something. The solemnization of marriages, their dissolution and such, is supposed to require, and be invalid without, the officiation of suitable ministrants, interestingly, those of the exarch's particular faith. They wish to seize power over all forms of life. Indeed, the exarch, again in virtue of the supposed superiority of the *koos* to the fist, will claim the exclusive right to crown emperors, without which act the coronation will be accounted illegitimate.

"So," said Julian, "the crown will be bought and sold, and the merchant will be the high ministrant, the Exarch of Telnar."

"Precisely," said Iaachus. "All is lost."

Otto reached within his cloak, and pulled forth an object. With a rattle of chain and metal, the object was flung upon the desk of Iaachus.

"What is that?" asked the Arbiter of Protocol.

"It is an artifact, a medallion and chain," said Julian. "It was obtained by Ottonius, on Tenguthaxichai, from the hall of Ingeld, the Drisriak, one of the princes involved in the projected marriages."

"So?" said Iaachus.

"We believe it to be the medallion and chain stolen from the *festung* of Sim Giadini on Tangara, delivered to Ingeld, most likely by some agent of the Exarch of Telnar."

"I recall we spoke of such a thing, a medallion and chain, long ago," said Iaachus.

"It is a symbol of the Vandal nation," said Julian. "It can rally the tribes of that nation to unity. The empire, united with the

Vandal nation, could turn back the Alemanni. It was delivered to Ingeld, of the Drisriaks, that he might rise to unexampled barbarian power, uniting both the Alemanni and Vandals against the empire. To prevent this I had duplicates smithed and distributed to a hundred worlds. Who would then know the true medallion and chain? This stratagem confounded Ingeld's plan."

"You suspect, I gather," said Iaachus, "that this object before me, the first of its kind I have seen, is the true medallion and chain?"

"We think so," said Julian, "as it was found in the hall of Ingeld."

"I see it as worthless," said Iaachus, "indeed, worthless by your own hand, for who, after your plentiful distribution of surrogates, could attest its authenticity?"

"I have explained that to Ottonius," said Julian.

"Still," said Otto, "I would not have it housed in the hall of a Drisriak."

"Surely," said Rurik, "there must be some who could tell the true artifact from its duplicates."

"Many years ago, as I understand it," said Julian, "a Herul delivered it to the *festung*, but I know little of him other than his name, Hunlaki. It was all long ago. Too, Heruls seldom live long lives, as younger Heruls frequently kill them for their wagons, their horses, and weapons. Too, even if he should be alive, we do not know his camp, nor would he be likely to remember the object with fidelity. Too, it is dangerous to approach Heruls."

"You say, a Herul?" said Iaachus.

"Yes," said Julian. "Why?"

"Nothing," said Iaachus.

"What of the guardian of the artifact?" asked Rurik. "He must have lived with it for years."

"He is dead," said Julian.

"How so?" asked Rurik.

"He was an Emanationist brother," said Julian. "The *festung* was attacked, and demolished."

"It was done by imperial cruisers, to eliminate a nest of heretics, according to the empress mother," said Iaachus.

"And perhaps to cover a theft as well," said Julian.

"The brother perished in the destruction of the *festung*?" asked Rurik.

"Yes," said Julian.

"If this brother should have survived, and could recognize the genuine artifact," said Iaachus, "why would anyone take him seriously?"

"Otungs would take him seriously," said Otto. "He was of the high, remote, glorious, and holy *festung* of Sim Giadini, which had stood for a thousand years, commanding the heights of the Barrionuevo Range. This is known in the forests of the Otungs, and on both sides of the Lothar. It is known on the Plains of Barrionuevo, and amongst even the Heruls, on what they call the Flats of Tung. Even in the provincial capital, Venitzia, the *festung* is known. And the trustworthiness, the truthfulness, the honesty, the holiness of the brothers is legendary."

"What was the name of this brother," asked Iaachus, "he who was the guardian of this artifact, of the medallion and chain?"

"Brother Benjamin," said Julian.

"He is in Telnar," said Iaachus.

"Take me to him!" said Otto.

CHAPTER FIFTY-NINE

"So," said Iaachus, "the great day has come."

"All is in readiness," said Julian.

"I would things were otherwise," said Otto. "Better to be hunting on Varna, riding on Vellmer."

"What will become of Sesella, Gerune, Renata, Flora, if we fail?" asked Tuvo Ausonius.

"Little," said Iaachus, "they are women, and marked. New collars, new chains, new selling platforms, new Masters to serve and please."

Elena, at the serving table in the office of Iaachus, trembled, and her hands shook on the decanter, the *kana* a small, golden storm in the vessel.

"Be careful, girl," said Rurik. "If you spill the wine, you will be whipped."

"Forgive me, Master," whispered Elena.

"Do not concern yourself, noble Rurik," said Iaachus. "She is my property. Her skin is mine. She is mine to discipline as I might please."

"Of course," said Rurik.

"Your troops, of the Farnichi, are prepared," said Julian.

"They are in position," said Rurik.

"The Farnichi," said Iaachus, "owe the empire much."

"The bargain was struck," said Rurik. "The Farnichi abide its terms. My presence here is an attestment to that fact."

"But unofficially, covertly, of course," said Iaachus.

"Of course," said Rurik.

"Cohorts loyal to me await our signal," said Julian, "elements of the guard, chosen army units, selected landing units of the imperial navy."

"But much, locally, I fear," said Iaachus, "depends on *comitates*, brought from Tangara, ostensibly to witness and assist in the celebration of the royal nuptials."

"I would think, dear Arbiter," said Rurik, "you would view the presence of Otungs in Telnar with apprehension."

"I do," said Iaachus. "One gambles."

"The *comitates* are allies," said Julian, "auxiliaries in the imperial forces."

"They are barbarians," said Rurik.

"So is our noble Ottonius," said Iaachus.

"I am aware of that," said Rurik.

"It behooves you to pretend confidence and trust, dear Rurik," said Julian, "even if it does not exist. Beware of offending allies, or their commander."

"More is at issue here," said Rurik, "than the loyalty of Captain Ottonius, with whose secret thoughts I am perforce unacquainted. There are others, as well."

"Each company," said Otto, "is commanded by a pledged man, each an Otung, Vandar, Ulrich, or Citherix."

"Barbarians, all," said Rurik.

"I am sure of them," said Otto. "I am less sure of Telnarians."

"I am a Telnarian," said Rurik.

"I am aware of that," said Otto.

"Crossroads will be seized, guard stations, public buildings, the house of the senate," said Julian. "The new order will be publicly announced."

"We can hold the palace only briefly," said Iaachus.

"If we can hold the palace," said Julian, "we will hold Telnar, as well."

"Not against the summoned, marshaled forces of the empire," said Iaachus.

"As the palace goes, so goes the empire," said Julian. "Many a coup has overturned a dynasty and was scarcely noted in the empire. One need not have generals marching on Telnar, foreign armies in the streets, cities sacked, worlds burned, alien fleets overhead. Many revolutions are quiet, moving on soft feet in the night, taking place in bedrooms and halls. Daggers and goblets of poison have emptied more thrones than wars. In time new names are sung, and new statues, scarcely noticed, appear in public places. Life continues as it has, and will. What ambassador from far worlds, what bureaucrat from afar, recalls vanished flags and banners? What master of what trading commission, what visiting potentate, questions what he finds?"

"I fear it is true," said Tuvo Ausonius. "I was employed on Miton, in the financial division of the first imperial quadrant. I often suspected our work would go on much as usual regardless of what might occur in Telnar, let alone in the palace."

"Much would be different," said Iaachus, "if the empire collapsed."

"Surely," said Tuvo Ausonius.

"I fear," said Iaachus, "we will soon hear the bells, the music, the acclaim of the crowds."

"There will be jubilation," said Julian. "There will be singing, and dancing, in the streets."

"And, the marriages done, the great triumphal procession, on flower-strewn streets, will approach the palace in stately pomp," said Rurik, "bringing the brides and grooms, in royal carriages."

"Should the ceremony not be done by now?" asked Otto.

"I suspect, soon," said Iaachus, "but we must not disallow our friend, the exarch, his hour of glory. He will draw from it what he can. Consider the prestige, the fame, the renown, the esteem, accruing to his office, his post, and faith. Is this not sub-tle, potent wealth in the sacred strongbox? Will not his Floonian cult now reign over other Floonian cults? Will it not seem to be endorsed by the empire, to represent the empire? Indeed, the empress mother is in attendance, and prominently enthroned. That will much please her. Will not this deed set a precedent for future claims and demands, for future control and power? Con-sider the spectacle, the impressive pageantry. The great temple is decorated, lit, and filled. A choir of a thousand ministrants sings. The very walls and windows of the edifice will rattle with their impressive blaring. The wafting of incense will linger for days."

"I regret that the empress mother is present at the ceremony," said Julian.

"It is natural," said Iaachus, "the brides are her daughters. Fear rather that she, who is currently taking instruction from the exarch, be converted, be anointed with the holy oil, imported from the sacred oil pools of Zirus, would that someone put a match to them. She should then, as a devout Floonian, submit herself to the will of Floon and Karch, who are the same and yet different."

"I take it," said Rurik, "that the will of Floon and Karch is made clear by the exarch."

"That seems to be the arrangement," said Iaachus.

"It would be an invisible emperor," said Julian.

"It would seem so," said Iaachus.

"What if there are other exarchs?" said Rurik.

"There are other exarchs, but not of Telnar," said Iaachus. "Telnar is the capital of the empire. Thus, the Exarch of Telnar has a certain advantage in possible competitions. One emperor, one exarch, and so on."

"It seems there could still be trouble," said Rurik.

"In the future, doubtless," said Iaachus. "But I think such things could be managed. Those who lose out can be accounted false exarchs. Perhaps it could be done by extermination, too, rather as one Floonian cult seems willing to exterminate other Floonian cults, the losers being accounted heretics, or such."

"Where is the emperor?" asked Otto.

"He is in his quarters, playing with his toy animals," said Iaachus.

"He is eighteen years old, is he not?" said Rurik.

"He was born eighteen years ago," said Iaachus.

"The ceremony must be nearly done," said Tuvo Ausonius.

"Yes," said Iaachus.

"Time is short," said Tuvo Ausonius.

"Yes," said Otto.

"I am uneasy," said Tuvo Ausonius.

"Be eager," said Otto.

"I tremble," said Tuvo Ausonius.

"Tremble," said Otto, "but not like the fleet one, with fear, but like the vi-cat, who prepares to pounce."

"I have heard little of Abrogastes," said Julian.

"It is peculiar," said Iaachus. "My spies made it clear that he accompanied his sons, and the princesses, to Telnar. But he seems to have disappeared. Surely it seems he should be present at the wedding. But it seems he is not. And, as far as we know, he has not left Telnaria."

"Interesting," said Julian.

"As I understand it, my dear Ottonius," said Iaachus, "you have met this Abrogastes."

"Yes," said Otto.

"Perhaps you have a sense of him?"

"I think so," said Otto.

"What is he like?" asked Iaachus.

"He would stand aside for no man," said Otto.

"Not even the Exarch of Telnar?" asked Iaachus.

"No," said Otto.

"Perhaps that is why he has disappeared," said Iaachus.

"Dear Ottonius," said Julian. "Much culminates. We trained long, and well. The hour is near. *Comitates* are at your side."

"It would not be so," said Otto, "save for a small, gentle creature."

"One guarded by, and protected by, a savage monster," said Julian.

"Not a monster," said Otto, "a Herul."

"Clarify this," said Rurik.

"You know something of the medallion and chain which Ottonius brought from Tenguthaxichai," said Julian.

"Yes," said Rurik. "Vandals would rally to it."

"Yes," said Julian, "if it were believed to be the one, true medallion and chain. Its guardian was an Emanationist brother, the salamanderine, Brother Benjamin. It was stolen from the *festung* of Sim Giadini, and Brother Benjamin left the *festung*, pursuing the thief, though unsuccessfully. Shortly after his departure from the *festung*, it was destroyed. He, much later, starving and ill, was found by Heruls on the Plains of Barrionuevo, and nursed back to health. He, and a Herul, Hunlaki, by name, on various grounds, suspected that the medallion and chain had been transported to Telnar, eventually to be received by the Exarch of Telnar. They journeyed to Telnar to confront the exarch and demand the return of the medallion and chain. The exarch, after denying knowledge of the medallion and chain, or of its theft, and curtly dismissing Brother Benjamin and his servant, the Herul, Hunlaki, from the temple precincts, set thugs on them, to follow and beat them, perhaps to kill them. Four of these six thugs, much to the dismay of Brother Benjamin, were killed by his servant, the Herul, their throats bitten through, and the other two fled. Our colleague, the Arbiter of Protocol, learned of this incident by means of the report of guardsmen, who took the pair into custody. He investigated, and was intrigued, having heard something of the medallion and chain. He arranged for their release from custody, and concealed them in a private dwelling in the city, to protect them from the attentions of the exarch. What then occurred was that the medallion and chain taken by Ottonius from Tenguthaxichai was shown to Brother Benjamin, who identified it as the true medallion and chain. It was then only necessary to transport the medallion and chain, Brother Benjamin, and his Herul servant, Hunlaki, to Tangara, where contact was made with Otungs."

"And *comitates* are now with us," said Tuvo Ausonius.

"Where is the medallion and chain?" asked Rurik.

"On Tangara," said Julian, "where it remains, to be kept in safety."

"I think," said the Arbiter of Protocol, "while we are waiting, a light collation, with *kana*, might be in order. The wine is at hand, atop our table, and I shall send my lovely Elena to the next room, to fetch some readied viands."

Elena slipped from the room, and soon returned, bearing a tray, which she placed, beside the wine, already on the table.

"Eating," said Rurik, "is always more pleasant, and food tastier, in the presence of slaves."

"True," said Julian. "Slaves stimulate the blood, and whet the appetite. Who can enjoy food so much as a Master, with a naked, or half-naked, slave at his feet? How the sight of a woman in a collar, on her knees, in her place, stimulates the appetite! The nerves come alive, the digestive juices flow. Let nature reign. Let the world be rightly ordered. Let there be Masters and slaves!"

"Master?" said Elena.

"Retain your gown, lovely Elena," said Iaachus. "If we should survive the day, you may crawl to me in my chambers, as is your wont, whimpering, a switch in your teeth, and serve me at the foot of my couch."

"Yes, Master," said Elena.

"Pour the wine," he said.

"Yes, Master," she said.

Rurik, turned about, and faced the door to the chamber. "Cornhair!" he cried.

The door was flung open, and Cornhair stood there, unable to kneel, held erect from behind, by the arms, by a guardsman, who then flung her to all fours in the portal, and she looked across the room, at Rurik, of the Larial Farnichi.

She was briefly tunicked, in what was little more than a rag.

Her Master had not yet seen fit, since the delegation to Tenguthaxichai, to accord her a suitable tunic, however brief.

She was content.

It was the will of her Master.

"Crawl here, collared Calasalii bitch, and get under the table," said Rurik.

Soon Cornhair was on her knees under the table, looking up.

Rurik dragged a chair near her, but did not take his seat.

The other guests, too, Otto, Julian, and Tuvo Ausonius, drew chairs near the table, but, like Rurik, remained standing.

"Gentlemen," said Iaachus, lifting his glass, "I propose a toast—to the brides and grooms, to the Princesses Viviana and Alacida, and to the princes, Ingeld and Hrothgar!"

This toast was drunk.

"Now, gentlemen," said Iaachus, "I propose a second toast, one to this day, a day which is public and a day which is secret, a day which is visible and a day which is invisible."

This toast, too, was drunk.

The guests then seated themselves about the table.

They ate little, they spoke little.

"I fear," said Iaachus, "our repast is insufficiently festive, even with slaves about."

"There is a time for the doings of men," said Otto. "There is another time for the grasping and handling of females."

From time to time, Rurik put a bit of food into Cornhair's lifted mouth.

"Listen!" said Iaachus, raising his hand.

"I hear it," said Otto, pushing back his goblet of *kana*.

"The bells," said Julian.

"I hear, far off, the shouting, the cries of gladness," said Tuvo Ausonius.

"The ceremony is done," said Iaachus. "The guests, the brides and grooms, will be issuing from the temple."

Otto, Julian, Rurik, and Tuvo Ausonius, with the Arbiter of Protocol, rose to their feet, and regarded one another.

"It is not too late to disengage," said Iaachus.

There was silence.

"I take it," said Iaachus, Arbiter of Protocol, "we are resolved."

"Yes," said Otto.

"Yes," said Julian.

"Agreed," said Rurik.

"Yes," said Tuvo Ausonius.

"I shall order the signal given," said Iaachus.

"Few are likely to notice the unfurling of another banner, amongst the many celebratory banners adorning the palace walls," said Tuvo Ausonius.

"Some will notice," said Otto.

Bells were pealing throughout the city.

"The sounds of the crowd, the cheering, grows louder," said Rurik.

"Street by street," said Tuvo Ausonius, "the procession, the wedding party, the carriages, grow ever nearer."

"Perhaps they will be surprised, when they are turned back, at the palace steps," said Julian.

"I think, my dear Ottonius," said Iaachus, the Arbiter of Protocol, "it is time for us to go to the throne room."

"And I think it fitting, friend Ottonius," said Julian, "if you should lead the way."

"Will this act save the empire, or destroy it?" asked Tuvo Ausonius.

"We do not know," said Iaachus.

Rurik turned back to the table, and snapped his fingers, and gestured to his side. Cornhair then emerged from beneath the table, and hurried after the men.

In the throne room, Otto took his place on the throne.

ACKNOWLEDGMENTS

It is interesting, and flattering, that an author is commonly given the credit for one book or another. As an author, I suppose I should welcome this practice, but, as an author who tries to see the world as it actually is, at least occasionally, wisely or not, once in a while, for better or for worse, I think it would be a bit more honest, at least on some occasions, of which this is one, to recognize the debts, never to be well repaid, which an author owes to others, many friends, most of whom he will never meet or know. First, novels are, clearly, a collaborative enterprise, as, in their way, every reader is a coauthor, creating, from a set of marks on a page, a vivid, marvelous, personal world, replete with its own colors, passions, winds, seasons, and weathers. Many roads lead from Rome. Beyond this, there are always the countless contributions, too often unremarked, without which a book, as it is normally thought of, would not exist. These far transcend the technologies of reproduction, involving an awesome compass of skills and talents, both artistic and practical. One thinks of such things, in particular, as artwork, packaging, marketing, and distribution. I have been very fortunate in many ways, and I am very grateful. I would also like to use this brief occasion to express my gratitude, however inadequately, to many individuals who have for years, with diligence and affection, largely by means of the internet, supported me and my work. Their commitment, and that of their sites, has been unapologetic and determined. Attention has been called to my work, and, in many instances, it has been honestly and salubriously promoted. Their aid, in various cases, has ranged from the friendly but exacting review of manuscripts, which is much appreciated, to galleries of artwork and platforms for research and discussion. These people understand diversity as diversity; integrity as integrity; and a free market as a free market, which is refreshing. Amongst these individuals, most of whom are unknown to me, I would like to cite three in particular, Mr. Mark Collins, Mr. Jon Ard, and Mr. Simon van Meygaarden. I would also like to take this occasion to thank my friend, and agent, for many years, Mr. Richard Curtis. To all my friends, known and unknown, with respect and affection, I wish you well.

John Norman

TELNARIAN HISTORIES

FROM OPEN ROAD MEDIA

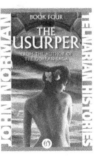

Available wherever ebooks are sold

OPEN **ROAD**

INTEGRATED MEDIA

Open Road Integrated Media is a digital publisher and multimedia content company. Open Road creates connections between authors and their audiences by marketing its ebooks through a new proprietary online platform, which uses premium video content and social media.